THE
WOODEN
MAN

THE WOODEN MAN

CHILD OF FIRE

GAME OF CAGES

CIRCLE OF ENEMIES

Harry Connolly

FANTASY

CHILD OF FIRE   Copyright © 2009 by Harry Connolly
    Publication History: Del Rey mass market, September 2009
GAME OF CAGES   Copyright © 2010 by Harry Connolly
    Publication History: Del Rey mass market, August 2010
CIRCLE OF ENEMIES   Copyright © 2011 by Harry Connolly
    Publication History: Del Rey mass market, August 2011

First SFBC Fantasy Printing: September 2011

Published by arrangement with
Del Rey Books,
an Imprint of The Random House Publishing Group,
a division of Random House, Inc., New York.

Visit The SFBC online at http://www.sfbc.com

ISBN 978-1-61129-770-6

Printed in the United States of America

CONTENTS

INTRODUCTION   vii

CHILD OF FIRE   1

GAME OF CHANGES   255

CIRCLE OF ENEMIES   505

INTRODUCTION

The first thing I want to say about this introduction is that you shouldn't read it before you read the novels. Yes, I know, an introduction should ease you in to a book, but I personally think these books work best when you come to them knowing as little as possible about them.

So flip past this part and go right to page one of the first book. You can read all this later, if you want. It'll still be here. Seriously. Just dive in.

Back again? Okay. Let me talk a little about these books and what they've meant to me.

The protagonist of the Twenty Palaces series, Ray Lilly, has been called a lot of things: a felon, a thug, a ruffian, a "grunt boy" (don't ask me what that last one means because I don't have a clue), and worse, too. But to me he'll always be my first attempt at a sympathetic character.

For years I'd written stories about anti-heroes and fools, thieves and killers, cheats and villains. The plots were dark, the character motivations darker still, and the endings resembled the inside of a bank vault during a power outage—utterly pitch.

Wow. I get wistful just thinking about it.

But of the many things that will bore a writer, the two worst are: 1) using the same tricks over and over and 2) never selling anything. Eventually I decided to expand my horizons a little; I sat down and tried to work up a sympathetic protagonist.

Another writer—a smarter writer—would have chosen a social worker with an overwhelming caseload. Or a grandmother of six who worked for Doctors Without Borders. Even easier would have been to file the serial numbers off a character like Peter Parker. But no, I had to come up with a former car thief who went to prison for a bar fight that got ugly—a guy who wanted to go straight, but whose misguided sense of loyalty and pride kept getting him into trouble.

Then I wrote a story for him, and the plot and setting was just as dark as you'd expect. The big difference from my previous work was that Ray was trying to do the right thing. His chief obstacle was himself. His second biggest was Annalise.

It's fairly common for mystery/thriller protagonists to have a Badass Friend (which is why you often see it in urban fantasies, too). The Badass Friend is more violent and more skilled with violence than the hero (and is often a more colorful, interesting character), and the hero calls on them when things get a little rough.

I wanted to turn that on its head. Annalise isn't the occasional helping hand in this team, Ray is (or he's supposed to be). And not only is she the one in charge, she doesn't like Ray all that much. She's a combination of ally and antagonist.

As it turned out, she's very like the protagonists of those pitch-dark stories I *used* to write: a ruthless killer with a screwed-up inner life. What can I say? I like having cake, and I like eating it, too.

So I heaped miseries on poor Ray all throughout the book, ran him through his paces, and at the end of the first draft, I killed him off.

It's funny to look back on that decision, which seemed so inevitable at the time. Obviously, once I realized there was still gold to be mined from these characters, I revised the ending to spare his life, but I remember at the time that I couldn't imagine any other legitimate resolution.

And that's not because I believe some old Comic-Code style moralizing like "Characters should suffer the consequences of their misdeeds." In fact, I wanted to get away from that. The moral absolutes that are so evident in other urban fantasies are deliberately absent here: Characters can not use a religious symbol to ward off capital E "Evil".

Magic in the Twenty Palaces setting is as morally neutral as a drill, a saw, a hammer, or any other tool. The otherworldly beings of great power and alien intelligence that come to our world are not immoral; they're new links at the top of the food chain, no more interested in doing "evil" than a tiger or a shark.

Then there are the human antagonists, people who do terrible things in the service of high ideals like Community, Mercy, Freedom, and Order. And who opposes them? The members of the Twenty Palace Society, who have their own reasons for doing terrible things.

So without an externally validated Good or Evil, what's left? Well, power is what's left, and the will of the powerful to do whatever seems fitting.

Which brings me back to that revised ending and what a huge change it was for me. It wasn't bright and happy, by any means, but it also wasn't pitch black. Call it grayish. Call it a willingness to believe power can be wielded with restraint.

I'm happy to have the chance to follow these characters for the past few years and I'm glad I spared Ray. In a world of impersonal forces and dangerous choices, it's nice to imagine we can come face our troubles and survive, ready to take on the next challenge.

—Harry Connolly
April 2011

CHILD
OF
FIRE

CHAPTER ONE

It felt good to sit behind the wheel again, even the wheel of a battered Dodge Sprinter. Even with this passenger beside me.

The van rumbled like a garbage truck, handled like a refrigerator box, and needed a full minute to reach highway speeds. I'd driven better, but I'm a guy who has to take what I can get while I'm still alive to get it.

The passenger beside me was Annalise Powliss. She stood about five foot nothing, was as thin as a mop handle, and was covered with tattoos from the neck down. Her hair was the same dark red as the circled *F*'s I used to get on my book reports, and she wore it cropped close to her scalp. It was an ugly cut, but she never seemed to care how she looked. I suspected she cut it herself.

She was my boss, and she had been forbidden to kill me, although that's what she most wanted to do.

"Where are we going?" I asked for the fourth time.

She didn't answer. She wasn't talking to me except to tell me where to drive. To be honest, I didn't blame her. She had good reason to hate me.

At the moment, though, she and I had a job to do and all I knew about it was this: Annalise was on her way to kill someone. Maybe several someones. I was supposed to help.

Because she wouldn't talk to me, I was not entirely clear who had ordered her not to kill me or why they would bother. I was just the driver, and I didn't even know where we were going.

"Quarter tank," I said as we approached a gas station. I hated to drive on less than a half tank of gas, but so far the boss had refused to let me fill up. Since she had the money, the title, and the physical strength to tear my arm off, she made the decisions.

She glanced down at the scrap of wood in her hand—unpainted and unfinished except for the twisted nonsense shape made of several colors on one side—and said nothing. I stifled my irritation and drove past the pumps.

We were westbound somewhere on the Olympic Peninsula. There were no other cars on the road. The streets were slick with misting rain, and the sky was growing dark as evening approached. After my years in Southern California, I'd forgotten how long it could take for night to fall in this part of the world.

The road was one of those rural highways with one lane in each direction and a speed limit of fifty-five. I was staying below the limit because the van, with its balding tires, whining brakes, and load of equipment in the back, wasn't equipped for the twists and turns of backwoods driving.

I was enjoying the drive anyway. I had a key to the door and I could see the sky. It felt good to be a free man again.

Up ahead, I saw a big cedar right up close to the road. Annalise was not wearing her seat belt. I was wearing mine. The speedometer on the Sprinter shuddered at the fifty-miles-per-hour mark. All I had to do was swerve. She and her little scrap of lumber would fly through the windshield and slam against the tree, while I would be safe in the arms of the shoulder harness and air bag.

I didn't try it. It wasn't just the motorcycle Annalise kept on flimsy mounts in the cargo area behind me. In truth, I doubted that slamming face-first into a tree trunk would do more than muss her thrift-shop clothes. And piss her off. She'd survived worse. I'd seen it.

I was pretty sure Annalise wasn't a human being. She had been, once, I thought, but I wasn't sure what she was now.

A Volvo station wagon with luggage strapped to the roof drove eastbound toward us. As it passed, the painted scrap wood in Annalise's hand flashed like a camera flashbulb. The design painted on the face of the wood began to twist like a nest full of snakes.

Annalise lunged toward me. "Turn around!" she yelled. She had a high, funny voice more suited to a cartoon squirrel than a grown woman. "Turn around and follow that station wagon!"

I was already doing it. I hit the brakes and twisted the wheel, letting the clumsy van fishtail as much as I dared. I heard crashing noises from behind me as Annalise's things toppled over. We came to a rest, and I threw it in reverse.

"Let's go! Goddammit, hurry up!"

"Keep your shirt on."

I backed up onto the shoulder, swung the wheel all the way around, and stomped on the gas. We crept after the station wagon.

"Goddammit, Ray," Annalise growled. She was very close to my ear, and I could hear the hate in her voice. "If you let them get away, I'm going to tear you apart."

"Oh yeah? Who are you going to find who can reach the gas pedal?" I said. My voice betrayed too much fear. When Annalise threatened to tear someone apart, she meant it literally. "This is your broken-down van. If we don't catch them, you can blame yourself for not buying better wheels."

She settled back into her seat and glared through the windshield at the empty road ahead.

I forced myself to smile at her. "Isn't this nice? Our first job together and we're getting along so well." It was stupid and dangerous to taunt her, but I was afraid of her and I hated to show my fear.

She ignored me, for which I was secretly grateful.

We picked up speed, rounding curves and topping hills the van could barely handle. Night was coming and the forest around us was filling with shadows. I switched on the headlights, but Annalise snarled at me to turn them off.

A red light flashed from between the trees on the right. I slowed. Annalise started to protest, but I shushed her. She didn't look pleased about that.

We came to a break in the forest—a gravel parking lot with a row of abandoned wooden stalls at the back. It looked like it had once been a roadside farmer's stand. The station wagon was parked at the far end, red brake lights glowing.

I parked a couple of car lengths away from the vehicle and jumped from the van as quickly as I could. Annalise was a little faster. She walked toward them, holding the fist-sized scrap of wood in her hand like a Geiger counter. The design on it writhed wildly; something about the car or the people in it was setting it off.

All the wagon's side doors stood open. A man and woman had their head and shoulders in the back doors, and they were working frantically at something. I checked their stuff. Among the things strapped to their roof was a vacuum cleaner in a clear plastic trash bag beaded with rain. These people weren't on a camping trip. They were skipping town.

All I could see of the man was a pair of extra-wide Dockers and the pale skin that peeked above his sagging waistband. *Office worker,* I thought. He must have heard us approach, but he didn't turn to look at us. Was he completely engrossed, or did he have a weak survival instinct? Out of unshakable habit, my next thought was: *Victim.*

No, no. I pushed the thought away. That was not part of my life anymore.

From what I could see through the car windows, the woman was also wider than strictly necessary and also dressed for casual day at the office. They continued to struggle with something in the backseat.

I felt a pressure against my chest, just below my right collarbone. Strange. I tried to ignore it and said, "Do you folks need any help?"

The woman glanced up, noticing us for the first time. She had a terrified look on her face, but I knew it had nothing to do with Annalise or me. Her husband glanced back as he came out of the backseat. His glasses were smeary from the drizzle. "No," he said too quickly. "We're fine."

The pressure against my chest increased.

Then their little boy climbed out of the car.

He was a good-looking kid, maybe eight or nine years old, although I'm no judge. His hair stuck up in the back, and he had scrapes on both elbows. "I feel funny, Dad," he said. He laid his hands on his chest and pressed. "I feel squishy."

Flames erupted around his head.

I felt light-headed suddenly, and the pressure against my chest vanished. Before I could think about it, I ran toward them, stripping off my jacket.

The woman screamed. The flames around the boy's head spread downward past his crotch. In an instant, his whole body was ablaze.

The father fumbled for a jacket draped over the driver's seat. I heard Annalise's footsteps behind me.

"Wow!" the boy said. "It doesn't hurt, Daddy. It doesn't hurt at all."

The father lunged at his boy with the jacket, knocking him to the gravel, then beating at the flames. I got there a half second later and slapped my jacket over the boy's face and head.

Rain steamed off the burning body. Beside me, the father made a noise like a strangled dog. I tried not to think about that. I tried not to notice the black scorch marks where the flames touched the ground. I tried not to think about what was happening. I just worked at the flames. I slapped at them, smothered them, wrapped them in my jacket.

It was no good. The fire flared up and my jacket erupted in flames. I threw it aside and started to drag my shirt over my head.

The kid laughed as though we were tickling him. Then his skin turned silver-gray and his whole head came apart.

The flames roared. A wave of heat forced me back. The father rolled back onto his padded behind, almost bowling over his wife as she rushed around the car toward us.

I let my backward momentum roll me onto my feet. Annalise stood nearby. She had unbuttoned the fireman's jacket she always wore, revealing colored ribbons alligator-clipped to her clothes. She pulled a green one free. The small sigil drawn on the bottom glowed with silvery light.

I turned back to the family. The boy's head, arms, and chest had come apart and been transformed into a mass of fat, wriggling, silver-gray worms, each about the size of my pinkie. Then his stomach came apart, then his hips. It happened so fast I had no chance to think about it. I saw the worms twisting themselves against the packed gravel, trying to burrow into the earth. They swarmed over one another, heading west. Everything they touched turned black with scorched, greasy soot.

I felt a tightness in my throat that might have been the urge to vomit, but there was nothing to bring up. I was completely hollow inside.

The father struggled to his feet, and his wife tried to move around him to her son. The expression on her face told me she already knew the truth, already knew her son was gone, but she could no more stay away from his disintegrating body than she could leap up into the clouds.

I tackled them. My shoulder sank into the father's broad, soft belly, and I grabbed the mother around the waist. With all my strength, I pushed them away from the car.

I didn't look back at Annalise. I didn't have to. I knew very well what those green ribbons did and how little she cared about collateral damage.

The father and mother stumbled backward and fell over each other, hitting the gravel hard. I landed on their legs.

I heard a *whoosh* of fire behind me. Annalise's green ribbon had hit its target. I glanced back and saw flames, green ones this time, roar up around the wriggling mass that had once been a boy's body. Where the flames touched them, the gray worms burst apart.

The sphere of green fire expanded. I pulled in my legs, trying to get away, but I was too late. The cold green fire washed over me.

I sucked in a lungful of air to scream my life away. It was too soon. Too soon. I looked down at my legs, expecting them to burn away to blackened, smoking bones.

It didn't happen. There was no pain, no damage to my legs, nothing. My clothes didn't even burn. I felt nothing more than a slight pressure below my collarbone—a place the flames did not even reach.

The flames receded. I was undamaged. So were the parents. I had pushed them out of range just in time.

The worms had not fared so well. There was nothing left of them but gray slime.

"Holy God," the mother said, her voice thin and strained. Her face was slack and her eyes were glassy. If I hadn't pushed her away, she would have been killed along with her son—another person struck down for no other reason than she was next to someone Annalise wanted to kill.

Annalise took another ribbon from beneath her jacket. This one was blue. I had no idea what the blue ones did, but I knew it wouldn't be good.

Before she could use it, a *force* passed through me. It wasn't a physical push. It struck my mind, my consciousness, whatever you want to call it, and it felt as though I was standing in heavy surf. It almost toppled me.

At the same moment, I felt a twinge high on the right side of my chest again.

Annalise staggered and winced; her blue ribbon fell from her hand. She felt it, too. The mother and father didn't stagger. Their expressions went blank.

Then it was gone.

The couple stood and began to straighten their clothes. "You didn't have to knock me over," the man said. "I was only trying to help."

"What?"

"We pulled over to help—oh, forget it." He slapped at the dust on his pants.

His wife clutched at his shirt and looked at me worriedly. "Douglas, let's just go."

They started walking toward the car, glancing back at me as if I was a stray dog that might bite.

They did not look the least bit upset by what had just happened to their son.

After they got into their car and slammed the doors, Douglas started the engine. His wife leaned into the backseat and fussed with a baby sleeping in an infant seat. I hadn't noticed the baby until then. Douglas turned on the music. Bobby McFerrin. Gravel crunched under the tires as they began to drive away, as though they were leaving behind nothing more important than some old fast-food wrappers.

Annalise charged past me, lowered her shoulder, and slammed into the car's front panel, just above the wheel. Her legs pumped. The fender crumpled and the car slid sideways like a tackling dummy until it tipped into a ditch.

She stood and straightened her jacket, a scowl on her delicate little face. I had seen her strength before, of course. She could have flipped the car onto its roof or torn the door off and pinched off Douglas's head. I assumed the only reason she hadn't done either was that she hadn't finished with them yet.

Douglas jumped out of the car to inspect the damage. He looked at the crumpled metal, then at Annalise, then all around.

"What . . ." he started. He couldn't finish the question. He ran his hand over the ruined fender, reassuring himself that it was really bent metal. He looked at Annalise again. "What hit my car?"

"I'm not done with you," Annalise said. She stepped toward him.

The wife leaned toward his window. "Douglas, get back in the car," she said. She leaned into the backseat to check the baby. Still sleeping.

Douglas let the keys in his hand jangle and backed toward the driver's door. My own hands were shaking. I felt hysteria building in me. That little boy had called him Daddy, and now he was going to drive away as though he'd just stopped for a piss? They'd shrugged that kid off as if he was roadkill. I had never even met the kid before two minutes ago, and what I'd seen made me want to weep and puke my guts out at the same time.

I didn't do either. Instead, I got angry.

"You're just going to drive away?"

The woman's eyes widened. "Douglas . . ."

"What about your kid?" I stalked after them, determined to see some sign of grief from them. I needed my anger. Without it, I thought I might shake myself apart. "He called you Mommy and Daddy! Don't you care what happened to him?"

Douglas would have to turn his back on me to climb into his car. He wasn't going to risk that. "Sir," he said, "I don't know what you're talking about."

"He called you Daddy! And he just . . . your own son!"

My anger was growing too large for me, but I couldn't stop myself. I needed to see a reaction from them. These people were going to show some grief if I had to wring it out of them with my bare hands.

The man rounded on me. "My son didn't call me anything! He's only three months old!" he shouted.

"Ray," Annalise said.

I ignored her. I just stared at Douglas, stunned and horrified. "You don't care at all, do you?" There was no more anger in my voice, no accusation, only amazement. I was building toward something terrible, and I had no idea how to stop myself.

If I had Annalise's strength, I would have stripped the flesh from his bones. If I had her arsenal of spells, I would have burned him alive.

"Ray."

I turned toward Annalise. Her thin, girlish voice sounded pinched. Even she had been rattled by the boy's death. "Settle down," she said. "They can't remember. Something took their memory away."

It took a couple of seconds for that to sink in. The wave. The wave I'd felt after the boy fell apart must have hit them, too. It must have erased their memories.

Why hadn't it erased mine?

Douglas was leaning back, one arm reaching toward his wife. There was a smack of metal slapping into a soft hand, and he came at me.

I was distracted and off-balance; if he'd been faster, he would have killed me. But he wasn't fast—he was an overweight office drone. A victim. I instinctively raised my arm to protect my head, and he slammed a tire iron onto my tattooed forearm.

I felt no pain and barely even any pressure. Annalise was not the only one with tattoos. Like hers, mine were magic. Hers covered her entire body, but mine covered just a couple of spots, including the outside of my forearms and hands.

Douglas thought he'd scored a winning blow. He smirked and waited for me to cringe and clutch my arm. Instead, I snatched the tire iron away from him and racked him up against the car.

Annalise stepped up to him. "Wallet," she said.

He barely glanced at her. Annalise was a far greater danger to him than I was, but all of his attention was on the big, tattooed man, not the tiny woman. She had to repeat herself.

His wife called out. "Douglas! For God's sake, give her your wallet!"

He produced the wallet and Annalise took it. " 'Douglas Benton,' " she read. " '144 Acorn Road, Hammer Bay, Washington.' "

"We don't live there anymore." Douglas sounded a little frantic. "We're leaving town."

I shook him. "Why?"

His mouth opened and closed several times. He couldn't think of an answer.

"He's forgotten that, too," Annalise said. She pulled a card from his wallet. It was white with a magnetic strip across the back. "Hammer Bay Toys," she read. "This where you work?"

"Yes," Douglas said.

"But you're not going back."

"No. Not planning to."

"You didn't return your security card?"

"I—I forgot." Sweat beaded on his lip. He glanced at each of us, trying to think of a phrase that would placate us and let him drive away. He thought we were crazy, and the way I felt at that moment, he wasn't far wrong.

"Hmm," Annalise said, as though she was unsatisfied with his answer. There was a moment of silence. Douglas couldn't bear to leave it unfilled.

"Look, I don't know what the problem is," he said. "I'm sure we can do something to work all this out. Right? I'm sure it's just been a misunderstanding or something."

Annalise seemed thoughtful. "Maybe you're right, Douglas."

I wondered if this was the moment she would kill them both.

That made him a little bolder. "Sure, sure, I understand. We're just a little confused. All of us. The baby didn't call me Daddy, right, Meg? He's too young for that.

"Meg and I have always wanted a son, but we were never blessed until just this winter. See? We're all just a little mixed up."

"One of us is," Annalise said. "Because you have a front-facing car seat in there."

We all looked into the backseat. A plastic car seat was buckled onto the far side of the infant's seat. A small one. The boy who had just . . . I wasn't ready to approach that thought yet, but he was too big to be sitting in such a small car seat.

Had they lost more than one? Had they forgotten that, too?

Douglas and Meg looked to each other for an explanation. Silence. Douglas turned to us and said: "We're bringing it to my sister?" As if he was guessing.

"There are scorch marks on it," I said. They were the same sort of marks on the ground where the boy had . . .

The Bentons didn't seem to know what to make of that. The blank confusion on their faces was fascinating. They really were enchanted. My anger was still going strong, but it wasn't directed at them anymore. I was beginning to pity them.

Meg went to the backseat, unbuckled the car seat, and heaved it toward the woods. It bounced once on the gravel and disappeared into a patch of nettles.

Douglas glanced at me nervously. "I don't know who put that there. Really." Then he turned toward Annalise. "Do you want money? Is that it?"

Annalise gave him a sour smile. She took the scrap wood from her pocket and laid it against the station wagon, then against Douglas's ample belly. The designs twisted, but more slowly than before.

"Does this hurt?" Annalise asked.

"No," Douglas replied.

"Tell your wife, because I'm going to do this to her, too."

She walked around the car and laid the scrap of wood on Meg's palm. Douglas stared at something fascinating in the gravel at his feet.

That's when I noticed his hands. They were red, swollen, and shiny wet. Burned. He didn't seem to be in pain. If I pointed them out to him the way we had pointed out the car seat, would he suddenly "remember" them? Would he suddenly be in terrible pain?

Annalise leaned into the Volvo and yanked on the gearshift. Then she walked to the front of the car, laid her tiny hand on the bumper, and shoved it. It rolled out of the ditch onto level ground. She started toward the van. "Ray, let's go."

"Get out of here, Douglas," I said.

"Yeah, Douglas," Annalise said. "Get far away from Hammer Bay, and don't come back."

We didn't need to tell him twice. Douglas jumped into his car and peeled out of the lot.

I watched them go, feeling my adrenaline ebb. I couldn't stop thinking about that little boy, or how fiercely hot the flames had been. I looked down at my own undamaged hands. I felt woozy and sick.

Annalise called my name again. I turned away, ran to the edge of the lot, and puked into the bushes.

When that was over, I had tears in my eyes from the strain of it. They were the only tears that little boy was ever going to get. I tried to spit the acid taste out of my mouth, but it wouldn't go away.

I wiped my eyes dry. My hands were shaking and my stomach was in knots. That kid had no one to mourn for him except me, and I didn't have that much longer in this world, either. Something had to be done for him. I didn't know what it was, but as I wiped at my eyes again, I knew there had to be *something*.

I heard footsteps behind me. "Don't get maudlin," Annalise said.

I told her what she could do with herself.

"Enough with this weepy Girl Scout routine. Drink this." She shoved a water bottle into my hands.

I rinsed my mouth and spat. As long as I did what she told me to do, she wasn't allowed to kill me. I did it again. "Thanks."

"Don't thank me," she said. "I just didn't want you to stink up the van with your puke breath."

We walked toward the van. I wondered how many dead kids Annalise had seen. Maybe the number was so high they barely registered anymore.

I climbed behind the wheel and buckled in. Annalise never wore her seat belt. She had other, less mundane protections.

"When the boy burned, he turned into something," I said. "It was, like, gray maggots or something, and they started burrowing into the ground. What were they?"

"Start the van."

"Why weren't my hands damaged by the flames? I don't have tattoos over my fingers. Why wasn't I hurt like Douglas?"

She didn't answer.

"What was that wave I felt? I know you felt it, too. It was like something pushed against my mind." The words coming out of my mouth sounded ridiculous, but Annalise had just seen me crying like a baby. It's not like I had any pride left. "And I felt this twinge on my chest—"

"Start the van," she interrupted.

I did. Once we hit the road, Annalise took a cell phone from the glove compartment. She hit speed dial. After a few seconds, she said: "It's Annalise." She told the person at the other end of the line Douglas's name, address, and license number. "Check him out," she said. "And I'm still waiting for a current report." She snapped the phone shut without waiting for a response.

At least I wasn't the only one she was rude to.

I focused on the road. The long, slow descent into an overcast northwest night was well under way. I turned on the headlights just in time to light up a sign that said HAMMER BAY 22 MILES. This time, Annalise didn't protest. Aside from the rumble of the van, it was quiet. Suddenly, I didn't like the quiet.

"Who did you call?" She didn't answer. "Your mom?"

She shot a deadly look at me. Oops. Sore spot.

"Why didn't you kill Douglas?" I asked. "Isn't that our job? To kill people who have magic?"

Her response was irritated and defensive. "The Bentons didn't *have* magic. Were they carrying a spell book? Had they cast a spell on themselves? Were they hiding a predator?"

"Guess not."

"Someone cast a spell on them. That's who we want. Those people were no threat. They're victims."

I didn't say, *That's what I thought, too.* I didn't think the word meant the same thing to her as it did to me.

We were silent for a couple of minutes. I kept seeing the boy's face as the flames erupted around it. I kept hearing him say it didn't hurt. I needed to keep talking, or I was going to start weeping again.

"Why are we going to Hammer Bay?" I asked. "Not for Douglas. What's going on there?" She didn't answer again. "Come on," I persisted. "We're supposed to be doing this job and I don't know anything about it. Tell me what's going on. Or don't you know? Flames that don't hurt. Boys that turn into maggots. People who forget their dead kids. Something that pushed against our minds." She was silent. "Aren't you going to explain any of this?"

"No reason to."

"Why not?"

"Because you'll be dead very, very soon."

We drove the rest of the way in silence.

We passed over the crest of a hill, and the Pacific Ocean suddenly appeared below us. Then I saw the town of Hammer Bay. We drove down the hill, straight toward the heart of it.

CHAPTER TWO

Annalise wanted to visit Acorn Road immediately. Rather than drive aimlessly around reading street signs, I insisted we fill the tank and ask directions. The middle-aged clerk behind the counter tried to help, but when he told me to take a right turn where the bowling alley used to be, I snatched a map off the display rack and added it to our bill.

As I filled the tank, I noticed a young mother pull in next to us, with a little girl and a little boy in the front seat beside her. Her car was full of groceries. "For God's sake," she said, exasperated. "Sit still for five minutes! Please? Five minutes?" I finished refueling, trying not to look at the kids. Every time I did I imagined them crowned with flames.

The streets were sprinkled with potholes and dark from burned-out streetlights. We passed a lot of battered, rundown pickups and rattletrap station wagons.

We drove by three houses having their roofs repaired and two that were being landscaped. The town looked like it had just started to pull itself out of a long decline.

It turned out that Annalise was not good with maps. She sent me in the wrong direction twice. We had a lovely but useless tour of Hammer Bay's downtown. We drove past antique shops and small, family-owned hardware stores. There was a sign above a storefront that read THE MALLET. The newspaper box at the curb had the same name across the front.

We drove uphill. The waterfront road was on the top of a cliff that grew higher the farther south we went. There were several restaurants: pizza, diner, Mexican, Italian, Chinese, brew pub, and a couple of high-end places that had prime cliffside locations. Sadly, the sports bar was the only place that showed signs of life. A glance through the window at the big screen inside was all I needed to see that the Mariners game was on.

I had the sudden urge to pull over, but I ignored it. Baseball wasn't part of my life anymore, and it hadn't been for a long time. Just thinking about it reminded me of friends I'd lost and times when life seemed much simpler.

Maybe Annalise was right. Maybe I was being maudlin. What the hell, I was going to die soon, wasn't I? I had a right.

By this time my hunger had returned with a vengeance. I slowed as we passed a Thai restaurant.

"Are you buying dinner?" I asked. I didn't have any money. I didn't even have a change of underwear or a toothbrush. If she was going to kill me, she could at least buy me a meal first.

"Not right now, I'm not."

That made me hopeful.

I took the map from her. It was a cheap tourist map, covered with little icons showing the locations of local landmarks and restaurants that had paid for the privilege. Crude squiggles represented the cliff. Behind us, to the north, was the bay the town was named for. Ahead of us in the dark at the south end of town was some sort of lighthouse, supposedly, although I couldn't see any lights.

Acorn Road was at the northeastern end of town. We were at the southwestern end. I made note of the route we needed and started off.

So far I had not seen a single cop. That struck me as a little strange. Most small towns station at least one car near the bars. I didn't know if they were busy with an emergency or were kicking back at a doughnut shop somewhere.

Now that she was not burdened with the map, Annalise picked up the scrap wood again and stared at it. The design churned slowly. It didn't slow down or speed up. It didn't change much at all. It just kept moving and moving.

Whatever this meant, Annalise didn't like it.

As I drove through the neighborhood, streetlights lit up three more black marks just like the one the gray worms had left in the gravel lot. One started at the top of a bright yellow plastic slide. Another lay across an asphalt driveway beside a skateboard and helmet. The last began next to a pile of windblown, rain-warped schoolbooks.

Not beside a riding mower. Not a Harley or a pickup. Only kids' things.

I found the Bentons' house and parked on the street. There were only five or six other cars on the block, and Annalise's Sprinter stuck out like a sore thumb. I didn't see any lights switch on or any curtains draw back. No one peeked at us. It seemed we had come to a small town where the neighbors were not particularly nosy. In other words, the Twilight Zone.

Annalise strolled up to the front door and rang the bell. When there was no answer, she rang it again. No answer. She lifted her foot to kick the door down.

"Wait," I said. I took the ghost knife from my pocket.

The ghost knife was nothing more than a small sheet of notepaper covered first by mailing tape, then actual laminate. On one side of the paper was a sigil like the ones on Annalise's ribbons or our tattoos. This one I had drawn myself.

It was a spell. My only one.

The ghost knife slid into the door as if the wood was only smoke. I drew the mark down through the deadbolt latch and pushed the door open. The dark house lay waiting for me.

The first time I went to jail, it was a trip to juvie for a handgun accident that had crippled my best friend. There hadn't been any formal charges over that, but it set a sort of precedent.

The second time was when I lived in Los Angeles. I'd been working as a car thief, stealing popular models and driving them either to a chop shop or else down to the docks at Long Beach to be shipped and sold overseas. It was fun, sort of. I was in a crew of jack-offs and morons I could almost rely on, and I didn't have to carry a gun, which was a big plus considering my history. When I was busted for a bar fight, and wouldn't testify against the jack-offs and morons, the cops made sure I did a couple of years.

The third time was last year. That didn't go well, in part because it was how I met and made enemies with Annalise. The cops arrested me following that fiasco, too, but after a couple of months the charges were dropped. I had a lawyer hired by the society to thank for that, along with a lot of forensic evidence that appeared to have been tampered with and/or incompetently handled.

It hadn't been, of course, but no one in the legal system was ready to recognize the aftermath of supernatural murder. Even the lawyer the Twenty Palace Society hired thought I was being framed and tried to convince me to sue the Seattle PD.

I didn't bother. When I'd walked out of the courthouse just this afternoon, Annalise was waiting for me. Now I was here in this town, and I wasn't expecting to see the end of the week. What was the point of filing a bunch of legal papers?

The point of this digression into the not-so-distant past is that I had a history with cops and jails. I didn't want to go back. Also, I'd never broken into someone's house before. Not a stranger's house, at least.

So I felt an unfamiliar chill as I pushed the Bentons' front door open. The house was quiet. I hesitated before entering.

There's a feeling of power that comes from invading someone's space. I'd felt it when I'd stolen cars as part of Arne's crew. I'd sit behind a steering wheel, beside their fast-food wrappers or whatever, and know I was taking something very personal. A simple action like readjusting the seat—

"Would you hurry up?" Annalise snapped. "I don't want to stand here all night."

"Sorry," I said. "I've never done this before."

"Well, don't step in that," she said, pointing.

There was a long black streak on the carpet that led to the door. I hopped over it into the living room. The streak led out the door and turned left toward the sea. I was glad I hadn't stepped in it.

Annalise shut the door and surveyed the room. She laid the scrap wood against the wall. The design continued to churn.

I looked around the empty house. Could there be a predator somewhere here?

"What do we look for?" I asked.

"Start by following this snail trail to its source. I want to know what happened here and why. Look around. Be thorough. Don't turn on the lights. And keep your ghost knife handy."

That seemed straightforward. Annalise went into the kitchen while I knelt beside the streak.

An opening in the curtain allowed light from the streetlamps outside to shine on the carpet. I got down on my hands and knees beside it. The carpet fibers appeared to have been scorched, and although I couldn't smell smoke, I could smell the nasty, sterile tang I'd smelled in the gravel lot.

The streak went up the stairs. So did I. There were three bedrooms and a bathroom on the upper floor. The streak led to the back room, where it ended in the middle of the floor, surrounded by a heap of scorched blankets.

There were Kim Possible posters on the wall and little pink ponies on the dresser. A third child for the Bentons. A daughter.

There was a certificate on the wall that said she'd won her sixth-grade math bee. I didn't read it. I didn't want to know her name.

The room was cluttered and disorganized—she wasn't a tidy kid—but there were a couple of blank spaces. One was on the wall beside her certificates and awards. Another was a rectangular space in the center of her bureau, among the piled clothes and school papers. Everything had two or three months' worth of dust on it.

The nightstand beside her bed was a nest of photos in cheap frames, except for a blank space at the front edge. Four or five more photos lay on the carpet beside the bed. I picked them up, wishing that Annalise had given me gloves.

Most of them featured a dark-haired girl on the verge of puberty. She was small-boned, like Meg, but she carried a lot of flab, like Douglas. She wasn't a kid I would have noticed, but standing in her bedroom, knowing that the scorch marks on the floor probably marked the spot where she died, I felt a profound sense of loss.

The pictures showed her smiling with a group of friends. She was, if you believed the photos, a happy kid. I saw the cowlicked boy in one of the pictures and looked away.

There was a second dresser in a corner of the room. Beside it, a mattress and box spring stood against the wall. This dresser was older and held fewer mementos. A photo on the back corner showed the same younger daughter with an older girl with the same narrow glasses and pointy chin. A sister? I liked the challenging, mischievous expression on her face.

I noticed that there was no dust on this dresser or any of the knick-knacks. Someone had been cleaning it. Could Meg have been walking past the younger daughter's things to clean the older one's? It seemed so. Obviously, they still remembered the older sister.

The middle room was larger and had two beds. There was a definite clash of styles in here—the Wiggles versus Giant Japanese Robots.

On the younger side of the room, I noticed several more empty spaces amid the clutter. The older boy's things, however, had been torn apart. Drawers had been yanked out of the dresser and dumped on the floor. The closet had been ransacked, toys and books scattered.

Someone had packed in a panic.

I went back into the hall. The scorched black mark was still there. I noticed something funny about it and crouched down on the floor.

At the edge of the streaks were a couple of smaller burns. It was like a river that had one main channel and some small channels that separated for a short while and then rejoined the main flow.

The silver worms had made this trail. I'd suspected it, of course, from the moment I saw the trail leading out the door, but now I was sure.

I hopped over the scorched carpet and checked out the bathroom.

It was also in disarray. Toothbrushes had been scattered across the sink and floor. There were a lot of personal effects in here, from expensive salon conditioners to a paperback beside the toilet.

The hall closet was filled with towels and cleaning supplies. Everything was neatly folded and arranged. This had obviously been passed over during the frantic packing.

Last was the master bedroom, which looked like it had been tossed by the cops. I walked on the clothes on the floor because there was nowhere else to step. An abandoned crib at the foot of the bed was loaded with winter clothes. The end table had a pair of cheap paperbacks on it, along with a pair of alarm clocks and a pair of eyeglass cases. Behind the clocks sat a little box coated with a thin film of dust. I disturbed the dust opening the box. Inside was a pile of unused condoms.

The Bentons had skipped town like a drug mule who had been caught dipping into the product.

At this point, I started to feel dirty. This was too private, and there was too much grief and tragedy here. I was ashamed of the tingle of excitement I'd felt at the door.

And yes, it made me angry. Angry at Annalise for forcing me to come on this job. Angry at Meg and Douglas for having these problems. Angry at whoever had cast the spell that had burned these three kids.

I kicked the clothes on the floor into a pile in the corner but found only ordinary carpet underneath. No circles, sigils, or other signs of summoning magic.

I opened the bedroom closet and dug around. If I was going to do something I hated, I was going to do it quickly. I pulled stacks of clothes out of the back of the closet and uncovered a small safe. It was locked.

Annalise could probably tear it open, but I didn't need her help. I took out my ghost knife and sliced off the steel hinges and the lock. The safe door fell onto the floor.

Inside I found a long, slender box and a folder full of papers. I opened the box, revealing a diamond necklace.

I don't know much about jewelry, but it looked old, like necklaces I'd seen in old movies. It was probably an heirloom, and it was probably worth a lot of money, yet the Bentons had abandoned it in their rush for the county line.

I held on to the necklace longer than was strictly necessary. I had no job and no food in my belly. My bed and board were in the hands of a woman who hated my guts and wanted me dead. It would have been easy to slip this jewelry into my pocket. I needed money of my own if I was ever going to be free, and it wasn't like the Bentons were coming back for it.

I put the necklace back into the box and put the box back into the safe. I didn't think about it or try to reason it out. I just closed the box and moved on.

The folder was full of investment papers. Douglas had a 401(k), some stocks, and a house in Poulsbo that he rented out. There was a lot of money tied up in these papers, but they'd been abandoned, too. It looked like the Bentons were too busy saving their kid to worry about their investments. I was starting to like Douglas and Meg, tire iron or not.

Considering the find I'd made in the closet, I decided to check the closets in the bathroom and the rest of the bedrooms, too. None of them held anything of importance, and nothing otherworldly bit my arm off. I supposed I shouldn't have worried about the danger. If there was a predator in the house, Annalise's piece of scrap wood would have detected it.

Whether she would have told me about it is another matter, of course.

Once, not too long ago, I'd cast a spell from a stolen spell book to give myself a vision of a vast expanse of mist and darkness. The Empty Spaces. The Deeps.

There I'd seen predators moving through the void: colossal serpents, huge wheels of fire, groups of tumbling boulders that sang to one another and changed direction like a flock of birds. All of them were searching for living worlds to devour.

Then I came face-to-face with a predator that had come here, to our world. It was a parasitic bug the size of a house cat, and it had a hunger for human flesh. If I hadn't stopped it, it would have brought the rest of the swarm here to feed like locusts.

Before she'd discovered the truth about me, Annalise had told me a little about them. They were not demons or devils, with pitchforks and horns and contracts you sign in blood. They were simply creatures hunting for food—predators—and we were the food.

They were drawn to certain kinds of magic the way sharks were drawn to blood. People summoned and tried to control them for all sorts of reasons—to destroy enemies, to grant power, to guard, or even just to learn the secrets of the world behind the world. That house-cat-sized predator I'd destroyed had been brought here for its supposed healing powers.

The only thing the predators wanted was to be brought to a world where they could feed. *They love to be summoned,* Annalise had said, *but they hate to be held in place.*

She had told me that the second predator she'd ever seen was a strange, spongy lattice that was difficult to see even under bright light. The creature was only clearly visible when it was filled with the blood it fed on.

The man who had summoned it had killed derelicts and petty criminals for years to sustain it, prompting the press to call him "the Mad Butcher of Kingsbury Run" and "the Torso Killer." Annalise said she had no idea what that weird predator had done for him in return for all that blood, but she had personally burned them both to ash.

She wouldn't talk about the first predator she had seen.

Any of those predators, summoned to Earth and allowed to run loose, could scour the planet of life. That was why we had come to Hammer Bay—to make sure that, whatever was happening here, it was stopped.

I thought about that old friend of mine again, the one I'd crippled and who'd loved the Mariners. I had loved him like a brother and I'd nearly helped him—and the predator inside him—destroy the world.

My hand fell against my jacket pocket, feeling the laminated paper inside. Of the three spells I'd cast from that stolen book, the ghost knife was the only one I still had. I had a copy of that stolen spell book hidden away, but I hadn't decided what to do with it. There was power in it, absolutely, but spell casting was painful and dangerous, and if Annalise or one of the other peers found out that I still had it, they'd execute me on the spot. For the Twenty Palace Society, stealing magic was a capital crime.

I couldn't think of anything else to do on the second floor and went downstairs, stepping carefully around the marks on the carpet.

There was a message on the answering machine. Since Doug and Meg didn't seem likely to be coming back, I pushed Play. It was only thirty minutes old and was from someone named Jennifer. She sounded about fifteen. The message was for "Mom and Dad" and made clear her outrage that her parents were planning to pull her out of school—and away from all her friends in the dorm now that she'd finally made some—with only three weeks until finals. This, apparently, would ruin her chance to get into a decent college. Can anyone express contemptuous disbelief as purely and cleanly as a teenage girl? I pressed the Save button on the machine; I liked Doug and Meg too much to erase a message from their daughter.

Annalise stood in the dark kitchen, staring out the window. Her face was utterly blank. Something about her made me give her some space.

I looked away and noticed a crumpled sheet of paper in the corner. I picked it up but there wasn't enough light to read it.

Annalise glanced at me, her expression still inscrutable. I approached her and looked out the window, too.

In the next house over, a woman sat at her kitchen table, crying over a small, framed photo. I wondered how long she'd been sitting there, and how long Annalise had stood silently in the darkness, watching.

"What did you find?" she finally asked.

"Douglas and Meg, who think they hadn't been blessed with a boy until last whenever, have actually had five kids. Three boys and two girls. It sounds as if the older girl is at a boarding school somewhere. The younger girl died upstairs in her room, and the worms marked up this carpet as they made a run for the soil outside. I suspect the middle boy died in his car seat a while ago. They packed in a frantic rush, but only for the middle child. We saw what happened to him.

"They rushed off in such a hurry that they left jewelry and financial documents in the safe upstairs. It looks like they threw a bunch of clothes and crap into their car and took off.

"I didn't find any evidence of a spell, or a spell book, or predators. Nothing except that scorched streak in the carpet. That . . ." I wasn't sure how to continue. "Those worms that came out of the boy . . . those were predators, weren't they?"

Annalise didn't look at me. "Did you take the jewelry?"

"No," I said.

She started to pat me down. Without thinking, I drew away from her. That was a mistake.

Annalise grabbed my upper arm and squeezed—not hard enough to break the bone, but enough to remind me she could. I held myself very still.

I still had the ghost knife, of course, but I wasn't confident enough to try it against her. Maybe later, though. Maybe soon.

She searched me and I didn't do a damn thing about it. When she was done, she went back to the window without a word. I moved next to her and stared at the woman, too. Whatever Annalise was seeing, it didn't entrance me the way it did her.

Eventually, Annalise went upstairs to the master bedroom. I followed. She took the jewelry from the safe and laid the wood scrap against it. The sigil twisted at the same steady pace. The necklace was no more magic than anything else in the house. Annalise didn't seem surprised.

"So, boss," I finally said, "do you want to see what picture she's crying over?"

"Yes," she answered. Her funny little voice sounded small.

"Does it have anything to do with the job?"

She looked up at me. Her tiny eyes were shadowed and impossible to read. "I'll know soon enough, won't I?"

I walked out the front door, up the Bentons' walk, and down the sidewalk to the next house. The mailbox had the name FINKLER on it in gold stickers.

I rang the front doorbell. After about three minutes—a long wait, but I knew she had to wipe away tears and check herself in a mirror—I heard her turn the knob. I stepped down her front step, giving her space and putting myself below her. I wanted to be as nonthreatening as I could.

She opened the door without undoing a lock. I'd have placed her in her mid-forties, although she could have been older. She had grim lines around her mouth and eyes, and her face was puffy.

As I looked at her, her expression changed. The traces of sorrow vanished. Within a few seconds, she was as pleasant as if she had just been watching a dull sitcom. "Yes?" she said.

I wanted to tell her to lock her doors. What if some ex-con came by with some song-and-dance story? Instead I said: "I've been trying to reach the Benton family next door? I'm a day early? No one seems to be answering, though?" I let my voice rise at the end of each sentence, turning everything I said into a question.

"I saw them loading up their car. It looked like they were taking a trip."

"Really? They were expecting me. Aunt Meg was going to help me find a job."

"At the toy plant?"

"She didn't say. I guess so."

"And she's your aunt?" She looked at me carefully, measuring me.

"We haven't met. Our family is pretty spread out. I'm still not sure what I should call her. 'Mrs. Benton' sounds so formal, but I'm not comfortable yet calling her 'aunt' when we haven't even met." I kept vamping, wondering how much time Annalise would need.

"When you see her," Ms. Finkler interrupted, "ask her what she wants to be called. People should let people pick their own names."

"Welp, that makes a lot of sense."

"But they went on some kind of trip. You say you're early?"

"Only by a day."

"They looked like they were going to be gone longer than that. I don't know what to tell you. But if you want a job, you should go to the toy plant tomorrow. They're always hiring lately." She looked me up and down. "Wear something decent."

I smiled at her. It took an effort. "Thanks. I appreciate the advice."

"You're welcome." She closed the door.

I walked back to the van and climbed behind the wheel. Annalise hadn't told me where to meet her, but I hoped she knew better than to think I was going back to the Bentons' house. I drove around the corner, parked beside the alley, and waited.

The streetlight was overhead. I took the piece of paper I'd found on the floor of the living room and held it up to the light. It read:

> I'm putting this where you will find it. This is the only way we can talk about the truth. Every time I try to talk to you . . .
>
> We need to get away from here before we lose Justin and Sammy, too. I sent a postcard to my sister asking her to invite us for a visit. I told her to make it seem like an emergency. When she calls, let's run and never come back.
>
> I'm terrified and I don't know what to do. When I'm alone, I remember them just for a couple of minutes at a time. Do you remember them, too, in the middle of the night when no one else is around?
>
> I miss them terribly. I don't know what's happening. I just want to get away. I don't think I'm crazy. Am I crazy?
>
> I love you.

That was it. The note was unsigned, but it looked like a woman's handwriting.

They'd lost three of their kids, and while I didn't have kids of my own, a lifetime of Hollywood movies had convinced me it was the worst thing that could happen. Except they only knew it had happened in odd, lonely moments.

Why the Bentons? Who had targeted their kids, and why?

The passenger door swung open. Annalise climbed in.

"Everything go okay?" I asked.

"I'm hungry. Let's find someplace to eat."

I started the van. "What did you find out?" She didn't answer. I drove toward downtown.

Her silence annoyed me, but then I had a scary thought. What if I hadn't distracted Ms. Finkler for long enough? What if she'd caught Annalise in her kitchen?

Annalise had spells that could deal with people without taking their lives—I'd seen them in action—but she didn't always use them. She hadn't been all that concerned about catching Meg and Douglas in her green flame. They had survived only because I had knocked them back.

Annalise only cared about one thing: she searched for people who cast magic spells, especially those that summoned predators, and she killed them. Nothing else mattered to her. Certainly not innocent by-standers. They were expendable.

And, to tell the truth, I'd seen a little bit of her world, and I understood her. I'd seen what predators could do. With their appetites, they could devour every living thing on the planet.

Maybe we needed people like Annalise—people who were willing to do whatever it took to protect us. Without her, and others like her, maybe we wouldn't even be here now.

But I really hoped she hadn't killed that sad woman.

Annalise held the scrap wood in her hands, staring at the designs as if they were tea leaves. Whatever she could read there, it was pissing her off.

I turned into the business district and pulled into the parking lot of a Thai restaurant. I didn't know how good it would be, but pad thai wasn't rocket science and I'd been craving it for months. They didn't exactly let you order in from a jail cell.

"What are we doing here?" Annalise asked.

"Grub."

"I don't eat this. Find a place that serves burgers or steaks."

I sighed to let her know how disappointed I was and found a diner just a block farther down the road. As we entered, Annalise placed the scrap wood on the doorjamb. As far as I could tell, the designs continued to churn slowly, without any change. We went inside and found a booth.

By the clock above the counter it was nearly eleven. We'd had a busy day.

There were three or four other customers. All of them thought we were worth a good, long look. I couldn't blame them. Annalise was quite a sight in her oversized firefighter's jacket, tattoos, and clipped red hair. Standing next to her, I looked almost reputable.

The waitress came to our table. "New in town?" she asked. Annalise grunted.

"Just drove in," I said. I smiled politely, knowing what some wait-staff do to the food when they don't like a customer.

"Looking for work at the plant, I guess?"

"They really need people, huh?"

"Sure do," she said. She took our order. Annalise asked for iced tea and a grilled steak. When she was told they were out, she ordered a cheeseburger with bacon. It sounded so good I ordered the same thing but with a cola. Maybe the sugar would keep me awake.

As the waitress started to turn away, Annalise grabbed her hand.

The waitress tried to wrench herself free but couldn't break Annalise's grip.

Annalise laid the scrap wood on the woman's wrist, then let her go. The waitress quickly retreated behind the counter.

Great. I hoped I wouldn't be eating her spit later.

Annalise stared out the window. She looked distinctly unhappy.

I smiled. "Nice little town, huh?"

"I've been to some that were nicer. Smaller, too."

"So what's be—"

Annalise abruptly stood and moved toward the counter. The other customers had turned back to their own conversations, but one of the men at the counter tapped his companion. They watched her approach. Both were in their fifties and wore blue overalls smeared with machine oil.

"Excuse me," she said to them. She laid the wood against the first man's arm, then the second's. She moved to a booth in the corner and the last of the diner's customers: a pair of ladies who must have been in their seventies.

"Excuse me," Annalise said again. She laid the block against one woman's shoulder. After a second, she moved to the next.

The second woman flinched. "I don't—"

"It's all right," Annalise said, and laid the wood against the woman's arm. After a moment, she started back toward our table.

The first mechanic caught her eye as she passed. "If you're looking for something radioactive, honey, you put your hand on the wrong body part."

His buddy chuckled. Annalise walked by without comment. As she settled back into her seat, the waitress returned. She didn't seem terribly happy with us. "If you keep bothering other customers, I'm going to have to ask you to leave."

Annalise didn't acknowledge her. "Understood," I said.

The woman moved away from the table while keeping a wary eye on us. I wondered how long it would take for word about us to spread around town.

"I expected you to keep a lower profile," I said.

Again Annalise didn't acknowledge the remark.

"What's the matter? Turn off your emotion chip?"

She stared at me as though she was imagining me dead. I've seen that look before, but it's not something I've ever gotten used to.

I settled back in my seat and was silent. Annalise didn't need to talk to me. I was going to be dead soon.

I remembered the way the boy had split apart into a mass of worms and my stomach flip-flopped. Why had I ordered a cheeseburger with the works?

I didn't have the guts to keep pestering her. The peers of the Twenty Palace Society might have forbidden her to kill me, but I had no idea how or if they would enforce that rule. I knew very little about her society except that, like Annalise, they were sorcerers. Like Annalise, they killed predators and people who toyed with magic. Like Annalise, they hunted for copies of spell books.

One thing I did know: as powerful as Annalise was, she was one of the weaker peers in her society. It was a scary thought.

Our drinks arrived, then our burgers. Despite my queasiness, I tore into my food, my body's needs taking over. All my concerns about dead children and murderous sorcerers receded just far enough for me to fuel up.

Spit or no spit, the eating was good. I could see that Annalise was enjoying it, too.

"So," I said between bites, "do you think the Benton family was targeted specifically?"

Annalise looked at me like I was a bug that needed squashing. She took another bite of her burger and kept chewing.

"I found a slip of paper on the floor of their living room," I said. I took another bite of food, making her wait for the rest. Eventually, I said: "They could remember their kids when they were alone. They could see their kids' things and remember what happened to them. It was only when they were with other people that the memories were wiped away."

Annalise took another bite. I set my burger on the plate and leaned toward her.

"Is that what you found in Finklers' kitchen? A photo of her with her kids? Or maybe her grandkids? Was that why you were so entranced by her? A mother all alone, grieving over her children?"

Annalise became very still. She stared at me with all the warm gentility of a shark.

"I'm not trying to push your buttons," I lied, "but I can be useful. I want to help."

"I don't need your help," she said.

"If I'm going to be dead soon, it won't matter if you answer my questions."

"I don't want your help."

"I work for you," I said. "Your peers in the society, whoever they are and whatever that is, put me here to help you."

"You agreed to be my wooden man," she said. Her tone was even and low. "You lied to me and betrayed me. I attacked a peer because of you, and the closest friend I have ever had in my long life is dead. Because of you."

"I'm sorry about Irena," I said. "I liked—"

"I don't want to hear you talk about her. At all. If you say her name to me again, I will splinter every bone in your body, peers or no peers. Am I clear?"

At that moment, before I even realized it was possible, I stopped caring what she would do.

I'd spent the whole day in the van with Annalise, knowing she would eventually kill me. Before that, I'd sat in a jail cell for months waiting for someone in the society to collect my head.

People become accustomed to their circumstances. It was one of the many unpleasant truths I learned in prison. We can't be afraid all the time; our bodies can't sustain it.

I was getting used to Annalise's hatred and to my quite sensible fear of her. What I was not getting used to was my own ignorance. I didn't like stumbling around in the dark. I didn't even know what a "wooden man" was. I was pretty sure it involved more than just driving around.

So, against all common sense, I pressed on. "The way you've been frowning at your scrap of wood makes me think the Bentons were not specifically targeted. The design on that scrap moves when magic is nearby, right? And does other stuff when predators are close, right?

"But you've been frowning at it wherever we go. I think it's telling you the whole town is enchanted. It's picking up a lot of background static but not directing you to the source. Maybe those two mechanics have lost their kids, too. Maybe that waitress cries herself to sleep at night, thinking about the son who never came home from school."

Annalise sighed. "I usually drive around until the spell registers magic, then I home in on foot."

"What does it mean that the magic is so spread out?" I tried to keep my voice reasonable and calm. Professionalism breeds professionalism.

Annalise sopped up some ketchup with a fry. "It means I don't know what to do next."

The window beside us shattered. I covered my head as shards of glass rained over me. Annalise turned toward the window, her hand reaching under her jacket.

Broken glass covered my half-eaten burger. Ruined.

I turned my attention to Annalise. She was standing beside the broken window, staring into the street.

"What happened?" I asked.

"Him," she said.

I looked into the dark street. I couldn't see anyone, but I heard a voice. "Where are my daughters?" a man shouted. "Who stole my little girls from me?"

Then I saw him. He was tall and stooped, with lank hair hanging past his shoulders and a bare scalp on top. He was so skinny he looked like his skin had been shrink-wrapped around his bones.

And he was carrying a rifle.

It looked like a bolt-action hunting rifle, but he was all the way across the street just beyond the glow of a streetlight, so I couldn't be sure.

"Who took my daughters?" he shouted. A man and woman bolted from the cover of a parked car, sprinting for the corner. I clenched my teeth as the tall man noticed them. He aimed the rifle at them but didn't fire. The couple reached the corner and safety.

"Where are they?" he shouted again. "Who stole my little girls from me?"

"He remembers," I said to Annalise. "Just like we do. How can he remember his kids?"

"I don't know," she said. "Go ask him."

CHAPTER THREE

She wasn't joking. She wasn't smiling. She just looked at me, waiting to see if I'd flinch.

I did. Hell, who wouldn't?

But I still made my way toward the front door. When it came down to a choice of facing a gunman or my boss, it would be the gunman every time.

One of the two mechanics had ushered the old ladies out of their booth and led them into the kitchen. The other mechanic and the waitress crouched beside the door, peering out into the street from the dubious cover of a foam-padded wooden bench. The cook left the relative safety of the kitchen and joined them.

The waitress swore under her breath. "Old Harlan has finally gone round the bend."

The mechanic dared a glance into the street. "I thought Emmett Dubois confiscated his guns."

The waitress let out a contemptuous grunt. She didn't think much of Emmett Dubois.

"Whose guns?" I asked as I crouched beside them. We were all keeping our voices low.

"Harlan's," the waitress said. I glanced out the window. Harlan sighted along his rifle, slowly turning toward us. I ducked back down before he saw me.

"This Harlan guy," I said. "I take it he's local color?"

The mechanic snorted. "You could put it that way."

The cook came up behind me. "He fell off a ladder in '97 putting up Christmas lights. Hit his head. He ain't been right since."

"He was never a bad guy, though," the mechanic said.

The cook scowled at him. "Tell that to my window, and these customers he nearly killed."

"What was he shouting about?" the waitress asked.

"His daughters," I answered her. "He wants to know who took his daughters away."

"Why, that's just crazy," she said. "He doesn't have any little girls. He never has."

"What the hell?" the cook said. His sour breath was right next to my ear. "Your girlfriend is just sitting in her booth like a duck in a shooting range. Don't she care about her own life?" He scrambled across the dirty floor toward her.

"Care about her own life?" I said. "Where's the fun in that?" Before anyone could stop me, I opened the front door and bolted into the street.

I didn't look at Harlan. I looked at the Corolla I was planning to use as cover.

I hit the pavement and rolled behind the wheel. I heard a shot and more glass breaking in the diner behind me. Someone cursed up a storm, which I'm sure was directed as much at me as at old Harlan.

I scuttled across a patch of grass and put my head right against the hubcap. There was a tree beside me, but the trunk was no wider than my hand. I wasn't counting on it for protection. "Stop shooting!" I shouted. "I'm trying to help you!"

"Can you tell me where my girls are?" There was a dangerous edge to his voice.

"No," I said. "I'm—"

"Then butt the hell out!"

I heard another rifle shot. The bullet punched a hole through the car door beside me and tore bark off the skinny tree. I hunkered down lower.

"I can help you," I shouted. I looked back at the diner and saw Annalise sitting by the window. She stared at me blankly. My situation meant no more to her than a dull television show. I saw the top of the cook's head as he beckoned her to safety.

"I can help you!" I shouted again, louder this time. If Harlan came toward me, I'd be screwed. My tattoos only protected part of me. I wasn't sure how well they'd hold up against a rifle.

"How?" he answered.

"Look, let me stand up and talk to you. My name is Ray. I came here to find out what's happening to the kids in this town."

"You did?"

"I'm standing up now. Hear me out before you shoot me, okay?"

I stood. Harlan had moved toward me into the street. He aimed his rifle at me.

No matter how hard you try, there's really no steeling yourself to see a brain-damaged redneck point a gun at your face.

He saw my hands were empty, and he started glancing from side to side as if he suspected I was a decoy.

"Harlan, my name is Ray."

"You said that already."

I had, but I hoped he would be reluctant to shoot me if he had a name to go with my face.

Harlan was younger than I expected, barely into his mid-thirties. His face was narrow and gleaming with sweat. His long nose curved over a thin, unhappy mouth. His clothes looked like they hadn't been washed in weeks. He'd have been scary without a gun.

"Harlan, do you know who Justin Benton is?"

"Nope," he answered. He shifted his grip on his rifle and looked up the street. He was getting antsy. Where were the police sirens? It had been more than two minutes since that first shot.

"He was a little boy who lived in this town. Earlier today, I saw him burn up."

Harlan burst into tears. The barrel of his gun wavered, then angled toward the asphalt. "My girls," he said, his voice small and broken with pain. "My girls."

"Is that what happened to them?" I asked.

"I don't know. The Monday after Thanksgiving, Lorelei didn't come home from school. I went nuts looking for her. But . . . but . . ."

"But the people in this town acted as though they'd never heard of her. They acted as though she didn't exist."

"They're liars!" he shouted, his grief flaring into anger. He didn't point his gun at me. "And the next week, my little Marie disappeared from her bed. Right in the middle of the night. And . . ."

He couldn't go on. I helped. "And there was a black mark on the floor. A long, scary mark. It led to the door—"

"The window." He approached me slowly. There was no threat in the way he moved.

"And it disappeared into the dirt. Now no one in town remembers either of your girls."

"They don't remember any of the kids! Not even their own!" His face was slack with astonishment. He'd apparently forgotten that he'd just accused the whole town of lying to him. Maybe he'd never really believed it. "Even after they saw it happen with their own two eyes! They still have tricycles sitting in their front yards and Happy Meal wrappers on their dashboards, but it's like they can't see them!"

"*You* saw it, though, didn't you? You saw it happen right here in town."

"Five times."

"Is it always kids? Does it happen to adults, too?"

"Only kids. Never adults. My God, every single person in this town must have seen it, but I'm the only one who remembers." His eyes welled up with tears. The rifle hung loose in his hand. "Why am I the only one who remembers? And why do I feel this pressure in my head! It's been there for months, since before my Lorelei vanished. It's driving me wild!"

"Harlan, I'm new in town but I came here to find out what's happening in Hammer Bay. I can't promise that I can get your girls back, but I'm going to find out what's going on."

I saw hope in his expression. He was a tired man, with a heavy load of grief. He'd been carrying it for nearly half a year, but he wasn't so far gone that he couldn't recognize a helping hand when it was offered.

"Can you do that?"

"Man, I don't know," I told him. "But I intend to try. I have some questions for you, and I'm going to want to check out the black mark in your house, but I'm not going to be able to do any of that if you shoot me."

Harlan looked down at the gun in his hand and blinked.

I kept my voice low. "Can I have that gun, please?" That was when we heard the sirens.

Harlan backed away and lifted the rifle. "I'm not crazy," he yelled. "I was married. I had two little kids!"

Goose bumps prickled on my neck. "I know, Harlan. I believe you."

"Someone in this town is going to tell me where they are. Someone knows what's happened to them."

"Harlan," I said. His expression had become hard and distant. "You're that someone. None of these people can remember. Only you."

A police car turned the corner and stopped in the road, lights flashing.

Harlan looked at it like a man nearing the end of a big job. Suddenly, I understood. He was done. His kids were gone, and he was going to commit suicide by cop.

"Harlan, don't do it. There are other kids in town," I said, thinking of the two kids at the gas station. "You could help me put a stop to this. You might be the only one who—"

He leveled the gun at my chest. His face was calm. "Why don't you go back into the diner now," he said in a resigned voice. "Before something bad happens to you."

He was aiming at my chest. Would the tattoos there protect me if he squeezed the trigger?

I had no idea how to talk him down. I imagine cops and paramedics are trained in that sort of thing, but I was just an ex–car thief.

I laid my hand against the pocket containing my ghost knife. I could feel it there, thrumming with life. If talking wouldn't work . . .

Harlan turned away from the flashing lights on the patrol car and looked up the street. His eyes narrowed. I followed his gaze.

A wolf stood in the road. I'd never seen one outside a zoo before, but I recognized it immediately. The fur along its back was tinged with red, and it stared at us, standing sideways as though it wanted to present the largest possible target.

It was big. I don't know much about wolves, but it looked much bigger than I'd have expected. Then again, when Harlan had pointed his rifle at me, it looked like a .90 caliber. Fear can do that.

Harlan swung the rifle to his shoulder and fired. I saw the bullet chip the asphalt between the animal's legs. The wolf bolted, running down the street and out of sight.

Harlan worked the bolt of his rifle. I slid my hand into my pocket and took out my ghost knife.

Harlan saw me out of the corner of his eye. He spun and slammed the butt of his rifle against my hand, smashing it against my hip. The ghost knife fell onto the street, and I staggered a few feet away from it.

He aimed the rifle at my face. I didn't have any tattoos to protect me there.

"It was just a piece of paper," I said.

Harlan glanced at the ghost knife and confirmed that what I was saying was true. Without a word, he swung his weapon around and sighted down the street, looking for the wolf.

I had cast the spell that created the ghost knife, and I could sense it there on the asphalt. I opened my hand and *reached* for it. The laminated paper flew into my hand, and in one motion, I threw it at Harlan like an oversized playing card.

According to the spell book I'd copied it from, a ghost knife cuts "ghosts, magic, and dead things." The wood and metal locks of the Bentons' front door were dead things, and the ghost knife cut through them easily. It could also destroy magic spells like my tattoos or the sigil on Annalise's scrap of wood; the results weren't always pretty.

But every living person has a ghost in them. At least, the spell thinks so, because when I use it on people, it passes through their bodies as though they aren't there and cuts at their "spirit."

And that's all I know about it. Even though I cast the spell myself from an old book I'd acquired under less-than-honest circumstances, and even though I'd used it a few times against people who were trying to kill me, I had no idea how it worked or what it truly did. As with so much else having to do with magic, Annalise, and her society, I was in the dark.

The ghost knife zipped across the few feet separating us and entered Harlan's body just below his armpit. His shirt fell open where the ghost knife sliced through it, but the laminated paper plunged into his body without leaving a visible mark. A moment later, the spell exited through the other side as if he wasn't even there.

Harlan sagged. His eyes dulled, and whatever was driving him to shoot up the town dwindled away. That's what the ghost knife did; it stole away aggression and vitality for a while. The effects of the spell were temporary—at least, they seemed to be.

Harlan lowered his rifle. I stepped toward him, ready to take the weapon away. The left side of Harlan's rib cage burst open. I never heard the gunshot. I only saw the exit wound. Blood splattered my left hand, and I felt the bullet whiz past me.

Harlan collapsed, falling onto his face on the street.

I looked up and saw a cop moving toward us, his revolver pointed at Harlan. "Move away!" the cop yelled. "Move away from the body!"

I was frozen in place. The cop pointed the gun at my face. He asked me who I was, and I told him.

He told me to move back again. I took a step back. The cop kicked the rifle just like they do on TV. It slid away up the street.

I heard a faint sucking noise and looked down.

"He's alive," I said.

"An ambulance is coming," the cop said. "Don't move."

The cop was in his mid-fifties, with a good bit of muscle and a little paunch. He had long, slightly graying hair, which he combed back like a European movie star. His face, though, was scarred and rounded as though it had been punched too many times. His jaw was long and heavy, and the look in his eyes was slightly feral.

He looked down at Harlan and smiled slightly, as though the dying man was a nifty bit of entertainment.

"Where's that ambulance?" I asked. I couldn't hear sirens.

He looked at me as though he thought I might be his next fun project. "*On its way,* I said. Who are you again?"

"Raymond Lilly," I said again. "Harlan has a punctured lung. He needs help right now."

Someone said: "Did you get him?" I looked up and saw two more officers approaching. One bore a close resemblance to the first cop—a younger brother, I assumed. Except this new arrival hadn't shaved in about a week and was chewing the ragged end of a burning cigar. The other cop had too much flab pressing down on his belt, and his face was red and shiny with exertion.

"I surely did," the older cop said.

They stood around Harlan's body, looking down at him as if he was about to turn into candy. I still couldn't hear ambulance sirens. The fat one licked his lips in a way that gave me chills. None of them moved to help him.

So I did. The three cops jumped back and trained their weapons on me, but I didn't look at them. I laid my hand over the wound on Harlan's back, then slid my other hand under him, searching for the exit. When I found it, I covered it with my palm. I tried to seal the wounds with my hands. Harlan seemed to be breathing a little better. Maybe it was my imagination.

"What are you doing there, son?"

I wasn't sure which of them was talking to me. "Trying to save his life."

"Why?"

"I thought you might want to shoot him again later."

I heard chuckling behind me. Someone thought that was funny. Ambulance sirens came next, finally.

Harlan tried to say something but couldn't manage it. Kneeling in the street, I tried not to think about what I was doing. A crazy man who hadn't bathed in weeks was bleeding all over my hands, and three cops were pointing their guns at me.

I heard more voices. The folks in the diner had come out into the street to gawk, and the sports bar up the street was emptying, too.

Annalise came near. "Boss," I said, catching her attention. "I think I dropped a piece of paper around here somewhere. Would you find it? It might be our map."

She understood immediately. We couldn't leave a spell lying out on the street for anyone to pick up. I could have called it to me again, but an awful lot of people were watching.

She moved off toward the far side of the street. The older cop followed her. They talked, but I couldn't hear them. The waitress and the mechanic were loudly telling the fat cop what I had done, and how I had almost talked Harlan into giving up his rifle. They were split over whether that meant I was brave, stupid, or both; their voices drowned out whatever the older officer was saying to Annalise.

The ambulance finally arrived and the EMTs gently shouldered me out of the way. I scuttled toward the curb, happy to sit and watch professionals at work. A chubby little guy with too much beard taped plastic over the gunshot wound. Beside him, his lean and hairless partner snipped the finger from a latex glove and then slid a long needle through the fingertip. They rolled Harlan onto his back. The bearded guy covered the exit wound with more plastic while his partner searched Harlan's ribs for a place to insert the needle.

I didn't watch. Weariness washed over me as my adrenaline ebbed. I was tempted to lie back in the street and go to sleep.

I wondered if I was going to be sleeping in jail tonight. I hoped not. It was too soon.

The older cop with the movie-star hair and the roadhouse face crouched beside me. "Your, uh, companion there tells me you came out to talk old Harlan out of shooting up the town."

"That's right," I said. I wanted to stand, but I didn't want to smear my bloody hands against the street. It was a weird impulse, but it was a day for weird.

I glanced at the man's badge. He was the chief of police. The name tag beneath read E. DUBOIS. This was Emmett, I guessed, who hadn't confiscated all of Harlan's guns.

"Hold on there a moment," the cop said. He stepped over and conferred with the fat cop standing just a few feet away. The fat cop walked away, and the older one came back. "That wasn't the smartest thing in the world to do," he said. "Why did you do it?"

"I didn't think about it, really," I lied.

"Good Samaritan?"

I didn't respond to that. The fat cop returned with a plastic squeeze bottle and a wad of paper towels. The bottle was labeled "waterless cleaner." I thanked him, squeezed the bottle over my hands, and started washing the blood away. The cleaner felt like jelly and smelled like rubbing alcohol.

"Witnesses said you'd just about talked him down when we showed up."

I understood where this was going. He didn't want people saying that I'd almost handled the situation diplomatically when he'd come in with guns blazing.

"I hadn't talked him down from anything," I said. "I had the impression that he was planning a suicide by cop."

"That's better. Much better than a smart mouth. I didn't much care for your remark about shooting Harlan again. I didn't like having to shoot him."

I remembered the way he'd smiled at Harlan's bleeding body and knew he was lying. "Sorry about that," I told him. "I was all worked up with adrenaline."

He smiled that same smile. "Fine," he said. "That's just fine."

He asked where I was from and why I was in town, but he seemed distracted and his questions were careless. I managed to avoid saying that I'd been in jail that morning. He didn't seem to care about me, now that I'd apologized.

I watched the ambulance drive away. "Where are they taking him?"

The cop eyeballed me, as if trying to decide whether answering my question would undermine his authority.

"County hospital," he said. "You planning to visit?"

"Yep. I'm a Good Samaritan."

"Fine. That's fine." A brown, rusted Dodge Dart parked at the intersection, a little too close to the police car already there. A fourth cop, this one tall and slender, moved out of the shadows to intercept the driver. As he stepped into the light, I saw bright red hair on the top of his head.

"That's our local paperboy," the cop said. "You better go now if you don't want to be here all night answering his questions. But stay in Hammer Bay for a couple days, understand?"

"I intend to."

Annalise stood on the sidewalk a few yards away, the broken windows of the diner behind her. Her eyes were hooded and her face expressionless.

As I approached her, the cook stepped up to me. "You cost me a door," he said. "Harlan busted my glass door because you wanted to be a hero. What if one of my customers had been shot, huh? What then?"

"Don't you pay any attention to him," the waitress said. "Anytime you want, you come back and have another burger. On me."

The cook turned on her. "What about my window?"

She told him that's what insurance was for, and the cook grumbled that all the different kinds of insurance in this town were going to put him in the gutter.

I edged away from them and stepped up to Annalise. I could feel the ghost knife on her somewhere. Good. I didn't want it to fall into just anyone's hands, and I didn't want to stick around here any longer.

She held out her hand. "Keys," she said. "You're not driving my van until you wash your hands."

I hesitated, hoping she would offer me the ghost knife. She didn't. I could feel that it was nearby, probably right in her pocket. I wondered how long she was going to keep it, because I sure couldn't take it from her. I dug the keys from my pocket and gave them to her.

There was a change in the noise behind me. I turned back toward the crime scene.

New people had arrived, and Emmett Dubois was speaking with them. They were four men: one was very tall, very lean, and somewhere in his late fifties; beside him was a younger man, also tall, also lean, with a thick head of dark hair. Another was a short man with a shaved head, and the last was a fat man with long, graying hair. Dubois's body language had altered. He didn't look imposing. I only caught a glimpse of them before they moved out of view behind a parked van.

Then I felt a twinge under my right collarbone. There was no wave of force this time, but I knew what that twinge meant. Another kid had caught fire somewhere.

One of the men talking to Emmett Dubois fell to the ground and flailed around. My view was partly blocked by the wheels and fender of the van, but I could see he was having a seizure. It was the tall young one with the dark hair.

Dubois bent down to him. "Medic!" he shouted, his voice worried.

"Let's go," Annalise said.

"Look," I told her. "At the same time that I felt the—"

"I know. Let's move."

She dragged me toward the van and drove away from the scene. I glanced back and saw the little reporter trying to climb back into the Dart. The officer was blocking his way.

"Well?" Annalise said as we pulled into the street. There was very little traffic. Men walked down the street, guns in their hands. They didn't look like citizens protecting their own. They swaggered and looked bored.

I told Annalise what I'd learned from Harlan. I mentioned that he had a black mark on the floor of his home, too. Annalise asked a lot of questions I couldn't answer, like where he lived and how old his kids had been. She didn't like that I hadn't gotten those answers, and his punctured lung wasn't a good enough excuse.

I knew she was just riding me, so I let it pass. I was too tired to be angry anyway.

I said: "Sorry I didn't get killed."

"There's always next time," she said.

CHAPTER FOUR

Aɴɴalise drove aroᴜɴd until we found a motel. She had to circle the block twice before she turned down the right street, but we got there eventually.

It was a small place, one story, just a parking lot ringed by rooms, all their doors facing inward.

My shirt was speckled with blood and my jacket had greasy black smears down the back. Annalise made me wait in the van while she rented our rooms. While I sat, I saw that one of the rooms had a black streak on the front walk. It came from under the door, turned forty-five degrees to cross the pavement, and disappeared at the muddy lot.

That was interesting. Going that direction, the worms had to travel farther before they could tunnel into the earth than if they'd gone straight—at least ten feet farther. Were they being drawn toward something in the west? Maybe it was the Pacific.

Annalise emerged with the room keys. Thankfully, I didn't have the room with the black streak. "Clean up," she said. "We're getting an early start tomorrow."

She went into her room and I went into mine next door. I stripped off my clothes in the bathroom and examined them in the bright lights by the sink. My jacket, shirt, and pants were nasty. I needed a laundromat and some industrial detergent. I wasn't going to get them. I took the clothes into the shower, washed off the waterless cleaner and blood, then scrubbed at every spot of blood on my clothes I could find. The blood was still wet, and the clothes came clean fairly well. I tried not to think about what sort of diseases Harlan might have had. I just wanted to be clean.

Eventually, I ran out of steam. I hung the clothes on chairs by the heater and turned it on low. Then I fell onto the polyester bedcovers and disappeared into dreamless slumber.

It seemed like an instant later that Annalise thumped on my door, hitting it hard enough to rattle it in the jamb. I climbed out of bed, wrapped a blanket around me, and opened the door.

She had changed her clothes, switching her fireman's jacket for simple brown leather. Her pants were black and her shirt a white button-down that looked a size too big for her. Her boots had been exchanged for simple black leather walking shoes.

She barely glanced at me. "Get dressed. We have a lot to do today." She tossed the keys to me.

My clothes were still wet, but they were all I had. There were traces of Harlan's blood that I had missed the night before. Damn. I put the nasty clothes on my clean body and went out to the van. I left the jacket in the garbage.

It was just after 7 A.M. The sky was gray, and there was a steady drizzle. I was hungry but I couldn't picture myself sitting at a restaurant with wet, bloody clothes. I just drove, hoping to find a drive-through somewhere.

Instead, Annalise had me turn into a side street beside an outdoorsman's store. Aside from the diner, which had cardboard taped over the broken windows, it was the only place open at this hour.

Annalise led me inside and bought me new clothes. They weren't fancy—four pairs of jeans, four black long-sleeved pullover shirts, four pairs of white socks, one pair of black hiking boots, one windbreaker with a zip-out lining.

The clerk held open a trash bag and I threw in all my old things, including my sneakers, which were rimmed with Harlan's blood. I hadn't even noticed. He threw all that old stuff away, and I walked out in new clean clothes.

It felt good. I wondered if the four pairs of clothes meant she expected me to live another four days.

Next, we stopped off for breakfast. We chose a different diner this time. Annalise ordered very rare steak with eggs and a side of ham. The waitress looked dubious, but Annalise packed all of it away.

Her tattoos were visible above the open collar of her shirt and at the edges of her sleeves. They looked like mine, which meant they were made with a paintbrush and a spell, not a needle and ink. They were just as permanent, though.

I didn't know who had given them to Annalise, but I wondered if she'd been conscious for it. I'd been awake for part of my own tattooing, and the pain had been worse than anything I'd ever experienced in my life, with the exception of casting my ghost knife spell.

I absentmindedly touched the spot below my right collarbone where I'd been feeling twinges for the last few hours. My fingertips registered the touch of normal flesh, but my chest registered nothing at all. The parts of my body marked with spells couldn't feel a thing.

And those spells had come from Annalise. I wondered if she could sense them—and me—the way I could sense the ghost knife. I also wondered if my tattoos had been as painful for her to cast as my ghost knife had been for me. When I'd created the ghost knife, channeling all the energy needed to power it had been like dousing myself with gasoline and setting myself on fire.

It was possible that I'd cast the spell incorrectly, but what if I hadn't? Annalise might have had to go through that same pain when she'd put these marks on me, and when she created each of the ribbons she carried. I didn't want to think about that.

Her abilities went beyond the marks though. Her strength was incredible, and she could heal herself by eating meat, the more raw the better. She also wore that vest full of spells, which was probably back in her room with the fireman's jacket.

I wondered what effect all those spells had on her. Was she still human? Would she still be human even if her body changed into something monstrous, as long as she thought like a human? I wondered how much her quest to hunt down and destroy dangerous magic had changed her. I wondered how it would change me, before she put an end to me.

Of course, the only reason my mind was wandering this way was because I had no one to talk to. Annalise sawed at her food and shoveled it into her mouth, one bite after the other.

The silence became annoying. I asked Annalise why Harlan was the only one who remembered his kids. She didn't answer. She didn't even look up from her plate. I asked her if she thought we'd find someone else like Harlan in town. No answer. I asked her where she grew up.

She stopped eating and looked up at me. It was not a friendly look. Fine. I dropped the subject. I got a Seattle newspaper off the rack and began to read it.

Hammer Bay was too far away from the city for Harlan's shooting to make the paper, but surprise surprise, I found a small mention of me in the local news section.

It was strange to read about myself in the newspaper. It was like being in a crowded room where everyone else suddenly sat down but

I didn't have a chair. I felt exposed. Maybe that was absurd, but that's how it felt.

The article was on the fourth page, and it was barely one and a half column inches. It said, simply and quickly, that Raymond Lilly, convicted felon, had been released from police custody in the matter of the several slayings, followed by a list of the dead. It was quite a laundry list of names. The official reason given for my release was insufficient evidence to charge me with murder, attempted murder, kidnapping, drug trafficking, assault and battery, and breaking and entering. They left out grand theft auto and discharging a weapon within city limits. Maybe they'd been short on space.

What the article didn't mention was that certain prominent local citizens claimed that I had saved their lives while those crimes were being committed. It also glossed over the forensics reports that stated the people I had supposedly killed seemed to have been dead for days or weeks before they met me.

I looked over the list of names again. Some were strangers to me, but there were several I had known all too well. It still made me heartsick to think about them, even after all these months.

Irena's name wasn't on the list. I wondered if her body had been tidied away by the society, and I wondered if they would do that for me when my time came. Would people think I'd left the country or changed my identity? I didn't have much in the way of family or friends anymore, but I had an aunt who'd opened her home to me when no one else would. I'd hate for her to think I wasn't grateful or wanted nothing to do with her.

Annalise finished her meal. I showed her the article, but she didn't care. I finished my breakfast while she paid the bill. I didn't feel like eating anymore, but I'd need the fuel later.

We got back into the van, and Annalise handed me a slip of paper with an address on it. I consulted the ridiculous tourist map and saw that it was near the toy factory.

We drove there through the mist and drizzle, and I realized that it *was* the toy factory.

The factory was actually two buildings. The first was a glass office building, four stories high, with curves instead of corners. If it had been in a corporate campus or an urban downtown, and if it had been ten stories taller, it might have seemed sleek and prosperous. Here it looked rinky-dink.

The second building was an old warehouse. It stretched from the edge of the office building toward a thick stand of pines and a steep slope that could have been the outer reaches of the Olympic Mountains. The warehouse was three stories tall, although I doubted there were actually floors inside. It was ringed with cars, mostly new, inexpensive models—Kias, Hyundais, that sort of thing.

There was no guard at the entrance to the campus. I pulled in and found a space at the west end of the lot.

I climbed out. The ocean lay before me, just within the limits of visibility in the misty weather. It had been a while. To the south I saw the shape of the lighthouse marked on the tourist map. It was also obscured by fog, so I couldn't see much detail, but it was certainly picturesque.

Annalise and I walked to the front of the office building. The two spaces closest to the building were reserved. There was a Prius parked in Charles Hammer's parking spot. He was a man who drove with a conscience. A black S-class Mercedes was parked beside it.

I opened the door and held it for her. She carried a worn leather satchel like she knew what we were doing; I followed along.

The lobby was simple and elegant, if a little low-budget. Annalise stalked up to the receptionist, told the woman her name, and said she had a meeting with Charles Hammer.

The receptionist wore a name tag that read CAROL and had a burning hoop with a squiggle of black lines inside that, at first glance, looked like the sigil on my ghost knife or on Annalise's ribbons. After a second, I realized it was a stylized HBT, for Hammer Bay Toys. Carol looked at her schedule, then picked up her phone and told the person at the other end of the line that Mr. Hammer's ten o'clock had arrived. She hung up, smiled at us, and told us it would be just a moment.

The lobby had a slate floor and walls lined with something stained to look like unweathered cedar. A wide flight of concrete stairs swept up to the next floor. I toyed with the idea of asking the receptionist for a job application. Everyone in town seemed to think I should, so why not? It would certainly annoy Annalise. I was wearing clothes she'd bought, had a belly full of food she'd paid for, and had slept in a room she'd rented. I felt like her personal toy, one she would break at her whim. The urge to annoy her was strong.

The elevator dinged, interrupting that dangerous train of thought. A man of about sixty walked out. He wore a six-hundred-dollar suit, three-hundred-dollar shoes, and a twelve-dollar haircut. He had a wide, playful smile on his face. His eyes reminded me of twinkling plastic.

"Ms. Powliss," he said, extending his hand. There was a little hitch in his smile as he took in Annalise, then his grin redoubled. "I'm Able Katz, vice president of operations. How was your flight?"

"I drove. I don't like to have my head in the clouds. It's nice to meet you, Mr. Katz."

Able turned to me, waiting for Annalise to introduce us. She didn't. "I'm Ray Lilly," I said, to end his discomfort.

"That's a familiar name. Have you been to New York?"

"I haven't," I confessed. He shrugged, smile still in place.

"Shall we?" He stepped toward the elevator. Annalise didn't order me back to the car, so I followed them.

We rode to the top floor in the tiny elevator. The cramped space made us all stand slightly too close together, so we said nothing. The elevator dinged again and Able led us out.

I looked around the office as we walked through it. There were desks everywhere but no cubicle walls. Carts and shelves were packed with stacks of papers, disorganized jumbles of folders, and assorted toys. Many of the toys were posed in various positions of everyday life. Heroic action figures sat around a tiny table holding flowery teacups. Barbie-type dolls dressed as Marie Antoinette posed like country-western line dancers. A tiny soldier seemed to be pondering a spreadsheet of sales figures, and another passionately embraced a coffee cup.

The toys made me smile. In fact, they made me feel damn good. I suppressed the urge to pick one up and put it in my pocket.

All the employees were middle-aged women. Every few seconds one of them would stop typing or whatever and touch one of the toys—just lay a finger on it or adjust its position slightly—with an absent expression that suggested it was an old habit.

An action figure dressed as an ancient Greek warrior but mounted on a huge eagle sat on the edge of a file cabinet. I ran my finger along the front edge of its wing and felt a sudden contentment. I could have played with that toy all day.

Three of the office workers were watching me closely. I left it where it was.

"I'm afraid my office is a little cluttered right now," Able said. "But we have a conference room set up."

"That's fine," Annalise answered.

I tried to study her face to see if she was drawn to the toys, too, but I couldn't get enough of a glimpse to tell. Able Katz seemed to be perfectly fine, and the workers around us seemed basically normal. One woman burst out laughing as we walked past. Able glanced over and saw that she was looking at a toy train with hands that were holding a jump rope. Suddenly, all the women began to handle the toys and smile.

Able grinned. That was just what he wanted to see.

He opened a glass door and stepped aside to let Annalise and me into the conference room. The windows were large and scrupulously clean. I couldn't see the ocean from here, but I could see the town. Hammer Bay spread out before me, stretching north toward the hills.

"I was surprised to hear from Jimmy Larson," Able said. "I haven't spoken to him since we were at Mattel. How do you know him?"

"Excuse me for one moment," Annalise said. She drew the scrap wood out of her satchel and held it so that only she and I could see the moving design. The lines seemed to be moving more quickly than usual. It wasn't a big difference, but it was there. She turned to Able Katz and said: "Will Charles Hammer be joining us? My meeting was with him."

"Mr. Hammer was unavoidably detained," Able responded. For an absurd moment, I thought he meant that he'd been arrested. "When one of his creative jags comes on, he goes into seclusion to work out the new toy."

"I'm disappointed," Annalise said.

"I understand. I'm sorry. However, I can pass to him any information you give me here."

"Before we do that," Annalise said. "I'd like you to indulge me in one favor. Hold your hand out, as if you were stopping traffic."

"And why would I do that?"

"Because I'm rich and eccentric and I'm asking you to."

Able looked at us for a moment, then shrugged. He held out his hand, fingers pointing toward the ceiling and palm facing us. Annalise laid the scrap wood against him. The moving design didn't change. She scowled and returned the scrap to her satchel. "Thank you."

Able laughed. "Jimmy warned me you would be a creative type. In this business, you get used to odd things."

"It's funny Jimmy would say that about me. He's never met me. And I'm not creative at all. What I am is an activist."

"Okay. What cause?"

"Human survival."

"I can get behind that," Able said. He snuck a glance at his watch. "But I don't know why you've come to me."

Annalise began her pitch then. It was about the clothes they made and sold for some of their fashion dolls. Annalise knew they made them locally, and she had a company in Africa that could do the work cheaper and where the people needed the wages more. She was calm and articulate, and I'd had no idea she could string so many words together at once.

"I wish I'd known this was what our meeting would be about. I could have saved you the trouble. Mr. Hammer is adamant about sending work overseas. He won't do it under any circumstances. He started this company, in part, to revitalize Hammer Bay. See, he's also an activist, but his sole cause is the survival of the town his great-grandfather founded."

Annalise pressed him. She knew he had more orders than he could fill, and that he'd turned buyers away at the last toy fair. The company—

Able interrupted her. He understood and respected her passion for her cause. He'd had her checked out before the meeting, but if he'd known *this* was what she wanted, he would have saved her the trip. Mr. Hammer would rather burn the company to the ground than outsource the work.

Able looked at his watch again. I could see it was a lost cause. The absent Mr. Hammer had made his feelings known, and Able Katz didn't have the authority to make this decision and didn't want it. He just wanted to get on with his workday.

"I'm sorry," he said. "I have another meeting to prepare for. I sympathize with you, I really do, but I can't help. Here." He took a pen from inside his jacket and wrote on the back of a business card. Then he passed the card to Annalise. "Chuck is an old friend from New York. Talk to him about the problems he's been having with the clothes for his snow ninja line. Okay?"

Annalise took the card from him. "I still want to talk to Charles Hammer."

Able's smile faltered. Not even a thank-you from her. "He's in seclusion working on a new line. He can't be disturbed." He stood to show us out.

We stood, too. "You're protective of him," I said.

Able turned toward me. His smile was a little strained. "Absolutely," he said. "He's earned it."

"How?" I asked. "I don't mean to pry, but I'm really curious. Why did you leave New York to come to Hammer Bay, Washington?"

Able shrugged. "Four years ago I was bringing down six figures with my own marketing-and-consulting firm. We designed ad campaigns for promo toys and ran the best focus groups in the business. When I saw the Hammer Bay Toys exhibit at the toy fair, I thought they were a joke. Everything about them was wrong, according to the conventional thinking."

Able opened the door and led us back into the main office. "I mean, fashion dolls from the seventeenth century? What little girl would buy Marie Antoinette outfits? Every toy fair has a couple of exhibitors that seem a little wacky. We were all snickering at Charles behind his back."

We slowly walked across the office toward the elevator. Able was on a roll. There was a light in his eye and a note of desperation in his voice. He sounded like a convict who'd found Jesus and wanted you to understand why.

"But we were wrong and he was right. Those old-fashioned dolls flew off the shelves as fast as he could make them, even though the price point was too high, and the profit margin was nearly nonexistent. I was supposed to be the expert, and as far as I knew, kids just *didn't want* that sort of thing.

"By the next year, when he came out with the Eagle Riders, Robo-Zombies, and Helping Hand Trains, I didn't know what to think. The toys were still all wrong and they were priced too high, but this time I was *drawn* to them. I *wanted* them, just like all those kids did."

I noticed a woman walking the length of the office toward us.

"So I left New York and my six-figure job to work for someone who believes in ideas instead of focus groups. With every new line we release, I expect the company to come apart. But it doesn't happen. Every knockoff line out of Mattel or Hasbro flops, even though their prices are lower and they can fill the shelves. I can't explain it, but it's been an amazing ride. And this year we're releasing more toy lines than ever."

He pushed the elevator button. The woman reached us. "Excuse me, Able," she said. "Charles is ready to meet with you now." We looked across the office. A tall, angular young man with a thick head of dark hair stood at the far end of the row of desks. He watched us, apparently waiting for Able.

It only took me a moment to recognize him as one of the four who had met with Emmett Dubois beside the van. He was the one who'd had the seizure.

Annalise turned and looked at me. Her face was blank. It was the same expression I'd seen on her face dozens of times, but at that moment goose bumps ran down my back. The elevator dinged and the door opened.

Annalise casually pushed Able and the woman aside. "Stay," she said, and walked toward the dark-haired man.

I guessed she'd found the person she'd come to kill.

Able didn't stay. "Excuse me," he said. There was anger in his voice. "Excuse me, but that area is off-limits."

He started after her. I grabbed his arms from behind. He tried to shake me off. I shoved him at a desk, and he fell into the lap of a woman with a stack of files in her hands.

"She told us to stay," I told him. Able didn't understand how dangerous it was to cross Annalise. The woman dropped the papers she was holding and grabbed on to him to keep him between her and me.

Annalise was halfway down the rows of desks. "Charles Hammer?" she asked.

"Yes?" he said. I couldn't see Annalise's face, but I guessed that something in her expression made him uneasy.

A woman at the desk at the end of the row stood and stepped in Annalise's path. She was a big woman and she looked like she was used to getting her way. She grabbed Annalise's shoulder. Annalise smacked the woman's arm away. The woman gasped and grabbed her elbow, holding it as though her arm was broken.

Annalise grabbed Charles Hammer's left hand and laid the scrap wood on his palm. A shower of dull gray sparks and a jet of black steam blasted from the design toward the ceiling.

Everyone gasped. Hammer tried to pull away, but Annalise didn't release him. She tucked the scrap under her arm. "Your spell book," she said. "Give it to me."

"I'm sorry, what was that?"

Annalise sighed, then tore off his index finger with as much effort as it would take me to break a stalk of celery. She tossed the bloody digit over her shoulder.

Hammer screamed in pain. The women working in the office screamed and cringed against their desks. Hammer tried to yank his hand away, but Annalise held him as tightly as an iron vise.

She spoke to him in a clear, quiet voice. "I can ask you that question nine more times." Hammer drew his right fist back and threw a haymaker at the side of Annalise's face. He screamed again when he connected, then cradled his hand against his chest as though it was broken. Annalise's face was unmarked, and she kept talking as though nothing had happened. "You're not going to like it if I have to ask again after that. Spell book. Where?"

The sigil below my collarbone twinged. Again, there was no wave of force, but maybe that only come the first time. The room grew slightly dark, and the HBT name tags the women wore flared with yellow flames. Then the office workers dropped their arms to their sides and stood up in perfect unison.

They moved toward Annalise and Hammer like automatons. Annalise didn't see them.

"Boss!" I called.

Annalise turned, and just as one of the women drew in a huge breath as though she was about to scream, Annalise grabbed the front of her sweater and kicked her legs out from under her. I could hear bones break from where I stood. Annalise tossed the woman over the row of desks.

I didn't see her hit the floor, but I thought she'd survive. I hoped to God she would survive.

"Enough of this," Annalise said. She struck Charles Hammer with the back of her hand. His head tore away from his body and bounced into the corner.

I brought her here, I thought. *I helped her kill these people.* The thought made me sick.

A flat-faced woman stepped forward and took a deep breath. Annalise looked at her, obviously surprised that Hammer's death had not restored the women to normal.

With both hands, Annalise slammed the scrap wood over the woman's mouth just as a jet of flame blasted out of it. The fire engulfed the enchanted wood and Annalise's hands, billowing over her wrists and setting her jacket alight.

Annalise screamed.

The scrap of wood exploded. Annalise fell backward, holding her burning hands in front of her face. As for the flat-faced woman, her head was gone. The stump of her neck was still ablaze as her body collapsed onto the carpet.

The women glided toward Annalise like ghosts. A tall redhead took a deep breath, and Annalise dove toward me and rolled. The jet of fire missed her and struck another woman, who went up like she was covered in gasoline.

The jet of fire stopped flowing from the redhead's mouth. Her lips and tongue were charred black. She clutched at her throat and collapsed.

Annalise curled up beside the top of the stairs. Her hands were still on fire and were blackened and shriveled. Her face was pale and her whole body trembled. I grabbed a jacket off the back of a chair and charged toward her.

The women surrounded her. A gray-haired woman took a deep breath. I shoved a woman aside to get to Annalise and was startled to realize it was Ms. Finkler.

Finkler knocked the gray-haired woman aside. The woman turned toward me.

I ducked low, grabbed her leg, and spun her.

I didn't have much leverage, but I managed to topple her just as the fire blasted from her open mouth. I felt the same scorching heat that had burned Justin Benton as the jet of flame passed over my head. I also had the strange feeling that it had somehow already happened.

It was as though I was remembering the fire at the same time I was experiencing it.

The woman fell against a desk, blasting a jet of flame against her computer.

I threw the stolen jacket over Annalise's hands and hauled her into my arms. For all her power, she was tiny, barely a hundred pounds, and while I didn't have her strength, I did have adrenaline. A lot of it.

Then I saw Charles Hammer standing at the far end of the room. His clothes were bloody, but he was whole and healthy. His expression was one of pure, innocent astonishment.

Someone nearby took another breath. I carried Annalise to the stairs and leaped for the lower landing. I heard flames cut loose behind me. I felt the heat but no pain.

I hit the stairs about two-thirds of the way down. By some miracle, I didn't twist my ankle or crack open my head.

Annalise slipped from my grasp and bounced against the concrete steps. I jumped down beside her and yanked her off the floor. I glanced back and saw a column of flame scour the steps. I threw her over my shoulder and ran for the second flight down.

The fire trailed me, always striking where I'd been. If one of those women—and I knew very well they weren't in control of themselves, but I had no idea what was—had led me a little, she would have burned me to a cinder. That didn't happen.

I ran like hell to the next floor down, where the jet of fire couldn't reach me.

Figures moved down the hallway toward me. Cradling Annalise in my arms. I ran down the next flight of stairs. I reached the next landing, then the second floor. It took just a few seconds, but that was long enough for my adrenaline to ebb. It was also enough time for me to wonder why I'd gone to so much trouble to save a woman who wanted to kill me.

Too late to turn back now.

I ran down the last flight of stairs into the lobby. There, blocking the only exit, stood Carol, the receptionist. Her name tag was ablaze, and she stood stiffly, with her hands curled into claws at her side.

She was too far away. I could never knock her aside before she burned me alive.

She took a deep breath.

I willed the ghost knife into my hand. It flew out of the inside breast pocket of Annalise's jacket. In one motion, I caught it and flung it.

Carol had just finished inhaling when the spell entered her throat, passed through, and exited the back of her neck.

I darted to the left. Although the ghost knife had left no mark, a jet of flame spurted out the front of Carol's neck, then a second shot out the back. Fire curled out of her mouth, but the pressure behind it was gone. The flames touched off her face and hair. She buckled. Fire blasted down the front of her clothes, the flames spreading. She didn't make any sound at all as the fire engulfed her.

I ran around the flames and pushed through the front door into the morning drizzle. The ghost knife lay on the sidewalk as though waiting for me. I hoisted Annalise higher on my shoulder and *reached* out to my spell. It flew into my hand.

Sprinting across the lot toward the van, I did my best not to jostle Annalise, but I doubted she could feel my shoulder bouncing against her stomach. But her hands . . . She let out a tiny whimper and pulled her knees closer to her chest. Unfortunately, my rib cage was between them.

"Ease up on me," I said gently. I had to gasp for air between every word, and I wasn't sure she could hear me through her pain. "Ease up."

She did. We reached the van. I unlocked the passenger door and lifted her into the seat. I pulled the shoulder strap of her satchel over her head and threw it onto the floor, then clicked her seat belt over her.

At the same moment, I felt the now-familiar twinge against my chest. Memories were being erased. Was it because of the fight we'd just lost, or was another kid being killed across town?

I ran around the front of the van, got in, and started it up. Within seconds we were on the street.

"Annalise," I said. She didn't respond. Her hands were blackened and shriveled. Her face was pale and covered with sweat. I touched her cheek. Her skin was cold. She was going into shock.

I pulled over. We were only a block and a half from the plant, but I needed to get her feet elevated or she was going to die on me.

"What are you doing?" she said. She didn't look at me. "Remember the supermarket we passed on the way into town? Go there."

I did remember it, but only vaguely. I pulled back into the street and drove north until I hit Main Street, then turned right. It was only another half mile or so to the gas station where I'd bought the map, then another few hundred yards to the market.

I parked as close to the entrance as I could and took the plastic from Annalise's glove compartment. She told me the PIN and said to buy lean beef for her. Lots of it. I laid her down between the seats and wadded my sweaty windbreaker under her feet. "Hold on," I told her. "I'm going to be back as soon as I can."

"We can find you," she said, "if you don't come back. I put those spells on you and they don't come off. Any peer in the society can find them, and you."

I closed the door.

With a couple bucks' worth of items from the housewares aisle, I could have stolen any of the cars in the lot in less than twenty seconds. I'd done it hundreds of times before. I could have been halfway to Oregon in an hour. Leaving Annalise to die—and I had no doubt that without help, she would die, and very soon—would solve many of my immediate problems, whatever her threats. But I wasn't going to do it. It wasn't just that I had no idea what would happen to the spells she had put on me, and it wasn't just that the peers would hunt me down and tear me apart, although both of these were damn solid reasons. And it wasn't just the power Annalise had, although power like hers was irresistible to me.

It was also Justin Benton. Someone had to stand up for Justin Benton.

I followed signs to the meat department, then started loading beef into my basket. I didn't know much about choosing cuts, but I knew the white stuff was fat, the hard stuff was bone, and the red stuff was meat. I picked packages that were mostly red. I selected about ten pounds' worth, then grabbed a wide plastic cutting board from a hook above the case and hurried to the checkout line.

There were two people ahead of me. I had a little too much time to think.

Hammer knew we were coming after him now. He would either move against us right away or withdraw to somewhere safe, maybe somewhere out of town. If I were him, I'd be trying to figure out a way to kill us before the hour was up, but judging by the way Hammer had looked as Annalise had done her thing, I didn't think he'd be that together. I figured he'd run.

It was my turn at the register. "Nice town you have here," I said to the middle-aged cashier.

"Thanks!" she said.

"Isn't there a family somewhere still around here, the one who founded this town? The Hammer family?"

She looked immediately suspicious. "Maybe."

"They live in town? Where would I find them?" I asked, figuring that the town wasn't small enough for everyone to know everyone, but it would be small enough for everyone to know their first family.

"What do you want with the Hammers?" the man behind me said. He was about forty, with a thick biker's beard and heavy muscles in his arms and shoulders.

I hadn't thought this through, and it was turning sour. I swiped Annalise's card and punched in her PIN. "I just wanted—"

"Don't bother," the cashier said. "I know exactly what you want."

"And you ain't gonna get it." Biker Beard stepped up very, very close to me. "Ain't nobody in this whole town gonna answer a question like that for you."

The cashier glared at me. "Time for you to go." She held the bag out to me, then dropped it on the floor.

I turned back to the big guy. My adrenaline was too high and I'd spent too many years behind bars to back down from him. Annalise was dying out in the van, and her medicine was lying on the floor beside me, all spilled out of its flimsy plastic bag, but I couldn't turn away. I was risking everything, but I couldn't turn away.

A little old lady came around the end of the counter and picked up my groceries. "Oh, enough of that, you two," she said, and took hold of my elbow.

Her grip was strong, but she couldn't have pulled me away unless I let her. I did. There were half a dozen good reasons for me to back down from Biker Beard, but the one that really mattered was that I didn't want to be the guy I was in jail. I wanted to be someone better.

The old woman had tiny half-glasses perched on the end of her

nose and a thin, pinched mouth like a snapping turtle. I took the grocery bag from her when she handed it to me and I followed her outside. "You must be having a barbecue or something?" she asked.

"Thank you," I said.

"Of course, dear. Which one is yours?" I waved in the direction of
Annalise's big white van. "Wonderful. You just get in that van and drive
right out of town, understand, dear? There's no reason for you to stay
here. We protect our own, and we don't want you here."

I glanced at her and back at the cashier and the small crowd that
had gathered by the door. So much for smalltown hospitality. At least
I knew how to pick a fight, if I needed to. I nodded to the old woman
and rushed back to the van.

Annalise was still alive. I pulled out of the supermarket parking lot
with them still watching me. I drove a block toward town and parked
beside a dry cleaners. Then I crouched behind the passenger seat with the
front wheel of her motorcycle poking me in the back. I laid a hunk of
meat on the cutting board and shaved off a slice with my ghost knife.
Ghosts, magic, and dead things. Then I cut crisscrosses through the meat,
being careful not to touch the cutting board. The ghost knife could cut
straight through the bottom of the van and I wouldn't even feel it. The
board was only there to keep the raw beef off the metal deck of the van.

I had to feed the bits of meat to her, of course. She took them almost
blindly, like a baby bird. After she had eaten a pound or so, the color
started to come back into her face. After three, her face no longer felt
cold.

She rolled onto her side. She was more alert but also wary. I kept
cutting meat, kept feeding her piece by piece. She watched every mor-
sel move from the board to her mouth as if watching for some trick.

After she'd eaten half the meat I'd bought, Annalise said: "Help
me up."

I did, lifting her by her elbows so she wouldn't have to lean on her
injured hands, then opened the side door and supported her as she
climbed down. She let me.

She turned toward the van, putting her back to the parking lot,
hunched over, and held her hands out of sight. She flexed them slightly.
Flakes of black skin broke off her fingers and fell to the pavement.

My whole body tingled and I closed my eyes. Of all the things in
the world I didn't need to see, that ranked pretty high.

With my eyes closed, I suddenly remembered Carol the receptionist. I remembered the way my ghost knife had cut through her neck,
and the way she had burned away because of it.

I opened my eyes. The blackened skin of Annalise's hands had peeled off like burned paper, mostly. Beneath was raw, wet red flesh, and not much of it, either. Her hands looked scarily reduced. She touched her fingers together and gasped.

"Go back in," she said, not looking up. "Get more meat. Then we'll get out of here."

I did. I drove back to the supermarket and bought most of the lean meat remaining in the case, along with a box of plastic forks. I didn't speak to anyone and stood in a different cashier's line. No one threw me out. When I got back to the parking lot, Annalise had returned to her seat.

I put the groceries in the back, closed the passenger door, and buckled Annalise in, taking care not to touch the seat belt to her raw hands. She looked at me strangely, but I didn't think about that.

We pulled out of the lot.

"What happened back there?" I asked.

Annalise didn't answer at first. Finally, she said, "I don't know. Charles Hammer was the source of the magic in Hammer Bay, but I don't think he knew what was going on." She was quiet for a moment, as though the effort of speaking exhausted her. "Did you see the look on his face when those women all stood up at once?"

"I didn't."

"He was surprised. Bewildered. He was the source of the magic, but he didn't control it."

"You mean he doesn't control it."

"What do you mean?"

"He's alive. I saw—"

"Bullshit. I took his head off."

I shook my head. "Just before we got out of there," I said, "I saw him standing by the desk. His clothes were soaked in blood, but he was whole and alive."

"Shit. It fits, I guess. I just hate it when they won't stay down."

"Do you think Charles Hammer has someone behind him, pulling his strings?" I tried to imagine him with his own Annalise sending him out to fight and die.

"It's possible, but the spell I touched to him shot sparks. That means predator, and a powerful one." After that she was quiet.

I thought about that column of fire on the stairway, always striking where I had just been, never anticipating me. I mentioned it to Annalise.

"Some of the predators don't have concrete understanding of time, or three-dimensional space. It can be a weakness for them sometimes."

She fell silent again. I didn't press her for more information. I didn't want to push my luck.

We arrived at the motel. I fished Annalise's key out of her jacket pocket and opened her door. She collapsed onto the bed, exhausted from the effort of walking into the room.

I fetched the meat and cutting board from the van. The room had a small, round table, where I put the supplies down. I locked and barred the front door, then made sure the curtains were fully closed and began cutting the meat.

This time I fed Annalise with a plastic fork. It was more dignified than using my fingers. She watched me the whole time, her gaze wary and measuring. Obviously, she expected me to betray her again.

"Will this be enough?" I asked after she had eaten the first ten pounds I'd bought. I couldn't believe she'd eaten so much. Her stomach should have been swollen, but it wasn't. I assumed her body was using the meat to heal her injuries. I glanced down at her hands. It was a slow process.

"It should be," she said. "It had better be."

"What do you mean?"

"I've never . . . this should have been enough already. My hands should have been back to normal by now. Hell, a couple of years ago I only needed eight pounds to regrow an entirely new left foot. But we're past that now and I can still barely use them. Something's wrong."

I didn't like the sound of that. I kept cutting. "That was the same kind of fire that burned the little boy. I'm sure of it."

"I know what kind of fire it was," she snapped. "And we should have been protected. That spirit fire should not have been able to get past our iron gates."

We. I had run into Annalise's iron-gate spell before. It had once protected me from her green fire. I put my hand on my chest, just below my collarbone. That twinge I'd felt . . .

"That's right," she said. "I put an iron gate in the tattoos on your chest. It's supposed to protect against certain kinds of spirit attacks."

"Like the pressure waves that make people forget the dead kids?"

"Yes," she said. "Or fires channeled from the Empty Spaces."

"So why didn't it work?" I speared a piece of meat on a fork and offered it to her. She glared at me, then accepted the food without answering my question.

I kept cutting meat and offering it to her. I didn't ask any more questions. Eventually, she was able to flex her hands into claws, then into fists. I could see that they still hurt, but she could move them. After I'd fed her eighteen pounds of beef, her skin looked healthy but still pale. That's when she took the fork from me and began to feed herself. She didn't ask me to stop cutting the meat, and I didn't.

She ate all of it. It was a little more than twenty pounds of beef, and she'd eaten it in a little less than three hours. She sat on the edge of the bed and flexed her hands. Her face was stoic, but I knew something was wrong. She kept testing them, moving them, staring at them. I suspected they still hurt her, and that she had expected them to be fully healed by now.

"I need to sleep now. And I need time to figure out what's happened to me."

She looked like she was about to say more, but she hesitated. I didn't care. "No problem," I told her, and started toward the door.

"Thank you," she said.

I knew it wasn't easy for her to say, and that it didn't mean she was ready to trust me. I didn't care. "You're welcome."

"Before you go," she said, "there's something I want you to leave behind."

I stopped and turned around. "Is that right?"

"Leave it, Ray. Give it to me."

"It's the only weapon I have."

"Do you think I can't take it? Right here and now?"

"I know you can," I said. "I just don't understand—"

"Give it to me," she said. She lifted the corner of her pillow.

I took my ghost knife from my pocket, crossed the room, and slid it under her pillow. Annalise watched me closely, her whole body tense. I got the message. I should have left her in the parking lot.

I went to my own room. There was next to nothing there that I had bought myself, except the jacket in the trash can. This wasn't my room; it was hers.

I took a shower, then changed into clean clothes. I kept expecting the local cops to kick down the door, but it didn't happen. They must have had their memories wiped, too. Neat trick. I opened my wallet and saw Annalise's debit card inside. Good. I was hungry again. At least I wouldn't have to sit in this room and starve.

I had the keys to the van, too. I considered driving it to a secluded spot and thoroughly searching all of Annalise's gear. She hadn't worn her ribbon-covered vest to the toy plant this morning, so she must have stashed it somewhere.

And there was the matter of her spell book. I knew she had one, but I didn't know where she kept it. Would it be nearby, so she could create more ribbons as needed? Or would it be hidden away somewhere back in Seattle, in a safe-deposit box, or buried beneath a concrete floor, or sealed in a crate and sunk in Elliott Bay?

Or it could be stashed in the back of the van.

I didn't believe it. Annalise wasn't careless enough to leave it lying around.

And while I didn't know much about this society of hers, I knew they had rules about their books: reading another peer's book was a killing offense. If I did find the book in the van, it would be because Annalise had left it there to tempt me. It would be the perfect excuse for her to break my neck.

Inside the night table was a phone book. Hammer Bay was small enough that the white and yellow pages were combined into one book, but no one with the last name of Hammer was listed. Figured. That would have been too easy.

I left the motel and walked past the van without peeking inside. I was too hungry for games. I went to the office and asked the nervous manager where I could get a bite to eat. He recommended a place.

It was only a couple of blocks down the road. I strolled over to it. The misty drizzle had lessened, but the heavy clouds still obscured the sun and dimmed the town. It was only about six in the evening, which meant I had another two hours of sunlight, at least. The thought lifted my spirits.

The place was a bar, but that was fine with me. I went inside and sat on a stool.

After a few moments, my eyes adjusted to the darkness. The bar ran the length of one wall, with a wait station near the door. The rest of the room was divided into booths. There were no dartboards or pool tables. There was no jukebox. The place was pretty empty. An elderly man sat at the bar, head bowed over his tumbler. Three men sat at the other end of the room, arguing in the relative privacy of a booth.

The bartender approached me. She was tall and lean, with glossy black hair that hung long past her shoulders and dark eyes that suggested she was at least partly Hispanic. Her long face had a no-nonsense friendliness that I liked immediately. "I didn't see you come in," she said. "What can I get you?"

I glanced down at her left hand. She wore two rings. Oh, well. "Let's start with a beer and a glass of water."

"That's fine," she said. "What kind of beer?"

"What do you recommend?"

"We have a terrific Elephant Stout on tap."

That sounded like an up-sell if I'd ever heard one, but what the hell, Annalise was buying. "Sounds great," I told her. She went back to the taps, and I looked around.

The older man looked over blearily and then turned back to his drink. He wore a modest suit that bulged at the middle, and he had carefully combed his hair over his bald spot.

Victim, I immediately thought. I could have rolled him for his wallet if I was desperate for chump change. A couple years back I'd have rolled him for his car keys, then driven his car straight to the chop shop.

That chapter was closed now. I didn't steal cars anymore.

I killed people. People like Carol the receptionist.

I wondered what was going to happen to the bodies of those women. Was it a crime scene now, with police tape, coroners, and witnesses who couldn't remember a thing? Or had those dead women been erased from the memories of everyone around them? I imagined the surviving office workers moving like automatons as they carried the corpses away. Or worse, walking past them like they weren't there, the same way people ignored the black streaks.

A gray-haired woman walked into the bar. She had a sensible work-and-church vibe that made her seem instantly out of place. She went over to the old man with the comb-over and set some papers on the bar beside him. They exchanged terms of endearment in a tone that suggested it was a habit for them and little more. The man tapped the papers. "What's this?"

"Financial papers and a birthday card for Paul," she said.

For a moment he looked as if he was going to ask for details, but instead he shrugged and picked up the pen. When he got to the card, he said: "Ten years old already? Is he coming home this summer?"

The woman sighed. "His scholarship covers a summer program in Atlanta, and he's going."

The man sighed, too, and signed the card.

As the woman walked out of the bar, the three men in the booth burst out laughing. They sounded loud, raw, and somewhat drunk. One called another a "fucking moron."

The bartender was just about to place my beer in front of me. She turned toward them, bared her teeth, and said: "Keep it down or take it somewhere else!" She didn't have to raise her voice.

They quieted down. The bartender set the beer in front of me, then served up a big glass of ice with a splash of water. "Sorry about that. Sometimes it's like a chimp house in here."

"I like noisy chimps. You know where they are. It's the quiet chimps you have to watch out for."

She smiled at me. "I'm Sara," she said.

"Ray."

"New in town?"

"Absolutely."

"I guess you came to apply at the toy plant?"

I shrugged. "Everyone keeps suggesting that."

"Well, don't," a man behind me said.

One of the three men from the back booth had come to the bar with an empty pitcher. Sara took it from him without comment and began filling it from the cheap end of the tap.

He was tall and rangy with a small scarecrow's head, and he stood closer to me than he needed to. I guess he wanted to look down on me while we talked.

"You're the first one to suggest I stay away," I said. "Something wrong with the company?"

"Not a thing," the scarecrow said. "I just don't want to see some stranger blow into town and take something that belongs to a local." Sara set the pitcher in front of him. "Thanks, little lollipop. If you get tired of these two, I have some prime lap space reserved for you back at the booth."

"Boy, you are one word away from being tossed out like trash. Don't make me call the Dubois brothers."

Brothers? Thinking back to the cops I'd seen at Harlan's shooting, they certainly could have been brothers, with Emmett the oldest. I filed that information away.

The scarecrow winked and sauntered back to the booth.

Sara grimaced. "I ought to ban them for good."

"Is this your place?"

"Yep," she said. She absentmindedly twisted the rings on her left ring finger. "Ever since Stan died."

"How long ago?"

"Nearly two years now," she said. "He was a good man. We worked hard. But lately the whole town's been going to hell."

"Why? It sounds like there's lots of work up at the toy factory. My boss and I were up at the offices this morning." I watched Sara and the old man closely. Neither reacted to that last statement at all. Neither said, *This morning? When all those women burned to death?* Apparently, neither knew about it, hours after it had happened. "They bring a lot of jobs here, don't they?" I continued. "Shouldn't the town be thriving?"

She shrugged.

"We're a timber town," the victim at the end of the bar said. "We're not a toy town."

"How do you mean?"

"A job isn't just a job," he said. His voice was thick and his words slow. Sara stayed close to him, listening just as closely as I was.

"A job is an identity," the man continued. "You don't put down a chainsaw and then pick up a sewing machine. Making doll clothes isn't the same as clearing trees. If you switch from one job to the other, you turn into a different person." He stumbled over that last word, but he was at least making sense.

"Why don't you guys cut timber anymore?"

"Lots of reasons," the man said. "The main one is that we've cut pretty extensively on our land already. There just aren't that many trees out there worth harvesting anymore, where we can get them."

"And there's the environmentalists," Sara put in.

"That's right. Charlie Junior knew what to do about them. So did his father. But the latest Hammer doesn't care about any of that."

"To be fair," Sara put in, "Junior had let the whole thing slide the last ten years or so."

"It was his health, I think. When times got tough, he had break-downs—"

"More like seizures," Sara said.

"Yeah, seizures. He worked like crazy to get through tough times, and he paid the price. But for the last ten years or so, he had the tough times without the working like crazy."

"Not that you can blame the man. He would fall on the ground and thrash like a flounder in a boat."

"Really," I said, just to contribute something.

"Yes," the man said. "Charlie Three seems to have inherited the family condition."

"And he's a helluva success, too," Sara said.

"I'll give him that," the man said. "Now, Cabot has a clean bill of health. No seizures, near as anyone can see, but he did get the family timber business, and it's sinking fast." The old guy slid off his stool and moved closer to me. "My name's Bill Terril. What's yours?"

"Ray Lilly," I said. We shook hands.

"Lilly, huh? That's kind of a girly name."

"Sure is," I said. "I'm the delicate type."

Bill chuckled as he looked me over. "I'll bet."

"So, this Charlie Three," I said, "he live in town?"

Sara and Bill were instantly suspicious. "Why do you ask?" Sara said.

"Whoa. It was just a question."

"We're pretty protective of our own around here," Sara said.

"Especially of the Hammers. We look out for them. I don't know a body in this town who wouldn't. So, again: Why do you ask?"

I shrugged. "I dunno. Rich guy, little town. It sounds like he could live wherever."

"Nope," Bill said. "The Hammers created this town, and they stick by it."

I wondered how deep and widespread the support for the Hammer family extended. If Charles Hammer's memory wasn't wiped after this morning's fight—and I'd have bet it wouldn't be—he'd have gone into hiding. He might be tough to find without local help. I needed a way to drive a wedge between our target and the town.

Amazing, really, how quickly I'd gone over to Annalise's side.

"Huh." I didn't know what else to say. "So who's Cabot? Another one of the Hammers?" I asked.

"He . . ." Bill paused. He thought about how he wanted to answer.

Sara chimed in. "He's Charlie Junior's little brother. See, this town was founded by their grandfather, also named Cabot. He came out here with a crew of men and started cutting trees. He decided that the little Chimilchuk Inlet ought to be larger. He dredged it, widened it, and called it Hammer Bay.

"He had a lot of people rushing here to find work. Built the town right up. He ran a tight ship. He owned the newspaper, the grocery, the speakeasies, all of it. If he could have paid everyone in company scrip, he would have."

"But he was fair," Bill interrupted. "Everyone respected him."

"None of them were fair," Sara said. "None of them. All they cared about was themselves and what they'd built. The only one who's any different is Charlie Three."

"Dammit!" Bill snapped. "Charlie Senior was a great man! He brought down governors and senators, and gave jobs to men who needed them. Men like my father."

"Don't go all wacky on me, Bill," Sara said. She waved as though he was a puff of smoke she didn't want to smell. "Charlie Three is trying to put a foundation under this town. He could do it, too. We'd have decent incomes without having to worry about what happens when the trees are gone. Charlie Three is bringing us into the next century."

"I don't much like it."

"Well, you're pretty much the only one."

The old man laughed. "Ain't that the truth. Most of the people in this town won't even talk to me anymore. Criticizing Charlie Three around here is like badmouthing the pope in Vatican City, even though he ain't a patch on what came before."

"Don't talk to me about Senior and Junior," Sara said. "You know how hard they made things for Stan and his own father."

"I . . . I'm sorry, Sara." Bill swirled his drink around in his glass. "You know how much I liked Stan."

She patted his hand. "I know, Bill. You slow down on that stuff, okay?"

Bill lifted his glass and then set it down without drinking. "It's not that the older generations didn't have their quirks. Remember that Scottish thing? But it's this latest one that's . . . he gave up on the trees and started making toys. And he gave up the reins."

"What do you mean?" I asked.

"When you have a stagecoach," he said enthusiastically, as though he'd spent a good bit of time thinking about this analogy, "when you have a stagecoach, you hold on to the reins, right? You have to control things. But what happens if you drop the reins, huh?"

"You stop moving," I offered.

"No. The coach tips over and everything spills out. It's ruined. Broken. The horses charge off in different directions, fight each other, eat each other. They tear each other apart, that's what happens. Someone has to have control."

Sara suppressed a smile. "Bill, I don't think horses eat other horses."

My beer glass was empty, and so was my water glass. I ordered refills and asked for a menu. Sara told me that they didn't serve food anymore. She was all alone. I was disappointed, but she offered to dial a local pizza joint. I ordered a medium pepperoni.

I turned to Bill. "I hope you like pepperoni. On me."

"Well!" he said, shuffling back to his stool beside me. "That's fine. Just fine."

"You're welcome to have a slice, too," I said to Sara.

"I'll pass. I don't eat cheese." She lifted a tray of dirty glasses and carried them into the back.

"She's a good woman," Bill told me, keeping his voice low. "There's lots of fellas in town who'd like to get next to her. Especially since she got herself this bar."

I tried to picture myself standing behind the bar pulling beers, or frying burgers in the back. It was a nice idea, but it wasn't going to happen. "Is that so?"

"Her husband was a good man, too. Older than her. He hired her to wait tables and then a year later gave her a ring and a half-ownership in the bar."

"What happened to him?" I asked.

"Nothing she did," Bill said quickly. "He was killed by dogs."

"Did you say *dogs?*"

"A pack of dogs. And he ain't the only one. In the last six years or so, eight or ten local folks have been torn apart that way. Very mysterious."

"I don't get it. A pack of dogs? Are there feral dogs in the woods? Or does someone keep them?"

"There's no way to hide a pack of dogs in a small town like this one. Emmett Dubois tried to trap the dogs several times, but he never caught nothing. Me, I think they've had their vocal cords cut. That's why nobody ever heard them barking."

I remembered the wolf that had stood out in the middle of the street. "Are the cops in this town really all brothers?"

"Sure," Bill said. "And it was their own daddy who hired them for the job. It might seem strange to an out-of-towner, but being a cop is a family business in Hammer Bay. And it was never a problem while one of the Hammers was giving the orders."

"Does that mean it's a problem now?"

"Heh. Well . . ." Bill rubbed his face. I guessed he would rephrase that if he could.

"Let me put it another way: Are they good cops? Honest?"

Bill lowered his voice. "Emmett keeps a lid on things in this town. And on his brothers, too."

"So I should be careful, then?"

"Yes. Emmett is smart, and Sugar has always been a good kid. But don't be left alone with Wiley. Just be careful with him."

The pizza arrived. I paid for it with Annalise's card and offered Bill the first slice. He took it gladly. The conversation turned religious after that. Bill was sure I was a good Christian, and that the dog attacks were the work of Satan.

It went on that way for a while. The three of us talked about all sorts of things, and Sara accepted a slice after all. It was very friendly. I pried here and there about their personal lives but didn't learn much. Bill had one daughter and one grandson, Paul, who was at a boarding school in Georgia. Sara said she and Stan had never been blessed with kids. Of course. Bill started in on Charles Three again, but Sara told him to lay off.

After a while, the topic turned to me. Bill asked again if I'd come to town to work at the toy plant. The scarecrow was standing at the bar, getting another pitcher. I decided it was time to try to drive that wedge between the town and the Hammers, so I told them why we had met with Able Katz that morning. "My boss wants Hammer Bay Toys to outsource some of its manufacturing to Africa. Sewing doll clothes, I think."

Sara looked as shocked as if I'd slapped her. "What? He'd never do that."

"It was only a first meeting," I said with a casual shrug. "So nothing was decided."

The scarecrow stared at me for a moment, then left the empty pitcher on the bar and went back to the booth.

"Sewing . . . Three of my aunts work in sewing. Aunt Casey needs that job to keep her house. We need those jobs here in town! Do you know how many of our older folks support themselves with a sewing machine now? What'll they do if the jobs go overseas?"

"People need jobs all over."

Sara collected my glass. "You know what, Ray? I don't want you in my place anymore."

The scarecrow and his two friends walked out the front door. They watched me silently as they passed. I didn't like that look.

I stood. Bill protested. "Aw, don't be that way, Sara. It's not his fault."

"It's all right, Bill," I said. "It was time I was leaving anyway. Sara, do you have a back door?"

She folded her arms across her chest. "Why?"

"Because I expect those three guys are waiting for me outside."

Bill struggled off his stool. "I'll go have a look-see."

"You stay right there, Bill," Sara said. "I'll check the parking lot if Ray here is feeling nervous."

She walked to the front door and went out. Bill lifted the lid of the pizza box. It was empty.

"Well," Bill said, "thanks for the grub and the company."

"It was my pleasure."

"Is . . . is it really true about Africa?"

"Times are harder there than they are here, Bill."

Sara came back in and told me that the parking lot was empty. So was the street.

She stood by the door. I walked across the room, matched her scowl with a smile, and went outside.

I had only taken three steps when I saw them leaning against a pickup truck. They smiled. The short one was holding a knife, and the other two were carrying tire irons. Scarecrow held a snub-nosed .38 in his off hand.

Behind me, I heard Sara close the door and throw the bolt.

CHAPTER SIX

"Hey, stranger," the knife holder said. "We're here to welcome you to Hammer Bay."

"Really?" I said. "Because I don't see a muffin basket. You wouldn't be lying to me, would you?" The bar blocked one side of the lot, and a cinder-block wall of the business next door blocked the other. There were no stairs, windows, or gaps that I could use to get away. Behind me was a chain-link fence with struts blocking my view of the other side. A Plymouth Reliant was parked up against it. If I was going to run, that was the way, but there was still that gun.

The one who had spoken was average height and wore large tinted glasses. The other was well under six feet and built like a fireplug; he held a beer in his off hand. Both were thick with muscle that comes with hard physical labor and the flab that comes with fried food. The short one wore a construction worker's helmet, and all three wore steel-toed work boots.

Glasses took a small box from his inside pocket. He lifted out a couple of tiny bundles wrapped in tissue or toilet paper and handed them to the others. Each man wet the bundle on his tongue, popped it into his mouth, and passed the beer back and forth to wash it down.

The short one nodded toward me. "Look at his tattoos. He's the one who set up Harlan for Emmett Dubois."

"Izzat right?" Glasses said, then threw the empty bottle at me. I ducked. It shattered against a fence pole behind me. "Well, well, well, now I'm double happy we waited for him."

The tall one bared his teeth and came toward me. He kept the barrel of the gun pointed at my stomach while he raised the tire iron. What was it with tire irons in this town?

"Don't you run from me," he said with all the practiced bullying of a wife beater. "Don't you run!"

I wished Annalise had let me keep my ghost knife.

He lifted the tire iron and swung for my head. I raised my left arm and caught the blow on my tattooed wrist.

It didn't hurt, but I did my damnedest not to show that. I cursed and clutched at my wrist as though he'd broken it.

The other two laughed. The tall guy wasn't in a mood to be entertained. "Harlan is my friend, and he's in the hospital because of you."

He swung the tire iron again. This time I caught the blow on my right arm. I made a small, strangled noise and cradled both arms against my chest.

The scarecrow sneered at me and dropped the revolver into his pocket.

Perfect. He stepped toward me and raised his tire iron again.

I laid a quick, right uppercut on the point of his jaw. He went limp and my left hand was in his jacket pocket before he hit the ground. I yanked the revolver free and fumbled it into the proper position. The scarecrow's tire iron clattered to the ground.

Glasses and the fireplug stepped back.

I pointed the gun at them. They froze in place.

"All right, kids. This doesn't have to get interesting. Let's make a deal. You never come near me again, and I won't kill you."

"Forget it," the tall guy said, struggling to his feet. "The gun's not loaded."

Glasses turned on him. "What do you mean, it's not loaded?" I wanted to know the same thing. "I told you what we needed to do."

The tall guy shrugged. "You're my friend, Wyatt, but . . . I left the bullets at home."

While they hashed that out, the fireplug grinned. He hefted his tire iron and stepped toward me.

I threw the gun onto the roof of the bar and jumped onto the trunk of the Reliant. Then I stepped onto the roof and leaped for the top of the fence. I hit it at waist level and rolled over the top. There was a Dumpster below me. I twisted and landed on it. I heard cloth tearing. I jumped to the ground and ran for the street, wondering if Annalise would spring for more clothes.

When I reached the street, I sprinted toward the left, away from the business district into a residential neighborhood.

I heard them shout behind me and kept running. I was confident I could take any one of them, especially with the protections Annalise had given me. But three was too many. Too easy for one of them to knife me in the armpit or smash in my skull while I was dealing with another.

So I ran. I passed one block, then another. As I started on the third, I looked back. All three were chasing me, and the tall one seemed to be gaining. That was fine. Wyatt and the fireplug were falling back, puffing and straining to keep up.

I rounded a corner and was suddenly sprinting right beside a police car. The fat officer sat behind the wheel drinking Mountain Dew from a two-liter bottle. The engine was off. He watched me run past but didn't reach for his keys or the radio. Great.

In the next block, I nearly stepped on a thick black streak on the sidewalk. I jolted to the side at the last minute, running into the street to go around it.

The beer and pizza began to weigh on me. I stopped beneath a streetlight and waited for the scarecrow.

He didn't keep me waiting long. And he wasn't stupid, either. He ran straight at me, then dodged to the side as he passed, swinging that tire iron.

I feinted a lunge at him, then stepped away from the swing. It missed.

The guy slapped his feet on the sidewalk as he tried to stop himself. I charged him. He turned and tried to leap back. With a weapon and a longer reach, I'm sure he was hoping to avoid a clinch.

He feinted a swing for my head, then went for my ribs. I barely managed to get my elbow in the path of the iron. It glanced off my arm without any harm but thumped into my hip. That one hurt.

I grabbed the tire iron as he tried to pull it away. My grip was stronger, and I ripped it from his hand and tossed it into the street. The scarecrow backed away into the streetlight, right where I wanted him.

I spared a glance at Wyatt and the fireplug. They were still half a block away, puffing toward us.

The scarecrow threw a solid left jab followed by a long, hard, circling right. Both were respectable efforts, although neither connected. I ducked under his right and landed a hard left against his floating ribs. I felt something crack.

He woofed and bent sideways. I threw a right into his midsection and slid a left hook over his shoulder against his jaw. He dropped.

I turned toward Wyatt and his remaining friend. We'd been standing in the light, and they had seen the whole show. They stopped running. After a second of indecision, they started walking away. I watched them go for a second or two, then went back to the man I'd just beaten.

I'd known guys who thought winning a fight was cause for celebration. They'd laugh and cheer and spread around high fives. I didn't feel like cheering.

I took the guy's wallet while he was coming around. His driver's license said he was Floyd O'Marra. I also found thirty dollars inside. Good. Eventually, Annalise was going to want her plastic back. I decided to charge Floyd for the important life lessons I was teaching him. I pocketed the money.

"Damn," Floyd said, rousing himself. "Where am I?"

"Look around," I told him. "Tell me if you see anything familiar."

He looked up at me. "Oh, hell."

"How's Harlan doing, by the way?"

Floyd didn't quite know how to take that question. "He'll probably live." *No thanks to you* hung at the end of that sentence, unspoken but clear.

He started to sit up, but I shoved him back down. "Where do you work, Floyd?"

"Henstrick Construction."

"What kind of construction do you do? What do you build?"

"Whorehouses," he said, sneering a little.

"Is that so? Where can I find me a girl? All this exercise made me a little anxious."

"Outside of town," he said. "A couple hundred yards behind the bowling alley. The Curl Club. Ask for me and I'll get you a real warm welcome."

He tried to move away from me. I pushed him onto his back. "Do you want to help your buddy Wyatt?"

"He's my buddy, ain't he?"

"Do him a favor. Tell him to keep away from me. In fact, you and him should hop in your truck and take a little vacation. Vegas or something. Go have some fun. Because if I see any of you again, I'm going to spoil your whole fucking day."

Floyd had come around enough to start getting angry again. He tried to roll away from me but winced at the pain in his ribs. He swore. "Next time I'm going to load that damn gun."

I couldn't take that lightly. I slugged him once on the nose. Not so hard that I'd break bones, but enough to make him taste blood. I held up his license. "Floyd O'Marra. 223 Cedar Lane. That sounds like a nice little neighborhood. Am I going to have to come to your house, Floyd? Am I going to have to burn it down? While you're sleeping there?"

He swore at me again. He was still feeling defiant.

Damn. Floyd just wasn't getting with the program. I couldn't let this guy go after he'd promised to kill me. I knew very well how easy it was to get shot.

I stomped on his hands, one after the other.

He howled. Lights started turning on in the houses around the block. I didn't care anymore. He swore at me some more, and each word was a half sob.

It wasn't a pretty thing. It wasn't a nice thing. But I couldn't have some guy running around after he'd threatened to shoot me. I'm not that brave.

I knelt beside him and lifted him off the ground. I knew it made his ribs hurt. I wanted him to hurt. I wanted him to get his thirty bucks' worth.

"Shut your mouth," I snarled at him. "In case you haven't figured it out yet, you're one word away from being a corpse, because the next thing I'll stomp on is your neck. Get it? Keep away from me. Next time I won't be such a sweetheart."

This time Floyd understood. He nodded frantically, his eyes closed. I dropped him onto the sidewalk and collected his tire iron.

I walked toward the bar. The police car was still parked in its spot, but I circled around the block to avoid passing it again. My hip felt tender where Floyd had hit me with the iron.

On the way back, I saw another black streak from across the street. Damn. The town was full of them.

I pushed open the door to the bar and strolled in like an old friend. Sara's mouth fell open. She backed toward the cash register, probably wishing she'd kept the door bolted. I dropped the tire iron on the bar. Loudly.

Bill was still sitting there. "Damn," he said. "Not a mark on him."

Sara lunged under the counter and pulled out a shotgun. The barrel was several inches too short to be legal. "Get out," she said.

"I don't care about you, Sara," I said. "I don't care what you've done. But I've come to Hammer Bay to do a job."

"Whatever," she said. "Get out."

She was scared, but not of me. I wasn't sure if that was a good thing or not. "Does Wyatt buy meth or does he make it himself?"

"What are you talking about?"

"Please. You can't tell me you don't know what's going on."

Bill chuckled. "Sure she can. She's a tough girl, but she's a little naïve."

I turned to Bill. "Which is it, then?"

"Wyatt buys it somewhere south of here, then sells it in the lot at his night job."

"Are the cops clueless or paid off?" I asked.

"Paid off, I bet," Bill said. "Considering."

"What night job?"

Bill laughed. "The Curl Club. He keeps it low-key, though. I don't think Henstrick has worked it all out yet."

"Wyatt isn't a customer there, is he?"

"No, he's a bouncer, like Floyd and Georgie. Most of her boys work the club when they're not working on job sites. Especially when times are hard."

"Who is this 'her' you mentioned?"

"Henstrick."

"Ah." I felt embarrassed to have to be told.

Sara was getting impatient and I was done. I backed toward the door. "Thanks, Bill."

He said he was glad to help. Sara asked me if what I'd said about Africa was true.

"Be sure to lock the door behind me." I left.

If I had played my hand right, Sara would begin asking around, spreading the rumor. Annalise was going to have to go after Charles Hammer again, and Hammer would know we were coming. I wondered how much it would take to truly isolate him.

A police car was parked across the street. Inside I saw the silhouette of the same fat officer I'd seen earlier.

I heard a clatter nearby. I turned toward the sound.

Something low and gray moved out from the side of the Dumpster. At first I thought it was a dog. Then I saw the tinge of red fur. It was the wolf from the night before.

It stared at me. The hairs on the back of my neck stood up.

The door to the bar opened. I whirled around and saw Bill limping toward me. He wore an eager, fevered expression.

"You're here for something, aren't you?" he asked.

I glanced back at the mouth of the parking lot. The wolf was gone. "Yeah. A couple beers and dinner."

"Sure, sure. I understand. Listen, have you talked to Pete Lemly yet?"

"Who's he?"

"Our local newspaper guy. He knows a lot of the local chess pieces, and how they like to move."

The police car across the street started up and pulled away. Bill glanced over at it, noticing it for the first time. His expression grew fearful. "Oh, Lord. I gotta get." He hustled back into the bar.

Apparently, I was not a person to be seen with.

I started walking. Two couples passed me headed for the bar. They walked close together as though huddling against the darkness, and when they laughed, their voices were too loud and full of strain.

I heard a woman scream. The couples heard it as well. They stood still, looking at one another as though waiting for someone else to make a decision.

I ran toward the sound. The woman, whoever she was, kept screaming. I sprinted around the corner and heard them following me.

About twenty yards ahead, I saw a woman standing on the far side of a Dodge Neon. Her face was lit by a fire in the car. She wore an expression of utter horror.

Then the fire went out. She staggered against a tree planted by the curb. A wave of wriggling silver shapes spilled out the back door, swarmed onto the nearest lawn, and burrowed into it.

I was just a few yards away when I felt that sudden *twinge* against my iron gate.

I slowed my pace. The woman brushed at her coat and then dragged a little girl from the backseat, urging her to hurry because it was already so late.

I stood ten yards away and watched her. Damn. Her child was gone, and she'd already forgotten. She noticed me and started to hurry. I had scared her.

The whole town was scaring me.

I walked around the block. By the time I reached the Neon, the woman and her child were gone. A black scorch mark on the sidewalk led toward the lawn, where the dirt was loose and shiny black in the streetlight. Another dead kid.

I walked toward the motel. At the last minute, I turned up the road and walked to the supermarket again. It took me an hour, but I eventually returned with a sack full of the last lean beef in the store. It was only four pounds, but if Annalise wasn't healed, it would be better than nothing. At least I didn't run into that cashier again.

As I walked across the parking lot, I noticed that the lights were on in her room. I went into my room next door, set the food on the table, and thumped lightly on the wall.

She knocked on my door within a few seconds. I let her in, then went into the bathroom to wash my face. I hate the feeling of dried sweat on my face.

"How are your hands?" I asked her.

"They're a little worse," she said. "Not too much worse, but they aren't good. I'm not sure what I should do."

Neither was I. I finished washing up and joined her in the other room. She was tearing the plastic off a skirt steak. Her hands were stiff and awkward.

"What about the rest of the Twenty Palace Society?" I asked.

She stopped and looked at me. "What about them?"

I knew I was about to tread on a sensitive spot, but it had to be said. "What if you called for help? You—"

"I don't need their help," she said evenly. "I don't need anything from anyone. I've been doing jobs like this since before you were born. Since before your father was born."

"Okay. Okay. I get it. You're a rock." I noticed that she had set my ghost knife on the table. I picked it up and started cutting the meat.

It felt good to have my ghost knife again.

Annalise ate all the meat I cut for her. When she was finished, she held up her hands and flexed them.

"Better?" I asked.

"Yes," she said. "But not healed. I've never had such a stubborn injury."

"We've pretty much bought out the local market."

"In the morning we'll try to find a butcher." She sighed. "The longer it's been dead, the less potent it is for me."

That kind of talk makes me nervous. Would she need to eat something alive soon? Maybe we should pick up a dozen oysters.

The door to my room slammed open. I threw myself to the floor. Someone shouted, "Police! Nobody move!"

Then I heard a gunshot.

"Luke! LUKE!" a man shouted. "Easy, now! Easy!"

I realized I was holding my ghost knife. I didn't want the cops to have it, so I set it on its edge and pushed it through the carpet. It disappeared into the floor.

"Nobody move!" someone else shouted. This voice was young. I wanted to glance at them, but I held myself completely still. I didn't need to see their faces. Not until they put away their weapons, anyway.

"Is anyone hurt?" the first voice asked. I recognized it as Emmett Dubois.

"I'm unhurt," Annalise said. Her voice was cool and relaxed.

"Good, good, now don't move."

The fat cop knelt on my back and cuffed me. I was hauled to my feet. Annalise stood beside me, her hands also cuffed behind her back.

"I'm sorry, Emmett," one of the cops said. He was the one with the seven-day beard. He'd apparently left his cigar in the car. I guessed this was Luke. "It's that *smell*."

"I know," Emmett said. His voice was soothing, an older brother talking to a younger. "We'll talk about it later."

They made us stand by the window while they tossed the place. They found my clothes but not the ghost knife. Emmett Dubois seemed pretty interested in all the meat wrappers, but he didn't ask us about it directly.

Then they took us to Annalise's room and let us watch as they tossed it, too. She didn't seem to have brought anything of her own into the room.

Finally, we all watched as Luke and the red-haired cop searched the van. They threw everything onto the asphalt, even rolling out Annalise's dirt bike and searching under the seat, inside the exhaust pipes, gas tank, and handlebars.

A little man came out of the manager's office and watched. He crossed his arms and stood well back in the shadow of the door as though he was afraid to be seen.

They didn't find her vest of ribbons or her spell book. The only thing that seemed to interest Emmett was the satchel she'd brought to her meeting with Able Katz. He pulled the papers out, shuffled through them, and shoved them back.

If Annalise was bothered by the way they ransacked her stuff, she didn't show it.

"All right," Emmett finally said. "Let's load them up."

Luke came over to drag me into a waiting police car. The fat cop took Annalise. I saw him lean down and whisper something to her. I couldn't hear what he was saying, but I knew he wasn't offering her a private suite with cable TV. Not that Annalise seemed to be bothered by anything he said. They sat us in the back of the cars and drove us away.

I didn't like being in the back of a cop car again. It smelled bad. I had to sit against my handcuffs, and they hadn't even belted me in.

We drove north through the downtown, passing the parking lot where Wyatt had tried to ambush me. The police station was on a small side road at the edge of the water. Huge, irregular black rocks lay on all sides of the station and the tiny road leading to it.

We parked outside the station. Three Dodge Ram trucks were there, one gleaming black, one fire-engine red, and one painted gunmetal gray with flames on the sides. They were tricked out with fog lights, chrome wheels, ski racks, and who knows what else. Beside them was a vintage Bentley, black, although I couldn't see enough of it to guess the year.

These were expensive cars, far above the level of the usual pickups and station wagons I'd seen around town or the dinged-up, rusted Celica parked at the far end of the lot.

They brought me inside but didn't process me. No fingerprints, nothing. Luke just walked me into the back and stuck me in a cell. Alone. He made me back up and stick my hands through the bars so he could uncuff me. He took his time about it.

"That girlfriend of yours isn't much of a looker," he said.

A chill ran down my back. I tried to turn to look at him, but he yanked the chain on my cuffs.

"She's got all them tattoos, though," he continued. "I'd guess she's a wild one. Am I right?"

I imagined Annalise backhanding Luke's head off his shoulders. "Watch your step with her."

Luke grabbed the back of my collar and slammed my head against the bars. My eyes filled with stars. I spun and fell against the metal bench. When I looked at him again, he had a nine-millimeter pointed at my head.

"A little caution might be a good idea right now, son. A little common sense, if you get my point."

I felt my head. There was no blood, but I'd have a fine lump in a couple of hours. And it hurt like a bastard.

Part of me wished he'd pull the trigger. I was sick of being chased, threatened, and left in the dark. A bullet, at least, would be a clean end.

"Common sense has never been my strong suit," I heard myself say.

Luke holstered his weapon. "Guess we'll have to work on that together," he said. He smiled at me and left.

I could, with a little concentration, summon my ghost knife, but I'd never tried it from farther than a few yards. I wondered if I could call it from all the way across town.

I closed my eyes and tried to shut out the pain in my head. The ghost knife had power, and that power recognized me. I didn't understand it any more than your average stickup man understands the chemical composition of the gunpowder in his nine-mil, but I knew how to make it work. I closed my eyes and concentrated.

I couldn't feel it. It was too far away.

Crap. With my ghost knife, I could have cut myself out of this cell in a few seconds. I planned to try again when my head cleared, but I wasn't hopeful.

The door opened and a woman walked into the hall. She looked past sixty, and she wasn't handling the years well. Her face was pale, and the pouches under her eyes were the color of storm clouds. Her hair looked as though she'd cut it herself without looking in a mirror.

Her mouth moved ceaselessly: she licked her lips, chewed them, pursed them, twisted them into a frown. She carried a stack of files.

"You're the fellow who . . ." She broke off. I waited for her. "Why did you help Harlan Semple?"

I didn't say *Because my boss told me to.* Instead I said, "Is he somebody to you?"

"My nephew." She glanced at the door behind her. She didn't want to be caught talking to me.

"How is he? I wanted to visit him, but I haven't had time."

"He's stable now, after a bad night and day. They said you saved his life. Why did you do it? Did you know him?"

"No, I don't know him, and I'm not sure why I did it."

"Did he . . . did he say why he was doing what he was doing?"

"You mean shooting up the town?" She didn't flinch. She just stared at me with the blank eyes of a hungry bird. "He said it was because of his daughters. He said he had two daughters, but they disappeared. He said kids have been disappearing from the whole town, but he's the only one who remembers."

She shook her head. "That poor, crazy-headed boy."

"Did he have two daughters?" I asked her.

"He didn't have anyone. His wife took up with . . . someone else after he was hurt. He was all by himself."

I didn't believe a word of it, but I was sure she believed it. She reached up and wearily wiped her eyes. I noticed a nasty scar on her hand.

"Is that a bite mark?" I asked. "A dog bite?"

She became flustered and started toward the exit.

"Wait a minute," I said. "Do you want to help your bosses?"

That stopped her. She glanced nervously at the door, then came back toward me.

I didn't get off the bench. I had to present this next bit carefully. She was obviously terrified of the Dubois brothers, and being so close to them every day meant she was probably desperate to keep them happy. She wouldn't pass on any information that might irritate Emmett or his boys.

"I don't care what you folks here get up to, understand?" I used a high voice and kept my head and shoulders as low as I could without breaking eye contact. She still stared at me dubiously. "Honestly, I don't care. The only thing I care about is avoiding trouble."

"You're not very good at it, though, are you?"

I smiled. "I'm trying. Listen, I'm just a driver. Annalise, my boss, is the one in charge. And she's rich. Very rich."

Her mouth twisted. "She doesn't look rich."

"She's eccentric, you know what I mean?"

She folded her arms. "Why are you telling me all this?"

"Just make sure your bosses know to be careful around her. If something happens to her, her people will be all over Hammer Bay. Politicians, lawyers, state cops, private investigators, newspaper people, the whole works. They'll start talking to everyone in the town, auditing tax records, the whole deal. I've seen it happen."

"I still don't know why you're telling me," she said stubbornly. "Everyone here is completely professional. She doesn't have anything to worry about."

Of course she didn't have anything to worry about. But I didn't want to deal with the fallout if Annalise pinched off Luke Dubois's head.

"Come on, ma'am," I said. "Don't kid a kidder. Luke Dubois stood right outside this cell and made a crack about her. He needs to know."

"So you're trying to help him, too?"

"Luke Dubois burst into my motel room and shot the place up, then he banged my skull against these bars. I wouldn't piss on him if his hair was on fire. But I don't want to sit through another deposition, or give more statements to state cops and private eyes. I just want to get through the next couple of days without some damn catastrophe falling on my head."

She stared at me for a moment, then said: "I'll get Sugar." She left the room.

A few minutes later, she returned with the tall red-haired cop. He was all knobby muscles and bulging Adam's apple. His name tag said s. DUBOIS.

"Is there a problem, sir?" he asked, just like a real TV policeman.

I went through the whole spiel again, but it was a little more polished this time. Sugar listened without expression. Finally, he held up his hand. I stopped. "I'll be right back, sir," he said. Then he left the room.

The woman watched him as though she didn't know whether Sugar wanted her to follow or stay where she was, and that it was an important question. She decided to stay.

A minute later, Emmett came in. He looked relaxed, smiling like the host of a well-planned dinner party. "I understand there's a problem of some kind?" he said.

I went through it a third time, making it much shorter and much less emotional. I did my best to make it sound like Annalise was a land mine. I didn't want to sound like I was threatening anyone.

Emmett cut me off after I'd barely touched on the points I wanted to make. "Nothing is going to happen to her. This may not be the Ritz, but my brothers and I are professionals."

I rubbed the goose egg swelling on the back of my head. "Then there aren't any problems at all, I guess."

He looked at me. I looked at him. He didn't seem to like me much.

"I know who you are," Emmett said. I didn't answer. "Come along, Shireen." He led the others through the doorway and bolted the door from the other side. The lights switched off.

I lay back on the bench. It shouldn't have bothered me that Emmett Dubois knew me and my history. It was part of the public record. Anyone with an Internet connection and the correct spelling of my last name could dig up the newspaper articles in a few seconds.

But it did bother me. He knew about the time I'd served, the enemies I'd made, and the people who were dead because of me. I didn't know a thing about him, except that he was hiding something. I wasn't sure what it was, but it was all over his face.

I wondered, not for the first time, why he'd picked us up. My fight with Floyd was reason enough, but had Sara called him, too? And there was the incident at the toy company to consider.

Somehow, I doubted it was the latter. The further that morning's fight slipped into the past without comment, the more convinced I was that no one could remember it. The Dubois brothers didn't strike me as the souls of restraint—one of them would have said something. Also, Sara and Bill hadn't heard about it hours after it happened.

One person I expected to remember everything was Charlie Three. The fires at the toy offices tied him and his company to the burned kids, but how was he doing it and why? And according to Bill, the latest Hammer patriarch—although it was funny to call him that since he was barely older than I was—had cut the Dubois brothers loose. His father and grandfather had used the police to control the town, but they were on their own now.

And there were the seizures to consider, too. Bill said they ran in the family.

Actually, he'd said they came on when the patriarch was successful. That was something to talk about with Annalise, if I ever got the chance.

Had Hammer made a phone call and had us picked up? It was possible, but if I had a whole town under my thumb, I wouldn't have the cops bring my enemies to a cell. I'd have them run out of town or shot.

Of course, the Dubois brothers might march in like automatons and breathe fire on me, but I didn't expect it. They could find a better place to kill us than their cells.

Then again, maybe Hammer hadn't sicced the cops on us after all. Maybe Floyd and Emmett were bowling buddies, and I was going to get stomped by the rest of the league before morning.

It wasn't a pleasant thought, but I'd been around scary people before. I was a light sleeper, too, especially when people were thinking naughty thoughts about me.

I stayed awake a good long time. When a suspect falls asleep quickly in a cell, cops see that as a sign of guilt. No one came to check on me, though, and eventually, I slept.

I heard the lock on my cell door clank open very quietly, and I was sitting up before I was even fully awake.

"Skittish, ain't he?" Luke Dubois smiled down at me. His fat brother stood beside him. It occurred to me that I'd never heard him speak. "Stand up and turn around," he said.

I did. He cuffed me and led me to an interrogation room. Emmett was waiting.

"Welcome, Mr. Lilly," Emmett said. "Have a seat. Wiley, set up the video, please."

Luke shoved me into a chair and left the room. Wiley, the fat cop that Bill had told me to be careful with, pulled a video camera out of a corner and set it on a tripod. The camcorder was a new model.

Emmett smiled at me as we waited. He had a pair of folders on the table in front of him, but he didn't open them.

Wiley started the camcorder, then sat in the corner. He pulled his gun from his holster and held it in his lap, staring at me as if he was trying to come up with a reason not to shoot me then and there.

Emmett recited the date for the benefit of the camera, then his name, Wiley's, and mine. I glanced at his watch. It was 3:15 in the morning. I wiped sleep out of my eyes. I needed to be alert.

"So, Mr. Lilly," Emmett said, smiling and leaning forward. "Tell me what you know about the murder of Karoly Lem."

CHAPTER SEVEN

"Uh, Carol E. Lem? Who's she?"

Emmett sighed as though I was being deliberately difficult.

"Are you stating, for the record, that you don't know a man named Karoly Lem?"

"Yes," I said.

"Are you sure that's the answer you want on the record?" Emmett asked.

"If I met some dude named Carol, I'd remember it."

Emmett chuckled. He slid the top folder to the side and opened the one on the bottom. "Karoly Lem," he read. "Born in Poland in 1962, moved to the U.S. with his family in 1980, became a naturalized American citizen in 1981. He lived in Portland for most of his life—"

"Is there going to be a test?" I interrupted.

"He came to Hammer Bay three weeks ago. He told Arlen, the manager at his motel, that he was scouting locations for Big 5 Sporting Goods. Six days ago, his body was found behind the library."

Emmett stared at me, waiting for my reaction. "Why are there so few children in Hammer Bay?" I asked. "I see lots of couples, lots of station wagons and plastic swing sets on people's lawns, but not many kids. Why is that?"

Emmett's eyes narrowed. He didn't seem to know what I was talking about. "Mr. Lem had been torn apart by some sort of wild animal." And yet, he'd called it a murder.

I knew better than to say the word *dog*. "Six days ago? You know, I have the most incredible alibi," I said. Wiley was still staring at me from the corner. My skin prickled where I imagined a bullet going in.

"I know you do," Emmett said. He opened the other folder. "You were still in jail, awaiting arraignment for . . . how many murders was it?"

That wasn't a question I felt any need to answer.

"Well, the number changed every time they found a new body, right? And the charges were dropped, weren't they?"

I didn't answer.

"In fact, some people were calling you a hero."

"I'm not a hero," I said, too quickly. A hero would have done more than kill a few predators. A hero would have saved his friend.

"Find any designer drugs in Hammer Bay, Mr. Lilly? Have you seen anything that can make the lame walk, and turn them into crazed killers, too?"

"Not yet."

"And your relationship to Mr. Lem?"

"I don't have one."

Emmett nodded at me. "I think we should take a break. Wiley."

Wiley shut off the camera. Emmett collected his folders and left the room. Wiley led me back to my cell.

It was still dark outside. Alone in the cell, I lay down on the bench and let myself drift off to sleep again.

I awoke to the sound of the cell being opened. This time it was Sugar Dubois letting me out. He didn't handcuff me. I glanced at the window and saw daylight.

"What . . ." Sugar said. He seemed almost shy. "Why did you have so many meat wrappers in your apartment?"

"I'm a collector," I said. "A rare cube steak can fetch a couple hundred bucks on eBay."

Sugar didn't think that was very funny. He led me out into the front offices. Annalise was already standing by the front door with Emmett. Shireen, Luke, and Wiley were nowhere in sight.

"You folks can go," Emmett said. "If you intend to leave town, let me know about it first. Understand?"

I looked at Annalise. She shrugged dismissively and walked toward the door. I heard Emmett make a low growl in his throat. He was used to being treated like a big shot.

I followed Annalise into the street. The Celica and the black and red trucks were gone. There was nothing to do but walk back to our rooms. My stomach grumbled, but food would have to wait. I wanted my ghost knife.

I noticed a silver Escalade parked on a side street near the station. It looked out of place, but I put it out of my mind. I had other things to think about.

"Did you know Karoly Lem?" I asked Annalise. She didn't answer. She was walking with her hands held out a little from her body. It wasn't a big change in her body language, but I noticed it. I spoke in a low voice. "Do you need a trip to the butcher shop?"

"Yes!" she hissed.

We walked quickly through town. "Why hasn't the meat cured you?" I asked her.

"I don't know. It always has in the past, but this time a little piece of pain remains, and I can't make it go away. The pain grows back."

"What should we do?"

She frowned up at me. That word *we* had just slipped out, but she didn't like it. "The longer a piece of meat has been dead, the less use it is to me. We need something as fresh as possible, and a lot of it."

A man walked toward us. He was dressed as a county electrical worker. I looked him in the eyes to catch his attention. "Excuse me," I said.

He checked us out. He didn't like the way I looked, but seeing Annalise beside me seemed to reassure him. "Yes?"

"We're not local—maybe that's obvious—but we're looking for a butcher shop. Is there one in town?"

"Well, I always go to the supermarket," he said.

"We've been there," I said.

"Okay. There is a place. It's expensive. It's at the other end of town just off Ocean Street. Look for a New Agey crystal and book shop and turn right. It's just a couple of doors down. You can't miss it."

"Thanks," I said.

I turned to Annalise. "That's just a couple of blocks past our motel. Do you want another ten pounds?"

"Twenty," she said.

We walked the length of Ocean, found the New Age bookstore, and walked up the side street. The butcher shop was closed and wouldn't open for another hour. At my suggestion, we walked back to Ocean and found a place to eat breakfast.

The silver Escalade now sat parked on the corner while we went into a seafood restaurant. I wasn't happy to see it again so much closer to us.

After we sat at a table, Annalise ordered for both of us. Apparently, we both wanted the fried-fish omelets, with a side of fish. After the waitress left, I excused myself.

I slipped out the back door of the restaurant. The alley smelled of old fish bones and was apparently home to a clan of feral cats. I made my way to the corner.

A quick trip up the side street showed me that the Escalade was still on the corner. Someone was sitting in the driver's seat. The engine was off, but the brake lights were on. Keeping a foot on the brake was a good driving habit, but it was bad for a stakeout.

I walked casually toward the vehicle. I would have liked to have a hat to pull down low or a different jacket to put on, but I didn't. I hoped that being casual would cut it.

It didn't. When I was still a full car length away, the engine started and the car jolted into the street. I ran toward it, hoping for a glimpse of the driver, but the SUV squealed into traffic, turned a corner, and was gone.

So much for my ninja skills. I went back into the restaurant and joined Annalise at the table.

"Where have you been?" she asked. The waitress approached our table with our food.

"Checking out a car."

Annalise grunted. She took my plate, scraped the side order of fish and half of my omelet onto hers, then returned the rest to me. She used her hands cautiously, tenderly, but her expression was calm. I took her toast.

We ate slowly, killing time. We didn't talk. Annalise watched the street, so I bought the Seattle newspaper and scanned it for my name. There was nothing, thank God. While I read, Annalise ordered another plate of fish. I didn't ask if it helped.

Ten A.M. finally arrived. Annalise and I strolled over to the butcher shop and bought five whole beef tenderloins. The butcher wrapped them all up in one package. It weighed twenty-five pounds, and I carried it.

At the motel, Annalise stopped in at the manager's office. I followed.

The manager was the same nervous little guy I'd seen while the Dubois brothers were ransacking our things. He gaped at the big package wrapped in butcher paper on my shoulder, then opened his mouth to ask a question. Annalise didn't give him the chance.

"Have there been any messages for me?" she asked.

The manager looked down at his desk and shuffled some papers. He rubbed his nose and said: "Nothing. I'm sorry."

Annalise swore under her breath and turned toward the door. She was going to walk out.

"Hey," I said to her. She stopped and looked up at me. "You do know he's lying, right?"

She seemed startled. She turned back toward the manager. If he had kept his cool, he might have bluffed his way through it. Instead, he began to stammer and protest with all the sincerity of a hack politician.

"Now, hold on," he said. "I . . . I don't want to . . . um . . . want to be rude, but I . . ."

Annalise yanked the package of tenderloins from my hands and walked over to the counter. She lifted the beef over her head and slammed it down on the counter like a sledgehammer.

The wood cracked. Instead of a flat counter, it was now a sagging V shape. The manager screamed out, "Jesus!" as he leapt backward. Annalise tossed the slab of meat to me. It nearly knocked me on my rear end.

"You lied to me." Annalise's voice was quiet. I was standing behind her, but I knew the expression on her face very well. Annalise had a way of looking at people as if they were something small and disgusting and in need of stepping on.

The manager retreated toward the back wall. There was a door behind him, but he seemed to have forgotten it was there. If he had a weapon in the place, he'd forgotten about that, too.

"I . . . I . . ." was all he could say.

"Where is that message?" Annalise said. Her voice was rising. "It belongs to me."

"I don't have it," the manager squealed.

"Who does?" Annalise hissed. "Who took it? Was it Able Katz? Charles Hammer?"

"What? No!"

"It was Emmett Dubois," I said. The manager looked at me, his fear suddenly doubled. "The message was from a Polish guy who stayed here, right? And just before he was killed, Chief Dubois came by here and collected the note. Right? Or was it just after he was killed?"

"I can't tell you anything," the man said. "You don't understand."

"I understand," I assured him. "You're afraid for your life, right? How much are you paying Dubois every month?"

"I can't," he said. "I can't talk about it."

"Give me the figure. That's all I want. How much?"

He looked at Annalise. He was afraid of us, sure, but he *wanted* to tell. We all want to tell. We all want to air our grievances and spread our gossip. Dubois had scared him pretty well, but Annalise and I were all the excuse this little guy needed.

"A hundred dollars," he said.

"That's fine. Now, did Emmett collect that message from you before Mr. Lem was killed, or after?"

"You said the figure was all you wanted. You said—"

"It was all that I wanted. She"—I nodded toward Annalise—"wants something more."

He sighed. "Before," he said.

"That's what I thought," I told him. "Don't worry, no one needs to know that we heard it from you."

Annalise folded her arms across her chest. "What did the message say?"

"I didn't read it," the manager said, his voice nearly pleading. "I just put it in an envelope like the foreigner asked and set it aside for you. I didn't even know it was important until Emmett came by asking about it. I swear."

"That's fine," I said. "That's fine. Annalise, will we be moving to new digs?"

"No, we won't," she said.

I set the meat on the edge of the manager's desk. Red juices dripped through the torn butcher paper onto a stack of papers. "Well then," I said to the little guy, "It looks like you're stuck with us for a while. Let's go into the back."

He needed a little convincing, but eventually I led him through the door into his back office. As I suspected, he had a hidden camera at the front desk. I collected the VHS tape, wondering if the Dubois brothers were on one of these cassettes, too. A hidden stash of bribe videos would be good insurance, if he had the wit to play his cards right.

But we were here for the fire and the dead kids. We were here for Charlie Three. Dubois wasn't any of my business.

"Listen," I said as I tucked the videotape under my arm. "That message was important. More important than you realize, and you put a lot of people in danger by turning it over to Chief Dubois."

"What are you, then? FBI?"

"Of course not. And don't ask that question again. We're going to be staying here for a few more days, then we'll be moving on. Keep your head down and you'll be fine. Understand?"

We walked back out into the front office. He looked at his ruined desk and groaned. "What am I going to tell my wife?"

"Tell her that two disreputable-looking people came in here and lost their tempers," I said. "Try to stay as close to the truth as possible. You're not much of a liar."

Annalise and I went outside. She checked the van. Everything that the Dubois brothers had thrown into the parking lot had been carelessly thrown back inside.

We went into my room. I retrieved my ghost knife from the cut in the floor and pocketed it. It felt good.

I dropped the beef onto the table and unwrapped it. I cut a long strip of meat and then cut that into tiny slivers. Annalise started to pick them up with her fingers and gulp them down.

"How did you know Dubois had the message?" Annalise asked. "And what difference does it make when he got it?"

"When the chief asked me about Karoly Lem, I figured he had something to do with you, even though I'd never heard of him before. He stayed at this motel, right?"

Annalise nodded while she chewed.

I kept the meat coming. "Not good. With all of us staying at the same place, it's too easy for someone like Dubois to connect us. Anyway, Lem is dead, and Dubois has to investigate, or at least make it look like he's investigating it."

"Do you think he killed Karoly?" she asked, her mouth full.

"I can't really tell, but I'd bet he did. What was Karoly here to do?"

She didn't answer me right away. She slid another piece of raw beef into her mouth and chewed.

I sighed. "I can guess, but it would be better if you just told me. Was he another one of your wooden men?"

"No," she answered quickly. "You're my wooden man. I've never had another."

"Okay," I said. I still didn't know what a wooden man was. "Then what was he doing? Casing the town?"

"Pretty much," she answered. "There aren't enough peers in the society to check out every strange report, so we have investigators who check things out. Hammer Bay . . ." She trailed off. Then she ate a piece of beef. With most people, you could let the silence play out and they'd eventually feel the need to fill it. But Annalise wasn't a people person. She was used to long silences.

"What about Hammer Bay?" I asked.

"We've investigated Hammer Bay before," she said. "We never found a reason to do an action, but we've had people here."

"What made you send them?"

"This time it was the success of the toy company. 'Toy Company Breaks All the Rules to Succeed' was the headline, I think. I have the clipping in the van." She lifted a hunk of beef and gulped it down. "We end up investigating a lot of that sort of thing—businesses that should fail but rake in tons of money instead. People who get rich quick. People who win lotteries."

"Lotteries? Really?"

She shrugged. "There are still a couple of luck spells floating around. They mostly don't work anymore, but when they do a lottery is usually involved."

A dozen questions presented themselves. Before I could choose one, she spoke up. "A hundred dollars doesn't sound like a lot of money. How did you know?"

"Something the cook at the diner said about all the different kinds of insurance he has to carry. And the Dubois brothers didn't buy those trucks on a small-town cop's salary. Besides, if they extort too much, eventually someone calls the state cops or the FBI. A hundred bucks is irritating, but not enough to fight the local bullies over. And if you're tapping twenty or thirty businesses, it adds up."

"I guess so."

"At Hammer Bay Toys, did you notice anything strange about the fire?" I asked.

"You mean aside from the fact that it shot out of the mouths of a bunch of middle-aged paper pushers?"

I laughed. This was practically a bonding moment. "Not just that. When the fire came near me, it felt like it had already happened. Do you know what I mean? It was like I was watching the fire right in front of my eyes, but at the same time the fire was something that had happened to me a long time ago. Kinda."

"Like you were feeling it and remembering it at the same time," Annalise said.

"Yes," I said. "I felt the same thing when I was standing next to the boy, Justin. It was as though the fire was reaching around the moment I was in and coming at me from the side."

Annalise stared at her hands and flexed them. She moved them pretty well, but she would have stopped eating if the pain was gone completely. "Not just in that moment. The fire seemed to strike at me in the past," she said. "It might have gone back and struck when I was just a kid, before Eli, before I had any of these protections."

I mentally filed the name Eli away. "It attacked you in the past to hurt you now? Is that even possible?"

She shrugged. "If it happened, it's possible."

"But then, wouldn't you have had this pain all of your life? Wouldn't you remember having chronic pain?"

She waved off my objections, tossed another piece of meat into her mouth, and spoke while she chewed. "I'm just guessing, but I'm not saying the fire burned me while I was a little girl at the butter churn. I'm saying it came at me from the past. Maybe the future. Not everything experiences space and time the way we do. Some predators can be pretty strange."

"Butter churn?"

"I'm older than I look, remember?"

I remembered. She looked to be about twenty-three or twenty-four years old. "Are we talking *Little House on the Prairie* old or Ye Knights of Olde old?"

She shook her head and looked away. "Just keep cutting." Her voice had a ghost of humor in it.

I wasn't sure what exactly had changed between us, but I was glad of it. Not just because I didn't want Annalise to kill me, although I'd be a liar if I said that didn't matter. The truth was that I wanted her on my side. She knew more about magic than I could ever guess, and she could handle herself.

She had power. I had to admit, I was drawn to that power. It was alluring. I wanted to be next to it, maybe leech off some of it for myself.

I tried to picture us in thirty years, when I was in my late fifties, still driving her around. Would she still look like she did now? I'd probably look like her father.

Unless she did for me whatever it took to make a person stay young . . .

No. I shook that thought away. Annalise wouldn't even tell me who she talked to on her cell phone. She certainly wasn't going to share the secret of her long life with me.

I was not going to spend my time daydreaming about something I would never get. That was poison.

And yet . . .

I looked at her again. She was so small. With her jacket off I could see her tattooed arms poking out of her short-sleeved shirt. They were so skinny that they made me queasy. She looked like she was wasting away. Her thin muscles rolled back and forth under her skin as she lifted a piece of beef to her mouth. Her elbows were like knots in a rope.

She had been scrawny from the first moment I saw her, but she looked worse now than ever. I wondered if her injury was burning the flesh off of her.

How long would she live with the pain in her hands? Would she have to go centuries like this, devouring a side of beef every day?

If the fire was coming at her from the future as well as the past, if it was always a second or two ahead of whatever cure she administered, she might never be free of it. Unless it killed her.

Annalise cleared her throat. "I'm going to tell you a story," she said.

CHAPTER EIGHT

"Okay," I said. I kept cutting meat, although it was nearly gone now.

"A long time ago, before most of the world was writing down its history, there was a powerful sorcerer. He was a primary, a dreamer, and his power was immense. I'm not much for history, so I don't remember his name. Let's call him Simon.

"Simon lived on a mountainside, in a huge palace. There were fertile fields all around, and Simon had a lot of villages and farmers working the land and paying him for the privilege. He wasn't a good man by today's standards, but for the time I suppose he was. And he protected his people.

"On the other side of a mountain range lived another sorcerer, Thomas. He wasn't a primary, but he still had a lot of power. And he summoned predators. Lots of them.

"At the time, the custom between sorcerers was live and let live, but Thomas was getting on Simon's nerves. His predators were killing Simon's villagers, turning them into vampires and other nasty shit, and stealing them away to work for him.

"Simon grew pretty annoyed, right? He sent a message to Thomas telling him to leave his lands and his people alone and get rid of his predators.

"Thomas, not surprisingly, refused. He said that he needed his predators for protection, and that he was doing nothing wrong himself. If some of his creatures roamed into Simon's lands to feed, there was nothing he could do about it.

"However, he did offer to leave the area, if he could take a copy of Simon's spell book with him.

"Simon immediately decided to kill Thomas."

I realized that she had stopped eating. I kept cutting and piling the meat on the butcher paper.

"So Simon gathered up a bunch of his spells and headed out. His lands were ruined and his people scattered. When he reached the edges of his enemy's lands, he began to fight.

"Now, Simon was powerful, but he couldn't get through. Before he could reach Thomas's palace, he was swarmed by predators: Floating Storms, Claw-in-Shadows, all sorts of things, not to mention his own villagers under the influence of Puppet Strings or transformed into vampires.

"He was driven back three times, each time expending more of his spells. He realized that he wasn't going to be able to take out Thomas this way, so he went into the forest and cut down a stand of poplar trees. Then he lashed the pieces of wood together. He put a spell on them to make them walk like men and swing their arms in a feeble imitation of an attack.

"When he had made enough, he sent them against Thomas's defenses. The predators swarmed them, destroying them wherever they found them.

"And in the confusion, Simon snuck into Thomas's palace and faced him one to one. Thomas didn't have a chance."

I had finished cutting the meat. It was there for Annalise whenever she wanted it. I wiped my ghost knife against the edge of the butcher paper. It didn't come very clean, but I didn't care. I dropped it, still wet with raw beef, onto the table.

I didn't look at her. I just stared at the pile of cut-up meat.

"Simon himself was never part of the Twenty Palace Society, but his student and heir was one of the founding members. And he shared the tactic of using wooden men with the rest of the peers. It's a tactic that has continued down through the centuries."

And that was the end.

Right about then, I thought, would have been the time for her to say, *Do you understand, Ray?* or *I'm sorry, Ray* or *But it doesn't have to be that way for you, Ray.*

She didn't say any of those things. She just picked up another piece of raw beef and started chewing.

"Excuse me," I said, and I went out of the room.

The fresh, salt air was bracing. *Stupid, stupid, stupid.* I must have been an idiot not to have seen it sooner.

The worst part was that I had volunteered. I'd asked to work for her. I hadn't understood at the time that it meant I would be a decoy, that I would be cannon fodder, but I had volunteered.

She had asked if I would be her wooden man, and I had said yes. She'd never explained what it meant. She had tricked me.

But of course, that was bullshit. I had been bluffing from the moment I met her and had pretended to know more than I did. And I had been lying to her in other ways as well, all to save my friend. If I was up to my neck, it was my own damn fault.

I was a decoy. Expendable. I had thrown my future away to save someone that I'd been forced to kill anyway. Damn.

I noticed the Escalade again, this time parked across the street. It would be harder to approach this time. I'd have to circle around two blocks to come up behind it, but what else did I have to do?

I went back into the motel room and asked Annalise if she had a second scrap of wood with a magic-finder spell on it. She took it from her satchel and handed it to me without a word.

I held it up to the light by the window. It flared, all of the designs freezing in place and turning silver. Then it returned to its normal shade of black, with the designs slowly turning.

I touched the wood to the tattoos on the back of my hand. Annalise's magic made it glow with silver light, but after it acclimated to my touch, it returned to its normal slow churning. No powerful magic was close to us right now.

I picked up my ghost knife, rinsed it clean in the bathroom sink, and slipped it into my pocket.

I left Annalise in my room. I didn't have a way out the back, but I bet I could go through the manager's office to a back door, then an alley, then I could try to come up behind the Escalade again. This time I'd get close enough to check it for magic. If Charles Hammer was watching us, I suspected he'd make the scrap of wood pop like a string of firecrackers again.

I walked slowly toward the office, wondering what I could offer Annalise to get her to release me from my promise. If I took out Charles Hammer by myself, or found a permanent cure for her hands, or pieced together the whole story of what was happening in Hammer Bay, maybe she would let me go home, or promote me to tin man or something.

That pointless line of thought was interrupted by a white cargo van that rumbled into the parking lot. It was a Dodge, and it looked remarkably like Annalise's, except that it was newer and had a pair of battered ladders lashed to the top. The back door opened.

Floyd's fireplug friend crouched there. He pointed a snub-nosed .38 revolver at me. "Hey, there, jackrabbit," he said. "This one is loaded."

Two more guys crouched in the back of the van. My mind

registered that they were there, but I couldn't look away from that damn gun.

"Your gun is drunk?" I said. My voice sounded much more calm than I felt.

"Get in. Someone wants to meet you."

I climbed into the van. They slammed the doors and my brain kicked in. They were all wearing construction boots. I looked directly at the fireplug. "Georgie," I said, "if Henstrick wanted to talk to me, she should have called. I would have liked a visit."

"Know my name, do you?" Georgie said. He smiled. "But you don't know everything."

The van bounced out of the parking lot. I glanced at the two other guys. Both held mean-looking hunting knives. If I knew everything, I wouldn't be in the back of this van.

"Get his wallet," Georgie said.

One of the other two, a trim ex-Marine type with dark bags under his eyes, placed the edge of his knife against the side of my neck. The third man sat well back out of everyone's way. The ex-Marine yanked my wallet out of my pocket.

"Raymond Milman Lilly," he read. "And here's Floyd's thirty bucks." He took the money out of my wallet and stuffed it into his breast pocket.

"Floyd is my bud," Georgie said. "I didn't like the way you left him."

"Really? Then why did you turn and walk away when I was beating his ass?"

Georgie didn't take my bait. "Conditions were unfavorable at the time. I like them better now."

"I'll bet you do."

The ex-Marine pulled the wood scrap out from my jacket pocket. We all looked at it. The design turned as slowly as ever. There was nothing magical about these fellows.

They stared, entranced. I tensed to spring at Georgie, but he sensed it, raised the gun, and leveled it at my face. "Be still," he said quietly.

"Whoa," the third man said, still entranced by the wood scrap. "That's cool."

The ex-Marine rubbed his finger along the design and yanked it back. "Tingles," he said. "How does it do that?"

"Trade secret," I told him. "We're trying to convince Hammer Bay Toys to manufacture and market them under their banner."

The ex-Marine shrugged and set it down next to me, apparently forgetting that I was being held at gunpoint. He pressed the blade more tightly against my neck as he jammed his hand into my jacket pockets.

"How we doing back there?" the driver called.

"We're fine," Georgie answered. "How far are we?"

"Halfway," the driver said. He turned sharply to the right. The ex-Marine lost his balance and his blade bit into my neck.

"Watch what you're doing," I snapped at him. He pulled the knife away slightly. I felt a thin trickle of blood on my collar, but I knew it wasn't serious.

"Sorry," the ex-Marine said. He pulled out my ghost knife and held it up. Everyone looked at it. It was just a sheet of notepaper covered with mailing tape and laminated. I could sense the power there, but none of them appeared to.

"What's this?" Georgie asked.

I held up my hand. "It's just a piece of paper," I said. "Toss it here."

I *reached* for the spell and called it to me. It shot out of the ex-Marine's hand, passing through a couple of his fingers on the way. As always, it passed through his living flesh as though he was not there.

The knife moved away from my throat. The ghost knife had done its work on the ex-Marine. I caught the spell and immediately threw it.

Georgie was taken by surprise, but not by much. The ghost knife went right where I wanted it to go, cutting through the top of his trigger assembly just as he began to squeeze it. The gun didn't go off, and a second later I heard the trigger clatter against the floor of the van.

In the time it took the broken trigger to fall, I called the spell back to me and slashed it through Georgie's leg. It cut a long slit in his pant leg, but the cut through his leg was bloodless.

I turned toward the ex-Marine. He was slumped and sagging, all the vitality drained out of him. For safety's sake, I slid the ghost knife through his arm one more time. It never seemed to matter where the ghost knife struck a living person—it always had the same effect.

Georgie and the ex-Marine slid to the floor as though they were fainting. The third man lunged at me, his hunting knife aimed at my throat.

I threw the ghost knife at him and batted at the knife with the protected part of my forearm. The spell disappeared into his chest. The strength went out of him, but there was still a lot of momentum behind that knife. I mistimed my block and felt the tip of the blade slice my unprotected upper arm.

The third man fell against me. I *reached* for the ghost knife again. If the spell went through the wall of a moving vehicle, I could be a block away from it very, very quickly. I wasn't about to leave my only real weapon behind.

"What the hell?" the driver said. I closed my eyes.

The ghost knife flew back into the van, cutting a slit in the wall and letting in a sliver of light.

The van swerved to the right and lurched to a stop. The third man fell on top of me, knocking me to the floor. I was pinned beneath him.

The driver climbed from his seat. I heard him open the glove compartment. I didn't try to free myself. I didn't have time. I switched the ghost knife from my pinned left arm to my free right arm. The driver turned toward me, gun in hand. It was another .38.

If I hadn't been lying under one of his friends, he would have had plenty of time to shoot me. We were at point-blank range, but he didn't have a clear shot. I threw my spell at him.

He tried to slap the ghost knife away but missed it. It entered just above his navel, and as soon as it disappeared I *reached* for it again. The spell boomeranged back to me, passing through the driver a second time. He collapsed.

I caught it. I'd never tried that trick before. I liked it.

I shoved the man off me and struggled to my knees. All four were still awake, but they were bleary-eyed and listless. I took both knives, Georgie's revolver, and the driver's, too. Both guns were identical to the one I'd taken from Floyd outside the bar. Maybe the construction workers in Hammer Bay bought in bulk.

Georgie looked up at me with glazed, pleasant eyes. "Sorry about the way I treated you," he said. "I don't know why I was so rude."

"Yeah, yeah," I said. The ghost knife didn't just take away their strength, it also cut out a person's rage and aggression. Temporarily.

I checked the cuts on my neck and left biceps. The one on my neck was barely a scratch. It had already stopped bleeding. The one on my arm would need a couple of stitches and had come way too close to my brachial artery.

I took their wallets. The four of them had a grand total of thirty-seven dollars on them. That's how it goes in the age of the debit card. I also took back the money Floyd "paid" me. I didn't bother with the IDs this time.

"All right, you clowns," I said to them. They all stared up at me with wet, docile eyes. I aimed the .38 at them. "Get on your knees beside the side door."

They did.

"Put your hands flat on the floor. Get them next to each other."

They pushed and nudged against one another, trying to position themselves.

"I'm sorry about all this," the ex-Marine said. "We were just—"

"Shut up," I said. I slid the ghost knife into my pocket and picked up the disabled revolver. I slid the cylinder release forward and dropped the rounds onto the floor. Then I picked up Annalise's scrap of wood and put it in my pocket. "Where are the keys?"

The driver spoke up. "In the ignition."

"What were you guys supposed to do with me?"

"Bring you to the Curl Club," the driver answered, "so Phyllis could talk to you."

"Phyllis?"

"Phyllis Henstrick. She runs the place, and Henstrick Construction."

"Why does she want to talk to me?"

"She didn't say," the driver answered. He crouched beside the others like a little lamb. All of them stared at the barrel of the pistol in my hand. They couldn't look away.

"I think," Georgie said, "that it had to do with a rumor she heard about Charles Hammer sending jobs overseas."

Of course, I thought. "Okay, boys," I said to them. My voice was low. "Live or die?"

Georgie understood right away. "Live," he said. The others agreed.

"Fine," I told them. "I'm only going to be in town for a couple of days, I hope, and I don't want to see any of you again. So I'm going to take out some insurance. Hold still. If any of you yank your hands away, I'm going to assume that means you've changed your answer." I turned the revolver around and held it like a club.

"Please," the ex-Marine said. "Please don't."

"It's gonna hurt," I said, letting some of my anger show, "but not as bad as a bullet in the guts."

I slammed the butt of the revolver onto the backs of their hands, aiming for the knuckle of their index fingers.

It wasn't the smartest move, but the smartest move would have been to kill them all. I didn't want them shooting at me from a moving vehicle tomorrow. I had to take them out of the game somehow, and I had to teach them, and whoever pulled their strings, not to mess with me. Breaking their hands was gentle compared with what I should have done.

They cursed and whimpered like scolded boys. When it was done, I slid open the side door.

"School's out for the day," I said, and kicked Georgie through the open door.

He tumbled out onto the curb, and the other three scrambled after him on their knees and elbows. They crouched on the sidewalk, blinking in the drizzle, holding their arms across their chests just as I had outside Sara's bar. I slammed the door shut.

The keys were, in fact, in the ignition. I laid the guns in my lap, started the van, and pulled into traffic.

At the first red light, I picked up the driver's revolver. I took out my ghost knife and cut off the hammer, then sliced through the cylinder. I tossed it into the back of the van. Georgie's gun was already ruined.

I have my reasons for not liking guns.

On impulse, I opened the glove compartment and peeked inside. My curiosity was rewarded with an envelope filled with five $50 bills.

Things were looking up.

My arm was bleeding pretty freely. It was annoying and I'd need to have it taken care of. I took the tourist map from my inside jacket pocket and consulted it. Looking around the neighborhood, I oriented myself to the two main roads in town. The hospital was behind me and to the east. I turned at a corner, then did it again.

I was a couple of blocks from the hospital when I saw a McDonald's. Half an omelet and toast hadn't held me, so I pulled into the drive-through. If I was going to wait in an emergency room, I might as well have lunch with me.

And wooden men don't have to worry about cholesterol.

I ordered the biggest, sloppiest burger they had, along with fries and a milk shake. In for a penny, in for a pound. As I pulled up to the pickup window, a pretty teenage girl with a splatter of pimples over her face leaned out the window.

"Hi, Uncle Ethan!" she said.

Then she saw my face. Her mouth dropped open, but she didn't say a word. "Hello yourself," I said. I paid her with Georgie's money. She gave me the food.

"That looks like my uncle's van," she said.

"Really? Weird," I said to her. I set the bag of food on the seat next to me and drove to the emergency room.

To my surprise, there were no other patients. To my further surprise, I didn't need stitches. The doctor cleaned the wound, glued it shut, and packed a bandage against it. It cost me three hundred dollars. Luckily, I hadn't bought two milk shakes. Uncle Ethan paid my bill for me, leaving about six dollars in my pocket. Easy come . . .

I thanked the emergency room staff and walked toward the exit to check on the van. Through the glass doors, I saw the Escalade slowly cruising through the parking lot. I stepped away from the glass. The SUV circled Uncle Ethan's van, then drove around the building.

I turned away from the doors and hustled through the hospital, moving as fast as I could without attracting attention. I had planned to visit Harlan Semple while I was here. That would have to wait.

I passed bare corridors with no doors. For a moment I felt lost, then I burst through some double doors and found myself in a storage room filled with plastic tubes in plastic bags, and IV stands. Feeling relieved, I broke into a sprint, running to the loading dock I knew had to be at the end of the hall.

There was a small panel van backed against the loading dock, and an eighteen-wheeler backing up beside it. A man in jeans and a polo shirt called out to me, telling me I wasn't supposed to be there, but I jumped off the loading dock and ran to the street beyond.

I reached the sidewalk. The street was nearly empty, and the Escalade was nowhere in sight. I was standing at the exit of the parking lot. Nothing there, either.

Wait. There it was. The Escalade pulled into view, then stopped, as if the driver was looking around. I ducked behind a tall hedge, bumping against the stop sign that controlled traffic entering the road.

The vehicle turned toward the exit and puttered toward the spot where I was hiding. I watched it through a break in the bushes, trying to get a glimpse of the driver. I couldn't. The overcast clouds reflected off the windshield, blocking my view. Still, I was sure it was Charles Hammer in there.

The Escalade pulled a little past the stop sign and paused on the sidewalk. I knew the driver would be watching the traffic to the left, so I stepped from my hiding spot, yanked open the passenger door, and hopped into the seat.

"Hello," I said.

The driver cried out in a high-pitched voice, and for a second, I thought Charles Hammer looked much shorter behind the wheel than he had in his offices.

Of course, it wasn't Charles behind the wheel. It was a well-dressed, dark-haired woman. She had broad, even, lovely features, hair that reached just below her ears. Her legs were thick with well-toned muscle. She looked to be about thirty.

And I had just jumped into her car like a carjacker.

"Oh!" she cried. "Oh, I . . . um . . ."

"Is there something you wanted to talk to me about?" I asked her.

She glanced at the cell phone holstered beside her car radio. "Do you want to call the police?" I asked. "Go ahead. I think that's a terrific idea."

"Look," she said, shrinking fearfully against the door, her hand inching toward the door release. "I'm sorry about following you around. You met with my brother, and—"

"Who's your brother?"

"Charles Hammer. At Hammer Bay Toys." I nodded. I could see the resemblance. "I wanted to talk to you—"

"Then why did you pull away when I approached you the first time?"

"I wasn't sure then. I just decided this morning."

She'd laid her hand on the door release, looking like she was ready to throw herself out of the car at any moment. I noticed a diamond tennis bracelet on her wrist. It was tasteful and worth more than Uncle Ethan's van. When she grimaced, I saw that her teeth were as white as pearls.

"Whatever," I said. I felt sour. I didn't want to terrify some woman. I didn't like the way she was looking at me. "Whoever you are, stop following me around. I don't like it."

I opened the door and slid out of the vehicle.

"Wait!" she called. I waited for her, both of my feet on the concrete and my hand on the door, ready to slam it shut.

"I'm sorry. I really do want to talk to you. I think you can help me. Would you meet me at this address in an hour?"

She held out a business card. I didn't take it. There was no point in getting distracted in my search for Charles Hammer.

Unless she was willing to help me.

"Please?"

I shrugged and took the card. She thanked me and apologized again. I shut the door. She pulled away.

I looked at the card. It read *Cynthia Hammer*. Below that was an address on Hammer Street. That was the right last name. I turned and walked back to the parking lot.

The fright I had given Cynthia Hammer had taken all the fun out of being a bastard. I returned to Uncle Ethan's van and tossed the keys on the floor by the brake pedal. I was tempted to wipe it down for fingerprints, but I noticed drops of blood on the driver's-side door and decided not to bother. Uncle Ethan, Georgie, and their two buddies should be turning up soon to have their hands worked on. They might as well find their ride waiting for them, even if they couldn't drive it home.

I walked around to the front of the hospital into the reception area. The very polite matron working there told me that visiting hours had just started. It was one in the afternoon. When I admitted that I was a friend of Harlan's, not a family member, she told me I would need permission from the family to visit.

She called a volunteer over and spoke to her in low tones. The volunteer then said, "Follow me, sir," in a shy voice. She led me to the elevator.

The inside of the elevator was stainless steel polished as bright as a mirror. I saw my dirty, rumpled pants and bloody, torn shirt. I didn't like the way I looked.

The elevator doors opened, and the volunteer led me down a quiet hall to a little waiting area. Shireen sat alone, reading a tattered copy of *Redbook*. She was wearing a WSU Cougar sweatshirt.

The volunteer spoke to her in a voice barely louder than a whisper. "This gentleman would like to visit Harlan. Would that be all right?"

"Yes," Shireen said. She turned to me. "Maybe he'll talk to you. I'm his only family in the entire world, and he treats me like an enemy."

The volunteer had already started back toward the elevator. Shireen returned to her magazine. "Which room?" I asked.

She tossed her magazine onto the vinyl couch with an irritated sigh. "This way," she said.

She opened the door and stepped into Harlan's room. I heard a rasping voice before I saw him. He said, "Out," in a raw, strained voice.

"Someone is here to visit you," Shireen said. "Try to show him more courtesy than you've shown me."

Harlan lay in the bed. He had tubes in his nose, his arms, and his chest. He looked smaller, than I remembered him, but everyone looked smaller lying in a hospital bed. Everyone looked smaller without a gun, too.

Shireen pushed by me and shut the door behind her. I pulled up a chair and sat next to the bed.

Harlan looked pale and exhausted. He might have been getting good care, but no one was going to make him live if he didn't want to.

"Having a bad week?" I asked. Harlan made a wheezing sound that might have been laughter. He winced in pain. "Sorry, man," I said. "No more jokes. I promise."

He settled down. I went to the foot of his bed. There was a chart hanging there, just like they show on TV, but I couldn't make heads or tails of it.

"How you doing?" Harlan rasped.

"How am I doing with my . . ." I almost said *investigation,* but that's a cop's word. I didn't want to say it. "I'm further along," I said, "but this town is a mess. And it's scary. But I've got nothing to lose."

And that was true. Harlan and I were both pretty close to death. Despite his injuries, I figured it was even money to see which of us would live longer.

"How long ago did this start?" I asked. "The kids, I mean."

Harlan held up his hand in a peace sign. Two.

"Two months?" I asked. He frowned. "Two years?!" He relaxed. I'd gotten it right.

Two years. Christ.

"Did something else happen around then? Something that seemed strange or . . ." Harlan's eyes grew dim. He was exhausted, and I had pushed him far enough. "Relax, dude," I said. "And hold on. I'm going to need to ask you more questions when you're better. I need your help, okay?"

He nodded faintly. I didn't really think he could help me much more, but I wanted to give him a reason to hold on. I stood and left him lying there, alone. I heard him struggling to breathe.

Shireen had company with her in the waiting room. Standing beside her was a short, fat man in a stained polo shirt and brown shorts that reached just below his hairy knees. He held a tape recorder in his hand. I disliked him on sight.

"Come on, Shireen," he said, his voice an annoying whine. "I'm going to find out . . ." Shireen's face was set in a scowl. She was not about to answer anyone's questions.

He glanced over at me, and his face lit up. He turned to me. "Hey! I've been trying to catch up with you for two days. I'm Peter Lemly with *The Mallet*. What's your connection with Harlan Semple? Is it true that you've come to town to outsource some of the Hammer Bay manufacturing jobs?"

I stared at him. He stared back, holding the tape recorder out. I leaned toward the microphone and said, very clearly, "You're just about as wide as you are tall, aren't you?"

He yanked back the recorder, but he didn't turn it off. He looked flustered and aggravated. "I know who you are," he said, trying to make it sound like a threat.

"So does she." I jerked my thumb at Shireen. "Now why don't you go away so I can express my sympathies in private."

"Are you a friend of the family, then?"

"Nope. Never met any of them before two days ago."

"What about the jobs at the toy factory?" he asked.

"I don't know what you're talking about." The rumor would work for us while it was a rumor. As soon as it appeared somewhere official, Able Katz could refute it and it would lose some of its power.

"Actually, I think you do. I'm the only media this town has, and I'm not going to be pushed around. I'm going to get some answers myself." He turned to Shireen. "Do you hear what I'm saying? I'm going to find out."

"I'm not going to talk to you, Peter." She wouldn't look at him. "I'm never going to talk to you. Now, excuse me, I think my visit is over."

She turned to leave. Peter started to follow her, but I stepped in his path.

"The lady wants to leave," I said. "Leave her be."

"So macho," he sneered. "So chivalrous. You have no idea who you're protecting."

"What story are you following?" If he had said *missing children,* I would have swallowed my bile and bought him a drink. With my last six bucks.

"Town corruption," he said.

"You're after . . ." I let the sentence trail off. Lemly was eager to finish it for me.

"The Dubois brothers. And the mayor, too, if he's involved. And the town council. The whole town knows what's going on, but no one will stand up to Emmett Dubois. Except me."

"Good luck with that." Shireen had already entered the elevator at the end of the hall. The doors closed over her unhappy face. I turned away from my companion.

"Wait!" He grabbed my elbow. "What are you doing in town? What have you come here to do?"

"Good luck with your story," I said. "I hope you don't get anyone killed."

I turned my back on him and walked toward the elevator. He followed me, peppering me with questions. He wasn't very good at it.

The elevator opened again. I stepped inside and shoved Peter away from me. He didn't fall, but he did keep his distance while the doors closed.

I rode down the elevator, thinking about my own behavior in the last hour. I'd driven around in a stolen van, jumped into an SUV and menaced a woman, and shoved a guy in a hospital hallway.

I'd never been this reckless and aggressive, even back when I was part of Arne's crew. I knew the cause of it, of course. I was a dead man. I had agreed to be cannon fodder for Annalise's war. Despite her recent gestures of friendship, she had promised to see me dead, and it felt very, very close.

I laid my head against the cool stainless steel wall of the elevator. The best I could hope for was that I would be there when Annalise took down Charlie Three. I wanted to see her put an end to that bastard and avenge those children.

I didn't know when and how she would make her next move.

Could she take out Charlie Three alone, injured as she was? What if she failed?

That pleasant thought was interrupted by the elevator doors opening. I walked into the lobby and asked the woman at the reception desk for directions to Hammer Street.

I got them. Of course Hammer Street wasn't on my tourist map, but it was near the toy factory, on the inland side of the plant, about as far south as the lighthouse.

I left Ethan's van where it was. Then I headed out onto the sidewalk, oriented myself, and started walking.

What I should have done was call Annalise. My destination was an address on Hammer Street—it could very well have been Charles's home. If I found him there, it would be best if she was with me. But she hadn't given me her cell phone number and I didn't want the motel manager to share my message with Emmett Dubois.

If Charles Hammer the Third really was at this address, was I going to kill him? Could I do it? It made me a little sick inside to think it, but I suspected the answer was yes.

Considering.

An even bigger question was whether Hammer would stay dead. That I didn't want to think about too much. I would take my shot at him, if I got one. If it didn't turn out well . . .

I *really* didn't want to think about that.

Of course, I wasn't exactly conducting myself like a sensible hitman. I'd just asked a hospital receptionist for directions to the victim's street, for God's sake.

Maybe I wouldn't have to kill Charles Hammer. Maybe I could find a better way.

I heard the sound of children screaming.

There was a long stretch of green grass on the corner ahead of me. Before I realized what I was doing, I was running toward it, ghost knife in hand.

Kids scattered in every direction, running off a junior-sized basketball court. On the asphalt, I could see a four-foot-high plume of fire with a little figure inside.

I ran into the street and sprinted toward the park. A hugely fat woman rushed toward the child, screaming. Then the flames sputtered out and the figure inside fell to pieces onto the asphalt.

I felt the twinge against my iron gate.

The fat woman stopped running. The few remaining children that hadn't disappeared also stopped. Parents began to call their kids back to the playground.

I reached the court. The fat woman turned and started walking back to the bench where the other parents were sitting. I was alone at the foul line.

As I'd seen with Justin Benton, this child had broken down into a mass of fat, silvery worms. They crawled across the asphalt court, shiny and revolting. Where they touched the ground, they left a trail of black soot.

I had no rational reason for what I did next. All I knew was that I had to destroy as many of those creatures as I could.

I swung the ghost knife at the trailing worms. Ordinarily, the mark would not hurt living things, but I suspected these were predators—creatures from the Empty Spaces, partly physical and partly magical. And the ghost knife cuts magic.

My spell slashed through the hindmost worm. There was a second's delay, then the worm split open and burst into flame.

I watched as the tiny creature was consumed by fire. Good. They could be destroyed.

I swung my ghost knife at another. Just before I made contact, a tiny cut appeared on its back and a tongue of flame erupted from it. I changed the direction of my attack just in time to avoid the fire, and my altered swing touched the worm in just the right spot to create the tiny cut I'd already seen.

I drew back from the fire. Damn. That time the wound had appeared before the ghost knife had connected. That meant something, I knew, but with my blood pounding in my ears, I couldn't work it out.

Both worms were still burning. I moved toward the side of the wriggling mass, striking at the tiny creatures at the edges. They flared and burned as I nicked them, but the flames never grew strong enough to combust the others. Maybe this spirit fire, as Annalise called it, didn't burn that way. It didn't matter. I crouched beside the mass, striking here and there, moving along its bulk away from the flames.

When the entire side was ablaze, I moved across the front, careful to avoid the tiny creatures as they crept forward. I imagined one of them leaping at me, burning me the way Annalise had been burned, but I kept up my attack.

Within seconds, the entire front of the mass was blazing. I began to work my way down the other side. The worms I had cut burned in the black streak behind the rest, and the creatures at the front crawled through the pyre of the others without apparent harm.

I crouched low and kept close, inflicting tiny nicks on the worms, watching for times when the little creatures flared up from my attacks before the attacks had actually landed.

We had gone ten feet. Then fifteen. Then twenty. Eventually, I stopped circling the mass. The spirit fire burned so fiercely at the edges and tail end that I couldn't get a clear shot there. I hopped to the front of the mass, dropping to my hands and knees directly in its path.

I struck at the worms as they tumbled through the wall of flames at the front. I backed away. I was destroying the creatures, but the mass was still advancing. I couldn't stop it.

My feet touched grass. There were many fewer worms than there had been, maybe only 10 percent of the original mass, but I wasn't going to get them all. I cursed at them, swore at them as I killed them. Eventually, I had backed all the way onto the grass, and the first of the worms tumbled off the asphalt. Fewer than a dozen hit the soil and started tunneling, but that was still too many.

I jumped to my feet and rushed back onto the court. The worms had vanished beneath the earth, and I didn't like the idea that they might tunnel up from beneath me.

I looked at my ghost knife. There was no residue on it, no blood, no black soot, nothing. It was as clean as the day I'd made it. I slipped it into my pocket.

A long skipping rope lay on the basketball court with a discarded baseball cap beside it. The cap was lavender. It had been a little girl this time.

I looked at the streak. The northern edge of the court was not ten feet from the spot where the fire had started, but the worms had turned toward the southwest. They'd gone a long way, exposed to danger, to head in that direction.

I turned and looked along the path of the black streak. It pointed in the general direction of the Hammer Bay Toys plant. It headed toward Charles Hammer the Third.

At that moment, killing Charles Hammer seemed like the most important and most natural thing in the world.

I walked the rest of the way to Hammer Street in a daze. I kept trying to picture the face of the little girl that had just burned away, but all I saw was a rotating series of faces, all absurdly angelic. At that moment, I would have knifed Charles Hammer in a police station, in front of forty cops and a dozen TV-news cameras.

This was my mind-set when I finally reached Hammer Street. It was a single block long, curving westward with no sidewalks. I walked up the middle of the street. There were stone walls on either side of me, and thick blackberry vines growing over the top. The road sloped upward, and as I reached a cul-de-sac, I saw three houses.

The smallest sat on the north lot. It was made of brick and had pretty white balconies. The second house, on the southern lot, was made of mortared stone. It was low and wide, and was probably very modern forty years ago. Both were shuttered and dark.

The largest house occupied the western lot. It was made of wood and stood three stories tall. It had a nest of slanting roofs, mismatched balconies, and clusters of stone chimneys. On the southern side of the house, a tall, round tower loomed above the rest. It was the oldest of the houses, and it dominated the street. I turned around and saw the town of Hammer Bay laid out before me. Maybe the house was meant to dominate the town, too.

I checked Cynthia's card. Of course her address matched the large house.

I wondered if Annalise would be grateful if I killed Charlie Three myself, right now. I wondered if her hands would heal.

There were three cars parked in front. One was the silver Escalade. Beside it was a fifteen-year-old BMW, a good car and pricey when it was new, but it had suffered rust and salt corrosion and the damage had been allowed to spread. The third car was a blue Tercel. It was such an ordinary, unassuming car, it was nearly invisible beside the others.

The street was empty. There were lights upstairs at the large house, but everything seemed still. I assumed all three houses belonged to the Hammers, although I wasn't sure what gave me that impression. Maybe it was the way the street had been laid out for maximum privacy. Maybe it was that I didn't think anyone would share an address on Hammer Street in Hammer Bay with the Hammer family.

An instinct for caution made me approach the brick house first. I circled it, looking for an unblocked window. There wasn't one. The stone house, though, had a broken shutter on a back window. I peered in.

Nothing. No furnishings, no art on the walls, nothing. It was an empty shell. I went to the big house and rang the bell.

To my surprise, Cynthia answered. She looked aggravated, and several strands of her dark hair stuck out in random directions. "You're late," she said. Her tone wasn't friendly.

"Where's your brother?" I asked. The anger in my voice surprised me.

She ignored the question. "I'm afraid I'm a little busy right now. I'll have to ask you to wait in the library."

"Where's your brother?" I asked again. "Where's Charles?"

"I don't like the way you're asking that question."

I imagined myself throttling the answer out of her.

No. I turned away and stared back over the town. The cold, furious sense of purpose that had driven me across town began to fade. I was not going to start killing everyone between me and my target. Annalise would have, but I was not going that far.

"I'll wait in the library, then," I said to her.

She stepped backward to let me enter. "I don't like that you're late. I expect people to be punctual. I'm not a person who likes to wait for others." She sounded flustered and annoyed, and I wasn't sure if she was trying to put me in my place because I'd scared her in the car, or if something else was getting on her nerves and she was taking it out on me. Either way, I didn't care.

She led me into the library and shut the door. I looked out the window. I saw a wide green lawn with a winding white stone path laid across it. The sight was soothing.

I held up my hand. It was trembling. I wondered how I could find out the name of the little girl I had just seen killed. No one would remember her. No one would go looking for her. There would be nothing in the news. I could look for that fat lady, I guessed, under the assumption that it was her daughter, but what good would that do? She wouldn't remember her any better than anyone else. I could break into their house and search the place for a photo . . .

I laid my hands on the window frame and pressed my face against the glass. I was not going to break into that woman's house. That little girl was never going to be more to me than a small bonfire, seen at a distance. I didn't need her name.

There was a small door to my right. I ran to it and yanked it open. It was a bathroom, thank God. I would have hated to vomit into one of Cynthia's closets.

I washed my face and rinsed out my mouth. My emotions were back under control, and I felt better. I felt like myself again. I didn't want to be some angry hard-ass who bullied his way toward his enemies. I didn't want to be Annalise.

That gave me pause. How many dead bodies had Annalise seen? How many dead children, killed by some jackass with a spell book? No wonder she acted the way she did.

I heard a man and a woman start shouting at each other, and I headed toward the door. On the way, a small picture in a silver frame caught my attention. It was a black-and-white photo, taken a long time ago.

On the left side of the picture was a man in a dark waistcoat. His face bristled with white whiskers, and he had the satisfied look of a man who fed himself well. In the center was a tall, angular man in a long, road-worn coat with a walking stick in his hand. His hair was a little too long and needed combing, and he smiled out of the side of his mouth. He looked like a smooth talker and a bit of a con man, the sort of friend you keep for a lifetime but never, ever trust. Both wore hats and old-fashioned clothes. I guessed the picture was taken in the thirties.

On the right was a young girl in a pretty white dress. Her hair was bobbed, and her little shoes pointed slightly inward. I could see, at the lacy cuffs and collar of her dress, a faint spider's web of black lines. Tattoos. She had turned her solemn little face to look up at the con man, and I could see by her profile that she was Annalise.

I stared at the picture, dumbstruck. She looked eight or nine years younger than she looked now, but I was sure the picture was taken at least seventy years ago. Who was the man she was looking at? A second glance at him showed tattoos covering the back of his hand. I squinted at Annalise's face. She looked love-struck and slightly awed. Was this her teacher?

The shouting started again. I set the picture down, opened the door, and went out into the hall. There were doors all around and voices were coming from behind one of them. I walked toward the sound.

"Now, Cabot," a man said. "There's no reason to be so upset. Cynthia didn't—"

"Don't tell me what she did!" a man shouted. I guessed it was Cabot. "I know what she did! I have eyes!"

"Well, here's a good idea for you," Cynthia snapped. "Use them."

"Things are going to come around again," Cabot said. "Things are going to be made right. You watch, and you *watch out*!"

I had almost reached the heavy oak door when it flew open. A man in his mid-fifties with a heavy paunch and a blotchy face stormed past me. His thick, dark hair was speckled with gray.

There was something in his expression that I didn't like. He looked like a man who didn't care anymore.

I watched him stomp off. His clothes had been expensive once, but the heels of his boots were worn away and his jeans were frayed at the bottom.

"I thought I told you to wait in the library." Cynthia had moved up next to me. She looked irritated. "Well?"

I heard the front door slam.

"I'm nosy."

She glared at me. After a moment, she said: "Come into my office. Please."

I followed her into a small room. The floors were hardwood, and a large desk dominated the far corner. The only adornments on the walls were a pair of kimonos set in wooden frames.

A fat little man sat on the couch, rubbing his face wearily. His long, graying hair hung over his shoulders. "That man exhausts me—"

"Frank," Cynthia cut in, "this is Raymond Lilly. Mr. Lilly, this is our mayor, Frank Farleton."

Frank lifted his face from his hands and looked up at me in surprise. He didn't look pleased to see me. "I know who you are. What are you doing here?"

I turned to Cynthia. "Call me Ray. I've seen the mayor before but didn't introduce myself. He was too upset about your brother's seizure. Isn't that right, Mayor Farleton?"

"What are you doing here, please?" he asked again. At least he was polite.

"She invited me. How long has Charles been having seizures?"

The mayor struggled off the couch. He had to huff vigorously to lift his bulk onto his feet. "What do you mean? Who invited you?"

I heard the front door slam again. No one else seemed to notice it. The office door was behind me to my left, the desk in front of me to the right. I backed against the wall and slid my hand into my pocket next to my ghost knife.

Cynthia strode behind her desk and offered me a strained smile. The mayor sat on the corner of her desk. "I don't think Frank means who invited you to my house. I think he means who invited you to Hammer Bay." Her pretty smile betrayed a touch of scorn. Her hands were shaking. She was having a bad day. "But," she continued, "you're here to answer my questions, not his. And if you don't feel like answering, all I have to do is call Emmett Dubois. Once I tell him you broke into my car and tried to take the keys—"

The office door burst inward and Cabot charged in. I was ready for him, but I was still too slow. He lifted his arm. He was holding a pistol.

Time seemed to slow down. Cabot aimed at Cynthia. His teeth were bared, his cheeks flushed red.

The mayor stepped in front of her, his arms spread wide, his fat cheeks puffed out in an almost comical way.

I swung the ghost knife at the gun. Cabot squeezed the trigger. The hammer drew back. I was too slow. The gun fired. A bare second later, the ghost knife swept through it, slicing it apart.

The mayor flinched as the bullet struck him just above the collarbone.

Cabot squeezed the trigger again, but the gun was already coming apart. It didn't fire. He turned toward me, his mouth opening in what I imagined would be angry protest. He looked at the remains of the gun in his hand in utter shock.

I slid the edge of the ghost knife into his chest and, before he had a chance to go slack, threw an overhand left. I was off-balance, but the punch landed just in front of his earlobe. Cabot dropped like a marionette with his strings cut.

I turned toward the others. The mayor was holding the top of his right shoulder with his bloody left hand. He stumbled away from Cynthia and looked at her. Then he collapsed onto the floor. The bullet appeared to have only grazed him, but he was bleeding profusely. His face looked pale.

Cynthia looked at me. Her mouth hung open in a little O, and her face was slack and pale.

I don't like guns. I stared down at the mayor for a moment too long, wishing the whole thing hadn't happened.

His face grew more pale by the second. Cynthia gaped at him.

"Call an ambulance," I said. Cynthia turned her empty gaze toward me. She seemed to be in a trance. "Right now!" I shouted.

She jumped and lunged for the phone on her desk. She wasn't used to being yelled at.

I grabbed an arm cover off the couch and knelt beside the mayor. I confirmed that the bullet had grazed him just above his collarbone, well away from the arteries in his neck. If he'd been less fat, it might have missed him altogether.

I wadded up the arm cover and pressed it against the wound. "Well, well," I said, trying to keep my tone light, "look what you've managed to do. This doesn't look too bad, though."

"It hurts," he said.

"Being a hero usually does."

"What? I'm not a hero. I wasn't thinking. I just—"

His face was getting paler. I grabbed a cushion off the couch and slid it under his feet. "Of course you didn't think," I said. "Who would jump in the path of a bullet if they were thinking?"

Cynthia spoke into the phone, asking for an ambulance. She spoke so quickly she was on the verge of babbling. I called her name to catch her attention, then told her to speak as calmly as she could. She took a deep, shuddering breath and recited her address into the phone. She told the operator on the other end that the mayor had been shot.

"I don't want to die," the mayor said. His voice was small and childlike. He squeezed his eyes shut, and I saw tears running down his face. "My wife . . ."

"I'm no doctor," I told him, "but I think you're going to be okay. Harlan was shot much worse than you, and he's recovering. Just try to take deep breaths and stay calm. The ambulance is on the way." The color came back into his face just a little.

Cynthia hung up the phone and stared down at the scene in utter befuddlement. "What happened to Uncle Cabot's gun?"

"Come over here and make yourself useful," I said. She circled around her desk and knelt beside the mayor. "Put your hands on this cloth and keep a steady pressure on the wound."

She looked at my bloody hands and balked.

"This man just took a bullet for you," I said. My voice was low and edged with anger. "Now do it."

She did.

The mayor looked up at her. "I'm sorry," he said. "I'm so embarrassed—"

Cynthia burst into tears.

I watched her for a moment, to make sure that she kept her hands on the wound. She did. The mayor began to comfort her, and his color definitely improved. It helped him to have someone to comfort.

Cabot lay in the doorway. I wiped my bloody hands on the front of his shirt, then began to pat him down. He didn't have another gun. He moaned and began to come around.

My ghost knife was in my pocket, although I didn't remember putting it away. I slid it through his hand. It wouldn't keep him unconscious, but it would make him docile.

I heard sirens. "You two sit tight," I said. "I'm going to open the front door." Cynthia and the mayor kept murmuring to each other. They didn't seem to hear me.

I dragged Cabot into the hall. Docile or not, I didn't want him waking up in the same room as them. Then I walked over and opened the front door.

The EMTs were already jogging up the steps, a stretcher in their hands. Behind them was Emmett Dubois, his hand on his holstered weapon. Emmett squinted the length of the hall and saw Cabot lying at the far end, his shirt smeared with blood. Cabot shifted his leg, barely on the edge of consciousness.

"He's right this way," I said to them, pointing to the open office door. They rushed past me.

When I turned around, I saw Emmett Dubois pointing his gun at me. "Turn around, put your hands behind your head, and drop to your knees."

"I'm getting sick of having guns pointed at me."

"Ain't that too bad." He pushed me onto my stomach and began twisting my arms behind me. Cynthia stepped out of the office and saw us.

"What are you doing?" she said. "He didn't hurt anyone. He *saved* us."

She told him what happened. Emmett uncuffed me and helped me to my feet. He offered a brief but insincere cop apology and made a beeline for Cabot. Cabot had come around enough to rub the side of his jaw. Emmett rolled him on his stomach and cuffed him. Cabot didn't resist.

Cynthia stepped close to me. Her hands were shaking. "I have to go to the hospital. Will you drive me? I don't think I can manage it right now."

"Sure," I told her.

The EMTs emerged with the mayor on a stretcher. They didn't seem to be in a hurry. Emmett dragged Cabot to his feet and led him toward the door.

"I'm sorry," Cabot said. "I'm sorry, everyone. I shouldn't have done that."

He went on and on like that. Hearing his meek, whining voice seemed to set Cynthia on edge, so I held her back to let the others get ahead. We stood on the front porch and watched them load the mayor into the back of the ambulance, and Cabot into the back of Emmett's police car. They started their engines but didn't turn on their sirens.

After they had disappeared around the corner, Cynthia turned toward me. "Do I look terrible?" she asked.

Her eyes were red and puffy from crying and her lip twisted down on one side as she fought back her tears. Her makeup was still perfect. "You can check yourself on the way. Do you have everything you need?"

"No, I'll be right back."

She rushed back into the house. I took the scrap of wood out of my pocket and laid it against the doorjamb.

Nothing. The design churned at its normal slow pace. The Hammer house was no different from any other. I looked at the other two on the cul-de-sac. If I were Charles Hammer the Third, heir to a timber fortune and owner of a wildly successful toy company, which would I live in? A tiny brick house or an empty stone one?

Neither, really. I started toward the brick house for no other reason than that it was slightly closer. I had only gotten a couple of steps when the door opened behind me.

"I'm ready. Let's go," Cynthia said.

She gave me the keys and I drove. She flipped down the passenger-side visor and studied her face. I tried not to pay too close attention as I wound my way through traffic, but I could see her hands trembling slightly.

"Are you all right?" I asked her.

"Yes. I think I'm going to be fine. What about you? Are you all right?"

The question surprised me. For a second I thought she'd known about me in the library toilet. *Hanging on,* I wanted to say. Then I realized she was talking about Cabot and the gun. "I'm fine. Maybe I'll freak out later, but I'm fine right now."

"You're not really going to freak out, are you?" she said. "You're just saying that to be nice." I shrugged, and she laid her hand on my arm. Just for a moment.

It was my turn to shiver. Damn, it had been a long time.

We reached the hospital. I was glad to see that Ethan's van was gone.

The receptionist told us that the mayor was in intensive care. Cynthia seemed to shrug this off, but I was confused. "I didn't think his wound was that serious," I said. "It looked like it just grazed him."

"Well . . ." The receptionist looked around and then began shuffling papers on her desk. She looked up at Cynthia as though she was one of her supervisors. Maybe that's what it meant to be part of a founding family—everyone treats you like you're in charge. "I shouldn't have told you that much. HIPAA rules."

Cynthia leaned forward and said, "Look—"

"Is there someplace we can wait?" I interrupted. The receptionist called a volunteer, who led us to a waiting room on the third floor. We sat on a plastic couch beside a stack of bland supermarket magazines.

"His wife hates me," Cynthia said. "She hates me already. I just hope she doesn't take another swing at me. I wouldn't be surprised if she brought a hatchet. Good thing we're already in a hospital."

She went on and on like that. Cynthia rambled, mostly about how much Farleton's wife hated her. She didn't mention Cabot at all, and I didn't bring him up. Misery was pouring out of her, and I didn't want her to shut me out. Not when I needed her to point me toward her brother.

The door at the end of the hall opened, and Emmett Dubois entered. Trailing along behind him was a tall blond woman, probably just a year or two older than Cynthia. She was long-legged and wore way too much makeup on her lovely face. She looked utterly distraught.

Cynthia jumped up. "Miriam, I'm so sorry."

"I don't want to hear it," Miriam snapped. "I just want to see my husband."

Emmett stepped between them. "Let's find Frank's doctor. Would you come with me?"

Miriam shot a withering look at Cynthia, then followed the chief down the hall.

Peter Lemly rushed in. He was red-faced and sweating, and I could hear him panting from down the hall. He followed the chief and Miriam Farleton.

"Did you see that?" Cynthia said. "She hates me." I didn't say anything. "She's always hated me. Ever since high school. She was three years ahead and she dated Charles for a couple of weeks. He wouldn't turn his life over to Jesus, though, and he got tired of hearing her talk about it. He broke it off with her, and for some reason she blamed me. She thought I was making fun of her behind her back."

"Were you?" I asked, although I was pretty sure I knew the answer already.

"Hell, yeah. But Charles didn't care what I said. He never cared. He always had to do things his own way."

"Your brother sounds like an interesting guy."

She didn't take the bait. "I saw the way you were looking at her," she said.

I shrugged. "She and the mayor don't exactly look like a couple, do they?"

She laughed. "The whole town, men and women, felt the same way when they started going together. Frank was ten years older and even fatter than he is now—she's worked on his weight over the years. He's a good man, even if he's kind of a wimp." I didn't mention that a real wimp wouldn't have taken a bullet for her. "I think he'd be scooping ice cream in the back of a truck if he hadn't married her. She's the ambitious one. But they sure do seem to love each other," she said. "No one really understands it."

"Maybe he cast a spell on her."

She turned and looked at me. She was measuring me, trying to see if I had dropped the word *spell* casually or if I was hinting at something. The way she looked at me told me what I needed to know. I wondered what would happen if I laid Annalise's magic-detecting scrap of wood against her skin.

I shrugged. I wasn't ready to show my hand yet. She blinked and then shrugged, too. I wondered how much she knew about what was happening to the kids in town.

"Where's your brother?" I asked her. "I'd like to meet him."

She leaned back in her chair and looked at me sideways. "I'm supposed to be asking you questions, remember?" She had a half smile on her lovely face. It looked good on her, but it was too practiced. "I asked you to come to my house so I could shine a bright light in your face and pepper you with questions."

"Okay, but let's leave out the badge-wearing goons."

"I think we can go goonless for now."

We smiled at each other.

She asked me a couple of questions about Annalise's meeting with Able Katz. I answered with harmless lies. The questions she asked told me more about her than she realized. I figured she must not have friends in the company or any pull with her brother or she would already know the basics.

Emmett Dubois arrived. He told us that he would need statements from both of us. Strictly routine, he assured us. Cabot had already confessed.

This time, I wanted to put him off until I could talk to a lawyer. Maybe Annalise would hire one for me, but Cynthia turned to me and said: "Why don't you go first? I want to wait and explain things to . . . you know. Be nice to him, Emmett. He saved my life. Frank's, too."

"Of course I will, Cynthia," Emmett said.

We left the waiting area and walked into an empty room. Emmett set his folder and his hat on the bed, then took a tape recorder from his pocket.

"Do you mind if I tape this?"

"I guess that'll be all right."

He turned on the machine and recited his name, my name, the date, and other information. Then he asked me what happened.

I told him, with a couple of modifications. I didn't tell him about the fire on the basketball court. I didn't tell him that I had gone there looking for Charles with the intent to kill him. I didn't tell him that I chunked into the toilet, and I didn't tell him that I'd cut the gun with the ghost knife.

I did say that the gun fell apart after it fired that first time. I said I felt lucky that I hadn't been killed, and that I personally didn't think I'd saved anyone's life. Cabot's gun was defective, and I coldcocked him. Even if I hadn't been there, I said, he couldn't have done more than he did.

We went over it again, this time focusing on why I was there, why Cynthia had invited me, and why I had gone. I had sensible answers for everything, and he didn't seem concerned.

It was the friendliest conversation I'd ever had with a cop. It made me a little nervous, but I did my best to smile and act friendly in return.

Finally, he shut the recorder off. "That jibes with what Cabot told me, although he claims that you broke the gun with your bare hands."

"Heh! Really? Weird. Someone should tell him guns are made of metal."

Emmett chuckled. "That's what I figured. We did take the gun into evidence, though. It was in a strange condition."

"How so?"

"It didn't explode, the way guns do when the barrel is jammed. It was sheared apart. Like it was cut."

"Is that unusual?" I asked, being careful to look him in the eyes— but not too closely—and not to touch my face.

"I've never seen a weapon fail that way. Never heard of it, either."

"Weird. And lucky."

He looked at me for a moment, then smiled. He was a friendly guy today. "It sure was lucky." He began to gather his stuff. Then he stopped and looked at me again. He knew something he wasn't saying.

There was something else going on here. There was something I wasn't seeing.

And honestly, I didn't like being on such friendly terms with Emmett Dubois.

"Excuse me, Chief," I said. "Can I ask your opinion on something?"

"Okay. What is it?"

I opened my jacket wide, so that when I reached into it he would see there was no gun. I drew out the scrap of wood.

"This is a little something that I'm trying to sell to Hammer Bay Toys. I think it's a neat little trick."

I set the scrap of wood on the bed beside his folder. The design on the front continued its slow, implacable churning.

"Well, I'll be damned," he said. He looked down at the moving paint, obviously intrigued. Then he looked up at me. "May I?"

"By all means," I said.

Emmett picked up the scrap of wood. As soon as he touched it, the design went dark. A tiny flare appeared on the wood, and then a jet of black steam and iron-colored sparks erupted from the design.

The chief had a predator inside him.

Emmett dropped it and jumped back. He laid his hand on his weapon. "What the hell was that?"

"This," I said, "is a Geiger counter for magic." I picked it up. My tattoos and ghost knife made the design flare silver for a second. "You have some kind of nasty spell on you, Chief. What is it?"

He stared at me, his eyes wide. I stared back. Was he involved in the deaths of those children? Did he even know about them?

"Come on, Chief. Tell me what's going on here. What's happened to you? What's happened to your town?"

"Who are you? What are you doing in this town?"

"You already know who I am. You read all about what I did last fall. As for what I'm doing here, there's something wrong in this town. I'm here to fix it. Party's over, Chief. *We* know about you now."

He sniffled. I had spooked him. He wasn't used to that. "Maybe I should take you in—"

I laughed. "You don't have any idea *what I am,* do you? I'm not going anywhere with you this time. You're going to have to tread carefully."

It was a bluff, but I wasn't going to put myself at his mercy. He was infected and had to be destroyed. Once Annalise found out, she'd pinch his fat head off.

But was Emmett an underling? The secret source of Charlie Three's seizures? Or was he another victim?

Emmett glared at me and backed toward the door, his hand on his weapon. I just smiled at him. He left.

I sat for a moment, thinking about Cynthia, the mayor, and Cabot. Was Cynthia in on it with her brother and Emmett? Was Farleton in on it, too? Maybe Cabot was trying to put a stop to the deaths. It was something to think about.

I walked back to the waiting room. Cynthia was still sitting on the plastic couch. I was startled to see Annalise on the other side of the room, incongruous in her oversized fireman's jacket, steel-toed boots, and tattered pants. For one absurd moment, I thought she'd come to be treated for her burned hands.

Cynthia stood when she saw me. "Was he decent to you?"

"He was fine."

She rubbed her hands on her pants, looking uncomfortable. She wanted me to keep her company, but Annalise was already moving toward me. Cynthia sat again. Annalise took my elbow and led me down the hall out of earshot.

"What have you been doing?" she asked.

"Making enemies. Friends, too. The chief of—"

"That girl said you saved her life," Annalise interrupted. "Is that true? Who is she?"

It seemed funny that Annalise was calling Cynthia a girl. Cynthia looked to be six or eight years older, but looks can be deceiving. "Sure, it's true. And she's Cynthia Hammer, sister to Charles Hammer the Third. She's the one who was following us in the SUV."

Annalise glanced back at Cynthia, making sure she was still on the couch. "I want you to fuck her," she said. "Then find out everything you can, especially where her brother is. I can't track him down."

"You're a real class act, boss."

"Just do it. I have work to do in the morgue."

She turned on her heel and stalked away. I wondered again how many dead bodies she had seen, and how long it had taken her to become what she was.

And she hadn't even given me a chance to tell her about the predator in Emmett.

I ran into the hall, calling her name. She stopped and turned toward me. A passing nurse shushed me forcefully.

"What is it?" Annalise asked.

"Predator," I said, my voice low. She tensed and leaned toward me. I had her attention. "Inside Emmett Dubois. I don't know what it is, but I'd guess his brothers are infected, too."

"How do you know this?"

I removed the scrap of wood from the inside of my jacket. She frowned and took it from me.

"Did he see this?" she asked, holding up the slowly moving design.

"Yep."

Annalise nodded and pocketed the scrap of wood. "You have your next assignment," she said, and walked toward the elevators.

I went back to Cynthia. She was, apparently, my next assignment. Spending the night with her wasn't the worst thing that could happen, but I didn't like that Annalise had *ordered* me to do it. I didn't even like the idea that she would know. It was creepy. I sat a little farther away from Cynthia than I had before.

"Is that your wife?" Cynthia asked. "Your girlfriend?"

I was honestly confused for a moment. "Who?"

"That redhead. The one you were just talking to."

I laughed. "Sorry," I said. "But that's funny. She's actually my boss, and she hates my guts."

"Oh."

"It's complicated."

"Well," she said, "I'm glad she's not your girlfriend."

That was my cue to say something smooth. Before I could think of something, the door to Frank's room opened and Miriam stepped out.

"Are you Ray?" she asked me.

I stood. "I am. Is there something I can do?"

"He wants to talk to you." Her lips were pressed together in disapproval. She pointedly did not look at Cynthia.

I moved toward her and the door. "Is he well enough for that?"

"No, he isn't. The gunshot wound was minor, but he had a heart attack in the ambulance. The surgeon is on his way to the hospital now. But he insists on speaking to you."

"I'll be quick," I said, and went into the room. She shut the door behind me, remaining in the hall.

Frank lay in the hospital bed, tubes running out of his nose. Peter Lemly stood by the side of the bed, and another man stood beside him. He must have arrived during my interrogation, because I didn't recognize him. He was tall, straight, and serene, with graying hair carefully styled. He was the third of the four men who had met with Emmett Dubois beside the van when I saw Charles have a seizure. He turned toward me without meeting my gaze, and I saw that he was wearing a clerical collar.

It made sense for the reverend to be there. But I didn't understand why Lemly was in the room.

"We meet again," Frank said. His voice was hoarse and weak.

"Let's do it without the ambulance next time," I said. "Shouldn't you be resting?"

He gasped between breaths. "I wanted to thank you."

"Forget about it. Relax. You're going to undo all my hard work."

Miriam had entered the room just in time to catch that last word. She narrowed her eyes at me. No one else seemed to care. Ah, well, I'm the bane of respectable women everywhere.

"Anything I can do for you," the mayor said.

"When you're stronger, I want to talk about Hammer Bay."

"He needs his rest," Miriam said.

"Of course." I backed toward the door. I was trying to think of a way to compliment him, to tell him, in front of his wife and a reporter, that I thought he was a damn brave man, but he spoke before I could.

"Hammer Bay," he said. His voice was low and a little angry. "My town. So rotten and corrupt. It's time I did something about it."

Miriam glared at me. Peter Lemly lunged forward, his tape recorder in hand. "Would you repeat that, Uncle Frank?"

Miriam snatched up a clipboard and thumped Peter on the top of his head. He wasn't deterred. The mayor began to say something else, but the reverend grabbed Peter's elbow and steered him out of the room after me. Within a couple of seconds, we were both out in the hall.

Cynthia was not sitting on the couch. She wasn't anywhere in the hall that I could see. Had she stepped out for a second, or had Miriam shooed her away while I was in Frank's room?

"Did you hear what the mayor just said?" Peter asked me. The door closed behind us. "Did you hear?"

"I heard that the mayor is your uncle," I said.

"Never mind that." He paced the hall. "The mayor is going to fight corruption in this town." He sounded excited, as though he was in a thirties gangster movie.

"Tell me about the town."

"It's pretty straightforward," he said. He was a guy who loved an audience. "The Hammers control the jobs. They're the first family around here, and they've always had a nose for the next thing. The next move to make. Until Cabot, that is.

"The Dubois brothers keep the peace, maybe a little too much. And lately they run a protection racket. I've been trying to get someone in town to go on the record about this, but no one will."

"Not since Stan, the bartender."

"How did you know about Stan Koch? He was supposed to bring me a bunch of records showing how much he'd been paying to Wiley Dubois over the years, but he was killed."

"Attacked by wild dogs."

"There really aren't a lot of dogs in town. Never have been. Someone gets a dog, it barks all night and all day, and within a couple of weeks it vanishes. That was a dull story to track down, let me tell you."

"The Hammers and the Dubois brothers. Is that it?"

"There's the reverend in there. Thomas Wilson. His church is the largest in town. There is a small Catholic church behind the Bartells Pharmacy, and there are some folks who speak the language of the angels in living room services, but Wilson's is the biggest. He doesn't do much, though. He cares about souls, not works."

"Who else?"

"I guess Phyllis Henstrick. She runs the vice, and some of the jobs, too. When business is good, her boys build and fix. When it's bad they get a little something from the whorehouse. A whorehouse is pretty recession-proof. That's pretty much everyone."

"What about drugs? There are always drugs."

"Sure, there's a little weed to be had here and there. No one much cares about that. Everything else, the Dubois brothers have some trick where they hunt them down."

"They take them over?"

"Actually, no. Their mama had a little trouble with pills back in the day. Mama's little helper, if you know what I mean. She cracked up their car, killing herself and their little sister. They don't much like drugs. When someone goes into the woods with a trailer to start up a meth lab, they don't come back. They just disappear, and Emmett drops by to give their friends little warnings. You know what I mean?"

"Subtle things, under the guise of investigating the disappearance, right?"

"You *do* know what I mean. So, is Hammer Bay Toys moving its manufacturing overseas?"

"If I wanted to talk to Charles Hammer the Third after business hours, where would I find him?"

"Probably at his home."

"And where's that?"

"Oh, no. We're protective of our patrons around here, Mr. Lilly. You're going to have a hard time with those sorts of questions."

"What if I ask about his seizures?"

"The Hammer family, er, *condition* is a private affair, which means the whole town knows about it. Not that there's anything to tell. Now, is Hammer Bay Toys moving its manufacturing overseas?"

"No comment."

"Oh, come on! I just laid out the whole town for you, and you don't pay me back?

"I have something for you. How much do you know about the shooting at the Hammer place?"

"Cabot took a shot at his niece after they argued about the family business. He hit Frank instead. You coldcocked him and saved them both."

"Not quite true," I said. "The truth is, the mayor saw the gun and stepped in front of Cynthia, protecting her. He stepped in the path of the bullet without even thinking about his own safety. Sure, I slugged Cabot, but I was standing right next to him when he came in. I don't think he even realized I was there. And I didn't really save anyone; Cabot's gun came apart after one shot. Frank is the real hero."

"Is this true?"

"Ask Cynthia."

"Don't think I won't. What else?"

"First, don't put anything in the paper about the mayor and Emmett Dubois. Not yet. Give Frank a chance to recover and prepare for the fight."

"He's had three terms to prepare for a fight."

"If you publish too soon—"

"I hear you. Anything else?"

"Leave town. Go to Seattle and sign on with a big daily. Or a weekly. But go. This town is dead already."

"So it's true, then? The jobs are going to China?"

"I'm not kidding. It's time to leave Hammer Bay while you still can."

"*Pft.*" He waved me off. "I'm not giving up on my town."

The door to Frank's room opened and Rev. Wilson stepped out. He managed to look down at us without actually looking at us. "I wonder if it would be possible," he said, his tone stuffy and superior, "for you to converse elsewhere. These rooms are not soundproof, you know."

Peter wedged his bulk between the reverend and me. "Are you going to support the mayor in his fight against corruption?"

"The mayor is in a terribly weakened condition. He won't be fighting anything or anyone for quite a while. It would be irresponsible for you to claim otherwise." He turned to me, glancing at me briefly before turning his eyes to the side. "And why are you still here?"

That was a good question. I walked away while Peter tried to get a statement from the reverend about what he was already calling the mayor's "new initiative."

I walked to the elevator. Beside it was a hospital directory, which told me that the morgue was in the basement. I entered the elevator and pressed the button. Cynthia hadn't returned, so I decided to stick close to my boss.

Why was Annalise in the morgue? I hoped it had something to do with Karoly Lem. I didn't want to go down there and see the corpse of someone I knew.

The basement was practically a ghost town. I wandered through the halls, looking for a sign that would point the way. Eventually, I found one. I followed the arrows.

I expected gray paint on the walls and rows of metal tables with bodies lying on them. I was glad to be wrong. What I found was a small reception desk in a little waiting room. Annalise stood beside the desk, filling in a form on a clipboard with her sharp, jagged writing. Her face was pale and her thin lips were white. She had a sheen of sweat on her forehead. Opposite her was a morose-looking woman with nothing to do but watch.

"Someone will contact you about the body," Annalise said as she handed over the clipboard. The woman accepted it and slunk through the door behind the desk. She was gone.

Annalise hefted a blue canvas bag from the edge of the counter. She winced. Then she turned to me.

"What's in there?" I asked.

"Karoly's things. What are you doing here? I gave you a job to do."

"While I was looking for a club to hit her over the head with, she slipped away. I'll have to drag her back to my cave some other time."

She scowled at me. I saw something in her expression I hadn't seen before. She looked vulnerable.

"Hey," I said. "Are you okay?"

"I'm fine."

"Don't lie to me," I said, amazed that I was genuinely worried. "How bad are your hands?"

She walked around me toward the doors, stuck her hands into the handles, and sucked air through her teeth. She was hurting. Bad.

I pulled the doors open for her. She didn't like receiving my help, but she didn't have a choice.

We walked up the hall together, turned a few corners, and pushed through a couple of doors. I had no idea where we were going. I decided to change the subject. "Did you find out what Karoly's message was?"

"I have his laptop in here," she said. "I'll read through it when we get back to the room."

"They let you have his laptop?"

"They searched it and didn't find anything. Who picked you up in the van?"

"Saw that, did you? Thanks for getting me out of trouble, boss. They worked for a player I haven't met yet: Henstrick, the woman who runs a construction firm and a brothel."

"Oh, yeah? Well, stick with the job I already gave you."

"I didn't say I . . . forget it." She stared at the floor as we walked. I wondered how well she knew Karoly, and how hard she was going to grieve for him, if at all. "While I was in the Hammers' house, I saw a picture—"

"I have an idea," she interrupted. "Go to the parking garage and get the van. I'll wait out front for you."

The look she gave me was angry and dangerous. Her face was paler and more sunken than before. I backed off. She held out the blue canvas bag, and I took it, being careful not to brush it up against her injured hands. She stalked away.

My life would become a lot easier if she were killed here in Hammer Bay. At least, I assumed it would. Maybe, when a peer in the society died, her wooden man was killed, too, like a pharaoh's slaves. Maybe the wooden man was reassigned to another peer, or traded around like a punk.

Or maybe they were cut loose. Maybe they were told to go away and not come back.

It sounded thin, but even so I didn't want anything to happen to Annalise. She hated me and would probably engineer my death, but the power she had was fascinating.

And I liked her.

Christ, I needed to get laid.

She hit a metal panel on the wall with her elbow, and the double doors in front of her opened. She stepped through, and the doors closed behind her.

I hustled back up the hall and reentered the morgue. I wanted a look at that clipboard Annalise had filled out. I wanted to see if it had an address on it, or a phone number. I wanted anything that I could use to track down some information on her or the Twenty Palace Society.

The reception area was empty. I rang the little bell on the counter. No one came. I rang again. I was all alone with the cracked plastic chairs and the slowly ticking clock.

I set the canvas bag on the floor. I'd seen the woman carry Annalise's clipboard into the back, but that didn't mean she hadn't brought it out again. I leaned over the counter and searched. There was an outdated computer, a steaming cup of coffee, a small collection of Pez dispensers, and a big framed picture of some sort of picnic. There was no form clipboard.

I vaulted over the counter and shoved the chair under the desk. There were file drawers below, but I didn't go for them yet. I figured that I'd have better odds in the back, and I had to do this quickly, before Annalise noticed the delay.

I laid my hand against the door. If there were metal tables and corpses on the other side of this door, I hoped they'd be covered with a nice, big cloth.

I pushed the door open.

The first thing I thought was: *That body should be on a table, not the floor.* Then I noticed a pool of blood slowly creeping toward me.

It was the morgue attendant, of course. Her throat was a raw, red mess, but her face looked utterly peaceful.

There were, indeed, tables in here. Two of them had sheet-covered bodies on top. I saw a phone on the wall and decided not to use it.

I couldn't see the clipboard anywhere.

On a table in the corner of the room I saw a pile of dark blue clothes set beside a pair of shiny black shoes. There was a holster and pistol on top of the pile. Cop clothes.

The blood had almost touched my shoe. I stepped back.

From somewhere in the room I heard a low growl.

CHAPTER TEN

I jumped backward, pulling the door behind me. I caught a glimpse of something large and low rushing at me. It struck the door hard, slamming it shut.

The door banged open again, and I fell backward onto the desk. The swinging door revealed a wolf, its hackles raised, teeth bared, red eyes glaring at me. This one was black, tinged with gray, and bigger than the reddish one I'd seen on the street. Or maybe it seemed that way because it was looking at me like I was lunch.

I snatched the steaming cup of coffee off the counter. The wolf moved toward me, and I threw the coffee, splashing some onto my hand. Damn, it was hot. The black liquid struck the creature across the face. It let out a high-pitched whine and drew back.

I rolled the chair forward, ramming the wolf while it was off balance and knocking it back into the morgue.

I grabbed the door handle. There was no lock on this side. I reached around and slammed my palm on the handle on the other side. Something clicked. I hoped it was a lock.

The wolf found its feet and twisted in my direction. I leaped backward, pulling the door behind me. I saw long white teeth straining toward me, and then the door was shut.

I vaulted back over the counter and landed on the canvas bag. I slipped and fell on my backside. Hard. Damn. I was going to be eaten alive because I was a clumsy idiot.

I grabbed the cloth bag, rolled to my feet, and rushed into the hall. I didn't expect the locked door to hold for long, and I was pretty damn sure that was not an ordinary animal. In fact, I was pretty damn sure it was Emmett Dubois.

I could have run after Annalise, but the wolf might have followed me through a hospital filled with patients and staff. I wasn't that ruthless yet. I wasn't Annalise. I ran in the other direction, toward what I hoped was the parking lot behind the hospital.

I pushed through the double doors and sprinted down an empty hallway. There were no doors on either side, but there was a turn up ahead. I saw an exit sign and bluish light shining there. I ran faster.

I was halfway down the hall when I heard the double doors open behind me. Over my shoulder I saw the wolf padding toward me. Its teeth were bared and its tongue hung out. Its eyes glowed, for God's sake, even in the harsh fluorescent lights.

The wolf paused about a third of the way down the hall. It seemed to be showing me more of its teeth. Was that a smile? Whatever his doubts about me during my interview, I was running from him now. He'd called my bluff and he knew it.

I turned the corner, headed for the exit. The fire doors leading to the parking lot were right in front of me. They were chained shut.

I was trapped. Or, I was supposed to be trapped.

I took out my ghost knife and cut the chain. Its weight pulled it to the floor with a loud rattle. I pushed open one of the doors and slid the ghost knife through the other one, just beside the latch.

I heard the clatter of sharp nails on linoleum. The wolf was losing me, and he knew it. I slipped through the door and slammed it behind me, then slid the ghost knife through it right next to the latch.

The wolf rammed the push bar on the other side of the door. The latch mechanism I had just cut made a grinding noise but didn't open. Thank God.

I backed away. The doors would hold for a little while, until Emmett finally hit them hard enough to bust the latch or decided to go back for his uniform and gun.

Emmett Dubois was a werewolf.

I ran to the far end of the lot where the van was parked, then drove to the front of the building. Annalise was waiting at the curb, scowling at me as I approached. Had I just said that I liked her? I decided it was time to stop being stupid and start hating her again.

I opened the door for her. She climbed in. She didn't put on her seat belt. "What took you so long?"

I was not in the mood to share information. If she wanted something from me, she was going to have to give something. "Tell me about the last time you were in Hammer Bay. Tell me about the last time you met with the Hammer family, and about the tall man with the walking stick."

She didn't answer. She looked at me closely for nearly a minute. I realized that I was still breathing hard, and my hands were shaking. The adrenaline had not left my system yet.

I began to get uncomfortable.

Finally she said in a low voice: "The tall man with the walking stick was named Eli Warren. He was a peer in the society."

"Were you his wooden, um . . ."

"No," she said. "I was his apprentice. And his toy."

Saying that cost her something. I could hear it in her voice. But I pushed. "Where is he now?"

"I killed him," she said. "He betrayed the society. He sold spells, then used the society to hunt down his customers. I figured out his game and told the society. They told me to kill him. I did. As a reward, they gave me his spell book."

"Do you think the spells we're facing here came from Eli's book? Could he have sold them to the Hammer family way back when?"

"I don't know. Each spell book is unique. Even if they contain the same spells—and most have at least a couple of spells in common—the marks are never identical. But the society excised a lot of Eli's book before they passed it on to me. I certainly don't have a spell that would make people around me breathe spirit fire. But he and I did come here, just before I puzzled out his scam."

"Do you have a spell that could turn a person into a werewolf?"

"That's a pretty specific question. The answer is no, but I do have a spell that makes my sense of smell as keen as a wolf's for a short while. To track people. I never use it, though. Now I ask why you ask."

"While I was getting the van just now, I was stalked by a wolf. Right down in the morgue. The woman you were talking to was dead. Her throat was torn out."

Annalise's eyes narrowed. She didn't say anything.

"I think it was Emmett Dubois," I said.

"How certain are you?"

"Well, not terribly certain. I saw what looked like a police uniform on a table near the body, all neatly folded, and I did just make an enemy of him. And the magic detector went nuts when I touched it to him."

"But you didn't see him change? He didn't say, 'I'm going to change into a wolf and rip your heart out'?"

"No. Does he have to?"

"No," she said. "We can kill him anyway just to be safe. But if he's carrying spells or infected with a predator, we should watch him to see if he's not alone."

I nodded. "Thanks for trusting me."

"You're earning it," she said. "And you're useful. But remember whose side you're on."

We stopped at the supermarket again and bought more beef, a roll of aluminum foil, and a leg of lamb. This time, Annalise came inside with me and picked the cuts she wanted. As we were walking back to the van, I asked: "Is the pain getting bad?"

"You don't understand."

"Okay. Very bad? What if we got you some painkillers? Even something as lame as ibuprofen ought to help."

"You don't understand," she said again. "I'm dying."

I stopped and stared at her. "What do you mean?"

"Inside the van," she said.

We climbed in, and I shut the door.

"There's a spell called golem flesh, right? It's a protective spell, like our tattoos, only better. For some reason, it shows up in almost all the spell books. No one is sure why, but pretty much everyone gets it."

I wasn't sure what she was talking about. How did spells "show up" in books? But this wasn't the time to interrupt.

"When Eli first recruited me, he laid these tattoos on my skin. I wasn't his wooden man, but . . ." Her voice trailed off. "When I was my own person again," she continued, "I cast golem flesh on myself. As I said, nearly everyone in the society has it. It protects your whole body, not just the parts that are marked, and you can still feel things."

She paused. I knew what she meant. The tattoos on my chest and arms were numb. The enchanted skin in those areas couldn't feel anything—not pain, not cold, not heat, not a human touch. And Annalise was, as far as I'd seen, nearly covered with them.

"You just have to eat meat to survive. That's the tradeoff. Any kind will do, and the less cooked the meat is, the more recently you've killed it, the better."

"And the meat will heal you," I prompted.

"When I'm injured, the meat tries to heal me. That's all it does. Nothing I've eaten has sustained me. I'm eating and eating—"

"And the food is going to a wound you can't heal."

"And I'm starving."

Most people could go weeks without food, but Annalise wasn't most people, and this was not regular food. "How long?" I asked.

"I don't know."

I started the engine and pulled into traffic. I wanted to reach out and lay a hand on her shoulder, to comfort her somehow, but it didn't feel right. Despite the fact that she had begun to trust me, there was still a gulf between us. There was a gulf between her and the world.

"What do we do, boss?" I asked.

"Finish the job," she said. "Afterward, we may know enough to heal me. If not, I'll go to the society and see if they can help."

"Why not go to the society right now? Why wait?"

She shook her head and would say nothing more on the subject. Conversation ended.

We reached the motel. I suggested that we move to a new motel, or at least change our rooms. She turned that idea down. She'd searched all over for Charles Hammer and come up with nothing. No one in town would talk to her. She was in pain. She was tired of searching for our targets. Maybe, if we stayed put, they'd come to us.

That didn't strike me as the most sensible idea in the world, but I wasn't in charge.

We went into her room. She picked through the things in Karoly's bag. It was mostly mundane personal effects, unless the ballpoint pen was enchanted to shoot fireballs, or the comb could turn french fries into hundred-dollar bills. It didn't seem likely, though; I couldn't see a sigil on any of them.

She took out the laptop and plugged it in. I didn't know much about computers. I'd had a PlayStation before I did my time, but I never had much use for the spreadsheets, email, or the Internet.

Annalise didn't look like an expert either. She pecked at the keys with one finger. After a minute or so, she picked up a teddy bear wearing a shirt that read WE MISS YOU, DAD! and popped its head off.

Some sort of computer plug stuck out of its neck. Annalise connected it to the back of the laptop. It looked as though its head was stuck inside the computer, and I couldn't help but smile. I'd bet Emmett Dubois hadn't found *that*.

I took out the meat and started slicing it up. I was pretty good at it by now. I also took out the box of plastic forks and began spearing little pieces of meat on the forks and setting them on a piece of aluminum foil beside her.

Annalise took out her cell phone and pressed a speed-dial number. She held the phone to her ear. "Karoly is dead," she said after a moment. "I have his drive, but not his password."

She took a bite of meat while she listened to whoever was on the other end of the line. *Click click tap tap.* The room began to feel stuffy.

"Got it," she said. "Thanks." She shut her phone and began scrolling through files on her screen.

I finally finished cutting the meat. I arranged it into a pile, then went into the bathroom to wash my hands and the ghost knife. When

I returned, she was still staring at the screen. I sat opposite her and speared pieces of meat with the forks.

The quiet began to make me antsy. "Find anything?"

"Nothing useful," she said. She took another bite of meat and laid the empty fork down. I picked it up and stabbed it into a new piece, then set it beside her. I was beginning to feel like a manservant. This was not exactly the straight job I'd envisioned when I got out of prison.

I decided to earn more of her trust. "I still have your plastic, you know."

She didn't look up from the screen. "I know." She continued staring at the screen. I should have brought a book.

Annalise looked at her watch. "It's getting late. Why don't you get some food? I may be at this all night."

I lunged out of the chair and went out. It was still daylight, but my stomach was grumbling. I went into the office and smiled at the woman behind the desk. She scowled at me. Apparently, the other manager told her all about us. She gave me directions to a bookstore in town.

I drove out there and bought a detective novel, then drove across town and ordered my pad thai. I was tempted to eat in the restaurant window and read my book. We were stirring up the town, trying to see what would float to the top. I should be visible for that, just to see what shook out. But I didn't like leaving Annalise alone, not if she was dying. I ordered takeout.

I drove back to the motel, and as far as I could tell, no one was following me. No one had staked out the motel either. After checking in on Annalise, I went to my room, ate, read three chapters, then fell asleep.

I dreamed about fire all night.

I awoke to a thumping on my door. It was Cynthia, and she looked terrified.

"I'm sorry to bother you. I'm sorry," she said, glancing back toward the street nervously. Everything cast long shadows; it was very early, probably no more than an hour past dawn. "But I don't have anyone else to turn to."

"Er, come in." I stepped away from the door to let her in. I had fallen asleep wearing my pants, but I didn't have a shirt on. I could feel Cynthia watching me as I dug out a clean one.

I retreated to the bathroom to wash my face. I used cold water. I was sure she hadn't dropped by for a quick roll in the sheets.

When I returned, I gestured for her to sit at the table. I sat at the foot of the bed. After a moment's hesitation, she lowered herself into the chair. She was wearing a long-sleeved, chocolate-brown dress that just reached her knees, white stockings, and little, flat-soled brown shoes. Simple, but she looked very good.

I made a point of looking at her eyes. "What's the problem?"

"It's Cabot," she said. "Emmett let him out of prison this morning."

"Ah, shit. Who told you this?"

"Does it matter?"

"I asked, didn't I?"

She looked at the floor. "I'm sorry, I—"

"Hold on," I said. "I didn't mean to snap at you." I noticed the tiny coffeemaker on the table beside her. "Hey, do you want a cup of probably terrible coffee?" I stood.

She jumped out of her chair. "I'll get it. I need something to keep me busy."

She went into the bathroom to fill the pot, and I went to the window and peered around the edge of the curtain. Cynthia's silver SUV was parked beside the manager's office, but everything else looked the same.

She came out of the bathroom with a pot full of water, poured grounds into the filter, and filled the brewer halfway.

"Why don't you fill it up," I said. "I'm going to need it."

"You don't have enough coffee. Too much water and you get bitter coffee."

I shrugged and sat on the foot of the bed again. I thought all coffee was bitter. What did I know?

"Where did you get those tattoos?" she asked. "Behind bars?"

There was something in the artificially casual tone of her voice that I didn't trust. "No. After."

"So you have been to jail."

"Yep. Prison, too."

She looked at me, trying to decide if that was a joke. She was still undecided when she started the coffeemaker.

"Why . . . what did you . . ."

I decided to help her out. "What did I do to get sent to prison?"

"Um, yeah."

"You have an awful lot of questions for me all of a sudden. Or are these the questions you meant to ask me yesterday?"

"Well, I came here to see you, so—"

"You can go if you want. The door's right there. But don't think I'm going to answer a lot of questions if you won't answer mine. Who told you that Emmett released Cabot this morning?"

"Okay. That's fair." She set the two cups on the table. The

coffeemaker had stopped brewing, but I could see liquid still dripping into the pot. "It was Sugar Dubois."

"Why did he do that?"

"He didn't say, but we were in high school together. We knew each other a little, and he was always nice. Deferential, even, like some boys get when they have a crush."

"He warned you because he had a crush on you in high school? Is there more to it than that?"

"Not to the crush. We never dated or anything. He was too far below me then. Don't make that face. It was high school. You know what that was like."

Actually, I didn't. I never stayed in school for more than a couple of weeks at a time, although I'd gotten my GED in prison. Not that I was going to tell Cynthia that. "High school is over. Is he making a move on you right now?" It made sense, if the Dubois brothers wanted to consolidate power in the town.

"Ugh. I think he knows better."

Okay. I'll bet he did. "Do you think Emmett put him up to it?"

"Why do you ask that?"

"Questions with questions." Before she could apologize, I said: "It seems strange to me that he'd go against his own brother because of a schoolyard crush."

"I don't think it's that simple. Sugar loves his brothers, but he's always wanted to be a cop. Actually, I think he always wanted to be a cop on TV, and I don't think the setup his brother has here in Hammer Bay is what he had in mind. He has to accept some of what they do—they're his brothers—but letting Cabot go when he might take another shot at me . . . I think they went just a little too far this time."

I didn't say anything to that. Emmett turned into a wolf and tore people's throats out, and I suspected his brothers were the same. Setting Cabot free was small potatoes for them.

I wasn't sure what play Emmett was making by setting Cabot loose. Was he hoping Cabot would take another shot at Cynthia, or was he trying to keep things as chaotic as possible, just as I was?

Cynthia passed me a coffee cup. She'd filled it while I wasn't paying attention. I took a sip. It wasn't bitter. How about that? There's a right way to do things after all.

"That's what I think, anyway," Cynthia said. She sipped her coffee and winced. It was obviously below her standards. To me, it was wonderful. "Now, how about you?"

I shrugged. "I went to prison because I was in a fight."

"That must have been some fight."

"Actually, it wasn't much of a fight at all. And it's not something I'm proud of."

"I'll drop it."

"Thanks. Why were you arguing with Cabot yesterday?"

"That doesn't really matter, does it?"

I sighed. I took a long sip of coffee and savored it. It took a few moments of silence for her to take the hint.

"We were arguing about the family business, if you think that's important. Charles inherited the timber company from Dad, but he wasn't interested in it. Uncle Cabot rounded up some capital and bought it. Charles used the money to start the toy company, which everyone thought was nuts, but it's Cabot who's going bankrupt and Charles who's thriving."

"So . . . what? Cabot felt cheated?"

"He wanted more financing from Charles to take some of the pressure off. And he wanted Charles to . . ." She paused, searching for the correct phrase. She had suddenly become very careful with what she said. "Charles has access to some resources that Cabot wanted to use. Advice, really. Cabot wasn't sure which way to jump."

That rang a bell. I couldn't quite remember why, but I'd heard something like that before. "Charles wouldn't help him."

"I'm not sure why, but no, he wouldn't. Charles wouldn't even meet with him. Uncle Cabot began to get really intense about it. I guess he was in more trouble than anyone realized."

"And he came to you, because?"

"He wanted me to help him with Charles. I don't know what he expected. I don't own any part of Charles's company, and I barely see him myself anymore."

"What do you live on?"

"Trust fund," she said carelessly. "The interest is more than I need, so I invested some instead of blowing it. I'm doing pretty well right now."

"Does Cabot know that?"

"Hell no, and don't tell him, either. I'm not throwing my money down his rat hole."

"So he thinks Charles has all the money. And you don't have any pull with your brother. Did you explain that to him?"

"Sure, but he didn't believe me."

I shrugged. "Neither do I."

"Excuse me?" She sounded irritated.

"People shoot each other for all kinds of stupid reasons. I mean, really stupid. I bunked with a guy who shot his brother-in-law over who deserved the biggest piece of chicken. But what you're describing is all wrong. If Cabot was going to shoot anyone, it would be Charles, for refusing to help him. Why would he pop one off at you? Charles is in town, right? I'll bet Cabot knows where to find him. So, either he knows you have a good-sized nest egg, or there's something else going on."

"He must know about the nest egg," she said, a little too quickly. Her voice sounded shaky, but I didn't ease up on her.

"I still don't believe you. Let's cut the bullshit. Cabot wanted to use you against your brother. He had a plan, and he made an offer to you—I don't know, more money or control of the toy company or something, right? He wanted you to help him with a hostile takeover."

"That's for publicly traded companies. Hammer Bay Toys is privately owned."

"Fine. I don't know a thing about high finance. In that case, he wanted you to have your brother declared incompetent."

Cynthia blinked. Bingo.

"Right. Charles has been having seizures. Has he been to a doctor? I'd guess not. He's too busy with his company, and he brushes off anyone who asks about them."

"Who told you about his seizures?"

"Everyone knows. I saw one the night Harlan Semple shot up downtown. What did Cabot promise? You file commitment papers on your brother, and he'd support you? You'd get control of the toy company and he'd get an infusion of cash? Or you'd sell the company and split the proceeds? And Charles would get the medical care he'd need. I'll bet he told you this was the best thing for Charles."

She stared at me. The look on her face told me that I wouldn't be doing the job Annalise had given me anytime soon. "Okay. Yes. That's the pitch he made, basically."

I didn't push that *basically*. I suspected that Cabot knew about Charles's spell book and that he wanted it for himself.

But did Cynthia know about it? And if so, how much? I couldn't be sure, and I didn't want to push too hard and shut her down. She'd just been shot at, and I could see the fear in her. Besides, I had more important things to worry about.

"Where's your brother?"

"What does that have to do with my uncle?"

"Questions with questions," I said.

"Tough shit," she snapped. Her anger put some strength back into her voice. "What does it have to do with Uncle Cabot?"

I shrugged and drained the rest of my coffee. It made me hungry. "Nothing. My boss and I want to meet with him."

"About what?"

Fine. I set the cup down. "Why are you here, telling me about your uncle?"

Suddenly, she wouldn't look at me. "I'm afraid . . . I think he might come after me again. I can't ask Emmett for help. Or Sugar, either. Not now. I want . . . I need someone to help me."

Damn. She wanted me to kill him.

CHAPTER ELEVEN

"And how exactly am I supposed to do that?"

"I don't know," she said, still not looking at me. She knew very well what she wanted, but she wouldn't say it.

"Why don't you leave town? You could be in Sea-Tac in less than three hours. From there, you could go anywhere in the world. I hear New York is nice in the spring."

"I can't leave my brother."

"The brother you never see? Please. Tell this story to Able Katz. He strikes me as a smart guy. He'll square things with the Dubois brothers. He could help more than I could. But neither one of us is going to commit murder for you."

The word *murder* didn't make her flinch. "I have money."

"So buy a gun. I'll bet you can afford a nice one."

"I'm sorry I bothered you." She stood and turned toward the door.

"I didn't say I wouldn't help you. Just that I wouldn't kill him for you. What if I talked to him? Maybe I could make him back off." And maybe I could get him to tell me where Charles the Third was hiding.

"Would you do that?" she asked.

"Sure." I couldn't help smiling. "In exchange, all you have to do is show me how to make a good cup of coffee."

We went out of the room. The shadows were a bit shorter and the air noticeably warmer. Cynthia took out her car keys, but I wanted to stop in and tell Annalise where I was going, and also to make sure she didn't need me.

I knocked. She told me to come in.

She was in the same position she'd been in the night before. She looked a little paler, and her eyes looked watery. Her bedcovers were rumpled, so I knew she'd had some sleep. Or at least had tried.

"Any luck?" I asked.

"I opened his files. Understanding them is something else."

"What do you mean?" I slipped into the room, and she turned the screen toward me.

"Have a look."

I squinted at the screen. "Is that some kind of code?"

"It's Polish. Karoly made his notes in his native language. Which I should have expected, but damn. I'm going to ask for English-speaking investigators from now on."

"Well, it answers one of my questions, at least."

"What's that?" she asked.

"Why didn't Emmett know about your investigation as soon as we hit town? I'm not sure what was in the note Emmett took—"

"The note isn't on here. I checked. He must have written it by hand."

"I thought so. We didn't find a printer in his stuff."

"I'm uploading the files to the society. Someone there will translate and prioritize them."

"That's cool. Can I see them when they come back?"

She stared at me a moment. "Maybe. It depends on what—"

The door opened. Cynthia stepped inside and shut the door behind her. She stood as close to the door as she could without being on the other side of it. "I'm sorry," she said. "I didn't feel safe out there alone."

I turned to Annalise. "Emmett let Cabot out of his cell. I'm going to go have a talk with him. Cabot, I mean."

She looked me in the eyes. There was something in her look that I didn't understand, but it seemed to be full of meaning. It unsettled me. It was as if I was becoming something she hadn't expected.

Or maybe she was trying to tell me to go get laid.

"Do you need anything before I go?"

"No," Annalise said. "Leave the van, in case I need to run out for something."

"Understood." We left. In the parking lot, Cynthia turned to me. "I thought you said your boss hates you. She doesn't look like she hates you."

"I know," I said. "Ain't that something?"

I thought about Annalise, sitting listless when Cynthia opened the door. Was she dying? Was I watching her die?

I realized Cynthia was talking to me. "Whoa. Back up and start over please," I said "I was somewhere else."

She looked at me like *Are you serious?* "I said that my uncle is probably at his office by now. He goes there every day, no matter what."

"Let's try there first. But I expect he'll stay at home. Does he live in one of the other houses on Hammer Street?"

"Uncle Cabot? No. He has a studio apartment in town now."

That surprised me, but I didn't say anything. We drove downtown, and Cynthia turned up a narrow side street. She parked. "That's it."

She pointed toward a run-down warehouse. I had to look at it twice to notice the HAMMER BAY TIMBER sign above the door. The outside was made of rough, unpainted wood. The walls had warped from the damp. This was a company that had fallen on hard times.

I opened the door.

"What should I do?" Cynthia asked.

"Go have breakfast. Or lunch. Or a cup of coffee. Park a block away from wherever you end up. I'll come and find you."

She told me where she'd be. I stepped out.

"Wait! What if something happens . . . if you don't show up?"

"New York is nice in the spring." I shut the door and she drove away.

I walked around the building first. I didn't see anything except a back door beside an empty Dumpster, some tall weeds, and a high, dirty window with a pale light shining inside.

A gentle drizzle began to fall. I tried the back door, but it was locked. My ghost knife was in my pocket, so that wasn't an obstacle for me, but I didn't cut my way in. I walked along the other side of the building, ducking under the fire escape and running my hand along the rough wood.

I reached the front door. The warehouse loading ramp was just a step up from the ground. I peered into the windows, but they were too dirty, and the inside too dark, for me to see anything.

I felt a twinge below my collarbone. Another kid was gone. I looked around, trying to find the source of the feeling, but of course I couldn't see anything. It could have happened anywhere in town. I gritted my teeth and pulled on the door. It was unlocked, and it creaked as I opened it.

The floor groaned as I walked on it. Enough light shone through the dirty windows that I managed to cross the floor without breaking my nose against a wooden post or tripping over the odd piece of furniture.

There was a flight of stairs against the side wall, and dim light shining from the top. I climbed them, and they groaned under every step. I took out my ghost knife—I wanted to be ready for anything.

"I can't pay you!" someone shouted from the top of the stairs. "Whoever you are, I don't have your money!"

I'd heard that shout yesterday. It belonged to Cabot.

I reached the top of the stairs. There was no doorway; the stairs simply opened into his office. I could smell the sour stink of old cigarette smoke.

Cabot was sitting at his desk with his head down on the blotter, a cigarette burning in an ashtray beside him. He didn't look up. If I had been sent there to kill him, I could have put a bullet into the top of his head and been gone again with no trouble.

I looked around. The floorboards were warped, and the walls seemed to be buckling with age. A huge map of the Olympic Peninsula was tacked to the wall. It was yellowed and curled at the edges.

"Go away," Cabot said again. He still hadn't looked up. "I don't have anything to give you."

"Don't be so sure," I said.

He started and looked up at me. His eyes widened with shock, he yanked open a desk drawer and stuck his hand inside.

"HEY!" I shouted. My voice boomed inside the room. Cabot was startled and froze in place. "If I wanted to kill you, you'd be dead already. Leave the gun in the drawer. You've been stupid enough with guns as it is."

I walked toward the desk, pulled a chair around, and sat opposite him. "You should have locked the front door," I told him. "What will you do if Peter Lemly comes here for a story? What if the mayor's wife decides to pay you a visit?"

"Christ. Frank. I didn't want anything to happen to him. I like Frank."

"Oh, shut up. Every jackass that shoots the wrong guy talks that way. It makes me sick."

He looked sheepish. He had the same thick dark hair as Cynthia and Charles, but it was shot through with gray. His chin was weak, and rimmed with folds of fat. His eyes were large with dark circles. He was just as rundown and creaky as this building, and just as depressing.

His hand was still in his desk drawer. He began to slowly move it, still searching for that gun.

I lunged out of my seat and slammed the drawer on his hand. Then I grabbed the top edge of the drawer and yanked it out of the desk. It flew backward and smashed the corner of his window before falling. Papers and pens scattered to the floor, but I focused on the heavy clunk of a handgun.

Another pistol. Cabot started toward it, but I shoved him back with all my strength. He fell against the chair and crumpled into the corner.

I picked up the handgun. It was a .45, and a little old-fashioned. Pulling back the slide, I saw that it was loaded but hadn't been cleaned recently. Sloppy. Everything about this guy was sloppy.

"Go sit down," I told him.

He moved like a little kid being sent to the corner, but he did it. "Who are you? What do you want?" he asked.

It was a relief to find someone who did not already know my whole history. "Just a guy doing a favor for a friend. What are you going to do, Cabot?"

"Nothing," he said. "I'm going to go to jail. And I'm going to go bankrupt. I'll probably have to sell the house on Whidbey and . . ." He was withdrawing into himself as he talked.

"Cabot," I said again. He looked at me. "What are you going to do about Cynthia? About Charles? How many more guns do you have?"

"Oh," he said. "Will you apologize to Cynthia for me? I'd been drinking, and I was desperate, and . . . and I was worried about Charles—"

I laughed. "So worried that you shot at his sister?"

"Charles is sick," he said resentfully.

"How sick?"

"He's got a tumor or something. He's lost a ton of weight—have you seen him recently?"

I thought about the tall, slender, dark-haired guy I'd seen at the Hammer Bay Toy office. I nodded.

"Well, he used to be fat. Big, porky fat, like a Samoan or something. But he's just melted away. And he's been having seizures."

"What? Like epilepsy?" I pretended not to know anything. I wanted to see what he would tell me.

"Don't know. He hasn't been to a doctor as far as I can tell. We have the same doctor—the whole family does—and I know Charles hasn't been to him. And he hasn't left town, either, so he hasn't been to see anyone else."

"How long has this been going on?"

"About two years, I guess. It started right around the same time as . . ."

"As what?"

Cabot rubbed his nose. "As, um, the play-offs. We were watching the NBA finals, and he fell down in the bathroom. He wouldn't let us take him to County. I think that was the first time. He looked surprised and kind of shocked, like it hadn't happened before."

"Is that why you tried to have him declared incompetent?"

"If he's seriously sick," Cabot said, his gaze sullen and his face stubborn, "he needs to see a doctor."

"And if you get a couple bucks out of the deal, that's just a happy side effect, right?"

"That's not how it is."

"If you say so."

My needling got a rise out of him. He leaned toward me, his voice getting higher and more petulant. "You don't know what you're talking about! You're not even a part of this family!"

"Thank God for that. I didn't bring my Kevlar."

He opened and closed his little fish mouth several times, then the wind went out of him. He sagged against the back of his chair.

"How do they do it?" he said. "My brother always knew just the right thing to do. He always made the right move. It was like he knew just what would happen. I've never been able to do that. I just follow my nose and try to do the smart thing, but I have no idea where it will lead."

"You wouldn't make much of a chess player," I said.

"I suck at chess. Is that the secret? Chess?"

"I wouldn't know."

"It doesn't matter now. I've been sitting here, trying to decide if I should kill myself. I don't think I have the guts for it."

"Good. Prison is bad, but you can survive it."

"God. At least I wouldn't have to look at this anymore." He shifted some papers on his desk and pulled out a slender newspaper. It was a copy of *The Mallet*. The headline at the top read CABOT HAMMER ARRESTED FOR ATTEMPTED MURDER!

I took it from him and scanned the front page. It was a special edition, run especially to cover this story. The article was written by Peter Lemly and told the same basic story that Cynthia had been spreading. Cabot and Cynthia had a big argument; Cabot tried to shoot her but struck the mayor instead when he shielded her. Cabot was then subdued by a "visiting businessman." For a few moments I was peeved that some other guy had gotten credit for what I did. Then I realized I was the businessman.

"Did you know," Cabot started, talking to me like a friend—didn't the guy have any friends?—"my brother could make people do what he wanted. My father, too."

"*Make* how?"

"It wasn't like he voodooed their minds or anything. And he never blackmailed them, as far as I could tell. He just wanted something and other people wanted him to have it. When he bid on a plot of forest, whoever was handling the parcel awarded it to him. It was like he made them want what he wanted them to want. He just bent them to his will, without any effort at all. And he always knew how to handle people. He knew how to use the Dubois brothers, and when to hold them off. He could play Reverend Wilson like a radio."

I twisted that around in my head until I sorted all the wants. "Isn't Charles the Third doing the same thing with his toy company? Isn't he putting out products that people are snapping up?" I remembered what Able Katz had told us: Hammer's toys weren't supposed to be a huge hit, but they were. I could have gone further, talking about the way the local townsfolk defended him like he was their king, but I wanted to see Cabot's reaction.

"Yeah. Yeah, I guess so. You know what's funny? I never would have pegged little Charlie to be the tycoon type. Now he's this reclusive business genius, spending all his time hiding in the tower, but I never thought he had it in him. He was such a fat, dorky little kid."

I remembered the high, round room I'd seen at the top of the Hammers' house. That must have been the tower. If I'd known, I would have slipped out of the library and confronted him. I made a mental note to tell Annalise about it. "Fat kids grow up," I said.

"No, no, I don't mean it like that. He wasn't just fat. He was lazy and stupid. He never got a joke unless you explained it to him. Kids bullied him on the playground. He was that kind of kid. He used to talk about helping the poor or saving the whales, but he never had more than a vague idea how to go about it, and he never . . . okay. Once, he decided that he was going to help some of the older folks in town. You know, retired lumber workers and their wives, they get sick or property taxes go up, and it's trouble.

"So little Charlie decided to start a food drive. He must have been fourteen or so, and he's as big as a whale. Everyone jokes that he's going to be eating half the food himself, though not to his face, of course. But most people like the idea and chip in. We stored the food right downstairs in this building. It was quite a stack—I was surprised by how much support the kid got.

"But Charlie lost interest as soon as it started to be successful. He spent his afternoons playing video games on the couch while the cans and stuff collected dust.

"In the end, I distributed it myself. Those folks were really grateful to get the deliveries, and a couple of them asked when there would be another. I had to tell them that I thought it was a one-shot deal. They were pretty disappointed. Poor folks. Stuck in this town. This fucked-up town.

"So, I didn't think the kid had a successful company in him. But he's just as good at it as his father."

"Why didn't you continue the drive yourself?"

"What's that?"

"The food drive. If it helped so many people, why didn't you take over?"

"Well . . . that's not the point I wanted to make."

"I understand your point. Your nephew was this big loser who suddenly turned into a successful guy, and you didn't."

"Well, not that I'm a loser . . . wait. Scratch that. I *am* a loser. I've always been one. But I've had my family to back me up. Until now. Crap."

"What changed for him? What changed for your nephew?"

I didn't expect him to say *Must be that spell book his daddy gave him,* but I hoped for something more than this extended bout of self-pity. Instead, he said: "God only knows. My kids certainly don't have it."

He was wearing a wedding ring. "You're divorced?" I asked.

"No. No, I'm still married to their mother. We love each other very much."

I wasn't interested in that. "How many kids do you have?"

"Four. Ages eight through fifteen."

"Cynthia said you live in a studio apartment."

"Well, yeah, I do, but they don't. They live on Whidbey Island."

"Is that right?" I asked. Cabot shifted in his chair uncomfortably. He didn't like the way I was looking at him. If he'd known what I was thinking, he'd be even less pleased. "When did this happen?"

"A couple years back after school ended. My wife has never been happy here, so I bought her a place up there. Everyone is transitioning nicely."

"Why do they live so far from you?" I asked. I was pretty sure I already knew the answer.

He scratched at his chin. "They have a good school district there." He shuffled some papers on his desk. "I want my kids to grow up in the best environment possible."

I leaned forward. A dangerous spark of anger had caught in my belly. "Cabot, you want to know what you should never do? You should never lie to me. Especially when I have this gun in my pocket."

He blinked a couple of times. "I don't know what you're talking about."

"*This town. This fucked-up town,*" I mimicked. "Charles the Third has his first seizure, that you know of, in what—April? May? And a couple weeks later you ship your kids to the other side of the mountain."

"Well—"

"While your company is gasping for its last breath."

"Okay—"

"You bought your wife a little place on Whidbey Island, where the real estate costs—"

"All right! All right! That's not the whole story."

"Tell me the whole story."

I could see that he wanted to tell me to get lost. He glanced at the pocket of my jacket. I still had the gun, and I had slugged him unconscious once already. "It's for their own safety," he said. "I have enemies in town—"

I slammed my hand down on his desk and jumped from the chair. I stood over him, and he stared up at me with wide, startled deer's eyes.

I could see it in those eyes. He knew about the kids. He knew about the fires. He remembered them.

Two years it had been going on, and he hadn't done a thing except move his own family to a safe place.

"I think . . ." I didn't know what I was going to say. It was like I had another person inside me, making all my decisions for me. "I think I'm going to kill you."

"What?" His eyes grew wider.

"I've got the gun. I'll lay the newspaper in front of you and put a bullet into your head. Everyone will think it was suicide."

"Now, wait a minute—"

"You wait a minute. You're spreading bullshit like it's sweet butter, and you think I should sit here and gulp it down?"

He lunged for me. I punched him in the throat.

He fell back against his chair, choking and gasping for air. I could have killed him with that punch, but I'd pulled back at the last moment. Had I pulled back enough, though?

"Don't—" Cabot wheezed at me. I figured that if he could talk, he would live. I was a little disappointed.

"That's just the start of what I'm going to do to you if you lie to me again." Cabot looked up at me and I saw it in his face. He was ready to tell me everything. "Tell me about the kids."

"There . . ." His voice was hoarse. He took a deep, shuddering breath. "There isn't much to tell."

"Tell me anyway."

"One day, my youngest came home early from school crying. She said that one of the kids in her class caught fire and burned to death, right before her eyes. This was the middle of May." He paused to rub his throat and take another deep breath. "I thought she was playing a game, but she insisted it was true. Her friend Carrie had caught fire while sitting at her desk.

"I went to her teacher and spoke with her in the classroom. One of the desks in the back of the room was scorched black, and there was a black trail leading out of the room and down the hall. The teacher acted like she couldn't see the scorch mark. She claimed that the desk had been empty all year long, and that there was no student named Carrie in her class.

"I'd met Carrie. She'd come over for playdates. There was a drawing on the wall signed with her name, in scrawling Crayola letters. The teacher couldn't see the black marks, couldn't see the drawing, and didn't remember the little girl.

"I thought she was crazy. I went to the school board, but they told me the same things the teacher had, and asked me if I had seen a doctor lately.

"Well, I went to Carrie's house to speak to her parents. Neither one of them could remember their own daughter. It was as though I'd had this memory of a little girl with bobbed red hair inserted into my brain. And my daughter's brain, too.

"It wasn't the last time it happened. Two weeks later, my kids started telling me that their friends were disappearing, and no one remembered them. Finally, I brought my lunch to the school and sat in my car, watching the playground. In the week I sat there, I saw two kids burn up. The other kids would freak out when it started, and then, when it was over, go back to playing as if nothing had happened."

"What about the worms?"

"I don't know. I don't know what they are, or what they mean. But I was freaking out, so I sent my wife and kids away, hoping they'd be safe. So far, they are."

"Are you so sure about that? What if you had five kids before, but you just can't remember one?"

"Do you think I haven't thought about that? But I'm sure. I'm sure."

I didn't like the sound of that. "That's it? That's all you did about those kids? You talked to a couple people?"

"That's all I could do! I talked to Emmett and Frank and Reverend Wilson. They looked at me like I was losing my mind. My kids were getting into fights in school because people thought we were going nuts.

All we could do was to wait for it to blow over. What else was I supposed to do?"

Something, I wanted to say, but I held my tongue. "And you swear you don't know anything about those worms?"

"Nothing. I don't know what they are. How do you know about this? Everyone else forgets all this."

I wished Annalise had left me her scrap of wood. I would have liked to know if Cabot was infected, enchanted, or brain-damaged like Harlan. "Stand up."

He pushed his chair back and stood.

"Empty your pockets."

He began to turn them out, dumping everything inside them onto the desktop. Wallet, key ring, gas receipt, bottle opener . . . all very bland and boring. But none of it looked like magic to me.

I leveled the gun on him. "Strip," I said. "Start with the shirt."

He started to grumble, but he did it. He unbuttoned his shirt and hung it over the back of the chair. As he turned, I saw a tattoo on his back.

"Hold it," I said. I turned him toward me. Well, well. There, tattooed on his back, was an iron gate. It was identical to mine.

"Where did you get this?" I asked.

"My father put it there when I was a baby. He put it onto all my kids, too, before he died."

"Why?"

"I don't know. It's supposed to be some kind of good luck. It bugs me sometimes, though."

I thought about the twinge I'd felt outside the building just a couple of minutes ago. "When does it bug you?"

"Every couple of days, I guess. It feels like someone pokes it with a stick or something."

"Did it bug you when you saw that little kid catch fire?"

"Well . . ." He hesitated. I knew he was going to lay out another lie. "It's possible, I guess. I don't remember."

"What about when Charles had his seizure?"

"How long is this conversation going to take?"

"We're getting to the important stuff right now. What about Charles?"

"Nothing that I remember." If he was lying, he was getting better at it.

"Where's the book?"

"What book?"

"The book! *The* book!"

"I don't know what book you're talking about!"

I shoved him over the desk and slammed his head against the blotter. He started to resist, but I placed the barrel of the gun against the back of his head. I hoped no one was going to walk in at that moment.

"Please!" he said. "You're not really going to do it, are you? You're not really going to kill me?"

"What do you think about all those burned-up kids?"

"I think it's horrible. I have nightmares—"

"But not so horrible that you kept trying to stop it."

"What was I supposed to do? People thought I was crazy! I'm a Hammer—I can't be the town joke!"

That was almost it. That last sentence almost made me squeeze the trigger. I wasn't even angry anymore. I just felt cold and bitter. Cabot seemed like a dirty little mess that needed to be wiped up. All I had to do was squeeze the trigger.

"Please," he said simply.

I pulled him off the desk and shoved him into the chair. "You have a chance to live, if you really want it."

"I want it! I do!"

"We'll see. Where's the book?"

"I don't know about any book! I swear!"

He made it sound like the truth, but I wasn't convinced. "Wrong answer. Let me explain something, Cabot. I'm here to put a stop to these fires, and I don't care who I have to step on to do it. If you're not going to answer, you're in my way."

"But I really don't know. I swear."

"Tell me about your father and the thing he put on your back."

"I was just a baby! I don't remember that!"

"What about your own kids? You weren't a baby then, were you?"

"He took each of them for one night. He sent Carla and me away. In the morning, they had this mark on their backs. Carla didn't like it, but I told her to stuff it. It's family tradition, and I was afraid we wouldn't get a penny out of him otherwise."

"What about the Dubois brothers?"

"What about them? They certainly don't have any book. I'm not even sure they can read."

This was getting nowhere. I took the ghost knife from my pocket.

"What are you doing?" Cabot asked.

"Hold still." I slid the ghost knife through Cabot's arm. He collapsed, struck the wooden floor hard, and began whimpering. Then he curled up into a ball.

"Please," he said in a half-choked whimper. "Please please please please."

I'd seen the ghost knife take away people's vitality and hostility, but I'd never seen a reaction like this. I'd meant to make Cabot more docile to get honest answers out of him. Instead, I'd cut away his bravery and uncapped his fear. I'd broken him.

The ghost knife was a spell I'd cast. My first. It was a part of me, and there was still a lot I didn't understand about it.

"The book. Who has it?"

"I don't know! I swear I swear I swear I swear—"

"Enough." He shut up.

What was I going to do with this guy? He'd recover if I left him, but was I allowed to leave him? What if he was also carrying a predator, like Emmett Dubois? What about his iron gate?

I didn't know what Annalise would do with him if she caught him. I didn't know if carrying a spell, even one he didn't cast himself, was reason enough to murder him. If it was, his whole family would die, too.

Could I do that? Could I tell Annalise about Cabot's iron gate, and the iron gates on his kids, knowing it meant she might hunt them down and kill them? Hell, she might make me kill them, as a kind of initiation.

Or should I keep my mouth shut, let them walk away, and betray Annalise again?

I looked down at Cabot. He didn't look dangerous, but I couldn't leave that spell active. What if Annalise laid her scrap of wood on him? I reached down and slid the ghost knife through the iron gate.

The mark burst in a shower of black steam. Cabot bucked, kicking the desk. Papers fluttered to the floor.

I felt something go out of him as the spell came apart. It was like a third person in the room had walked out and I hadn't noticed its presence until it was gone.

Cabot moaned and wept, laying his face against the floor. He looked miserable and pathetic, but I wasn't done with him yet. I had to make sure he didn't have any more spells on him.

I pocketed the gun and dragged him out from behind the desk. He didn't resist. I wasn't sure he could resist, even if he'd had the guts for it. All he did was cover his face with his hands and plead in a voice so small that I couldn't make out anything he said.

There were guys I'd met in prison who would have gone stiff as a rod to see a man break down that way, but it made me feel queasy. Still, I had to be sure there were no more spells on him. Annalise would want to know.

I rolled him over. I slid the ghost knife through the top front of his pants, cutting the belt and zipper wide open. Then I grabbed his pant cuffs and pulled.

I *really* hoped no one would walk in on us now.

I studied him long enough to confirm that there were no other marks on him. I kicked his pants to him.

"Humiliating, isn't it?" I said. "Some guys would be so furious at being treated like this that they'd get themselves a gun and come after me for revenge. Don't be that stupid. Understand?" He nodded. "I want a couple things. First, tell me where the book is. And don't lie. If you lie, I'll know."

"I swear," he said in a pathetic voice. "Please, I swear I would never lie to you. I don't know. Maybe Cynthia has it—"

"Second, keep away from Cynthia."

Cabot shut up and nodded. His eyes were as big as saucers.

"Third, you aren't protected anymore. I don't know when the next kid is going to die, but I do know you're going to start forgetting them soon. Maybe you'll be happy to forget. But don't forget this: I don't want to see you again.

"Last, get out of town. Don't go back to your apartment. Just get in your car and go to Whidbey. Tomorrow, go see a lawyer, but tonight go be with your kids. You may still end up dead or in prison, but at least you'll get to see them."

That was it. I couldn't look at him anymore. I couldn't look at what I'd done to him. I backed away, quickly scanning the room. I didn't want to leave anything behind. I didn't want to come back here ever again.

I walked to the stairs and went down. They creaked and groaned. I could hear Cabot behind me, quietly weeping to himself. The ghost knife had destroyed him in a way I'd never seen before. I took it out and looked at it in the semidarkness of the stairs. I could feel the power in it, and I could feel that power was partly mine, but only partly. How would it feel to have the spells on my body destroyed?

More important, what would Annalise think of what I'd done? We were here to destroy predators and steal spell books. Spells were too powerful to circulate out in the world. The scorched black earth all over Hammer Bay was proof enough of that.

The only exception, as far as I could tell, was the Twenty Palace Society. From talking to Annalise, I knew they had strict rules about the use of their magic, and if they were a little too ruthless with it, it was only out of fear and a desire to protect us all.

Even so, I felt like a hypocrite. I'd done a lot of stupid things in my life. Who's to say that it was okay for me to walk around with spells all over me, but Cabot couldn't? And who says the Twenty Palace Society should be the ones who decide?

I walked across the wooden floor toward the door. I was going to tell Annalise about Cabot and his kids. If she decided they had to die, or if that was some sort of rule for the Twenty Palace Society, so be it. Maybe I would be the one to do the deed. It would serve me right.

I hoped we could let them go, though. Cabot didn't have any spell book. I was sure of that now. I would just have to ask Cynthia next. And Charles the Third.

I stepped through the doorway into the dim daylight. Four men were standing on the curb. They pointed snub-nosed .38s at me.

"That's him," someone said. Another man was standing behind the first four. His hands were wrapped in casts. It was Floyd.

I didn't recognize the others. I realized that I should have been afraid, but my adrenaline glands had apparently not gotten the danger message yet.

The door to the warehouse was still open behind me.

"Don't do it," one of the men said. "Hear me out first."

He was medium height and built like a decathlete. He had a thick mustache and goatee, but his head was shaved. Finally, I'd met the fourth man who had spoken with Dubois, Charles Hammer, and the mayor when Harlan had been shot.

His expression told me what I wanted to know most: he wasn't jumpy, wasn't nervous, wasn't uncomfortable. He would kill me if he had to, and then he'd go on with his day. I shrugged. "Okay. What do you have to say?"

"Our boss is interested in you. She would like to invite you to have lunch with her."

His expression was cold. All four guns were still pointed at me.

"I accept."

CHAPTER TWELVE

This time we rode in a Chevy Sport van. It had plenty of space for the goons to sit around me and keep me covered.

Floyd sat in the front passenger seat. The guy who extended the invitation sat on the bench behind me. Another sat beside me, and the last two were on the seat in front of me. They twisted around to aim their revolvers at me.

The one beside me held his gun too close to my arm. I could have wrestled him for it, if he didn't have three armed friends backing him up.

"Bobby?" the one next to me said.

"Do it now," the man behind me answered. "And don't use my name, dipshit."

I looked at the guy beside me. I'd known dozens of guys just like him inside, and the one thing I couldn't do was show them my fear. "Why can't you use his name but he can use yours?"

If the guy took offense, he hid it well. He pocketed his gun and started to search me. He did a pretty terrible job of it, even if he did manage to find everything useful I had on me. He took Cabot's gun, my wallet, Annalise's keys, and my ghost knife and handed each one back to Bobby.

"What's this?" Bobby asked me, holding the ghost knife over the back of the seat so I could see it.

"My good-luck charm."

"Yeah? What's this squiggle?"

"My doctor's signature. I copy it when I'm forging a prescription."

"Not funny. Give me the real answer."

"Okay. Really, it's the last signature Kurt Cobain ever gave. He died the day after he signed it."

"Whoa," one of the guys in front of me said. He was a scrawny black guy with bad teeth. "I want to see that."

I couldn't help it. I laughed.

"Shut up up there. It's nobody's signature. And it sure ain't no good-luck charm, otherwise you wouldn't be here."

"You just wait." I winked at the scrawny guy in front of me and sat tight. As long as I didn't make a break for it, I figured I'd live long enough to eat lunch.

I sat quietly and watched the town pass by. I could feel the ghost knife behind me. I knew I could call it, but this wasn't the time.

We approached the supermarket. I told the driver I wanted to stop in and pick up a bottle of wine—I hated to show up at someone's house empty-handed. He slowed at the entrance to the parking lot, unsure if he should stop. Bobby cursed at him and told him to pass it by.

I didn't laugh this time, but I did smile. The guys were liking me less and less all the time. Bobby, unseen in the backseat, griped and mumbled about the amateurs he had to deal with.

"Don't be an idiot, *Bobby*," I said. The vehicle was suddenly silent. "Professional criminals are the stupidest people in the world. I know. I've been one of them."

We drove the rest of the way to the Curl Club in silence.

The first thing I saw when we approached the club was a high wall. It looked freshly painted. Tall, flowerless stalks had been planted along the cinder block. I wondered what sort of plant it was.

We pulled up to the wrought-iron gate. The driver lifted a remote control, pressed a button, and the doors slid apart.

Inside, I saw a big lot with a line of cars along the far wall, parked out of sight of the road. The club itself was off to the right, nestled into the side of the hill. It was four stories high, and judging by the long windows, the bottom floor was some sort of auditorium.

To the left, there was a smaller building, only two stories, with a loading dock in the front. Finally, at the far end of the lot sat a little cottage. It had a little weather vane on the top and a mailbox in front. A homey little sign above the door said simply OFFICE.

We didn't drive to the office, as I expected. We pulled right up to the double doors in front of the big building. A small sign above the door said CURL CLUB. It, too, was freshly painted. The rest of the guys began to pile out, momentarily forgetting that they were supposed to be threatening me. I felt the barrel of Bobby's gun tap the back of my head, so I climbed out of the van like a good boy.

"Watch him," Bobby snapped. Two of the gunmen turned their weapons on me again. Floyd smirked like a kid who was going to see his big brother get a spanking. The Kurt Cobain fan opened the doors. Bobby stayed behind me.

The sport van pulled away. I turned to watch it go, thinking about that remote control. I felt a hand shove into my back. "Move." I did.

We walked into the building. The first thing I noticed was that the main floor was even bigger than I'd thought. Not only was the ceiling twenty feet above me, but the floor was sunken.

"Come on," Floyd said. He was still smirking.

We descended the stairs. The room was done up like a bumpkin's idea of a casino, but done on a budget. The wallpaper and carpets were whorehouse red, which was appropriate, I suppose. I saw a pair of roulette wheels, a handful of craps tables, and a lot of blackjack tables. In the corners were a couple of lonely, neglected-looking slot machines. Judging by the number of customers, business was slow. Maybe these were just the all-day die-hard gamblers.

Against the far wall was a mezzanine with green felt tables. Poker, I guessed. At the end of the mezzanine I saw a fire door marked EXIT.

We turned left and walked across the floor toward a flight of stairs. The boys accompanying me were relaxed, and I didn't do anything to spoil their mood.

We climbed the stairs. One of the men was gasping for breath by the time we reached the hallway at the top. The corridor seemed to run the length of the building, with several doors on the left side but only one on the right. At the far end, a second flight continued up. The Cobain fan rapped on the first door on the left, and someone inside threw the latch. The door opened.

We all walked into a little restaurant. At first I thought it was a bar, but this place had no booths and no dark corners anywhere. At the back I could see a little stage with a brass pole.

Only a single table was occupied. Bobby and I walked toward it, but the others hung back by the door. Seated at the table was a young woman of about twenty, slightly plump, with dull yellow hair, black eyebrows, and pale skin. She smiled at me with painted lips, and her gaze was intense and slightly intimidating. She was plain-looking at best, but she had an aura of furious vitality.

Beside her, a woman of about seventy, with dyed-red hair piled on top of her head and a shapeless dress over her shapeless body, sat slightly hunched. She stared up at me with narrow, suspicious eyes, picked up a long, white cigarette, and took a deep puff.

I assumed I was looking at Phyllis Henstrick.

"This is him," Bobby said.

"Thank you, Bobby," the old woman said. Her voice was raw from years of smoking. "Have a seat." I wasn't sure which of us she was talking to. Bobby pulled out a chair for himself and pointed at the one he wanted me to take. We both sat at the table. She didn't object.

She watched me for a couple of seconds. The silence dragged out. "Thank you for coming," she said finally.

"Thank you for inviting me so politely."

"You're welcome." She was so deadpan I couldn't tell if she was being sarcastic or if she really was unaware that I'd been brought here at gunpoint. She stuck the cigarette between her lips and sucked on it. Bleh. I'd only spent a couple of seconds with her and I wanted to get away. "We have a lot to talk about," she said, "but it's a little early for lunch. Maybe you'd like to go upstairs. Tiffany can show you the way, and keep you company for a while, if you're feeling a little tense."

I looked at Tiffany. She still had that dangerous glint in her eyes. It had been a long time for me, so of course I was tempted, but the ugly old woman took an ugly puff on her ugly cigarette, and I found the common sense to resist. "I'll pass. Sorry, Tiffany. I'm sure you're very good at your work."

"Not your type, eh?" the old woman said. "I don't have any boys on the premises."

"I'd turn down anything you offered me, except a ride into town. Or breakfast."

She turned to Bobby. "Would you ask Arlo to fix us some turkey sandwiches? And cole slaw." She turned to me. "Do you like cole slaw?"

"Not really."

"Bag of chips for him." She turned to me again. "Do you have any food allergies? You aren't going to fall over dead if you bite a tomato, are you?"

"Well, I do prefer my arsenic on the side, thanks."

She chuckled and waved Bobby off. He stuck his hand in his pocket, presumably where he had stuck his gun, and gave me a nasty look. He was leaving me alone with this woman, and he didn't want me to try anything stupid.

The old woman stared at me again. "Poison is a little too hifalutin for us, I'm afraid. We don't go into that fancy stuff. Too easy to screw up."

"Uh-huh."

"You did a real number on Floyd and some of my other boys."

"Floyd can't take a hint."

"Well, that's the God's honest truth. But Floyd is a workingman, too. He has a nut to make, just like everyone else. How is he supposed to pay his bills while he can't work?"

"Since he was hurt doing a favor for Wyatt, Wyatt ought to give him a cut from his meth money. If Wyatt doesn't take care of his people, he's not going to have them for long."

She blinked. It was a small thing, but I'd surprised her. She covered it up well, though.

"I know all about taking care of people. The folks in Hammer Bay look out for each other. We need each other. If one of us gets into trouble, all of us suffer."

"Is that why the Dubois brothers are shaking down the local businesses for protection money? Is that why you're running a casino? To help the good folks of Hammer Bay?"

"Emmett and I don't get in each other's way. That's how it has to be. And this place does help the community."

"By taking their money?"

Bobby returned to the table. He sat beside us without comment, his hand still in his pocket.

"And the money from people in Sequim, Port Angeles, and Port Townsend, too. Most of the boys who work here are on my construction crews. When there's a boom time, the boys practice their trades: wiring offices, patching roofs, hanging Sheetrock. Frankly, during a boom this place is a pain in the ass. We're understaffed and too busy. But during a bust this place keeps bread on the table for a lot of local men."

"You convinced me. You're a town hero."

"I'm not a hero, smart-ass. I'm an employer. Communities need employers, no matter what you think of the business they do. When my husband passed, God rest his soul, this place was falling apart. No one was building. No one was playing the cards. The whores were walking petri dishes. You know what it's like to sit in a room with a bunch of whores no one wants to touch? It's depressing. They're not typically great at the art of conversation. No offense, Tiff."

Tiffany shrugged. She was still watching me. She looked like she wanted something from me.

"I turned this place around. Me. I rehired the men my husband, God rest his soul, turned out onto the street, along with a few Cabot let go, too. Do you know how I was able to do all that?"

"Do I have to guess until the food arrives?"

She ignored that, bulling on with her little speech. "Because of Charlie Hammer. Little Charles Hammer the Third opened up a plant and a big office and started putting people to work. Those paychecks went into home repairs and new builds. In other words, to me. And I put a bunch of that money into the pockets of my boys. So you'll understand if I get a little squirrelly when some prick blows into town and threatens to ruin things."

"Am I the prick?" I asked. "I hope so, because I was waiting for you to get to my part in this."

"You had a meeting with Charles. Now your little girlfriend is stalking him, trying to follow him around. I know. You can't keep secrets in a town like this."

I laughed. I couldn't help it. I laughed right in her face.

"What's so funny?" she asked. "I know all the secrets around here. I know the mayor's, the reverend's, the chief's—"

"You know Emmett Dubois's secret?" I asked. I wondered if she meant that he was a shape-shifter, or that he liked to have Tiffany dress him in a diaper and spank him.

"I told you he leaves me alone, didn't I?"

"If you know his secret," I said, "you know he should be stopped."

"If by 'stopped' you mean 'killed,' I'm not sure I can. I have a basketful of questions about him still, and I'm not sure I could take him out clean."

Tiffany turned her gaze on Phyllis as if she was about to volunteer for the job. Phyllis spoke to her as if she could read her mind. "Now, Tiff, I don't want you or Bobby or anyone else going near Emmett Dubois. You're good people, but you're not tall enough to ride that ride."

"Yes, ma'am," Tiffany said. Bobby sat quietly, serenely confident that he could do whatever Phyllis asked of him.

I shifted in my seat. My stomach grumbled. "So you know how he manages to take out his enemies with a pack of dogs when he doesn't actually have a pack of dogs."

She eyed me keenly. "I do. It's pretty obvious to anyone willing to believe. It's that willingness that most people can't manage."

I smiled at her. "I'm willing. For good reason."

"Then I suppose you noticed the plants surrounding the wall out front?"

"I saw them, but I'm no botanist. Wait a minute. Are they wolfsbane?" The old woman nodded. I almost laughed again but I held it back. "Maybe we could help each other. We seem to have a common enemy."

"That doesn't make us friends. I want to know why you're interested in Charles Hammer. Until we get that straight, you're nothing."

A man in kitchen whites entered with a tray. He set a plate with a turkey sandwich and an ice cream scoop of soggy cole slaw next to Phyllis. He set a second plate next to me. The sandwich was identical, but I had a tiny pile of supermarket potato chips. We each received a tall glass of iced tea.

Phyllis gestured at the food. "Tuck in, Nothing."

We picked up our sandwiches. Mine was as dry as plasterboard and just as flavorful. It didn't matter. I hadn't eaten all day. The tea tasted like sour water, so I didn't have more than a sip.

While I chewed, I thought about Phyllis. She was loyal to Hammer, and she had a lot of muscle and cash. One of her men probably had a brother-in-law who worked night security at Hammer Bay Toys, or a wife who worked in his office. She probably also had blackmail material on half the town. She was connected, and I had to figure a way to turn her to our side.

I finished half the sandwich and felt full, but I ate a chip just to keep busy. Phyllis was still working at her sandwich. She reminded me of a bear I'd seen on a nature show—it was tearing into a picnic, hunched over, holding a balled-up pizza in its claws and ducking its head to tear off bites.

I looked over at Tiffany just to have something more pleasant to look at. She stared at me with a creepy insect expression. I got the impression that she was imagining herself having great fun with me, but not in a way I'd especially enjoy.

"So," Phyllis said, then swallowed a lump of dough and meat. "Why did you meet with Able Katz at the toy offices?"

"I thought the whole town knew that by now."

"I want to hear it from you."

"My boss owns a factory in Africa that could handle some of the manufacturing work."

"Outsourcing."

"Sure. I hope you're not *surprised*, Phyllis." I tried to sound worldly, which I wasn't. "That's how the game is played."

She slapped her hand down on the table. "This isn't a game!"

"And it's his company, not yours. Maybe he started it as a charity, but I don't think he's going to keep doing that forever. His margins are too thin—"

"His company is a success. It's turning a profit, because of our work."

I didn't disagree, and I noticed that she had thrown herself in with the old ladies who were sewing Eagle Rider outfits. "And his ideas. Hard work he can get anywhere."

"He turned you down, didn't he?"

"Able Katz turned us down, on standing orders from Charles. He also agreed to meet with us again. The door's not shut. They're turning a profit now, but everything is boom and bust, just like you said. What happens when they hit a bust period? According to Able, they're over-due. And if they don't sign with us, it'll be someone in Malaysia or the Philippines. In fact, there's a prison in China—"

"Prisoners!" She slammed her hand down on the table, making the plates jump.

I ate another chip while she fumed. I had no idea if anything I'd said made sense. It was a jumble of news stories I'd heard mortared together with bullshit. It seemed to be having the desired effect, though.

I leaned closer to her. "That's not the end of it." I waited a moment for her mind to clear. When I had her full attention again, I continued. "You know what Emmett Dubois is." I paused again, making sure that she kept up with me. "Well, near as I can figure, Charles Hammer is something worse."

"What is this? What bullshit is this?"

I was losing her, but I had to risk it. "How do you think he's been so successful? Even Able Katz doesn't understand it. You remember when I said every business has a boom and bust? Katz knows that Hammer Bay Toys should have had a bust by now. Even a little one. But they haven't."

"Where is this going?"

"The guy is making his success happen *another way,* and the whole town is paying the price."

Bobby was looking at me like I was old fish. I couldn't read the look in Tiffany's eyes at all. Phyllis was squinting suspiciously at me again. "What price is this supposed to be?"

I sat back in my chair. "Where are the kids? Where are the kids in your town? The school yards are empty. The parks, too."

Bobby turned to Phyllis. "This dude is out of his mind."

I watched Phyllis's face. "Imagine what they'd say if you told them about the Dubois brothers."

Phyllis kept staring at me. "Are you saying he's made everyone sterile or something?"

"Worse. I'm saying the kids were here, but now they're gone and no one can remember them. How many girls do you have who have kids? It seems like it should be a pretty common thing for working girls to have a couple of kids. How many do?"

"We look after our girls here," she said. Her jaw was thrust for-ward, stubbornly refusing to acknowledge what I was saying, but her eyes looked troubled.

"What about your boys? How many of them are married with kids?"

"There's Ty, and Thomas, and, uh, Richard."

"That's it? Ty, Thomas, and Richard? Three guys out of how many? And how many of those men drive station wagons or minivans—cars no guy would own if he wasn't a father? Your future is almost gone, and you don't even realize it."

Tiffany turned toward Phyllis. "I don't like what he's saying." She stood and circled the table toward me. I tensed, putting both feet on the floor.

Bobby slipped his hand into his pocket. I stayed put.

Tiffany bent over me and patted my face. Her hands were soft but clumsy. She smelled like baby powder. "You must have been having a bad dream or something." She tilted my face up and looked into my eyes. She had the stare of a praying mantis. After a few seconds, she saw what she wanted to see and went back to her chair.

"Do you see those men behind you?" Phyllis asked. I turned and looked at them. "Any one of them," she continued, "would put a bullet in your head if I asked them to." Behind me, Bobby coughed. "We could drop your body in the rain forest. No one would find you. No one's found any of them."

I turned back to her. "Killing people is easy," I said. "It doesn't impress me. What would impress me is if you could wake up and see what's going on."

"All that talking must have left you parched," Tiffany said. "Why—"

"Tiff," Phyllis said sharply. "The boys over there are getting bored. Why don't you talk to them for a while?"

Tiffany looked a little stung as she retreated toward the door. I didn't pay much attention.

"So," Phyllis said, "How is it that you can blow into town and see what's going on, but we can't?"

I couldn't tell her anything about Annalise or the spells she'd put on me. "Willingness to believe," I said. It was the wrong moment to play coy with her, but I didn't have a choice. Annalise was already unhappy that I'd showed the scrap of wood to Emmett Dubois. I didn't want to repeat the mistake.

"What about your lady friend?"

"Never mind her."

Phyllis turned to Bobby, "Speaking of which, they're late."

Bobby took out a cell phone and started to dial.

Oh no.

Phyllis looked at me. "We'll ask her when she gets here."

"You didn't send men after her, did you? You didn't give them guns or anything?"

"Don't break a sweat, kid, I told them not to hurt her."

I didn't know whether to laugh or cry. The salty chips had made me thirsty; I took a swallow of iced tea just to bide my time. So much for recruiting Henstrick. I felt a little dizzy.

"No answer," Bobby said.

"Don't bother," I said. "They're dead."

Phyllis glared at me. "What do you mean, dead?"

"I mean, if you sent men to strong-arm my boss the way they've been trying to strong-arm me—with guns and knives and bad manners—they are dead. *Thirty* men couldn't kidnap my boss. Get it? If you want to talk to her, visit her yourself or send someone to ask politely."

My head started to feel light. The lights went dim. I suddenly felt very tired.

"Dammit," I heard Phyllis say. Her voice sounded far away. "Send someone after them. Find out what's going on."

Then, darkness. My last thought was that I was helpless now. They could do anything they wanted to me. I took that thought into oblivion.

CHAPTER THIRTEEN

I awoke suddenly. I was sitting up, leaning against a pile of pillows. My hands were bound.

I'd been handcuffed to the post of a bed. I rolled off the mattress. I didn't want to think about who had been on it before.

Each of my wrists had a handcuff of its own. One end was locked on me; the other end was locked tightly around the thinnest spot in the post, which was about the width of my two thumbs. It looked like a hack setup, but after ten minutes of trying I still hadn't managed to free myself. So much for hack.

The room was slightly more homey than a hospital room but slightly less homey than a Best Western. The wallpaper, curtains, and bedcovers were decorated with a dense, multicolored pattern that reminded me of a counter at a diner, like they were designed to hide stains.

A big LED clock on the bedside stand told me the time was 8:45. There were no windows anywhere, so I couldn't tell if it was morning or evening. I was hungry again. Damn.

No one had left any saws or key rings nearby. I wanted my ghost knife. I closed my eyes and *reached* for it, searching for the slightest tickle that would tell me it was close. Nothing. If I survived this, I'd have to practice sensing the ghost knife from farther and farther away.

I wrapped my arms around the post, stood on the box spring, and laid my shoulder into it, using my weight to try to break it off. No good. A better plan would have been to kick the top of the post, but that would have made noise. I didn't want to let people know that I'd woken up.

I lay back on the bed, set my heels on the top of the post, and grabbed the chain of the cuffs. Then I pressed with my feet, holding myself in place with the cuffs. I had leverage, but the strain on my wrists prevented me from using my full strength.

I heard a key turn in the lock. I redoubled my efforts, gritting my teeth against the pain, but I didn't hear the slightest sound of cracking wood.

The door opened. A voice said, "You were right. He's up."

"Hear hear," a woman said. "Stop that right now."

I let my feet drop to the ground and stood. A man and a woman approached me. They were in their late forties and looked as average as any supermarket shopper. He was balding and walked with a plump shuffle. She was heavily done up and carefully balanced on high heels.

She carried a tray with a platter of fish and chips on it. "Here you go, dear. You've been up here a couple hours, and I'm sure you're hun—"

I kicked the platter out of her hands. Greasy fish and dark vinegar splashed onto the ceiling and wallpaper opposite us. "Go fuck yourself."

The woman stepped back. "Well!"

The man became indignant. "You have some nerve," he said, huffing out his cheeks.

"Try it!" I shouted at him, my voice rebounding off the walls of the room. They were taken aback by how quickly things had escalated. "Even with my hands cuffed I'll stomp you."

The woman laid a hand on the man's shoulder. Her long, fake nails dug into his shoulder.

I shut my eyes, closing out as much of the rest of the world as I could. I *felt* for the ghost knife. Nothing. The supermarket shoppers weren't carrying it. They turned and left.

I rolled back onto the bed and returned to working on the post. The encounter with the shoppers had fired my anger, and I strained even harder, but I couldn't crack the damn wood. If they already knew I was awake, there was no reason to keep quiet. I lay on my back and started kicking the top of the post.

Kick kick kick. I wasn't being secretive or clever about it. I wasn't in the mood for either. Tools would have been great, but I didn't have any. If I could have tipped the bed on its side, I would have laid my weight against the frame and broken the post that way, but I couldn't move my hands far enough to get decent leverage on the whole bed. So I kicked and kicked, letting my anger block some of the pain as the cuffs dug into my wrists.

Finally, I heard wood crack. I began to kick frantically then, until the wood splintered enough that the post bent at an angle.

I rolled to my feet and put my shoulder against it, breaking it off. I was free.

I lifted the broken hunk of wood. The empty ends of the handcuffs swung free.

The lock on the door clicked and the door opened. Bobby entered. He held a .38 in his hand. "You've been making a lot of noise up here."

"Quietly waiting to be killed is too hifalutin for me."

He didn't seem to remember the reference, and I didn't care. He waved at me with the gun, encouraging me to follow him. I tossed the broken post aside and followed him into the hall. There were three more men waiting out there, along with Tiffany.

She was looking at me like a hungry dog eyeing a steak.

I knew right then, from the look on their faces, that they were taking me away to kill me.

"We found our boys," Bobby said.

"The ones you sent for my boss?"

"They were friends of mine."

I wanted to tell him that was the price of playing gangster, but there was no point. "Next time you want to talk to her, be sure to use the magic word."

"I think we'll send her a different sort of message."

I looked at the other men. They had guns but didn't look happy to be there. They weren't gunmen; they were carpenters or Sheetrockers or whatever. They looked like guys with an unpleasant job to do and they looked like they wanted to get it over with.

Bobby twisted my arms behind my back and clamped the empty ends of the handcuffs onto my wrists. I'd never been double-cuffed before. I guessed they were a little nervous about me.

There were doors along both sides of the hall. The carpet was deep red with faint brown stains.

Bobby turned to the fattest of them. "Bring the van around to the back."

"I hope that's not your personal van," I said to his retreating back. "Bloodstains don't come out."

Tiffany's expression was still, but her eyes were wide with wonder. "I want to do it. Is that all right? I brought my knife. I want to do it." She sounded a little breathless.

"Shut up," Bobby said. He wasn't taking any pleasure in this, but he was being professional about it.

"I'll make it quick, if you want," she said, and glanced back at me. "I can do it whatever way you want."

"Fine," Bobby said. "Just shut up about it."

We started walking down the hall. Tiffany was ahead of me on the left, leading the way. Her stride was measured and careful, as though she was hyperaware of herself and her surroundings. Bobby was behind me again, this time on my left as well. A young, clear-eyed kid who seemed barely out of high school was behind me on the right. In front of me on the right was the same tubby, middle-aged guy who had searched me in the Chevy van. I wondered if he was still carrying my things. I also wondered why I was cooperating with my killers.

I stopped walking and turned around. The kid nearly bumped into me. Bobby lifted his gun and pointed it at my heart. "Keep going," he said.

The kid followed Bobby's lead. He pointed his gun at my chest, although he was still much closer to me than he should have been.

I closed my eyes. I could *feel* the ghost knife behind me.

"Why should I make this easy for you?" I asked.

If Bobby had been smart, he would have lied. He would have told me that he didn't *really* want to kill me, that he was going to let me go if I promised to disappear so completely that his boss never found out. But he'd seen too many movies. "Because if you don't," he said, "you're going to hurt. A lot."

I *reached* for my spell. The ghost knife slid out of the chubby man's pocket and landed in my hand. At the same moment, I heard Tubby sigh and stagger. It must have passed through part of him on the way to me.

I looked at the ceiling. They did, too. I cut the handcuff chain with my ghost knife. My hands were free.

The next part happened very fast.

I swept my left hand upward as quickly as possible and struck the kid's gun arm, batting it aside. The gun went off, but the barrel was already pointing past me. I heard the boom of the shot and felt the rush of air as it passed my shoulder.

At the same time, I threw the ghost knife at Bobby's gun. Again, I was too slow. Bobby squeezed the trigger.

I felt the pressure of the bullet striking my chest, but there was no pain. *He killed me,* I thought. *Shouldn't it hurt if he killed me?*

Hot gas billowed over my neck, and a burning speck struck beside my Adam's apple. The spot where he'd shot me didn't hurt. I didn't feel anything there. There would be no wound, either, if Annalise's tattoos had held. I didn't look down to check.

The ghost knife slid through Bobby's gun, cutting it in two, then vanished into his chest. I heard him gasp.

My back was still exposed, and I'd left the kid too long. I lunged at him, punching him on the side of the head and ripping the weapon from his hand. I grabbed the back of his head, spinning him between me and Tubby and Tiffany.

I didn't have to worry. Tiffany was frozen in place; whatever she'd imagined would happen, this wasn't it. And Tubby was on his knees, a bloody gunshot wound in his chest. Then he fell onto his back. He wasn't going to get up again.

I don't remember a lot about the next few seconds. There was a feeling of tremendous pressure inside my skull. I know I didn't shoot the kid's gun. I know Tiffany was much quicker with her knife than I'd expected, and I hit her too hard on the side of her face.

What I do remember is standing over Bobby, Tiffany, and the other two and slicing the kid's bloody gun in two. One of Bobby's teeth was still wedged in the barrel.

I'd broken their bones, but at least they'd live. They were better off than Tubby. It took every ounce of willpower I had to keep from vomiting all over them.

Doors all along the hallway swung open and heads poked out. Geniuses. They hear gunshots and rush toward them. The peeping face nearest to me was Rev. Wilson.

I stepped around the bodies on the floor to the dead man. He had forgotten to shave that morning. I took Cabot's gun from him and pocketed it. I also took back my wallet and keys.

After a moment of indecision, Wilson rushed toward me. He was wearing long black pants but no shirt. "What is happening here?" He looked me in the eye for the first time.

"These guys need an ambulance," I said. "But I'm afraid this guy is gone." I was talking too fast. I wanted to be cool and collected, but I felt anything but.

"Why did you—" Wilson began.

I heard a commotion behind me. Three more men had appeared at the far end of the hall. They rushed toward me, guns in hand. One held a walkie-talkie to his mouth.

"Help them," I said, and rushed past him. Another man rounded the corner of the hall ahead of me.

The door nearest to me was the one Rev. Wilson had come out of. I ducked inside and locked the door. I had a gun, but I didn't want to use it. There were too many people around, and I wasn't some badass hitman. Also, I had already gotten more lucky than I deserved. If Bobby had aimed at my head instead of my heart . . .

A woman was standing next to me. She was stark naked and unashamed. I guessed she was about forty-five, with long, auburn hair and a simple, honest face. Wilson had good taste.

"What's going on out there?" she asked.

"General naughtiness."

She reached toward my chest and tugged at the bullet hole in my shirt. It was scorched with powder burns. "I see that," she said.

For a moment I thought she would panic just as I was about to. "I don't want trouble—"

"Of course not. Come this way." She led me through the room into a second, smaller room. She was very calm. "Bobby and the boys have been getting worse and worse over the last few years. They used to be working guys protecting their own. Lately they've been acting like thugs."

There was a second door, next to a window that showed the forest slope behind. It was the way out. She took a key ring from a hook. "Not everyone wants to come in through the casino. We have a couple of rooms with a back door."

She unlocked the door and swung it open. The sun had gone down, but there was still a little light in the sky. I stepped out onto a metal staircase. There was a little carport four stories down.

I turned toward the naked woman. "Thank you."

A shot ricocheted off the metal stairs. I didn't see where it came from, and I didn't hang around to find out. I pushed my way back inside and shut the door. I heard the faint sound of construction boots running up the metal steps.

Damn. So much for sneaking out the back.

I ran back into the bedroom. The knob rattled but didn't turn. Someone's meaty fist pounded on the door.

"Keep out!" the woman yelled. "He's got a gun!"

For a moment, I thought that she could see it in my jacket pocket, but then I realized that she was just buying time. She came close to me and said in a low voice, "The cops—"

"They won't be on my side," I said. "Get over in that corner. Get as low as you can."

She did. Someone was still pounding on the door. They'd be inside in just a minute or two, as soon as someone with a key turned up.

I leapt to the other side of the bed and knelt on the floor. I jabbed the ghost knife into the floor, holding it by the barest corner so it would reach as far as possible, then I slid it along the floor, cutting a rough circle.

The circle didn't drop through to the floor below. I heard jangling keys on the other side of the hall door. "What are you doing over there?" the woman whispered. I wished I knew her name.

They'd be inside in a moment. I could have taken Cabot's gun from my pocket, but I didn't. Instead, I jumped onto the circle I'd just cut. I heard the lock disengage.

Wood splintered, and I fell through the floor.

I fell about ten feet and struck a tiled floor. My knees jarred, and I rolled to the side. It hurt, but I'd managed not to twist my ankle.

I rolled against something soft. It was a big, soft pile of sheets and bedcovers, and I missed it by two feet. There was a smear of red blood on several of the sheets, and it took me a second to realize that it had come from me. My hands were covered in blood.

I was in a laundry room. Three big industrial washers and dryers stood against the outside wall. There were no windows.

"Sweet sainted Mary!" A tiny old woman with a thick brogue stared at me. I stood and ran past her toward the door.

"Keep away from the hole," I told her. "Men with guns are going to be coming through in a moment."

I ran past the dryers and saw that they ran on natural gas. I stopped. The gas line joined the machines at the top. I yanked open the dryer doors, shutting off the flames. Then I traced the gas line along the ceiling to where it disappeared into the wall. There was a shutoff valve there. I cut it out.

The old woman gaped at me.

"Gosh," I said to her. "You have a gas leak. Better tell those boys upstairs with the guns."

I saw shadows move in the space above the hole. I turned and ran through the double doors. The old woman was shouting something, but I didn't know who she was shouting at. I just hoped she had the sense to pull the fire alarm.

I recognized this hallway. Beyond the opposite wall was the little restaurant where Phyllis had drugged me. I ran toward the stairs. I would rather have avoided the casino, but that didn't seem possible.

Two men came up the stairs. One of them was Floyd. He pointed at me with his bandaged hands, and the guy next to him lifted his weapon.

I ducked to the side as the gun boomed. I didn't feel the bullet hit me, but there wasn't a lot of cover in the hallway.

There was a door next to me. I yanked it open and dove inside. Another shot boomed, and something tugged at my pant leg. I didn't feel any pain.

I was in a linen closet. Neat stacks of folded sheets lined the walls around me. I pulled the door shut, and the darkness gave my animal brain a moment's comfort, tricking it into thinking I was hiding.

I knew the wall in front of me led to the outside world, but it was also three stories from the ground. I wouldn't make that jump.

I lay down and cut another hole in the floor. This time, I angled the ghost knife outward so that it wouldn't catch.

Gunshots tore through the closet door. The sound was terrifyingly close, and splinters rained down on my back. I cursed and resisted the urge to draw Cabot's gun and shoot back. That would be a losing game for me.

I finished the cut, and the section of floor fell away. At the same moment, the fire alarm went off.

I looked down through the hole. As I'd hoped, I was just above the mezzanine. I slipped through the hole and landed on one of the poker tables.

The fire alarm was clanging loudly, and everyone stood around and looked at one another. No one wanted to be the first to head for the exit. Hadn't they heard the gunshots?

I jumped off the table, pushing aside a man in a UPS uniform who had a nice stack of chips beside him. I glanced over at the long flight of stairs. Rev. Wilson, still without his shirt, led several men toward the exit. They were carrying Bobby, Tiffany, and the dead chubby guy and walked straight across the floor in full view.

I turned toward the exit I'd seen earlier. There was one man standing there. He wasn't looking at me and didn't seem to have seen me come through the hole in the ceiling. I rushed toward him, taking out Cabot's gun to get his attention.

When he did turn toward me, he looked unhappy. For a second I thought he would jump the rail.

"Hold still," I snapped at him. "Give me your gun."

He gave me his .38. Henstrick must have bought them in bulk. "Hey, man—"

"Shut up and get these people out of the building. There's a gas leak. Hurry!"

I pushed past him and went through the doorway. The night was no darker than it had been two minutes ago. I started down the metal stairs, just as exposed as I was before, but as I'd hoped, there were no shots. The trip was shorter, too.

It would have been nice to lose myself in a crowd of people fleeing the fire alarm, but the patrons were too slow and I wasn't going to wait around for them. I ran along the back of the building, away from the gate. I needed a vehicle to get away, and a remote to open the fence. I could cut my way through the fence or the wall, but fleeing on foot would be suicide.

I ran around the building and spotted the sport van, still parked in the same spot. The gate was closed. They'd open it for the ambulance and fire truck, but I didn't want to wait. I sprinted for the van, cut a hole in the driver's window, and unlocked it.

Someone shouted, "There he is!"

Cynthia's Escalade backed toward me. "Get in!" she yelled, and the passenger door swung open.

I looked back at the minivan. The remote sat on the dashboard. I grabbed it and jumped into the open Escalade.

Cynthia gunned the engine. The door swung closed on my ankle. I cursed at the sharp pain and pointed the remote through the windshield. There was only one button. I pressed it.

A gunshot shattered the back window. Cynthia screamed and ducked her head. Out of habit, she slammed on the brakes, but before I could say anything she hit the accelerator. The gate slowly rolled open. The parking lot was long, and whoever was shooting was going to have plenty of time to get a bead on us.

I slid closer to Cynthia and draped my arm over her. With my forearm hanging beside her head and neck, my tattoos would provide her some protection, but not a lot.

A bullet punched through the front of the driver's side window and snapped a hole in the windshield. Cynthia cried out just a little. The gate slid farther open. I thought it would be wide enough for us to clear, but I wasn't certain. I saw a woman running toward the opening. Her course put her in line with our bumper. Cynthia eased off the gas pedal, as though she was afraid to hit her. Something struck the back of my chair, passing inches from my ribs.

I slammed my palm on the horn. The blare made the woman look at us with a startled, furious expression, then jump aside.

More glass shattered, and I heard bullets punching holes in the SUV. Cynthia ducked low, barely peeking over the dashboard. She spit out a stream of curses. I would have cursed, too, if I could have unclenched my teeth. Instead I held on to the dashboard, hating guns, hating Phyllis Henstrick, hating Annalise and everyone who had led me into this mess, including myself.

Just as I thought the barrage had gone on too long, and that our luck couldn't hold anymore, we were through the gate. Cynthia wrenched the wheel to the side and we skidded along the road. The bullets stopped.

An ambulance with flashing lights and blaring sirens raced at us. Cynthia swerved and slammed on the brakes, and the ambulance roared by. I turned around. Through the shattered back window, I could see a few people running through the open gate.

"Oh my God," Cynthia said, her voice shaky. "Oh my God."

I still had the remote in my hand. If I pressed it, the ambulance

might have trouble getting the injured people out, but Henstrick's amateur gunmen might be delayed long enough for me to get away. I didn't
press the button.

"Keep it together," I said. My voice sounded loud in my ears. "Keep
going. People are coming through the gates."

She turned the car and gunned the engine. We roared up the asphalt road, passing the supermarket. Cynthia bared her teeth. She had
tears on her cheeks.

There was a red light up ahead. She wasn't slowing down. "Light!
Light!" I shouted. I leaned over and stomped on the brake pedal. The
Escalade skidded to a halt.

A woman in a Volvo station wagon loaded with groceries was
waiting to pull out of the supermarket lot. She gaped up at the bullet-
ridden SUV.

The light changed, and Cynthia eased into the intersection, carefully turning the wheel with shaking hands. She checked her speedometer several times. She drove like it was her first time behind the wheel.
The car rattled and clanked.

"What should I do?" she asked me.

"Drive to your house."

She did. We got out of the car and walked around it. There were
two holes in the windshield. I hadn't noticed the second, even though
it must have happened right in front of me.

Three of the bullet holes were clustered low on the driver's door.
Those must have passed under our seats. Four more were sprayed
across the back panel, two very close to the back left tire. Someone
had tried to shoot it out. There were two more bullet holes in the front
fender. Judging by the way her engine had sounded on the way home,
I suspected her engine block had gone the way of the dodo.

"You're bleeding!" Cynthia said. She touched my shoulder blade.
I felt a tiny sting. I had no idea how I'd gotten hurt. "Come inside."

She led me toward her front door. I looked up at the round tower
room at the top of the house. Cabot had said that Charles spent all his
time at the tower now. I wondered if he was up there, and what I
would do if I found him.

Cynthia led me up the stairs to a large bathroom in the back.
While I sat on the edge of the tub, she took a box of Band-Aids and a
squeeze tube of disinfectant from the medicine cabinet. She took off
my jacket, felt the weight in one of the pockets, and reached inside.

"You had a gun the whole time? Why didn't you shoot back?"

"Someone might have gotten killed."

We started laughing. It was a release for her, I knew, but my own laughter only increased the pressure building inside of me. I thought about Bobby's tooth, and the chubby guy lying dead on the floor. I thought about the way Tiffany's face seemed to *give* when I hit her. I kept laughing, but the sound of it scared me. I was alive. I wanted to shout the word at the tile ceiling just to hear it bounce around me. *Alive.*

I clenched my teeth and forced myself to be quiet. I shouldn't have been laughing, because whatever I was feeling at the moment, it wasn't happiness. Hammer Bay was full of people doing terrible things for the best reasons. It made me furious. I made me feel dark and low to the ground and ready to kill. This town was making me into something ugly and dangerous. I had to get away, but I knew I couldn't. Not without setting things right.

Of course, Annalise and I were here to kill whoever we had to kill to stop the magic and save the kids in Hammer Bay. I was here to do terrible things for the best of reasons, too. I hated this town, but I knew it was a mirror image of myself.

I didn't like it. I didn't have to like it. I was here to be vicious, to beat, kill, or humiliate anyone I had to, and I wasn't going to stop until all the magic had been expunged from this place and things were set right. And God help me, I was finally ready to do it. I was ready to go as far as I had to go to get the job done.

Cynthia told me to take off my shirt. I did. She dabbed at my shoulder blade with a wad of tissues. "This isn't bad at all. It's barely a scratch." I didn't answer. "They were terrible shots, weren't they?"

"Most people are."

"No one has ever . . . do you think they knew it was me? Do you think they were trying to shoot me?"

I understood. She probably had the only Escalade in town, and most people would recognize it.

"No," I told her. "If they had realized it was you, I don't think they would have shot at us. Henstrick is still loyal to your family. I think they were just all worked up and not thinking straight. In fact, I think you should expect a call and an apology from Henstrick."

I could feel her rubbing something onto my shoulder blade. It stung. Her hair brushed my shoulder, and goose bumps ran across my back.

"Do you go there often?" I had a hard time keeping the suspicion out of my voice.

"No. After I dropped you off at Uncle Cabot's office, I didn't go for a cup of coffee like you said. I didn't realize how I would feel when I saw you go into that building alone—for me—and I couldn't just go off and eat a banana muffin or something while you risked your life.

So I stayed close just in case. I don't know what I was going to do, exactly, but I hated feeling like a coward.

"So, I was parked down the street when you came out. I saw those men grab you outside the office, and I recognized Bobby, of course. I followed you to the casino and lost two grand at the blackjack table waiting for you to turn up."

That made sense, and I was grateful that she'd come for me. "The gun is Cabot's," I told her. "He was planning to shoot himself, but I convinced him to get out of town."

"Thank you," she said in a quiet voice.

"You saved my life tonight."

"We're even, then." She taped a gauze pad onto my shoulder blade. It felt like a big pad, but the scratch didn't hurt much. I wondered again if her brother was in the house somewhere. She patted my shoulder with a dismissive finality. "All done."

I stood. She was very close to me, and she seemed so small. Her hands were still trembling. I took her hand and held it in mine. I still felt a sickening rage inside. It took all the self-control I had to touch her gently. "Thank you."

We held hands for a moment. She felt warm and soft and impossibly fragile. I could have squeezed that hand and broken it to mash. The thought terrified me. I was as gentle as I could be.

She let my hand go, and it fell to my side. She stared up at me. Her brown eyes seemed to have turned black. "What next?" she asked.

"What's in that round room at the top of the house?"

"That's my bedroom."

"Take me there."

She hesitated for a moment. It was just a moment. She looked up into my eyes, then took my hand and led me to the stairs. I carried my shirt and jacket.

We entered the round room. It was tastefully decorated, I guess, with a lot of muted green pastels. Every surface had at least one candle and, for some reason, a stuffed rabbit.

Charles Hammer wasn't here. As far as I could tell, he had never been in this room. I was vaguely disappointed as I laid my jacket and shirt on a chair. I was absolutely ready to shoot him dead. I didn't know if I'd ever find myself feeling so ready to kill someone again.

Cynthia stood a few feet from me. "This is it," she said, as if waiting to see if I approved of her inner sanctum.

I wasn't going to kill Charles Hammer today. "Take off your clothes," I said.

She did. I took mine off at the same time.

I saw what I knew I'd see. She had a tattoo on her shoulder blade right where Cabot had his. She had an iron gate, too.

She knew what had happened to all those kids. What was still happening.

She lunged at me and we kissed. We were wild and desperate. I was still filled with rage, but I tried as hard as I could to keep it from her. I liked her.

Even though she had known all along. She had known. She had known. She had known. She had known. . . .

We made our way to the bed. It was good to feel alive. It was good to touch someone. It was good to feel like a human animal, to smell and taste and hear and see someone close.

She responded to me more powerfully than any woman ever had before, but I could not stop thinking about those dead children, about the flames, about the pale, gray worms, and that she knew all about it. It made me furious and sick at the same moment that we were grasping at life.

When my own release finally came, my mind was full of images of murder, and there was no pleasure in it at all.

CHAPTER FOURTEEN

I woke up without realizing I'd fallen asleep. The gray sunlight was shining on my face, and the bed jostled slightly.

Cynthia was sitting on the other side of the bed with her back to me. She was wrapped in the top sheet. I could see the iron gate on her back. The thing that had made me sick with anger last night now seemed like another unfortunate fact of life in Hammer Bay. Who was I to judge Cynthia? Or anyone? I was not exactly pure myself.

I reached out to her and touched her shoulder. She let me, but she didn't respond. She didn't seem angry or resentful. She simply didn't react. I took my hand away.

"Last night was powerful," she said in a low voice. "It was wild and strange and very powerful, but I don't think I'm going to want to do that again. Not ever. It was good. It was great, in fact, but it scared me, too. I don't want to visit that place again."

"I understand," I told her.

"Are you sure?" she asked.

She turned toward me. The look on her face made me ashamed. I wished I could start over again, more gently this time, but her expression said it all. Never again. "I'm sure."

"Do you want some coffee?"

I nodded. She stood and dropped the sheet. I watched her put on pair of jeans and a T-shirt. I couldn't help imagining her on the floor, screaming, as black steam jetted from the iron gate on her back. She told me that she would wait for me downstairs and left.

Alone, I covered my face with my hands. I couldn't see or hear anything. I looked inside myself and didn't recognize what I saw.

I stood and dressed in the clothes I'd tossed onto the floor. My shirt still smelled of gunpowder, and there was a powder-burned hole in the center.

I followed the smell of coffee downstairs. Cynthia stood by the bubbling coffee machine with her phone to her ear. The clock on the wall said it was just after 11 A.M.

She hung up the phone. "You were right," she said. "Phyllis left me a message asking if I was all right and saying she was sorry her people were so stupid. She offered to pay for any damages."

"I thought as much."

"What about you? Is she going to come after you? I could call her and tell her to leave you alone."

"Thanks, but it's better if you don't get mixed up in that any more than you already have."

"God, I nearly got shot last night. It doesn't seem real."

"It will when your next car-insurance bill comes."

She laughed. I was glad to hear it. We stood beside the counter, about three feet from each other. We didn't touch.

"How do you like your coffee?" she asked.

"I'll have it however you're having it. I don't care."

"Soy sauce and horseradish, coming up."

This time we both laughed. She set our cups on the table, and we sat. I took a sip. It was very dark and very sweet. I liked it.

"So," she said to me. "You never did tell me why you met with Able Katz."

"Tell me about the seizures," I said. "Have you ever had them?"

The remnants of her smile faded away. She stirred her coffee. "Is it like that?"

"Like what?"

"Am I supposed to give you dirt on my family? On my own brother?"

"I think you misread me."

"It's just a toy company, for Christ's sake—"

"I don't give a damn about the toy company. I don't care about that."

"You don't care about a multimillion-dollar contract for your boss? Isn't that why you came to town?"

"No, it isn't. And you should know better than that." She didn't respond. "There are strange things happening in town, aren't there? People being attacked by mysterious packs of dogs, for instance?"

I let her think about that for a minute. She stared at me, trying to guess how much I knew. "Why are you asking about Charles's seizures? You think it has something to do with the people who have been mauled?"

"I won't know until I ask."

"Well, it doesn't," she said. She took another sip. "My father had them, and his father, too. Charles has them worse than Pop, but it's a family thing."

"Do you have them?"

"Not so far," she said. "It's always a possibility, though. Charles's episodes didn't start until two years ago. My dad never had them as a kid, either, according to Uncle Cabot. Scary thought, huh?" She didn't look up from her coffee when she said it and she didn't look scared.

"I've been having a lot of scary thoughts lately. What about the dogs?"

"It . . . I don't know. I wish I did. I'd tell Emmett if I knew who was using those dogs. It's a horrible, horrible way to go. I get shivers just thinking about it."

I didn't believe her. I wanted her to be on my side in this, and not only because of the help she could give me, and I certainly didn't want to fight with her. "Are you sure you don't know anything? Maybe there's something about the killings that you would mention if you had a little time to think about it. Something funny about each one."

"Like what?"

"Like, did these people have enemies in common? Did they die at the same time of day, or at the same sort of place? Anything in common? Anything unusual?"

"Stanley Koch died in the alley behind his bar. Wilma Semple ran off the road up the highway. That was just a car wreck, though, although they said a cougar got to her before the ambulance did. Henry the grocer was mauled on his loading dock along with his night custodian, a man named Johnson, I think."

"What's the town gossip?"

"When Wilma died, everyone thought it was Harlan. She had just divorced him and taken up with another man. And Stan had just barred him from his place for a month for bad behavior. But Harlan didn't even know Henry. He did all his shopping at the Safeway."

"Did Wilma own a business in town?"

"No, she didn't."

"Then who had she taken up with?"

"Luke Dubois."

"So you know the Dubois brothers are behind this."

"Lots of people think so. Only a couple will say it out loud. Luke had been after Wilma for years, though. He was pretty torn up when she was killed."

"You think she found out something that she wasn't supposed to?"

"Like what? That the cops in this town extort protection money? The whole town knows that."

"I mean, that the Dubois brothers are werewolves."

She flinched. "What?" She was honestly surprised. I was relieved to see it.

"Werewolves."

"Are you joking?"

"Phyllis Henstrick said it was obvious to anyone willing to believe."

She stared off into space for a minute or two, holding the cup half-way to her lips. I took a sip, enjoying the warmth in my belly. It felt good to sit here with her like this. I tried to imagine myself sitting here day after day, talking to Cynthia while we shared coffee. I thought it would be a good life.

It was never going to happen. Not while Annalise was around, and not while Charles still had his "seizures."

"Is that true?" she asked.

"I think it is."

"What should we do about it?"

"*We* aren't going to do a thing about it."

"Okay, then. What are *you* going to do about it?"

"I'm going to cure them, if I can."

It was the truth, but it wasn't the whole truth. As far as I knew, the only cure was the most permanent one.

"Wow." That was all she said. "There's so much ugliness in the world."

I looked down at the table. Some of that ugliness came from me, and it was only going to get worse. "Tell me about the kids."

The color drained from her face. She didn't answer. She just gaped at me.

"Tell me about the kids in Hammer Bay who have been burning to death. Yeah, I know about it. I have the same tattoo you do. It twinges whenever Charles has a seizure, just like yours. Tell me about them."

"I . . ." She wouldn't look at me. She wouldn't speak.

I reached out and gently took her hand. Whether that made her feel comforted, trapped, or both, I couldn't say.

"What do you want me to say?"

"Everything," I said. "Start wherever you have to, but I want everything."

She pulled her hand away, lifted her cup, and drained it.

"My best friend ever since I was six was Daphne. We went through grade school together, high school, everything. She's divorced now. Her ex is a creep, but she had the most wonderful little girl. She was bold and adventurous—she drove Daph crazy. Daphne couldn't keep up with her, but I loved that little girl, and I knew she'd grow up to be someone wonderful.

"One day I met Daphne for lunch, and she didn't have her little girl with her. I asked if she'd found a sitter, and Daphne said her dogs could play in the backyard just fine. Her dogs. I asked who was looking after her daughter, and she said, 'Who?' Just like that. 'Who?' As if her little girl had never existed.

"Then she started talking about leaving Hammer Bay. What did she have to keep her here, besides a best friend? She had no roots, no family. She was gonna pursue her dreams while she was young enough to do it.

"Eventually, we got into a fight about it. Believe me, that little girl was worth more than any dream anyone has ever had. It was an ugly fight, and some of the people in the diner who knew us butted in. They kept telling me that Daphne didn't have a daughter, that she'd never had one."

Cynthia's hands were trembling. She pressed them against the table. "Daphne started worrying about me. She thought I was having a psychotic break or something. She brought me to her apartment to convince me that she'd never had a kid. She walked me through the rooms, saying, 'See? No one lives here but me.' And all I could see were these little toys on the floor and Golden Books on the shelves."

Her voice caught in her throat. She took a deep, quavering breath. "Daphne left town a couple weeks later. I should have gone, too, but I couldn't. By then, I'd seen it with my own eyes." She stopped talking. She looked down at her empty cup. "There was a baby in a baby carriage . . ."

She stopped again. She had said enough.

I stood and refilled our cups. I brought the sugar to the table. She scooped and stirred but didn't look at me. After a few minutes, I asked: "What did you do about it?"

"I hired a private investigator. I told him that something strange was happening to the children in town. He thought I was crazy, but he was happy to take my money. He searched around, interviewed people, the whole thing. Emmett scared him away after a week. All I got out of it was a bill and a useless report."

"Why do you think you can remember and no one else can?"

"My tattoo. Isn't that what you already said?"

"I'm just making sure we're having the same conversation. Cabot said you got it from your grandfather."

"Why do you think he would put it there? So that we would know when something went wrong? If that's so, I don't think I've been much use—"

"I don't think that's why. I think it's there to protect you and the rest of the family from that fire. Your grandfather was playing with dangerous magic, and he took pains to protect his own in case things got out of control."

"I . . ." She couldn't finish that sentence, and she couldn't look me in the eye. "I don't want to believe that."

"But you do."

"Yeah, I guess I do. I don't have a choice anymore, do I?"

An idea occurred to me. "You're the one who gave the boarding school scholarship to Bill Terril's grandson, aren't you?"

She shrugged. "I started the scholarship after the private investigator flopped. Well, after the relocation assistance flopped, too."

"Hold on. Start over for me, please."

She sighed and sipped her coffee. "The investigator was a waste of time. I didn't know what to do. I knew people had to get their kids out of Hammer Bay, but how was I supposed to convince them to go? The truth sure as hell wasn't going to do it.

"I started a relocation fund. I offered ten grand to any family with kids who wanted to move out of town. Only fourteen families signed on. This was right as Charlie's toy company was taking off, and people thought I was trying to sabotage him. I got a lot of nasty looks, not to mention gentle lectures from concerned townspeople.

"It wasn't enough, though. The kids . . . it was still happening. So I started a scholarship fund for boarding schools across the country. I wasn't prepared for how popular that one was. I wrote checks for eighty-seven kids to go to Oregon, Massachusetts, even Canada. It's not easy to find spots for that many kids."

I remembered the empty house just next door to this one. "That sounds expensive."

She still wouldn't look up at me. "Not all of my assets are liquid. I had to scramble for some of that money, sure, but I could do more, if people were willing or if I knew what to do. I wish . . ."

"What? Tell me."

"Before Daphne left town, I convinced her . . . actually, I paid her to get one of these." She pointed to the iron gate on her shoulder. "I paid extra to have it copied exactly. *Exactly.* Daph didn't like it, but she had already enrolled at the University of Washington and needed money. She was already leaving me."

I knew where this was heading. "But it didn't work."

"No."

There was more to casting a spell than tracing a couple of lines. If she didn't know that, she didn't have the spell book Annalise and I wanted to find. Hell, she might not even know it existed.

I was glad of that.

"What else could I do?" she asked. "I stay here because my family built this town. I own a good chunk of it. These families only stay because the toy factory gives them jobs. I'd firebomb the factory—hell, the whole town, if I had to—but Charlie . . ." She let her voice trail off.

"What? What did Charlie do?"

"He said he could fix it."

That gave me goose bumps. "What do you mean?"

"He said he could turn the kids back into kids. He said he could cure them. He told me not to worry, that he was going to take care of it and that I didn't need to give everything away to stop . . . He said a lot of things about this town and our family. But he told me to leave it to him, that he could undo it. I believe him. Do you think he can do it?"

I suddenly felt sick. Could Charlie Three undo the transformations that had struck the town's children? If so, I'd made sure the little girl on the basketball court could never come back. If so, I'd killed her. "I don't know."

"Well, you can cure the Dubois brothers, can't you? Maybe Charlie can cure all those kids."

My fear and nausea turned into a hard little knot. I'd once tried to cure people of the predators inside them. I'd failed in the ugliest way I could imagine.

I looked into her eyes. Her face was full of hope that her problems were going to be fixed by someone else—someone with the power and authority to set things right. Mingled with that hope was the fear that she was passing the buck. I wished there was something I could do for her. "Maybe."

"You don't believe it, do you?"

"I won't know what to believe until I talk to your brother." She glanced at the phone on the wall. I shook my head. "Face-to-face.

"Do you think this is his fault? I know you do. You're not that good a liar. But it's not his fault. It can't be. He would never do something like this."

"Cynthia, his company logo has fire on it."

"That's not . . . when he was a kid, he had nightmares all the time

about a burning wheel, and it . . . he'd wake up screaming from them."
She stopped talking and looked all over the table as if she expected to
find a persuasive argument lying on it. "Can I tell you another story?
About Charles?"

Hammer Bay seemed to be made of stories. "Go ahead."

"Charles wasn't the kind of kid to have a lot of friends, okay? He
was a good kid, mostly, but it just didn't work out for him. He did
have the latest, most expensive toys, though, so a lot of kids wanted to
play with him. See what I mean?"

"Yeah."

"So he had these dreams, okay? And he and a couple of the kids
who played with him got the idea to roll these old car tires down the
hill behind our house so they'd bounce into the trees. Being a kid and
kinda dumb, Charles tried to impress everyone. He put something
flammable on them—I never found out what—and set a couple on fire
before he rolled it down into the woods.

"I don't know if it was because of his dreams or if he was just being a dumb kid like every dumb kid, but he started a huge fire. Three
families lost their homes, and Charles cried and cried. After that night,
he became very sensitive to his place in this family. He understands
what it means to be a Hammer in Hammer Bay. He put that burning
wheel into the company logo to remind himself of his responsibilities.
He would never do something to hurt the people in this town again. It
just isn't in him."

"What if he thought he was doing more good than harm?"

She opened her mouth to respond, but no words came out. Her
expression went far away for a moment, as if she was remembering
something. When she looked at me again, she seemed less sure of herself. "He would never do something like this."

"Cynthia, what if you're wrong?"

She laid her hand over her mouth and her eyes brimmed with tears.
I did not offer kind words or a gentle touch. There's no way to comfort
a person who suspects someone they love is a killer. Her secret fear had
been spoken aloud, and she needed to face the naked truth of it. Or
maybe I'm just a bastard.

"Is that really what's happened?" she asked.

"I'm not sure yet. But I want you to help me put a stop to this."

She nodded. I was glad. If there was anyone who could get me
close to Charles, it was her. I hoped she was ready.

The newspaper was lying on the table. I noticed the headline: TIME
I DO SOMETHING ABOUT IT. The subhead read: HERO MAYOR VOWS TO
TAKE ON CORRUPTION IN HAMMER BAY!

"Oh, hell. That idiot!" I stood without thinking about it. "Have you read this?"

"No, I never read it. Why?"

I handed the paper to her. She glanced at the headline, then skimmed through the article. "I don't understand. *Frank Farleton* is going to 'do something' about Emmett? From his hospital bed?"

"I need Reverend Wilson's phone number." I rushed to the phone and held it in my hand.

"The phone book is right in there." Cynthia pointed at a drawer beside my hip. I pulled out the thin directory and flipped it open to W. There was only one Wilson in Hammer Bay: Wilson, Thomas. I called him.

The phone was answered by a woman who sounded elderly, probably his secretary. She seemed to be terribly upset. "He's busy right now. He can't come to the phone."

"It's an emergency. A real emergency."

She sighed. She probably thought I was tempted by drink or that I was coveting my neighbor's car. "Who should I tell him is calling?"

"Tell him it's Raymond Lilly."

I heard the phone clatter onto a desk. The wait seemed interminable.

"Hello?" he said.

"Reverend, it's Ray Lilly. Listen—"

"Martha told me you didn't really hold a gun on her. In fact, she was surprised when I told her you had one." It took me a moment to remember what he was talking about. "You should know," Wilson continued in a slow, mopey tone, "that I'm composing my letter of resignation right now. It's for the best, I think. I love her, but my congregation—"

"Hey!" I shouted into the phone. "Reverend, I don't care. Understand? Don't tell me about it, because it doesn't matter. Have you seen today's paper?"

"Uh . . . well, no, I haven't."

"The mayor's life is in danger. Do you hear me? The mayor is going to die, if he isn't dead already. You can save him. Are you listening?"

I wished I could read his face. His voice was flat and steady as he said: "I am."

"This is what you're going to do. You're going to call four members of your congregation who own guns. They should be people with courage and faith in a reward in the next life, understand? Also, make sure none of them work for Phyllis Henstrick. You're going to send them to the hospital. Tell them to walk in the front door with their weapons in plain view. They are to walk all the way to the mayor's room. Two of them will stay inside the room and two will stay in the hall outside the door."

"I don't understand why—"

"You just told me, Reverend, that you're listening. Are you still listening?"

"Okay. I am."

"Get those people in position. No one, and I mean no one, is to go into the mayor's room with a weapon."

"Emmett Dubois is going to take a statement from Frank this afternoon—"

"Emmett is at the top of the list. If he tries to enter that room with his gun, your people are to shoot him. Understand me? This isn't a joke. No one who works for Henstrick should get in to see him, either."

I heard him rustle paper on his end of the line. "Lord preserve us," he said in a low voice. "Peter Lemly has thrown a rock at the beehive. But can't we just have Frank taken to another hospital? Emmett is—"

"We're going to have him moved, yes, but that's going to take time."

"But guns in a hospital . . ."

"Reverend, listen to me. Last night, you could have gone out that back door. You could have slipped away from all that trouble and run. You didn't. You stepped up and took charge. This is another opportunity for you. Dubois, Hammer, and Henstrick have been running this town into a shit hole; it's time for you to step up and take your place. Hammer Bay needs you, and to hell with that letter you're writing. That's just another secret back door."

It was a corny pitch, but I could hear Wilson's breathing change. I had him hooked. I just needed him to follow through.

"You're right," he said. "Of course, you're right. I'll make some calls."

We hung up.

Cynthia gaped at the newspaper. "I should have realized right away—"

I took the paper from her. "Do you have another car?" I asked. "One that doesn't have bullets in the engine block?"

"Of course."

The other car turned out to be an Audi TT. It was smaller than I would have liked, but I didn't have a lot of choice.

Cynthia revved the engine. I slid the passenger seat back as far as it would go and climbed in beside her. I still had Cabot's gun in my pocket.

"Where to?" she asked.

"The mayor's house. You know where it is, right?"

She threw the car into gear and sped into town.

At the first red light, she turned to me. "Can I ask a stupid question?"

"Sure. I'll bet I have a stupid answer."

"Shouldn't Wilson's people have silver bullets?"

"Christ, I hope not."

"You don't know? What if they shoot Emmett and nothing happens? Won't Emmett kill them?"

"I'm hoping Emmett won't go that far into the open, but people do unexpected things when they feel cornered."

"What about the silver? Do we have to have it?"

"I don't know. And I'll bet Emmett doesn't know, either."

The light turned green, and Cynthia peeled into the intersection. "What do you mean?"

"He's probably never been shot with a regular bullet. I'm sure he knows all about the silver bullets and full moons and stuff, but that's the movies. I don't think he'd trust his life to something he saw in an old movie. I'm willing to bet he doesn't know if he's bulletproof."

"Not know? How could he not know?"

"You've had a tattoo on your back your whole life. What can you tell me about it?"

"Um, it's magic?"

"What's the spell called? What does it do? Where did it come from?"

"Okay. I don't know anything about it, except that it hurts when Charles has his seizures. But do you think Emmett is the same way? Just doing what he's doing in the dark?"

"We'll see."

Cynthia swerved her car suddenly and slammed on the brakes. We skidded to a stop next to the curb. There were a lot of cars parked behind us.

"Frank and Miriam's house is a couple doors back."

We climbed from the car and walked toward a modest two-story house with a tidy flower garden in the front. The bay window was blocked by cream-colored drapes. It looked like a little old lady's house. The car in the driveway was a huge Yukon that someone had painted tangerine orange.

I walked to the front door and rang the bell. Beside me, Cynthia sighed. "I'm not looking forward to this."

The door swung open, and I found myself looking down at a little woman with steel-gray hair and a pair of cheap, safety-goggle sunglasses over her regular glasses. She shifted her position to bar my way.

Cynthia leaned toward her. "We need to speak to Miriam right away."

"Who is it, Cassie?" a woman called. Cassie took one look at me and started to close the door.

I hit it with my fist, thumping it open.

I walked into the living room. Miriam Farleton sat on a little chair at the far end of the room. Seated all around here were seven old women, all dressed in what looked like their Sunday clothes. Cassie, at the door, made eight. Miriam's eyes were red from crying, but her cheeks were dry. I guessed these were friends who'd come by to comfort her. Not one of them was less than thirty years her senior.

The ladies gasped as I bulled into the room, which was full of lace, delicate furniture, and little ceramic figurines. I was afraid to touch anything—I might have put a grubby manprint on it. "I'm sorry to barge in this way," I said, "but there isn't a lot of time."

She didn't respond. The woman sitting next to her struggled to her feet. She was a stocky little lady, and her hands were large and strong. She stepped between the mayor's wife and me. "I don't think you were invited here today," she said, glaring at Cynthia. "Either of you."

I tried to talk past her, acutely aware of the bullet hole in my shirt. "Have you seen today's paper? I think your husband is in danger."

"Threats, is it?" the stocky woman said. "If you don't leave right now, I'm going to call—"

"Who?" Cynthia asked. "Emmett Dubois? Emmett is going to kill Frank if you don't let us help!"

This time the gasp from the room was followed by a lot of whispering. Great. The whole town would know what was going on by dinnertime. I turned to Miriam again and held up the newspaper. "Can we please talk privately?"

Miriam stood. "Yes."

"Miriam," the woman said, "you shouldn't be alone with strangers right now."

"Why don't you join us, Arlene," Miriam said. "If that's all right?" I nodded. Arlene and Miriam led us through a swinging door.

The kitchen was pastel blue and decorated with duckling wallpaper. I wondered if there was a room somewhere in this house for Frank.

I showed the headline to Miriam and Arlene. "This," I said, "is essentially a declaration of war against Henstrick and the Dubois brothers. Lemly put your husband's neck in the guillotine. Yours, too."

Miriam held the paper, skimming over the story. "Oh, Peter," she said. She looked tired.

"What do you aim to do?" Arlene asked. I suddenly recognized her.

She was the one who'd given Bill Terril a birthday card to sign in Sara's bar—she had a grandchild at boarding school in Georgia. Small town.

"Reverend Wilson is already putting people outside Frank's room to protect him, but that's a short-term solution. We need to get him out of town to a place where they can't find him. And we need to do it secretly."

I glanced at the doorway. Miriam and Arlene followed my glance and understood. Arlene patted Miriam's hand and started toward the door. "I'll shut down the rumor mill for a little while. I'll be right back." She stepped through the door way.

Miriam looked me in the eyes. "Why don't we call the state police," she said quickly, "or the FBI?"

Call the cops, I thought. It wasn't an idea that came to me naturally. "We will," I assured her, "but that's the long-term solution. They're a bureaucracy and they move too slowly. Let's get your husband to safety first, then worry about who to tell."

"He'll go to prison, you know," Miriam said. I could hear Arlene reading the riot act in the next room, but I couldn't make out what she was saying. "Emmett opened an account in Frank's name in Oregon. He's been putting money in it every month, as though it was a payoff. Frank and I didn't even know until Emmett sat us down and showed us a bank statement. He made it look like Frank is part of the whole thing. The FBI is going to go after my husband just as hard as they go after Emmett."

There was a loud boom from the living room, followed by a crash of breaking glass. I charged through the double doors, almost knocking Arlene to the carpet.

The big bay window that looked out into the garden was shattered. The rod had fallen, and the drapes lay in tatters on the carpet. A woman sitting on the couch clutched at her shoulder. Blood seeped through her fingers. Another woman held her hand against the back of her head. I realized that people were screaming and that some of those screams were actually squealing tires.

Cynthia ran to the window. I pulled her away.

Arlene was examining the woman with the cut on her head. I went to the woman with a bleeding shoulder. "This isn't too bad," Arlene said casually, as though she'd seen much worse. "But we'll still need to go to the emergency room."

"This too," I said. The woman I was examining stared at the bullet hole in my shirt and the tattoos beneath it. "Is anyone else hurt?"

I didn't get an answer. I heard a door open. Two or three of the women, Miriam included, pushed through the doorway into the front yard.

"No!" I shouted at them. "Stay inside!"

They didn't listen. So much for my leadership skills. I turned to Cynthia. "Organize a ride to the emergency room for these two. We have someplace to go first."

I ran out into the yard. Miriam and her three friends stared up the street, trying to see who had fired at them.

As I came near them, I saw a long white van drive up from the other direction. The black barrel of a shotgun protruded from the back window. It pointed at Miriam.

I shouted at them to get down, but she and her friends simply stared at the van in bewilderment. They were as still as paper targets.

I was too far away from the van to use my ghost knife, but Cabot's gun was still in my pocket. I jammed my hand inside and wrenched it up. The hammer caught on my jacket, tangling the gun.

I had already lost my chance. The shotgun had her in its sights. She was not going to survive.

But the weapon never fired. The van passed us, then squealed away down the road.

I couldn't figure it out. Was this just a warning, or had someone lost their nerve? I hoped it was the latter; it would restore my faith in humanity a little to know that there were people out there who couldn't shoot a bunch of women in cold blood.

I dropped the gun back into my pocket and ran to Miriam. She looked shocked.

"He didn't shoot," she said, sounding amazed. "I looked right into the barrel of that gun and I prayed it wouldn't hurt too much, but—"

"Would you get back inside, please?" I couldn't keep the annoyance out of my voice.

That startled her. She and the other women turned and bustled back to the house. I watched for the return of the van and saw something small rolling in the street. I ran toward it, keeping an eye out for vehicles.

It was a yellow hard hat. The name "benny" was written in all lowercase letters on the inside lining. I sprinted back into the house.

Arlene was organizing the others into their cars. She had a brisk honesty that I liked. "These two will be all right," she told me as I entered. "Vera is going to drive them to the hospital to be checked up, but I think they're more frightened than anything."

"What's that?" Cynthia asked.

"I found it in the street. It must have come from the van."

A little woman I hadn't spoken to yet grabbed my wrist and looked at the lining. "That belongs to my little brother, Benjamin."

There was a general expression of astonishment. Arlene came over to us. "Vera, do you think he shot at us?"

Vera scowled down at the hard hat. "He's always losing things. I knew he was in debt to that damn casino, but I never thought he'd go this far, or that Phyllis would ask him to."

"We don't know who was behind that shooting," I said, "so don't start rumors. Now let's go. Vera, you're taking the injured to the hospital, right? Cynthia and I will take Mrs. Farleton there in a bit. We have a stop to make."

"I'm going with you," Arlene said. She had a stubborn look in her eye.

"There isn't room," I told her.

"My car can squeeze in four," Cynthia said.

"I know," I told her.

"I'm going," Arlene said.

"She is, or I'm not," Miriam said.

I threw my hands into the air. How could I argue with these people?

I took the gun from my pocket. One of the women gasped, and I felt a little twist of nausea at her fear. I led Vera and the other women to Vera's station wagon, where they all squeezed in beside one another. As they pulled away, I imagined Luke Dubois sneaking through Miriam's back door and killing them all while I was out front. I ran back to the house and found them waiting for me.

I stood facing Miriam. I had her full attention. "Your husband seems like a good man. Do you love him?"

"I do."

"What about all this?" I waved at the house, the furnishings, everything. "Do you love all this, too? Because it's time to choose."

"What do you mean?"

"It's time for you and your husband to get out. You're going to have to leave a lot behind. Artwork, knick-knacks, all sorts of stuff."

"I can do that," she said. "Staring down the barrel of a shotgun clarifies things."

"Get your financial stuff," I said. "Bank records, credit-card papers, mortgage papers, insurance stuff, whatever. And get photo albums and old love letters, too. Everything else you should leave behind. Expect it to be burned to the ground before you get back."

She nodded and hurried up the stairs. Arlene started to follow her, but I caught her arm. "I have two questions for you: Do you have a reliable car? And if so, can she borrow it? They can't run away in a tangerine Yukon."

"Yes," Arlene said. "Yes, of course." She went off to help Miriam.

Cynthia and I stood in the living room. She smiled at me and squeezed my hand. I took a deep breath and relaxed. I was glad that she was helping me. I hoped that I wouldn't have to cut the iron gate off of her, or worse.

Within five minutes, Miriam came back downstairs with a banker's box in her arms. On top of that was an old leather-bound Bible. "I'm ready."

"We'll put them in the back of Arlene's car. Arlene, we'll meet you at the hospital. Ready?"

We went out the front door and loaded up the back of Arlene's Forester. While Miriam pushed the box into place, Arlene tapped my elbow. "Who are you?"

"Raymond Lilly."

"That doesn't really answer my question."

"I'm aware of that." Miriam shut the hatch. "Go quickly, please."

Arlene climbed in behind the wheel and pulled away. I made Miriam get into the backseat of the Audi and stay low. I felt silly rushing around like movie spies, but being shot at changes things.

"Where to now?" Cynthia asked.

"We need Annalise."

"Your place, then." She pulled away from the curb, and we drove quietly for a few blocks.

Miriam broke the silence. "Do you think Phyllis tried to have me killed?"

"I'm not convinced it was her. The hard hat was a little too obvious. And from what I've seen, her guys all carry the same snub-nosed .38."

"I heard she got a deal on them because she bought in bulk," Cynthia said. "She's a real cheapskate."

"But it was her sort of van," Miriam said. "And I'm sure some of her men have guns of their own at home."

I knew how easily a vehicle could be stolen. "It's pointless to speculate. What matters is that we get you and your husband to safety."

Five minutes later we had arrived at the motel. My room had been tossed and all of my clothes torn to shreds. I would have to make do with the bullet-hole shirt for a while longer. My detective novel had been destroyed, too. Bastards. Now I wouldn't find out who the killer was.

Annalise's room was empty, but it had also been tossed, and

everything in it torn apart. Miriam peered over my shoulder into the room. "Mercy," she said. "Do you think something has happened to her?"

"I'm not worried about her," I said. "I'm worried about us."

The van was gone, too. I wished she had given me a damn cell number I could use. I needed her, and I had no idea where she was or what she was up to.

Cynthia tugged on my sleeve. "Are we done here?"

I could have asked the manager where she'd gone, but I didn't trust him to give an honest answer.

I was on my own.

CHAPTER FIFTEEN

"Here," I said. Cynthia pulled into a parking lot. "Leave the engine running," I said. "I'll run up and run back."

"What are you planning to do?" Miriam asked.

"If you see trouble, peel out of here without me, understand?"

Cynthia nodded. She and Miriam began scanning the street. I turned and ran into the building that contained the offices of *The Mallet* and Peter Lemly.

In the lobby, I scanned the directory. There was an actuarial on the second floor and marriage counselors on the third. The fourth was the editorial offices of *The Mallet*.

The elevator looked slow and confined to me, so I took the stairs, vaulting up them as quickly as I could. I nearly knocked over a middle-aged couple coming down from the third floor. I mumbled an apology and squeezed past them.

At the top of the stairs I saw the door for *The Mallet,* est. 1909. It wasn't locked, and I let myself inside. There were three doors along a short hallway. The farthest door was marked EDITORIAL. I put my hand on the knob and hesitated. The air was very still. Peter wasn't here, and I wanted to sprint back down to the car. Instead, I opened the door.

I immediately smelled blood. I walked toward the desk and window at the far side of the room. There was a pair of fresh blood splashes on the glass, and the desk had been knocked crooked.

Peter was behind the desk, mostly. His arm lay in the far corner, his hand still clutching a nine-millimeter. His head lay a few feet away beside a single spent bullet casing. I wondered if he had managed to hit his target.

I backed out of the room, wrapped my hand in my shirttail, and pulled the door closed, then wiped my fingerprints from the knob. I did the same to the knob on the door to the stairs.

I ran down the stairs, out the door, then hopped into Cynthia's car. "Any trouble?" I asked her.

"No. You?"

"Oh, yes. Peter Lemly is dead."

"Oh, shit," Cynthia said.

"Shouldn't we call someone?" Miriam asked.

"Like who? The cops are probably the ones who killed him."

"An ambulance, of course. What if he's just badly hurt?"

I turned around and looked in her eyes. "Miriam," I said. "He's very, very dead."

She snapped her mouth shut and stared out the window. Cynthia raced through town and pulled into the county hospital lot. She parked as close to Arlene's car as possible.

Within five minutes, we were all walking down the hallway toward Frank's room.

Just outside his door, I saw a tiny, bald black man of about seventy. The top of his head came up to the bullet hole in my shirt, and he wore huge, black-framed rectangular glasses that make his eyes look like apricots. He held a long, black rifle in both hands.

Across the hall, a bird-thin woman of about sixty sat on the same padded bench Cynthia and I had sat on the day before. She held a World War II–era carbine across her lap.

The tiny man thrust out his chin and slid his finger over the trigger. "Stop right there, young man," he said in a high, nasal voice. "You stop there."

"Lord in heaven, Roger," the thin woman said. "Can't you see that they have Miriam with them?"

He squinted at us through his gigantic goggles, then scowled. Letting people into the room must have felt like a loss of much-loved authority.

I glanced at the far end of the hall. Two hospital security guards leaned against a door. They were watching Roger and us but were obviously unwilling to approach closer.

At that moment, Arlene pushed past the guards, with Rev. Wilson and a doctor close behind. Miriam, Arlene, and the doctor bent their heads together for a conference. The doctor's voice was low but emphatic. He was unhappy about something, and I was pretty sure I knew what it was.

Rev. Wilson turned toward me but kept his gaze pointed off to my right. "Emmett was here just a few minutes ago, but he's gone now."

"He wouldn't surrender his weapon," Roger announced. "Or submit to a search."

"And he smelled funny," the bird woman said.

I imagined he would, if he hadn't had time to wash off Peter's blood. "What about his brothers?"

"There's been no sign of them," Wilson said.

I remembered the spent casing by Peter's body. I went to the doctor, who was objecting most strenuously to something. "Hey, Doc," I interrupted. "Have any of the town police been admitted to the emergency room today?"

"I'm a cardiologist."

"Don't be annoying, please. If one of them came into the ER, the whole hospital would have heard about it, right?"

The doctor obviously wanted to continue his argument with Miriam, but she was paying attention to me. He sighed. "Right, and no."

I hoped Peter had missed with his shot. "Thanks. Now run along and get us a wheelchair, would you? We're taking the mayor out of here." He blinked at me as he tried to generate a suitably outraged reply.

I heard a low growl behind me.

I turned. Luke Dubois stood by the door we had just come in. Standing next to him was a wolf.

Shit. Too slow. If only I hadn't stopped for Peter Lemly, I might have gotten them away in time.

"Everyone stand where you are," Luke said, looking pleased with himself.

The other wolves I had seen in Hammer Boy had been tinged with red or gray fur. The one beside Luke was black, and it was big. I remembered Wiley's dark mop of hair, and knew this one was him.

"Not protecting your secret anymore, Luke?" I said. "It must hurt to have killed Wilma over something you're just throwing away now."

Luke was startled, but he didn't break down in tears or anything. "I didn't . . . I would have never . . . we don't have to be afraid," he said, turning the subject toward something he wanted to talk about. "All this time we thought we had to be afraid, but we don't. And we're not giving away our secret. Not today, at least."

That wasn't good. We were in for a bloodbath. "Roger," I said, keeping my voice low, "shoot that damn wolf."

The gun went off almost before I finished the sentence. It was brutally loud in the tiled hallway, and despite myself, I flinched.

A bloody hole appeared dead center on the black wolf's head. Roger was a good shot. As I watched, the hole closed over. The wolf barely staggered.

"You see?" Luke said. "All this time we've been afraid, and we didn't have to."

Damn. Peter *had* shot one of them. We needed silver, and they knew it.

I heard screams behind me. A red wolf had knocked down one of the security guards and was tearing apart his forearm. The grayish wolf had already gone for the throat of the second man, who struggled weakly against the attack, red blood squirting onto the tile floor.

"Get into the room!" I shouted.

Cynthia barreled into the door. I heard her shouting at someone inside not to shoot her.

Roger worked the bolt of his rifle. His face was set, as though he was trying to work out a complicated puzzle.

The gray wolf charged us. The birdlike woman stepped toward it and lifted her rifle. There was another shot, but the wolf leaped on her, knocking her to the floor. It sank its fangs into her neck just below her ear. She didn't get a chance to scream.

Roger grunted. The black wolf had landed on him. I kicked it in the ribs just as it snapped at his throat. Roger's gun went off. Luke, still standing at the end of the hall, collapsed backward onto the tile floor. The wolf tore into Roger's throat.

I rushed at Miriam. The red wolf came at her first. Arlene and Rev. Wilson both lunged at the creature. Wilson and the wolf went down. The reverend was not going to last long.

Arlene grabbed Miriam and shoved her toward the door to Frank's room. They collided with me. Rather than fight my way around them toward the reverend I let myself be pushed into the room. I ran when Rev. Wilson, the guards, Roger, and the old lady could not, and I was glad to do it.

I slammed the door shut and threw my shoulder against it. There was no lock. Someone slid a chair under the doorknob. I looked up and saw that it was the cardiologist. I hadn't seen him enter the room, but here he was, holding the door with me.

"What's going on?" he asked me, his voice low and breathless. "What is that officer doing with those dogs?"

"Killing us, if he gets the chance."

I turned and looked around the room. Frank was lying on his bed, tubes up his nose. Standing beside him were a fat middle-aged man with rake-thin arms and a fat elderly man with a handlebar mustache. Both were carrying identical doughboy-era rifles. Along with them were Cynthia, Miriam, and Arlene. Miriam was fussing over Arlene's hand, but the rest were looking at me.

"Is everyone all right over there?"

"It's Arlene," Miriam said. "She's been bitten pretty badly."

"You have a patient, Doc."

Cynthia fetched a rubber doorstop from the corner and kicked it beneath the closed door. Blood started to flow under the door. "I saw what happened when the old guy shot the wolf. It wasn't hurt at all."

"I know."

"We need some kind of silver weapons, don't we? Silver bullets or something?"

"I don't know. I wasn't planning to fight them. That's why we were running away. But I don't know if silver will work."

"What happened out there?" the man with the mustache asked. He looked like he wanted to throw his gun down and run. The middle-aged man was even more spooked. "Where's Roger and Binky?"

"They're both dead," Arlene snapped. "So is Reverend Wilson."

"What?" Mustache said. "How—"

Everyone began talking at once, in high, panicked tones.

I felt someone try the handle. Someone pushed. Someone strong. I pushed back. I could hear sounds coming from the other side of the door, but I couldn't make them out.

"Hey!" I shouted at them. "Be quiet!" No effect. Everyone was still badgering Arlene for explanations. Frank began to look pale. Miriam rushed to him. "Shut up!" I shouted at them, but all I did was add to the noise.

From the other side of the door, a wolf howled. Then two, then a third. Everyone in the room fell silent.

"All right in there," Luke Dubois said. He didn't sound like a man who had just been shot. He sounded happy. "What say we talk terms?"

"Sure thing," I said. "Let everyone in this room leave unharmed, and I won't rain hellfire on your ass."

Luke chuckled. "Hellfire, huh? You didn't look like you had much hellfire on hand when you were scurrying into that hospital room. You looked like you had a load in your pants."

"You don't know who I am," I said.

"Don't care, neither. Not anymore."

"That's because you're stupid." I took the ghost knife out and threw it through the door. It cut a slit in the wood and passed through. I heard Luke grunt. Something metallic fell onto the tiled floor. I *reached* for the ghost knife. It flew back to me, cutting a second slit through the wooden door and landing in my hand.

"What . . ." Luke's voice was small and frightened. "What was that?" I knew the ghost knife had taken the fight out of him. Hopefully, it would give him pause, too.

"That was just the start. That was small magic for small potatoes like you. Where did you get this trick for shape-shifting, Luke? Straight from the Hammer family, I'll bet. I'll bet the first Cabot gave it to your grandfather, and he's passed it down over the years. I'm right, aren't I? Didn't you ever wonder where he learned the trick?"

"He's rich," Luke said, as if that explained everything.

"Please. He got his magic from the same place I got mine. From the same book, in fact. But he only taught the Dubois family that one trick, right? He only gave you that one spell. And you didn't even know enough about it to be sure the magic protected you. Not until Peter Lemly unloaded a round into one of you."

I just kept talking, hoping to stall him. I didn't know what to stall him for, but it was all I had.

"So what? What does that have to do with you?"

Cynthia came up to me and held out her hand. "This was all I could find," she whispered. She had a delicate silver chain in her palm. I took it. I hoped it would do some good.

"Damn, Luke," I said, "you fellas have been stumbling around in the dark for years. And now, when you finally realize what you have, you blow it by killing Karoly and Lemly, and now going after the mayor. You drew too much attention to yourselves. Now we're here to take the magic back."

"We're just protecting our own interests," he said, his voice almost complaining. "This is our territory."

I waved at the two fat men while Luke kept talking. They approached me timidly. Rake-Thin Arms was about to ask a question, but I held my finger to my lips. I gestured for them to throw their weight against the door. They did.

I ran to the window. We were on the fourth floor—too damn high to jump. But there was a ledge. I took out my ghost knife and cut a large hole in the window, as large as I could make it. Then I turned to Cynthia and the doctor. "Out onto the ledge," I whispered.

Cynthia didn't hesitate. She stepped through the window and climbed out. The ledge was only six inches wide, and there was nothing but parking lot below, but she inched her way along.

The doctor followed her after a moment's hesitation. Frank didn't have the strength for that kind of climbing, and Miriam wasn't going to leave him. Arlene wasn't going to leave Miriam.

I went back to the door and shoved the fat guys aside. "Go," I whispered. Whatever Luke had been saying, he was done saying it. I laid my arms against the door and braced myself, for whatever that was worth. I looked over my shoulder.

The two fat guys rushed toward the window. Mustache looked out at the ledge, then turned back to me. I could see he wasn't going to risk it. Rake-Thin shoved him aside.

"You have two choices, Luke," I shouted through the door. "You can stay in Hammer Bay and be hunted like animals, or you can run for it. Rio is nice, I'm told. I'd think that would be a good place for a murderer to lie low."

"No," Luke said. I could hear courage in his voice. Damn. He was recovering from the ghost knife too quickly. "I don't think so. I've been to Rio."

The door seemed to explode right in front of me. Splinters of wood struck my face. I felt a dead pressure against the tattoos on my stomach. Gunshot.

I fell backward. Splinters fell around me in slow motion. I fell in slow motion, too. I knew a second gunshot was coming, but it seemed to take a long time.

Then it boomed. I hit the floor and rolled to the side. A third shot slammed past me. Then a fourth. Mustache dove for the ground. Rake-Thin Arms toppled through the window like a sack of flour and vanished. Miriam screamed as more shots blasted through the wood. At first I thought she was screaming over the death of the middle-aged fat guy, but then I noticed a single round bullet hole just above Frank's right eye.

Arlene grabbed Miriam and dragged her to the floor. Mustache crawled toward me, holding the rifle.

Boom boom boom. The barrage seemed to be endless, although I'd guess there were no more than ten or twelve shots. When it ended, the door was Swiss cheese. I heard Luke eject a clip and replace it. He racked the slide.

I expected him to say something before he started shooting again, but he just jammed his pistol into one of the holes in the door and started shooting.

The barrel of the gun was only a couple of feet above me. I slashed at it with the ghost knife. The trigger fell free and landed with a *ting* on the floor outside.

Luke drew back the weapon and cursed. He kicked at the door and broke open a section with several bullet holes. His foot got stuck in the hole.

Mustache shot him through the ankle. Luke cursed violently as he yanked at his foot. Mustache and I saw the wound heal in seconds.

"Jesus wept," Mustache said. "What do we do now?"

I had an idea. "Gimme."

Mustache handed me the rifle. I took the silver chain from my pocket and cut it in half. Then I cut the halves as well. Might as well try it.

Luke pulled his foot free, and the black muzzle of a wolf jammed through the hole in the door. The wolf snarled and snapped at me, throwing itself against the splintering wood, forcing itself into the room.

I dropped a piece of chain down the barrel of the rifle. I held the shoulder stock low and the muzzle up, so the chain wouldn't slide out.

The black wolf lunged at me. Saliva splashed against my face. The creature's jaws gaped.

I jammed the rifle barrel down the wolf's throat, as deep as it would go. Then I tilted it up. I heard the chain slide down the barrel.

The wolf yelped. It froze in place for just a moment, its eyes widening, then started to pull back.

Before I could even think about it, the ghost knife flew into my hand. I slashed it across the wolf's throat. The gun fell backward and so did I.

The wolf tried to scream, but a solid inch of gun barrel was stuck in the back of its throat. It tried to retch. It wrenched itself back through the broken door and fell to the floor, shuddering.

"What do you know?" I said quietly. "It worked." The gun barrel was cut at a slant now. I felt a twinge of guilt at ruining what looked to be a family heirloom.

I tried to slide a second piece of chain into the barrel, but my hands were shaking too badly. Mustache reached over my shoulder and held the weapon steady.

My thanks were drowned out by howls from the hallway. Luke called Wiley's name. I glanced through the hole in the door and caught a glimpse of pale, blubbery flesh. Wiley had turned back into a human. Damn, it *was* like the movies.

I slid another length of chain down the barrel. "I'm sorry about the gun," I said.

"Forget the gun, boy," Mustache answered. "Just don't let those bastards in here."

"Fair enough." I slashed the ghost knife through the barrel, cutting it at a sharp angle. Then I shaved the leading edge until it came to a rough point. It wasn't as sharp as a spear, but it might do the job if I put my back into it.

Mustache gaped at me, the end of his rifle, and the ghost knife in turn. "What—"

"Don't ask," I said. "National security."

His mouth snapped shut. I glanced over at Arlene and Miriam, who were still crouching on the floor. Arlene's face was blank with terror, but Miriam, holding her dead husband's hand, looked at me with deep suspicion.

The Dubois brothers were still making a racket in the hall. I heard a slapping sound as Luke tried to revive his brother.

"I guess you have reason to be afraid again, huh, Luke?" I felt dizzy and manic. It felt good to have a weapon, even a hack one. A swatch of gray-flecked fur moved past the hole. I knelt and leaned toward it. A chance to kill Emmett was too good to miss.

A section of door burst open, and Luke's arm smashed through the damaged wood. Before I could react, he ripped the rifle out of my hands.

Shit. I rolled back on my heels and started to stand, and I bumped into Mustache's big soft belly. I reached for the rifle stock, but Luke ripped it through the broken door.

The ruined door splintered apart, and a flash of red and black burst into the room. I threw myself at it, feeling a chunk of wood strike my ear as I lunged. The wolf stumbled coming through the door, giving me the split second I needed.

Someone from the other side of the door shouted: "Sugar! Don't!" It wasn't Luke's voice. It was Emmett.

I landed on its back, plunging the ghost knife into the back of its head.

The wolf faltered but didn't go down, even with my full weight on it. I caught the ghost knife in my teeth, freeing my hands. I wrapped my arms around the wolf's neck.

It tried to turn itself around to snap at me, but I held on, refusing to let it turn. It tried to wriggle backward out of my grip, but I swung my legs against its hind legs, knocking it to the floor. It took every ounce of strength I had, and I knew I couldn't hold it for long.

I dipped my head, jabbing the ghost knife into the wolf's back. It weakened, but only a little. Its feet scrabbled against the floor, twisting its body away from me and threatening to steal my only leverage. I started to lose my hold on him.

"My God!" Mustache shouted from behind me. "They're cutting him wide open!" I had no idea what he was talking about.

The ghost knife wasn't working. The Dubois brothers had a greater resistance to my spell than anyone I'd ever met. I knew I couldn't stay in this position for long—the wolf would eventually scramble out from under me and I'd have no way to hold those teeth at bay any longer. I needed a plan.

The only idea that came to me was the open window. The fall wouldn't kill Sugar, I figured, but it would put some distance between us. Maybe I could get Miriam, Arlene, and Mustache to a safe place in the time it took the wolf to come at me again.

But I had no way of gaining my feet without losing my hold.

Then I felt something. It was a sensation of power, somewhat like Annalise's iron-gate spell when I first stole it from her so many months ago. I felt it just under my chest, in the wolf's back. I lowered my head and slashed the ghost knife toward it.

The fur on the wolf's back suddenly erupted in a jet of black steam and sparks. The wolf howled, and I felt the steam scald my left shoulder and neck. I tried to hold on, but the pain was too much. I shoved the wolf away from me.

It staggered back. It had blurred and become indistinct, as though some parts of it were appearing out of or receding into a fog. It was as if I was looking at two superimposed versions of the same being. The wolf was fading, and the man was reappearing.

The paws became hands. The fur became skin. The snout became Sugar's face. The magic was still pouring out of him in iron-gray sparks and jets of black steam.

I lunged at him, grabbed him by the arm, and rushed him toward the window. Arlene and Miriam had to pull their legs back as we passed. Sugar had difficulty keeping up with me, but he was dazed enough to try.

We reached the window, and I heaved him through it.

He was still changing as he vanished below the sill. I didn't hear him scream.

Mustache elbowed past me and looked out the window. "Sweet Jesus," he said, "please have mercy on this sinner, as you have mercy on all of us sinners."

I backed away from him. I didn't want to see Sugar's body, and I didn't want to pray for his salvation. I wasn't that good a person.

"Sugar!" Emmett yelled. "Sugar!"

"He's waiting for you outside," I said nastily. "In the parking lot."

I heard retreating steps. They were going. Thank God.

"We did it," I said.

"You did it, son." Mustache clapped me on the shoulder. "Good work."

I looked over at Frank. He was stretched out on his bed with the single bullet hole in his forehead. It didn't seem like good work to me. I felt like a screwup of the first order. If I'd skipped a visit to Peter Lemly's house, if I'd looked at the newspaper sooner, if I'd been more forceful when I'd told Lemly to hold off on the story, I might have saved Frank's life, and the lives of the others, too.

"What did I just see?" Miriam said. She struggled off the floor and helped Arlene up, too. "What was that? Was that Sugar Dubois?"

"I think we know what we saw," Arlene said. "I just have a hard time believing it."

I rushed to the window and looked out along the ledge. Cynthia and the doctor were not there. I looked down at the parking lot, but I saw only the bodies of Mr. Rake-Thin Arms and Sugar Dubois. Had Cynthia gotten away? I hoped so. I hoped I wouldn't see her again. I hoped she would go far away from here, and that I'd never have to cut the iron gate off of her, or use her to hunt and kill her brother.

Miriam approached me. She pulled the front of my shirttail, exposing two more bullet holes across my stomach. One was so low that it was almost below my tattoos—that bullet could have shattered my hip.

I also noticed that my right forearm was bloody. I glanced down and saw that wooden splinters from the door had jabbed through my skin on the inside of my arm. The cuts were few and shallow; I'd hurt myself worse shaving. Still, I was surprised that I hadn't even felt it. I began to pluck the splinters out.

"Are you one of them?" Miriam asked me. Her face was flushed and her eyes were wild. "Are you cursed?"

"I can't do what they did," I told her.

"But are you cursed? Have you sold your soul, the way they did?"

Mustache laid his hand on her arm. "Miriam, he just fought for us—"

"Be quiet, Walt! I have to know." She waited for my answer.

My adrenaline high was wearing off, and I felt shaky and exhausted. I was tempted to tell her what she could do with herself, but I'd promised to help her and I'd failed. If Walt could pray for the souls of the people who had just tried to tear him apart, I could at least comfort her with lies.

I'd spent enough time in a cell with a reformed preacher to know generally what to say. "I can't tell you very much," I told her. "I swore an oath not to. I was a sinner, like everyone, and I'm still a sinner, but an angel with a flaming sword and a crown of light appeared to me, and . . . I can't tell you more. I shouldn't even have said—"

She laid her hand on my arm. "Thank you."

"You should get out of town now."

Someone banged on the door. "What's going on in there? Open up!"

I spun toward the door, but it was only more hospital security guards peeping at us through the broken door. I moved toward it to unlock it, but Arlene grabbed my elbow.

"What about me?" she asked. "One of them bit me. Does that mean . . . am I going to become one of them?"

She looked at me as if I was an expert. I knew how it felt to want to *know* but not have answers.

But I didn't have any answers for her. Silver had hurt one, yes, but that didn't mean these were Hollywood-style werewolves. For all I knew, the Dubois brothers could change into ten different animals, not just wolves.

"I can't answer that," I told her. "I'm sorry. I honestly don't know."

Arlene turned to Miriam. "I can't go with you, dear. I can't go anywhere until I know."

Miriam clutched at Arlene's injured hand. Arlene winced, but Miriam was too rattled to notice.

I turned to Mustache. "Walt, is it?" He nodded. "I need you to drive Miriam out of town. You're going to take Arlene's car because it's already packed."

Miriam turned back to the hospital bed. "Frank . . ."

"I'm sorry," I said to her. "I'm sorry I didn't do better."

"My father hated him," she said. "Said he was a weakling. He even said it to Frank's face once. But he was such a sweet man, and so funny. He always knew how to make me laugh. Lord, how can I leave him like this?"

She moved toward Frank's body, but I caught hold of her and steered her toward Walt. "Take her now. Right away."

Arlene pressed the keys into Walt's hand. "Don't worry," Walt said. "This sort of trouble can be cleared up pretty quickly. Then we'll get you back to see about your Frank."

Someone had finally brought keys for the door. Security guards unlocked it and swung it open, peering carefully around the doorjamb as if afraid we might start shooting at them.

The hall was full of blood and bodies. Wiley Dubois was gone. Had they taken his body away, or had he survived the silver I had jammed down his throat?

"They cut him open," Walt said to me. "Emmett and Luke cut Wiley open like he was a fish and dug that bit of silver out of him. I guess the fat son of a somethin' must have survived."

"Guess so." I gently shoved the others toward the door, and we all walked into the hall. "Don't look at them," I said. "Just keep going."

Something heavy banged against my hip. I still had Cabot's gun in my pocket. I'd forgotten all about it.

"Hold it right there," a man said. He stepped through the bodies to bar our way. He was wearing a cheap suit and a name tag that identified him as head of security. "You're all going to have to wait for the police."

Miriam started laughing. It was a frightening sound.

Arlene stepped up to the man in the suit. "It was the police who did all this."

A young woman in a doctor's jacket came around the edge of the hallway and moved toward the bodies. She knelt down and began checking Rev. Wilson for life signs. She didn't look like she expected to find any.

"What are you saying?"

Arlene stepped up close to the head of security and read his name carefully. "Listen to me, Mr. Arnold Reyes. Luke Dubois just killed the mayor, and several of the people who tried to stop him. We're going to take the mayor's wife out of town until the FBI, state police, or an angry mob does something about the Dubois brothers. Hopefully, it will be something brutal that leaves them in lots of tiny pieces. And if you try to contact Emmett, or if you get in our way, you're going to be very glad that you're already in a hospital."

Mr. Arnold Reyes let Walt and Miriam pass. "Who's going to explain this?"

The young doctor stood. "They're all dead," she said. I gestured toward Arlene's hand. The doctor bent over the injury and studied it carefully with gloved hands. "This will need to be bandaged, but no stitches, I should think."

I looked up. Cynthia was standing beside me. The cardiologist was right beside her. He looked rattled. Cynthia was pale. I let out a deep, relieved sigh. They'd found a safe way inside after all.

"This dude is going to explain it all," I said to Arnold Reyes and waved to the cardiologist. "Come here, hero. You get to tell everyone what happened."

"But I don't know what happened." The tall doctor looked like he wanted to flee down the stairs and never come back.

"Did you recognize the cop that was here?"

"Um, yes."

"Did you hear him say what he came for?"

"The mayor."

"You're the spokesman. I'm going to see that these other people get to a safe place." I took Cynthia's arm and started to lead them away.

"Where's Frank?" Cynthia asked.

I shook my head at her, and she stepped back. "I'm going to stay here. That doctor isn't going to be able to explain it all."

"All right," I said. "Don't say anything that will sound crazy."

She smiled at me. She looked terribly fragile. "Give me some credit. I'm going to want to see you again later. My place?"

I nodded to her, then started to push Walt and Miriam through the doors. Arlene trailed behind, with the doctor holding her hand. No one spoke.

At the doors to the parking lot, the doctor made Arlene go to the ER. I led Walt and Miriam outside.

"I'm sorry," I said as Miriam was about to get in the car.

She threw her arms around my neck. I could feel her tears smearing on my face. "Lord bless you," she said.

They got into the car and drove away.

I walked back to the ER and watched Arlene get bandaged up. She filled out some paperwork, and then it was time to go. As we walked toward the parking lot, I looked through the glass doors and saw Annalise's van parked out there. Annalise stood beside it, waiting for me.

"Now what?" Arlene asked me.

"Call a friend and ask for a ride home."

I walked through the doors into the gray afternoon. Arlene followed closely behind. "No," she said. "I can't go home and wait. It would kill me. I have to know."

I didn't respond. We approached Annalise.

She stared at me as we approached. "You've been raising quite a ruckus, I hear."

"You could have joined in if I had a way to contact you. A cell phone number or something."

She shrugged. "You seem to have come through okay without me."

"People died." She didn't respond. She didn't even blink. "And the bad guys got away."

"How many bad guys?" she asked. "What kind?"

"Three, maybe four. Remember when I said I wasn't sure if Emmett was a werewolf or if he was alone? I'm sure now, and I'm sure about all three of his brothers. I may even have killed one or two of them."

"Really?" Annalise glanced at Arlene, measuring her expression.

"Yep. What about you? Have you found *him*? Did some of Henstrick's people visit you?"

"No, and yes."

"What happened to Henstrick's men?"

"They had a car accident. A terrible, terrible accident. None of them survived."

"Okay. What's next?"

"I've never killed werewolves before. That sounds like fun."

CHAPTER SIXTEEN

Annalise pulled open the passenger door and climbed in. I walked around to the driver's side.

"I'm coming with you," Arlene said in her most commanding tone.

"No, you're not." Annalise's voice didn't carry a lot of power the way Arlene's did, but there was a dangerous undercurrent to it that I doubted Arlene would recognize.

"I am," Arlene said. "I need to. There are some things I have to know."

Annalise had not yet closed the door. Arlene climbed onto the footrest and stepped up much too close. Maybe someone else would have been uncomfortable, would have yielded, but Annalise's girlish little voice just got very low. "Step back."

"Arlene," I said. "Get down. You don't know what you're doing." Reluctantly, she stepped back onto the parking lot. "Boss, she could be useful."

Annalise snorted. "How?"

"I can find them," Arlene said. "Emmett keeps the others close. They've never left the house they grew up in."

"What if the Dubois brothers aren't at the station? She could direct us to their house."

"So could a phone book."

Arlene smirked. "They're unlisted. You—"

"Fine," Annalise said. "But she's your baggage, Ray. You have to haul her around, and it's on you if she gets killed."

Annalise slammed the van door. Arlene huffed indignantly and began to walk around the front of the van.

I went to meet her. "Don't annoy my boss."

"She certainly seems to be short on manners."

"You're not listening. Emmett Dubois is nothing compared to the woman in that van. She's not going to show either of us any respect, and if you can't handle that, you can go back to organizing the cleanup at church socials."

"I . . . I understand." Arlene looked toward the ground.

"Climb in," I said. "You'll have to stand between the seats. We're not set up for hitchhikers."

She did. I strapped myself in behind the wheel and started the engine. "Where to first, boss?"

"Let's try their home. If you injured them, they might go to ground."

"North," Arlene said immediately. "They live on the north end of town, about three blocks east of the station."

I pulled out of the parking lot slowly. Even so, Arlene winced as she used her injured hand to stabilize herself. On the way, we passed a knot of people attending to a body on the sidewalk. It was Rake-Thin Arms, who had been shot and fallen out the window. I wondered if I would ever learn his name.

Sugar Dubois was nowhere in sight.

After a few minutes of driving, Arlene turned to us. "Can I ask a question?"

Annalise didn't answer. "Okay," I said. I had a question of my own to ask, but I wasn't going to do it in front of Arlene.

"If one of them bit me, does that mean I'm going to . . ."

She'd already asked me this question. I didn't know if Annalise was going to answer or not. After a few moments of silence, I said: "Annalise? Is she going to become a predator?"

Annalise turned and looked at Arlene. "If I knew for certain that you would, you'd already be dead."

"The silver hurt them," I said. "Regular bullets didn't do anything. And one of them had a sigil on his back. He turned into a human when I broke it."

Annalise didn't respond.

"Please," Arlene pleaded. Her voice was small. "Can't you tell me anything?"

Annalise turned and looked at her. "I can tell you this: if you're one of them, I'll make it quick, because Ray seems to like you. There's nothing more you need to know."

That was the end of that conversation.

We pulled up to the Dubois brothers' house a few minutes later. It was a large wood-frame house with a long front yard and a high chain-link fence around it. Behind the house, the ground sloped upward into wild terrain.

Arlene pointed to it. "Their grandfather bought that house. The men have always shared it. When you marry one Dubois brother, you marry them all. Not that any of them are married at the moment. Luke's first wife never left the house until she'd boozed herself to death. That was years ago, before Wilma. Emmett's wife—well, she disappeared one day with her kids. If anyone is there, it's one of the brothers."

Annalise opened her door and stepped out of the van. "Boss?" I called. "Do you need me, boss?"

"I doubt it." She slammed the door shut and walked toward the front gate.

"I brought this," Arlene said, holding up a slender letter opener. The blade was silver. "I stole it off the desk at the emergency room. Shouldn't I give this to her, just in case?"

I turned back to Annalise. She unzipped the front of her jacket, then stepped up to the padlocked gate. She grabbed the chain link and tore it off the frame. Beside me, Arlene gasped. Annalise shook her hands at her sides. They must have hurt her very much. She stepped through the gap and walked casually toward the front door.

"She doesn't need it," I said. "We'll keep it in case one of the brothers makes a break for it."

Annalise kicked the front door down. She entered the darkness of the house.

While we waited, Arlene laid the flat side of the letter opener against her wrist. I could see that the edge was pretty dull, but that wasn't surprising. Silver was not a metal for weapons. The tip seemed sharp enough, though.

Arlene lifted the blade from her arm. Welts had begun to form. She looked at me. "Are you going to tell her?"

"I have to," I said.

"Good." She held up the opener and stared at it. "I can't do it myself, you understand. That's a terrible sin."

"Under the circumstances—"

"It's a sin," she said with finality. "I won't let my last act in this world be a sin."

"If you could choose, how would you want it?" I asked. I knew Annalise could take Arlene's life quickly and simply.

Arlene stared at the silver blade. "Fighting. I want to go down fighting." Then she knelt on the dirty floor of the van and began to pray.

A few minutes later, Annalise emerged from the house. She walked down the front path and climbed back into the van. "They weren't there, but we already knew that."

"Then why did you go in?" Arlene asked.

I glanced at the house and saw orange firelight flickering in one of the windows. If there was a spell or spell book hidden there, it would soon be ashes. I started the engine and pulled away. "The police station, then."

"Don't you think they would want to find a doctor for Sugar?" Arlene asked.

"They were already at a hospital," I said. "They could have charged into the emergency room with their guns drawn and gotten whatever they wanted. I don't think they want doctors or drugs or stitches. I think they want their magic."

We drove the remaining two blocks in silence. All three pickup trucks were parked in front of the station, along with the Bentley and two police cars. One of the patrol cars was parked at an angle, as though it had skidded to a halt. The blinds on all the windows were closed.

I drove around the corner and parked a full block away. "What's the plan?"

Annalise glanced at Arlene, then turned to me. Her expression was unreadable. "You're my wooden man. I'll go around the back and wait for you to draw their attention. When you have, I go in through the back door and start doing my work. If you survive, that's nice, too."

"You know what would be nice?" I said. "Some gloves. I'd like some latex gloves or something. My fingerprints are already on file with the police. If I do survive, I don't want to spend the rest—"

"If you needed gloves, I'd have given them to you already," she said.

"What about me?" Arlene asked.

Annalise glanced down at the welts on Arlene's forearm. "I'll take care of you later." She got out of the van.

Arlene gripped my shoulder. "I'm coming with you. Is that okay?"

It wasn't, but I couldn't find it in myself to tell her so. "Come on," I told her. Guess I wasn't going to die alone today.

We climbed out of the van and walked down the block, passing the diner Annalise and I had eaten in that first night. The windows were still covered with cardboard, but the waitress spotted us anyway and came outside. "Aunt Arlene, what's going on? I heard there was a gunfight at the hospital, and Emmett and the boys just screeched into the station like they were starring in an action movie. Do you know what's going on?"

Arlene turned to her. "Emmett Dubois killed me," she said.

The waitress stepped back in surprise. "What? What do you mean?"

"He's killed a lot of people," Arlene said. Her voice was flat. I looked at her gray hair and wrinkled skin—she had looked about sixty when I first met her, but she seemed much older at the moment. I wondered if she'd led a good life, and if I would be ready to end my life at her age, or at any age. "He's been bleeding this town dry. Someone has to end it. And end him."

"What do you mean he's killed you?" the waitress asked. "Has he poisoned you?"

"Yes," Arlene said. "That's it exactly."

The waitress stepped forward. "Aunt Arlene—"

"Don't." Arlene waved her niece away. "I have something I need to do."

She and I walked the rest of the way toward the station. I told her to stand at the corner of the wall, beside the stairs, then I circled around behind the trucks. The red one was full of garbage and fast-food wrappers, so I broke into the black one.

With the ghost knife, I cracked the ignition lock and started the truck. I raced the engine loudly, threw it into reverse, and backed out of the spot.

The blinds rippled, and I stood on the brakes, making the tires chirp.

The front door flew open, and Luke lunged out, his face twisted with anger. Obviously, this was his truck. He lifted his revolver and aimed it at me.

I ducked beneath the dashboard, but I didn't hear any shots. Maybe he loved his truck too much to shoot at it.

Emmett yelled at him, and although his voice was faint, I distinctly heard him say, ". . . your own brother." I peeked over the dash and saw him go back into the building.

Obviously, I needed to do more to catch their attention. I threw the truck into drive.

The door flew open again, and Luke shoved Shireen into the daylight. She looked terrified. He pointed a revolver at her head, and she cringed and sank to the ground.

And began to change. Shireen seemed to recede from me, while a strange, hairy *thing* became visible. It was long and ungainly, with spindly, crooked legs and clawed fingers and toes. Its head was round and bristling with fur, and it had a short snout filled with brutally long teeth.

It stepped forward into the daylight, its gaze locked on me. It had its orders, and it was pretty clear who it was supposed to kill.

It moved toward the steps. It was clumsy on its spindly legs, but those teeth looked vicious. It went down on all fours, but that appeared to be even more awkward than walking upright, so it grabbed the railing instead.

Poor Shireen.

I revved the engine and shot forward. On her crooked legs, Shireen stumbled at the bottom of the stairs. The pickup slammed into her with its full force.

The air bag went off in my face, and I felt the truck bounce backward. The air bag deflated, and I threw open the door.

Shireen's arm and legs were shattered, and her rib cage was crushed. Before my eyes, her broken bones righted themselves with loud pops and cracks. She moaned and whimpered.

Maybe I could get into that red truck after all and park it on her.

Shireen growled at me. Her transformed legs weren't built for standing or walking upright, and she stood awkwardly. Steadying herself on the crumpled, hissing hood of Luke's truck, she lunged for me.

I ran around the back of the truck. Shireen followed me, growling and snarling. I held my ghost knife close to my chest and crossed my left forearm across my throat. The tattoos on my arm didn't cover enough flesh to truly protect me, but I had nothing else. I didn't know if her bite would carry the same curse as the Dubois brothers', and I didn't want to find out.

She lunged at me again. I leaped to my left. She tried to change direction and follow, but stumbled. Her flailing right arm tore through my sleeve. I backed away and circled her, and she turned to follow me.

I glanced up at the police station. No one was watching us. So far, I wasn't much of a distraction for Annalise's attack. I wondered if Luke and Emmett were trying to save Sugar's life in there.

Shireen snapped at me, then faked a little lunge. I jumped straight back, just to keep her honest. I looked over her shoulder and saw Arlene charging silently at Shireen's back, her silver letter opener high over her head. She wasn't moving quickly, but she was putting everything she had into the charge.

Arlene's foot scraped against the asphalt. Shireen hopped away and turned toward the sound. Arlene, still ten yards away, didn't slow her charge.

Shireen bent low, letting her hands touch the ground, then leaped forward, snapping her jaws on Arlene's wrist. The old woman screamed. The opener fell from her hand and bounced down Shireen's back. Shireen flinched when it touched her, then wrenched her whole body to the side. Blood spurted from Arlene's arm. She lost her footing and went down. Shireen caught hold of Arlene's hair with one spindly claw and released her wrist, then turned her fangs to the old woman's throat.

I heard screams from somewhere nearby. Someone was watching.

I forced myself to look away from Arlene's bloody murder and searched for the silver blade. It couldn't have fallen far, but I didn't see it anywhere. I dropped to my hands and knees and spotted it under Luke's truck. I scrambled between the back wheels. The truck was tricked out to have a high clearance, but I still had to scrape my belly through oil and antifreeze to reach the opener. I crawled to it, trying to be as quiet as I could. Arlene was dead already, I knew. Wooden man or not, I didn't want to be next.

I closed my hand on it, feeling the slipperiness of the antifreeze and oil on the wooden handle. At the same moment, Shireen stuck her head under the carriage of the truck and snarled at me.

I felt something grab at my jacket and begin to pull me out from under the car. Shireen had caught the gun in my pocket, which I had forgotten about again.

I slashed and felt the opener strike bone. Shireen yelped and let go of me. I slid away from her, not that it would do me much good. She could be on the far side of the truck before I could. She could even grab hold of my feet and drag me into the daylight. Then the best I could do would be to kill her just as she was killing me.

But she didn't do that. She came right back at me the same way, and this time she led with her face. Her mouth was open, and I could see blood smeared into her fur.

She was moving slowly. I held the letter opener tightly but didn't attack. She was presenting such an easy target, I figured there had to be some sort of trick.

But she didn't lash out at me. She kept creeping forward, getting closer and closer. It was almost as if she was daring me to strike—or she wanted me to. I couldn't let the opportunity pass. I stabbed her, plunging the silver blade deep into her eye.

She shuddered. I pushed the blade in as far as it would go. She collapsed and fell still.

I slid away from her. I wanted that letter opener, but I didn't want to take it out of her just yet. She became indistinct and Shireen's human face returned.

I rolled out from under the truck as slapping footsteps grew louder. Three townspeople had rushed over to us and stood around the bodies of the two women, gaping. I ran around the back of the truck and shouldered a man out of the way. It took me a moment to realize that he was the cook from the diner.

"Everyone get out of here," I said. I tried to sound commanding, but fear and adrenaline make my voice squeak.

"She changed," the cook said. Shireen still lay half under the truck, her torn clothes partly covering her wrinkled flesh. She looked very human and frail. I tried not to think about that. "Did I really see that? Did I really see her change?"

"Nope," I said. The two young women standing beside the cook stared aghast at the ruined bodies at their feet. "Now get away."

I pulled Shireen out from under the car. Her head bobbled as it dragged across the ground. The handle of the letter opener scraped the asphalt. I felt a powerful urge to retch.

"You shouldn't do that," the cook said. I took the letter opener from the body and forced myself to stare into the bloody ruin that used to be her eye. It didn't seem to be healing the way her broken limbs had. She was dead.

I moved away and knelt beside Arlene. She lay still and cooling on the asphalt, but the ragged tears in her throat and arm were slowly joining together. She was dead but healing.

It seemed unfair that she had wanted to go out fighting but now wouldn't be able to. In just a minute more, she would be awake, and talking about how she wanted to die rather than become a second Shireen.

I slid the blade of the letter opener between her ribs. Her wounds stopped knitting closed, but she didn't groan or sigh.

Behind me, I heard a door open. I turned to see Wiley Dubois step out of the police station, a shotgun in his hand.

No time for squeamishness. I ripped the letter opener out of Arlene, then threw my shoulder into the nearest of the two women. They both stumbled away from me. I ducked toward the back of the truck. "RUN!" I shouted.

The shotgun boomed as I hit the ground. The cook called out to Jesus, then beat a quick retreat. The two young women were already way ahead of him.

I scrambled to my feet and raced toward the other side of the truck. I heard the terrible clicks of the shotgun being pumped and dove behind the truck bed. Then came another boom, and I felt fire scrape along the back of my left calf.

I hit the ground and rolled. For a moment I was sure that the bottom half of my leg was gone, but that was just my imagination running wild. I had caught a couple of pieces of buckshot in my calf muscle.

I immediately peeked over the back of the truck and saw Wiley huffing down the front steps, heading for the narrow space between Luke's wrecked truck and the damaged station wall. He pumped the shotgun again.

I held the ghost knife in one hand and the letter opener in the other. The gun in my pocket was useless. Damn. I didn't have many choices left. I could run away and be shot in my unprotected back. I could backpedal and get shot in the legs or the face. I certainly couldn't hide.

All I could do was charge him. Charge at a man with a shotgun, and hope I could get close enough to stab him before he killed or crippled me.

I took a deep breath. This is what a wooden man does. He plays decoy and he dies.

I stood. Wiley lifted the shotgun to his shoulder.

From inside the station came the sound of gunshots and a scream. Wiley turned toward the sound, and so did I. It was a man's voice, high-pitched with panic. The scream was cut off with a strangled sound, and Emmett shouted Luke's name. The gunshots continued, a dozen over the course of a few seconds.

The window shattered, and something the size of a soccer ball flew through it. It smashed into the windshield of Luke's car. Wiley gaped at it for a second, then hustled up the stairs toward the front door. He had bigger problems than me.

There was another flurry of gunfire from inside the station.

I rushed to the front of the truck, but I already knew what had broken the windshield. It was Luke's head.

Annalise had started her attack.

I couldn't resist one more look at Luke. Thankfully, his face was not much in view, but it suddenly became indistinct. It was vanishing right before my eyes. Damn. I should have stabbed it with the letter opener.

There were more gunshots from inside the station. Ducking below the windows, I ran toward the stairs. I saw a flare of green light, and Emmett began screaming "No no no!" at the top of his lungs. I burst through the door.

The desks we had walked past on our first visit had been smashed and knocked aside. Just beside the door, a pile of scorched black bones lay on the tile floor.

Annalise stood in the center of the room, her fireman's jacket wide open, ribbons hanging from her vest. Luke Dubois's headless corpse lay at her feet.

But his head was starting to appear on his shoulders. His head was coming back.

"This is amazing," Annalise said to me. "I've never seen anything like it. Look at the fat one."

I looked down at Wiley again. Raw meat was growing on his bones. It was repulsive. "Jesus," I said. "Everything about these guys makes me sick."

"No more," Emmett said. He stepped out of his office, a pistol at his side. The slide was back; he'd already emptied it. "Please, no more. We'll leave town and never come back. We have money we can pay. Anything. Just let me take my brothers away from here."

"The spell," Annalise said. "I want it."

"Wha . . . what do you mean?" Emmett said.

"Ray, do that one." She nodded at Wiley's corpse.

There was nothing much of him to stab with the letter opener, so I swept the ghost knife through the same place on his shoulder where Sugar had been marked with a sigil. The space where the spell would have been suddenly erupted with a jet of black steam.

Wiley's body stopped regenerating. The gory mess inside his rib cage sagged and began to spread out across the floor. I hopped away from him.

"Oh my God, Wiley." Emmett's voice was small. I felt a twinge of sympathy. Then I remembered the dead woman in the morgue, and all the bodies at the hospital, and my sympathy shriveled into cold hatred. He didn't have the right to grieve.

"You're right, Ray," Annalise said. "These guys are repulsive. Do the rest."

"No!" Luke yelled. "Don't do it!" He was alive again.

Annalise put her foot on Luke's back, holding him down. "I already did it," she said to him, "and I may do it again if you don't shut up."

I crossed the room and slipped the ghost knife through Luke's shoulder. There was another jet of steam and Luke screamed.

Emmett let his empty pistol fall to the floor. "We did some good here, too." His voice was feeble and small. "We protected the town, too."

I didn't care, and neither did Annalise. I walked toward him, being careful not to get between them. I cut his spell with the ghost knife, and he collapsed to the floor in agony. I didn't watch this time. I walked over to Sugar.

He was lying on the floor in the middle of a spell circle. Compared with the other circles I'd seen, this one was surprisingly simple. It was not drawn or painted on the floor, it was just a hoop of silver wire. There were no other marks or designs that I could see.

Sugar was in bad shape. His arms and legs were broken, and I could see where his skull had cracked and swollen. He looked like he was in terrible pain. His shirt had been cut open, and there was a new sigil on his chest. He wasn't healing, though. He didn't seem to be changing at all.

That seemed important, although I wasn't sure why.

I cut the silver hoop with the ghost knife. There was no rush of power or bolt of black steam. I moved toward Sugar and bent to cut the sigil.

"Don't!" Emmett pleaded. "Please. He'll die without it."

Annalise snorted in irritation and moved her foot to Luke's skull. Luke let out a little shriek.

"Boss, wait!" She did. I turned to Emmett. "Give me the spell, and tell me everything you know about it. Where it came from and who gave it to you. All of it."

Emmett looked nervously toward Annalise. He reached into his jacket pocket and took out an index card inside a plastic sleeve. He held it out to me. His hand trembled.

"Toss it." He did. I glanced at it. There was a complicated design on one side of it, and a four-line rhyming poem on the other.

"My father gave it to me." Emmett said. "He got it from the original Cabot Hammer, the man who founded this town, a long time ago. I don't know much more than that, except that I'm supposed to say the words while the person getting the spell sits in the hoop and looks at the other side of the card. That's the only copy, too. My father told me to never try to copy it.

"We didn't kill people every full moon or anything. It didn't work like that. We—"

Annalise stamped down on Luke's skull. At the same moment, I slid the ghost knife through the sigil on Sugar's chest. The magic rushed out of it, and his tortured breathing stopped.

Emmett's shoulders sagged. All the fight was gone from him. "Do it. Just go ahead."

Annalise looked me in the eyes. "Ray."

My turn at bat. I took Cabot's gun out of my pocket and pointed it at the back of Emmett's head.

In the movies, you often hear actors say it's hard to kill someone. They'll say it's the hardest thing in the world. Well, that's bullshit. Prison is full of people who thought murder was some kind of achievement—I lived with some of them.

And most of those guys wish they could take it back, because the truth is, the only thing a person needs to commit murder is a moment when they don't care about the consequences, when they don't think about what they're doing and what it means.

Most people spend their whole lives without thinking what it means.

I couldn't do that. I had done too much time and had too much conscience. I'd shot my best friend when I was just a boy, and I'd hated guns ever since. I knew exactly what would happen. I knew exactly what it would mean.

I squeezed the trigger anyway.

EMMETT'S corpse looked just the way I expected it to look. So did the room around me. So did Annalise.

I saw a flannel shirt hanging on a coatrack and used it to wipe down Cabot's gun. I tossed the gun onto the floor. It thunked as it landed. I wasn't worried about Cabot, though.

Everyone in town had seen me. There was no way I was going to avoid prison this time. I was a cop killer. He was a corrupt cop and a killer himself, but that wouldn't matter once the manhunt began.

But what choice did I have? I couldn't let him walk free. What if he had another copy of the spell somewhere? What if he went looking for more magic? He would just move somewhere else and start killing again.

With some difficulty, Annalise pulled a red ribbon off her vest and dropped it onto a stuffed chair. It burst into flame. She kicked over a desk, scattering a stack of papers onto the flames. The fire was already licking at the painted walls. Soon the station would be lit by orange firelight, just like the Dubois home.

I returned Annalise's debit card. I didn't want anything of hers, especially not her money.

"Stop moping," she said. "You did something useful here, even if the work makes you feel dirty."

"Let's just go."

I followed her toward the door. A small, framed photo hung on the wall, and while I didn't want to look at it, I couldn't turn away. It showed Emmett with his arm around Charles the Third. The youngest Hammer was about thirteen and tall for his age, but he was carrying an extra hundred pounds of flab. An older man with Charles's narrow face and unruly black hair flipped burgers on a gleaming barbecue. That must have been Charles the Second, Charles Junior.

While the fire grew behind me, I leaned close to the picture. The elder Hammer was the only one not smiling—his face was worn and sagging, his eyes rimmed with dark circles. He was a man with regrets. In the background, I could see the huge windows of an expensive modern house and a smooth, curved gray stone wall like the base of a castle.

The firelight cast flickering shadows over the photo. The flames had reached the ceiling. Annalise stood by the front door, waiting for me silently. Time to go.

We walked outside. The storm clouds had blown away, and I could see blue sky and sunshine for the first time in days.

A crowd of people stood across the street. The van was parked around the corner. We walked toward them.

"Next time, I'll park closer."

"Good idea. You look like a mess."

I pulled at my shirt. It was torn, sopping wet, and it stank of gunpowder and antifreeze. "I needed more than four changes of clothes, I think."

"I didn't think you'd live through that many. Are you going to vomit?"

"Oh, yes," I said to her. "But not right away, I think."

As we neared the crowd, the cook approached me nervously. I must have been quite a sight. "What's happening?" he asked. "What's going on in this town?"

"The Dubois brothers killed Reverend Wilson."

There were gasps of astonishment from the crowd. "What?" the cook said. "You can't be serious."

"Go away," I told him. We pushed through the crowd and headed up the block. No one tried to stop us. "Charles Hammer is next, right, boss?"

"He would be, if I knew where to find him. That's all I've been doing is looking for him. He hasn't been home or at his office since we were there last, and Karoly's notes don't tell me anything."

"Are your hands any better?"

"No," she said. "They're worse. I expect I won't be able to use them at all by tomorrow. They feel like they're burning, and I can barely bend my fingers."

We reached the van. I opened the door for her and helped her in, not bothering with the seat belt. I climbed in behind the wheel and started the engine. "We could stop off at the butcher again—"

"Don't bother," she said. "The last time it barely helped at all, and I don't want to spend all day on it. It's a waste of time."

"And your stomach?"

"I'm starving." She didn't look at me. She just stared ahead. "I feel a little weak and disoriented, to tell the truth. I'm going to have to rely on you a little more than I would normally. Can I do that?"

"Yes," I said. "I just killed a cop in cold blood for you. If that doesn't prove I'm on your side . . ."

Right then I felt like vomiting. Thankfully, I hadn't eaten in hours.

I pulled out of the parking space. I didn't have anywhere to go, but I didn't want to be near the scene of the fight any longer. I didn't know where I was going, so I just drove.

Hammer Bay was pretty in the sunlight. I thought of all the people who were not going to see this sunshine, from the woman in the hospital morgue to the reverend to Sugar Dubois, and I felt a twist of cold anger. I tried to aim it at Charles Hammer, or his grandfather, or Eli Warren, who had brought the spells to this town in the first place, but in truth, I was angry at everything, including myself. The world seemed to be full of killers and those who stood by and did nothing about them. I suddenly wished I was one of those who stood by.

"If I don't survive," she said, "I don't want you to go after Charles Hammer by yourself."

"Why not?" I sounded a little indignant, but she ignored it.

"Because he's too big for you, and I don't want him getting a close look at the spells you're carrying. If things go wrong, head out of town. One of the peers will track you down and debrief you."

"I'll be in jail by then, right? Will the society get me out again?"

She shrugged. She was dying, and she didn't much care whether I went to jail or not. I'd have probably felt the same way.

I drove toward Cynthia's house, glad that it was my left calf that was throbbing, not the one I drove with. Maybe we could get Charles's location out of her. Something was nagging at me. There was something I should have remembered but couldn't quite recall.

"You don't think he left Hammer Bay, do you?"

"I hope not," Annalise said. "I don't think so. He started this whole thing for his company and his town. I don't think he'd cut and run."

I nodded. Cynthia had refused to leave, too. "What about a boat or something? He's rich enough to have one."

"He does. Karoly's notes told me which one. I sank it last night. He wasn't there."

Then I remembered. "Cabot said that Charles has been spending all his time hiding in the tower."

"There's a high, round room at their house."

"That's what I thought, too, but no dice. That's his sister's bedroom."
She didn't react to that. "Did the sister tell you where he is?"

"She wouldn't. Not her own brother." This was the point where I could have told Annalise about Cynthia's iron gate, but we had more important things to discuss. "I want to ask her one more time."

Annalise didn't say anything after that. I wondered what she would do to force an answer out of Cynthia. Had I saved Cynthia's life so my boss could kill her?

Then it hit me—the gray stone wall in Emmett's photo, Cabot's remark that Charles had been hiding in the tower . . .

I switched off the turn signal and kept going south.

We passed out of the business district. I looked toward the ocean and saw the sunlight sparkle on the water. It was a beautiful sight.

And there, naked in the sunlight, was the lighthouse. Except that with no mist or fog around it, it didn't look like a lighthouse at all.

I pulled over and shut off the engine. "Where's that bad map?"

We searched the glove compartment and the spaces under the seats before I remembered that I had looked at the map in Ethan's minivan. I found it in the inside pocket of my jacket, folded up into a tiny square. I unfolded it. The lighthouse was marked with a number four. I turned the map over and found the entry for number four.

"What's all this about?" Annalise asked.

"A lighthouse that isn't a lighthouse," I said. "Here it is: 'In 1949, Charles Hammer the First bought a castle in Scotland and had it shipped to Hammer Bay, where it was rebuilt stone by stone. Sixteen years later, an earthquake toppled all but the southernmost tower, which still stands today.'"

I stared at the tower. It didn't have the battlements that I saw in old movies. It was slightly crooked, but it was a tower. This was the "Scottish thing" Bill had mentioned.

"That's where he is."

Annalise nodded. "Let's finish this job."

"Boss," I said. I wasn't sure how to say what I wanted to say next, so I just blurted it out. "Do you think there's a way to turn those worms back into kids? Do you think they can be cured?"

She did not like that question. "Anything is possible, Ray."

I thought that, if I'd asked her if we could fly a candy-cane rocket to Jupiter, she would have given me the exact same answer in the exact same tone. "Boss, I had to ask."

"I know you did." That was all she had to say.

I drove to the waterfront and parked behind a seafood restaurant.

The southward road turned east, away from the cliff and the ocean, leaving an unpaved driveway to go the last two blocks toward the edge of town. We walked toward it, seeing little more than a tumble of black volcanic rocks ahead. And the tower.

It stood alone, well away from the rest of town and a dozen yards from the edge of the cliff. At the base, I could make out a low, modern house, with huge windows along each wall. And there was a broad asphalt platform where a person could turn a car around. I couldn't see a driveway connecting it to the town, and I couldn't see the ruins of the rest of the castle.

"There," Annalise said. She nodded toward a pair of Dumpsters a few doors down. The driveway to the tower was hidden behind them.

We walked quickly back to the van. I pulled out of the parking lot and drove toward that driveway. We passed three identical burgundy Crown Victorias, but I chalked them up to someone's desire to keep up with the Joneses.

The gravel road was barred by a long gate. I stopped, climbed out, and cut off the lock with my ghost knife. The gate swung wide open. I drove down the sloping driveway and parked the van at the end. No one was going to be driving out of here unless they tipped the van onto the rocks, which, frankly, was not all that unlikely.

I climbed out and opened Annalise's door. We walked toward the house. It was much larger up close than it had seemed from the parking lot. The windows were all two stories tall. And none of the shades were drawn.

Something was wrong.

I slipped over to the garage and peeked into the window. Inside was the same elegant black S-class Mercedes I'd seen parked outside the toy factory door. It was a couple of years old. There were no other cars in sight.

"This isn't right," I said to Annalise.

She was too short to look in the window and didn't bother to try. "What do you mean?" she asked.

"There's a Mercedes in there. Charles Hammer drives a Prius."

"He's rich." She moved toward the front door.

Not right. Not right. Not right. I took the ghost knife from my pocket and threw it, cutting the phone line.

I was about to cut through the locks on the front door when Annalise clumsily turned the knob and pushed. The door swung open. It was unlocked.

We entered. Golden sunlight filled the room. I could see storm clouds down at the edge of the horizon, but the sunlit waters were beautiful.

I shut the door and noticed something hanging beside the hinges. It was a long, double-edged knife. The blade appeared to be made of silver. I suspected it was there on the off chance that the Dubois brothers turned on their masters. I took it off the hook and held it in my off hand.

I followed Annalise toward the far end of the room. There was a flat-screen TV hung on the wall and a very low couch facing it. The coffee table was littered with a dozen empty cans of beef stew, bread crumbs, and torn-open baguette wrappers. It looked as though someone had holed up here, but then why were the shades wide open?

"Through here," Annalise said. She kicked open a door and entered another long room. I followed her.

This room had plush carpeting. All the shades were drawn, and the air was thick. At the far end, about twenty feet away, was a long wooden desk. Heavy drapes hung just behind it.

The high leather chair behind the desk was turned away from us. It moved slightly. I saw the sleeve of a dark suit jacket on the armrest.

"Charles Hammer the Third," Annalise said, with the tone of a judge passing sentence. She pulled a ribbon from her vest. "You—"

"That's not Charles Hammer," I said. "That's Able Katz."

Able Katz swung the chair around. He looked quite smug.

The drapes fluttered, and four men stepped out. They were built like boxers, wore the brown uniforms of a private security force, and held Uzis in their hands.

A door to the side opened, and six more guards rushed into the room. They fanned out along the wall to our left.

"There are two more waiting for you by the front door," Able said. "So don't try to run that way."

I noticed a webcam on the desk, beside the computer. Charlie Three was watching us, but from where? I dropped the silver knife into my pocket.

"Oh, no," Able said. "Not your pocket, young man. That's not good enough. You'll have to toss that weapon away from you, onto the floor. In fact, please dispose of all your weapons that way." He smirked at us.

Annalise reached up and tugged a fistful of ribbons off her vest.

"Wait," I whispered to her. "They're just guys doing a job."

"Their job is to let a child killer go free."

"That's nonsense!" Able barked. "Charles has done nothing of the sort. You two are the ones who have been tearing this town apart."

I kept my focus on Annalise. "Emmett was a killer, but these guys were hired to protect someone. They aren't evil."

She turned to me. "Of course they're not evil," she said. "I'm the one who's evil."

The phone on the desk rang.

Everyone seemed startled except for Able. He answered it. "Yes, Charles?" He listened. "I will." He pressed the button on the handset and turned the phone to us.

"Can you hear me?"

It was Charles Hammer, talking over the speakerphone.

"Yes," I said. Annalise looked impatient, but I wanted to hear him out.

"Let me explain myself," the voice said, "and I hope we can avoid any unpleasantness. I really, really would like to avoid violence, if that's possible. More than anything."

I watched the guards. Hammer could have been delaying us until the state police arrived, or even more guards, but I doubted it. He had ten armed men in the room with us, and two more, if Able was to be believed, by the exit. "I'm listening."

"Able," the voice said. "Do you trust me? Some of what we're going to say will sound bad, and these people may make accusations against me that I don't deserve. I want you to understand—"

"There's no need for that, Charles," Able said. "I trust you."

"Great." Charles took a deep breath as though he was about to cliff dive for the first time. "First I want to explain—"

"Want want want," I snapped. "Don't tell me what you want. What about the kids you killed?"

"I never killed any kids! The missing children are still alive, and I can get them back. I've been searching for a way to get them back."

"Looking through your book, huh? The one Eli Warren sold to your great-grandfather?"

"How did you— It doesn't matter. Yes, I'm looking for a way to get them back. It's the number-one priority for me. The children are the next generation of Hammer Bay."

I laughed at him. "You're not running for office, are you?"

"Sneer if you want," the voice said, "but everything I've done is to help the people of this town. I've worked hard to bring jobs and dignity back to Hammer Bay."

"And you had help," Annalise said.

"Yes." There was a pause. "I did have help. A consultant, of a sort. A fortune-teller."

"The same one your father had, and your grandfather."

"My great-grandfather, too. 'Use it sparingly,' my father told me, but there were so many things I didn't know. And the people . . ."

He kept talking. He sounded very much like the weary activist, so burdened with the tasks ahead of him and so impressed with his own motives and ideals.

But something had struck me. *Fortune-teller,* he'd said.

What if he was not just looking into the future? What if the magic he was using was actually controlling the future?

It made sense if he was using magic that let him step outside of time in some way. Annalise's burned hands kept coming back, no matter what she did to treat them. The Dubois brothers could heal anything, even brutal, mangling death. Maybe they were simply backing up in time, to a point before they were injured. Maybe that's why the new sigil on Sugar Dubois couldn't heal his injuries the way his brothers had been healed. It could not restore him to a time before it was in place.

As for the Hammer family, I had assumed that the seizures they suffered during hard times, and the smart moves they had made to turn things around, had come from visions of the future. But what if they were more than visions? What if he was *making* good things happen?

How else to explain a successful line of toys about Marie Antoinette, for God's sake?

I tried to picture the power of a spell that could control whole populations of people. I couldn't. How could he be so strong that he forced people to love his products? How could he force people to forget the people they loved most?

Then it dawned on me. He wasn't doing it. His "consultant" was.

Goose bumps ran down my back. Annalise was right. This was completely out of my league.

I looked at Annalise. She was scowling at me. "Have you been paying attention to this crap?" Charlie Three was talking about siting a plastics factory.

"His great-grandfather summoned a predator out of the Empty Spaces, right?" I said. "And this dick has been communing with it somehow, using it to draw in customers for his fucking *toys.* And *it's* been taking the children for some reason, probably to eat them."

"That's what I figure, too," she said. "And I'll bet it was this predator that controlled those women in his office"—she held up her hands—"burning them all to protect him. *He* doesn't have the power or the guts for a move like that."

I turned to Able Katz. "Do you remember what happened after our meeting at your office?"

"What meeting?" he said, sounding irritated. "I've never seen either

of you before in my life." Charles was droning on, but I was focused
on Able. It was true. Just as I'd suspected, he couldn't remember meeting us any more than Doug and Meg Benton could remember their
dead kids. The predator was controlling people.

"Why hasn't the predator run amuck? Why hasn't it tried to kill
everyone on the planet?"

"It's probably bound somehow. Eli must have helped them summon and bind it."

"That was a long time ago. Do you think it's likely to get free?"

She looked back at Able Katz, who was scowling at us. He must
have thought we should pay more attention to his boss's speech. "It's
already free enough to kill."

I thought of the way the children had fallen apart when they
burned. They'd turned into little worms and crawled off to the southwest. To here, in fact, or somewhere close to here. I wondered if the
predator was feeding on those worms.

Hammer started talking about median home prices, and I couldn't
take it anymore. "Shut up!" I snapped. "You want to avoid violence?
I'll make you an offer. Send your guards away. Turn over to us all copies of the book Eli Warren sold to your great-grandfather. Take us to
your so-called consultant."

"But," the voice said, "the company can't continue without my, um,
consultant."

"The company isn't going to continue," I said. "And neither are
you. There's too much blood on your hands."

"I can find those kids again!"

I turned to the guards. "Hear that? I'm talking about missing children, and he's worried about his company. Is that who you're trying to
protect?"

"Don't bother," Able said. "These men are not going to turn against
us. They're professionals. That's why I hired them. They do their jobs."

Annalise turned to me. "And you had better do your job."

She dropped the fistful of green ribbons onto the carpet, then
grabbed my arm. She winced while she did it.

The ribbons struck the carpet and flared into green fire. Flames engulfed my legs, but I didn't feel any pain. Several of the guards gaped at
us in shock, and one cried out. They thought we were burning ourselves
alive.

The fire crawled up our bodies and billowed outward. As soon as
the flames reached above her head, Annalise charged forward.

Able Katz's expression went slack. He stood and inhaled deeply.

The tinny voice on the speakerphone shouted, *"No! No! No!"*

Annalise slapped the desk to the side. It smashed a window and tore the drape from the rod. The desk and drape fell outside and crashed to the rocks below.

The four guards who had been flanking Able opened fire on Annalise, drowning out Hammer's voice.

Annalise slammed into Able, knocking him into the wall with a sickening thunk. Blood-red fire blasted from his mouth, igniting the wooden beams in the ceiling. He had been about to breathe dragon breath on us, just like the officer workers at Hammer Bay Toys.

I dropped low into Annalise's green fire and rolled toward the far wall. The guns made an incredible racket in the enclosed room. I felt something zip past me. It must have been a ricochet off Annalise's invulnerable body.

I lifted myself into a crouch. The green flames were spreading toward me, and the six guards along the wall bolted toward the door they had entered through. Good. Let them run. At least they'd live.

One of them turned and saw me. He raised his weapon.

Without thinking, I threw the ghost knife at him. One of his partners bumped him in the rush to get to the door, and another stepped briefly into his line of fire. Then the ghost knife struck him over the heart.

The guard collapsed onto the carpet. The man behind him tripped over him and fell into the doorway, blocking it. The green flames reached them, and they disappeared within the fire. I could hear their screams.

I summoned my ghost knife. It flew into my hand. Of course I had killed them. Damn.

The door behind me opened. I spun, catching a quick glimpse of the two men entering through the doorway we had just used. Both held their Uzis at the ready. I threw the ghost knife again and ducked into the flames, throwing myself flat on the floor.

The bullets zipped above me. Then I heard a bang, as if one of the Uzis had jammed and backfired, and the two men cried out. All gunfire in the room stopped. Just then, the green fire evaporated. I looked around the room. The two guards who had entered behind us were smoking skeletons. One of the submachine guns in their hands had burst open.

"You did good," Annalise said, her back to me. The room seemed strangely quiet after all the gunfire, but there was a terrible stench of burned plastic and roasted flesh in the air.

"It doesn't feel like good," I said. I glanced over to where she had been fighting. The other four guards were also smoking bones. So was Able Katz.

I should have been sick, but I had already passed that point. Maybe if there had been one body, or two, I could have puked my guts out and cried like a little girl, but these were too much. It didn't seem real.

"At least for them, it was quick." Annalise turned toward me. Her right eye was gone. She had only an empty socket there. Just below that empty socket, in her cheekbone, was a second bullet hole.

"Holy . . . !" I shouted. I backed away from her. She had two bullets in her head, with no exit wounds, but she was walking around as if nothing had happened. What the hell was she? Was she even alive?

"I know," she said. "It sucks when this happens." She reached up and gingerly touched her face with her stiff, inflamed hand. One of her fingers slipped into her ruined eye socket.

That did it. I heaved a thin, acid stream onto the carpet.

"Oh, knock it off," she snapped. "You're not the one who got shot. Let's go."

She charged through the doorway, kicking the smoking bones out of her way.

Holy God, what was I doing here? What was she?

I was about to follow her, but I couldn't. I couldn't step over the bones of the men we'd just killed.

"What are you waiting for?" she snapped at me.

I didn't answer. I couldn't help picturing the guards' wives and children, their mothers and fathers.

The smashed-up computer lay in a heap beside one of the bodies. I strode over to it and lifted the webcam. The little red light was still on, but I didn't know if it was still sending images.

"This is your fault," I said to the camera. "You put these people here. You asked them to die for you. You—"

Something smashed the camera out of my hand. It was a scorched human skull.

"For God's sake!" Annalise hissed. "This is why you'll never be more than a wooden man, Ray. You're too fucking soft. Don't talk to the targets. Don't taunt them. Don't be their fucking friends. It just makes things harder. Be a fucking professional. Treat them like objects." She held up the skull and waved it in front of my face. "They're glass figurines, Ray, and nothing more—some are very pretty, some not so much. But it's your job to break some of those figurines, and you can never tell right away which ones that'll be."

I stepped away from the skull. "Don't—"

She stepped toward me, and for a moment I thought she was going to rub the blackened bone against my face. "Does this bother you? Get over it. This is what we do. We make corpses. And maybe, if we make enough of them . . ."

She broke off. Her hand was shaking. She let the skull fall to the floor and cradled her hand against her chest. Her pain must have been intense. She scowled at the floor. I saw anger in her expression, and resentment, too. And regret.

The overhead sprinkler system turned on. I looked up to see water dousing the flames Able had blasted onto the ceiling. Annalise and I stood in the downpour while brilliant sunlight shone through the broken window.

"Boss—"

"Could you kill a priest, Ray? Could you kill a priest who only wanted to help terminally ill children? Could you kill a mother who was trying to protect her kids? Could you kill a five-year-old girl whose only crime is that some idiot adult cast a spell on her? I could. I've done all those things."

"Annalise—"

"You're good at this, Ray. You're good at this job. And the society needs good people, more than ever. But you're useless if you stop right before the finish line to moralize. We have a planet full of people to save. Get it? If someone gets between you and your target, there's a planet full of people who will die if you can't bring yourself to do your job."

She clamped her mouth shut and turned away. I had the impression that she had a lot more to say, but she had to hold it back. She sealed it all off with anger.

Suddenly Annalise seemed very human to me, despite the grotesque injuries to her face. And she was right. If we stopped now, more little kids were going to die. Charles Hammer needed killing.

She marched into the hall. "Come on. We have to search the house." I bent and touched one of the unfired Uzis. It was, as expected, cool to the touch. I lifted it and draped the strap over my neck. It was a weapon, but it didn't make me feel any more confident about the coming fight.

I followed her into the hallway. There were three doors along the far side. I charged into the first one. It was an empty bathroom. Annalise opened the next. It was a laundry room and pantry. Farther down the hall was the kitchen, complete with gas range and walk-in fridge. Beyond that was a set of stairs leading to the second floor.

The upstairs was just a single room, broken up by a couple of support columns. There was a small cluster of exercise equipment, some bookshelves, some closets, a terrace with a monstrous charcoal grill, and an open futon against the far wall.

"This way," Annalise said. She kicked open a door. It led to a ten-foot-long covered causeway that connected to the entrance of the tower. We strode across it, looking down at the jagged black rocks twenty feet below.

The tower was made of gray stone blocks. It was dark inside, with only a single electric light burning above.

Annalise sprinted up the wooden stairs. I followed as closely as I could with my injured leg. She seemed to have forgotten that I was supposed to be her decoy.

We ran up the spiraling stairs, never pausing at the landings or glancing out the windows. Annalise tugged a ribbon free, but I couldn't see what it was. My shoe was filling with blood, and I started to fall behind.

Annalise finally reached the ladder at the top of the stairs. She climbed up, threw her shoulder into the trapdoor above us, and broke through it.

She flinched, turning her face down toward me. There was the boom of a shotgun. Annalise's head snapped back, and I knew she had taken the blast in the side of her face. The ribbon fell from her fingers, and she sagged toward me for a moment. I heard the gunman rack a new shell into the shotgun.

Instead of falling off the ladder and through the center of the tower, Annalise stood up straight again. She was still fighting.

"No!" someone shouted in disbelief. "No!"

Annalise was halfway through the trap. She covered her face as another blast struck. This time, she had braced herself and didn't even flinch.

Whoever was up there racked the shotgun once more. Annalise climbed out of the trapdoor. I was right behind her.

Charles Hammer backed toward the other end of the room. Annalise ran at him. He aimed the shotgun low, blasting at her feet. Her legs went out from under her, and she fell onto her hands. I heard her hiss in pain.

I gained the tower room. I saw books all around me, and another silver hoop in the middle of the room. This one was bent and twisted into a variety of strange sigils.

On the other side of that hoop stood Charles Hammer. He looked like a sick man. His skin was sallow, his hair was greasy, and he had bags under his eyes. The room smelled like old socks and gunpowder.

Annalise stood. I slipped my ghost knife between my teeth and lifted the Uzi. No sense in being fancy about it.

Hammer's eyes rolled back into his head. His mouth dropped open and he took a deep breath. My iron gate twinged painfully. It felt as though someone had reached under my skin and made a fist.

I squeezed the trigger. Nothing happened. It felt stuck. I squeezed it as hard as I could, but the weapon still wouldn't fire. I realized that the safety had to be on, but I had no idea where the safety was.

Charles blasted a column of fire from his mouth. Annalise threw herself at me, knocking me back through the trapdoor. I fell off the ladder just as the flames engulfed Annalise from head to toe.

I heard her scream. I was screaming, too. I tumbled down the stairs, wrenching my arm against the railing as I yanked myself to a stop. My legs dangled over the edge, with the long, long drop through the tower below them.

I pulled myself onto the steps, untangling the gun as I did. The fire still blasted over the top of the stairs. There was no way to enter the room above without charging straight through the flames. I held up the gun, found what looked like the safety, and flipped it. My iron gate throbbed.

Then the jet of flames stopped. I heard a sick, choking noise. What the hell, I thought. I charged up the stairs, screaming.

Everything in the room was charred and blackened. The acrid stink of smoke burned my nose and eyes. I couldn't see Annalise anywhere. Hammer stumbled back against the tower window, clutching at his throat.

The inside of his mouth was as black as the room around me. The fire had cooked him as it came out. But as I watched, his lips turned pink, and his mouth and throat healed as quickly as Arlene's ravaged throat had.

I shot him.

I tried to fire a short burst up the center of his body, from crotch to forehead, but the Uzi kicked like crazy, and the trail of bullets tore through his shoulder instead. Charles Hammer the Third stumbled back and fell out the tower window.

I ran across the room, feeling the burned wood wobble dangerously under my feet. I reached the window before he struck the rocks below. I saw him hit. Hard. He was still.

I noticed a piece of silver wire set into the windowsill. It ran from the hoop on the floor out the window and then down the side of the tower. I wondered what was at the other end. I also wondered when my iron gate was going to stop throbbing.

Then I saw Hammer lift his arm. Damn. The gun and the rocks hadn't finished him. He wasn't dead.

I turned back to the trapdoor, wondering if Annalise had managed to leap out a window, too, when I saw her. I had run right past her without recognizing her.

She was burned. Her skin and clothes were blackened and shriveled. She was not burned down to her bones, she was too tough for that, but her mouth gaped wide and her little hands were curled into fists. She held them as though she was about to knock my head off. She was absolutely still. She was gone.

CHAPTER EIGHTEEN

I knelt beside her and touched her face. Her skin crumpled like burned paper, and hot grease scorched my fingertips.

Damn damn damn. I wanted her back.

I ran down the tower stairs. I didn't know how much time I had before he healed himself, but I knew it wasn't much. My mind was racing, wondering why Annalise had deliberately sacrificed her life for mine, wondering whether the ghost knife or the silver blade I'd taken from behind the door would do the job the Uzi couldn't, whether my iron gate would ever stop hurting, and whether the pain from my iron gate meant that more kids were burning to death even as I ran after their killer.

I reached the bottom of the stairs.

Through the thick Plexi enclosure around the causeway, I saw Charles Hammer struggling across the huge black rocks. Then I noticed the tumble of broken gray stones among the volcanic black. That was where the rest of the castle had collapsed.

There was a twenty-foot drop below the causeway, and I knew I couldn't jump down onto the jagged black rocks. I slid the ghost knife through the Plexi, cutting out a section that was eight feet by five feet. It fell across the rocks.

I lowered myself out the hole and dropped onto the plastic. It bowed under my weight but didn't snap. I scrambled across it and out onto the rocks.

Hammer was a good thirty yards ahead of me. He seemed to be heading southeast, although I couldn't imagine where he was running. The town was to the northeast; if he wanted help or protection from the people of Hammer Bay, he was headed the wrong way. As far as I could tell, the only thing to the southeast was forest and mountain.

I kept after him, my ghost knife between my teeth, silver knife in my pocket, and the Uzi banging against my knee as I leaped from rock to rock. I considered dumping the gun. It had already proven less than useful, but I couldn't bring myself to do it. I needed all the weapons I could get.

Annalise had told me not to go after Hammer by myself. She had said he was too much for me. She was probably right. But I had just touched her burned face. I couldn't let that go. I couldn't run away.

I focused on the rocks, trying to increase my speed to shut off my thoughts. Now wasn't the time to think about my boss. Now was the time to figure out what Charles Hammer had become, where his silver wire led, and how hard I was going to kill him.

I looked up from the rocks I'd been navigating. Hammer had vanished. Cursing furiously, I tried to rush toward the spot where I'd seen him last. I hoped he had entered a cave or fallen down a well. If he had turned invisible or something, I really was out of my league, and I was headed in the wrong direction.

But I kept going forward, hopping from rock to rock, occasionally looking up to see if he had reappeared from behind some low hill of stones.

I jumped over a rock and stumbled across a flat pile of stones. It was a collapsed wall, and I could see a piece of gray, pitted wooden furniture jutting out from behind the rocks. Beside it was a small pile of broken crockery. I was standing on the collapsed castle.

I hopped the last few rocks to the spot where Hammer had vanished. Nothing. I couldn't see a thing there, except for a strip of faded red cloth and a smashed grandfather clock that had spent decades exposed to the weather. I looked all around. If he had turned invisible, he could come right up behind me and burn me to a cinder before I even knew he was there.

I noticed an open spot between two of the rocks. I leaped toward it.

And there it was. I was standing at the top of a stone stairwell that led down into the earth.

I leaped onto the stairs and started down. After about ten feet, the smooth gray stone walls became jagged cave. It quickly became very dark, and I didn't have any sort of light. Again I was reminded of Annalise's warning, and again I shut it out. She had just saved my life. I wasn't going to let this guy go.

I slowed a bit. The light became more dim. I could still see, but not well. How much farther?

I reached the bottom of the stairs. There were two tunnels, one off to my left, another to the right. I listened for the sound of Hammer's footsteps, but I couldn't hear anything except the ocean.

Damn. Which way? One tunnel went almost directly south, the other went west-northwest. The latter led toward a section of the collapsed building; the former led away from it. There were good reasons for choosing either.

I noticed a glimmer on the wall. It was the silver wire. It ran just below the ceiling and vanished into the darkness of the northwest tunnel. I reached up and ran my fingers over it, feeling the rusted U of iron that held it in place against the stone.

I followed it. As I moved into the darkness, I put the ghost knife into my pocket and slung the gun over my back. I trailed my left hand along the wire, making sure that it didn't turn down some unseen tunnel or vanish into a rock wall. I held my right hand in front of me and stumbled down the cave.

The floor was about as flat and smooth as a path in the forest, which was better than I expected. I wasn't sure if it was man-made or not. I had no way to know; I was just grateful that I didn't have to climb over jagged rocks in the dark.

The ground sloped upward, then turned downward again. Before I went below the edge of the slope, I turned around and looked at the entrance to the tunnel behind me. The golden sunlight of the afternoon still glowed there. I turned around and went down into the dark.

Moving through that tunnel was slow work. It annoyed me that I couldn't hear anything but ocean sounds echoing off the stone. I wanted to hear footsteps or the sounds of Hammer cursing as he bumped his head in the dark. I wanted evidence that I was on the right path.

I followed the tunnel as it curved to the right, then to the left, and sloped down. I thought I might be somewhere under the house, but it was pointless to try to map my progress. I just kept my hand on the wire and continued.

I suddenly stepped in hot water. I yelped in fear and jumped backward, striking my head against something. I listened carefully. The ocean sounds were very loud.

I stepped forward. The water sloshed over my shoe and retreated, then washed up again. *This* was the ocean. The waves were washing back and forth along the tunnel. I waded into it for a couple of steps, getting wet up to my knees. Why was the water so hot? Maybe there was some sort of volcano nearby.

I waded out farther. The water was hot, but it wasn't scalding. I told myself that some people spend a lot of money to submerge themselves in swirling hot water. The tunnel angled down and I quickly reached the point where it went under the water.

Damn. Had Hammer really gone this way? I didn't want to drown down here in the dark, but this was where the silver wire led. I also hated the idea of letting Hammer go because I didn't have the nerve to follow him. I took a deep breath, then another, then I ducked my head under the water and pulled myself along the rocks through the tunnel.

I didn't open my eyes. What was the point when I couldn't see anything out of the water, either? But I remembered all those little gray worms. I imagined them all around, trying to wriggle under my skin.

I tried to clear my mind. Too much imagination was not in my best interests right now. I kept moving, pulling myself along the bottom of the tunnel. My chest grew tight. If I didn't find air, I was going to have to turn around very soon.

No. I was not going to turn around. I was going to reach the far side or I was going to drown here and rot. If Charles Hammer came this way, so could I.

Unless Hammer had magic that let him see in the dark and breathe underwater. Or unless he took the south tunnel, because this one had been blocked by the collapsing castle.

I didn't want to think about that, because it was already too late to turn back.

My lungs were burning. I held on even though I knew it was too late. I had gone too far. I had gambled and lost.

I reached for the next rock, but it wasn't there. I panicked, letting air bubble out of my mouth. Then I found a handhold a little farther away.

The cave was sloping upward again. I pulled myself along the rocks, praying that I wouldn't slam my head against a stone and drown myself.

I broke the surface and took a gulp of stale, heavy air. It stank of salt and steam, and I didn't get enough oxygen out of it. I clung to the rocks, desperately sucking in air.

After a minute or so, my heart stopped racing and the spots stopped dancing in front of my eyes. The air was close here, but it wasn't going to kill me.

And I saw a light. There was a very faint light coming from somewhere above me.

I laughed aloud. Light. Just seeing it up there gave me strength.

The cave was vertical here. I grabbed the nearest rock and began to climb. The rocks were wet and slick, but I moved slowly and steadily toward the light.

Partway up, I caught the Uzi strap on a rock. I had a sudden chill thinking about what would have happened if it had caught while I was under the water.

I reached the top of the wall and crawled over the lip. Ahead, I could see the bend in the cave. Light was coming from somewhere around that bend, and I crawled to it. The air was fresher here, but it was also thick with steam. I stood. The roof was too low for me, but I hunched along, going farther and farther upslope. There, against the wall and spattered with mud, was the tarnished silver wire.

I followed the bend in the tunnel, checking my pockets for the ghost knife and the silver knife. They were both there. I tilted the Uzi this way and that, draining as much of the water out of it as I could.

The tunnel exit was narrow. I peered through it. Below me was a broad cavern made of volcanic rock. A thin stream of water ebbing back and forth along the far wall and clouds of steam billowed against the roof, just above my head. The whole place was lit by a bright, flickering source of light from somewhere to the left.

I squeezed through the opening into the cavern. Charles Hammer was not in sight. There was a second cavern to the left. Maybe he had already gone toward the source of the firelight.

Beside me a path ran along the upper edge of the cavern, but there didn't seem to be any way down except by free climbing the cavern wall or flying. I wasn't about to do either.

At that moment, I heard a pained grunt echo against the rocks. I stepped back into the narrow opening behind me. Charles Hammer climbed through a small opening in the far right wall of the cavern, then ran along a wooden walkway. He went straight for the second cavern on the left.

The bastard had taken the other path. He must have gone the long way around because he thought the way I went was impassable.

It was too far to shoot accurately with a submachine gun, even if I thought it would do some good. And he was definitely too far for me to throw the ghost knife.

I started along the high ledge, trying my best to match his pace. He was quick though, and the ledge was slick and precarious. Even with the shortcut I had taken, he was still ahead of me.

My biggest advantage was that he hadn't seen me yet. I lifted the gun and rushed ahead. Hammer reached the opening into the second cavern.

I came to the end of the path. Below me was a long flight of stone stairs chiseled into the wall. I started down. I could hear Hammer's sneakers thumping against the wooden boards.

After about fifteen feet, I came to a break in the wall. It was a little window into the second cavern. I looked through.

I saw it.

Not very long ago I used a stolen spell to reveal the predators that move through the Empty Spaces, searching for worlds full of life like our own. They were strange creatures made of stone or color or motion—terrifyingly alien creatures living in a terrifyingly alien environment. What I saw through that opening in the cavern wall gave me chills. I was looking down at one of those predators.

It was a huge wheel of fire, maybe 150 feet tall and partially submerged in a pool of ocean water. Steam billowed up around it, filling the cavern and dripping down the walls.

Charles Hammer approached the creature. From within the wheel, a huge flaming eye opened up and looked down at him.

I ducked down below the opening and held my breath. Goose bumps ran up and down my whole body. It was alive. The wheel of fire was alive and it was here, on Earth. I peeked through the opening again and saw what I'd expected to see—a thick circle of shining silver surrounded it. The silver was inscribed with sigils, and it was untarnished. From where I stood, it looked clean and new. I noticed the silver wire running through the opening, down the cavern wall, and toward the silver ring. By squinting, I could see where it connected. I jerked my hand away from the wire. What if the wheel could sense me touching it, the way a spider could sense movement on its web?

Christ, what was I supposed to do about this? I slid to the steps, ducking down out of sight. This was the source of Hammer's power, and I was sure it had been here for decades.

I took out my ghost knife and held it up. It was just a piece of laminated paper. What good would it be against that massive wheel of fire? The silver knife wouldn't be much better. And that assumed that I had the nerve to cross the silver ring that held it in place. What if attacking it also set if free?

Annalise was right. I was completely out of my league.

They love to be summoned, but they hate to be held in place. I peeked through the opening again. I couldn't see any sign of anger in that massive eye. I couldn't see any malevolence, just a tremendous power and tremendous *otherness*.

Charles Hammer stood before the ring, his arms raised above his head. He was shouting to it, imploring it the way a man might plead with a cruel god, but the echoes in the cavern garbled his words so thoroughly that I couldn't understand them.

I felt a sudden spasm in the iron gate on my chest, the most powerful one yet. I could feel waves of power flowing out of the wheel of fire, pressing hard against me.

On the cavern floor, Hammer had fallen to the wooden walkway. He writhed in agony, clutching at the same spot on his back where Cynthia had her iron gate. Then, suddenly, he relaxed, rolled onto his knees, and pressed his forehead against the boards. I might have thought he was praying if he hadn't been shuddering with gasps and sobs.

Something began to rain down from the ceiling, dropping through the steam and landing around Hammer. At first, I thought the roof was caving in, but the objects were small and the shower ended quickly.

Hammer looked around him as the fallen objects began to move, then he lifted his arms in helpless misery.

I realized what the falling objects were. Another kid had burned to death, and these were the gray worms created by the fire.

The worms scuttled across the uneven stone floor toward the far side of the cavern. I craned my neck and looked at the spot where they were heading.

There, I saw a second wheel lying on its side.

This one was not made of fire. It was simply a mass of wriggling worms in the shape of a wheel. It was much smaller than the burning wheel, and it was not surrounded by a silver ring. The worms crawled and wriggled in a clockwise direction, giving the impression that the wheel was slowly turning.

It was a child. The wheel of fire was using the bodies of the children of Hammer Bay to create a second wheel, one not held in place by a magical binding.

Hammer turned back to the burning wheel, pleading with it some more. The fiery eye did not react, did not seem angry. It just stared at him implacably.

There was no way those worms were ever, ever going to be turned back into human children.

Hammer kicked at a section of wood, flipping it over. Underneath was another silver hoop, very much like the one in his tower. He stepped into it.

My iron gate flared white hot. The world went dark.

I woke up slowly. I don't know how long I had lain there on the stone steps, but I hadn't soiled my shorts, and I wasn't dying of thirst. It couldn't have been longer than a couple hours, although it might have been only a few seconds. I jumped up and looked through the opening in the wall.

Hammer was out of the hoop, crawling across the rocky floor of the cavern toward the baby wheel. Gray worms clung to his clothes and hair as he laboriously scuttled from one jagged rock to the next. He moved dreamily, as though he was sleepwalking.

He reached the edge of a long slab beside the smaller wheel. Now that he was next to it, I had some sense of its scale. It was at least forty feet in diameter.

Hammer plucked the worms off of his clothes and hair and tossed them onto the wheel. Then he stood among the rocks and lifted his head as though taking a deep breath.

He was about to breathe fire onto the baby wheel. He was about to ignite it.

The Uzi was in my hand before I realized what I was doing. It didn't matter anymore that I was too far away. I had to try something. I couldn't let a living wheel of fire get loose on the world, and I had no other way to stop him.

I fired a short burst that chipped the rocks twenty feet short of where Hammer was. I adjusted my aim and tried again. This time I hit the small wheel itself, to no apparent effect.

I felt the monstrous wheel turn its attention to me. Waves of power washed over me. My iron gate burned and throbbed. I didn't dare look at the predator. I didn't have the guts.

A jet of fire erupted from Charles Hammer's mouth and sprayed over the baby wheel.

I unloaded on him. Bullets spattered against the slab he was standing on, and miraculously, one struck his ankle.

His foot flopped inward like a broken chicken neck, and he fell hard, sliding down among the rocks. The jet of fire from his mouth roared upward toward the ceiling, igniting nothing.

Fires sputtered along the baby wheel, but they quickly died out. Hammer was going to have to try again. I saw him clutching at his throat.

I threw the empty gun away and sprinted down the steps. I had taken out Carol the receptionist by venting the flames as she was breathing them. Maybe I could do the same to Hammer, or maybe I could stab him with the letter opener in my pocket. Either way, I needed to be closer to him to do it.

I leaped down the steps at breakneck speed, ghost knife in hand, my bloody calf aching. If I fell, if I didn't stop him in time, I'd be dead, and so would a lot of other people. I tried to avoid a fall.

At the bottom of the stairs I leapt across a fissure onto the wooden walkway. It broke underneath me. My foot slid down the side of a rock and jammed painfully between two stones. The broken plank flew upward and wedged itself against the inside of my thigh. Nothing was broken or sprained, but by the time I freed myself from the mess, Hammer had regained the lip of the slab. His ankle and throat looked completely healed.

He was fifty feet away, too far for me to throw the ghost knife. I'd failed.

He took a deep breath.

An idea came to me. If I could call the ghost knife toward me, maybe I could control it in other ways, too.

I looked down at the spell in my hand and imagined it going through Charles Hammer's throat.

A jet of flame shot from Hammer's mouth.

I glared at the tattered spell in my hand and willed it to move.

It shot from my palm and zipped across the cavern for Charles Hammer's back.

Hammer turned his head back and forth, playing the fire over the baby wheel. Spurts of flame began to shoot up from the wriggling worms. Hammer turned far enough so that part of his face was visible, and I saw his agony.

The ghost knife struck the back of his neck. A jet of flame burst out of the cut like steam escaping a ruptured pipe. Flames engulfed his head, and the jet of fire lost pressure, falling short of the baby wheel. It hadn't ignited.

His whole head burning, Hammer fell backward. He did not scream, although I imagined he very much wanted to.

I sprinted along the causeway. The huge wheel stared down at me. As I ran past the silver wire, the pain in my iron gate grew. It was reaching out to me, trying to destroy me. Only Annalise's spell held it at bay.

I leaped off the walkway and started bounding across the rocks. The pain eased as I put some distance between the silver wire and me. I reached the slab where Hammer had been standing.

He was lying on his back, wedged between two stones. As I watched, his skin turned from scorched and blackened to pink and healthy. I thought how much I wished Annalise could do the same, and I hated him all the more.

"Oh, God," he gasped, as though he'd been holding his breath. "No more."

"What a fantastic idea," I said. I slid down the slab of stone and landed on his chest with both knees. I pulled the silver letter opener from my pocket.

"No!" Hammer screamed. He struggled, his arms flailing and

batting at me, his legs scrabbling against the stones. I grabbed his arms and held them down.

His eyes rolled back in his head. He took a deep breath.

I jammed the silver blade under his chin into his brain.

He bucked twice. No jet of fire came out of him. He fell still and silent. He was dead.

I stood, leaving the letter opener in place. He didn't heal and he didn't wake up. I had guessed correctly. The wheel couldn't exert its power over him while he had the silver inside him.

At least, I hoped it couldn't. The silver ring that enclosed the wheel of fire was not enough to keep its immense power in check. I didn't know how long the knife would hold him.

I could have turned him over and destroyed his iron gate but decided against it. What would that have accomplished except to allow the wheel to erase his memory?

I looked up at it. I felt very small beside that terrible creature.

"Can you understand me?" I said. *Don't talk to the targets,* Annalise had told me, but I couldn't resist. "Can you understand? Can you see the future? Can you control it?"

/Yes./

It was not a sound, it was a pressure against my iron gate and my mind at the same time. I felt sick and small, like an ant who sees a boot moving above him.

"Can you make me do what you want, the way you controlled all those parents and toy shoppers?"

There was no answer this time. I took that as a no.

I walked across the rocks toward the hoop Hammer had stood in. It was connected to the main ring by a second silver wire.

"What do I have to do to get you to control the future for me? Do I have to be inside the silver hoop?"

/Yes./

"Well, then," I said, "that's some sad luck for you, you great big bitch."

I held up my hand. My ghost knife flew into it like a bird returning to its nest. I bent down and cut the silver wire that connected the wheel's binding circle to the hoop, then I cut the other wire that led through the tunnel to the tower. I didn't see any more wires.

Immediately, the pressure against my iron gate eased. I had isolated the wheel, partially reducing the power it could bring to bear on the world outside its silver ring. Hopefully, with the wire cut and the silver blade wedged in Hammer's body, the predator wouldn't be able to heal him again.

I climbed back over the rocks to the baby wheel. Tiny worms wriggled sluggishly in a circle. It was not ready to be born. Maybe our attack on Charles Hammer had rushed the birth process, forcing the wheel to turn the spirit fire on it before it was ready. It didn't matter now.

I held out the ghost knife, letting the crawling worms cut themselves on the edge of the spell. The worms broke apart, falling to the stones like windblown ash. I yanked my hand away from the tiny gouts of flame that erupted. Thankfully, the fire did not spread.

I felt a great, mournful wail wash through me. It was not something I could hear, but it seemed to fill me nonetheless. I was murdering the wheel's unborn child, and it couldn't do anything but watch.

It took a while to finish the job. There were thousands of worms, but I could kill four or five with a quick swipe of my arm. I could have struck more, but I didn't want to throw my spell in case the wheel could catch it somehow, and I didn't want to let the little worms touch my skin.

I felt the predator behind me trying to exert its will over me. It didn't work. Cutting the wires had limited the amount of power it could use outside the ring. Still, the iron gate on my chest throbbed and ached.

The baby wheel shrank as I killed it. Eventually, it was reduced to the point that the inner hole vanished and it became a disk. When that happened, the remaining worms fell apart and died on the stones around me.

I was hungry. I was thirsty. I wanted to get the hell away from Hammer Bay. I didn't know how far I would have to drive before the sigil on my chest stopped throbbing, but I was willing to gas up and find out.

The wheel of fire looming above me really was out of my league. I didn't even want to look at it. I'd collect Charles Hammer's spell book, if I could find it, and let a peer in the society figure out what to do about the wheel. Someone needed to destroy it, but that someone wasn't going to be me.

I climbed over the rocks toward the wooden walkway.

Charles Hammer was gone.

I cursed and turned toward the hoop. He wasn't there, either. I'd already broken the connection between the hoop and the wheel of fire.

I scanned the entire cave. He wasn't anywhere nearby.

I hopped to the walkway, trying to pretend the wheel of fire was not looming above me, watching my every move, and sprinted toward the outer cavern. I didn't know how long ago Hammer had come to and fled, but I expected him to leave by the same long tunnel. I climbed up the stone stairs. I was going for the shortcut again.

The trip back seemed surprisingly quick. Maybe it was because I was so focused on chasing Hammer, or maybe it was because I knew what lay ahead, but in no time at all I was climbing back into daylight.

There was a tiny drop of blood on the top step. I didn't need to look for a second. I didn't need a blood trail to track him. He would be at the house or at the cars. Either he was collecting his things or he'd had gotten them already and was running.

I leaped over the rocks toward the house, angling for the asphalt parking lot and garage on the eastern side. I didn't see any lights or movement through the house windows. That was bad. If he was already gone, I was never going to catch him. I didn't know anyone willing to hand me leads on him, I didn't have any idea what other properties he owned, and I didn't have any damn money. Once the tank of gas in the van ran out, I was stranded.

If Hammer managed to get to an airport, I was never going to catch him later. Maybe someone in the society could, but I had no way of contacting them. It was on me or no one.

I finally reached the asphalt parking lot and climbed up onto the flat ground.

There was a tiny drop of blood on the ground beside the garage. The van was still parked in the mouth of the driveway. Hammer hadn't driven out. I went past the garage and raced to the house.

The smell of burned flesh hit me hard. I held the ghost knife close to my chest as I crept through the house. Nothing seemed to be changed as far as I could tell. I moved through the rooms, past the piles of bones, up the stairs, and across the causeway.

I heard nothing. I didn't see any movement.

I stepped onto the landing. The wooden stairs spiraled above me. There was another drop of blood on the first step.

He'd come this way, obviously. Unless the blood was mine. Was he still up there with Annalise's corpse?

I heard soft fabric rustling. It was my only warning. I threw myself sideways.

Bullets streamed through the doorway. Hammer had come up behind me and fired a good long volley at me. I crouched on the stairs, hearing the shots ricochet inside the cylindrical tower. I covered my face with my tattooed forearms and waited. A ricochet tugged at the sleeve of my shirt, but that was as close as he got.

Finally, the shots finished. I knew he had more guns out there if he had the stomach to rummage through the bodies for them. If he had the nerve, he could charge in here and put a nasty end to me.

"You bastard!" he shouted, his voice high and desperate. "You can't kill me, and if I see you again, I'm going to burn you alive. I can still feel the power of the Great Wheel inside me. It's still inside me and you can't take it away!"

I moaned. "Call an ambulance," I said, trying to sound wounded and helpless. I held the ghost knife ready. "Please." Maybe, if I could lure him closer . . .

"Hah! Fuck you!"

I heard his footsteps as he ran away. I heard bones clacking. Then he was gone.

I peeked into the causeway. Nothing. I ran into the house. Bones had been scattered around the hall. The front door was standing open. I ran toward it.

Hammer was sprinting across the asphalt, holding a book in his left hand and a set of keys in his right. An Uzi hung on his back, bouncing around near his kidneys. In a just world, the gun would have gone off, blowing out his midsection and the family jewels, ending the line. It didn't happen. He ran around the van, leaping onto the rocks to go around it.

Keys. Dammit, that's why the bones were spread around the hall. He must have taken a set of keys from one of the guards.

That's when I remembered the three Crown Victorias parked on the street.

I ran back into the house, kicked the bones aside, and grabbed two of the Uzis. Whatever Hammer had, I wanted double. I looped both of their straps around my neck. Offering a silent apology to the unburied dead, I ran out of the house, climbed into the van, and started it up.

It took a moment to turn the van around in the parking lot, then I raced up the driveway and fishtailed across the gravel road, wishing I had more acceleration. A vehicle that didn't handle like a refrigerator box would have been nice, too.

I swerved out onto the street just as one of the Crown Vics screeched out of its parking space and took off down the main road. I stomped on the accelerator, hoping to T-bone it and trap Hammer inside, but it had already passed me. I caught a quick glimpse of him behind the wheel, his eyes wild and his neck covered with gleaming red blood.

My heart sank as I watched the vehicle accelerate down the block. There was no way I could keep up with him. Still, I pulled the shoulder harness over me and clicked it into place. I was going to ram him, if I got the chance.

A soccer ball bounced out from between two cars, and Hammer slammed on the brakes. He slowly drove around it, then sped up toward the corner. I roared after him and chased him through Hammer Bay. He crept through stop signs and red lights, blaring his horn, screeching to a halt when he came too close to another car. This was his town. He was not going to break anything in it—at least, not where anyone would see.

I managed to clip his taillight when he braked for a woman on a bicycle, but it wasn't enough to stop him. He raced past the supermarket, past the hospital, past the last biker bar at the edge of town, then he crested a hill and vanished onto the highway.

If I couldn't keep up with him in town, I was never going to be able to follow him on the winding highway.

I rumbled up the crest in the hill. Hammer was pulling away. I picked up the Uzi with my left hand and leaned it out the window. I didn't have any other choice now, and there were no innocent bystanders to worry about.

I fired on him, trying to keep my shots low, near the tires. My aim was crap and the gun bucked like crazy. His back windshield shattered, and he swerved as he ducked below the dash. I punched holes in the trunk, for whatever good that did.

The magazine ran dry. I was reaching for the second one when Hammer, still ducking below the dashboard, swerved across the center line. A pickup truck loaded with gardening equipment rounded the curve ahead, heading straight for him. The driver blared his horn.

The vehicles swerved away from each other. The pickup slid onto the shoulder of the road and rumbled through the gravel. Hammer overcorrected, angling across the road and over the shoulder. He hit the brakes too late and smashed into a tree.

The pickup driver slowed to a stop, and so did I. I saw Hammer's air bag deflate back against the steering wheel. Hammer was hurt, but I knew he wasn't out of commission. I tossed away the empty gun and climbed from the driver's seat.

"Did you see what happened?" the pickup driver said, not really looking at me. "He swerved right into my lane!"

He rushed toward Hammer's car, intent on helping him. Hammer shoved open his door and stumbled out of the car. He was holding the Uzi. The pickup driver stopped suddenly about ten feet away and said something like "Whoa, friend . . ."

Hammer pointed the weapon at me. I fired.

He blossomed with bullet holes and fell back against the car. He lay still. The driver fled back to his truck like a perfectly sensible person.

I rushed over to Hammer and took his gun away. The bullet wounds were already healing, but slowly. Without the silver wire, the connection between the man and the predator must have been faint.

Using the ghost knife, I sliced off his clothes. I found an iron gate on his shoulder, just where it had been on Cynthia and Cabot. I cut through it, letting the black steam and gray sparks arc into the air.

There was another sigil on his stomach. It was a circle with flames at the four cardinal points and a single eye at the center. This one didn't look like a tattoo, though. It looked, and felt, like a tumor that had grown under his skin. I slashed the ghost knife through this one, too. There were no jets of steam or sparks, but Hammer's bullet wounds stopped sealing over.

As an experiment, I slid the corner of the ghost knife through his wrist. His skin split apart as if I was using a scalpel. He was dead.

The pickup truck raced away. I climbed into the Crown Vic and found an old leather-bound journal. It fell open to a page that read "To Call and Bind a Great Wheel, Which Will Grant You Favorable Outcomes."

On impulse, I pulled out Charlie Three's wallet. I found five hundred-dollar bills and ten twenties. I took them all. This had been a valuable lesson for him.

I tucked the book under my arm and went back to the van.

CHAPTER NINETEEN

I drove back into town. I should have dumped the van, stolen a car, and made a run for it, but I doubted I would get far. Half the town had seen me at the casino, the hospital, the police station, and during the car chase through town. The FBI or the state police were probably already looking for me.

Besides, I had no choice. Charles Hammer might have left another copy of his spell book in his tower. I had to finish Annalise's work and burn it down.

I drove through town without incident. Traffic still seemed lighter than it had. Most of the people must have been on the north side of town, where two columns of black smoke rose toward the sky. I pulled into Hammer's driveway without attracting any apparent attention. There were no police cars waiting for me, and no one seemed to have come to the house. The front door was still wide open.

I went inside and let myself onto the terrace. There was no lighter fluid beside the barbecue, but there was a long lighter, a bag of charcoal, and a charcoal chimney. That would do. I tore some pages off Charles's kitchen calendar and squirted olive oil on them. Then I put the paper on the bottom of the chimney and the coals in the top.

I'd almost forgotten about the sprinklers. I followed the sprinkler pipes along the ceiling to the place where they joined the main water system beneath the kitchen sink, and turned the valve all the way off.

Then I stood and opened the fridge. I was hungry, sure, but I had another thought nagging at me.

On the bottom shelf of the fridge, Charles had left three porterhouse steaks. I carried them along with the lighter and chimney to the tower.

I set the lighter and chimney on the landing inside the door. Then I sprinted up the stairs with the steaks in hand.

Annalise was still there. One look at her and I knew my idea was crazy and useless. I opened the first package and, with the ghost knife, cut a long strip from the steak. Annalise's mouth was wide open in a frozen scream. I stuffed the piece of meat into her throat.

I did it again and again. If I was crazy, I was crazy. Maybe they would put me in a nice, uncomfortable psych ward when they finally nabbed me.

As I finished the second piece of meat, I felt something in the back of Annalise's throat move.

She breathed on me.

She still looked dead. Her skin was charred and blackened, her face shriveled, her eyes empty sockets.

I put my hand back up to her mouth. I could swear I felt a faint breath. Unless I had lost my mind.

I cut up the third steak as quickly as I could, jamming it down her throat. When it was gone, I picked her up, getting greasy ash all over my ruined shirt, and carried her down the stairs and out of the house. I opened the back of the van and laid her down as gently as I could.

Then I ran back into the house, lit the charcoal chimney, and set it on the landing beside the stairs. Soon it would be hot enough to ignite the wood.

I ran into the kitchen and disabled the electric pilot light on the gas stove, then turned all the burners on full. In the front room, I tipped the overstuffed couch against the wall and lit a pile of magazines beneath it. The magazines would light the couch, which would ignite the wall, which would still be burning when the gas reached it.

All of this took three minutes at most, but it seemed like forever. I finally ran back to the van and raced out of the driveway. There was always the possibility that someone would go to the house and be hurt or killed when the gas main went, but that didn't seem likely. Hammer liked his privacy, and the town gave it to him.

I drove through town again, pulled into the supermarket lot and parked beside the Dumpster, where the van wouldn't be visible from the road. My clothes were a mess.

People in the supermarket gave me some strange stares, but I limped as quickly as I could and paid with Hammer's cash. I bought another leg of lamb and forty pounds of pot roast.

Once back in the van, I started the engine. I didn't have any capacity for planning left. All I had was a buzzing, jangling urge to flee town.

I heard a loud *thoom* as I pulled out of the parking lot. A quick glance toward the water showed a heavy black cloud where Hammer's tower was supposed to be. People around me screamed or jumped into their cars to race toward the fire.

I turned the other way and drove out of town.

Several miles down the road, I came to the same empty lot where Annalise and I had confronted the Benton family. I pulled in and parked behind the abandoned stall.

I climbed into the back. Annalise was still breathing, but more faintly than before. Feeling her breath gave me chills. It was like feeling the breath of a ghost.

I opened the first package of pot roast. Just a few days before, I would have left her to burn in the tower, or I would have pitched her into the woods behind me and been glad to be rid of her.

Not anymore.

For the next hour, I sliced off strips of meat and fed them to her. She lived.

ACKNOWLEDGMENTS

First, I'd like to thank Ted Elliott, Terry Rossio, and all the regulars at the Wordplayer.com forums, most especially Bill Martell. I would never have learned how to put a story together without that site.

And thanks also go to Caitlin Blasdell and Betsy Mitchell for giving so much of their care, expertise, and precious, precious time to this book.

Finally, the largest share of my gratitude goes to my wife, Mary-Ann, who believed in me when believing in me didn't make a bit of sense. This book wouldn't exist without her.

GAME
OF
CAGES

For MaryAnn

CHAPTER ONE

It was three days before Christmas, and I was not in prison. I couldn't understand why I was free. I hadn't hidden my face during the job in Hammer Bay. I hadn't used a fake name. I honestly hadn't expected to survive.

I had, though. The list of crimes I'd committed there included breaking and entering, arson, assault, and murder. And what could I have said in my defense? That the people I'd killed really deserved it?

Washington State executes criminals by lethal injection, and for that first night in my own bed, I imagined I was lying on a prison cot in a room with a glass wall, a needle in my arm.

That hadn't happened. Instead, I'd met with an attorney the society hired, kept my mouth shut, stood in at least a dozen lineups, and waited for the fingerprint and DNA analysis to come back. When it did, they let me go. Maybe I'd only dreamed about the people I'd killed.

So, months later, I was wearing my white supermarket polo shirt, stocking an endcap with gift cards for other stores. It was nearly nine at night, and I had just started my shift. I liked the late shift. It gave me something to do when the restlessness became hard to take.

At the front of the store, a woman was questioning the manager, Harvey. He gestured toward me. At first I figured her for another detective. Even though the last press release about me stated I'd been the victim of identity theft and the police were searching for other suspects, detectives still dropped by my work and home at random times to take another run at me. They weren't fooled. They knew.

But she didn't have a cop's body language. She wore casual gray office clothes and sensible work shoes, an outfit so ordinary I barely noticed it. She walked briskly toward me, clutching a huge bag. Harvey followed.

She was tall and broad in the hips, and had long, delicate hands, large eyes, and a pointed chin. Her skin color showed that she had both black and white parentage, which in this country made her black. "You're Ray Lilly, aren't you?" she asked.

"Who's asking?"

"My name is Catherine Little. I'm a friend of your mother's."

That hit me like a punch in the gut. The last time I saw my mother, I was fourteen years old and headed into juvie. She was not someone I thought about. Ever. "Who are you again?"

"I'm Catherine. I work with your mother. I'm a friend of hers. She asked me to contact you."

"Where is she?" I peered through the glass doors into the parking lot, but it was pitch-dark outside.

"Okay. This is the hard part. Your mom's in the hospital. She's had some . . . issues the last few days. She asked for you."

I laid my hand on the gift cards on the cart beside me. They toppled over, ruining the neat little stacks I'd been working with. I began to tidy them absentmindedly. "When?"

Catherine laid her hand on my elbow. "Right now," she said. "It has to be right now."

Something about the way she said that was off. I looked at her again. There was a look of urgency on her face, but there was something else there, too. Something calculated.

This woman didn't know my mother. I knew it then as clearly as if she was wearing a sandwich-board sign that read I AM LYING TO YOU.

Her expression changed. My face must have given me away, because she didn't look quite so sympathetic now, but her expression was still urgent. "We have to hurry," she said.

Harvey laid his hand on my shoulder like a friendly uncle. "Ray, go get your coat. I'll clock you out."

I told Catherine I'd meet her out front and went into the break room. She had to be with the Twenty Palace Society; there was no one else who would want me. I had been dreading the day they would contact me again. Dreading it and wishing for it.

I grabbed my flannel jacket and hurried outside without speaking to or looking at anyone. I could feel my co-workers watching me. Just the thought of talking to Harvey—or anyone else—about my mom, even if it was a bullshit cover story, made me want to quit on the spot.

Catherine waited behind the wheel of an Acura sedan, one of the most stolen cars in the country. I sat in the passenger seat and buckled up. She had a sweet GPS setup and some electronic equipment I didn't recognize. I squinted at a narrow slot with a number pad on the side—I could have sworn it was a tiny fax machine. While I had been living the straight life, cars had moved on and left me behind. She pulled into the street.

"I'm sorry," she said. "That really hit you hard, didn't it? They told me to contact you that way. I didn't realize . . . Sorry." She seemed sincere if a little standoffish.

"Who's 'they'?" I asked, just to be sure. "Who are you?"

"My name is Catherine. Really. 'They' are the Twenty Palace Society. We have an emergency and I need help. You're the only other member in this part of the country at the moment."

My scalp tingled. It was true.

Part of me was furious that they'd dangled my mother in front of me like bait, but at the same time I wanted to lunge across the hand brake and hug her.

Finally. Finally! The society had come for me. It was like a jolt to the base of my spine. *Finally, something worth living for.*

"Are you okay?" she asked warily.

"I'm okay." I did my best to keep my voice neutral, but I didn't succeed all that well. Christ, she'd even said I was a *member* of the society. I belonged. "We need to go by my place."

There were no tattoos peeking from the cuffs of her sleeves and the collar of her shirt. She had no sigils on her clothes or the interior of the car. No visible magic. She might have had something hidden, of course. I was tempted to rummage through her pockets to search for spells.

She drove to my place without asking for my address. My hand was trembling and I gripped my leg to hide the adrenaline rush. I'd thought about the society often over the last seven months. Aside from a visit from an old guy with a brush mustache who'd debriefed me about Hammer Bay, I'd heard nothing from them. I hadn't even gotten a call from Annalise letting me know how she was. I had been telling myself I wanted to be cut loose. I had been telling myself I wanted to be forgotten.

But now they had come for me again and every traffic light and Christmas decoration seemed saturated with color. In fact, all my senses seemed to have been turned up to ten. I felt alive again, and I was grateful for it.

At my aunt's house, I had Catherine drive around to the back. I climbed the stairs to my mother-in-law apartment above the garage and let myself in. I went to the bookshelf and pulled a slip of paper from between two yard-sale hardcovers. It had been covered on both sides with mailing tape and had laminate over that. A sigil had been drawn on one side.

My ghost knife. It was the only spell I had, except for the protective tattoos on my chest and forearms. They didn't count, though; the ghost knife was a spell I'd created myself, and I could feel it as if it was a part of me.

I slipped it into my jacket pocket and looked around. What else did I need? I had my wallet and keys and even, for the first time in my life, a credit card. Should I pack clean underwear and a change of clothes?

Catherine honked. No time for that, I guess. I rushed into the bathroom and grabbed my toothbrush. Then I wrote a quick note to my aunt to tell her I'd be gone for a while and please don't worry. Catherine honked again before I was done. I carried the note down the stairs and annoyed Catherine further by running toward the back door of the house. I stuck the note on the backside of the wreath on the screen door, rattling it in the frame.

The inner door suddenly swung inward. Aunt Theresa was there, looking up at me. "Ray?" She wore a knit cap over her wispy gray hair and a bright red-and-green scarf around her neck. Cold, she was always cold. It was one of the many things about her that made me worry.

"Oh! I thought this was movie night. I was leaving you a note." She must have come to see who was honking.

She popped open the screen door and took the note with fingers bent sideways from arthritis. "Movie night is tomorrow, dear." She opened the note and read it. The note didn't mention my mother—it was Catherine's cover story, not mine, and I wasn't going to lie to my aunt about her little sister.

I glanced at the room behind her, expecting to see Uncle Karl in his badge and blue uniform, scowling at me. He wasn't there.

Aunt Theresa looked up me. "Will you be back for Christmas?"

The way she said it startled me. Of course I had gifts to give her and Karl, but I hadn't expected her to care if I . . . I felt like an idiot.

"I hope so," I said, and meant it.

She shuffled forward and hugged me. I hugged her back. She knew a little about what I did. Not about the society itself, and not enough to get into trouble, but enough to worry. "Be careful."

We let go. I backed down the stairs and hurried to Catherine's car. I should have said something reassuring to her, but it was too late now. Time to go.

I climbed into the Acura and belted up. My adrenaline was high, and I couldn't help but smile. Catherine didn't like that smile. "Do you have everything now?"

The ghost knife in my pocket felt like a live wire. "Yep."

She rumbled through the alley and pulled into the street. I thought it would be best to let her tell me what was going on when she was ready, but after driving in silence for four blocks, I couldn't hold back.

"What's the emergency?"

"Well . . ." she said, then fell silent while she negotiated a busy intersection. Her body language had changed again—she was irritated. I wasn't sure why; didn't it make sense for me to stop at home before I went on a job?

"Well," she said again, "earlier today we found out there's going to be an auction. Tonight. In fact, it might be taking place right now, although I hope not. I went an hour out of my way to pick you up, so you better be worth it."

This was a sudden change in tone. I wondered where it had come from. "I'll do my best," I said, but that made her scowl and blow air out of her nose. "What's being auctioned?"

"A predator."

That was the answer I didn't want to hear. Predators were weird supernatural creatures out of the Empty Spaces. I'd seen two so far, along with the pile of corpses they left behind. "Do you know what kind?"

"What kind?" She seemed to think this was an idiotic question, but I had no idea why. "No. I don't know what kind."

"Okay." I was careful not to snap at her.

"Who are you?" she asked. She looked me up and down. I didn't feel a lot of friendliness coming from her.

"I'm Ray Lilly," I answered, keeping my tone neutral. "Remember? You just pulled me out of work."

"I know your name," she said, leaving out the word *dumbass* but implying it anyway. "What were you doing at that supermarket? What are you doing in that apartment?"

"Working. Living."

"That's not cover for a mission? Okay. What I want to know is who you are in the society. Because you are definitely not a peer. Are you an apprentice? An ally?"

"I'm not any of those things," I said. "I'm Annalise Powliss's wooden man."

She exhaled sharply, then laughed to herself a little. "For God's sake," she said, then fell silent. After a few seconds more, she pulled into a Pizza Hut parking lot. She didn't turn off the engine. "All right," she said, and I could tell by her tone that I wouldn't like what she was about to say. "Somebody fucked up. You shouldn't be here, not with me, and I shouldn't have been sent a fucking hour out of my way to pick up a fucking wooden man, not on a supposedly emergency job. What's the point in having you along? I don't need you and I don't want you. Hell, I don't even like looking at you, knowing what you are.

"So here's the deal: you keep quiet and do what I say, or you get out right now. I have a long night's work ahead of me, and I don't need you getting in my way. So, which is it going to be? Because if following orders is going to be too much for you, you need to be out of my car and have yourself a nice day."

She stared at me, waiting for a response. It had been a while since anyone had spoken to me like that. If Catherine had been a guy . . .

Not that using my fists had ever turned out well for me. Old habits don't just die hard, they make living hard, too. "You must be part of the diplomatic wing of the society."

She sat back, rolled her eyes, and sighed. "What the hell did I do to deserve this?"

"I'll tell you what you did," I answered. "You talked to me like I ran over your dog. Whatever your problem is, it has nothing to do with me."

"Oh no?" She turned the key, shutting off the engine. "Bad enough to have a peer or an ally along. Then I would spend all my time praying the collateral damage doesn't hit me. But every wooden man I've ever met was either a stone-skulled thug, terminally ill, or a terminally ill stone-skulled thug." She made sure to look me straight in the eye as she said it. She had guts. I would have liked her if she wasn't so obnoxious. "Which are you?"

"Well, I'm not terminally ill."

She frowned. I'd lived down to her expectations. "Well, that's just dandy."

"If you order me to get out of your car," I said, "I'll hop out right here. I'm not going to ride with someone who doesn't want me. But that's the only way I'm getting out. When the friendly guy from the society turns up to debrief me, I'm not going to tell him I *chose* not to go. Understand?"

She turned away from me. The society had kept me out of jail, somehow. I had no idea what would happen if I refused to take a job. Would they kill me? Would they lift whatever spell kept the cops off my front door? I had exactly one person handy who I could ask, and she was trying to kick me out of her car.

Pizza-delivery guys carried red cases across the lot. They didn't seem happy about the way we were parked. I wondered how much they made a month.

"All right then," Catherine said. "We go on the job, and you take your orders from me."

"That ain't going to happen, either," I told her. As Annalise's wooden man, I went when she said *go* and I did when she said *do*, but that didn't mean I was going to take orders from everyone in the society. Not unless Annalise told me to. "If you have a good idea, I'll be happy to go along with it. If not, then not. That's the only deal you're going to get. If that's not good enough, *you* can explain why you gave the boot to the guy the society sent you an hour out of your way to pick up."

She chewed on that for a while, then pulled into the street and drove onto the ramp to the highway. We weren't talking, apparently, but I could bear it. At least she didn't want to kill me.

We drove to 520 and headed east toward the Cascades. Two hours and several increasingly narrow roads later, we turned off just before we came to a pass. We drove north for a short while, following a winding two-lane highway through the mountains.

It occurred to me that Catherine might have a report or a file about the job we were on. I asked, but she shook her head. Either she didn't have one, or she wasn't sharing. They came to the same thing for me.

We changed roads a couple of more times, weaving and winding through the Cascade foothills. We didn't play music. Catherine was a very good driver, although I doubted most people would recognize it; she had complete control of the car, held the same steady speed, and had excellent lane discipline. Nothing flashy, but she knew what she was doing. I wondered how much time she spent behind the wheel every day.

We skirted a small town, passing along a road in the hillside above it. It was late, but Christmas lights still burned in the town below. It felt strange to be traveling several hundred feet above a star, but I was probably just tired.

I didn't see the name of the town and realized I had no idea where we were. It didn't matter. By my watch, it was just past eleven. The road and rain forest looked fake in the headlights, like a TV show. I felt adrift in the darkness.

We curved south and quickly came upon a high black iron fence on one side of the road. Catherine pulled to the shoulder and checked her GPS against a slip of paper in her pocket. "This is it. The gate should be up ahead."

"I can cut through the fence," I told her. The long drive had eased tensions between us. "We could hide the car and sneak onto the property."

"That would take too long. The driveway from the gate to the house stretches three miles, and the terrain would be difficult. There's also a second road off the grounds that heads east-northeast toward town and a whole twisty mess of access roads and horse trails, otherwise I'd suggest we hide outside the gate and snap photos of drivers and license plates of everyone who leaves. We're going to have to risk driving it."

I nodded and kept quiet. After a few minutes we came to the gate. Catherine drove by, slowing slightly to allow us to look up the driveway. I didn't see any cars or guards, but a heavy chain held the two halves of the gate together.

She drove down the road a ways, turned off her headlights, then did a quick three-point turn. We approached the gate from the other side and stopped at the entrance. "I have a bolt cutter in the back," she said, reaching for the door.

"We don't need it," I said. I opened the passenger door and closed it as quietly as I could. The *chunk* sound it made was loud in the thin mountain air.

If there was an alarm system on the gate, it was hidden. There were no wires, electric trips, or warning signs. I took the ghost knife from my pocket. Holding it felt like holding my own hand.

I approached the chain snaked through the gate and laid the laminated edge of the ghost knife against it. *It cuts ghosts, magic, and dead things.* With a quick flick of my wrist, I slid the sheet of paper through the steel, slicing it in half.

Metal rods extended through the bottom of the gate into a hole in the asphalt. I cut those as well.

The chain came off in two pieces. They had been wrapped around the gate but not locked together. I hadn't needed the ghost knife at all.

I pushed the left gate open, making enough room for the Acura. No klaxons went off, no lights flashed, no Dobermans charged out of the darkness at me.

We drove up the driveway with our lights off. It was a winding road, dipping and curving around gullies and rock faces. I was glad Catherine had shot down my idea of crossing the estate on foot—it would have taken hours.

It occurred to me that, if the society wanted to get rid of me, this was the way to do it. Send a woman to pick me up. Dress her in bland, nondescript clothes. Drive all the way into the mountains. If this estate belonged to Annalise or one of the other peers, no one would ever find me.

I shook that off. A peer could just as easily throttle me in my bed and burn down my apartment. Or pull my head off with their bare hands. They didn't need to be clever.

Catherine and I gasped at the same time as a curve in the road revealed a pair of headlights shining from around the next bend. She braked gently. I laid my hand on the door handle in case I needed to bolt from the car.

"Don't," Catherine said. The headlights were not moving toward us. In fact, they weren't moving at all. We backed up a few yards and turned down an access road I hadn't noticed. The tires crunched on downed branches and muddy gravel. She drove twenty yards, then shut off the engine. Once the sun rose, anyone on the drive above would be able to spot the car, but I hoped we would be gone by then.

We shut the doors as quietly as we could. Catherine changed from her office shoes into hiking boots and slung a pack over her shoulder, then followed me back to the driveway. My own black leather low-tops slipped in the mud.

Once back at the driveway, Catherine laid a long pine branch across the shoulder. She then placed a pinecone in the center of the asphalt.

With the access road to the car marked, we crept along the shoulder, staying just inside the line of trees. I heard the wind blowing above me, but I was sheltered down in the hills. Unfortunately, we were heading up. My jacket was too thin for December in the mountains, but I'd be okay if I kept dry.

I reached the edge of the curve. A BMW sat on the shoulder of the road, grille facing me, but the headlights were off. The lights actually came from a second vehicle: a panel truck on its side, the windshield cracked and the low beams shining into the trees across the road. The truck was lit by the headlights of a third car that I couldn't see from where I stood. I watched for a minute or so, waiting for the drivers to show up. They didn't.

Catherine crept up beside me and peered around the trunk of a tree. I wished I knew the hand signals TV commandos use. I leaned close to her and whispered: "Let me check it out. If no one shoots me, you follow."

The reflected headlights illuminated Catherine's face clearly. I saw her nod gratefully.

I rubbed the tattoos Annalise had put on my chest and forearms, but I couldn't feel anything. That was how they worked: where the marks covered my skin I was numb, but those marks could bounce bullets.

It wasn't much. My neck, my face and head, my back, my legs, and a couple of other places I didn't like to think about were not bulletproof, but it was more than most people had.

I darted from one tree to the next. The headlights lit the accident scene pretty well, but anyone who might be standing guard was well hidden. Or there was nothing to guard. To hell with this. I climbed down the embankment and walked along the shoulder.

The BMW was an xDrive 50i in a lovely burgundy. An X6. It was also empty. The license plate holder showed it belonged to a "luxury" rental agency. Out of habit, I checked the ignition. No keys. The driver's door was unlocked, though. I had always liked stealing BMWs. They were fun to drive and valuable enough to ship out of the country. That wasn't my life anymore, of course.

I jogged toward the toppled panel truck. I was too close to creep around in shadows, and it would have looked suspicious if I'd tried. Instead, I strode directly through the headlights, trying to make my body language say *I am a Good Samaritan.*

The truck was lying on the passenger side, with the cab partly blocking the driveway. The mud beside it was smeared with footprints.

Standing by the roof, I pulled myself up and peered into the open driver's window. There was blood on the steering wheel and a bloody handprint on the side of the door.

Then I noticed the front driver's-side tire. It was dead flat, and there was a finger-poke hole in the metal rim.

A skid mark stretched from the middle of the road to just a few feet away. Uphill was a long, gentle slope, very unlike the terrain we'd passed on the estate so far. The trees were scant on that part of the hill, and at the far top I could see the lights of a house.

I walked around the front. There were no dents in the grille, so it was clear there'd been no collision. At the bottom of the truck, I could feel the drive train still giving off heat. Gas dripped out of a small rupture in the plastic gas tank.

Catherine jogged up beside me. "This accident just happened," I said.

"Did you notice the color on the roof?" she asked.

I followed her around the truck. Now that she'd told me it was there, I saw it immediately—there was a dark circle just under two feet in diameter on the part of the roof next to the ground. I knelt close to it. The blue paint of the truck was nearly black there, although it was difficult to judge color accurately in the moonlight.

Was this circle fresh paint? I picked up a stick and poked it.

"Don't—" Catherine said, but she was too late. One tap against the circle caused the whole area to crumble to dust, leaving a hole in the roof.

I jumped back, careful not to get any dust on me. "Holy shit," Catherine said. "What did that?"

"I was going to ask you," I said.

She took a flashlight from her bag and shined it down onto the pile of dust. It looked like fine metal filings. She turned the beam of light into the truck. "I can't tell what I'm seeing in there."

I walked to the back. The third car parked behind it wasn't a BMW. Something about it caught my attention, but the headlights were bright and I was too focused on the truck to think about it. The truck's double doors were unlatched. One door hung across the opening. Half of a bakery logo was visible on it. The other door lay open on the uneven ground. It would have been convenient if the headlights of the third car had lit the interior of the truck, but it had been parked at the wrong angle for that.

Catherine joined me but kept well back from the open door. She knelt and shined her flashlight into the darkness of the truck. Right beside the opening was a car battery. Beyond that, I couldn't see much detail.

I didn't see or hear anything moving inside. I stepped onto the open door. It groaned and bent under my weight. I knelt below the other door, not wanting to touch it in case it made more noise, and I crawled inside.

Catherine followed. Her flashlight illuminated the contents well enough. Beside me was the car battery. Only one lead was still attached.

At the far end of the truck bed was a Plexiglas cube, three feet on each side. It was still bolted to the floor, which meant it was now midway up the side of the tipped-over truck. There was a broken battery mount on it, and each corner of the cube had a floodlight aimed toward its center. With the battery broken off, presumably by the accident, the lights had gone out.

"What the hell is this?" Catherine asked. Her voice echoed off the metal panels.

"A cage," I said. I remembered something Annalise had once told me: *Predators like to be summoned, but they hate to be held in place.* I moved closer to it. There was a discolored hole on the "roof" of the cage.

"Don't touch that, please," Catherine said. "I have to breathe the air in here, and I don't want a lot of plastic dust floating around."

"Good idea."

"It looks like we're too late," she added. "It looks like the owner of this truck won the auction, then had an accident while they were driving away. The battery mount broke, the lights went off, and whatever was inside escaped. Seem right to you?"

"Sure, except about the accident. That left front tire was shot out. You can see the bullet hole on the metal rim."

She nodded. I had the impression I'd passed the first IQ test. "Okay. If the gunfire has already started, then we should gather up what information we have and get out of here. But what do you think about these discolored holes?"

"I think I don't want to get in this predator's way."

She handed me the flashlight, then stepped outside. I could hear her texting someone, probably reporting to the society.

I shone the light around the enclosure. There were small stones at the front of the truck bed. I got down close and saw they weren't stones at all. I picked one up. It was half a dog biscuit.

I climbed out of the truck just as Catherine shut off her phone. "Well?"

"They'll be on their way as quickly as they can. It'll take hours, though. Probably not until tomorrow night or later. Did you find anything?"

"Just this." I held up the biscuit. She frowned at it.

"Weird. Do you think they fed a dog to the predator?"

"What are the odds that this predator eats doggy treats?"

She gave me a look that told me I'd failed my second test. She held out her hand and I gave her the flashlight. As she stooped below the hanging door to enter the truck again, she said: "No offense, but I'm going to check your work. I'm the investigator here."

She was? That was useful information. I'd never met a society investigator before, but I knew they were supposed to look into suspicious situations, file a report, and get out. It was up to the peers—and their wooden men—to do the fighting.

She was inside the truck for just a minute or two, but it seemed much longer. Someone was going to catch us here if we didn't move on soon.

I looked at the third vehicle and stopped short. No wonder it had caught my attention: it was a Maybach Landaulet, roof closed, naturally. Christ. Someone was rolling in the cash.

Finally, Catherine climbed out of the truck. "I have an idea," she said. She walked around the truck to the hole in the roof, then began searching the muddy slope. "Look."

She pointed to an indentation in the mud. It was perfectly round and flat, as if someone had tamped down the earth with a big soup can. There was another nearby farther up the slope, then another and another. They were spaced out like footprints, and there seemed to be a lot of them.

"Are there two predators?" I asked.

"Either that, or it had more than two legs. And look at this." She shone the flashlight onto a separate set of tracks, this time made by men's dress shoes. They headed up the small rise and over it, the men chasing the escaped predator.

"Which way do we go?" I asked. "Do we follow the tracks or continue toward the house?" I nodded up the slope at the house lights.

"Can the spell you used to cut the chain out front kill a predator?" she asked, her tone making it clear she didn't have that sort of weapon.

"It has in the past," I admitted. To push away the memories that statement churned up, I kept talking. "Whether it will work on this one or not, I don't know. I don't even know what we're facing."

"Neither do I," she said.

We trudged through the mud after the footprints. At the top of the rise we saw a long, even, tree-lined slope headed downward. And four bodies.

"Oh, shit," Catherine said as she backed away. I moved toward the dead men, more out of a sense of duty than common sense. Apparently, searching the dead wasn't part of an investigator's job.

The three men whose faces I could see—one was facedown in the mud—were Asian, and they were all dressed very well. They wore wool three-quarter-length coats and dark suits. One suit had pinstripes, which was a stylish touch. Their hair was neatly cut, and they were all closely shaved.

The nearest man had been shot in the side of the head from very close range. Two others farther down the slope had been shot in the chest; they lay on their backs, Glocks in their hands. The fourth man, the one lying facedown, had at least eleven exit wounds in his back and one in his neck. He also held a gun, but the slide was back. His gun was empty.

There was a little white mark on the side of his face. I crouched down to look at it more closely. It actually looked like the end of a mark, as though someone had rubbed bleach on his face with the pad of a thumb. It ran from his temple down toward his cheek; the rest, however much there was, was covered by mud. I could have seen more if I'd wanted to move the body, but I didn't.

He had a wallet bulging in his back pocket. It ruined the line of his suit, so I pulled it out for him and opened it up. It contained American greenbacks along with a number of foreign bills. There was an identity card, but it was written in some kind of kanji and I couldn't read it. The picture showed a very serious Asian man with a crooked nose but no white mark.

Damn. Seeing him with his eyes open, even if it was only on a driver's license or whatever, gave me a chill. Images swirled in my mind—food, laughter, booze pukes, fucking, boredom in line at the bank—all the memories I imagined would make up his life, all reduced to this lump of dead meat on a muddy hillside.

Catherine was watching me. I held the wallet open to her. "Can you read Japanese, or Thai, or whatever?"

She shook her head and folded her arms across her chest. I closed the wallet and slid it back into the man's pocket. I didn't take the money, not even the U.S. bills. I wasn't going to pick a dead man's pocket in front of Catherine.

"Who shot them?" she asked.

"I think they shot each other," I answered. "I'm no TV detective, but this dude was shot at close range, and . . ." I opened the first man's coat. His weapon was still in the holster. "Yeah, he didn't even get a chance to draw his gun. Those two were shot from farther away, and they have their guns in their hands.

"And this bastard is lying here with an empty weapon and a good dozen bullet holes in him. Are there more footprints going down the hill?"

Catherine went around the bodies. The starlight was pretty dim, but our eyes had adjusted. "Yes," she said. "But there are fewer of them."

"I think Mr. White Smudge here shot the others. The ones who killed him probably stood around *what-the-hell*-ing for a while, then took off after the predator."

"Wouldn't they want to carry their friends back to the car? Or call the cops?"

I shook my head. These guys had expensive suits and identical weapons. I figured them for somebody's hired muscle—a crew. I'd been part of a crew once. We'd done everything together, but we hadn't been friends. Not really.

I looked at Catherine. "Do you want to turn around?"

"Let's keep going," she said. "We decided to chase the predator, and this doesn't really change things, does it?" Her arms were still crossed. I didn't suggest she take one of the dead men's guns. Her body language made it clear what she thought of the idea. Besides, it hadn't done them much good. She glanced at White Smudge as though trying to figure out what had turned him on his buddies. Then she looked away.

We followed the footprints down the hill, through a stand of trees into a meadow. Some of the bark was scorched black as though from a fire. The damage looked months old, though, and the forest was rebounding.

The weird soup-can footprints didn't pass through any of the trees.

At least, there were no dark circles on the trunks. I wondered why the predator didn't take shortcuts through them. Were they too thick? Too alive? Something else? I had no idea.

"Look at this," Catherine said.

The soup-can footprints headed straight across open ground, then clustered together as though the creature had turned to face its pursuers. Then the trail split apart.

One set of prints continued ahead down to the meadow. Another went to the right. A third led off to the left. The shoe prints also split up to follow the three separate trails.

"It's not cloning itself, is it?" I asked. Catherine shrugged.

I followed the trail of prints to the right. After about five feet, they vanished.

Catherine waved to me. "The prints stop here," she said. She was standing about ten feet away on the trail that led to the left. A quick check showed the same thing on the center trail. After about five feet, it vanished.

The shoe prints milled around, then split up and led away in those three different directions. What the hell was going on?

"Maybe it cloned itself and flew away," Catherine said.

I felt goose bumps run down my neck. The night sky above me was empty, as far as I could see. It gave me the willies to think that the predator might have been above us all along.

"What do you think?" she asked.

"I think I don't want this thing to swoop down on me."

"I meant what do you think we should do next."

Was this another test? I looked around. By the starlight, I could see trees, underbrush, uneven ground, and far, far down the slope ahead I saw a single burning bluish streetlight. I reminded myself that I was here with an investigator. A peer would have hunted the predator to kill it—a single predator on the loose could, in the long run, lead to the extinction of life on this planet. Investigators, though, collected information for the peers.

Who would be getting here soon. I hoped.

"Well," I said, shrugging, "there's nothing to be learned wandering around out here. And I definitely don't want to come up on those gunmen by accident. I say we should check out the house."

She half smiled, then led the way back up the slope. For a brief moment I thought the four dead men were gone, having been carried off into the night sky by whatever we were following, or even worse, having gotten up and shambled off. Then I saw that they were just a little farther away than I'd thought.

No one had come to check on the cars. Catherine didn't want to drive her Acura any closer to the house, and I agreed. A strange car pulling up at this time of night would attract the worst sort of attention.

Catherine insisted we hike along the driveway rather than take the direct route across the estate, and after a half mile I was glad of it. The slope was not as smooth as it had appeared. We kept to the shoulder, watching ahead and behind for headlights. We were ready to dive into the trees at the first sign of a car, but none came.

We rounded a curve in the road and saw the house up close.

I'd certainly seen bigger. In L.A., all you have to do is drive along a freeway and look up; huge houses are scattered on the hillsides. But this house was huge and isolated and completely out of place. It was three stories tall, with a high, slanted roof and tall, narrow, arched windows like a church. It had chimneys like a porcupine had quills, and I couldn't imagine the kind of person who would look around at this isolated patch of rain forest and decide it was the place to build a mansion.

There was a garland in the front windows and nets of tiny multicolored lights draped over the bushes along the front. Someone had made the effort.

We ducked off the road into the trees, pushing our way through scattered blackberry bushes and scraggly ferns.

The grounds around the front had been cleared, and the road had been widened into a little parking lot with a wide section at the end, probably to give delivery trucks room to turn around. At the moment, the lot was filled with cars, all pointed toward the gate. I saw another BMW to match the one by the truck, a pair of black Yukons, a black Mercedes, and finally a Passat, of all things. At the far end of the lot the asphalt narrowed again into a path leading to a multicar garage.

I stared at the cars, searching for movement or a human shape inside. The X6 had to-go coffee lids on the dash, and the Yukons had bright red-and-white cards in the front windows, but otherwise they were empty.

I moved close to Catherine. "Do we circle around?"

"To where?" She pointed toward the near side of the house, where there were twenty-five yards of lawn separating the tree line from the building. There appeared to be even more space around back. "Do you see any people?"

"Yeah." I pointed toward the door, where a man in a heavy wool coat and a furry Russian hat stood just out of the porch light. I thought he was dressed too warmly for the weather, but I'd been jogging up a long hill and he'd been standing around. Still, bulky coats made me nervous.

"Crap." Catherine pulled me back from the edge of the hill to a stand of trees. When we were out of sight, she let go of me quickly, as if she was afraid I'd take it as a gesture of friendship. "We need photos of the license plates."

"What if they're all rentals, like the one down the hill?"

"I still want them," she said. "But what's more, I don't want to kill anyone. Not everyone we meet is going to be part of some plot to bring predators here to eat our spleens, and I would like to kill as few of them as possible. Can we agree on that?"

I stared at her. Had the society told her what I'd done? I felt a sudden flush of shame, but not for the people I'd killed. I hadn't killed any innocent bystanders. At least, I didn't think I had. Annalise may not have cared about collateral damage, but I had been more careful.

But I still felt ashamed, because I knew the society was, at the core, vigilantes. I believed they had good reason for doing what they did, but their day-to-day work was finding people and killing them.

And not only had I taken part, I'd been eager to drop everything to come on this job, eager for the adrenaline rush, and I couldn't honestly say I didn't know what we'd be doing.

And I liked Catherine. Her heart and her head were in the right place, and if she was a little weird and distant with me, well, she was right to be.

"Agreed," I said. Standing still in this wind was giving me chills. "Around the side?"

"Not this side," she said. "I'd rather enter from the garage, in case there are more plates to photograph there."

We circled around the property. The ground near the garage was thick with trees and brambles, which gave us more cover but also slowed us down. And we made more noise than I would have liked. There didn't seem to be anyone to notice.

We moved toward the side of the garage. There were no footprints in the mud. There was a single window in the wall, but it was dark. I hoped no one was inside, watching us approach.

The backyard was even larger and more open than the front. The ground still sloped upward, but it was mostly a gentle rise. A bungalow sat well away from the house, in the middle of the meadow. Heavy black power lines ran out to it from the main building.

A guesthouse for a home this large? Maybe there was no such thing as "big enough" for some people.

I led the way toward the back door of the garage. More than one trail of footprints went back and forth from the house, so I couldn't tell if someone was inside. Fair enough. I turned the knob and pulled the door open.

Very little light shone through the dirty windows, leaving the inside nearly pitch-black. Catherine handed me her flashlight, and I flicked it on. There were four cars parked here, all packed close. Right beside me was a fifteen-year-old Civic hatchback. Next to that was a white Audi SUV, a Q7, with tinted windows, then a long black Fleetwood—maybe a '54, but I'm not an expert on vintage cars. Beyond that was a modern sedan, but all I could see was the line of the roof and back windshield. Huh. Maybe the Civic belonged to a servant.

Catherine took a camera from her bag. She focused on the license plate of the Civic. A little orange light illuminated the back bumper, and she snapped a photo. The flash lit up the room.

I moved away from her, wishing she had waited—maybe the windows had curtains I could draw or something. I understood her urgency, though. The predator, whatever it was, was on the loose.

She went around the car to snap a photo of the front plate, too. I walked to the far end of the room. The sedan was a BMW 745i. All of the cars were empty, thank God. There were garden tools along the walls and ladders, canoes, and ski equipment up in the rafters.

Meanwhile, Catherine snapped the front and back plates of the Audi. I crouched beside the BMW to cut the fuel lines. If we had to run, it would be a huge help if the cars were disabled.

The back door clicked open. I dropped to the floor.

"Um, excuse me?" a man said. His voice was high-pitched and gentle. "Who is in here?"

"Nothing's getting stolen!" Catherine said, taking an angry tone. The change in her personality was startling. "I just have a job to do, so you go ahead and go back where you came from." She sounded so offended that I half expected him to apologize, but he didn't.

"Ma'am, I have to ask you to look at my hands."

Catherine's voice became low. "You put that gun away."

"Ma'am," he said, his voice just as gentle, "I purchased this weapon not knowing whether I would have the chance to use it. Frankly, I find the prospect thrilling."

"Now, you just wait a minute . . ." Catherine sounded less sure of herself.

I lifted myself off the floor and shifted position, peering under the fender. All I could see of him was a pair of khaki pant legs tucked into rubber boots. This guy wasn't with the Asian men we'd found out on the hillside, not in that footwear.

"I will not wait," he said. His voice was still high and soft, but there was a breath of excitement in it. "If you don't do exactly as I say, I will shoot you right now. Then I will drag your body into the woods. No one on the premises will care except me, and I will only feel the secret satisfaction of knowing exactly what I am capable of."

"Whoa, now," Catherine said. "I'm unarmed! The *Times* sent me."

"Put the camera down," the man said. I heard something being set gently on the trunk of the car. "Turn around."

It wasn't doing any good to look at this guy's shoes. I kept my feet in place to avoid scuffling against the concrete floor and walked my hands backward until I was in a crouch. I peeked through the windows of the BMW and the Cadillac. Catherine was moving very slowly. Behind her, I saw a man in an orange parka so thick it looked like it had been inflated.

I took out my ghost knife and held it across my body like a Frisbee. "I'm a journalist," Catherine said. "That's all. No need to freak out. I'm just a woman doing a job."

The man leaned her against the back of the SUV the way a cop would, but he didn't make her spread her stance. He stepped forward and patted her down, moving behind the blind spot by the Cadillac's back window.

Then I heard the unmistakable sound of a pair of handcuffs.

"You're not putting those on me," Catherine said, her voice rising in panic.

"Stay calm," the man whispered.

"You're not putting those on me!"

I had to step in whether I was ready or not. I stood. The man in the orange coat started to turn toward me as I threw my ghost knife. He raised his pistol. At the last moment, the ghost knife swerved into it, cutting through the metal and the gunman's hand.

He gasped and staggered against the wall. Tools rattled as he bumped into them. The pieces of the gun fell to the floor. I *reached* for the ghost knife again, calling it back to me. It flew into my hand as I came around the back of the BMW. Before I could get there, Catherine spun and hit him with an elbow just below his ear.

The man staggered but didn't fall. I hissed at Catherine to make her stop. She did. A moment later I was beside the man, examining his hand. As usual, there were no cuts or blood—the ghost knife hadn't cut him physically.

"I'm sorry," he said. His high, soft voice was full of regret. "Holding that weapon—I should never have let that power go to my head. How awful for you, ma'am."

Good. The ghost knife had done its job. All his hostility and willpower had been cut out of him. The effect was only temporary, but there was a lot I didn't know about it—such as whether a beating would bring him back to himself.

"I'm tremendously sorry," he said again.

Catherine looked at me in disbelief. She shifted her stance, bumping something metal with her foot. I shined the flashlight on it, confirming that it was half of the gun. It looked like an old .45. She stared at it, then back at me. Guess she had never seen a ghost knife at work before.

"You can make it right," I told the man. "Start by lying down and spreading your arms. And tell me your name."

"Okay," he said as he did it. He didn't even sound afraid. Only contrite. "My name is Mr. Alex."

I searched him. His wallet gave his full name as Horace Alex and listed an address in New York State. He was a long way from home. He had keys to a rental car, house keys, a small backup gun, a fat Swiss Army knife, a cellphone, a little paperback book written by somebody named Zola, a spare clip for his .45, and a pack of gum. I dropped all of it into a plastic bucket.

He wasn't local, and he certainly wasn't working for the man with the Maybach. Now it was time to find out who he was.

"What are you doing here, Horace?" Damn if I was going to call this guy *Mr.* anything.

"I saw the camera flash and came to investigate."

"Why are you here, though, so far from home?"

"Several of the Fellows put together a kitty for the auction, but it wasn't enough." The way he said *Fellows* made it sound like a title, not a group of friends. "The bidding topped forty-two million very quickly, and we were left behind."

Catherine leaned down toward him. "What were you bidding on?" Her manner had changed again. Her voice was low and friendly, and her body language mirrored Horace's. She had become a different person.

"Some sort of creature from the Deeps. Only Professor Solorov was allowed to go up the hill to see it."

"The professor's full name?"

"Elisabeta Solorov."

"What about the other bidders?" Her voice was soft; it invited answers.

"I'm sorry, but there were no introductions, formal or otherwise. There was a Chinese fellow who spoke Cantonese. He won the auction and left a short while ago. There was also a fat, scruffy-looking Silicon Valley man who looked completely out of place. Finally, there was an extremely unpleasant old man who spoke German. That's all I know about them."

"Why didn't you leave when the auction winner left?" I asked.

"The rules state he gets a two-hour head start, then the rest of us can go."

"Does anyone know you've come in here?"

"No."

Catherine wasn't finished with him. "Did you hear anything about the creature? Was it big, small, furry, scaly?"

"I'm sorry," he said. "Professor Solorov will certainly tell us about it privately, but we haven't had a private moment yet."

"Fair enough. How many people are inside?"

Horace turned thoughtful. "Each bidder was supposed to come with no more than five people, but our party consisted of seven. Several Fellows refused to contribute to the kitty if they couldn't come along. I thought it was bad form to bring so many, but the gentleman from Hong Kong brought twelve. The German brought only two employees, and the fat Californian brought a single bodyguard. The hostess has only one servant that I saw and, of course, the handler. Plus the hired security men in those brown uniforms."

Catherine and I looked at each other. We hadn't seen any security. If we didn't count uniformed guards or the winning bidder, there were fourteen people, with the possibility of more servants. Great. I didn't care how big the house was, that was too many people for us to go wandering around the grounds. Someone was bound to look out a window and spot us.

I picked up the handcuffs. Catherine put her hand near my elbow but didn't touch me. "How did you find out about this auction?"

"Professor Solorov met with a man while she was in Los Angeles. Not the fat Silicon Valley person. He told her about the auction, and she brought the news to us. We were very excited. Forty-two million dollars is a lot of money for our group. Too bad it wasn't enough."

"What group?" Catherine asked.

"We call each other 'Fellows' but don't have a name," Horace answered. "We don't even have a charter. We're a social group with a common interest."

"Interest in what?" Catherine asked before I could jump in with the most likely guess.

"Magic."

That would have been my guess. Before I could respond, Catherine asked another question. "Do you have spell books? Artifacts?"

She was deliberately blocking my questions. What the hell. She was the investigator. I backed off to let her do her thing.

"No," Horace answered. "None. All we ever do is read magic theory and case reports. None of us have seen a creature of the Deeps, and we certainly haven't done any magic."

"Theory? What books?"

Horace began to recite a long list of titles. I couldn't follow them, but Catherine seemed intensely interested. She had her cellphone in hand. She was probably recording him. "There are some others I'm forgetting," he finally said.

Catherine asked where the books were kept, and he gave an address in a town I hadn't heard of. Then, at her request, he listed the other Fellows. They were just names to me, and I couldn't remember them.

When that was over, I looked at Catherine to see if she was finished. She only shrugged. "Okay, Horace," I said. "On your feet." I lifted him and handcuffed him behind his back.

The rear door of the Caddy was unlocked, and the seat was spacious. I loaded Horace inside, then emptied his backup revolver and tossed it into the nose of a canoe in the rafters. I slid the tip of the ghost knife through his ankle and told him to get some sleep. He thanked me and closed his eyes.

When I turned away from him, Catherine was standing very close. "What do you have there?"

I slipped the ghost knife into my pocket. "A spell."

"It made him answer all our questions. He didn't hesitate at all."

"Yeah," I said. "He also didn't want to kill us anymore."

She laughed a little. "That's a good thing, too. Okay. I think you should give that to me." She held out her hand.

"Um, what?"

"That spell. You should give it to me and show me how it works. I'm the investigator here, and that thing could really help me with my job."

"This is my spell," I said. "I cast it."

"I understand." She didn't pull back her open palm. "But you can see that this would be for the best."

I was surprised that she would even ask this of me. "It's my spell," I said again with more emphasis. "I cast it myself. It's pretty much a part of me. You might as well ask for my thumb."

"Oh." She let her hand fall to her side. "Is that how it is?"

"Yeah. You didn't know?"

"I'm just an investigator. People with spells don't usually explain anything to me."

"Let me explain this much, then: I can feel this spell like it's a part of my body. I don't know how to explain it better, but it feels like it's alive. And it's mine."

I could see that she had more questions, but all she said was "Thank you."

"Did you get all that," I asked, "with the list of books and people?"

When she answered, her voice was low. "Yes, but we don't need it. The society has a mole in their group. That's how we knew about the auction. I was just testing him to see how compliant your little spell made him."

Sure, now that she knew she couldn't have it, it was a *little spell*. "How do we find this mole? Maybe he can give us better information."

"He's not here, unfortunately. Not only did he give us this information at the last possible minute, he's gone into hiding. Probably ice fishing in Canada or something."

"So, this group without a name—"

"The Fellowship."

"Okay. This Fellowship: What do we do about them?" I wasn't sure whether the society wanted to dig into their secrets or if they wanted us to keep our hands off in case they flushed out their rat.

"Just don't kill them all," she said, her voice tight. Apparently, that was all she had to say.

She finished photographing the license plates, then we followed the path Horace had made in the mud to the house.

Catherine pulled herself up and peeped into a window. "Empty," she said. "Let's go."

She hurried to the back door. I saw a keypad on the wall and a sign announcing which security company would send a car if the alarm went off. Luckily, Horace had propped the door open with a hand truck.

She went inside and I followed. I didn't like it, but I followed. The oppressive warmth and bright lights made me feel like I'd been captured already.

"This way," Catherine said. She moved the hand truck quietly against the wall.

She led me through a mudroom into the kitchen. We passed a gas grill, a fridge that had a door larger than my bed, and a long stainless steel counter.

"There." Catherine hurried into the pantry and began inspecting aprons hanging from hooks. When she reached a white, double-breasted jacket, she yanked it down and held it against my chest. "Put this on. It'll let you get close enough to these guys to do your mind-control thing."

I stripped off my jacket and gave it to her. "It's not mind control, you know. All it does is make them sorta docile. They get all apologetic if they've been trying to kill me, but that's it."

"What if they're not trying to kill you?" She grabbed a tray off a metal rack and placed a plate on it. "What if you just need information from them?"

"I tried that," I answered. "But only once. I didn't like the results."

I pulled on the white jacket. It was too small; my wrists and shirt-tails stuck out. She picked up a silver tray, and then we heard footsteps. I slapped the light switch off, and Catherine swung the pantry door until it was just open a crack. She peeked through the opening, and I joined her.

At first we could only see an empty kitchen. We heard a rattling doorknob and a woman cursing under her breath, then she hurried into view. She was at least seventy, hollow-looking, with long, stringy hair. Her nightgown was dingy and speckled with food. It looked like she hadn't bathed in a long time.

Heavier footsteps followed her. She grabbed a ladle and held it in both hands. I didn't think she had the strength to hurt a squirrel, but she looked enthusiastic. "Keep away!" she said. Her voice had an air of lost authority.

Then the man she was warning off stepped into view. He was about thirty-five, with the pouchy face of a hard drinker. He wore sloppy nurse whites and had just enough muscle to push around old women.

"Regina," he said with warning in his voice, "you know better than this."

"You keep away," Regina said, her voice high. "You're fired!"

"Regina, if you come peacefully—"

She swung the ladle, hitting him on the fat part of his shoulder. The blow didn't have enough force to dent a stick of cold butter, but the nurse bared his teeth. "How many times do I have to teach you this lesson?" He snatched the ladle out of her hand and tossed it clattering into the sink. Regina cowered, but he wasn't in a merciful mood. He grabbed her wrist and pinched the skin of her upper arm viciously. Regina's face contorted with pain, her mouth making a silent *oh oh oh* as she tried to slump away from him toward the floor.

Cold revulsion flooded through me and rekindled a fire that I'd been lacking for months.

Catherine must have sensed something because she held her hand in front of me, trying to keep me in hiding. Unfortunately, I wasn't made for investigating.

I pulled a skillet off a hook, not caring how much sound it made, and stepped forward. Catherine backed away from the door and let me pull it wide. She knew there was nothing to be gained by scuffling with me.

When the nurse noticed me, his smugness turned into astonishment. I charged at him. He shouted "Hey!" An instant later I was on him. He threw his hands up and flinched, but it was all instinct. Instead of swinging the skillet in a wide arc, which probably would have killed him, I jabbed with it, angling it between his elbows. It struck the side of his jaw.

He tumbled backward onto the floor. He was out like a light, and I felt no satisfaction in it.

Regina was still crouched beside the sink. I offered her my hand, and she looked at it as if it might burn her. She stood without my help.

More footsteps came toward us.

I offered her the skillet, and her eyes lit up. She took it gratefully. I put my finger to my lips and slipped back into the pantry.

Catherine had taken up a position behind the door. I left the door open just enough to peek out at Regina.

I heard people rush into the room. Regina raised the skillet over her head. "Don't come any closer!"

"It is all right, ma'am," I heard a woman say. "There is no need to be violent." I liked the careful way she pronounced every word.

Regina glared. "What have you done with Armand?"

"Not a thing, ma'am, I assure you," Well-Spoken Woman answered.

"Madam," a man's voice said. "May I approach this man? I fear he might be dead." He had a Russian accent.

"I hope he is dead." Regina still held the skillet high, but she was getting tired. A hiking boot and a gray pant leg entered my field of vision, but I didn't widen the opening to get a better look. "I hope he's as dead as a . . . as a . . ." She sighed and let the skillet fall against her shoulder. It was late and she was tired. "He always did things to hurt me."

"I'm sorry for that, ma'am," Well-Spoken said. "And who are you, if I may ask?"

Regina straightened up. "This is my house."

Someone else rushed in with the clicking footsteps of high heels. "Aunt Reggie, what have you done?" another woman asked. She had a high, harried voice and a slight southern drawl.

"I stood up for myself," the old woman said harshly.

"Oh, God, is he dead?"

"No," the man said. "He is unconscious and possibly has a broken jaw. He should be taken to a hospital."

"The two-hour grace period has not yet ended," Well-Spoken said. A woman stepped into view and took the skillet from Regina without kindness or cruelty. She was nearly thirty, with an orange tanning-booth tan. She wore a green suit with touches of gold at the lapels and cuffs. Something about her put me off. "She's right," she said. She was the one with the drawl. "It'll be another half hour before anyone can leave. We have to give Mr. Yin's truck the head start we promised."

They don't know. They don't know that, just a mile away, the truck was on its side and the predator was on the loose.

The gray pant leg and shoe moved out of my field of vision. "And if he dies?" Mr. Accent asked.

"Then his family will sue us." The niece turned to Regina. "Aunt Reggie, let's get back to your room. Please. I don't have time for this right now."

"What about Armand?" Regina asked as she let herself be led away. "What do all these people have to do with Armand? I want to see him! Why won't you let me see him?"

Her voice receded, and a man I hadn't heard before said something in a language I couldn't identify. His voice was harsh and low.

"There's no need to be rude," Well-Spoken said. "But I agree. The old woman can also identify us to the police."

The harsh voice spoke again. Was it German? The woman answered in the same language.

The Russian man cleared his throat. "I do not like the idea of killing a sick old woman. If it is necessary, of course I will do it, but she is very like my own grandmother. Why would we need to kill anyone? There is nothing illegal here."

The harsh voice answered with a short remark.

"I agree." Well-Spoken was still cool and relaxed. "It is one thing for us to know what was sold here, but the woman could raise an outcry, especially if she regained part of her fortune. I would hate to attract the wrong kind of attention."

The harsh voice again. Well-Spoken answered him: "Perhaps not, but they could harm *us*."

"We would also prefer not to attract the wrong kind of attention," the Russian said. "But I still do not like the idea of murder."

"Security has been inadequate from the moment we arrived," she said, ignoring the man's comment. "For instance, there is also the problem of Mr. Kripke."

"Yes," the Russian said. "He and the group he represents are not discreet."

The German man spoke. The woman sighed and answered: "I'm afraid I must say the same. Unfortunately, I must leave soon to meet Mr. Yin. Neither of us can linger long enough to take care of him." I wished one of them would step into my line of sight, narrow as it was. I wanted a good look at anyone who talked that casually about murder.

The Russian sighed. "We will do it. No one will find the body. But in exchange, we spare the old woman. This is America—no one will listen to her."

"Acceptable," Well-Spoken said. A pale man in a long scarlet ski jacket arrived. He was as tall and crook-necked as a stork. I figured him for one of Horace's Fellows. He lifted the nurse's legs. Unseen hands helped him carry the man away.

Then a man stepped into my view. He wore heavy canvas pants with a leather jacket. His hair was blond and wispy and his skin pale. He had the face of a man who'd taken a lot of beatings and the expression of one who'd given out even more.

But that wasn't what made me catch my breath. He had tattoos just like mine on his hands, neck, and even his face. I could see that they went up his sleeve, down his collar, and under his hairline. He didn't look like part of—what had Well-Spoken called him?—Yin's crew of pin-striped gunmen. But who was he with? Was he the German voice, working for the "extremely unpleasant old man"? Kripke's bodyguard turned traitor to his boss? Or was he one of the Fellows? I hoped he was part of the Twenty Palace Society. Or even—what had Catherine said?—an ally. I didn't like the look of him and didn't want him as an enemy.

He stared at the pantry door, his expression alert and calm. I knew he wouldn't be able to see me—the room was too dark and the gap too small—but then it occurred to me that I was assuming he had everyday human eyes. If one of those marks gave him X-ray vision or something, I was in for a fight.

Someone's cell began playing Mozart. I heard Well-Spoken answer it in a language I didn't recognize. Some kind of Chinese, maybe? Horace had said Mr. Yin spoke Cantonese, so maybe that was it. After a delay, she said: "My employer wants me to speak with our hostess. If you'll excuse me."

I heard her walk away. The tattooed man walked away too. I waited, listening to the silence. Tattoo hadn't acted as though he'd seen me, but maybe he had a great poker face. Maybe he was going to another room to get a shotgun.

Catherine came toward me, her eyes widened as if to ask *Are they gone?*

"I guess so," I said. No one heard me. No one shouted *Hey* again. I opened the pantry door on the empty kitchen.

Catherine slapped my shoulder. It wasn't a playful tap, but it wasn't meant to hurt, either. "Dumbass," she said. She kept her voice low. "You nearly got us killed for that old woman."

"Maybe so."

"Definitely so. I understand the impulse, boy, but bigger things are at stake here."

I didn't like being called *boy*, and I didn't need to be reminded of the stakes, but there was no edge to be gained squabbling over it.

Catherine wanted me to eavesdrop on Well-Spoken Woman's conversation with the host while she got into position to take photos of the bidders as they left. We agreed to meet in an hour at her car. If one of us didn't make the meeting, we would meet at nine A.M. in the parking lot of the post office in the town below. My flannel jacket didn't go with the white servant's coat, so Catherine promised to bring it to the car.

"Don't get killed" was the last thing she said before she left.

CHAPTER THREE

I had NO idea where Well-Spoken was going, but I knew how to follow voices. I picked up the silver tray and left the kitchen.

The halls had dark paneling and were hung with landscapes of sunny places thousands of miles away. The floor was hardwood with a strip of burgundy carpet down the center. The carpet had been plush once but had been worn thin down the middle and dotted with faint brown stains.

I walked quietly but not sneakily. I still had the too-small servant's jacket on. It would probably fool anyone who didn't actually live or work here, and I hoped that was good enough. I held the tray in front of me to hide my shirttails.

Well-Spoken Woman and the Russian had talked about *attracting the wrong kind of attention,* and I knew they were talking about me. They wanted a predator; the Twenty Palace Society kills people who have predators.

And while I'd killed people, I'd always known who I was killing and why they deserved it. I tried to picture myself kicking open the pantry door and shotgunning those strangers, but I couldn't. That wasn't me.

The corridor ended at a T intersection, and as I approached, a small group of people walked by. The man in front was the tall man with the stork neck who'd carried the nurse by the legs. Behind him was a blond woman of about fifty with salon hair and makeup. Two more men walked at the rear. Both were balding, one short and skinny, the other short and fat. Both had big square glasses and porn-star mustaches.

The men were dressed like Horace—they had ugly winter coats and cheap boots. Stork Neck was wearing rubber galoshes, and between the three of them, their haircuts couldn't have cost more than fifteen bucks.

The woman was different. She wore a stylish brown leather coat that reached to mid-thigh. Her boots were also leather and trimmed with fur. In the seconds I had to look at her, she gave the impression of being very carefully put together, very exacting and self-aware. She drew my attention the way the men with her did not.

Was this Well-Spoken Woman? The three men were obviously Fellows, but—

The woman and the two mustache guys glanced at me. They saw my servant's jacket and looked away. I was invisible. I was help.

When I reached the intersection, I had the choice of turning right and following them or turning left toward the direction they'd come from. To the left was a pair of heavy doors, both shut tight. I didn't know what was behind them. I turned right.

Ahead of me, Stork Neck's party turned left. I hustled after them and peeked around the corner just in time to see them file into a room.

I walked to the door. The woman was speaking, and her voice was deeper than the one I'd eavesdropped on from behind the pantry door. She wasn't Well-Spoken Woman after all. "It's a surprisingly small library," she said. She had an accent like a Kennedy.

A man's thin, nasal voice answered: "But the quality is excellent, if you are interested in road building, Bigfoot, or Ayn Rand. Otherwise—"

"Now," the woman said.

I heard the rustle of clothing and peeked around the edge of the door. The woman stepped backward, allowing the Mustaches to pull sawed-off double-barreled shotguns from under their puffy coats. They pointed them at two men seated in the corner. One was a pudgy young guy with Larry Fine hair, and the other was a huge-bellied biker in riding leathers.

The biker looked startled, then let his hand creep toward the waistband of his pants. Something he saw in the expressions of the Mustaches changed his mind. Stork Neck came up behind him and patted him down.

From my position, I couldn't see Larry Fine's expression. "What the hell are you doing?" he said.

Fat Mustache answered him: "The other bidders here have asked us to kill you both." He was the Russian-speaker. I'd followed the wrong party.

"You can't do that!" Larry Fine blurted out.

"Of course I can," the woman answered. Her voice was mild. Stork

Neck removed a little revolver from the biker's belt. "However, I'm tempted to let you live, if you cooperate."

I crossed the doorway to have a better view. No one saw me. They were all paying very close attention to one another. Larry Fine had a look of blustering outrage, as though he had been told he couldn't have nutmeg in his latte. "This doesn't even make sense—"

"Don't be dense, Mr. Kripke. You did not come here to purchase this creature. You don't have the cash to bid or the resources to hold it."

"I didn't expect the price to start so—"

"Shut up," she said. Her tone wasn't harsh or angry, but he did it. "You came here to gather information for your little electronic circle of friends. You plan to put our names and descriptions into your database. Don't bother to deny it."

His mouth worked while he decided whether to take her advice. "You're wrong and you're right. I would have bought the creature if the price hadn't been so high, just like you. I'm also planning to make a record of everything I've seen, Professor Solorov, also just like you." Kripke had an edge of contempt in his voice, as though he didn't think they had the guts to kill him.

Biker looked uncomfortable and edged away from Kripke. I could tell he took the threat seriously, and so did I.

The ghost knife was still in my pocket, but I couldn't use it. Both Mustaches had their backs to me, and I couldn't see their guns. My spell would pretty much hit whatever I wanted it to, but I couldn't hit what I couldn't see. I also expected them to have backup weapons. Horace did.

I could have targeted the men rather than the weapons, of course, but I couldn't hit all of them together. Someone would have time to squeeze a trigger, and I wasn't protected well enough to survive a shotgun blast.

"Perhaps we will," Solorov answered. I wondered if she said *we* when her gunmen weren't around. "But there are crucial differences. First, we know everyone we will share this information with personally. Second, we brought more guns. You." She spoke to Biker for the first time. "You're his friend, correct? He didn't hire you as a bodyguard; he asked you to come along, right?"

"Right," Biker answered. His voice was hoarse.

"We thought so," she said. "We're going to split you up, but we're willing to spare your lives if you *both* cooperate."

Kripke let out a dismissive puff of air. "I wouldn't join your group if you—"

"I didn't say you could *join* us," Solorov said sharply. "You can *work* for us. I know someone has been feeding you information—recent information. If you share it with us—all of it—and if you report to your group in exactly the manner I indicate, you and your friend may survive."

Kripke looked over at Biker. The look on his friend's face drained all the insolence out of him. He nodded.

"You're lucky, Mr. Kripke, although I doubt you have the wit to see it. If Mr. Yin had been asked to get rid of you, two of his men would have walked in here, shot you both, and left you dead on the floor. And that crotchety German bastard would have cut you open and *eaten you*. At least I—and the rest of the Fellows, of course—have given you a chance to live and be useful."

Stork Neck and Skinny Mustache waved at Biker. He stood. They were leaving.

I slid away from the door as quietly as I could. There was one other door in the hall, but it was locked. The rattle of the latch sounded as loud as an alarm bell. I hustled away, holding the tray in my left hand.

The corridor ended at a door with a dead bolt. I didn't bother to rattle the knob. To my right was another mudroom and a door into the backyard. To my left was a flight of stairs. I walked up the steps.

The library door clicked shut. At the top of the first landing, I heard Biker's hoarse voice say: "You guys don't have to kill me, you know."

"We know." I didn't recognize that voice.

"You . . . you wouldn't really do it, though, right?" I could hear the question in Biker's voice: *Are these guys really killers?* "Have you ever done this before?"

"I wanted a monster," a new voice said. It sounded high and thin, as though the speaker was under terrible strain. "I came here to get a monster, but we weren't fucking rich enough. Do you know how long I . . ." He let that sentence trail off as though he was swallowing all his disappointment and resentment. I wouldn't want to be on the ugly end of his gun.

"We won't do anything we don't have to do," the first man said calmly.

They went outside. I climbed the second flight and came to a huge back window. Through the drapes, I saw Stork Neck and Skinny Mustache lead Biker toward the woods, away from the garage.

According to Horace, the guesthouse was where the predator had been kept. That was my next stop.

There was a muffled *chunk* of a slamming car door. I crossed toward the front of the house. The nearest door was unlocked and the room inside was filled with furniture covered with white sheets, just like in the movies. The musty smell made me wrinkle my nose.

More heavy drapes hung over the windows at the front of the house. Each window was taller than my apartment. I pulled the drape open a crack. The X6 backed up, trying to make its way through the crowded lot. When it was as close to the door as it was going to get, the guy in the furry Russian hat climbed out of the driver's seat and hustled around the front. He opened the back door like a chauffeur.

A small woman slipped into the backseat. From above I didn't have the best view of her, but I saw that her very dark hair was parted severely down the middle and curled into a librarian's bun. She had a dark complexion and wore a gray suit.

The chauffeur closed her door, got behind the wheel, and sped off. If she was leaving before the others, she worked for Mr. Yin, which meant she was the Well-Spoken Woman who was so casual about asking other people to kill for her. I hoped Catherine was in position to snap a photo.

I mentally ran through the list of bidders Horace had given us: Yin's people were all out on the hillside hunting for the predator. I hadn't seen Yin himself, only his gunman and Well-Spoken Woman, who was his representative. Kripke and his biker bodyguard were accounted for and not doing very well. I'd seen Professor Solorov and about half of her mismatched, badly dressed Fellows; on their own, they didn't impress, but their guns were dangerous enough.

And there was Tattoo, who had to be the German with the harsh voice. I didn't like the look of him, especially since Horace had said he was one of the "old man's" people. The professor had said the old man would have eaten Kripke, and based on previous experience, I knew there was a good chance she meant it literally. I didn't want to meet that old man.

That meant I'd had at least a glimpse of each of the four groups of bidders. Hopefully, what I'd learned would be useful to the society.

I went back into the hall and heard the faint jabbering of a radio. I peered into the darkness and noticed a tiny sliver of light shining from under a door. I had a hunch I knew who was behind that door, and if I was right, the guesthouse could wait.

"I can hear you out there!" Regina shouted. "You can't fool these old ears."

Fair enough. I opened the door and went inside.

The bright light hit half a second before the smell. Who ever brought Regina up here hadn't expected her to sleep. Maybe they didn't care. Three halogen lamps filled the room with an acid-yellow light—there was no way to nod off in here without a blindfold.

The room also stank of unwashed bedpans, sweat, and neglect. My initial impulse was to flee back into the musty shadows of the hall.

"I know," Regina said. I guess I wouldn't have made much of a poker player in that moment. She switched off a small transistor radio on the bed beside her. Her niece had buckled her left wrist to a bolt in the frame. She was still wearing the dirty nightgown, and I wished she would pull it down over the black-and-blue patches on her legs. They gave me goose bumps. "It sickens me, too. Just be glad you don't have to live this way."

"I am. My name is Ray."

"I'm Regina Wilbur. When I was a girl, my father would have had you thrown out of this house for introducing yourself to me. You'd have left with a muddy boot print on your derrière."

"Things have changed," I said, for lack of anything more profound to offer.

She rattled the short chain on her restraint. "So they have. What have you done with Armand?"

"I'm sorry, but I don't know who that is," I said, hoping it would prompt her to explain.

Instead, she sighed bitterly and looked around the room. "This house was mine once. My father built it with timber money. My husband built four more just like it all over the country, and one in the Italian Alps, too. He took my father's fortune and doubled it five times. Trucking lines, at the beginning, then tires and road building. He was a bastard, but most are. At least he had the decency to die young.

"But now Stephanie has taken it all, and the little bitch didn't even have the good manners to wait until I had dirt over my face. She's going to sell it, just like the ones in Carolina and Maine, so she can live in *California*." She said that word with special distaste. "All auctioned off! All the history here. All the gifts from politicians and people desperate to do business. Even from enemies who wanted my blessing . . ."

Her voice trailed off and she stared across the room. Her eyes were like dark river stones. The whole situation made me uneasy.

She seemed to have forgotten me. To prompt her, I said: "Was Armand one of those gifts?"

"Yes," she said, savoring the word like it was candy. "He was a gift from one of the most powerful and dangerous men in the world, Nelson Taber Stroud. Dead now, of course. He and I clashed over all sorts of garbage over the years, especially mining rights, but that changed once Armand arrived. Nothing else mattered after that. Armand was *everything*."

What is he? I wanted to ask. That seemed too direct. Regina may have been in a bad spot, but she was still sharp. And she hadn't asked for my help, hadn't even hinted that she wanted it. She was either tough as hell or completely crazy.

"It sounds like you loved him very much."

"You bet I did. I made sure Ursula kept his cage clean and stayed with him in his house. He was *loved,* and I made sure he knew it."

She looked at a nightstand loaded with pictures in silver frames. I circled the bed toward it. I had to move in front of a window, but the glass was so dirty that I wasn't worried about being spotted. The closest picture, though still out of her reach, was of a much younger Regina holding a Scottish terrier to her face. The dog wore a diamond necklace. "Is this Armand?"

She twisted her mouth in disgust. "That's the first Armand. Give me that."

I handed the picture to her. She snatched it with her free hand and flung it across the room. It smashed against a radiator with a noise I thought the whole house could hear.

Damn. Now I understood why it had been out of her reach. I slid my hand into my pocket next to my ghost knife, just in case someone came to investigate.

"That's what I think of that," she said with finality. She turned back to the other pictures.

Regina was much older in these. Every picture showed her crouching beside an empty Plexiglas cage similar to the one in the wrecked truck, only much larger. Flood lamps lit the interior, and the cage was spiderwebbed with electrical wiring.

But all I could see inside the cage was a blurry blue smear. Whatever it was, I couldn't make it out.

I looked at the other pictures. There were at least a dozen, all showing Regina posing with the empty cage. Her hair was longer in some pictures than in others, but she had the same creepy, ecstatic smile in each. Something about them bothered me, though. The smile was the same, but the expression was not. It seemed that the longer her hair was, the more ferocious her eyes became.

I studied the background of the images. They had been taken indoors; there was a couch, a ski jacket, and skis against the wall in one photo, a tiny stove in another. The space looked pretty cramped, and I guessed it was the guesthouse out back.

One picture showed a different woman who didn't smile at all, but her face glowed with smug contentment. She was younger than

Regina—maybe in her early fifties—with a pale, stolid look about her. Her eyes had the same fierce glint as Regina's.

"I can't see Armand. Was he in the cage when this was taken?"

"We didn't *cage* him," she snapped, forgetting that she'd already told me she kept his cage clean. "We kept him safe. But yes, he was there when we took those. He doesn't turn up on film. He isn't a regular animal, you know. He's special."

Now we were getting to it. "How is he special?"

"He is *beautiful*!" she cried. "He's the most beautiful thing on God's green earth. His eyes are like the stars of the Milky Way, and he's as delicate as thistledown. He's the only dog of his kind in the world. A sapphire dog, Stroud called him. He's as beautiful as a dream at twilight. Like holding the sky in your arms."

I wondered how she could hold the sky in her arms while it was inside a plastic cage, but it didn't seem polite to argue. "That's a pretty way to describe him."

She waved my comment away. "I didn't write it. Some college professor did. I held a poetry contest years back to find someone to capture Armand's *essence,* if you know what I mean. The winner had retired up here from some southern university to start a winery, and he won the cash prize hands down. Then I invited him to the house.

"He didn't think much of writing a poem about some rich broad's dog until he met Armand, of course. Then he fell in love, just like anyone would. He spent six months here, sleeping on a cot, watching Armand—staring at him. What I said before is all I remember of the poem he wrote. You'd think it was sap if you'd never *seen.*"

Her tone had changed. Something told me I should probe further. "What happened?"

"He refused to *leave,*" she answered, her mouth twisting with anger. "He even told me that he loved Armand more than I did. That I wasn't 'sensitive' enough to appreciate him. Ursula had to taser him to keep him from breaching the cage. Hah! I appreciated Armand enough to take care of that old fool."

The way she said that gave me a chill. "What did you do?"

She bared her teeth. "I . . ." Then she stopped. It was pretty clear that she'd been about to confess to a crime. "Well, I paid him off," she said, in the least convincing way possible. "Also, I had the sheriff run him out of town. Out of the country, actually. He'd committed a crime against me, stolen books out of my library, if you have to pry. I warned him that I was going to call the police the next day, and he was gone before morning. To Canada, maybe. Or Fiji. That's all and nothing more."

She lifted her nose and looked away from me. Most people are terrible liars, but she was the worst I'd ever met. She could contradict herself all in one breath. "I'm not a cop," I said. "I'm not going to arrest you. You killed him, didn't you?"

"Yes," she said, smiling at me with open contempt. "Yes, of course I did. I knifed him and pulled him out into the woods on a big old sled all by myself." She looked at me as if she might like to cut me open and gulp down my heart. "And I'll do the same to anyone who tries to come between me and my Armand."

"Is that right?"

"It is. It's very right. And don't lie to me—I'm not fooled by that big silver tray and that tiny jacket. I know you're one of the people that bitch brought here to buy him. Stephanie doesn't understand. She's never been close enough to really see, to really *feel it*. But if I thought you had my Armand, I'd cut your pathetic little johnny off and stuff it down your throat until you choked on it!"

I nodded. I had gotten the message. Of course, if she found out what I really wanted to do to her pet, she'd come apart at the seams. The bidders only wanted to buy him.

The urge to throttle the miserable life out of her made my hands shake. I went into the hall, closed the door, and walked away. It wasn't my place to put people out of their misery or dish out punishment for old crimes. I wasn't pure as snow myself. Besides, no matter what she'd done, I didn't want to see the expression she'd made when the nurse had pinched her.

I went back to the stairs. Voices echoed up from the bottom floor, so I went farther down the hall to a narrow set of steps at the end. I paused at the top, but the only sound I could hear was a TV announcer droning away. I crept down.

There was a short hallway at the bottom of the stairs that led to an exterior door. There were also three interior doors, one of which was open. The announcer's voice and a flickering TV light came from there.

I looked around, wondering how I was going to pass that open door without alerting whoever was inside.

An old woman in a maid's uniform stepped into the doorway and stared at me. She glanced at my white jacket with contempt; she wasn't fooled for a second.

While I considered what I should do, she rolled her eyes and shut the door. Apparently, she wasn't being paid to be security.

I walked to the exterior door. There was a dead-bolt key on a hook by the door, but I left it. As long as I had my ghost knife, I didn't need keys. I set the tray against the wall and went outside. After the musty warmth of the house, the cold made my skin feel tight on my face and hands.

The cottage sat at the top of the bare slope. When I crossed to it, I would be in full view of anyone looking out of a back window. I wished I had some cloud cover to darken the lawn; the thick black power line that ran from the house to the guesthouse cast a moon shadow on the lawn.

I jogged across the damp crabgrass. *He's the only dog of his kind in the world,* Regina had said. *A sapphire dog.* I wondered if she was being literal or if that was more rotten poetry. I still imagined something with wings.

Maybe it was a bad idea to imagine anything. Whether it had wings, was shaped like a dog, or was just a blue smear of light, I was going to have to destroy it. If I could. Better to keep an open mind.

A stairway of mortared stone led up the muddy slope. I jogged up. The cottage faced away from the main house, and all but one of the ground-floor windows were shuttered. I peeked inside. A desk lamp shone onto scattered papers and a closed laptop, but the room beyond was dark. I circled around.

There was a huge metal tank and a generator against the building. I rapped on the tank. It was nearly full. Regina had enough fuel to run that generator for weeks.

The front of the cottage was pretty much what illustrated fairy-tale books had taught me to expect. There was a heavy wooden door with an even heavier lintel. On either side was a window split into four panes with a window box underneath. At the far side of the building, I saw the front of a parked ATV.

By the floodlight above the door, I saw muddy footprints smeared on the stone walkway leading to the door. I knocked, then knocked again. No answer.

The door was locked. I slid the ghost knife between the door and the jamb, then put it into my back pocket. The door creaked open.

"Hello?" I called. The room was silent. I reached for a light switch, then stopped myself.

A ceramic tile hung on the wall just above the switch. It was about the size of my palm, and it was painted white with an emerald-green squiggle on it.

Out of habit, I glanced down at my hand. The squiggle didn't look exactly like the marks on me, but it was similar enough to make me nervous. I took out my ghost knife again and sliced through the tile.

It split in two, but even before it fell, the broken squiggle released a jet of black steam and iron-gray sparks. I jumped out of the doorway to avoid the spray.

A magic sigil can throw off a lot of energy when it's been destroyed.

After it died down, I stepped back into the room. Whatever that spell had been created to do, it was just a mess on the floor now. I flicked on the light.

The cottage was a single room with very little furniture. A narrow bed was set into the back corner with a small dresser beside it. Next to that was a narrow desk with a lamp still burning, and beside that was the tiny stove from Regina's photo. The shelf above the stove was filled with can after can of Dinty Moore beef stew.

I saw no TV, no stereo, no bookshelves, and no Charlie Brown Christmas tree strung with lights. There was one thing in here to occupy a person's attention.

A large Plexiglas cage was set into a recess in the floor. It was larger than the one in the truck, maybe five feet on each side. It, too, had powerful floodlights at four corners, all aimed inward. Tiny electric fans were set on opposite sides of the cage, one to blow in, I guessed, and one to blow out. The black electrical wires powering them were strung all around the Plexi and held in place with peeling yellowed tape. There was also a plastic hatch along one side with an additional light shining through it.

Hanging from the ceiling was a smaller Plexiglas cube that could be fitted to the hatch. I guessed it was a holding tank so the main cage could be cleaned.

But there was nothing in the cage that needed cleaning—no bowls, blankets, litter boxes, or squeak toys. There hadn't been any of that packed in the truck, either.

A rocking chair was set at the edge of the recessed section of floor. I imagined Regina sitting and staring into the cage.

The door banged open behind me. I spun. A woman was silhouetted by the floodlight. She was almost six feet tall, broad in the shoulders and hips and dressed head to toe in white ski gear. Her plump face was pale and puffy. It was Ursula.

I felt the edge of the ghost knife in my pocket. "Don't move!" she shouted with an accent I couldn't place. She extended her arm, and I realized she was holding a gun.

It was a Colt .45, very old, very intimidating, and very aimed at my head. Someone who knew more about guns would have aimed it at my chest, where I had protective tattoos. I didn't have any protection on my face.

"Put that away," I said, sounding much more calm than I felt. "I've come to offer you a job."

"Hands up!" she barked. "Take your hand out of your pocket slowly. It should be empty, or I will shoot. Yes?" Her accent was northern European—Swedish maybe. I left my ghost knife in my pocket and showed her my empty hands.

"How did you get in here without . . . ?" She glanced back at the wall and saw that the tile was gone. She didn't think to look on the floor. "Who are you?"

"You should hear me out, and quickly. I'm not kidding about that job."

"I think you are kidding. Even if you were not, I would never work for a man dressed as kitchen help. Besides, I already have a job. I will be traveling with Armand early tomorrow, and I do not have time to waste."

I smiled. "Armand isn't going to Hong Kong with Yin."

She smirked at me. "Do you know something I don't?"

"Everyone knows something you don't. Why don't you close that door? This jacket isn't worth a damn."

I held open the servant's jacket so she could see I was unarmed, then stripped it off and tossed it onto the top of the plastic cage. She stared at me in shock. Apparently, touching the cage was Just Not Done.

She entered and pulled the door shut. The latch didn't engage because I had cut it off. "This is my home," she said.

I felt a twinge of guilt at that. I had done a lot of rotten things and I'd broken my share of laws, but I didn't like scaring women. Not that she looked scared.

Too late now. "I'm sorry for barging in, Ursula," I said, trying to keep any genuine regret out of my voice. I didn't think she'd trust a sympathetic face. "I had to see this setup for myself. It's not much, is it?"

"What is it that you know that I do not?"

"That Asian fellow offered you a job, correct? To keep caring for Armand?"

She nodded. "Of course. I have cared for him for years. I am the expert."

"Well, he doesn't have Armand anymore."

Her expression didn't change. "What do you mean? Who has him, you?"

"No one has him, as of an hour ago. He's running loose on the mountainside."

Her expression still hadn't changed. I didn't like the way she was looking at me. It reminded me too much of Regina's flinty stare. "Why should I believe you?"

"Because I'm here." I sat in the rocking chair and didn't let my smile fade. "I wanted to see whether he came back here. This is his home, isn't it?"

"It has been for twenty-two years." Both of us stared into the empty cage.

"Do you think he will come back here eventually? His home doesn't look very comfortable."

"He does not need comfort. He is not like other kinds of dog. At first, we gave him chew toys and soft blankets, but he never bothered with them. He never ate, either. Never drank water. I'm not even sure he ever breathed . . ." Her voice trailed off. I wanted to keep her going.

"Never ate?" I prompted. "What kind of dog is he?"

"He is not a dog, of course. Not a real one. He is a spirit. We fed him with our love. That was all he needed."

We heard a pair of gunshots. They were far away, faintly echoing off the mountainsides. Maybe Biker wasn't going home after all.

"My God!" Ursula said. "Are they hunting him?"

"No one is going to shoot him, not when he is worth so much," I said. "It was probably—"

She turned toward me and raised the Colt. I threw myself and the rocking chair to the side as the gun went off. I rolled onto the floor, wondering if she'd hit me.

The ghost knife was already in my hand. I threw it.

The gun went off again, splintering the wooden floor. A moment later, the ghost knife sliced through the Colt's barrel and hammer. Then the spell passed through Ursula's shoulder.

Her ski jacket split open, but I knew the flesh beneath would be unmarked. The top of the pistol fell to the side, and the spring in the magazine flung the remaining rounds into the air. I *reached* for the ghost knife, and it returned to me, passing through Ursula's stomach.

She stared in amazement at the weapon in her hand. I relaxed a bit and checked myself for bullet wounds—I'd heard people could be shot but not feel it. I didn't find any blood. She'd missed. A little shiver ran through me; I'd been lucky.

I kicked the rocking chair away and felt it wobble. The gun or the fall had broken it. I rolled onto my knees.

The floorboards shifted. On impulse, I raised my arm just as Ursula body-slammed into me. I heard an electric crackle, then felt a sharp, burning pain on my biceps.

My whole body jolted as an electric current ran through me, making all my muscles fire at once. We hit the floor together, and the impact broke the connection. I twisted, reached up with my other arm, and caught her wrist.

She'd burned me with a stun gun, and if I hadn't raised my arm, she would have zapped me in the eyes.

Her face was close. Her teeth bared, her eyes wide with a killing urge. Damn. The ghost knife had passed through her. Twice. Why hadn't it worked?

I tried to push her off me, but she was too big and too strong. She raised herself up and put her whole weight behind the stun gun, forcing it toward my face.

I didn't have the strength to hold her off with just my left hand, and my right was numb and weak from the shock. She grinned at me, and I could see triumph in that smile.

I forced the stun gun to the side and heard it crack against the floor by my head. Ursula cried out and dropped it. I twisted against her, letting her body weight roll over me. She fell onto the broken rocking chair and hissed in pain.

I tried to get out from under her, but she lunged toward me, mouth gaping. I leaned away as she snapped at me, her teeth clamping down on my collar inches from my throat.

To hell with this. I put my knees against her hip and kicked. She fell back and I rolled away onto my feet.

Ursula grabbed the stun gun and lunged at me, arm extended. She was a big woman, but she was slow. I caught her wrist and pulled her toward me, knocking her flat on her stomach. I pinned her elbow and quickly knelt on her shoulder. Now she was the one without leverage.

"Damn," I said. "You're a pain in the ass." I wrenched the stun gun out of her hand. One of the metal leads was broken. I doubted it still worked. "Hold still, or I'll use this on you."

She didn't. The thick ski jacket made it tough to control her. If she didn't settle down, I was going to have to either let her go or hurt her. I laid the stun gun against the back of her neck and shouted at her to be still.

She answered in her native language, whatever it was. I couldn't understand, but I knew she wasn't asking how I take my tea. I tossed the broken stun gun away.

The ghost knife was nearby. I could feel it. I *reached* for it and it flew into my hand.

Ursula grunted from the effort of trying to throw me off. In a few moments she would have her knees under her and I'd have another fight on my hands.

I slid the ghost knife through the back of her head. She didn't react at all. The spell was supposed to "cut ghosts, magic, and dead things"; it could destroy the glyphs that sustained spells, cut through inanimate objects, and damage people's "ghosts." I didn't know exactly what that meant, but everyone else I had cut with it had stopped trying to kill me. Why didn't it work on Ursula? Did she not have a "ghost," whatever that was?

Ursula nearly bucked me off. She was still cursing at me, and I had no way to control her except by throwing punches.

I wasn't going to do that. I had fought in the street for the Twenty Palace Society. I had broken into homes and burned them to the ground. I had shot men in cold blood. But I wasn't ready to punch this woman.

She kept thrashing. "Let me go," she said, her voice vicious with rage. "I have to check on Armand."

"No one is going to hurt Armand, not if he's worth so much."

She kept fighting me. I wasn't getting through.

I was going about this all wrong. I leaned close to her and spoke quietly. "This isn't his home, is it? If it was, he'd have come back here as soon as he was free." She stopped struggling, although her breathing was still harsh. "I came here to see if he'd return to the people who loved him. But he won't, will he?"

A low moan escaped her throat. I kept talking. "You love him, I know you do. But now that he has his freedom, he's never coming back. He doesn't want to be your prisoner anymore. All these years you've kept him trapped in this little room, giving him your love, and now you know what he's always wanted."

She made a terrible, heartrending sound. It was the sound a mother might make over a dying child. I let her buck me off.

We both scrambled to our feet. She looked at me, her eyes brimming with tears. Then she looked at the Plexiglas cage, turned, and ran out the door.

I looked around one more time. The place made my skin crawl. I'd spent time in prison, but this disturbed me in ways I wasn't ready to think about.

I heard Ursula shouting outside. I hurried to the window. She was lumbering toward the house, screaming and pointing back to the cottage. Back to me.

CHAPTER FOUR

DAMN. I raced out the door. The tree line wasn't far, but I didn't want to run into the woods. Not when Catherine's car was in the other direction.

The ATV had a key in it. I grabbed a bungee cord from behind the seat and strapped the handlebars down. Then I started it up and sent it on its way.

As I came around the edge of the cottage, Ursula ran through the servant's entrance of the house and slammed the door behind her.

I sprinted down the hill toward the house. I had nearly reached the doorway, still stupidly planning to follow her inside, when the back light turned on. She had roused the house faster than I expected.

The corner of the building was just a few yards to my right. I ran around it and ducked out of sight, staying in the muddy tracks Biker and his two killers had made.

The only tool I had was my ghost knife, but I was pretty sure I could crack a steering column with it. Unfortunately, the cars in the garage were on the other side of the house. Horace had distracted me before I could disable them, but I couldn't get to them right now. I could have gone around the front, but if the guard at the main entrance had been replaced, that wouldn't turn out well.

I peeked around the corner. Six Fellows streamed through the back door, each carrying a shotgun. They fanned out across the yard, one particularly fat one moving toward me. Dammit. The ATV had overturned on a tree root across the yard; hadn't they noticed it?

I leaned away from the corner of the house. The tree line was not close enough for me to risk it, especially considering how much noise I'd make in the undergrowth. I'd end up like Biker, a rotting corpse with a bullet in my back. But there was a basement window at my feet. I dropped to my knees in the freezing mud and cut through the latch. The window opened toward me, but the gap was too narrow for me to fit through. The man with the shotgun would come around the corner at any moment. I cut both hinges and slid through the opening, pulling the frame in after me.

The basement was pitch-dark, except for the yard light shining through the narrow windows along the ceiling. I landed on something flat and solid. It didn't tip over and crash onto the floor. I pressed the window frame in place—it was upside down and didn't fit properly, but I tried to hold it absolutely still.

The fat man in the parka walked in front of the window. His puffy face was already red from the cold, but something in the way he scanned back and forth made me wary. He was calmer than the others. More in control.

Luckily, he was looking toward the trees opposite the house, not at his feet.

My ghost knife was in my back pocket, but I wasn't sure it would work on him any better than it had on Ursula. Was it running out of power, or did she have a protection spell? My ghost knife didn't *feel* any weaker, and it had cut the window readily enough.

Someone shouted, "There!" and the fat man trotted back toward the others. I blew out a long, relieved breath and fitted the window, carefully squeezing it into the jamb. A strong wind would knock it out again, but I planned to be long gone by then.

I climbed down to the floor. The low dresser I'd been crouching on had a white cloth draped over it. Each window was about ten feet from the next one, and by their faint rectangles I could see the shape of the room. It was obviously the size of the house above, but the weird silhouettes and broken shadows showed me it was full of clutter.

My eyes were not accustomed to the darkness, so I moved slowly, my hands guiding me around chair legs, discarded bicycles, and other junk I couldn't identify by touch alone.

At first I intended to go to the front of the building to steal a car, but I heard shouting from the back of the house and moved toward it.

The window closest to the back entrance was blocked by a tangle of what appeared to be broken garden equipment, but the next one over had two steamer trunks stacked beneath it, along with a pile of lacy dresses. I climbed onto them, probably ruining them with my muddy clothes, and peeked out the window.

There were shoes just a few feet from me. One pair were green Chuck Taylors, soaked through by the mud. Beside those was a pair of hiking boots fresh from the sporting goods store. The third pair was the professor's fur-trimmed leather boots. The man in the Chucks fidgeted back and forth but let himself be hemmed in by the other two. It was Kripke. It had to be.

Beyond them, I saw the two Mustaches marching across the open meadow toward the ATV. A third man was with them. He had a lean, hollow look and was dressed completely in cold-weather bicycling gear. He was another Fellow, I was sure. No one else would dress so badly.

I couldn't hear them. I slowly, quietly unlatched the window and eased it open.

"He had a gun," Ursula said. "He threatened to shoot me if I didn't tell him everything I knew about Armand." Just as she finished the sentence, she came into view, walking across the grass with Stephanie beside her, followed by the tattooed man and a frail-looking blond man I hadn't seen before. They walked toward the professor.

"Have you ever seen this man before?" Frail asked. He had a German accent, and his voice was high. Ursula shook her head. "Think carefully. You may have seen him in town or while running errands. Could he be a local?"

"No, he—" Ursula began, but Stephanie interrupted.

"Where are the goddamn guards? I hired a security team to protect the grounds. Where are they?"

"Ms. Wilbur," Solorov said. "Shut up. We have questions to ask."

"Don't you tell me to shut up! I *paid* them. Now I find that they all ran home to their mommies! I'm going to sue them for so much money—"

"Shut up, Ms. Wilbur, or I will have you shot," Solorov said. Stephanie gaped at her.

I heard an old man's wheezing laughter. They stopped and glanced back as he shambled into view. He wore a bulky black coat and a black fur cap with the earflaps down, and he leaned on a gnarled black cane that had been heavily carved. A pair of black bird-watching binoculars hung around his neck. Frail rushed to him and gently took a black leather satchel from his hand.

I realized I was staring, just as the others were. There was something arresting about him, although he appeared completely ordinary in every way.

Frail walked beside the old man as though he was ready to catch him, but he continued his questioning. "Please, explain why you are so sure he is not a local."

"It was the way he spoke," Ursula said. Her tone was flat. "Some things he said. He said Mr. Yin didn't have Armand anymore. He said that Armand had escaped."

"That's a lie," Stephanie blurted out, apparently forgetting the professor's threat. "I just spoke with Mr. Yin ten minutes ago, and they are en route without incident. He must have been trying to trick you." The contempt she held for Ursula was clear.

"What did he look like?" Frail asked.

"He was a little over six feet tall. Slender and handsome with a knife scar on his cheek. He was wearing a stolen servant's uniform. And he had tattoos on the backs of his hands."

The old man spoke up, his voice raw and low. "What sort of tattoos?"

"Like his." Ursula pointed at Tattoo.

They fell silent.

"What?" Stephanie asked. "What does that mean?"

The old man turned toward Frail and spoke in a soft grumble of German. Frail rushed away on an errand, then exchanged a meaningful look with Tattoo. "Professor Solorov," the old man called. "Bring your people back to the house, please. This is something I will have to take care of, I think."

I heard a cellphone being dialed. "Come back to the house" was all she said. I heard the phone snap shut.

Then I heard her say in a low voice: "Tell me why those tattoos might be important."

The voice that answered was Kripke's. "I thought you people knew—"

"I do know, Mr. Kripke. Now you have to impress me with what you know."

"Well, the tattoos are spells. The part that shows, anyway. Most are probably protection spells."

"So far you haven't impressed me."

"For instance," Kripke continued, emphasizing the words to show his annoyance at being interrupted. "That one there, on the German muscle's forehead, that's the guiding hand. It's supposed to make others feel something, depending on the little variations. A really common version makes people attracted to you. Sexually, I mean. His is a little different, but judging by how I feel every time I look at him, I suspect it's supposed to intimidate people."

There was a brief pause. Finally, Solorov spoke in a low, urgent, dangerous voice. "You will turn over your spell book to me, along with all copies, or I—"

"I don't have a spell book," Kripke snapped.

"—or I will kill you and everyone in your family. I'll burn their houses down while they sleep at night. Do you understand me?" Her voice was urgent and, unlike the others in her group, completely free of *oh boy I get to be naughty* breathlessness. She was fierce and cold and sharp.

"I don't have a spell book," Kripke said. "I really don't. If I did, I'd be a badass like them. I wouldn't be letting you hold a gun on me."

"Then where did you get this level of information? Or are you fabricating it?"

Kripke sighed. "A guy dropped by the server uninvited. He baited his way in, but before we could ban him, he offered up good information—very good."

"What good information did he give you?"

"It's too complicated to go into it now. Honest. We can review that later, if you want, but one of the things he gave us was a write-up of a couple of dozen spells and the outward glyphs that go with them. Mostly, they were protection spells like golem flesh and iron gate, but he also included odd things like the twisted path and the second word. No summoning spells. He listed the things the spells could do when they were fresh and when they weren't."

"I want to see that."

"Okay."

"And everything else you have."

Kripke sighed again. "Okay. It goes against our TOA, but okay. Another thing: I know where the security guards went. I saw Mr. Yin approach the one at the front door, the lead. Yin flashed ID and ordered them to leave. The guard called someone, and after a couple of seconds, he shrugged and ordered all his men into their Expeditions."

"The harpy hired one of Mr. Yin's companies to provide security?" Solorov sounded amused.

"More likely Yin found out who she hired and bought them out. He's really, really rich."

The old man's assistant returned. Everyone stopped talking. He handed a metal bar to the old man, who shuffled out onto the lawn.

I wondered who had given Kripke his information. I knew the society would be interested in that. I also wondered what he'd meant when he said spells could be fresh. Until Ursula shook off the effects of my ghost knife, it hadn't occurred to me that it might have an expiration date.

I couldn't help but think of my boss, Annalise. She wouldn't have hidden in a dark basement, eavesdropping. She would have bashed heads together.

Would she have killed Kripke and the professor? The Twenty Palace Society killed people who used magic. Did they kill people who were just searching for it, too?

Not that it mattered right now. I wasn't going to kill anyone I didn't have to, and not just on Catherine's say-so. I did need to grab hold of Kripke, though. Like the professor, I wanted information from him.

Tattoo returned with the sour-faced old housekeeper. He held her hand as they walked across the grass. Her scowl had been replaced by an empty, dreamy smile. Someone needed to give her a coat.

Tattoo steered her onto the lawn. The old man waited at the bottom of the slope, twisted iron bar in his hand. I had a bad feeling about that damn bar. I took out my ghost knife.

The old man was about fifty feet from me. I could have thrown my ghost knife and hit him easily. It goes where I want it to go—I don't even really need to Frisbee it, although it moves faster that way. Still, the Fellows had shotguns. And I would have bet every penny I had that the old man was a sorcerer. My little ghost knife couldn't take out all of them, but maybe I could disrupt things and get away.

Assuming it worked on him better than it had on Ursula.

Men crowded around Solorov to ask her questions, and their legs completely blocked my view. I could hear them muttering to one another, half excited and half envious. I needed to get to another window to see what the old man was going to do. I couldn't throw my spell without aiming it, and if I was going to stop him, I'd need to hit the bar—and him—with my first shot.

The window to my left was blocked with garden tools. The window to my right was blocked by an old couch on its end. I leaned back to see if there was a better option farther down the room.

"Christ!" one of the men outside shouted.

I turned back to the window. The men had stepped to the side, clearing my line of sight.

The old woman lay on her back in the grass. The old man had just stabbed the metal bar through her chest into the ground. He stared at a carving on the top of the bar.

"He did that right out in the open," one of the Fellows said. "Right in front of us."

"Be quiet," Solorov said.

I had expected him to consult a spell book, say a few words, maybe draw a circle. Something. But he hadn't, and I had missed my chance. I should have just cut my way through to him, and to hell with what came of it.

Frail ran toward the house, putting a lot of distance between himself and the body. The old man only stepped back a few feet. He looked to the sky, but I couldn't see anything up there besides night clouds and stars.

The metal bar wobbled. It was adorned with a variety of shapes, but at this distance I could only make out the one on top, a large eye.

There was a sudden flash of light. The Fellows leaped back against the building wall. A bolt of lightning had flashed out of the clear night sky and struck the trembling bar—a lightning rod, that's what it was—engulfing the old woman in crackling light.

Her body lifted off the ground as the power poured out of the sky. The lightning—tinged with red now as though stained with blood—curled around her, shaping itself into a ball. The Fellows cursed in fear. A woman screamed—it sounded like Stephanie. I felt like screaming myself. Then the light became too bright to look at.

After a couple of seconds, the light faded enough for me to squint at it again. It had formed a sphere about three feet across. It rose into the air, drawing itself off the lightning rod as if unimpaling itself. The old woman had been reduced to blackened bones. The grass where she had lain was not even singed, although the lightning rod glowed white hot.

The churning ball of burning gas and lightning hovered above the old man.

"Sweet Jesus," someone said. "What did he do?"

I knew the answer already. He'd summoned a predator right in front of me.

I looked at my ghost knife. My spell was written on laminated paper. Even if it could kill that creature—and that was a big if—I was sure the heat and power of the thing would destroy my spell.

I wasn't ready to do that. It was my only weapon, the only spell I'd created myself, and I didn't have the spell book anymore.

The old man shouted something at the predator in German. "He's telling it to search the woods around the house," one of the Fellows said. "He's telling it to kill everyone it finds between the house and the iron fence."

"But what the hell is it?" Russian Accent asked.

It was Kripke who answered. "I think it's a floating storm."

The predator floated toward the cottage. The old man shouted at it, then shouted again, his voice more insistent and aggravated.

"He's telling it to hunt," Kripke said, volunteering information like a good little employee.

The floating storm did not change direction. It hovered above the spot where the thick black power cable connected to the guesthouse. Blue arcs jumped from the wires into its body. The old man shouted at it again, sounding like a grandfather trying to control a toddler from the comfort of his easy chair. The predator ignored him.

The porch light suddenly went out, and the blue arcs stopped. A couple of flickering tongues of flame appeared on the cottage roof.

Once the power was off, the floating storm glided toward the woods. The old man scowled at Tattoo, who responded in German. The old man shrugged. They both laughed and shook their heads like boys who had launched a firework in the wrong direction. The predator was out of their control, and they thought it was funny.

Tattoo walked up to the lightning rod, which had cooled to merely red hot, and grabbed it with his bare hand. Both men started toward the house.

The predator floated over the bare trees, making shadows sweep across the grass. "Professor," one of the Fellows said, "I think we should be getting inside."

She didn't move. "It's beautiful, isn't it?"

"Um, can we go now?" Kripke said. "It's not safe to be out here." No one moved. "Please?"

Professor Solorov sighed. "Let's go inside and find some candles. We may be here awhile."

They stepped back, leaving me a clear view of the predator as it moved away from the house. Had it sensed Catherine and the gunmen searching the grounds of the estate? It didn't even have any eyes.

Catherine needed to know this thing was hunting her. She had a cell, but I didn't know her number. I had to risk going into the woods to warn her, and I didn't have much time.

I pushed the window closed. I heard a muffled "Hey!" Footsteps came toward me. Damn.

I backed off the steamer trunks and crouched behind a little round table that smelled of mold. A man knelt by the window and shined a flashlight inside. The light was too dim to illuminate the pitch-blackness of the basement, but it didn't matter. I'd been spotted.

A second man knelt by the window. I heard one of them tell the other that he'd seen the window close. While I silently cursed my stupidity and impatience, they yelled for more people. I couldn't keep hiding here. If I was going to warn Catherine, I'd have to move before they got organized.

I pivoted away from the window and bumped into something sharp and metallic. It clattered to the floor, then a stack of somethings crashed in the darkness. Not that it mattered now.

I reached the window I'd cut open and pulled it from the frame. The way looked clear. I climbed up, sticking my head and neck through.

A foot squelched in the mud nearby and I threw myself backward.

A shotgun blast tore through the window frame, spraying wood splinters like shrapnel.

I fell back onto the legs of a chair, rolled to the side, and ducked behind a stack of copper pots.

Fat Guy knelt beside the open window and peered in, shotgun in hand. "I saw him," he said to someone over his shoulder. "I didn't get him, though."

I had the sudden urge to leap forward and punch him in the face with every bit of strength I could muster. The son of a bitch had shot at me. I clenched my hands into fists to calm my trembling and hung back in the darkness like a coward.

Whoever he was talking to grabbed his shoulder and tried to pull him back. "The fat lady said he had a gun."

Fat Guy shrugged the hand away. "I saw his hands. He didn't have no gun. Get inside and get down there."

I threw my ghost knife at him.

He must have seen movement because he threw himself back. The ghost knife struck the shotgun, shearing off the front of the barrel and the pump, too. The cut part of the weapon fell through the window into the basement.

I *called* the ghost knife and it zipped through the open window into my hand. It still worked on *dead things,* at least.

Fat Guy held up half of his weapon. "Well, I'll be damned."

"What could have done that?"

"I don't know, but I will soon. Gimme your shotgun."

The other Fellow didn't like that suggestion, and both men moved away from the window to talk about it. The other man eventually agreed to stand guard.

I inched forward, peering around the edge of the window jamb. The Fellow stood about ten feet away, the shotgun against his shoulder as though he was about to shoot skeet. He was the one dressed in biking clothes.

"Hey in there!" he yelled. "Come out with your hands up, and I won't shoot."

He snapped the barrel of the gun to the right, then left, looking very trigger-happy. I didn't want to throw my ghost knife directly into the path of a blast of buckshot. I moved toward the front of the house. The garage offered more cover, but it was too far away. Had they posted a new guard at the front door? I'd have to risk it.

Heavy footsteps clomped overhead. The Fellows were coming—with guns—and I didn't have time to wait around. My only real hope was that they were all coming after me, leaving the area outside unguarded.

I banged my head against something that made a solid wooden *thunk*. I laid my hands on it—it was smooth and curved, but I had no idea what it was. What I could tell was that it completely blocked the path. I had to turn back.

Footsteps stumbled down the stairs somewhere to my left. By the echo, I judged they were coming from the center of the room.

I crept back the way I'd come, keeping low so they wouldn't spot my silhouette against a window.

One of them said something in another language. Russian, maybe. Another answered: "Just one, I think. A guy." The Russian-speaker answered. He didn't sound confident. Someone flicked a light switch several times. Nothing happened.

Damn. I wished I could pinpoint where they were.

"I don't like it down here," another one said. The Russian-speaker said something that seemed like agreement. "I mean, what was that thing outside? We didn't try to buy something like *that*, did we?"

"Shut up, Gregor," another said. I recognized his voice. It was Fat Guy. "You're gonna talk yourself out of the Fellowship."

"I'm just saying," Gregor continued, ignoring the other man's advice. "You saw that old woman die. You saw her spirit, or whatever that was, float away into the woods. What if it comes for us? Are we supposed to use shotguns against it?"

"Then let's find this guy," a new voice said, "so we can go home."

They were spooked. I just wished they'd been spooked by me. I sure as hell didn't want to fight all of these guys. One at a time, without guns, was bad enough, but like this it was too chancy.

Then I had an idea. I threw the ghost knife into the darkness.

I waited, feeling it move away from me. No effect. The Russian-speaker was talking, and the others were listening quietly. I *called* it back and threw it again in a slightly different direction.

This time I was rewarded by a loud crash across the room. The spell had cut part of an unsteady stack somewhere.

"Christ!" Gregor shouted. There was a barrage of gunfire. I dropped to the ground, but I was pretty sure it wasn't aimed at me. After a few seconds, the shooting stopped. I *called* my ghost knife back, my ears still ringing.

"Goddammit!" Fat Guy yelled. "I'm standing right here!"

The trigger-happy one was breathing hard. So was I. The ghost knife settled into my hand.

"Reload that weapon," Fat Guy said. "And if you shoot one of us, I'm going to kill you and your mother, too. Get me?"

"Sorry," Gregor mumbled.

I slowly got to my knees. My shoe scuffed against the floor, but the Fellows were breathing too hard to hear it.

"We should fan out," Russian Accent said.

"We're not fucking fanning out. Not with this crew. I'd prolly bump an old mirror, and Gregor here would empty a clip of soft-points into me. Stick together and cover each other."

One of them flicked on a flashlight, and I knew just where they were. I sidestepped to get a clear shot.

"What do you think is down here?" Gregor asked.

I threw the ghost knife at them. Please work. Please.

One of the men screamed. It gave me chills—he sounded like I'd cut off a body part. I heard someone fall and a clatter of breaking glass. The flashlight beam swerved around and pointed at the floor. Shapes moved in the light.

"It touched me!" Gregor screamed, his voice stripped of all courage and dignity. "It touched my soul! Don't let it happen again! Please, God, don't let it happen again."

I felt a tremendous relief. My ghost knife still worked. I wondered if Ursula had some sort of special protection against it.

"What happened?" the new voice said. He sounded spooked. The Russian-speaker answered him in the same confused, frightened tone.

I *called* the ghost knife to me. One of the men screamed, "Look out!" then the spell returned to my hand.

"It came from over there!" Fat Guy said, and then a volley of gunshots rang out, all facing away from me. I dropped low anyway. The floor was concrete and the walls were cinder block; I didn't want to be killed by a ricochet.

The shooting stopped after a couple of seconds. One of them let out a high, quavering whine, like a fan belt about to give. "Dammit," Fat Guy said. "Gimme a clip. Somebody gimme a clip."

But it was too late for that. Their morale had been broken. There was a cascade of stomping footsteps as they fought one another up the stairs. No one wanted to be the last to get out of the darkness.

I crouched in the dark, listening. The basement was quiet, but I could hear footsteps above me, shuffling around. I felt a little smug. Those guys had been afraid of me—well, they'd been afraid of what they'd imagined was in the darkness.

There was probably a lesson in that, but whatever. Someone was moving toward the front of the house, so I headed toward the garage. I still needed to find Catherine. I held my hands in front of me as I went. Although I had to backtrack out of a couple of dead ends, I didn't run into anything dangerous.

The windows on the garage side of the house were about fifteen feet away when a metal shelving unit toppled onto me.

I raised my arm to shield my face, feeling for a moment that the whole building was falling onto me. Something slid off the shelf, bounced off my forehead, and shattered at my feet. I fell back against a second metal shelf, and the two frames closed on my head. I cried out as I scraped myself free.

"Got you!" someone said. It was Fat Guy again.

The shelves struck something and stopped falling. I slid close to the floor where the gap between them was widest.

A sharp pain in my knee froze me in place as a huge shadow moved toward me, black against not-quite-as-black. I'd knelt on something, but I'd worry about that later.

I could hear him breathing through his mouth. He had emptied his gun and asked for a clip. Had he gotten one before his buddies ran upstairs? I lunged for him, hoping to end this quickly. Trickery wasn't going to help me now.

I threw a punch at the general area where his head should have been, holding back a bit in case I missed and struck a piece of furniture. I connected. Lucky.

He took the blow in stride and grabbed my collar. Like a lot of big, slow, tough guys, he wanted to grapple. My shirt rippled. He'd hit me on the protective tattoos on my chest where I couldn't feel it.

Now I knew exactly where he was. I hit him with a right to the side of his jaw and, when he staggered, a left to his temple.

My left hand—which had never fully recovered from an old gunshot injury—throbbed, but the strength went out of Fat Guy. He rolled and fell flat on his back. I heard flimsy metal clatter around him in the dark.

I knelt and patted him down. He carried his wallet in his breast pocket. I took it. I also took his handgun from his shoulder holster and, after checking that the slide was back, pitched it into the darkness.

It only took another minute or so to reach the windows on the garage side of the building. I peeked outside. No one in sight.

By the light of the window, I searched Fat Guy's wallet. He was from Chicago and had two hundred dollars in twenties. How considerate of him. I took the cash and tossed his wallet into the clutter.

I cut a window out of the frame and pulled it free as quietly as I could. Cold, clean air rushed in. I boosted myself up and squeezed my shoulders through the gap.

A familiar voice said something in German. Tattoo was standing by the corner where he could watch this side of the house and the front. He began to stroll casually toward me.

I squirmed through the window and scrambled to my feet. He was smiling and his limbs swung loose. He said something else, sounding almost friendly, and gave a pointed glance at my stomach.

I absentmindedly wiped my hand down the front of my shirt. There was a long slash in the cloth, starting beside my solar plexus and going down and to the left.

Damn. Fat Guy hadn't punched me in the gut. He'd had a knife and I never knew it. The Fellows had been frightened of what they couldn't see, but I'd nearly been killed by the same thing.

Tattoo was just a few paces away from me now. He was smiling like a guy who was going to walk all over me and enjoy the hell out of it.

The ghost knife was still in my pocket. I left it there. Tattoo made me nervous and I needed to keep something in reserve. The marks on his body could mean all sorts of things. Maybe he could breathe fire. Maybe he could shoot tear gas out of his armpits. I wanted him to play his hand before I played mine.

Also, I didn't want to go for my weapon right away. I hate to show my fear.

I started toward the garage, but he stepped lightly into my way. His smile grew wide and he clucked his tongue. That wasn't allowed. Hell, if he was going to *tsk tsk* me, he was going to get the fight he wanted. We moved toward each other.

He was fast. When he threw the first punch, I almost didn't see it coming and barely got out of the way, staggering back. He looked surprised that I'd avoided his jab but not particularly worried.

I leaned into him, moving my head to the side while throwing a jab of my own. I hit him full on his tattooed nose while his counterpunch went just wide.

Now it was his turn to stagger back. He kept his balance and his smile. *"Gut, gut!"* he said, as though advising me to try body blows. My left hand stung from the shot I'd landed, but his nose didn't look damaged at all. Damn. His tattoos seemed to be the same as mine, more or less, and he was completely covered by them—even his face. Probably even his scalp. This guy was better protected than my boss.

He came at me again. I went on the defensive, blocking and weaving. I'm pretty quick—I was a promising baseball player once, and I've always had a sharp eye and fast hands.

Tattoo was fast too, but he wasn't unnaturally fast. He wasn't superstrong, either. I wondered just how complete his protection was. He threw a low right hand that I let hit my ribs while I extended my left, fingers out, toward his eyes.

He dodged sideways, almost losing his balance in his haste. In that moment, I landed a solid kick to his crotch.

We backed away from each other. My lunge at his eyes had wiped the smile from his face, but the kick had brought it back. It'd had no effect on him.

"Oh, hell no," I said. "Your johnson, too? That's just not right."

His smile turned sour. Whether he spoke my language or not, he understood what I was saying. Suddenly he wasn't having quite so much fun.

I kept backing away from him, my left hand still aching. I wasn't focused on the fight the way I needed to be. If my head was in the right place, I wouldn't feel my hand until after. My adrenaline was trailing away—I'd wasted it in the basement and I needed it now.

He caught up to me, feinted low, and hit me on the side of my jaw.

I managed to roll with it at the last moment, but the world still blinked dark. I felt something cold against the side of my face—mud? It felt solid. I pushed away and crumpled into the mud for real. As I fell, Tattoo's fist hit the side of the house where my head had been.

I tried to shake my mind clear, but I was still feeling fuzzy. My ass was wet. My hands were muddy and leaching heat, but that soothed the pain in my left.

Tattoo was talking again. Someone who didn't know about my protective tattoos would have kicked me in the ribs, but he circled behind me. The idea that he might return the favor of a kick to the nuts gave me a much-needed burst of adrenaline.

I rolled onto my hip and held out my forearm. That punch to the face frightened the hell out of me. If he did it again, I might never wake up. His kick struck my wrist. In a desperate grapple, I grabbed his right foot and twisted it with both hands. He yelped in surprise and pain, rolling against the steps Catherine and I had used to enter the house and falling into the mud to avoid a dislocated knee. His other boot scraped painfully across my scalp, but there was no power behind it. He got his arms under him. I didn't have much time. I jammed his foot behind the other knee, then folded his leg over it.

I remembered that sour-faced housekeeper. The old man had sacrificed her without a second thought, and Tattoo had laughed about it.

I rolled over his ankle and broke it.

He screamed. It was a high, girl-in-a-horror-movie scream, full of fear and unaccustomed to pain.

He reached back for me. I twisted his thumb too far, and he screamed again. I loved that sound. It was like a church choir to me. This bastard was faster than me and he hit harder, but the tattoos that protected him from cutting and impacts didn't protect against twisting.

And I couldn't leave him alive. He'd come after me again someday, and I didn't think I could take him a second time.

He swung with his good arm, stinging my ear. I let the momentum of his swing carry him onto his back, but I stayed close. I shifted my weight onto my feet, grabbed his wrists, and stood, lifting him off the ground with his head hanging down.

The stairs were made of stone. That should do. I waddled over there, pinning him with a bear hug. He struggled, but I could hold him long enough to break his neck.

Something came at me from the top of the stairs and slammed into me. The sudden impact broke Tattoo from my grip, and I wanted to cry out like a terrified child. I smelled a lemon aftershave as I sprawled in the mud.

It was the old man's assistant, Frail. I flipped him up and off me, letting our momentum roll me clear of Tattoo. He scuttled off, his hands over his head. Tattoo crawled away from me, dragging his crooked ankle behind him.

I heard shouting and footsteps through the open kitchen door. Tattoo's screams had brought help. My head still hadn't cleared—all I could think about was guns. I turned and ran around the garage into the woods.

I fled blindly, pushing through a break in the blackberry bramble and dodging through the trees so they wouldn't have a clear shot. It wasn't until I tripped at the bottom of a steep slope that I realized they weren't chasing me.

I leaned against a tree, fighting to catch my breath. Why hadn't they come after me with their shotguns? I rubbed my aching hands and face. My head began to clear.

And I remembered the floating storm.

Damn. I scanned the woods around me. I didn't see any floating balls of light, but my visibility was pretty limited. Damn and damn again. I'd planned to steal a car and drive to Catherine's. We could have gotten off the property in a few minutes.

I looked back up the slope. The cars were still there, of course. I could try to sneak back.

No. They knew I was out here. And even if they weren't going to chase me, they were probably watching from the windows. It's what I would have done.

I really wished I'd killed that tattooed bastard.

I jogged along the base of the slope, watching the treetops for any trace of the reddish light I'd seen the floating storm give off. The ground was covered with moss, fallen branches, and a few scattered ferns. I made a lot of noise, but it was better than pushing through brambles. After a few minutes, my head had cleared. There was still no sign of the creature.

Predator, I reminded myself. That old man had summoned a predator out of the Empty Spaces. And the Twenty Palace Society existed to kill people like him.

I had bought into that mission. Not an hour ago, I had wondered if I could bring myself to kill again. Now I had a list.

I thought about the people caught up in this mess: Regina and her staff, the Fellows, the old man and his dangerous little crew, and the well-dressed Chinese gunmen. The society was just another gang after the same prize, and Catherine and I were the only ones here to represent. Maybe that should have bothered me, but it didn't. I had bought in. I knew what predators could do, and I was ready to do whatever it took to destroy them.

And God! This was what I'd missed since Hammer Bay. I'd thought it had been the excitement and the danger, but it was really *this* feeling. I had a clear purpose. I had important work. I would do whatever I had to do to stop these people.

But no. That wasn't true. If I'd done to Ursula what Annalise would have done—if I'd killed her—I wouldn't have been trapped in the basement and I wouldn't have fought Tattoo. Hell, the old man wouldn't have summoned the floating storm. That maid's death was partly my fault. Annalise was ruthless but she wouldn't have gotten herself into this situation. It was something to think about.

The wind had picked up, and my wet pants and sleeves were leaching body heat. I wished I'd kept my jacket. I moved forward, scrambling over uneven ground and fallen wood, hoping I was headed toward the long asphalt drive.

I came across a trail of footprints in the mud and stopped. Was someone out here hunting me? I couldn't see anyone. There were actually three pairs of footprints. Two headed toward the house, and the third went back the other way.

They were mine, Catherine's, and Catherine's again. Perfect. At least I was on her trail. I followed the footprints to the long drive and then down the hill.

A thunderclap echoed from somewhere up ahead. Had I failed Catherine already? Had the floating storm killed her? I kept running. I wasn't going to give up on her until I saw her corpse.

That little thought prompted a quick series of ugly mental images that didn't do anything but slow me down.

I reached a steep part of the hill and crouched at the base of a tree. The crashed truck lay on the road below. The Acura was close, and I couldn't see anyone.

I fell once going down the slope. My pants were already as wet as they were going to get. No one shouted or shot at me. A few minutes later, I came to the stand of trees where Catherine's car was hidden.

It was still there. I approached cautiously. Catherine wasn't around. Damn. I peered inside. Nothing.

I circled the car, hoping to find a second trail of footprints to follow. Something moved out from behind a tree. I jumped and cursed before I realized it was Catherine.

"Sshh!" she hissed. "There are still men out here, hunting around. I saw you coming but couldn't tell who you were. So I hid. I sent the license plate photos already, and I've been waiting for you. What did you find out?"

"Stuff," I answered. "But the most important thing is that one of the bidders in that house summoned a predator."

"What?"

"They stuck a lightning rod through an old woman's heart and there was this flash of light and . . . the old man sent it out to kill everyone on the property."

"Well, let's get out of here then."

She unlocked the car and we climbed in. My flannel jacket was lying on the front passenger seat. I put it on, getting mud on the lining; my shoes and pants smeared mud on the car seat. "I'm sorry," I said.

She clipped her seat belt and turned the key. "You're wearing wet clothes on a winter night? Not smart. You'd last longer with nothing on."

I imagined myself lying out in the bramble, shot to death and wearing only smears of mud and underwear. To hell with that. I'd rather freeze.

She backed toward the road, taillights glowing. When all this was over, maybe I'd install a kill switch on her lights so they wouldn't light up the mountainside.

At the driveway she turned toward the gate and hit the gas.

We came around a twist in the road and saw two men blocking our way. Both were Asian, dressed in dark, expensive suits, and held pistols. Yin must be desperate, if he was having his men search every vehicle leaving the estate.

The taller one had no hat; maybe he didn't want to muss his high, moussed-up hair. He held out his hand like a traffic cop, expecting the weapons to make us obey.

Catherine gunned the engine and flicked on her headlights. The men scurried aside. The taller one shouted something to the other and fired two quick shots into the grille.

"Shit!" Catherine shouted. "Those bastards shot me!"

They didn't fire again. It took a moment to realize Catherine hadn't really been hit, just her car. The engine rattled. We began to slow down. I glanced back and saw that the two gunmen were following us, but they didn't appear to be in a hurry. "We were lucky," I said.

"Lucky? I love my car and those bastards killed it."

"We weren't going all that fast," I said. "They could have shot us both in the head. Easily. We're lucky they still haven't found the predator."

We crested the top of a hill and started down. The engine suddenly made a loud grinding noise. The car was dying.

Catherine put the car in neutral so we could drift to the bottom of the hill. "Shit!" she said again. She sounded close to tears. "Those ass-holes shot at us! Should I have stopped for them and let them search the car?" For the first time, I heard uncertainty in her voice.

"No," I told her. "After they searched, they would have held on to us, and I don't think we would have liked it."

She took a deep breath. "Right. Of course. I knew that." The Acura reached the bottom of the slope and lost momentum against the next rise. Catherine twisted the wheel so it blocked the road. "I'm sorry. The gunfire has me a little rattled. We run for the gate, don't we?"

"I think so. Those guys will be coming up behind us, and the old man ordered the floating storm to kill everyone it found between the house and the fence. Although . . ."

"Although what?"

"He didn't seem to have complete control over it."

She sighed again. "Let me get my jump bag." She grabbed a small, stuffed duffel bag from the floor behind her and got out of the car. Then she began jogging up the road. I followed her but spared a glance behind us. The two gunmen hadn't made it over the hill yet. We didn't sprint because we weren't sure how far we had to go, but we did hustle.

"Ray," she said. She was not breathing hard, but she didn't look comfortable. "I'm sorry for what I said. You've been a solid guy. You didn't have to come out here to warn me, but if you hadn't . . ."

"Thanks," I said, feeling a tremendous sense of relief that I couldn't really explain. It was hard to admit how much I wanted her accep-tance, and through her the acceptance of the society as a whole.

And that hadn't been easy for her to say.

"Too bad you're a wooden man."

"Let's save our breath, okay?" But I knew what she meant. A wooden man didn't come with a long life expectancy.

The treetops cast long shadows across the road. The woods around me seemed to become more clear. My eyes were adjusting, I thought, but something didn't seem right. The shadows were too sharp. I grabbed Catherine's sleeve and pulled her to a stop. She cringed just a little, and I let go of her.

The long, crooked shadows of the trees were slowly moving toward us. I glanced up. Ahead and to the left there was a light in the sky. It was dimmer and smaller than a full moon, but it was growing brighter.

"Lord above," Catherine said. "It's coming right toward us."

I heard hissing, like water drops boiling in a skillet. It was, in fact, coming right toward us.

Catherine bolted for the downhill slope at the edge of the road. The bramble was thick there and the ground uneven. "No!" I shouted. "This way!" I ran back up the road.

I glanced back once to see that she had followed and that she could keep up. The floating storm passed over the trees onto the road. We ran around the Acura and up the hill.

"Where are we going?" Catherine called.

I slowed down to let her get next to me. An old joke popped into my head about running away from a bear, but I didn't think she'd find it funny. Catherine's mouth was set in a determined frown, and her forehead was a mass of wrinkles. She already had streaks of sweat down the side of her face.

Ahead of us, the two gunmen had reached the top of the slope. They had already seen the floating storm, of course. The tall one with the elaborate hair was talking very excitedly on his cell. His partner was short and round, with a Moe Howard haircut that made him seem like comic relief. He didn't have a fearful expression; he looked like he was seeing the awful end he'd always expected.

I risked one glance back at the creature behind me. It was traveling along the road now, but I couldn't tell if it was gaining or not.

The gunmen glanced at Catherine and me. I could see their indecision.

"Run for your lives!" I screamed at them, letting my face show some of the terror I was feeling. They shrank away from me, understanding the tone of my voice if not the words. Fear is contagious. The men in the basement had proved that.

They turned their attention back to the predator. Haircut pulled his cellphone away from his ear and winced as though it had stung him.

We were fewer than ten yards from them now. I grabbed Catherine's elbow and shoved her toward a deer path on the side of the road.

It was a steep drop-off. We hopped partway down the hill until I slipped in the mud and fell, body-sledding into the back of Catherine's legs and knocking her on top of me.

We struck a tree trunk at the bottom of a shallow ravine and tumbled into the mud. I jumped up, pulled Catherine to her feet, and followed her up the slope ahead.

Gunshots. We both stopped at the top of the little slope and looked up at the road.

The two gunmen were holding their ground, standing in two-handed firing stances: shoulders squared, legs spread, one hand supporting the other. The shots went quickly, *popopopop*—it takes surprisingly little time to empty a handgun.

The floating storm was about fifteen yards off the ground and nearly above them. Moe Howard dropped the magazine out of his pistol and slapped in a new one with well-practiced speed. He started shooting again, and I knew he was hitting his target even though I couldn't see any effect. Haircut didn't bother to reload. He began to back away.

Beside me, Catherine said, "Oh, God. No."

The floating storm was above Moe now. There was a tremendous flash of reddish light and a thunderclap louder than anything I'd ever heard in my life. A blast of air staggered me. Haircut was close enough to be knocked down. When I blinked away the lights in my eyes, I saw him struggling to his feet, still half stunned.

The floating storm moved straight toward Haircut. He didn't have a chance.

I turned to run and saw Catherine giving me a withering stare of raw hatred. I was startled, but when she took off downhill, I followed.

We ran, aiming mostly northward because it was downhill. Where the ground was rough, we angled toward one side of the path or the other, trying to keep to flat ground. We also kept to the trees, hoping they would force the predator to stay high and out of range. And the ground was clearest where the trees were thickest. Where they were thin, the way was choked by vines and bramble.

It stayed on our tail, never getting too close and never falling far behind. Would a ball of churning gas and electricity toy with its prey? I figured not.

So we ran. The light from the predator cast long shadows ahead of us. Whip-thin tree branches, nearly invisible in the dim electric light, stung my face, neck, and arms. As we topped a ridge and slid down the other side, the light the predator gave off was suddenly blocked. We had to pick our way through the moss-covered branches by touch until the floating storm came close enough to light the way again.

We were never going to survive this way.

We came to a little stream—not deep, but the banks on both sides were pretty near vertical and too far to jump. Catherine bolted to the right, running along the gap until she came to a place where the bank on the far side was more gentle.

She jumped, hitting the ground with a loud *whuff*. I landed beside her and a little farther up. I grabbed her jacket to help her up the hill, but she shook me off angrily and ran by me. Her breath was coming in labored heaves.

I glanced down at my shadow and realized how short it had become. I sprinted after Catherine, trying to keep close without passing her.

I watched her. It was obvious that she was tired, but she never let up the pace. She ran on willpower, hurdling broken branches and exposed roots. It was barely running—more like hopping through an obstacle course. I didn't think either of us had the stamina to outrun the predator. I glanced back at it again. If it was becoming tired, I didn't know how I'd tell. At least we were putting a little more distance between it and us.

Catherine suddenly angled to the right, and I followed. She'd found a footpath that was clear of broken branches, although the moss was still slippery. The wind chilled the sweat on my face. We made better time on the footpath, and the forest grew darker around us.

"The town is down there," Catherine wheezed. I looked in the direction she pointed. Through the trees, I could see a cluster of faint, distant lights.

We could never run that far. We kept running anyway.

Then we came to the thing I was most afraid of—the ground dropped away in front of us. We had reached the edge of a fifty-foot cliff.

At the bottom was a little pine forest, all laid out in perfect rows. A Christmas-tree farm.

"Shit," Catherine said. "I can't run any more. Boy, you said you had a weapon that could kill a predator."

"I said *maybe*. And it won't work on this one. My spell is made of paper, and that thing is made of lightning. My spell would just burn up."

"Are you sure? You won't even try?"

Of course I would try—as a last resort. To the left of us, there was a section of cliff that had collapsed, making a very slight slope. A couple of trees grew nearly sideways out of the dirt. "Can you climb down this cliff?"

The electric hum of the predator was growing louder, and the woods were growing brighter. "Not fast enough," she answered.

"I'll give you time. Get down to the farm. Find something to kill an electricity monster. I'll lead it to you."

She ran to the left. "What if it catches you?"

I almost answered: *Then when it comes for you, I won't be leading it,* but the predator was close and it was time to run.

I followed the path along the top of the cliff, lengthening my stride to stretch out my legs. I'd already run a couple hundred yards over rough ground, and I didn't have a lot of gas left in my tank. The predator fell behind, but at least it was chasing me, not Catherine.

The woods to my right became steeper, sloping higher and higher until it was a wall of ferns and mud above me. If this trail dead-ended, I would be dead-ended, too. I was too damn tired to run uphill.

A couple of the trees ahead looked strange—too regular, and stripped of their branches. As the floating storm lit the woods around me, I realized they were power poles.

I picked up the pace. The power line came up the cliff below at a slant, ran along the trail for a few hundred feet, and then continued uphill to the right at a rocky point. The nearest pole on the trail was just ahead. The cliff drop to the left was still steep but looked manageable if I had a little time to work at it. I stepped around the pole and backed away from it, gasping to catch my breath.

As I'd hoped, the floating storm went for the power line. It moved carefully through the trees, avoiding branches when it could, setting them alight when it couldn't go around them. It reached the top of the pole and began to draw power slowly, sipping instead of gulping. Blue arcs flashed out of the top of the pole to the predator.

At the edge of the cliff, the muddy ground beneath me shifted. I fell, sliding with the mud down the slope. I had a sudden image of myself lying at the base of the cliff with a broken back while the predator moved toward me.

I managed to grab hold of a cluster of woody brush and stop my slide. I struggled to my knees, but the angle of the slope was too steep for me to hold myself in place, so I let go and stretched out flat. I slid slowly down the hill, finding one foothold after another in tree roots, trunks, and clumps of bushes. There were a couple of sketchy moments, but I survived.

At the bottom of the hill, I scrambled to my feet. The wind was gentle, but it still chilled me. Maybe Catherine was right, but I left my shirt on. I didn't like throwing away resources.

I crossed under the power line. The predator was still up there at the top of the cliff, still feeding. It had apparently learned that it could trip the breaker by feeding too fast. I didn't like that. I wanted it to be like a shark—dangerous but basically stupid. The smarter it was, the harder it would be to kill.

It looked like it was growing larger. Would it stop hunting me if it fed enough from the power pole? I didn't know what to do, so I jumped up and down and swung my arms, trying to keep my muscles warm for the next leg of the chase. All I was sure of was that I was giving Catherine extra time to prepare.

Then I imagined the predator growing large enough to split in two like a dividing cell. That thought scared the hell out of me.

Five quick cuts with the ghost knife on the nearest power pole made it topple—away from me, thank God—and snapped the power line. The blue arcs stopped popping under the predator. Dinner was over.

The floating storm didn't move for a couple of seconds. It bobbed up and down as if it was trying to puzzle out why the juice had stopped. I picked up a rotten hunk of branch and threw it.

The predator was too far away for me to hit it. The branch landed in the bushes near the base of the electric pole, and a sudden crack of red lightning blasted the ground at that spot. The sound startled and frightened me, and clumps of dirt and burning wood chips showered down over me.

The floating storm started in my direction. I turned and ran like hell toward the tree farm. The chase was back on.

CHAPTER SIX

There were no trees here, and the landscape between me and the tree farm was a wall of bramble and bush. I sprinted around the edges, hopping over downed trees in some places and pushing blindly through tall grass in others. My shadow began to shorten. Then I hit a rocky little stream and ran along it, picking up speed. I knew it was stupid to have my feet in water, but it was the only place I could run.

The stream disappeared into a drainage pipe. I scrambled up a dirt slope and ran straight into a chain-link fence.

With my ghost knife, I cut a hole in the chain link and pushed through. My shadow was short—too short. Behind me the creature was humming like a transformer, and I expected to feel lightning any moment. I sprinted out into the neat rows of trees. Flat ground. Hallelujah.

The old man had ordered the predator to patrol within the iron fence, but the chain link was made of steel. Obviously, he didn't know that the black iron fence along the road didn't ring the property. Or he didn't care. I had a moment's hope that the floating storm would turn back at the fence anyway, but that didn't happen. Damn. I kept running.

The trees themselves were just over two feet tall and offered no cover at all. I was glad. I needed to see.

My shadow slowly stretched out before me. I saw a small cluster of buildings way off to my right and angled toward them. There was a figure waving a long cloth back and forth over its head. Catherine.

I tried to put on extra speed, but I didn't have it. I didn't look back at the predator. I didn't need to. I could feel it back there like a high-tension wire, and I was flagging.

There were three buildings: One was a yellow farmhouse well off to the left. The others were a pair of big wooden barns, both painted red.

Catherine stopped waving her jacket at me, backed toward the red buildings, and ducked between them, making sure I'd seen where she'd gone. I was not far behind her.

"Through here!" Her voice came from the darkened doorway on the right. I staggered toward it just as the shadow of the other building swept over me. The floating storm was close behind.

I rushed into the darkness, barking my shin against something low and wooden. I tumbled onto my face, and the pain in my leg made me curse a blue streak. Something wet sloshed onto my leg.

The ground was packed earth and smelled of pine needles. I scrambled away from the doorway until I struck my head against something metal.

The barn lit up with a flickering electric red light.

I turned around. The floating storm had followed me to the doorway but had stopped at the entrance. It bobbed up and down, as though it didn't want to enter an enclosed space.

I glanced around, trying to see what Catherine had planned aside from the water-filled trough across the entrance, but the predator was too bright. I couldn't see into the shadows cast by the doorway.

I had not been this close to the floating storm before. It seemed to be swirling and churning from inside, like a sped-up lava lamp. The outside was a bluish-white cloud of brilliant light, but in the spaces where the swirling gases were thin or parted from one another, I could see a dark red color that swirled like blood in oil. In the center of that was a white-hot fire.

I laid my hand on an old, rusting truck. Would grounding myself lure it inside? Apparently not. To my left I saw a small pile of wooden disks. I grabbed one. It had been cut from the base of a pine trunk and was still sticky. I threw it at the floating storm like a discus. It struck almost dead center, but nothing came out the other side but a little burp of flames. So much for using my ghost knife.

"What are you waiting for?" I yelled. "Didn't the old man order you to kill me? You want to pose for a picture first?"

There was no way to tell whether it understood. I kept throwing hunks of wood at it. One grazed the bottom edge and landed, burning, on the ground outside. The others never made it all the way through.

After the sixth piece of wood, it ducked under the lintel and floated into the room. It must have decided I didn't have anything more dangerous than slices of Christmas trees.

I took the ghost knife from my pocket.

The shadows receded as the floating storm entered. Tucked back into the corner on the right, I saw Catherine against the wall. She had a long wooden pole in her hands.

As the predator moved by her, she dropped the pole and something heavy swung out of the ceiling—chains, it was chains. They fell against the floating storm's body and splashed into the water.

What happened next happened without a scream or a moan or any of the sounds you would expect from a living creature. It seemed to bleed light and heat into the hanging chains. The water below boiled. That lasted a few seconds until the creature's core had deformed into a teardrop shape as the power flowed out of it.

The glowing chains melted apart and dropped into the boiling trough below.

The predator flew erratically for a few seconds, seemingly disoriented. It was very much reduced in size, but for a split second I was sure that Catherine's trap would have killed it if I hadn't let it drink so much power from the electric lines. *My fault,* I thought. *All my fault.*

Then the water sprinklers turned on.

Steam blasted off it. The floating storm sank toward the ground and passed near the door on the left side. Sparks shot out of its body onto every metal object within ten feet—door handle, hinges, nails in the wood, even the still-glowing chains.

A wave of flame billowed up the wall. The predator struck a pair of metal trash barrels, releasing the last of its life and energy in one sudden blast. I was knocked flat near the rear wall, my ears ringing. Aside from the flickering firelight of the burning doorway, the room was dark.

The predator was dead.

Flames climbed the walls on either side of the door, and even the trough was on fire. I wouldn't be getting out that way. I couldn't see Catherine anywhere.

I hopped up onto a table saw and cut a circular slash in the wall above it with my ghost knife. The flames had already covered both side walls and had spread to the loose pine needles and sticky pitch on the ground. The sprinklers were not going to stop this fire.

I pushed the cut section and jumped out, running far away from the building. My scalded skin cooled quickly in the night air, and I knew that soon my wet clothes would be stealing body heat.

But I was alive. A predator had chased me halfway down a mountain, and I had survived.

Catherine came around the edge of the building, giving it a wide berth. We jogged toward each other.

"Thank you!" I said.

"No one has come out of the farmhouse," she said, ignoring me. Her expression was blank, but her hands were trembling. "Either they're really deep sleepers or there's no one home. Normally, I'd suggest we knock and ask for help, but since we just burned down their barn, I think we should get the hell out of here." She was still all business.

"Fine." About fifty yards away, I could see a line of streetlights. We headed for it. She took out her cellphone, scowled at it, and put it away. No reception.

"It looked bigger," she said.

"It was," I said. "While I was leading it away, I came to a power line—one that led to the mansion up on the hill, I think. It fed from that before I could stop it."

She didn't respond. The closer we got to the road, the stronger the wind became. I began to shiver.

"We need to get out of this wind," I said.

"Good idea," she snapped. "Let's chop down some trees and build a log cabin."

We didn't say anything else for a while.

On the road, we came to a sign that read WASHAWAY 2 MILES. We headed in that direction, jogging along the shoulder. The wind was strong at my back.

The road narrowed ahead, and the wide, gently sloping area where the trees had been planted gave way to steeper ground. People lived here, although we could only see their mailboxes and driveways.

A pair of headlights came up behind us. Catherine moved to wave the car down, but I grabbed her elbow and pulled her to the drainage ditch. We crouched behind a tree, watching.

Two black Yukons passed. Both had red-and-white cards in the front window. They were bidders, but which ones?

"Don't grab at me again," she hissed.

We kept going, moving more carefully now. We stayed off the road when we could and hid whenever we saw a pair of headlights. After about ten minutes, a fire truck came toward us from town, lights flashing. We ducked behind a thicket of blackberries just as it rounded the curve and drove by.

We started walking again. I was shivering and my legs were chafed from the drying mud on my pants. My ears were burning cold, and I squeezed my hands in my armpits to keep them warm. Still, I felt elated. I'd faced a predator and survived. Again.

I wanted to thank Catherine in a way that broke through her anger, but I couldn't see a way to do it. She made a point of staying several paces ahead of me, and she didn't want to chat. It was too bad, but it was her choice.

Still, there were things we *had* to talk about. "Hey," I called. "We need to get our story straight."

She was so used to working alone that it hadn't even occurred to her. We settled on a rough carjacking narrative. The barn fire would be a problem; there was no way to deny that we'd passed the building at the time it burned, but what should we say? Catherine wanted to claim we hadn't seen anything, but I'd never met a cop who would be satisfied with *I don't know a thing about it.*

In the end, I convinced her to say it had been fine when we passed it, but we'd looked back and seen the flames from down the road.

Traffic began to flow out of town toward us. Morning was coming. My elation over our victory began to wear thin, and my morale dropped. Catherine and I stopped hiding from traffic, and eventually a battered pickup pulled up beside us.

"What brings you folks out here?" the driver asked as she rolled down her window. She was in her sixties, with a thick head of wavy gray hair and a deep, no-nonsense voice.

"My car was stolen," Catherine said in a high, helpless voice. She had a personality for every occasion.

"Out here?" She sounded skeptical. "What'd they look like?"

"Like Chinese fellas," Catherine answered.

"If that don't beat . . . Hold on. Lemme give you a ride into town."

She climbed out of the truck and grabbed a blue plastic tarp from the back. Catherine thanked her and said of course she wasn't offended to be asked to sit on the tarp, considering how muddy she was, of course not. The driver asked me to hop in back with Chuckles, a sleepy Rottweiler. I looked Chuckles over carefully first; he wasn't made of a blue streak and he wasn't even a little beautiful. I decided he wasn't Armand with a fake ID.

The driver introduced herself as Karlene, then climbed behind the wheel and did a U-turn.

Chuckles and I weren't all that interested in each other. I watched the houses go by—big farmhouses with crooked foundations and peeling paint. We crossed a bridge over a narrow river, and the lots became smaller. More of the houses were decorated with Christmas lights and lawn displays. I slumped down out of the wind. Chuckles leaned against me.

Eventually, we did another U-turn and stopped at the edge of a gravel path. Catherine opened her door, so I hopped out of the bed.

"Chuckles keep you warm?" Karlene asked.

"Other way around, I think."

"Hah! You have to watch out for him. There's a motel way other side of town, but these people are nicer. You can shower and call the sheriff here. And I'm in a hurry, so tell them—wait a minute." She glanced at a pickup driving down the street. "What's Phil doing driving back into town so early? With an empty load? Anyway"—she turned back to us—"you folks take care." She sped off.

At the top of the path was a huge rambling farmhouse on a tiny lot. "One moment," Catherine said. She took out her phone again and pressed the dial button. Then she held up a hand and moved far enough away that I couldn't hear what she said. She spoke a few words, then shut the phone. I might have thought she was bad-mouthing me to the society, but her message wasn't long enough.

We walked onto the porch. The sign by the door said this was the SUNRISE BED AND BREAKFAST. Catherine rang the bell, and a slender woman of about fifty let us in. The warm, dry air burned my face and ears.

The woman led us into a living room with a fire crackling in the fireplace and twinkly white lights on the mantel. Catherine told her we'd been carjacked.

She sized up the situation quickly. "We've only got one room left."

"We'll share, if we have to," Catherine said with the brisk efficiency of an executive.

"And no luggage, right?"

"Not anymore, except for my bag."

"Would you like to borrow some things to wear until the stores open?"

Catherine shook her head and looked at me. I almost said no out of habit. Then I looked down at my clothes. I wasn't in Chino anymore. I could accept an offer of help. I said: "Yes, thank you," but it was hard.

She seemed to understand. "Don't fret, hon. Everyone needs help now and then." She went through a door behind the counter, leaving us alone.

Catherine turned to me. "We're going to hole up here for a little while, but you'll have to pay for it. They have my car, which means they know who I am and could trace my credit cards. They don't know you, do they?"

I took my MasterCard out of my wallet and handed it to her. My dirty hands made it sticky. "No, they don't."

The owner returned from the back room with two short stacks of folded laundry. I held up my hands when she tried to give one to me. "Huh," she said, then led me into the back.

She explained that these were her private rooms and I wasn't to come back here without her say-so. I told her that was fine with me, and she passed me off to a tall, heavy man with dull gray hair and a heavily weathered face. He was big enough to be a pro wrestler, if he had been thirty-five years younger and dosed with steroids.

She left, shutting the door behind her. The man examined the side of my face for a moment, then began to unbutton my jacket. I tried to help, but my hands stuck to the fabric. They were still covered with pine pitch.

"We'll get them clean in a second." He sounded like someone's grandfather. He got my jacket off and I lathered up my hands. The mud rinsed right off but not the pitch. "It's all right," he said. He splashed a little bath oil on my hands, and that worked.

I looked at my face in the mirror. "Shit," I said. "He hit me pretty hard, didn't he?"

"I guess so," Wrestler said. "But it's no excuse for that kind of language."

"Sorry."

"You can take a shower in your room. Take the clothes—heck, you can keep them. They don't fit me anymore." He led me back into the living room.

The woman returned with a receipt on a little black tray. I signed it and kept my copy. The place cost less than I had expected but more than I wanted to give up.

Wrestler handed us keys. "Your room is upstairs on the right. Breakfast is served until eleven. Checkout's eleven, too. If you need anything, just ask Nadia or me."

"Thanks."

He left. Catherine suggested I get a shower first, then come back down to meet her. I accepted.

The room was pretty, with floral prints on the bedcovers and little wooden picture frames on the night table. The lampshades were edged with lace and the floor covered by a throw rug woven out of rags. Nadia and Pro Wrestler took pride in this place, but I would never feel comfortable here.

My shower was quick and hot. Pro Wrestler's clothes were a little too roomy, but the pants had a belt, so I was fine with it. There was even a cotton sweater in the stack. I wouldn't have to put on my muddy flannel jacket again. After I rubbed the pitch off them, I transferred my wallet, keys, and ghost knife to the new clothes. Unfortunately, in all the excitement I'd lost my toothbrush.

When I returned to the living room, Catherine was sitting by the fire, a little plate with a half-eaten bagel beside her. "All yours," I said.

"Ray," she said. "Give me your key."

Was she kicking me out in the street? "Why?"

"Because I'm going to take a shower and change. I can't do that knowing you have a key."

I nodded and gave her the key. She took it carefully so our fingers wouldn't touch.

"Thank you. Don't come upstairs."

I took her spot by the fire. It felt nice to sit. I'd been up for nearly twenty-four hours, and the last few had been way too exciting.

The next thing I knew, someone was gently pushing my shoulder to wake me. I didn't even realize I'd fallen asleep.

"Hey there, son," he said. "I'm sorry to disturb you, but I need to talk to you about last night."

I sat up straight and rubbed the sleep from my eyes. "How long have I been out?"

"I'm told it's been about three hours." I rubbed at my eyes again and got a good look at him.

He was wearing a wool cap and a red plaid hunter's jacket. He was small, a little older than Pro Wrestler, and he had a genial face that seemed used to smiling.

"Are you a cop?"

"No," he said and laughed a little. "Washaway is too small to have a police force, and the county sheriff has his hands full, apparently. My name is Steve Cardinal. I'm part of the neighborhood watch around here."

"What do you want from me?"

"Not idle gossip," he said, holding his hands up. "If there's a criminal loose in town, we have an email list we need to notify so what happened to you won't happen to anyone else. I'm not an officer of the court, just a citizen, but anything you tell us could be helpful."

What the hell. I told him the story Catherine and I had cooked up: We came upon a big BMW by the side of the road. When we slowed to ask if they needed help, they pointed guns at us and ordered us out of the car. One of them slugged me.

While the two men were arguing in a foreign language, Catherine and I ran for it. They didn't shoot at us or anything. We ran through a big iron gate, hoping to find a house. Instead, we saw another BMW and more men. We couldn't go back, so we went cross-country.

We followed a trail to a tree farm. No one answered at the house, so we went to the road and walked into town.

It sounded fishy to me, but I told it straight, my voice flat from exhaustion. Cardinal asked what the men looked like, but he didn't ask any cop questions, like *Did anyone see you?* or *What time was that?*

Then he asked me why we were hiding along the side of the road when cars passed. I guessed we'd been seen sooner than I'd thought. I told him that we were afraid the guys in the BMWs would come back. In fact, one of the first cars we hid from was a BMW headed toward town.

He didn't like that, but he forced himself to smile. I gave him a description of the car. He said he'd ask folks to keep their eyes open.

I wanted to ask about the fire, but curiosity is dangerous. Instead, I told him I was glad and let my eyelids sag. He took the hint.

On his way to the door, I heard Nadia speak to him in a low, urgent tone. I couldn't make out what she said, but he did his best to reassure her before he left.

Nadia had a note for me from Catherine. She was going to sleep until at least eleven, and I shouldn't bother her until then. The clock said it was only 10:45, which meant there would still be breakfast. I piled three scones and a mealy apple onto a tiny plate and carried a full coffee back to my chair by the fire.

Once my belly was full, I got restless. I couldn't stop thinking one thing: Where was the sapphire dog?

We had taken on the floating storm, and now I was ready for the main event. I also needed to figure out what, if anything, to do about Tattoo, Frail, and the Old Man. They had killed someone to summon a predator, and that memory brought back clean, welcome anger. Someone needed to do something about that group, and I wanted it to be me.

I did my best not to think about Regina, Ursula, Biker, and Kripke. They complicated things and I wanted simplicity. I grabbed another coffee and went to wake Catherine. We needed a strategy session.

She answered the door on the second knock. She had changed into a pair of dark jeans and a black sweatshirt, which fit too well to be charity like mine. Her eyes were red. She'd been asleep, too.

I felt awkward. "Can we talk about what we do next?"

She stepped back to let me in.

Catherine walked to the far side of the bed and started stuffing things into her bag. Her head hung down to hide her face, and her shoulders were hunched. She zipped the bag closed with a sudden, angry swipe of her arm. Then she wiped her face with her hand and sat by the window. She wouldn't look at me.

I guessed we weren't going to jump into bed and celebrate last night's victory.

"I'm leaving now," she said.

I sat across from her. "We haven't found the predator yet."

"I don't find predators. I don't kill them, either. I don't fight sorcerers and I don't face down gunmen. I'm an investigator. My job is to confirm that something bad is going on, then contact the society. I give them enough information to get started, and I get out of their way. I shouldn't even have gotten this damn job."

"You already sent the photos of the license plates?"

"Yes. Even though most of those cars were rented, they'll still be able to trace them. Pictures of the people would have been better, but that didn't happen. Now we have a predator on the loose and a sorcerer summoning more. We need a peer to handle this. Maybe more than one."

My heart skipped a beat. Annalise was a peer. "Is Annalise coming?"

Catherine gave me a careful look. "I don't know who they'll send."

My whole body grew warm. I wanted Annalise here with me. I needed her. She had power and she didn't falter. Everything was simple for her. She would have dummy-slapped Ursula into next week, and I would have never even heard of a floating storm.

Catherine said: "You should leave, too."

"What? Why?"

"For a lot of reasons. You're not trained for this. You have that one spell in your pocket and whatever is all over those tattoos of yours, but that's it. Hell, we don't even know what we're facing."

"Regina Wilbur said it was a sapphire dog."

"She did?" Catherine seemed startled. "Why didn't you tell me before?"

"Because a predator was trying to kill us," I answered, which didn't make a damn bit of sense. I should have told her everything in case she made it but I didn't.

Damn. She had asked me what I'd found out, and I'd answered *Stuff*. She was right. I wasn't trained for this. "I should have, though. I'm sorry."

"Anything else?"

I took a deep breath and told her everything that happened after we'd split up. When I finished, I asked her: "What's a sapphire dog?"

"I heard about one once. A . . . friend of mine said it was a beautiful creature that destroyed anyone who saw it. That's all I know."

"Isn't there a book or website or something? Shouldn't there be a database or an encyclopedia with pictures and—"

"No," she answered. "There isn't one and there never will be one, for good reason. The society doesn't share information."

"We could do our job a whole lot better if they did."

"Information shared is information leaked. Any secrets the society shares with the rest of us would eventually be sold, or be scammed or tortured out of us."

"Tortured?"

She sighed heavily. I was annoying her and she wanted me to know it. "This isn't a low-stakes game we're playing, Ray. Anyone who finds out what we are will want to know everything we know. Everything. And they won't be gentle about it, either. The more people hear about sapphire dogs and floating storms, the more they'll want one. That's when they start searching for spell books."

I didn't answer right away. Of course she was right. I'd already heard Professor Solorov and Kripke say that very thing.

And it wasn't as though this was my first encounter with magic. Both previous times had been bloody and awful. Catherine had a point.

"You said I should leave town for a lot of reasons," I said. "And you've been angry with me since we faced the floating storm. What happened? Should I have used my ghost knife against it?"

She let out an exasperated laugh that turned into another sigh. "I'm not angry with you, Ray. Okay, I was, but not anymore. You mean well. It's this Annalise that pisses me off. She's the one who put those spells on you, am I right? And she has you thinking she's such hot shit that you're practically creaming in your pants over her."

I suddenly felt very still. "Watch it," I said.

"Or what?" she snapped, straining to keep her voice low. "What are you going to do? Feed me to a predator?"

"What the hell are you talking about?"

"See? This is what I'm talking about. This! When this Annalise brought you into this life, what did she tell you about the predators?"

"They love to be summoned but hate to be held in place," I said. There was some other stuff she'd explained, but I didn't think Catherine was pissed off about where they came from or whether they were angels, devils, or, as Annalise said, neither.

"And that's it?"

I didn't like the way this was going. It was one thing to have her angry with me, but this was worse. She was treating me like a fish just arrived on the cellblock.

It made me want to lose my cool with her to make her back down, but part of me knew her anger was justified. I didn't know why, but I trusted her enough to assume it. "And we have to destroy them. Kill them," I added, because she was being honest with me, and I wanted to be honest in return.

"That's what I thought. What about feeding them? What about serving them a late-night snack?"

I felt my face flush. I'd let the floating storm feed from the power lines for too long, and she knew about it. "I'm sorry," I said. "I cut the power pole as soon as I realized, but—"

"Power pole? I don't care about a power pole. I'm talking about people."

I stared at her, trying to figure out what she meant. "Do you mean the two assholes who shot at us?"

"Of course I do, Ray. You led the predator to them and let it feed."

"It zapped them with lightning. Red lightning. It didn't *feed*."

"Predators feed in all sorts of ways. . . . Okay. Listen up. When I first signed on to this damn job so-and-so years ago, I was investigating a string of overeating suicides. People were eating and eating and they could not stop themselves. Eventually, they ruptured their guts and died in agony, but if anyone tried to restrain them, they howled like starving dogs. Nobody could figure out what the hell was going on, but I did. It turned out that it was a tiny little predator that looked like a songbird, sort of. People were killing themselves because they heard this birdsong, and somehow this predator was feeding off of that."

"What happened to it?" I asked.

"I don't know. I sent my report and skipped town before it noticed me and sang outside my window. No one ever tells investigators how it turns out. We're not secure."

"You think the floating storm fed on them, somehow?" I asked, still doubtful.

"I don't know how it works," she said. "They're not like us. There's a different physics where they come from. A different reality. All I know is that they don't kill for fun, and they don't waste their time."

I looked down at the woven rug. The weave was complex, all twisted around itself and bound tight. I wondered what I would have to know to be able to make a rug like that and how much it paid, because I wasn't as ready for this life as I thought.

And while Annalise had been shockingly ruthless sometimes, she had never allowed a predator to kill anyone.

Catherine stood and straightened her sweater. "Don't be too hard on yourself. You screwed up in a big way, but you didn't know any better and we fixed it. And I wouldn't have survived the night if not for you. Besides, when I said I didn't want to see people killed, I was including you. None of this will be in my full report."

"Don't lie for me," I said.

"Okay then." She took out her cellphone and dialed a number.

"Catherine Little, supplemental report," she said. Then she repeated what I'd told her but much simpler and faster than I had. She'd had practice, I guess.

She also told them the floating storm had taken two victims at my instigation because I had an "all enemies" outlook.

She paused to listen to their response. She looked at me and said, "Absolutely not. He just needs someone willing to explain how all this works."

That gave me a chill. I was grateful to her for having this conversation where I could hear.

Catherine explained that she was leaving the site and hung up. She went into the bathroom and returned with a couple of small bottles, which she jammed into her jump bag. "Ready to go?"

"I want that phone number."

She smiled at me. There was a trace of kindness in it. "So many do. If they want you to have it, they'll give it to you."

We went downstairs. Catherine suggested I check out, but I surprised us both when I said I wouldn't. She studied my face for a moment, but nothing needed to be said.

On the street, the air was brisk and damp, and I thought we'd have rain soon. There was no sidewalk and we had no car. We walked along the shoulder of the road, watching for careless drivers and Yukons, BMWs, and Mercedes.

A couple of pickup trucks drove by, and a man with a thick, dreadlocked ponytail pedaled by us in a recumbent bike decorated to look like Santa's sleigh.

Catherine seemed to know where we were going. She led me through an intersection with a four-way stop, then turned left at the next. At that, we'd entered the business district, such as it was.

The first building we passed was a visitor's center, which was closed, then a bagel shop and a general store. After that, we passed a bar, a bank, and a beauty shop, all decorated with tasteful white lights. There was a single sporting goods store behind the beauty shop. I noted the location in case I needed another change of clothes.

A banner strung above the street announced the upcoming Christmas festival.

Just beyond a pizza place, the neighborhood turned residential again. The road twisted and turned up ahead, with a steep hill behind the homes on one side and a long drop behind the homes on the other. Washaway was laid out in the flattish spaces that followed the twists of the ravines and gullies.

We turned the corner and approached an auto mechanic shop.

The building was painted nausea green, and the sign above the door was obviously old but kept in meticulous condition. The front door was open despite the time of year. It looked like any other garage I'd ever seen, maybe cleaner.

There was only one person there: a short guy in green overalls working under the hood of a Dodge Aries. I scuffed my feet so he wouldn't be surprised by our approach, and he stood up. He was Asian, and for a stupid moment I thought he was one of Yin's men, waiting to ambush us.

He had a broad, tranquil face that showed the ravages of teen acne. His hair was cut into a buzz, and there was a smear of black grease on his nose. He picked up a rag and began wiping his hands, presumably so we wouldn't offer to shake his hand. "Hey, now," he said, his voice surprisingly deep. "How you folks doin'?"

His name was Hondo, like the movie, not the motorcycle, he said. With the flat, clipped tone of the executive again, Catherine asked if he had cars for rent, and he answered yes. He put his tools away carefully and led us around back, explaining that he did a decent side business renting to folks while he worked on their cars.

There were three to choose from. Catherine went with an Acura again. I nixed a Corolla hatchback and picked a Dodge Neon. I'd have preferred something bulkier, just in case, but those were the choices.

We went into the office, which wasn't as clean as the rest of the garage. We filled out the forms, and he ran my credit card through his little machine to put down a deposit. He told Catherine how to get to the train station and offered to pick up the car there for an extra charge. I bought all the insurance he offered, which made him nervous.

Catherine and I went out front while Hondo brought the cars around. "You should change your mind," she said.

"I can't." A Volvo station wagon puttered down the street. There was a Christmas tree stuffed in the back. "What's an 'all enemies' outlook?"

She looked at me evenly. "*All enemies are equal*. It's someone who thinks serial killers, business competitors, pedophiles, or abusive fathers-in-law are just as bad as the predators from the Empty Spaces. To the society, there's only one true enemy, along with the humans who summoned them. No feeding the monsters, no matter whose head you put on the platter."

I nodded. She presented so many different faces to so many people, I couldn't help but wonder whether she was acting for me, too. Normally, I wouldn't care—if she acted roles, she had a reason for it. It wasn't up to me to peel back that disguise.

But we'd killed a predator together. We'd been a team. I was grateful to her, but even though she was right beside me, she was still remote. I was afraid that my gratitude wasn't getting through the defenses she kept.

Maybe it was selfish of me and unfair to her, but I wanted a glimpse of the real Catherine Little before she drove out of my life forever, so I said: "How did it feel to kill that predator?"

Her expression softened and became thoughtful. A smile turned up the corner of her mouth.

The Acura arrived. She tossed her bag into the backseat. "See you again sometime, Ray." She was still smiling as she got into the car.

I watched her pull away. Part of me thought I should have gone with her. Neither of us was qualified to face a predator. She was doing the smart thing. A peer was coming, after all. This job was best left to them.

Except I had no idea how long that would take. It was one thing if a bidder captured the sapphire dog and got away. They could be tracked down. But what if none of them captured it?

And really, what did I have to do that was more important than this? Stock shelves at the supermarket?

Hondo gave me the keys to the Neon, and I got behind the wheel. If I was going to run back to the straight life I'd once wanted so badly, now was the time.

I couldn't do it. I couldn't go back to facing cereal boxes while a predator was on the loose. The idea was absurd.

Besides, Annalise might show up at any time.

I pulled out of the lot with no destination in mind. Maybe the sapphire dog would run into the street and under my tires. Maybe I would come up with a real plan. Each possibility seemed as likely as the other.

There was a gunshot from somewhere nearby. I stopped in the middle of the intersection and rolled down my window. There were two more shots. The echo seemed to come from the center of town, so I did a U-turn and drove into the residential area.

There was some other traffic, but I didn't see anything unusual. I didn't hear any more shots.

Then I saw a house with the side door standing open. I parked and got out of the car.

The house was white with black trim. Above the third-floor window, someone had painted a black-and-white checkerboard. The front door was shut and the drapes drawn tight.

I went around the side of the house, my shoes sloshing through the mud. There was no one at the windows. For a moment, I thought

I had come to the wrong place. Then I reached the open door and peered in.

It was a kitchen, also done in a black-and-white checkerboard. On the floor, a woman lay stretched out, a pool of bright red blood spreading around her.

I drew my ghost knife and stepped inside. If a phone was handy, I'd call 911 for her, but I didn't think it would do much good. Her belly had been cut wide open.

The kitchen was a mess. Loose mail and newspapers were stacked on the counters, and the table was dusted with crumbs and splotches of purple jelly. I spotted the phone on the wall beside the fridge and started toward it.

"Clara!" someone called from outside. It was an old man's voice. I put my ghost knife into my back pocket. "Clara!" he called again and stepped into the doorway. "Oh my Lord!" He moved toward the body, splashing the toe of one rubber boot in her blood. He had a double-barreled shotgun in his hands. Then he saw me.

"Hands in the air!" he shouted. I complied. "What the hell did you do here, huh? What did you do?" His voice trembled with rage, and I thought he might twitch hard enough to shoot me accidentally.

"Don't pull that trigger." I kept my voice calm. "The police will be here soon if we call 911."

"I already have, smart-ass." He smirked at me fiercely. He straightened his shoulders and brushed back his wispy white hair. He was posing like a hero. "Don't wet your panties. I'll just hold you here until the sheriff comes. Unless you try something stupid. Get me?"

"Got you," I answered. He didn't like my tone. He wanted me afraid, but I wasn't going to give him the satisfaction.

"Why shoot you when you can get the needle, eh? I hear that's real painful, like burning to death on the inside. A man who murders a woman don't deserve no better than that."

He was a terrible bluffer, and I wasn't spooked. He decided to drop it. We both looked at the woman on the floor. She was wearing a fleece pullover decorated with poinsettias. There was a little Santa pin on her collar.

She also had a white mark on her face, just like the well-ventilated gunman on the Wilbur estate. Because she was on her back, I could see the whole thing; it started near the point of her chin, ran across her lips, up her cheek, and onto her forehead. It was about the width of the pad of my thumb, and it looked very much like a bleach stain on cloth.

I had no idea what it meant, but I was pretty sure it hadn't killed her. If it had, she wouldn't have needed so many stab wounds.

Still, where had it come from? It could have been a birthmark or an old scar, I guessed, although the odds that a woman in a small town in the American Northwest would have the same mark as a hired thug from Hong Kong weren't worth taking seriously.

Then I noticed the revolver in her left hand. It was big, clunky, and black, the sort of gut blaster home owners prefer—no concealment necessary.

There was a china plate on the floor by my foot. A raw porterhouse had been placed on it, but it was untouched.

So, the woman and the gunman were both armed when they were killed. The plate on the floor suggested a dog, and the expensive, untouched steak suggested even more.

My arms were getting tired, but I had no intention of asking permission to put them down. After a few minutes, Steve Cardinal stepped into the doorway. "My God," he said when he saw the body on the floor. "Isabelle! What happened?"

"About time someone got here," the old man said. He sagged, letting his shotgun droop, and slumped into a dining room chair. It hadn't occurred to me that he would be getting tired, too. "I caught the feller. He was still standing over the body. Almost shot him, too."

Cardinal looked down at the body, then at me. "Oh, Preston, he's not the killer. Isabelle has been stabbed, and he doesn't have a drop on him."

"What?"

"Unless you found a spear in his back pocket. But thank you for calling me. One moment." He took out his cell and went outside. It was only a minute before he came back in. "Bill and Sue are on their way." Cardinal looked at me. "You can put your arms down, son. What are you doing here?"

Now he was ready to play the cop. "I heard gunshots and came out this way. I saw the open door and found her on the floor."

Cardinal turned toward Preston and laid a friendly hand on his shoulder. He managed a smile, but it was strained and his face looked pale. They were two old men trying to find the strength to do an unpleasant job. "Preston, I need to ask you a favor. Go out to the street and look for the ambulance. If Stookie is driving, we'll have to send up a flare to get him to the right address."

Preston took a little white pill from a pill bottle and put it under his tongue. "I can do that." He shuffled out the door.

Before Cardinal could start questioning me again, I asked: "She doesn't live here, does she?"

Cardinal put his hand in his pocket. "Now, how did you know that?"

"When Preston came in, he was calling 'Clara,' not 'Isabelle.' She lives nearby, though? Lived, I mean."

"I'm the one with questions that need answering, son. Having you pass the Breakley place just as it burned down—and that's the only way you could have gotten into town from the estate—was quite a coincidence. This is too much."

"You know something of my history, don't you?"

"I can Google," he said. "I know about the arrest in Los Angeles and the time you served. I know about the incident in Seattle last year, although some of the details don't make much sense. Drugs, wasn't it? Some kind of designer drug made a friend of yours go on a killing spree."

He wasn't even close to right, except about the killing spree. I felt a flush of shame at the memory, though. Not only had Jon killed people, he'd eaten them, too. I was grateful Cardinal hadn't mentioned that, because if he'd read news reports on the story, he knew about it.

Still, "drug-induced psychosis" was the official explanation for the events of the previous fall when I tried to save my oldest friend from the Twenty Palace Society—and from himself—and ended up killing him instead. But that official explanation could be useful.

"That's pretty much it," I said.

"Well, what's happened here doesn't have anything to do with that, does it?" A siren grew louder.

I hesitated before I answered. "I don't know."

He sighed and drew a small revolver from his pocket. "If you won't talk to me honestly, son, I'm going to have to do things neither one of us likes." He took a pair of handcuffs from his back pocket. "I'm going to make a citizen's arrest. I'm not going to have trouble with you, am I?" The siren was close.

"Me? I'm Mr. Cooperation. You don't have to cuff me."

"I'm afraid I do. I have to look around now. I'll be back in a few to let you loose, but I can't rightly take any chances. Not with what's been going on today. Hold your wrist next to the handle there."

He pointed at the oven door. It was an old-fashioned black iron handle and attached pretty solidly. I put my wrist beside it so he could cuff me easily.

If Cardinal was nervous about me, he didn't show it. I didn't let my nervousness show, either. I doubted he'd be convicted if he "accidentally" shot me. Hell, he probably wouldn't even be arrested. I was an ex-con from L.A. Who cared about me?

And he hadn't said a word about the things I did in Hammer Bay.

The siren fell silent. Cardinal went outside and waved to someone, then returned to the house and walked through the other rooms.

The first paramedic was a black woman about my age with unruly hair pulled into a ponytail. She was squat like a fireplug and had broad, strong hands. The man who followed her through the door was a six-foot-four white guy with a wool-lined hunter's cap and a bushy gray beard. They carried a gurney.

"Holy . . ." The woman let her voice trail off.

"That's Isabelle, all right," Bushy Beard said. "What a fucking day."

Ponytail stepped up to the body. I could hear her shoe splash in the blood. "Damn."

Bushy Beard had a clipboard in his hands, but he wasn't writing anything down. Instead, he was looking at me. "I knew her."

"I'm sorry for your loss," I said. That made his eye twitch. "I'm the one who found her."

"Yeah, right," Ponytail said. "That's why you're in cuffs. This woman went to grade school with my mother. She drove our whole family to my grandfather's funeral."

They were angry and trying to talk themselves into letting it go. It wasn't a sudden anger, though. They seemed more tired than shocked. I wondered what else had happened that day. Had they been to the Wilbur estate? Had someone been hurt at the burning barn?

"You shouldn't have done this," Bushy Beard said.

"Shouldn't have done what? Find a body?" I was getting annoyed. Everyone was so sure I was guilty just because they didn't recognize my face.

"Yeah," Ponytail said. "Right."

"What did you want?" Bushy asked. "Money?"

I took a deep calming breath and tried to shrug it off. These people had just lost a friend, I told myself. There was nothing to be gained by losing my temper.

But he wasn't done. "How did it feel? Did you get off on it?"

That was my limit. "Go fuck yourself," I said. "You think I'd come to fucking *Washaway* if I wanted money? Or to get off?"

That was what he wanted. He moved toward me. "It must have been something else, then."

"Kick his ass, Bill," Ponytail said.

I had the ghost knife in my pocket but no way to use it without both of them seeing. I was glad that I'd offered my left to Cardinal. If I was going to fight one-handed, I wanted to use my right.

He lumbered toward me. I threw a right jab at his chin. He was expecting it and caught my arm. Grappling, we fell against the stovetop, his massive weight bearing down on me. I wriggled my right arm, trying to get it in a position to gouge at his face, but he was too heavy and too close. His breath smelled of cheap teriyaki and expensive mints.

He hit the side of my face with a huge, heavy left. It hurt, but I'd been hit harder in the previous twenty-four hours.

The punch loosened things up between us. Before Bushy Bill could close in again, I drove my knee into his crotch. He hissed, doubled over, and staggered back a couple of steps. I threw a right elbow toward his face, but he felt it coming and leaned away from it. He threw a wide, swinging right at me. I couldn't block it with my left, so I ducked and caught it on the crown of my head. It hurt, but I knew it hurt him more.

"For goodness sakes!" a thin voice yelled. "What's going on here?"

Cardinal stood in the kitchen doorway with a swaddled baby in his arms. He had a diaper bag over his shoulder and an unhappy look on his face.

Bill shuffled to the opposite counter and stared at the floor, looking as if he would back all the way through the wall and out of town if he could.

Cardinal marched up to him and laid the baby in his arms. I caught a glimpse of its tiny, perfect little face. Cardinal folded the blanket over its eyes to block the light. "Don't wake that baby, Bill. Take him out to the ambulance and check him over, you hear me? Check him over good. Now."

Bill waddled to the door. Cardinal turned to Ponytail. "For goodness sakes, Sue! Don't you know any better?"

"We saw him handcuffed next to Isabelle's body, and we thought—"

"No, you didn't think! Gosh darn it!" Cardinal's voice was high and thin, more of a whine than a shout. Sue looked ashamed. "You'll be lucky to just be suspended. This man could press charges against you."

"Him?" She sounded startled and outraged. She glanced back at the cuffs. "But Isabelle and the Breakleys—"

"He's an innocent man, Sue. Innocent. Can I tell you how I know that? Because no one has proved him guilty yet. Even that befuddled old Lutheran from the public defender's office could get him sprung now. When the sheriff comes, he may have to arrest *you*. Do you understand why we can't have this sort of malarkey?"

"I'm sorry, Steve."

"Have you pronounced yet?"

"Yeah."

"Good. Go out to the ambulance and try to figure out where we're going to find two paramedics to replace you."

Sue went outside. Cardinal took a deep breath and took out his handcuff keys. "Mr. Lilly, I'd like to apologize for myself as a man and as a citizen of the town of Washaway. I expect better from our people, and I certainly don't want you to think I put handcuffs on you so Bill could . . . do what he did. I'm truly sorry." He opened the cuffs and put them away.

"I know you didn't," I said.

"Will you press charges?" he asked reluctantly, as though he would have to do the paperwork.

"I don't know yet," I said. I didn't have any interest in suing the town, but the threat was leverage I wasn't prepared to give up. "What did she say about the Breakleys? Did the fire spread to their house?"

"No." I was tremendously relieved. "The whole family is dead, though. A seven- and a nine-year-old girl, both parents, and the girls' grandmother. Sue and Stookie just came from the scene," he added, trying to get a little sympathy for them.

"What happened?"

"I can't really talk about that. Did you or your lady friend know them?"

"No, not at all." I shut my mouth, hoping Cardinal would fill the silence.

He didn't oblige. "What did you see on their farm, Mr. Lilly? Why did you rush toward the sound of gunshots? Does it have something to do with what happened to your friend?"

"Can I call you Steve? Because my name is Ray."

"Sure, Ray."

"Shouldn't the cops be asking these questions, Steve?"

He took a deep, weary breath. "They should, if they would answer our calls for help. The fire truck came for the Breakley fire, but the sheriff hasn't showed up yet. Maybe he had a car accident or something. But yes, it should be the police asking these questions. We're going to have to make do. Does this have anything to do with what happened to your friend?"

"Maybe," I said. "Did the Breakleys look like they'd been eaten?"

Steve looked back at Isabelle and the untouched porterhouse on the floor. "No, they didn't. Now tell me why you ask."

I knew I should keep my mouth shut, but I talked anyway. "Last night, while those guys were carjacking us, I got a weird vibe off them. Something about them reminded me of that friend of mine who died last year."

"What was it, specifically?"

"I don't know," I said. "Something about the way they talked and acted. Something about the look in their eyes. Maybe it doesn't make sense, but I thought they were high in the same way that Jon—that my friend was."

Steve took that in with a thoughtful nod. I could see that he still didn't like my story, but he believed it. His cell rang. He answered, listened for a moment, and said, "I'll get out there right away."

He turned to me. "Ray, we seem to be having quite a busy day today. I think you and your lady friend should stay in town for a while. When he does finally get here, the sheriff will want to talk to you. I'll contact you later at the Sunrise."

Obviously, he was used to throwing his weight around town. I nodded and he rushed outside. I followed.

Bill and Sue gave me a sullen glare as I passed their ambulance, but Preston was gone. Good riddance to him and his shotgun, I thought. Steve climbed into his car, an old Crown Vic, and started the engine. I lagged behind, acting as if I was in no rush.

He pulled into the road. I followed him as he drove into a less populated area. Traffic was sparse, so I let him pull way ahead. Eventually, he stopped by the side of the road behind a charcoal-colored Honda Element. By the time I pulled in behind him, Steve was standing by the Honda's driver door, talking into his cell. There was an Escort parked on the other side of the road.

Steve didn't look pleased to see me. A woman came toward me as I climbed out of the rental. She was about thirty-five, with a pixie cut and a runner's physique. She wore wool pants and a pink jacket, and she looked pissed. "Keep your distance," she said as I approached. "This is a crime scene."

"You're not a cop," I said as I walked by her. "I think I know what I'm going to see here, but I have to see it for myself."

I stepped up to the window. A woman of about Isabelle's age was slumped in the driver's seat. She had dyed red-gold curls that looked like they cost a lot of money. A long white mark ran up her cheek and across her nose. Her lap was drenched in blood. She had been gut shot. A bloody butcher knife was in her hand, and there was an off-color circle on the passenger door.

It was feeding, I suddenly realized. Whatever the sapphire dog was doing to these people to make them kill one another was how it fed itself.

And it had just spent more than two decades in a plastic cage. I bet it was *starving*.

"I can't understand it," Steve said, ending his call. "The hospital is back the other way."

"This is Clara, isn't it?" I asked as I went around the front of the car. The engine was still running.

"Yes," Steve said. "Why did she leave her grandson? Why didn't she call 911?"

"What's out on that road?" I asked.

The runner stepped into my field of vision. "Who are you?"

"I'm Ray Lilly. Who are you?"

"Justy Pivens. I'm part of the neighborhood watch. What do you know about this?"

"I know people in your town are starting to kill one another. What's out at the end of this road?"

Steve was too shaken to play cop for a moment. "Nothing. The camp and fairgrounds, and a feeder road that connects to I-5, eventually, but there's nothing out there for a woman with a bullet in her. Not for miles."

I went around the car. There was another discolored circle on the outside of the passenger door. Steve and Justy hadn't noticed it, so I didn't point it out. There was another line of soup-can footprints in the mud leading away from the car.

"What are you looking at?" Steve asked. He came around the car. "What the heavens could those be?"

Justy frowned at the prints. "They aren't animal tracks," she said. "They look like stilts. Four-legged stilts?"

The tracks went up a bare hillside toward a lonely farmhouse.

"Is your gun loaded?" I asked.

Steve hesitated before he answered. "Yes, it is. I loaded it this morning."

"What about you, Justy?"

"In the car."

"Get it and follow us, if you want."

We went up the hill, following the footprints in the mud.

"Ray, I need you to tell me what's going on. I can't just go on this way without knowing what to expect. And we've had more deaths in town today than we've had in the last three years. Gosh darn it, don't keep me in the dad-blamed dark!"

He was whining again. I wondered what it would take to drag a little profanity out of him. "I'll be honest with you," I said. Justy had followed us, and I made sure to address her as well. "I don't know. Let's go up to the house and see if anyone is still alive."

It was only about twenty yards to the front porch, but Steve was an old guy. I tamped down a tangle of scraggly bushes and steadied him over an old log. He was slowing me down, but he and Justy were locals. I wanted them with me.

The porch was made of unpainted cedar, weathered until it was as gray as Steve's hair. A small stack of fertilizer in plastic bags gave off an unpleasant farm stink. The strings of lights around the porch were dark. The boards creaked loudly under our weight.

Steve walked up to the front door and slammed the knocker three times. I was a bit surprised at that; I'd been peeking in windows and breaking into houses since last night. Actually knocking on a door seemed quaint.

Heavy boots clumped toward us, then the door was yanked inward and a woman leaned out. She was in her mid-thirties, plain-faced, and had what looked to be permanent bedhead. She was dressed head to toe in fleece sweats. A set of keys jangled in her hand.

A long white streak ran from her jawline over her ear and up into her hair.

"Penny, have . . . are you okay?"

"I'm fine, Steve," she answered. "What do you want?"

"There's been some trouble in town." Steve's tone was cautious. "It led us out front."

Justy said: "What's that on your face?"

Penny shifted from one foot to the other, obviously anxious to get back to whatever she was doing. "Nothing's on my face. And there's no trouble here. Okay? Gotta go."

She glanced at me without interest and started to close the door. Steve blocked it with his foot. "I'm sorry, Penny, but you do have a white something on the side of your face. Where did you get it?"

"I was baking earlier," she said, her voice flat and unpleasant. "It's flour."

"Is Little Mark here? I'd like to come in to talk some more. To both of you."

"It's a bad time, Steve."

"Please, Penny?" he persisted. "Folks have died."

That didn't interest her at all. "It's a bad time for me. Maybe to-morrow."

"Now, Penny, I'm afraid I have to insist."

She sighed again. "Fine. Give me a moment." She glared at his foot until Steve drew it back, then she closed the door.

Damn. This wasn't right. She wasn't curious about me, the trouble in front of her property, or the deaths in town. Something was very wrong.

"It's okay," Steve said, maybe sensing my unease. "Penny's my cousin and we get along very well." He wrung his hands nervously, looking from me to Justy and back again. Justy looked pinched and skittish. She stayed close to the top of the stairs.

In the window behind the fertilizer, I saw a curtain move. It was a boy, maybe fifteen years old, with brown hair in a ragged bowl cut. His eyes were big and brown and empty. He had a white mark on his face, too.

The door swung open suddenly. I heard a low growl and lunged forward.

Penny heaved herself through the doorway, swinging something over her shoulder at Steve. I caught hold of it even as I realized it was an axe and pushed. The blade passed over Steve's skull and thunked against the doorframe.

Steve cried out in a high voice. Footsteps thumped on the wooden stairs, leading away.

Penny jabbed the butt end of the axe at me. I ducked. The handle whiffed by my jaw. I put my shoulder against her hip, wrapped my arms around her knees, and upended her onto the floor.

The axe flew out of her hands and bounced across a dingy throw rug. She reached for me, hands curled like claws, but I caught her wrist and pulled her onto her stomach, then planted a knee in her back.

Steve was still standing in the doorway, his mouth hanging open. Justy was nowhere in sight.

"Bring your cuffs in here before someone gets killed!"

That jolted him into action. He fumbled at his back pocket.

I took my ghost knife from my pocket and slipped it through the back of her head. It passed through without leaving a mark the way it always does with living people. It didn't even cut her hair.

But it didn't stop her thrashing. It didn't cut away her anger and hostility the way it had for Horace. Damn. She was immune, just like Ursula. Was it something to do with the stain on her face, which Ursula didn't have? I didn't know, but I was pretty sure it wasn't my spell.

I glanced around, worried that the boy would come at me with a kitchen knife, but I couldn't see him.

Penny tried to wrench her arm out of my grip. I didn't want to hurt her, but I wasn't going to be able to hold her for long if I didn't do something drastic.

Which was the same choice I'd faced with Ursula. People had died and I'd nearly gotten myself killed because I couldn't be ruthless with a woman who wanted to murder me.

I leaned my body weight onto her, pinning her arms to her back. I could have broken them, hit her behind the ear, or stomped on her, but I held back, and my refusal to make that choice became my choice. If that made things difficult later on, so be it.

Steve knelt beside her but didn't cuff her. He pleaded for her understanding, apologized for what he had to do, and generally irritated me by trying to be reasonable with a person who had lost all reason. "Just snap them on!" I barked. I bent her arms behind her back, and he did it.

We heard a car engine rev outside.

"No!" Penny screamed. "Don't take him from me! You can't take him away from me!"

I sprinted through the door and across the porch. A dirty white pickup roared across the yard, heading downhill toward the street. It lurched and swerved in the mud. I raced after it.

The truck skidded on a steep part of the yard and slammed against a tree.

I ran around a thicket toward the truck, ghost knife in hand. Maybe the spell was useless against these people, but it made me feel better to hold it. The truck bed was empty, so I circled toward the driver's side. There was a strange sound, like a high-pitched keen mixed with a metallic scrape. I had never heard anything like it; I figured it was a damaged fan belt.

I reached the driver's window. The brown-eyed kid was behind the wheel, holding his bloody forehead—the pickup was too old to have air bags.

"Sit still," I said. "We're going to have someone take a look at that head."

He looked at me, his expression still empty. "I'll kill you," he said. "If you try to take him from me, I'll kill you."

I glanced over at the passenger seat. It was empty. The plastic lining on the passenger door had a discolored patch.

Goose bumps ran the length of my body. The sapphire dog was very close.

I stepped back and looked around. I couldn't see anything but trees, leafless bushes, and mud. Justy laid rubber peeling away down the street. Steve was running toward me as fast as he could, which wasn't fast at all. He had almost reached the back fender when he looked toward the passenger side of the truck.

And stopped. He gaped at something on the other side of the truck that I couldn't see.

I walked toward him. My guts were in knots, but I refused to be afraid. I had come here for exactly this moment.

You're not trained for this, Catherine had said. *It destroys anyone who sees it.*

Steve stood and gaped as I came around the back of the truck and saw the sapphire dog.

CHAPTER EIGHT

It was walking away from us, and I didn't think it looked like a dog at all. It didn't have fur, and its skin was a brilliant electric blue. Its body swayed as it moved, as though it was part cougar and part python. Its four legs extended and retracted in a disturbing, boneless motion, like a set of tentacles or springs. It didn't have wings, but it did have two rows of dark spots running down its back. A second glance showed that they weren't spots at all but actually faceted blue crystals embedded in its flesh. Its long, slender, whiplike tail snapped and wavered the way a stream of water might move as it flowed over a pane of dirty glass.

Then it reached a patch of grass about a dozen feet away from us, turned, and sat on its haunches. Suddenly, it looked very much like a dog. Its broad, oversized head tapered at the front to a snout that had no opening. There were more blue crystals on its forehead and around its impossibly narrow neck. Its ears were long and floppy, almost long enough to be rabbit ears. And its eyes . . .

Its eyes were huge, as large as a cartoon animal's. Its pupils were shaped like eight-pointed stars, and there were five of them in each eye, all shining gold and arranged in a circle.

It stared at us with an unfathomable expression while its pupils slowly rotated. The effect was hypnotic.

The sapphire dog was beautiful. That's a simple word I've used to describe anything from a new car to a moment of karmic payback, but it could never capture the impact the sapphire dog had on me. Framed in bare trees and mud, the otherworldly beauty of it hit me like a punch in the gut. It didn't look solid. It didn't look real. I thought I might be having a vision.

"Lord, thank you for this day," Steve said. He was a few paces to my right. It took an effort to look away from the animal, but Steve was just as stunned as I was. He stepped toward it, and so did I. I didn't want him to be closer to it than I was. I didn't want to share.

The sapphire dog looked at Steve, and I felt a twinge of jealousy—I wanted it to look at me. I wanted to punch the old man in the back of his head and knock him cold, so the sapphire dog would want me and only me.

There was a familiar pressure against a spot below my right collarbone. It meant something, but I couldn't quite remember what it was.

The tip of the sapphire dog's snout began to recede, the way a person might suck at their cheeks to make them hollow. The snout changed color—first to a dark purple, then to shit brown. A nasty, puckered opening appeared—round, wrinkled, and toothless like a shit-hole.

We were in danger. I remembered that the twinge under my collarbone was a warning that I was under attack. There was a tiny feeling of unease deep inside me, but thoughts of the sapphire dog had crowded it out.

This wasn't right. I knew it wasn't right, and if I didn't wake up, I was going to be dead.

It lifted its snout toward Steve. I bolted toward him and knocked him into the mud just as the sapphire dog's long, bone-white tongue snaked out at him.

The tongue passed over us, swiping through the air near my shoulder. I felt Steve hit the ground hard, the air *whuff*ing out of him.

A second wave of love-struck longing washed over me, but this time I recognized the twinge under my right collarbone. My iron gate, one of the protective sigils on my chest, was trying to block a magical attack.

These weren't my feelings. I had to focus on that. The animal—no, the *predator*—across from me was trying to control how I felt.

It turned its attention on me. I rolled to my knees in the freezing mud and cocked my arm to throw the ghost knife. Its eyes widened.

I threw the spell.

The sapphire dog seemed to move in three directions at once. It slid to the left and right at the same moment, and shot straight up from the ground. It was almost as if it was a still image that had split apart.

The three afterimages vanished. The ghost knife passed through empty air.

I jumped to my feet, stepped between Steve and the ghost knife, and *called* it back. Hopefully, he wouldn't see.

The sapphire dog was gone. Although it had split into separate still images before it vanished, there were footprints in the mud heading to the left and right for a few feet. Damn. At least it wasn't cloning itself.

I scanned the area around the house. The predator was nowhere in sight. I ran around to the other side of the truck, but it wasn't there, either.

I laid my face against the cold metal cab. I felt empty. I had a raw, hollow space inside where my adoration for the sapphire dog had been. I knew those feelings weren't mine. I knew they'd been forced on me, but I still felt their absence as a terrible ache. And I knew that, because of them, I'd missed my chance to kill a predator.

Steve was still on his back in the mud. He stared up at the overcast sky and muttered to himself.

A few seconds ago, I'd been about to put his lights out, and I'd been partly protected by the iron gate Annalise had given me. How much worse had it been for him?

I heard a crash from inside the house. The front door was still standing open, but I couldn't see Penny. Damn. Of course she couldn't just wait quietly to be taken to prison.

I kicked the bottom of Steve's shoe. "Get up," I said, my voice more harsh than I'd intended. "You have to call those ambulance assholes for the kid in the truck. You have to take your cousin to jail, too."

I jogged toward the house. The predator might have hidden inside. I didn't think it was likely, but I had to check. It's what I was there to do, after all.

Penny was not in the living room, but the axe still lay where she'd dropped it. I stepped carefully inside. I couldn't see anyone, but I did hear the far-off rasping of metal on metal.

I walked toward the sounds. The throw rug in the middle of the floor and the dingy brown sofa were coated with a fine layer of white cat hairs. Beside the sofa was one of those structures built of flimsy wood and cheap gray carpeting that are supposed to be fun for cats. This one was four and a half feet tall and three feet around.

A dead cat lay on the floor beside it. It had been stomped on, probably by someone with a heavy boot. Someone like Penny.

The kitchen was also coated with cat hairs. The smeary fridge had book reports and pop quizzes held on with magnets. The kid out front was a straight-A student—exactly the sort I used to beat up in my own school days.

Maybe, just maybe, the white stain on his face was temporary.

On the far side of the fridge was a set of stairs leading down to the basement. The sound of metal-on-metal sawing was coming from there.

The wooden stairs creaked under my weight. "Get out!" Penny screamed. "Get out of my house!"

The basement had a concrete floor and a low ceiling. There was a long workbench at one end and a stretching mat at the other. The mat had been repaired many times with duct tape.

Penny was beside the workbench. She'd managed to clamp a hacksaw into a vise and was rubbing the chain of the cuffs up and down the blade.

"Your son is outside," I said. I had a pretty good idea how she would react, but I had to be sure. "He's hit his head and is bleeding pretty badly."

"Get out!" she screamed again.

"An ambulance is on the way to pick him up."

"Get out of here before I kill you!"

Just as I'd thought. When she'd screamed not to take "him" away, she was talking about the sapphire dog, not her own son. It had touched her face and made her fall in love with it. It had fed on her.

She fumbled for a screwdriver on the bench. Her hands were still pinned behind her, and her charge was awkward and slow.

I yanked the screwdriver out of her hand and kicked her behind the knee. She fell onto the padded mat. I took a claw hammer off a hook on the wall. "That was a pretty little animal, wasn't it?"

"Are you a fucking moron? It was the most beautiful thing I've ever seen. If you try to keep me from it, I'll chop you into tiny pieces."

"Yeah, sure. It needs a ride out of town, right? I'll bet it wants to go to a city. Right?" She didn't answer, but the hateful look in her eyes was all the confirmation I needed. "Now listen to this: I'm going to put you in the back of Steve's car. If you fight me"—she began cursing at me, so I raised my voice—"if you fight me, I'll break both your legs."

I slammed the hammer on the concrete floor. She stopped shouting.

"Then," I continued, "you won't be able to take anyone anywhere, and the sapphire dog will find someone else to be with. Get me?"

She glared at me, her breath coming in harsh gasps. Just the idea of losing her precious pet made her eyes brim with tears. "Bide your time," I told her, "or you'll lose any chance you might have had."

Penny let me lead her out of the house to Steve's car. He told her an ambulance was on the way to check her son over, but she didn't even look at him. She didn't care. She sat in the back and I closed the door.

Steve rubbed his face. "We have a jail cell in the basement of the town hall. Sheriff uses it sometimes. The mayor's on her way here with the key."

"Good." As long as she hadn't picked up the predator's knack for walking through solid objects, Penny would be out of the way for a while.

"Now. What in the Sam Hill was that thing?"

Before I could answer, the ambulance arrived. Steve waved Bushy Bill and Sue toward the crashed truck.

"That's the first I saw of it," I said.

"It . . . it was beautiful. And it vanished into thin air, didn't it? I felt . . ."

"You loved it," I said. "You loved it and you wanted it all to yourself."

He squinted up at me. He'd come into contact with the world behind the world, and he didn't even know what questions he should ask. *Information shared is information leaked.* But he'd seen the predator, so he already had the most damning information. And I knew he would talk to Penny soon enough; I didn't want her version of the sapphire dog to be the only one he heard. I had enough enemies as it was.

I said: "This is how it started last year with my friend. Understand? There was a creature that could make certain things happen. In my friend's case, it healed his back and let him walk." There was no need to mention Hammer Bay, so I didn't. "This is something else, though."

"I loved that animal."

"It's not an animal," I told him. "It's smart. It may be smarter than us."

"By golly," Steve said. He rubbed his neatly shaved chin. "Today I don't think that would be too hard."

"Not any day for me," I said. "I've never been smart. But that doesn't matter. What matters is that we have to kill it."

"Can't we just capture it?" I could see the *wanting* in his expression.

"For Christ's sake," I said. Steve winced at my language, and I was glad I hadn't said what I'd originally meant to say. "Look at your cousin. Was she a bad mother before today? Did she hate her son?"

"No," he said. "She loves that boy."

"*Yesterday* she loved that boy. Today all she can think about is that damn sapphire dog." That seemed to stagger him, but I wasn't finished. "And you already know that Clara and Isabelle killed each other over it, don't you?"

Steve stepped away from me, his shoulders slumping forward as if he suddenly bore a heavy weight. "Oh my heavens."

"Maybe it's temporary," I said. He shot a look at me; he hadn't even considered how long it would last. Of course, I'd seen predators at work before, and when they destroyed people, they didn't do it on a temporary basis. "But our first job has to be to find that thing and kill it."

"You made it vanish," he said. "What did you throw at it?"

Now he *was* asking for too much information. "A credit card." I pulled my MasterCard out of my pocket and showed it to him. "I scared it off. I don't think it knows very much about this world."

"Who brought this devil into our world?"

We were getting close to another subject I wanted to avoid. If Steve started talking about Jesus, I wouldn't be able to turn him away from it, and judging by the way he talked to the paramedics, he had a lot of authority in this town.

Annalise had explained that predators and magic had nothing to do with God or hell, angels or demons. Magic was a way of controlling reality, and predators were just what the name suggested—hungry things from a place *outside*, sometimes called the Empty Spaces and sometimes called the Deeps.

If Steve started telling the people of Washaway that they were facing a devil, they might try to protect themselves with prayer and crosses, which was as effective as stopping a sniper's bullet with a hopeful thought.

"It's not a demon," I told him. "It's an alien."

"Oh."

"It didn't come here in a ship. It's just here. And it's been here a long time."

"It has? Where?"

"In Regina Wilbur's house."

"Regina? Why, she . . ."

His voice trailed off. I could see him reconsidering everything he knew about her in light of what he'd seen today. "But she doesn't have a mark on her face."

"No," I said. "She's kept it prisoner. It's been hidden on her estate for all this time. But it can affect us at a distance. I think it did exactly that to her for decades. And I think it's getting stronger."

"What do we do?"

The paramedics were loading the boy into the ambulance. Sue had a bandage on her wrist; from the way the kid was lunging and snapping at them, I guessed he must have bitten her.

"How many roads lead out of town?"

"Just two," he said. "This one, which leads to I-5, and Littlemont Road, which goes past the Breakleys' to the pass."

"We need to block them off. The predator is trying to get to a heavily populated area. Can you block the roads without causing too much suspicion?"

"No," he said, "but the state police can. I'll tell the mayor to call.

Heck, considering everything that's happened, it would be suspicious if we didn't block them. But we're going to do more than that, aren't we?" He looked stricken and miserable. I couldn't help feeling sorry for him.

"We'll try," I said. "And help is coming."

"I'll take your word for it. Just tell me one thing, son. You didn't cause this, did you? You didn't let this thing loose on my town?"

The question startled me, although it shouldn't have. "No."

He sighed in relief. He believed me, although I had no idea why. "I'll take Penny . . ." He trailed off as a battered yellow pickup screeched to a halt at the edge of the road. "Looks like you're going to meet the mayor," Steve said.

The driver's door opened and a burly, gray-haired woman bowled out. She wore a Santa cap and a red-and-green coat covered with snowmen. She bustled up the hill toward us.

Steve turned to me. "What should I tell her?"

"You know her. I don't. Would she believe the truth?"

He sighed. "Not a chance on God's green earth."

"Like I said: you know her. Tell her what you have to."

"Good Lord, Steve, what's going on?" she said when she was a few paces away.

"People are going crazy, Pippa, and the crazy is spreading."

I kept my mouth shut, letting Steve take the lead. She stopped next to us, breathing hard. "Explain. No, wait. First, who are you?"

She stepped close to me. She may have been past sixty and barely five feet tall, but she looked at me with the same bullish challenge I'd gotten from cops and prison-yard toughs.

I didn't answer. "Ray Lilly," Steve said, "this is Pippa Wolfowitz, mayor of Washaway."

"Nice shiner you got there. You're the fellow who got himself car-jacked last night."

"I am."

"Funny how all this happened just as you came to town."

I was about to tell her it wasn't funny at all, but I didn't. For all I knew, one of the bodies I'd found today was a member of her family. She was entitled to be a little testy.

"Pippa, Ray here saved my life. Penny tried to chop me down like a tree, but he stopped her."

"Big Penny?" Pippa looked at the back of Steve's car. "What's she got against you?"

"Not a thing as far as I know. It's like I said: everyone is going crazy. It started at the Breakley place, then somehow got to Isabelle's house. Isabelle brought it here, and it got to Penny and Little Mark."

"It? What *it* got to all those people?"

Steve looked at me, his mouth working. "We don't exactly know yet."

"Don't play games with me, Steve Cardinal. I'm too old for that stuff."

"Sheriff get here?"

"No, and don't change the subject."

"It's all the same subject. You need to call the state police and have them block the roads. We can't let this spread."

"Block the . . . ? The festival is tomorrow! People here *need* this festival. They have bills to pay!"

"Pippa—"

"Is this about November, Steve?"

"For goodness sakes, would you listen to me?" His voice got high and whiny when he was angry. "This has nothing to do with the election."

He was losing her, and the more I thought about it, the less it seemed to matter. What could she do, anyway? Organize a posse? Warn people to stay indoors? I wasn't even sure how useful a roadblock would be.

What I did know was this: I was wasting time listening to these people. I backed away from them and looked up at Penny's house. It was dark and quiet.

I went inside and took out my ghost knife.

I searched the house from basement to attic but didn't find anything out of the ordinary. The sapphire dog certainly wasn't hidden there, and Penny didn't have any spell books I could find. The only things I found were a pair of tabby cats cowering under the bed and an old police-band scanner in the kitchen.

When I went back outside, Pippa and Steve were standing at the back of Steve's car, talking to Penny.

I walked toward the Neon. Pippa heard me coming and held up her index finger, signaling me to wait. I ignored her and kept walking to my car.

Pippa frowned and followed me. "So, this is your dog?"

"Nope."

"But you know about it," she said. "What's wrong with it? Rabies? Why is it blue?"

"Steve and Penny both saw it. Why not ask them?"

She stepped too close to me again. I'd have suspected she was clueless about personal space if it hadn't been for the look on her face. "I have. Now I'm asking you."

Steve had felt the effects of the sapphire dog. I'd talked to him because he already knew enough to get killed. With Pippa, things were different.

And I didn't like or trust her.

The ambulance siren chirped as it pulled out.

"Come on, Pippa," Steve said. "He saved my life and he's trying to help."

She ignored him. "I don't trust you. When the sheriff gets here, I'm going to have you locked up until the real truth comes out."

"Well, you should call him, then."

"I think I will."

She walked away, putting her cellphone to her ear. Steve came close. His expression betrayed his embarrassment, but he didn't apologize.

"Once Penny's locked up," he said, "we'll talk again. Go back to the Sunset, okay? You look like you could use some sleep anyway."

"You'll block those roads, right?"

"Right," he said. "Pippa will order it. I'll make sure."

He started toward his car, but I wasn't finished. "Steve, what happened to the Breakleys?"

He glanced around to make sure Pippa was still on her cell. "They were home when the fire broke out," he said. "The fire chief said he saw them in the basement window while the crews were dousing the barn. They wouldn't come out, though. A couple of hours later, I went back to check on them.

"There was a hole in the stone foundation of the house, like someone had tunneled through. They were all dead. They'd killed each other, starting with the little ones."

"Any white marks?"

"The parents each had one, and the grandmother."

"But not the kids?"

Steve shook his head, got into his car, and did a U-turn to head back to town.

Parents killing their own children. I tried not to think about that. The sapphire dog hadn't touched the two little girls. Maybe it hadn't gotten the chance, or maybe they were too young. Steve had said the girls were seven and nine, and while Little Mark had a white stain, he was at least fourteen or fifteen. The baby Steve had given to the paramedics hadn't been marked, either. Maybe the predator needed its food to be ripe.

After a quick circuit of the rental car to make sure the predator hadn't materialized in the backseat, I drove farther out on the road.

There were no more houses or buildings out this way. I passed several signs telling me the highway turnoff was coming up, and I saw a couple of scattered businesses, a campground, and a turnoff for the church and fairgrounds. Another banner told me the Christmas festival was taking place at the fairgrounds, and a little sign below told me the church was having a benefit lunch . . . well, it was happening right then, as it turned out.

I drove by, passed the school grounds, and entered the town from the other side. I hadn't seen the turnoff for the highway. I did a U-turn and drove back. I missed it a second time. Maybe some joker had moved the signs.

This time I pulled into the fairgrounds. The church was off to the right on a low hill; it looked like exactly the sort of church I'd expect in a little town: small with a peaked roof and a steeple. I parked below the church in the fairgrounds parking lot, a wide asphalt patch that overlooked the fairgrounds below. The grounds were slightly larger than a football field, which I thought surprisingly small until I realized that level ground must be a pretty scarce commodity around here.

I shut the engine off and sat in the car. The sapphire dog had not come this way by accident. It was possible that Clara had chosen the route, but I didn't believe it. Little Mark had tried to chauffeur the predator, too, and I remembered the way it felt to be near that thing. Whatever it would have wanted, I would have wanted, too. The sapphire dog was the one in control.

But why this way? Maybe it wanted to go camping. Maybe it wanted to go to church. Maybe it wanted to get on the feeder road—which I couldn't find—to the highway and then hit the big city, where there were hundreds of thousands of people to make crazy. But it had failed.

Now I was looking across the fairgrounds at a cinder-block building. The door kept swinging open as people went in and out. Why go all the way to Seattle to feed when it could stop off right here?

I climbed from the car and walked along the parking lot. I passed an old fire engine; the firefighters had probably stopped off for lunch after the Breakley fire.

To catch this predator, I'd have to figure out what it wanted. *Eat and reproduce* was the simple answer, but Catherine and her songbird story had made me realize that this wasn't as simple as it seemed.

Maybe it just wanted its freedom. Maybe the most important thing to it right now was not to be captured and starved in a cage again. Then, once it was far away, it would do its thing. Maybe it would call more of its kind here. Or start a cult. Maybe it would create an army and install itself as Pet Emperor.

Unless I destroyed it first.

The cinder-block building was painted white, and I walked inside feeling like a man with a bomb strapped to his chest. I had come eagerly to this little town to kill and possibly be killed, and none of the old ladies smiling at me as I dropped fifteen dollars of Fat Guy's money into the food-bank kitty had any idea how dangerous I felt. There was a second door right in front of me, and behind the welcome table on the right was a long hall filled with lawn equipment.

I accepted a tray in exchange for my donation and went into a much larger room. As I moved down the line at the kitchen windows, a heap of mac and cheese, a pair of chicken drumsticks, succotash, home-baked rolls, and broccoli-cheddar bake were put on my plate. I said thank you. No one had white marks on their faces, and no one seemed likely to go on a murder spree.

The sapphire dog hadn't come here. Not yet.

As I stepped away from the serving line, I scanned the room. There were a dozen round tables set up and ten chairs at each table. Most of the seats were full. At the center table, a half dozen firemen were holding court. They were tall, well-muscled men ranging from their mid-twenties to mid-fifties. Several women—two dozen or so in all—sat at their table or chatted with them from an adjacent table. I wondered if I could sit close enough to hear what they knew about the Breakleys.

"Oh, please join us," a gray-haired woman said from the table nearest me, at the edge of the room. She was sitting with three people: an Asian woman who looked just a few years younger; a brown-eyed toddler wearing tiny earrings; and a woman I assumed was the toddler's mom, plump, with dark hair and a lot of eyeliner.

The gray-haired woman, who had the whitest skin I'd ever seen, introduced herself as Francine, then went around the table and introduced Mai, Estrella, and Graciela. I told them my name was Ray, and Mai immediately asked me if I was the one who had his car stolen. I retold that story, because it would have seemed odd to refuse. The women clucked their tongues and made a fuss over my black eye. Then conversation turned to the Christmas festival.

Just as I was about to steer the topic toward the Breakley fire, another woman stopped by the table. The others called her Catty, which startled me. For a moment, I thought they had copied my habit of giving descriptive names to people, but no, it was just an unfortunate nickname. They traded forced pleasantries until Catty left, then Graciela admitted that she felt obligated to buy some of Catty's jewelry at the festival because Catty had helped her out so often.

Mai kindly told me that Graciela's husband was serving overseas, and while the whole town was happy to help her out, only Catty hinted that she deserved some sort of repayment. Graciela listened to this without looking up from her plate.

They chatted about the display Catty would have and how much Graciela should spend. I wasn't a part of the conversation, but it was too late to move to another table. I was not getting any closer to finding the predator.

I had looked into the sapphire dog's eyes only an hour before. After I'd seen something so alien and beautiful, the everyday chatter around me made me feel utterly out of place.

Then Hondo stopped by. He greeted everyone enthusiastically, especially little Estrella. Turning to me, he said: "I take it your lady friend decided not to leave after all."

Someone on the other side of the room laughed uproariously. People were having fun. "What do you mean?" I said.

He was a little surprised by my tone. "Your friend. She paid me a pickup fee for the train station, but it only takes a half hour to drive out there. I'm still waiting for her call."

Francine noticed the look on my face. "Maybe she has a problem with her phone," she said in a soothing tone.

Now Hondo was looking concerned, too. "I don't think so. Arliss at the station knows my cars. He says it's not there."

Catherine didn't arrive at her destination. I dropped my napkin onto my plate. "Excuse me."

"Hey, man," Hondo said, "do you need help?" Everyone at the table looked ready to jump up and join the search.

"Thanks, but no. I'm sure she's fine. I just need to make certain for my peace of mind."

I pushed my way toward the door. As I passed the firefighters, I heard one of them say he had to get back to his family for Christmas, then they stood, too.

I made my way back to my car. It was nearly three-thirty, and Catherine had left around noon. I had to find out what had happened to her.

CHAPTER NINE

I parked across the street from the B and B. Two people on stilts came down the shoulder of the road. They were dressed in silver costumes, with white masks over the top half of their faces and delicate dragonfly wings on their backs. The costumes were decorated with snowflakes and reflective tape. The rented Acura was nowhere in sight.

I went into the Sunset, still feeling like a bomb ready to explode.

Pro Wrestler was sitting at the little desk in the living room entering figures into a computer. He hunched over the keyboard, carefully tapping the keys with thick fingers, and I felt a startling yearning to be like him. To hell with feeling like a bomb. I'd rather be a human being. I walked up to him and extended my hand. "Thank you for your help this morning," I said. "I'm grateful. My name is Ray."

He already knew my name from my credit card, of course, but he took the hint. "I'm Nicholas. Those clothes look a little loose on you."

We were smiling. "Yeah, but they're warm."

"Good to hear. Staying for the festival?" He looked around the little lobby. I did, too. A man in a long tan coat and a wide-brimmed tan hat sat by the fire. Nicholas's expression was slightly disappointed. Obviously, he'd hoped for a bigger crowd. "Sure," I said, because why not? "Sounds like fun."

I was about to ask if he'd heard from Catherine when Nicholas said: "I almost forgot." He took a manila envelope from the bottom drawer of his desk and handed it to me. My name was written on it in sweeping lines of delicate brown ink. The envelope held something bulky and small.

"Where did this come from?" I asked.

"Nadia found it on the front porch."

I tore open the envelope. It was a cellphone wrapped in a sheet of notepaper. It was Catherine's, but I turned to Nicholas and said: "Someone found it. That was nice of them."

"Does it say who?"

I said the note was unsigned, thanked him, then went to my room. Once the door was locked, I sat on the corner of the bed and opened the slip of paper. It read PRESS REDIAL in the same sweeping hand.

What the hell. I'm good at following directions. The phone rang twice. "Hello?" It was Well-Spoken Woman, and she had me on speakerphone.

"Thanks for the phone," I said. "I have a pal in Tokyo I'd like to call."

"We know your name, Mr. Lilly, and we know why you are here. If you would like your friend to live through the night, come to the Grable Motel. It's out past the Breakley farm. Come right away."

"Give me an hour or so to wrap up."

"Unacceptable."

"I have to wash the blood off," I said testily. If they really did know why I was here, they would believe that.

"All right then." She sounded hesitant, which was what I wanted. We hung up.

The bed smelled like laundry soap, and the plug-in pine scent made the air close. God, how good it would have felt to lie back and close my eyes . . .

There was a knock on the door. I opened it, figuring Nicholas must have another envelope for me.

It was the man in the tan coat. He was a little shorter than me, even with his hat still on, and his skin and hair were the color of sand. "You're Raymond Lilly, aren't you?"

I didn't like the way he was smirking at me. "Yeah. Who are you?"

"I'm Talcott Arnold Pratt. The society sent me here to clean up this mess."

His coat was open, presumably to give me a glimpse at the sigils burned into the lining. A peer! An honest-to-God peer had finally come.

I must have let my relief show. He gave me a sour, condescending smile and pushed into the room. "Shut the door," he said. I did.

Everything about the guy gave off contempt, but I was glad he was there. A peer in the Twenty Palace Society ought to have the power to take out the sapphire dog, not to mention the bidders.

"The investigator who brought me here is—"

"I know who she is. I've read her report and don't need to talk to her."

"You don't understand. She's been kidnapped. I need your help to get her back."

"I don't rescue people. I kill predators."

Of course not. I hated this guy already, but there were bigger things at stake than my feelings. "Okay. What can I do—"

"I don't answer questions from wooden men. Are we clear?"

I felt the skin on the back of my neck prickle. Was I going to have to throw down with this guy right here? "We're clear."

"Has anything happened since the last supplemental report?"

"I don't know when Catherine made the last supplemental report," I answered. I kept my tone neutral.

"It was this morning."

"Then yes."

Pratt was getting annoyed, too. "Yes, what?"

"Yes, something more has happened since the last report."

He glowered, then looked away and laughed a little, shaking his head. He loosened his coat, probably to give me another look at his sigils. "Has she told you what's at stake here?"

"Wait . . . let me guess. End of everything that matters to us, right?"

"That's right. Creatures from the Empty Spaces are terribly inefficient predators. They invade a habitat and hunt it to destruction. They don't have any balance about them."

"The sapphire dog isn't killing anyone—just making them crazy."

He continued as if I hadn't spoken. "But you want to put your pride above all of that, don't you? You want *respect*." He gave me a thin smile. I'd seen that look before. It was a cop's expression—a look of superiority so complete he would never think to question it.

"Sure, sure," I said. "The stakes are so high you get to do whatever you want and I have to take it. Let me give you an update so you can make your big exit."

I gave him a quick rundown of everything that had happened since Catherine and I rented the cars. I described the predator, the way the victims had looked, and how it seemed to split apart when threatened. He asked what I had threatened it with, and I told him Steve's gun; I wasn't going to tell this jerk about my ghost knife.

When I started telling him about the cellphone and the kidnapping call, he lost interest. When I got to ". . . then I opened the door and was insulted by you," he was already walking out.

He stopped in the hall and smirked. "You're done. Run along home now, if you can." He left.

There was a moment when I could have booted him in the ass, but I let it pass. If Pratt was anything like my boss, he could have pinched my head off with one hand. Peers were strong and tough—they had to be to face predators. And the guy killed for a living.

I checked my pockets to make sure I still had everything, then went outside to the Neon. I didn't know the names of any of the streets in Washaway, but I knew how to get in and out. I followed the road to the bridge, drove by the burned-out Breakley farm, then kept going. I passed the Wilburs' black iron gate and finally reached a shopping center. A road sign promised to connect me with a state route just down the hill, but I didn't see the road.

The Grable was set in the back corner of the shopping center. All that was visible of it was a cinder-block wall painted the same color as the field house and an entry arch with a sign at the top. The NO VACANCY sign was lit.

As I cruised by, I saw an open courtyard/parking lot with just enough space for cars to drive down the center and angle park in front of the units on either side. In fact, there were three BMW X6's in there now, all parked in front of units at the far end of the lot. The Maybach was in the last slot.

There was no possibility of getting in the front way without being exposed to every unit. I drove across the lot.

The shopping center was laid out in the shape of a U. At one end was a drugstore. At the other was a supermarket. In between was a variety of little shops and storefronts—a small bookstore, a pitch-dark bar, a dentist, a drive-up burger joint, a teriyaki restaurant, a Subway, and several darkened windows with FOR LEASE signs in them. All were one story tall, except the drugstore and supermarket, which had peaked roofs. The Grable sat in the back corner of the U.

All the windows were papered with sale prices, garlands, and religious displays. There was a huge inflatable Santa and reindeer on the roof.

Santa gave me an idea. I parked beside the drugstore and went inside. I bought a newspaper, a lighter, and a votive candle with Fat Guy's money, then went around the back of the building.

The alley was strewn with trash and smelled like old piss. It was wide enough for a trash truck to squeeze through. The paint on the buildings was peeling, while the guardrail on the other side of the alley, where the ground dropped away to a nettle-ridden slope, was dented and rusty.

At the far end of the alley, I came to more white cinder block. I'd found the edge of the Grable. I stepped onto the guardrail but couldn't see over the wall. I could see the broken glass cemented into the top, however. The Grable had been built for privacy.

Turning around, I saw a young woman in the doorway, puffing on a cigarette and watching me. Her hair was a dull, fake black that she brushed into her raccoon-dark eyes. She was positioned beside the Dumpster, and I'd been so intent on the motel grounds that I hadn't noticed her.

"Uh . . . ," I said, trying to think up a plausible lie. She rolled her eyes, stubbed out her cigarette on the scarred edge of the Dumpster, and turned her back on me. She couldn't have cared less.

After she went inside, I laid a wooden pallet against the building and, with a running start, used it to jump up and get a grip on the edge of the roof. Thankfully, there was no broken glass here.

I pulled myself up and lay across the tarred paper. If I made too much noise, stood too high, or walked onto a section that couldn't support me, I was going to spend the night in jail. At best. I kept low, crawling on my hands and knees toward the edge of the building and the white wall of the motel.

I wondered how Catherine had been caught. They probably staked out the only place where we could have rented replacement cars. I should have tried to look more interesting; maybe they would have taken me instead.

The top of the motel wall was even with the drugstore roof. I swept the ghost knife through the glass shards, slid belly-down over the wall, and dropped between it and the nearest unit. There wasn't even enough space for me to turn all the way around. I edged toward the back of the building.

Each unit had a small window at the back that would have shown nothing but wall. Maybe it had once offered a view of the forest. I knew that peeking in a window with a big white background was a good way to be spotted. I peeked anyway.

The walls inside the unit were yellow and the bed-sheets a slightly darker yellow. It looked like an invalid's room. At the far end, a slender, dark-haired man in a black suit sat in a chair. He hunched forward to peer through a crack in the curtains into the courtyard. He had a Glock in his hand.

I ducked down and hurried to the next room. This one was empty. There were two more units in the row, but only the end unit was occupied.

I went back to the first empty room, cut the window out of the wall, and climbed through.

I took a towel from the bathroom and set it on the bed with the candle, newspaper, and lighter. One of the things people don't realize about prison is that it's vo-tech for criminals. The trick I was about to set up had been taught to me by a college kid who liked fire a little too much. I'd never tried it myself, but I remembered his instructions. At least, I hoped I did.

I set things up and climbed out the window, then used the narrow space between the end unit and the wall to scramble back over to the drugstore roof. Night was falling.

My hour was up. I lowered myself into the Dumpster alley and hustled around the buildings. The cellphone in my pocket vibrated. I didn't answer. The motel entrance was just ahead of me, and they could talk to me in person in a minute.

I paused at the arched entrance and slid my ghost knife into the stone. The only evidence that it was there was a paper-thin slot in the cinder block. No one would find it, and maybe it would be close enough for me to *call* if I needed it.

In the front office, the clerk looked up at me in surprise. He looked like he would appear surprised by the arrival of lunchtime.

"Which room is Mr. Yin's?" I asked.

A newspaper rustled behind me. A short, athletic Chinese man stood, stepped toward me, and dropped a comics section onto the floor. He didn't pull out a gun, but he did gesture toward the door with a slight bow and a polite smile.

We walked through the courtyard. Mr. Yin, of course, was staying in the room farthest from the entrance. It was a well-defended spot, but it didn't leave him an escape route—not unless he had a pogo stick that could bounce him over a ten-foot wall.

Drivers inside the BMWs and the Maybach started the engines and drove out of the lot.

My guide knocked on the door and led me inside. This one had a genuine painting on the wall. It showed a man in robes sitting on a hill between some twisted trees. It had been painted on something thinner than canvas, but I didn't know enough to identify it. The painting obviously didn't come with the room.

"Ah!" a middle-aged man said. He stood at the far end of the room, six bodyguards standing near him. This had to be Mr. Yin. He had a thick neck, a black suit, a placid smile, and a gold ring on every finger. His eyes were wide, almost bulging out of his head, as though he was studying everything around him. This was a billionaire?

A dark-skinned woman in a gray suit stood beside him. By the way she had wrapped up her hair in a bun, I figured she was Well-Spoken Woman.

I glanced over at the painting again. Maybe he took it with him everywhere. "You have an eye for quality!" Yin said. "Your attention goes directly to the most arresting object in the room. Excellent."

His English was better than mine. "Where's Catherine?"

"Close by," Mr. Yin said, "but not so close that you could kill us all and take her away unharmed." He was smiling at me. What the hell was he talking about?

He turned to the woman beside him. "Well?"

She was staring at the backs of my hands where my tattoos were most visible. Her eyes were shining, and she looked like a pirate who'd found buried treasure. "*Mowbray Book of Oceans*, I'd say. I'd need to see more to be certain."

This was not going as I'd expected. These were the nicest kidnappers I'd ever met. And that remark about killing them all . . .

Of course.

I sighed and chuckled, mostly to buy myself time to reset my body language and tone. "I'm not here to play games," I said. "And I'm sure as hell not here to strip for you. I have a predator to kill. Give me my investigator, and I'll let you all get into your cars and drive away."

One of the gunmen drew his pistol and aimed it at me. It gave me goose bumps, but I kept my smile in place. Mr. Yin said something to him in Chinese. I couldn't understand the words, but the tone said *Don't bother.*

Yin thought I was a peer, which meant he also thought I was damn near bulletproof. I'd hate for his bodyguard to prove him wrong all over the cheap carpet.

"You must understand," Mr. Yin said. "I spent a hundred twenty-eight million dollars last night for the rights to that unusual creature. Then someone shot at us, allowing it to escape. I can't allow you to kill my dog, Mr. Lilly."

"You know it's making people murder each other. Parents have killed their own children. Do you really want to bring that thing into your house?"

"Ah, but *these* people are *bumpkins*, and Americans, too. I will exert more control."

His body language was still utterly self-assured, although he was wary of me, too. I knew my body language wasn't as confident as his, and I knew he'd noticed that.

I looked over at the man who had drawn his gun. He hadn't put it away. "What do you want for Catherine?"

The gunman and I looked at each other. He wasn't impressed with me, and I wanted to punch him right in his stupid smirk. I hate to be afraid.

"I propose a trade," Mr. Yin said. "I will return to you the woman, unharmed, if you will give me everything you brought with you for this mission: your computer, your files, your research books, and any enchanted artifacts you have on you."

He wanted my ghost knife. "You have to be kidding me."

"I also want safe passage out of the country and your personal assurance that you will not try to kill me or any of my descendants, ever."

"Do you want my left foot, too?"

"If your left foot is of value, then yes, I want it. I want everything a man can want."

He smiled, waiting for my answer. I didn't have any research books, of course. I didn't own a computer and I didn't have any files.

And my ghost knife was a part of me. I *couldn't* give it up, not even for Catherine.

Mr. Yin fussed with the lapel of his jacket. "You appear distressed," he said.

"Because you're wasting my time with this MBA negotiating crap. This isn't a boardroom where you ask for a long list of things you know you're not going to get so we can whittle all the way down to what you actually want. You're not getting away with the sapphire dog. The mayor has already asked the state police to block off the only two roads out of town."

Two of the gunmen seemed nervous about that—he had only brought two English-speakers. Yin wasn't nervous at all. "Another thing," I said. "You're not the only one out there looking for it. While we're chit-chatting, one of the other bidders could be capturing it right now."

Suddenly Yin didn't seem so smug. "The sapphire dog is mine. I paid for it."

I rolled my eyes. "Keep telling yourself that, because I'm sure if one of the others had won the auction and then let the creature get away, you'd totally return it to them. Let's cut the crap and get to what you really want for my friend."

Yin smiled again. His contentment was like a suit of armor. "Your computer, your files, your research materials, your enchanted artifacts, your assurance of safety for my descendants and for me."

Annalise would have already started killing. "Here's my counter-offer: your life, and the lives of all your people, for as long as it takes me to have a turkey and ham at the Subway. I'm in the mood for pep-peroncini. No guarantees after that."

He turned his lapel over. There was a patch of white fabric pinned to the other side, and it had a sigil on it.

I blinked. For some reason I was staring at the carpet from just a foot away. My iron gate felt as though someone was pushing a needle through it.

I was on my knees. Yin had hit me with a spell, and like an idiot, I had fallen for it.

I felt hands patting me down. They were searching me very thoroughly. Two men grabbed my wrists and cuffed my hands behind my back. I was too woozy to resist.

"You are not a peer," Yin said. His voice had a little twist of contempt. "At best, you are an apprentice, hm?" He kicked me in the shoulder, but my tattoos blunted the impact. "You dare try to bluff me? I admire your courage, but it will cost you your life."

"Okay," I said. "Okay." I tried to lift my head, but any movement at all made me dizzy. Instead, I pressed my forehead against the carpet and dragged my knees under me. With my hands cuffed, it was a struggle to keep from falling over. Still, I managed it.

It was the perfect position for one of these assholes to put a bullet in the back of my head. Just the thought made my guts watery. "Okay," I said again, looking up at Yin. "A sandwich and some chips. That's my final offer."

Instead of ordering his men to shoot me, he laughed. He said something in Chinese, and I was hauled into the bathroom.

Someone was already in there, sitting on the toilet. It was one of his own men, bound and gagged. Thank God his pants were up.

They spun me around and shoved me into the tub. They made a special effort to tear Nicholas's shirt.

I tripped over the rim and toppled back, smacking my head against the tile. I saw stars and the pain made tears well up. Damn, those tears made me furious. I was not going to let these bastards think—

"Mr. Lilly," Yin said. "See? This is the spot where your friend would be, if I actually had her. It seems we were both bluffing!" He laughed with a high, girlish giggle.

I blinked the tears away. Yin was waiting for a response. "You're full of shit," I said. "You had her phone. Where did you hide her?"

"I do have her phone, but not her. She is a clever woman. Your society has more wit left to it than I'd heard." He kicked the bottom of my foot. "Not in you, though. This fellow here"—he gestured to the man on the toilet—"is the one who let her escape, so he has taken her place.

"In many ways," Yin continued, "I am an innocent in this world. I'm merely a financier with a mania for collecting. Without my collection, I would have no use for my money or these good, brave men. And I would have no use for torture."

His tone was still calm and friendly. Nothing worried him at the moment. "Still," he continued, "we can hardly employ such methods here. But I have other options." He leaned close, wide-eyed and smiling. "I brought some of my collection with me."

He turned toward the door. Well-Spoken handed him something wrapped in a black cloth. It was smaller than a T-ball bat. He unwrapped it with reverence.

It was a long knife, or maybe a short sword. I don't know the difference and I don't care. The scabbard was black and gleaming like polished stone. Yin drew it with a sudden motion, then held it up to admire it. The blade was straight, and as wide as two thumb widths. It had been honed and polished, and it looked like an antique. Yin held it up to the light as though he was about to discuss its history, then he turned and stabbed the bound man through the throat.

I shouted something inane like "Hey!" Bound didn't have time to gasp. He froze, a grimace on his face. He looked around the room, finally stopping on me, and I thought how brutally unfair it was that I would be the last thing this stupid bastard ever saw.

Yin pushed the sword downward through his breastbone and stomach all the way to his belly button. He had to put his weight behind it, but it was not as difficult to cut through the bones as it should have been. Then he pulled the sword free. There was no blood, no cut, no wound at all. I stared at Bound, waiting for the blood.

Yin yanked off the man's gag. Bound looked up meekly and said something in Chinese. Yin seemed amused. "He has just apologized to me."

It's an illusion, I thought. Yin had a trick sword, and Bound was playing along.

But I had no idea why they would bother; I was already in cuffs and at their mercy. I looked back at Bound and realized I needed to change his nickname. The ropes he'd been tied with were lying on the floor in pieces. His clothes were cut open, too. I'd been so focused on looking for blood that I hadn't even noticed.

Bound slid down to his knees and hung his head.

"Do you see?" Yin asked, showing me the blade. There was a small sigil engraved near the hilt. "This mark is from the *Ketrivisky Book of Oceans*. This is a soul sword. It does not leave a mark on his flesh, but his will now belongs to me."

The bastard had a ghost knife of his own.

CHAPTER TEN

Yin studied the sword. "It is not as powerful as it was in the hands of the man who sold it to me. I'm sure you know what happens to magic each time it changes hands." He pointed it at me. "I wonder how many of the spells on your body I could cut before it shattered?"

Now was the time. "I don't have files," I said, not bothering to hide my hatred of him or my fear of that damn blade. "I don't have any authority to guarantee your safety or the safety of your children. I only have one thing to offer: I can give you a spell of your own."

Yin's eyes narrowed on me and the sword lowered. "A spell?"

Bingo. "It's the only one I know. Give me a big sheet of paper and a pen and I'll draw out both parts for you. Then you let me go and leave us alone. We pretend this meeting never happened. I can't offer more than that."

He smiled at me. He was terribly smug. "I agree. Understand, though, Mr. Lilly. If you betray me, I will make sure others hear about our deal. I know how your superiors respond to trading spells."

Two of his guys pulled me upright and unlocked my cuffs.

"Remember," Yin said, "do not—"

"Just give me the paper and pen so we can be done with it."

Well-Spoken brought them to me. I laid the paper on the bottom of the tub and wrote "for the mind" in the upper left and "for the hand" in the upper right. I'd only cast a couple of spells in my life, including the ghost knife, and while I couldn't have re-created them from memory, this was how they had been drawn in the spell book.

On the left side of the page, I drew a couple of squiggles that might have been a hole in the ground and maybe an eyeball. On the right, I drew a couple of short lines that suggested a campfire. I have never been much of an artist, but considering what real sigils look like, that worked in my favor.

I handed them the paper. They cuffed me again.

Yin laid his hand over the drawing on the left. He knew enough to recognize the danger in looking at that part of a spell before he'd learned the right-hand drawing.

"What does it do?" Well-Spoken hurried toward him and peered at it over his shoulder.

I glared at Yin. "Wait for it," I said.

It took less than a minute, but eventually the fire alarm clanged. His gunmen looked nervous, but Yin was greedily delighted. "An arson spell?"

"I don't recognize it, sir." Well-Spoken had to shout over the alarm. "I don't even recognize the style."

"Is it . . ." He searched my expression. When he strained his voice, his pitch went quite high. "I have heard that the *Book of Grooves* is in this part of the world. Is this from the lost *Book of Grooves*?"

I looked him straight in the eye. "I have no idea what you're talking about," I said truthfully.

He looked flustered for a moment, then his smug expression returned. "Of course. I forgot to bargain for its provenance. Have no fear, Mr. Lilly. My people are very good at their jobs. I'll have my answers soon enough." He waved his men out of the room and backed away. "Of course, you forgot to bargain for the keys to those handcuffs!" It was his parting shot, and I let him have it. I kicked the door shut.

Bound was still kneeling on the floor. Yin had abandoned him, but I couldn't bring myself to care. I bent low, passing the cuffs under my feet so my hands were in front of me, then peeked into the living room. No one put a bullet in my head. They were gone. Through the front window I could see black smoke pouring from one of the units across the way.

I was suddenly very tired. I glanced at my watch and saw that it was dinnertime. I needed sleep, and while I wasn't desperate enough to lie down here, it would have to be soon.

Bound was still crouching there. The fire across the lot was growing strong. I dragged him to his feet. Together, we hustled out the door.

We hurried toward the arched exit, keeping as far from the fire as possible. Glass shattered somewhere behind me. I shielded my face and dragged Bound past the office.

The fire engine screeched to a stop at the entrance to the motel, while the clerk waved at them with a windmilling arm. I pulled Bound through the arch and off to the side, but we'd been spotted. A firefighter jumped from the back of the engine and ran toward us.

"You two!" he shouted. "Get to a safe distance, but don't leave the area. We're going to have some questions . . ."

He noticed the handcuffs and stopped talking. Then he looked again at Bound's torn clothes and hunched, face-to-the-ground body language. He didn't know what to say.

"What?" I said. "We're consenting adults."

He frowned, then pointed to a place well away from the fire. "Go there. Stay." Then he turned and ran through the arch.

"How did you get here so fast?" I called, but he was already gone.

I laid my hand against the stone arch and *called* my ghost knife. I held it close and said, "Come on." Bound followed me.

We went farther than the fireman wanted, hurrying by the people filing out of the bar to watch the flames.

With the ghost knife, I cut the cuffs off—carefully. I didn't know what effect the spell would have on me, and now was not the time to experiment.

I dropped the cuffs into a planter. People were coming out of the stores, and I didn't want any more attention than necessary. Then I saw Yin step into the Maybach. His driver closed the door for him and got behind the wheel.

Movement off to my right caught my attention. It was Tattoo sitting on a Megamoto. I felt the sudden flush of fear that comes from finding myself too close to a guy who wants to kill me, but he was watching Yin. He hadn't even noticed me.

As the trio of BMWs rolled out of the parking lot, Tattoo stuck a piece of toast in his mouth and pulled his helmet on. He didn't have a cast over his thumb or ankle, and I was sure I'd broken both. Damn. All that work and nothing to show for it. He started his bike and followed Yin's people.

Without thinking about it, I bolted away from Bound and ran toward Tattoo, ghost knife in hand. Yin was a bastard, but Tattoo was worse.

It was no use. The cars were out of the lot and Tattoo was only fifty feet behind them, too far away for me to use my ghost knife.

Bound was standing where I'd left him. I pushed him against the wall and patted him down. His gun was gone. He let me take his passport and billfold. He had credit cards, foreign cash, even a notepad and pen. None of it interested me, and none of it was worth taking.

"Hey," I said. He wouldn't look me in the face. "Hey. Where's Catherine? Your boss said you had her, but she got away. Where did she escape? What did you do to her, you asshole?"

He said something I didn't understand. He repeated it again, and I realized he was saying: "Help me." Apparently, that was the only English he knew.

"Sure thing, buddy. Sure thing." I smiled and laid a reassuring hand on his shoulder. Yin's ghost knife didn't leave him enough vigor to smile in response, but he did look relieved.

I took the notepad and pen out of his billfold and wrote: *I don't speak English but I do like to start fires. Please arrest me.* Then I tucked the billfold back into his pocket, gently put the note in his hand, and gestured toward the men by the bar. He started walking meekly toward them, note held in front of him.

I didn't stick around to see how that would turn out.

As I approached the Neon, I passed a pair of old hippies watching the fire. It was still going strong. One of them turned toward me. "What happened, dude?" I couldn't see his mouth moving underneath his wiry gray beard.

I shrugged. "I just got here. Is there another motel in town?"

"Naw, just the Sunset, but that's a really nice place."

I smiled while he gave me directions, then thanked him and climbed into the car. I couldn't go back to the Sunset. Yin knew about it.

I pulled out of the lot and headed away from town. I would have to sneak around the roadblock and find a room at the next exit, whatever it was, and come back for my car when I'd gotten some sleep and food.

A green pickup drove toward me. Hadn't the roadblock been put up yet? Had the mayor decided not to call it in because of the festival?

The car in front of me was a Volvo station wagon packed to the windows with loose laundry. It was about a hundred feet ahead when its brake lights came on. I slowed down, too. My iron gate twinged, but that seemed unimportant.

The Volvo stopped. I slowed to parking-lot speed, the twinge in my shoulder growing stronger. After a couple of seconds, the Volvo did a three-point turn and drove back toward me.

I braked and took out my ghost knife. The driver was a bird-faced old woman who didn't glance at me once. She simply drove past me toward town with a pained expression on her face.

Weird. I took my foot off the brake and started toward the highway again. The first flare of a headache started, and I slowed again. I couldn't remember why I was driving out of town. It didn't make sense. Washaway was where I needed to be.

I stopped in the road. There was a reason I needed to leave, but I couldn't remember what it was. A beer truck came up the road toward me, but it stopped about a hundred and fifty feet away and turned around. I watched it drive away.

I touched my iron gate. It was throbbing, but there was no one else around, not even other cars.

I saw a blue tarp on the side of the road. I got out of the car, leaving the engine running, and walked into the weeds. There were actually several tarps. The closest was the smallest, and I knelt beside it, my headache growing stronger. The edges were tucked underneath the object it was covering. I took out my ghost knife to slit open the top, then thought better of it and just pulled it back.

It was a little girl. I won't describe her in detail, but she'd been beaten and strangled to death many hours before. She did not have a white mark on her face. I tucked the tarp under her again.

When I pulled back the tarp on the next one, I found Clara's red-gold curls. I didn't need to see more.

I stood and backed away, my head pounding. The other tarps were probably Isabelle and the rest of the Breakley family. I could have pulled them all back to see if Biker was there, or if the gunmen had been brought down from the Wilbur estate, but I didn't. I didn't want to look at more dead faces.

Sue and Big Bill had obviously brought the bodies out here and laid them by the side of the road. That seemed perfectly logical to me. The tarps would protect them from animals, and while it didn't make sense to take them out of Washaway, they had to be put *somewhere*.

I headed back to the car, instinctively understanding that I would feel better if I went back to town. I did a three-point turn and drove back toward the fire and the trucks. My headache eased and my iron gate stopped aching.

But I still didn't have anywhere to go. It wasn't safe to stay at the B and B, and the motel was gone. There were empty houses I could break into, but they were all crime scenes. Besides, I didn't really want to sleep in the Breakleys' bedroom tonight, knowing what had happened there.

If I couldn't sleep, I needed to find the predator quickly. I needed a plan.

I drove through town and pulled up in front of Penny's house. The pickup was still against the tree, but her front door was closed. Both had been surrounded with yellow tape. At first I thought the mysterious sheriff had finally arrived, but when I got closer I saw it was caution tape, not police tape.

I went inside. The house was dark, but the entry to the kitchen was lit by a nightlight. The police scanner was still there. I turned it on to make sure it worked, then pulled the plug and tucked it under my arm.

Something rustled behind me. I took out my ghost knife and crept into the living room, hoping I was about to catch the sapphire dog by surprise and not Penny's cats.

It was neither. Little Mark lay on the couch, sleeping peacefully. His head was covered in a big white bandage.

It looked like the same bandage the paramedics had put on him. Obviously, they hadn't taken him to the hospital. I could have taken him myself, but that didn't make sense; I couldn't leave Washaway. I needed to stay, and Mark probably did, too.

I left by the front door without waking him.

I needed to find a place where I could work on the scanner and connect it to the Neon's electrical system. Something private and well lit.

As I drove through town, Steve's Crown Vic came toward me in the opposite lane. He pulled left, blocking the road but giving me enough room to brake. A second car, a rusted Forester, stopped beside his.

He climbed out and came toward me. I could see he was angry. "I thought I asked you to stay at the Sunset."

God, I hated that whining voice. "I didn't have a choice. Can we leave it at that?"

The Forester's driver door opened and a short, plump woman climbed out. At first I thought it was Pippa, but as she stepped into my headlights, I saw that she was a black woman with Coke-bottle-thick glasses and a long, quilted yellow jacket. I guessed she was yet another member of the neighborhood watch. A man climbed out of the Forester behind her. He was a fat little cowboy with a Wilford Brimley mustache.

"No," Steve said. "Things have been happening pretty fast around here. Look at this." He took a sheet of paper from his pocket and held it up. It was already too dark to read it. "I'm the new chief of police in Washaway—temporary emergency position only. Pippa saw to it."

"The sheriff hasn't come yet?"

"No," Steve said, "and I've called him eight times today. But I was a patrol officer in Wenatchee for a few years, so Pippa figured I'm the best candidate for the job. Now, tell me where you've been, or I'm going to arrest you."

"At Penny's. Did you know that Mark is there right now? Sleeping?"

"With a head wound? Is anyone with him?"

"Nope."

He turned to the others. "We can't leave that boy alone with a head injury. Sherisse, Ford, would you go and collect him, please?"

They hustled back to their car. Steve turned to me. "You haven't been at Penny's this whole time, though, right?"

"No."

Steve sighed in irritation. "What about the other strangers in town? They're looking for this thing too, right?"

"Yes, and we can't talk about this here."

"Well, we *could* have talked at the Sunset, if you'd done like I asked, but *no*—"

"Oh, for . . . They found me there, okay? They know I want to kill it, and I'm not safe there anymore. I need a new place to crash." I rubbed my eyes. "I'm pretty much running on fumes."

"Okay." Steve rubbed the faint stubble on his chin. "Let's go."

I followed him through town, turning off Littlemont Road onto a winding asphalt street barely wide enough for two cars. He stopped in front of a clapboard, two-story house with a long garage, walked up the front lawn, and opened the garage door. I pulled inside.

"This is my house, if you haven't guessed." The walls were covered with tools on pegboards. There was a thick layer of dust on them. If Steve had been handy at one point in his life, it was long ago.

I followed him through a mudroom into a little kitchen, then a living room. Everything was perfectly clean and neatly arranged, but it was a depressing little house. It seemed to absorb light, but every scuff of our feet echoed as if we were in a drum. He led me to a threadbare couch and offered me tea and sandwiches. I said yes, thank you, and he went into the kitchen.

A four-foot tree stood in the corner. It was undecorated.

Steve returned and set a foldout table in front of me. There were two little plates on it, each with a white-bread sandwich and a handful of corn chips. Beside them were thick white mugs with steaming tea.

I thanked him again and took a bite of the sandwich. It was yellow cheese with mayo and iceberg lettuce. I was hungry enough to enjoy it.

Steve took a bite of his sandwich, more out of politeness than hunger, I could see. When he swallowed, he set it down and settled back in his armchair. It looked too big for him. "I think it's past time you give me the *full* rundown."

"Okay," I said. I set down my own sandwich and sipped some tea, just to buy time. "Regina Wilbur had this sapphire dog in the little cottage behind her house for decades. It was trapped in there, and she kept it all for herself."

He nodded. We both remembered how the sapphire dog had made us feel. "You said it was a gift?"

"That's what she told me. She was grateful for it, but I don't think the gift giver was doing her any favors."

Steve opened his mouth to respond, then paused. He knew the history of this town and the Wilbur family. "When she was younger, Regina Wilbur was a terror in this part of the county. She had very definite ideas about what had to be done and who should be allowed to do it. Then she simply stopped coming to planning meetings and became a hermit. Lots of folks were relieved."

"But something changed recently, right?"

"Well, her niece had her declared incompetent. There was a videotape of Regina pitching a fit in her drawing room, claiming that they were keeping her dog from her. A dog that died twenty-five years ago."

"Named Armand, right?" Steve nodded. "I thought so. She gave that name to the sapphire dog, too. You can imagine how she'd behave if they kept her from visiting it."

"The niece . . . Does she know?"

"She held an auction last night. She sold the sapphire dog to a Chinese guy for nearly a hundred thirty million dollars." It was hard to believe that all this trouble had taken place in less than twenty-four hours.

"Lord help us. I know about the men, of course. Washaway has been full of rumors that he was looking to invest nearby and had come to see the festival. But they were here for this auction?"

"Yeah, but the creature escaped. Now the Chinese guy—and the others who lost the auction—are looking for it. They all have guns, and they aren't squeamish about using them."

Steve winced. I described the groups who had been at the estate in a general way, leaving out the summoning of the floating storm and the spells on Tattoo's body.

"What about you? Did you come for the auction, too?"

"No," I answered. "With me, it's . . ." What the hell could I say? I couldn't tell him about the society. ". . . just bad luck."

He didn't look impressed with that answer. "And what does this have to do with what happened to you in Seattle?"

"Near as I can tell, nothing. It was similar to this, though—weird creature, people going nuts."

"You did solve that problem, though?"

I kept my face carefully neutral. "I did."

"How?"

I thought back to the last moments of that ordeal, when my best and oldest friend had pleaded for me to spare his life. The smells of spoiled blood and field turf came back to me, and so did his voice. The old injury on my left hand throbbed.

I opened my mouth to answer, but the words wouldn't come. I'd only talked about it to one other person, a peer in the society I had never seen before or since. At the time, I was still in shock and I'd expected him to kill me. Since then, I hadn't said a word about it.

And I wasn't going to start with a cop, even a temp cop, no matter how politely he asked.

"Never mind," Steve said with a wave of his hand. "I understand."

We didn't say anything for a while, and my eyelids began to droop. He noticed. "Let me set you up for some shut-eye. Any fool can see you need it, even this one."

The pillows and blankets he brought were pink and flowery. I stretched out on the couch, feeling awkward and vulnerable, but when I closed my eyes, I dropped into a deep, dreamless sleep.

"Get up."

I came awake suddenly, thinking that Yin's men had found me again, but it was Catherine.

"I mean it," she said again. Her tone was sharp. "Nap time is over."

I sat up and rubbed the bleariness out of my eyes. The VCR clock said it was almost ten, but was that the evening of the same day, or had I slept all the way into the morning? "It's nice to see you, too. Is it early or late?"

"It's still the same day, if that's what you mean. And I'm hungry again. Those bastards took my emergency food with the jump bag. Come on! Up!"

As a rule, I don't like being snapped at, but I was too damn tired to care. Maybe I was just glad to see that she was okay. "Don't talk to me that way," I said out of habit. "How did you find me?"

"Goddammit, Ray." She sat down on the edge of the couch and folded her arms across her breasts. "I *saw* you go into the motel to meet Yin. What kind of game are you playing?"

"I'm not playing any kind of game. Do you think he turned me? Do you think he bought me off?"

"It wouldn't be the first time."

"That's bullshit," I said with more anger than I'd expected. "He sent me your cellphone and told me he'd kidnapped you. I went there to free you."

She sighed and set her hands on her knees. "And I watched you go in, thinking you were collecting a payoff."

"He nearly killed me, but the fire made him back off."

"That was lucky."

"Not really."

She smiled and I smiled back. We had a moment. Then she looked away and her smile vanished. She held up her hands. They trembled slightly.

"I'm forty-five years old, you know. I'll be forty-six in August, if I live that long. This job isn't as exciting as it was when I was twenty-five. I'm better at it now, but ..." She rubbed her hands together and leaned back. "They did get me, you know. They stopped my car and dragged me out onto the asphalt. It seemed like a dozen of them, all smiling shit-eating smiles and holding their guns against my body. All over my body."

She was silent for a moment. I waited for her, and eventually she said: "They couldn't keep me, though. They underestimated me, and when I saw my chance I took it."

"I'm glad." It was a stupid thing to say, but I couldn't think of anything better.

Catherine just nodded. "How did you get into this? How did you get sucked into this life?"

Maybe she didn't know my history. Or maybe she was testing me to see if I shared information. I didn't care. "My best friend ... my best friend had a predator in him. Annalise was there to kill him, but I tried to save him. I took his side against her, but he was past saving."

She nodded. "With me it was my nephew. He was a little wild and very funny, but one summer day he could suddenly *do things*. When the society came hunting for him, the whole family hid him away. They protected him. Except me. I knew he was killing people, and I decided to turn him in. I had to do the right damn thing, no matter what it cost. My family ... isn't my family anymore. I'm married now, with two girls, but they've never met my mother or sisters. I don't want them to hear the things my family says to me—what they call me now. I got this damn job out of it, though."

I couldn't imagine how hard it was to do society work as a parent, and I said so.

She pulled away from me and let her body language become neutral. "I have ways of dealing. There are ways of doing this job that help keep a little distance. I don't do any of the violence, and I'm never around when it happens. There's no need for me to see that and carry it around with me, bring it home to my family. Not after what happened to my nephew. I take care of my own people and let these people take care of themselves."

That last bit was a little cold. *I don't rescue people. I kill predators.* But I did my best not to react. People have to cope the best they can.

She continued. "But . . . maybe it's just that I know more now. Maybe I just know more about the danger and the . . . the suddenness. It can be so quick. One minute everything is just fine, and the next you've lost all power and control. They only had me for about twenty minutes, okay? That's how long it took me to get away, but . . . When they have you, they can do anything to you. Kill you, rape you, torture you . . ." She paused while she ran through the possibilities in her mind.

I couldn't ask what Yin had done. I didn't have any real need to know except self-indulgent curiosity. What I needed to do was make her feel better. "Want to go kill them?" I asked.

"Yes!" she answered, but she didn't jump up and rush for the door. "But I'm not the type. And it wouldn't get me anything. I'm going to have nightmares about this, I think. I'm going to have nightmares for a long time about this. Christ, I'm collecting them like scars." After a moment, she added: "Do you really think we should kill Mr. Yin?"

I spread my hands. "Catherine, I bought him off with a fake spell. *Someone* is going to have to kill him."

We had a little discussion about that, where I explained what I did and how I did it. Catherine didn't like the idea on general principle but couldn't think of a specific reason to object. She even admitted that the society publishes fake spell books to discourage wannabes. Then she explained that Steve Cardinal had told her where to find me. It seemed that most of the town was looking for us, with instructions to call him if we were spotted.

"He seems to know more than he should," she said. She watched my response carefully, as if trying to decide whether I was sharing information I should have kept to myself.

"He saw the sapphire dog," I said. "In fact, it nearly fed on him. So yeah, he knows more than he should." I told her about the predator, how it looked and what it could do. She was motionless while I spoke, staring at me intently.

Then I told her about my visit with Pratt. She seemed to recognize the name.

"Did he give you his number?" she asked.

"He wasn't that into me. Actually, he was a complete asshole. He told me to go home, and he wouldn't help deal with Yin."

Wouldn't help rescue you was what I should have said. Catherine seemed to understand anyway.

She rubbed her face. "Well, we can't leave," she said. "It wouldn't make sense to leave Washaway now."

My head felt foggy and sore for a moment, probably from the effects of sleep. "Right, that doesn't make sense."

After that, she set up the police scanner. Steve was out, so I went into his kitchen. I couldn't find any coffee. We had to settle for black tea and sugar. His fridge contained nothing but condiments, Wonder bread, white cheese, and hamburger buns, and his freezer was packed with microwavable meat patties. I felt a little awkward raiding the man's kitchen, and the dismal selection made it easy to leave it all untouched. Maybe we should order out.

We listened to the scanner for the better part of an hour. It was extremely dull, but Catherine had an amazing capacity to focus on something that might become useful at any moment. I got up and moved around the room, swinging my arms and trying to keep loose. My face felt stiff, and when I checked a mirror I saw that my eye was not swollen anymore but was an ugly dark color. The spot where Bushy Bill had hit me was slightly red but not too bad. No wonder the women in Washaway weren't tearing their clothes off when I walked into the room.

There was squawking on the scanner when I came back. It barely sounded like human speech. "Do you understand any of that?"

"Fire at the motel is out," she said. "The whole thing is a loss. The neighborhood watch is supposed to find locals who can put the firefighters up for the night."

I wasn't sure why they weren't going home, but that didn't seem important. What was important was Steve's house; I didn't want to be there when he got home. I didn't like that clean, quiet, depressing little place.

"I want to get out of here," I said. "Do you want to stay and man the scanner?"

"No," she said quickly. "I'll come along."

That surprised me. "Are you sure?" I didn't say *This is a safe place* or *We might run into bad guys*. I didn't have to.

"They know about me, so there really isn't a safe place anymore. And I'm not the stay-at-home type."

She took the keys to the Neon and carried the scanner into the garage. While she fiddled with the wires under the dash, I went into the kitchen, boiled water, and poured it into a thermos. Then I added a tea bag and the last of Steve's sugar.

Back in the garage, I found Catherine sitting behind the wheel, the engine running and the scanner hissing. I opened the garage door and she pulled out. I closed the door and climbed inside.

The scanner sat on the floor mat beside my feet. I didn't dare move for fear of pulling out a wire. "I'm the one who rented this car, you know."

"Maybe, but I'm a better driver."

Fair enough. We drove back and forth through town, waiting for something to happen. At one point, a black Yukon passed us going the other way. The bidders had the same idea. After almost an hour, a thin fog billowed in, but nothing else came up. Finally, Catherine said what I'd been afraid to say. "Could it already be gone? Things wouldn't be this quiet if it was still in town, right?"

"Maybe," I said. "Except that the Breakleys were only discovered because we burned down their barn. Maybe it's holed up somewhere, feeding and biding its time."

"I don't know about that," she said. "The cage was surrounded by lights, remember? What if it only wanted a ride because it needed to avoid daylight? What if it set out cross-country once night fell?"

"Fuck." That hadn't occurred to me. The predator hadn't walked like a creature that could cover a lot of ground, but I wouldn't have guessed it could move through walls, either.

"Driving around is a waste of time," I said.

"I agree completely." Catherine did a U-turn in the middle of the street and headed back toward the shopping center on Littlemont.

The Grable was sealed off with more yellow caution tape. The arch was blackened on one side, and the building was a shell. I didn't like looking at it.

Catherine parked in front of the bar. "I'm going to socialize," she said. "You're designated driver, so you can have Pepsi. After I get inside, count to five hundred and come in. This works better if people think I'm alone."

She went inside. I sat and counted slowly. There was a Fleetwood parked a couple of dozen yards away. It took a moment for me to remember where I'd seen it before. I got out of the Neon.

I approached from an angle that would keep me out of the side and rearview mirrors, but I didn't need to bother. The driver was alone and asleep. It was Regina Wilbur.

She was wrapped in an expensive cashmere coat, and she'd managed to clean herself up. Her hair had been washed, at least. She had a duck hunter's shotgun in her lap.

The button for the door lock was up, so I yanked the door open and snatched the shotgun away from her as quickly as I could. She woke instantly. If I'd been any slower, I'd have been staring down the barrel. I was glad I hadn't underestimated her.

"Hello, Regina," I said. "It's kind of a chilly night to be sleeping in your car, isn't it?"

"Oh," she said. "It's you." If she had bothered to remember my name, she wasn't going to say it. "I know why you're in Washaway. If I get my hands on that shotgun again, I'll use it to part your miserable skull."

"You don't know as much about me as you think," I said.

That got a rise out of her, as I'd hoped it would. "That little German bastard told me everything I need to know. He says you want to kill Armand."

"And you believed him? You can't trust that guy. He murdered a member of your own staff in cold blood."

"Pfah!" She waved a liver-spotted hand at me. "Why should he lie to me? I'm just a helpless old woman!"

I almost laughed in her face. But that "little German bastard" wouldn't have been fooled by her any more than I was. "And I'll bet he offered to capture Armand for you."

"Not just for me," she said, sounding as if I'd insulted her intelligence. "He wants to bring in a team to study Armand, and he thinks the home I built for him would be the best place to do it."

"So he wants to share the sapphire dog with you? Like the poetry professor?"

"Yes!" she drew out the hiss at the end of that word with malicious joy. "He and I will share the same way I shared with the poetry professor, as soon as he catches Armand in one of those big, black Yukons of his."

I couldn't resist correcting her. "The Yukons with the red-and-white cards on the dash? Those aren't his. That's a different bidder entirely."

She smiled like a snake, and I realized I'd made a mistake. She started the engine and backed out of her parking slot. I had to jump out of the way of the open door. She gave me one last sneer before she pulled out, leaving me holding her shotgun.

Damn. I had underestimated her after all, but what should I do about it? I could have tried to call the new emergency chief of police, if I had his number, which I didn't. And if I followed her, I would be separating from Catherine again.

That hadn't worked well the last time, and I wasn't going to do it again. I tossed Regina's shotgun onto the roof of the teriyaki place. Maybe she had another gun, but I think she would have tried to shoot me if she had. And while she could certainly afford a new one, she'd have to wait until the stores opened. I had time. I hoped.

I decided that I'd waited at least a five-hundred count and went inside.

Catherine was sitting at the bar, chatting amiably with the bartender. She had a glass of white wine in front of her. Her body language was different from what I'd seen before—yet another personality. I wonder how she chose them, or if she went by instinct. I took note of where the bathroom was and picked a spot where I'd have to walk by her to get to it.

Two stools over from me was a guy of about twenty-five. He was slumped over a beer, reading the label as if it might make him happy.

In the corner was an older couple sipping from tall drinks with a careful, trembling elegance. They both looked shriveled and wasted on the top half of their bodies and thick with flab on the bottom half. They seemed like people who had once had much better uses for their time but would have been offended at the label "barfly."

A pair of young guys shot pool in the corner. They didn't talk, but I couldn't tell if that was because they didn't like each other or they were just intent on their game.

The last person in the bar was Pratt. There was an empty bowl and crumpled napkin in front of him—he'd come here for his dinner. I wondered if, like us, he was here to find information or if he was slacking off from his job. Which wasn't fair, but to hell with him. I didn't like him.

The bartender tore himself away from Catherine long enough to take my order. He was a middle-aged guy with a slouching belly and no ring on his left hand. His face had started to go pouchy, but his hair was thick and combed straight back as though he was proud of it. I asked for a root beer and a menu. He dropped them off and wandered back to Catherine.

I could overhear a little of their conversation: she was complimenting the town in ways that prompted the bartender to brag a little. He described the Christmas festival that would happen tomorrow, explained the history of it, and flirted with her shamelessly. She didn't encourage him, but she didn't back away, either.

Depressed Guy tapped his empty bottle on the bar and the bartender brought him a new one. He took my order, too. I went for the grilled cheese, figuring it was cheap and too easy for him to screw up.

Catherine went back to doing her thing. I couldn't hear everything she was saying, but it sounded like small talk. Whatever information she was getting was coming at a leisurely pace, and she didn't seem interested in speeding up the process. My grilled cheese arrived; I'd never had a better sandwich in my life.

Depressed Guy muttered something to himself. I glanced over at

him. He said: "Ever love someone or something so much you can't live
without them?"

I remembered the way the sapphire dog had made me feel. Depressed Guy suddenly had my full attention. "Yeah, man. I think I have."

Encouraged, he turned toward me. His eyes looked a little bleary
and he had trouble focusing, but he could talk without slurring. "It
hits so hard at first. It's like . . . all the love in your life is *ripped* away
from you all of a sudden. All you have left is this, like, little tattered
shred of something in your hand, because you tried to hold on too
tight. Ya know whutamean? You think I tried to hold on too tight?"

Catherine did this for a living, I thought. She drew people out,
listened to their stories, and found the information she needed. Not
me. Everything I'd ever learned about investigations had come from
being on the other side. I couldn't play this game her way; I had to do
it mine.

"I don't know, man. Who did you lose?"

"My wife." I immediately lost interest. Still, he kept talking. I
glanced away and saw that one of the pool players had joined Catherine's conversation. Whatever they were talking about, she seemed interested. Was she a good actress, or did she enjoy this? "She dumped
me over the phone. Can you believe that? After ten and a half months
of marriage."

I glanced around the room. Pratt was looking straight at me. I
looked back, and he didn't look away. In some places, that would have
been an invitation to brawl, but I haven't had much luck with bar
fights.

Depressed Guy wasn't finished. "Almost eleven months! I thought
we were in love."

"That's rough," I said.

He went back to his beer. "I'm keeping the damn fish tank, you
can believe that."

I imagined a tank full of dead fish, and it suddenly occurred to me
that Pratt might have completed his job already. Maybe this was his
victory meal, as pathetic as that sounded.

I slid off my stool and crossed to his booth. He was dipping his
spoon into a bowl of grayish chowder when I sat across from him.
Before he could tell me to get lost, I said, "Well?"

"Well, what?"

I met his stare. Apparently, he wanted me to talk out loud in front
of all these people. "Well, have you taken care of that dog?"

"I don't report to you." Which was true, but he struck me as the
boasting type, so I figured the job wasn't done.

"Fair enough. How about another supplemental report?"

"You don't file reports," he said. "I get those from the smoke."

For a moment I thought he was talking about smoke signals, or visions in magic smoke or something. Then I realized—duh—he meant Catherine. "You're a real charmer."

He stirred his soup. "Get out of here," he said without looking at me, "before I break both of your legs."

So much for warning him about Yin's ghost knife. I glanced back at Catherine. She was looking at me, and her expression was difficult to read. I stood and went to the men's room, washed my hands in the dirty sink, and walked toward my original spot. As I passed Catherine's stool, the bartender said, "Hey, man. Are you Clay Lilly?"

I stopped. "My name's Ray Lilly."

"Well, I'll be," Catherine said, her voice lilting. "I knew that was you. How is your mother?" She slid off her stool. "Excuse me, Rich," she said to the bartender.

I heard the bartender curse under his breath, but it was too late. Tonight's entertainment had walked off with another guy. I led her to the table and picked up my soda. "Did—"

She interrupted me right away. "Is your mother still working at that law firm?" We had a conversation about a woman I hadn't seen for years. While we were talking, Pratt laid a couple of bills on the table and walked out.

Eventually, I said I had my mother's phone number out in the car, and Catherine smiled as though I was learning the game. I paid for my food, and while we were waiting for the slip to sign, Depressed Guy looked blearily over at us.

Catherine couldn't resist. "How are you, honey?" Her tone was maternal.

"Alone," he said. "My wife just left me."

"I'm sorry to hear that. What happened?" If she was pretending to be interested, she was damn good at it.

"Thass the thing. I don't even know! This afternoon everything was great between us. An hour later, she called me and said that she didn't love me anymore. She said she'd found someone else. Someone with stars in his eyes."

Catherine looked at me. I looked at her. I fought down the urge to grab the guy and shake him until he told me more.

"That's terrible," Catherine said. Her voice was shaky and she'd lost her grip on the kind, maternal, cry-on-my-shoulder character she was playing. "Where did she call from?"

It was a crazy transition, but Depressed Guy was drunk enough to take it in stride. "She rides out at the stables three nights a week." He took a pull off his beer. "He's prolly a cowboy or something."

The credit card slip came. I signed it. Catherine and I walked calmly and slowly toward the door.

Once through it, we ran to the car. We had our lead.

CHAPTER ELEVEN

I scanned the parking lot. Pratt was already gone, dammit. "Do you know where the stable is?" I asked.

"I know how to find it." She took out a cellphone, dialed 411, and got the address from the operator. "There's only one in the area," she said. "Shit. I wish they hadn't stolen my cell."

"What's that in your hand?"

"The bartender's. He loaned it to me, without realizing he was loaning it to me. But I can't use it to file a supplemental report. The number would turn up on his phone bill."

I was feeling keyed up. "I'm sorry," I said. "The answer we needed was sitting right next to me, and I didn't realize it."

"Don't worry about it. That's my job, not yours. Not that I found out a damn thing. All those boys wanted to talk about was the festival tomorrow. They're worried that it may be canceled after 'what happened today.' I wasn't sure how much they really knew, but they were being careful."

I wondered what the festival would be like. If we destroyed the predator tonight—and did it quickly and cleanly—the town could have Christmas in peace: no more killings, no more people going crazy, no more burning buildings. Maybe there would be something nice I could pick up for Aunt Theresa and Uncle Karl. And maybe I could find a gift for Catherine, if—

"God, I hope we can finish this tonight," she said. "I want to spend Christmas with my family. Was that man in the tan coat who I think?"

"That's Pratt. He didn't want to talk to you at all."

She seemed to understand right away. "They're like that. A lot of them. They live a couple of hundred years, and everything they knew about the world gets turned on its head. They see a black woman alone at a bar, talking to men she doesn't know, and they immediately think *prostitute*. They're old-fashioned, squared. Some of them even talk about the good old days before the Terror."

I didn't know what "the Terror" was, but I got the point. "Do you know anything about him?"

"One of the other investigators said Pratt likes killing people, which doesn't exactly set him apart from the crowd. He should have talked to me. Now I can't even get a new report to him." She sighed. "So, we're going to check out the stables, right?"

"Oh, yeah."

She started the car and we rode through the dark town. I wondered how late the stables would be open, and if we'd have to break in.

We headed toward the fairgrounds but reached the turnoff well before the festival banner appeared. There was a split-rail fence, a gate, and a sign that said CONNER STABLES. The gate was bolted and pad-locked. I cut the padlock, opened the gate, let Catherine drive through, and closed it again.

She drove down the long path with the headlights off. Our plan was simple: Sneak in as close as we could without being spotted, just like the Wilbur estate. Locate the sapphire dog. Use the ghost knife on it, preferably from ambush.

Catherine wondered if we could use bright light to trap or stun it, but I didn't trust that idea. Sunlight hadn't bothered it at all, as far as I could tell. I suggested that its cage might have had special bulbs in it, and we agreed that we should have stolen a couple when we had the chance.

"Are you sure you want to come with me for this?" I asked. She gave me a look.

There were no turnoffs from the main drive where we could stash the car, so Catherine pulled all the way into the stable's parking lot and backed into a spot. There were three other cars already there.

I was getting a lot of practice closing car doors quietly. We walked toward the gate as if we belonged there. I was keyed up and jittery, and Catherine seemed to feel the same.

The muddy lot was ringed with trees and heavy scrub. Ahead was a wooden rail that looked just like the one at the edge of the property. It could have been part of a set in a cowboy movie except that the gate attached to it was made of welded aluminum pipes and locked with another Yale padlock.

There were two fenced-in areas for the horses to ride in; one was a muddy circle about twenty-five feet wide with a tall fence made of more welded aluminum. A second, larger area was bordered with low wooden rails to make an oval about seventy-five feet long. Cedar chips had been spread over the ground, and obstacles—long window planters without plants and uprights with crossbars that formed an X—had been left out. There was a Porta Potti and an overturned wheelbarrow to the left, but they couldn't have been the only source of the odor that made us wrinkle our noses. This place must have been stink heaven on hot summer afternoons.

Farther left there was a cluster of big, windowless wooden buildings decorated with pennants. I guessed those must be the stables.

I hopped the fence. Catherine climbed over it more slowly, but that was what I wanted. I had the tattoos and should be in the lead. I made my way toward the nearest stable. No one shouted a challenge at us. No waving flashlights came out of the darkness, no little squares of window light appeared in the distance. No one knew we were there.

There was a low, echoing rumble of thunder from somewhere nearby. It seemed to rebound against the mountains around us, coming from every direction and muffled by all the trees and brush nearby. Rain was coming.

· I walked along the building. A lamp was shining on the other side of the stables, and we made our way by indirect light. The wind hissed through the branches, but aside from our footsteps, there was no other sound.

At the corner of the building I peeked out. There were three more buildings, all four set two by two facing an open area about thirty feet wide. A single light glowed above the open door across the way. I peered into the darkness, searching for a human silhouette. I didn't see anything.

I stepped out of hiding. All four of the stable doors were open. Was that normal on a chilly winter night? I had no idea.

Catherine followed me into the yard as the mist thickened into a light drizzle. The stable beside us was dark and quiet. Then we heard steps from the stable across the yard. A horse slowly stepped out of the darkness.

I grabbed Catherine's arm. "It has a white mark on its face."

"Lots of horses have that."

This mark was completely off center, starting on the left side of its nose and passing under its left eye. "But can they be all crooked like that?"

"Maybe it's a paint," she said, which I didn't understand.

It stared at us. God, it was big. I heard Catherine back away. I was about to ask if we should just walk by it when she said: "Is it bleeding?"

I looked again; its ear was ragged and its mouth was bloody. It also had open wounds on its shoulder.

It lowered its head.

Catherine's voice was a low whisper in my ear. "Is that mud on its hoof?"

The horse stamped its foot. *Something* coated the hoof, but it looked too red to be mud. I raised my hands to clap. "Horses run from danger, right?"

Then it charged at us.

Catherine cursed and fled into the open stable behind us. I backpedaled after her, keeping the protected part of my chest toward the horse.

Christ, it was fast. Catherine yelped in pain and fear, but I couldn't turn to see why because the animal was already next to me.

It tried to bite me but missed. Even its mouth seemed huge. I ducked to the side, raising my arms to protect my face. My heel struck something and I nearly fell; in that same moment, the horse reared and kicked.

It caught me full in the chest. Already off balance, I tumbled back, feet flying over my head. I landed on my shoulder in the corner, my legs hitting the wall above me. The shin I'd bashed against the water trough flared with pain again. I fell with dirty straw in my face and long-handled wooden tools clattering around me.

I was exposed. A kick would cave in my skull, and—

Catherine screamed.

I rolled to my knees, shrugging off whatever had fallen on me. The stench of horse shit filled my nose, but I'd worry about that later. My hand fell on a thick wooden handle, and I grabbed at it like a lifeline.

The horse snorted and stamped. I jumped to my feet and raised my hands. I was holding a push broom.

That wasn't going to do me any good. Catherine cried out again, a sound more of fright than pain. I threw the broom underhand, hard, like I was throwing a shovel into the back of a truck. It struck the horse's hind legs, startling it. The horse jumped and kicked a little, turning its huge body toward me.

I reached back down into the straw, unwilling to look away from the animal. My hand fell on something thin and metal, and I dragged it out of the straw. It was a pitchfork.

The horse moved toward me. I backed toward the corner. There was a narrow pen in front of me to the right, and a second at my right elbow. Close on my left was the wall, and there was no back door. I was trapped.

I held the pitchfork high so the light would fall on it. Could the horse see what I was holding? I could. Would it understand and back away?

Apparently not, because it kept coming toward me, stamping its feet and snorting angrily. I yelled "Yah!" at it, just like a movie cowboy. It didn't have any effect. I pretended to jab at it, shouting "Hah!" each time.

I really, truly did not want to stab this animal. The thought of this dirty metal entering its flesh made me nauseous.

But it wouldn't back away. It was coming more slowly, more cautiously, but it wouldn't stop coming and I was running out of space. Soon it would have me pinned against the wall, the pitchfork would be useless, and it could kick my skull in.

"Yah!" I shouted again, half hoping that, even if the horse wouldn't back off, someone who worked here would suddenly show up and take control of the animal. There wasn't time for that, though. The horse reared back and kicked with its right hoof. I tried to pull the sharp tines away, but it struck the side of the fork and I nearly dropped it.

My nausea knotted into naked fear. To hell with this. I wasn't going to be killed just because I wasn't willing to defend myself. I jabbed with the pitchfork, just barely striking the horse's shoulder as I yelled "Back!" It wasn't enough to do real damage, I hoped, but it would break the skin and sting a little. Whether the horse could see well in the dark or not, it knew what I was holding now.

It suddenly made a high, hair-raising shriek and lunged at me, kicking with both front hooves. I jumped back and felt the pitchfork wrench upward, shivering, as a hoof nearly knocked it out of my hands. God, the *sound* the horse was making . . .

I tossed the pitchfork high, making the animal flinch and step back. I lunged to the right, into the pen. Running away from a horse was a lunatic idea, but if I stood my ground, I was going to have to kill it.

The horse followed—I could hear and feel it just behind me. I leaped up, grabbing the top of the wall between the enclosures. Adrenaline gave me the strength and speed I needed to practically throw myself into the next pen. I felt something snag my pants cuff—was the horse trying to bite me again?—but my momentum pulled it free.

The room suddenly darkened—not completely, but something big moved to block the light from across the yard.

I got my feet under me just in time, then jumped for the wall of this second pen. I didn't have the same quickness that comes from having a huge, hostile animal at my back, but I still had plenty of fear.

And I could hear the horse backing out. It didn't have room to turn around quickly, but I still didn't have a lot of time.

I dropped down on the other side of the wall, my weight pitching forward and my hands landing on something huge, soft, and cool right in front of me. It was another horse, this one dead and lying almost against the wall.

One of the front doors had been closed, and the other was scraping shut, cutting off my light and means of escape. I stumbled over the dead horse, half running, half falling toward the exit. I didn't look back. If those hooves were coming toward me, I didn't want to see it. I slipped through the doorway and sprawled in the mud just as Catherine slammed it shut.

The doors banged and jolted as the horse tried to kick them open. Catherine was knocked several inches away from them, then threw her shoulder against them again.

"Get something!" she yelled at me, and I jumped to my feet.

There was no way I could see to lock both doors—no bolt, no bar, no padlock. There was only a wooden catch, which I closed, but it was worn and fragile. It might not have held up in a strong windstorm, let alone a couple more kicks.

I turned, scanning the yard. What I needed was a truck or tractor I could drive up to the doors and block them with, but there wasn't one nearby, and I couldn't have gotten any of the cars in the lot through the fence.

Instead, I ran to the aluminum pen and cut off two lengths of pipe. As I ran back to Catherine, I shaved one end of each into a point, then staked them into the ground at the base of the doors.

Catherine stepped back carefully, ready to throw her body against the doors again if the stakes didn't hold. I stood next to her with the same thought.

The stakes held, but the doors still wobbled with every kick. And damn, it was loud.

"That's not secure enough," Catherine said, and I agreed.

I cut and shaved two more stakes from the aluminum fence. I had a twinge of guilt at destroying someone else's property, but I figured it was minor compared with what had happened to their two horses. I tossed them both to Catherine.

The doorway across the yard was built the same way, with two doors on two hinges each. With my ghost knife, I cut through the hinges on one of them and let it fall across my shoulders. I carried it across the mud, dropped it on its side, and tipped it against the staked door. Catherine drove the two stakes into the mud at its base, bracing it in place.

The *thump* of the doors slamming together must have startled the horse inside, because the steady *bang bang bang* of its kicks halted. We stepped back and surveyed our work again. Catherine turned to me. "Better," she said. She lifted her forearm and tenderly laid her hand against it. Was she injured?

"I'm sorry," I said. "I had a pitchfork in my hand, and maybe I could have stopped that horse without—"

"Ray, forget that shit. If you think I wanted you to kill that animal, you haven't been paying attention."

"No, I know that," I said. "We would have been safer, though, if I'd been willing to go all out. If I hadn't held back."

"I'd rather be good than safe."

With that, the conversation was over.

I crossed the yard and went into the stable the horse had come from. There was a trough filled with hay and two more dead animals. Both had their skulls crushed.

"A horse wouldn't . . ." Catherine's voice sounded tiny.

"Both of these have white marks, too."

So, the sapphire dog fed on animals as well as people. Hopefully, no one kept any lions around.

We searched the other stables. We found three more dead horses and a dead woman. She was dressed in dirty coveralls, but she'd applied her makeup with extraordinary care. She'd even plucked her eyebrows and drawn them back on. Her neck was crooked—broken by a horse's kick, maybe. And she had a white streak over her left ear.

Catherine searched her and produced a driver's license. She was Lois Conner, just like the name above the entrance. She was forty-nine, and like me, she carried a single credit card. I stood watch in the doorway while Catherine finished. I didn't have the stomach for another corpse. Instead, I stared at the braced stable door, watching it shudder under the trapped animal's kicks. They were slowing and growing weaker as it tired.

"She's been dead for hours," Catherine said. Apparently, there was nothing else about her that mattered to us.

Beyond the last stable was a bungalow with an OFFICE sign over the door. Behind that was a house that looked like an uneven stack of wooden boxes. The office was locked up and dark. A single light shone in the house.

We searched the office first, just in case. I held my ghost knife ready, but we didn't find anything.

The front door to the house was standing open. I entered first. We walked through the living room into a quiet little den with a sunken floor. The rooms were nicely furnished but filled with clutter: stacks of papers, pretty seashells, two dozen books all lying open and facedown on counters and coffee tables. Everything looked like it had been set in a random but convenient place and then forgotten.

Catherine got ahead of me and peeked into the hall. A light shone from a room at the far end, illuminating a body lying curled in the corner of the corridor floor. I caught her elbow and pulled her back. I was the one who was a little bit bulletproof. For once, she didn't cringe at my touch.

I turned the body over. He had long, graying hair like a hippie cowboy. He'd been shot in the chest and had fallen with his face to the wall and died. If he had a white mark, I couldn't see it.

"It isn't a very efficient predator, is it?" Catherine asked.

Pratt had said something similar. "What do you mean?"

"Well, its prey drives off or kills other prey. It's one thing if a cougar catches a sheep and the bleating frightens the rest of the herd, but in this case the sheep sticks around after it's been eaten, driving away other potential meals. I don't know why this thing hasn't gone extinct yet."

I remembered my idea that the sapphire dog might become Pet Emperor. "Maybe it's starving. It's been trapped for a couple of decades. Maybe it's feeding hard."

"Sure. Maybe."

We stood. I led the way around the corner into the lighted room. It was the kitchen. A huge refrigerator was lying on its side, and a little old gray-haired lady was trapped beneath it.

But I didn't notice that at first, because the little old lady was holding a big damn revolver, and I was looking right down the barrel. She had one eye squinted shut as she squeezed the trigger.

Click. It was empty. I stood in the doorway like a paper target at a pistol range. She let the end of the barrel fall onto the dirty tile floor.

"Damn," she said. "Wasted too many shots."

Catherine tried to step around me, but I held her back. I wasn't convinced it was safe yet. "What did you waste them on?" I asked, hoping she would say "A blue dog."

"Them," she said, and coughed blood onto her chin.

There were two more dead bodies by the stove: both young, tall, and slim, with long dark hair and short, upturned noses. Each woman had been shot multiple times. They looked enough alike to be sisters. Was one of them Depressed Guy's wife? I honestly didn't want to know.

The old woman reached for a box of ammunition on the floor beneath a kitchen chair, but it was out of reach.

"Would you hand that to me, sonny?"

I stepped into the room, allowing Catherine to follow. "I don't think so," I said quietly.

"Well, fuck you then. Get out of my house! You can't have him."

Catherine walked around the old woman, taking in the scene without expression. I wished there was a mirror nearby so I could see if I had the same composure. I didn't think I did.

The old woman looked very slender and frail, and her face was terribly pale. She had a streak across her forehead.

I felt very tired. "We should call an ambulance," I said.

"Don't you touch anything, you . . . *burglars*. Not even the phone. I forbid it."

"We will," Catherine said to me, ignoring the woman on the floor. "After we check the rest of the house."

I nodded. There was a set of stairs going up. I led the way, stepping over the two young bodies to get to them.

I wondered how long it would take to get used to seeing corpses. Maybe it was callous of me, but I wanted it to be soon. I wanted to stop feeling sickened by the blood and the slack, empty faces. I wanted to not care about the smell. I wanted . . .

I wanted all sorts of things I wasn't going to get. I took a deep breath and forced myself to focus on the job. The next old woman might not be holding an empty gun.

The upstairs had the same clutter, but there was no sapphire dog. I stopped in the bathroom to look in the mirror. I couldn't see any horse shit on me, which seemed like a minor miracle. Then we checked the back bedroom.

The walls were covered with posters of horses, and there were toy horses everywhere. Some people couldn't get enough, I guessed. Then I heard something scrape against the carpet. It was a tiny sound, but it made the hairs on the back of my neck stand up. I stepped in front of Catherine and held my ghost knife ready.

"Come out!" My voice was harsh and low. I knew it wasn't the sapphire dog—it had always fled, never hidden. "Come out right now!"

I heard a tiny, frightened gasp, then a little voice said: "I'm sorry!" The voice was choked with tears. "I'm sorry for hiding!" Behind me, Catherine gasped.

A girl slowly crawled from under the far side of the bed. She was about ten, thin as a rail, and she tried to make herself as small as possible.

She also wouldn't look at us, letting her hair cover her tear-streaked face. I couldn't tell if she had a white mark.

"Are you alone?" I asked, but Catherine pushed by me before the kid could answer.

"Oh, honey," she said, "what happened here?" Catherine went around the bed and took hold of the girl's hands.

"My granma tried to kill me," she said. I expected more sobs, but her voice seemed to hollow out and become steady. "That *thing* licked her and she went crazy."

"You saw it?" I asked.

"Yeah, it walked right by me. I saw what it did to my mom and gran. Then they turned against me." The girl's voice cracked. "They hated me. I don't know what I did, but they hated me so much. . . ."

"Oh, honey," Catherine said, and gathered the girl into her arms. "You didn't do a single little thing to deserve this. Not a single little thing."

The girl began to cry. Catherine held her close. I stood in the doorway, weapon in hand, feeling useless.

"We have to take her away from here," Catherine said.

"No!" the girl shouted. She broke Catherine's embrace and retreated to the corner. "My granma is still out there, and so is that *thing*. It's out there doing that to other people, and I don't want to leave here I won't go I won't do it—"

Catherine pressed her fists against her chest. "It's okay, honey. It's okay. You don't have to do anything scary."

"We can't bring her anyway," I said. "We're hunting." I was surprised by the sound of my own voice; it sounded flat and miserable. *I don't rescue people. I kill predators.*

The girl was willing to tell us her name, Shannon, but she absolutely refused to leave her room. Catherine promised to call emergency services for her. Shannon slid back under the bed, and we went into the hall.

"Oh my God, Ray," Catherine whispered. "That little girl . . . I wasn't ready for what happened to those horses, but that girl breaks my heart."

"The sapphire dog didn't feed on her," I said, trying to think about something, anything else, "but it did feed on Little Mark. What do you think is the age break where people become food? Puberty?"

"For Christ's sake, Ray." Her voice was harsh but still low. "Didn't you notice—"

I hissed at her to cut her off. It didn't matter that she was right. At that moment, I couldn't bear to be told that I wasn't feeling enough.

My misery and adrenaline turned to anger. "I may not be *trained for this,* but I'm trying to focus on the job. Maybe you . . ." I almost said: *should take care of your own people and let these people take care of themselves,* but it would have been too much. I wasn't going to turn something she'd told me in confidence into a weapon. I turned away.

"It's okay," she said. "I shouldn't have said that." Then she patted my hand briefly.

We went down the stairs into the basement. I led the way again, stepping around stacks of newspapers and old board games, trays full of glass candleholders, and other crap.

I switched on the light. The Conners kept their basement relatively clear, compared with the rest of the house. There was a leather saddle up on a stand and leather-working tools laid out on a workbench.

I remembered the rumble of thunder I'd heard outside. I hadn't heard a second one. The thunderclouds might have passed, or maybe I'd heard a rock slide and didn't recognize the sound. Still, something felt off about it.

My iron gate twinged. I knew that feeling, and I could feel where it was coming from. I turned toward the basement window behind me.

The sapphire dog was there, peering through the window at us from outside the house. It was lying on its stomach, its bright eyes almost pressing against the glass. Its star-shaped pupils seemed to be glowing.

CHAPTER TWELVE

Behind me, I heard Catherine say: "My God, it's beautiful."

I could feel those waves of emotion hitting me, but I was ready this time. Palming my ghost knife, I lifted my hands toward my face. Once my arm was curled, I would throw it as hard as I could right between that thing's eyes. If that didn't kill it, I'd fetch that revolver and box of ammo from the kitchen.

From behind me on the left, I heard the distinctive sound of a round being chambered.

I ducked down and to the right just as a gunshot boomed beside my head. I dropped to one knee, spun, and swept my ghost knife upward.

I missed the gun in Catherine's hand but hit her wrist. She gasped and her hand opened. The weapon clattered to the floor. I lunged for the pistol but I didn't need to rush. She didn't do anything but clutch her wrist and say: "I'm sorry." I could barely hear her above the ringing in my left ear.

It was a small stainless steel Smith & Wesson with a plastic handle. Where had she gotten it? I looked back at the window. The sapphire dog was staring at me.

I'd already thrown my ghost knife at it once, when it was much closer to me, and it had vanished. Now that I'd lost the chance to surprise it, I tried something else. I lifted the S&W and emptied the clip into it.

I saw the bullet holes in the glass, so I knew some of my shots had hit their mark. The sapphire dog didn't react at all. It didn't recoil or flinch, and no bullet holes appeared on it. It was like shooting a hallucination.

The old woman in the kitchen above thumped her gun against the floor. I glanced up, then back at the window. The predator was gone.

Catherine stared at me sheepishly. She apologized again. The ghost knife had worked on her, even though she'd been under the sapphire dog's influence.

"Where did you get this?" I asked, holding up the gun. I tried not to shout.

She handed me a spare magazine. "I took it off Lois Conner," she said, and in that adrenaline-fueled moment I had no idea who she was talking about. It didn't matter. The sapphire dog was gone, and I had to go after it.

"Go to the car," I said. She was already nodding obediently. "Drive to the fairgrounds and wait for me. Stay away from people, okay? If you can't avoid someone, don't do what they ask you to do. Just do what I told you."

"I will," she said. Her eyes were wide and blank. "What if I see the sapphire dog?"

"You can try to run it down with the car, if you think you can hit it." I ran for the steps, then stopped. She was still staring at me with a passive, helpless expression. "On second thought, don't try to run it down. Don't do anything. Just hide. Hurry."

I ran upstairs. In the drawer by the back door, I found a flashlight. I took the phone off the hook and dialed 911. I felt a stabbing headache so strong that I could barely understand the operator who answered. Could it have been a delayed reaction to the gunshot? I said what I needed to say and hung up. My headache eased up almost immediately, and I put it out of my mind.

I ran outside. When I reached the bullet-ridden window my ghost knife was in my hand, but I didn't have a target. The sapphire dog was gone.

The soup-can footprints were right where I expected, running along the edge of the house into the woods. I followed the trail.

Catherine came out of the house and lightly jogged toward the car. I guess that was the best version of *hurry* I could expect after the ghost knife had done its work on her.

She didn't have a white mark, like Penny, but neither had Ursula. So why had my spell worked on Catherine but not Ursula? Maybe the predator had used its influence on her many times over the years. Maybe, after all that time, she had lost her ability to feel anything else, just like the people with the mark.

But this wasn't the time to speculate. The footprints led to a horse trail. I peered into the woods, trying to see if the sapphire dog was hiding in the shadows, but I couldn't see anything. Was it behind a bush or tree, waiting to feed on me when I got close? The thought of that bone-white tongue touching my face made me shiver. Maybe my iron gate would protect me, but I didn't want to bet my life on it.

I turned on the flashlight. Lois Conner's reloaded gun was in my pocket, and my ghost knife was in my right hand. The tracks led straight down the center of the trail—almost as if it was avoiding the greenery. I started after it.

Of course, it wasn't native to this planet. Maybe it was *afraid* of the underbrush and the more mundane predators that it might run into there.

Which made me immediately think of Catherine. I couldn't help but wonder who she might run into. What if she met the bartender again, and he invited her back to his place? Had the ghost knife taken away her ability to say no?

Damn. Maybe I should have asked her to come with me, but after I saw the look on her face, I didn't want her anywhere near the sapphire dog. Catherine was smart and tough when she was herself, but the ghost knife turned people into victims.

The wind rustled the tree branches. I froze in place. Could the sapphire dog climb trees? It didn't have hands or claws, but underestimating it could get me killed.

I had to put Catherine out of my mind for now. If I'd made a mistake in sending her out on her own, it was too late to fix it. I had to focus on the job at hand.

Where the hell was Pratt, anyway?

The flashlight beam could reach about ten feet—a respectable distance but not enough to show me the tops of the trees. I crouched beside a tree trunk and played the light along the path. The weird round footprints continued for as far as the beam could shine.

Of course, I'd seen the sapphire dog's tracks lead in multiple directions—it might have left this trail for me to follow while crouching in the shadows to ambush me. I kept moving forward, putting all my thought, all my attention, into my sight and hearing. I examined every shadow, every rustle. My shoes had soaked through from the mud, and I spared a single, stupid moment envying the Fellows and their hiking boots.

Then I pushed that thought away. I crept forward, thinking about the sapphire dog, its glowing eyes, and its long, floppy ears. I didn't know how fast it could move or how far it could travel without rest. I just kept going, determined to destroy it or be destroyed.

It didn't ambush me, but I didn't catch up to it, either. It was fleeing and I was being careful. I was never going to catch up to it this way. I increased my pace, my feet squishing loudly in the mud.

At the top of a rise, the trees and underbrush suddenly thinned. After fifteen feet of gentle slope, the ground flattened into the fairgrounds. Farther out there was a ring of halogen lights on poles set in a circle, and all the lamps were on. The locals were setting up the fair, although my view of them was obscured by the whitewashed buildings and a set of bleachers.

To my left was the high-peaked church. The back door was open, letting yellowish light into the yard. From this angle, I could see a little house behind it.

To the right were more woods, open fields, and darkness.

I shone the flashlight down into the mud. The sapphire dog's trail split into three directions, just like on the Wilbur estate. On the left, the trail led across a muddy patch and then into the high grass beside the church. In front of me it led down the slope, and to the right it went through the bushes.

Crap. I ignored the footprints that led to the right into the underbrush—if the predator had avoided that sort of cover for this long, I doubted it would take it up now.

On impulse, I started down the slope toward the fairgrounds. The footprints were more difficult to find among the tree roots and hard soil of the hill, but they were there. They led straight out into the grass.

Maybe if I'd grown up a hunter, with weekend trips into the woods with deer rifles and orange earflap caps, I could have followed the predator's tracks across the newly mown lawn. But I'd grown up on baseball and video games. I couldn't find the trail or even tell if it ended suddenly like the ones on the Wilbur estate.

I didn't like the way this looked. So far, the sapphire dog had been drawn to people and buildings. It had fled from its captors, sure, but it had gone from one house to another, feeding and controlling the residents.

The only people on the fairgrounds were the ones out in the lights setting up. If the sapphire dog was going to go for them, it would have had to angle more to the left, not straight ahead into the dark open space of the lawn.

I scrambled back up the hill. The left-hand tracks pointed directly toward the church and the open, lighted door. I followed them.

After about fifteen feet, the tracks disappeared. As expected. The grass was unmowed and dripping wet. By the time I was halfway there, my pants were soaked from the knee down.

A pickup truck backed up to the open door, and a short, wiry man began unloading boxes from the bed and carrying them inside. I switched off my flashlight and I walked toward the open door, the ghost knife in my hand and the gun in my pocket. On the near side of the church was a neatly mown lawn. On the far side was a cracked asphalt parking lot.

The night must have been darker than I thought; the man unloading the truck didn't notice me until I was close enough to tap the edge of the truck. I startled him. He was wearing a clerical collar and had the quick, limber movements of a karate teacher.

He looked me up and down. I could see by the light shining from the inside of the church that his expression was carefully neutral. "If you're looking for money," he said, "we don't have any. We're a rural church. If you're hungry, though, you've come to the right place."

I looked into the bed of the truck. It was half full of grocery bags of canned food and boxes of premade stuffing. I glanced down at my clothes. I was still wearing the shirt Yin's men had torn, and I supposed my eye was still ugly.

"I'm not looking for food or money," I said. "I'm looking for a dog." Maybe it would have been better to say it was my dog, but the words wouldn't come out of my mouth. "It has fur that's been dyed blue, and it's sick. Contagious, actually."

"Contagious?" I had his attention. "I haven't seen any dogs running loose, and I've been driving around picking up donations. I can make a couple of calls, though. Help me carry some of this inside, and we'll see what we can do."

He grabbed two grocery bags in each hand and turned his back on me, confident I'd follow. I looked around but didn't see the predator. I picked up a crate filled with boxes of muffin mix and went inside.

It was a wide, shallow room filled with cheap metal shelving. Almost half the shelf space was filled with food donations. There was a second door nestled between the shelves. A dead bolt held it shut. A chipped wooden desk stood in the corner. A cheap portable stereo on the edge of the desk played seventies disco.

Had the sapphire dog come in here? The room was lit well enough that I could see the pastor didn't have a white mark, and there were no discolored circles on the walls.

The pastor reached up and scratched the ear of a pudgy, long-haired cat. "Those muffin mixes go there." He indicated a high shelf.

I set the crate there. "If you see that blue dog, don't go near it. In fact, stay far away. I'd be grateful if you would spread the word."

I started toward the door. One circuit of the church should tell me if the sapphire dog had gotten in through the walls; then I'd check the house. If I didn't find anything, I wasn't sure where I'd go next.

He took out his cell. "Let me make a couple of calls."

I nodded. "Be right back."

Outside, I played the flashlight across the lawn but didn't see anything interesting. I walked around the truck, then the church. There were no openings the predator could have used and no dark circles that indicated it had gone through the wall.

I was on my way to the house when the pastor came out of the church. "Are you Ray?"

"I am," I said, still walking.

"I'm Aaron," he said. It seemed weird to think of him by his first name instead of Reverend Surname, but what did I know? Maybe he'd invite me in to play Guitar Hero. "I spoke with the manager down at the fairgrounds. No one down there has seen your dog, but they'll keep an eye out. Also, Steve Cardinal asked you to wait here for him. He'll be over as soon as he can."

I nodded, but I wasn't about to wait, not if the sapphire dog was as close as I thought. I wished he hadn't said the dog was mine, though.

I walked around the porch, shining the light on the base of the walls. It wasn't until we reached the far back corner of the house that I saw it: a dark circle on the brick beneath a kitchen window.

"Crap."

"What is it?" Aaron knelt beside the mark.

"Don't touch it," I warned him as he reached out. "I need you to get away from here."

"Is it in my house? I have . . . I have family inside. Loved ones." He looked jumpy.

"Leave them to me," I said.

"You said your dog was contagious. Will they have to be quarantined? Does your dog bite?" His voice was going high with stress.

"Aaron, go to your truck and stay there."

He turned and ran back along the house, then vaulted over the porch rail with the ease of a gymnast. I shouted his name, but he was already at the door. I ran after him, but I heard the door close and lock before I could even reach the porch.

I climbed up over the rail after him, but much more slowly. Maybe I should take up parkour, if I survived.

I dropped the flashlight into my pocket and took out the gun. I slid the ghost knife between the door and jamb, then hesitated. The pastor and his family didn't know me; I didn't want to charge into his home with a gun in my hand. I put it back into my pocket and hoped I wouldn't get killed because of it.

I cut through the locks and pulled the door open. The house lights were on but the place was completely quiet.

"Hello!" I shouted. There was no answer. Had Aaron found the sapphire dog already? Maybe not. Maybe he was in his room hiding his porn.

I crept into the living room. The couch was covered with stacks of newspapers and old travel magazines. There was an uncluttered easy chair by the fireplace and an empty office chair beside the desk. The biggest piece of furniture in the room was another four-foot-high cat playground. The room smelled like damp carpet and cat litter. What family did the pastor have in here?

The kitchen was cleaner but didn't smell any better. The trash overflowed with pizza boxes and teriyaki take-out cartons. There were three kitty-litter trays in the corner.

The sapphire dog wasn't in there, either. The back door was locked and the basement door had a discolored circle at the bottom.

I twisted the knob and jiggled the door. The discolored circle collapsed into a billowing cloud of dust. The sapphire dog must have entered the basement and come up through there. I went back into the living room and found a flight of stairs leading to the second floor. I started up, avoiding stacks of cheap paperbacks by the rail.

I heard something slide upstairs and called Aaron's name. Again, no answer. Footsteps sounded above me.

I rushed to the top of the stairs. There were three doors up there, and one was partly open. That was the bathroom, and it was dark. I went through the door on the left.

It was the master bedroom. There were clothes all over the floor. Below the window was a double bed with piles of dirty laundry on one side. Three big cats stared at me from under a clothes bureau.

Damn. The pastor didn't have a family in this house. He had run toward a predator because of his damn cats.

I raced into the hall, then into the other room. It was storage, with banker's boxes stacked against the walls.

The window was open. I rushed to it. The pastor had climbed down the porch roof and was already on the lawn. He opened the door to his truck, and something low and blue slithered into the passenger seat.

I reached for the gun in my pocket, but it snagged on my jacket and clattered to the floor. I cursed at myself as I picked it up. It was only a second's delay, but it was long enough for Aaron to get into the driver's seat.

I looked down at him. He looked up at me. Just before he closed the door of his truck, I saw by the cab light that he had a single white dot on his forehead.

He started the truck and began to back away. I put two bullets into the grille, then two more into the front driver's corner, where the battery should be. Aaron slammed the truck into reverse and did a one-point U-turn onto the church parking lot. I emptied the gun at his tires, but I've never been what you'd call a crack shot. I was pretty sure I'd missed the battery, too.

The truck labored onto the street. I ran through the house and out the porch door. The pastor's taillights turned onto the road toward town. At least he'd left the fairgrounds. I sprinted across the grass and parking lot. I was never going to catch them on foot, but I hoped the truck would break down before the sapphire dog could reach another victim.

I ran out into the road and jogged after them, but the truck was already out of sight. Headlights appeared behind me and I stepped onto the shoulder of the road. An ambulance screamed by, with Steve Cardinal's car close behind. I waved to him, and he stomped on the brake, screeching to a halt.

Justy was in the passenger seat. She rolled down the window, but it was Steve who spoke. "What in heaven's name have you been doing?"

"I saw it! It just caught a guy in a blue pickup."

"My God. Who?"

"Aaron. The pastor. I don't know his whole name. I damaged his truck. We need to catch him before he finds another ride."

"Well, get in then."

I pulled the back door open and climbed in. He stomped on the gas before I could get fully into his car. I yanked my foot inside just as the car's momentum slammed the door shut. I fussed with the seat belt. Steve was talking. "Reverend Dolan's a good man. He's forthright and strong in his faith. He grew up here. When he was a boy—"

"Don't write his eulogy yet." I didn't say that the pastor wasn't important. It was the sapphire dog that mattered.

"It's not a eulogy. He's a strong man. Maybe he'll resist it." Steve was quiet for a couple of seconds, then said: "I've been to the estate."

"What?"

"I've been to the Wilbur estate. No one was there. Everything was locked up and dark, but I found where they've been holding it all these years. I found the plastic cage with all the lights. Was it the plastic that kept it trapped?"

"No," I said. "It can go through plastic."

"The lights, then. It was the lights that held it all this time?"

"Maybe. There are a couple of things you need to know about, though: there's a girl named Shannon at the Conner house. She's all alone there." Justy took out her phone and began typing out a text message. "The adults are all dead or . . . damaged like Penny. And I saw Regina Wilbur in town. She had a shotgun. You might want to—"

"There!" Justy suddenly shouted. "I saw brake lights." She pointed toward a gravel turnoff on the right.

Steve slammed on the brakes. "Are you sure?"

"Positive."

Steve backed up and turned onto the path. "Where does this lead?" I asked.

"Back to the fairgrounds."

The road curved to the right, then led downhill to connect with the fairgrounds parking lot at the opposite side from the church. Justy finished her text message without glancing down at her phone.

"There's the truck right there," I said, pointing into the lot. The blue pickup was parked crooked beside the cluster of vans, trucks, SUVs, and other vehicles. Steve slowed down, approaching the scene carefully.

Now that I was closer, I saw just how blindingly bright the fairground lights were. The workers—volunteers from town, I assumed—had already constructed two huge tents, not as large as circus tents, but still big enough to house dozens of disaster victims, with two more ready to be erected. The canvases had been painted in different designs: red with white snowflakes, white with green Christmas trees, that sort of thing.

Everyone was working. They were unfolding canvas, connecting pipes, uncoiling electrical cable, whatever it took. No one was standing around watching. No one was fighting. Two people stopped and embraced while a third person rested a hand on their shoulders, but that looked like grieving. The predator wasn't there.

In the far end of the parking lot, half hidden among the trees, was the Neon I'd rented. I hoped Catherine was there and that she was okay. I'd check later, if I had the chance.

I saw a shape move behind a van. "Stop. Stop!" I said, unclicking my seat belt and opening my door.

"Heaven's sake, stay in the car." Steve's voice was tense.

I didn't. He chirped the brakes as I climbed out, nearly dumping me on the ground. I ran around the edge of the parked cars, then dropped low.

Christ, the asphalt was cold. Why hadn't I used my plastic to buy gloves? I peered under the cars, looking for moving feet and, maybe, a glimpse of a blue leg. No luck. I scrambled to my feet and peered through the car windows. Still no luck.

Steve had circled around the cluster of vehicles. He was too close, only ten feet from the pastor's pickup. He should have known better. It occurred to me that I could use him as a distraction, as a wooden man, but I rejected that idea. I wasn't here to sacrifice innocent people. I wanted to save them, not destroy them.

Several of the builders had noticed me creeping around their cars and stopped working. "Hey! Fella!" someone shouted. Six or seven of the workers began walking this way. Crap.

I was about to ask about a dog when Steve's reedy voice cut through. "Have any of you boys seen Pastor Dolan?"

That question stopped them cold. The man in the front, wearing a wool-lined jacket and hunter's cap, waved an arm vaguely behind him. "His truck broke down. Esteban is giving him a ride somewhere."

I looked across the field in the direction Hunting Cap had waved. Midway down the tree line, there was a break in the woods. It was another feeder road.

"You saw that?" Steve asked him. "You saw the pastor get into his truck?"

"Yeah," Hunting Cap said. "He was carrying something in his arms, like a load of laundry or something."

I was already running toward the car when Steve called my name. Justy threw open the back door for me and yelled: "If you see either of them again, keep away! Let everyone know!" I climbed in and slammed the door shut. Steve raced down the slope across the grass toward the second feeder road.

The seat belt was difficult to click with the bumps and jolts of the uneven ground, but I managed it. "What kind of truck does Esteban have?"

"Cube truck," Justy answered. "He's a plumber." Her tone was clipped. Steve hissed as he jounced around behind the wheel.

We reached the feeder road without breaking an axle, and Steve slowed. This road was made of mud and ruts. We had to be careful, or we were going to be stranded.

I wondered whether we'd find Aaron or Esteban in the truck when we caught up with it. So far, none of the people who'd been marked by the sapphire dog had wanted to share.

We hit a deep pothole, and the whole frame jolted. Steve slowed even more, which frustrated me even though I knew it was the smart thing to do. I hoped that whoever was driving the truck was less sensible and had stranded himself.

It didn't happen. We eventually reached a two-lane asphalt road. There were no taillights visible in either direction.

"Town is to the left," Steve said. He turned that way, really giving it gas.

I knew the road to the right also led to town, although it was a longer drive, but fair enough. I sat in my seat, staring ahead. The road twisted and curved, but there were no turnoffs. Eventually, we came to the top of a rise and I could see the lights of Washaway below.

"There he is," Justy said. I saw a pair of taillights speeding toward town. Steve stomped on the gas, and for once I wished we were in a genuine cop car with lights, sirens, and everything. We zoomed down the hill, taking a long, slow curve at twice the speed the top-heavy truck could manage.

Justy turned around and stared at me blankly. "I'm sorry," she said. "At Big Penny's, I wasn't ready. I ran—"

"Don't worry about it. You didn't do anything wrong." I meant it. She looked grateful, then nodded and turned around.

Within two minutes, we were right behind him, honking our horn. Of course, the truck didn't pull over.

"Dad-blastit," Steve said. We angled across the double yellow line to pull alongside him, but the cube truck swerved, nearly smashing us off the road into the trees. Justy screamed, and Steve slammed on the brakes. I wished I could drag him out of his seat and jump behind the wheel.

"Esteban's not answering his phone," Justy said, snapping her cell shut. "I'm going to try Aaron now."

We hung back from the truck for a few seconds. The gun in my pocket was out of bullets, and I didn't think Steve would loan me his so I could shoot at the truck's tires. Hell, I couldn't hit the pastor's tires when he was pulling out of a parking spot. There was no reason to think I'd do better now.

Of course, I also had my ghost knife. It would hit whatever I wanted it to hit, but it was just a piece of paper. Cutting into the edge of a moving tire would probably tear it apart, and I'd lose the last chance I had for killing the sapphire dog.

Steve gritted his teeth and stepped on the gas again. "Hold on!" he shouted. He rammed the back corner of the truck as we came to a sharp turn.

God, it was loud. We were jolted harder than the truck was, but we were expecting it. The truck driver overcorrected toward the left, swerved into the other lane, then swung back too hard to the right.

Steve slammed on the brakes. The truck struck a fence, then, skidding, hit a tree.

Steve's car fishtailed to a stop. I opened my door and stepped out, ghost knife in hand. No one told me to stop this time.

I crept along the passenger side of the truck, half expecting the sapphire dog to jump on me. Instead, I heard the driver's door open and close. I moved back to the rear of the truck.

Steve opened his door and stood behind it, his little revolver trained on someone I couldn't see on the other side of the truck. "Drop that!" he shouted. "Esteban, you drop that or I will have to fire!" He sounded desperately afraid.

Steve didn't change position. I moved toward the corner of the truck as quietly as possible. Not quietly enough, though. A Hispanic man with a sizable paunch and the biggest monkey wrench I'd ever seen turned toward me. He was smiling.

He had a white circle just below his left eye.

Esteban was a lefty, and when he swung that wrench, it came at me in a high, slow arc like a Frisbee. It was so slow that I actually caught it and tugged him off balance. When he stumbled, I hit him once, quickly, where his jaw met his ear. He dropped to the asphalt.

Steve holstered his weapon. He looked relieved.

I knelt on the plumber's back while Steve handcuffed him. At least it wouldn't have to be a citizen's arrest this time. I jumped up and walked around the truck. There were no signs of activity in the cab and no dark circles on the sides. I hopped up to peek into the window.

Empty. I went around to the back. The latch was padlocked, but Steve had fished a fat, jangly key ring off Esteban's belt and was fumbling with the keys. I could have cut the padlock off in a second, but I didn't want to use the ghost knife in front of them. Instead, I stood and waited, holding my breath to hide my impatience.

He found a likely key and slid it into the lock. It sprang open. He drew his revolver and waved me back. I reached into my pocket and held on to my ghost knife.

Steve opened the door and shined a flashlight inside. The walls were lined with tools and shelves, and there was no place for the predator to hide.

"Esteban," Steve said. "Where is it?"

The man on the ground had come around enough to laugh at him. He tried to get his knees under him, but he was still unsteady. He fell onto his side and kicked at me, still laughing.

Steve and Justy tried to pressure him into sharing more information, but it wasn't going to happen. He laughed and jeered at everything they said, pleased that he had tricked us into following him.

I knelt beside him and held his face still. The mark was just a spot rather than a streak. The texture of his skin was unchanged—the pores and tiny hairs inside the mark were the same as outside—but the skin itself had become as white as a sheet of paper. I poked at it; it felt normal.

"Why has the sapphire dog decided to stay in Washaway?" I asked. "Why isn't it trying to leave anymore?" He didn't answer.

"He's not going to help us, is he?" Justy said. She didn't want to get close to him, and I didn't blame her. Esteban cursed at us and laughed again.

Steve sighed. "Help me put him into the back of the car."

I did, slamming the door shut. Esteban didn't fight me and didn't try to break out. He just sat and smiled.

"What do you think?" Steve said.

"Let me check something." I went to the truck and climbed into the cab. Hunting Cap had seen the pastor get into the truck with something in his arms. If Esteban had attacked him, it would have happened in here.

There was no blood. There was no evidence of a fight at all. And I didn't believe for a minute that Esteban could have taken that quick little pastor in a fight. I climbed out of the cab.

"Something's changed," I said. "The sapphire dog's previous victims fought one another over it, but this guy left it with someone else to lead us on a wild-goose chase, and he's *happy about it.*"

"And the mark is different," Steve said.

"Either it's learning how to control us better, or it's eating more carefully. Probably the latter. I bet it's still with the pastor."

"But where is he?"

A car whooshed by us. There were two people inside, but they were gone before I could catch a glimpse of them. "Pretty much anyone in town would offer a ride to the pastor, right?"

Steve sighed and rested his hand on the roof of his car. He looked tired. "Yes."

"We should see if he doubled back."

"What if he didn't?" Justy asked.

"Then we'll drive around town, looking for him or anyone else with marks on their faces."

Steve's car rattled and clicked as we drove back to the fairgrounds. He kept looking into the rearview mirror and talking to Esteban, trying to pry cooperation from him with reason and social connection. I watched Esteban's ironclad serenity and knew it was wasted effort. The sapphire dog had taken away the parts of him that Steve could appeal to.

The men and women working at the fairgrounds swore up and down that Pastor Dolan hadn't returned and that none of their cars were missing. They had to shout at us while we talked; a snow-making machine on top of the field house was running, and it was *loud*. We found the church and the house dark. We broke down the doors and searched together. Steve clucked his tongue over the mess in the house, but we didn't find any signs of life. Even the cats were gone.

We walked out into the yard. Steve offered me a ride back into town, but I declined. He drove away.

The Neon was parked in the same spot. Catherine opened the door for me.

"How are you?" I asked.

"I'm fine," she said, to my tremendous relief. "Thank you. I'm sorry I tried to shoot you."

She still had that look. I didn't like it and I had no idea how long it was going to last. She gave me the keys and slid into the passenger seat. She clicked her seat belt in place and folded her hands in her lap.

I started the engine. "Keep an eye out for hitchhikers. And for the predator."

"All right." Her voice sounded dull and thin. All the fire and sharp intelligence were missing. The ghost knife had done just what the sapphire dog did—it took away every part of a person's personality but one. In that way, we were alike.

But who gave a damn about that? The predator was feeding on people, and it was my job to stop it.

I drove toward the campgrounds, the school, and the possibly mythical highway feeder road. My high beams lit the greenery around me, but I didn't see any movement. I saw blackberry vines, ferns, and moss-covered trees, but no people hiding in the greenery. Certainly no pastor.

I rolled down the window. The air was bracing but Catherine didn't complain. I drove quietly, radio off, listening and watching.

Nothing.

After a couple of miles we came to the campground entrance, a wide dirt path leading off the main road. I decided to pull in.

"What's that?" Catherine asked.

The headlights had flashed on something bright red in the bushes. I put the car in park and stepped out. Immediately, I could see that it was a dead man.

CHAPTER THIRTEEN

I leaned close to him. It was Stork Neck. He'd been shot once through the chest and then fallen into the hedge. Had the sapphire dog gotten loose among the Fellows, turning them against one another? Or was something else going on?

I touched his hand. It was cold, but so was mine. I lifted the bottom of his ski jacket to feel his belly. It was still warm.

That was a bad sign. I glanced around quickly but didn't see any other bodies. I had no idea how close the shooter was or whether he was coming back. I should probably have gotten out of there, but I didn't. Instead, I got back into the car.

My headlights shone down the dirt path into the campground. Down the slope, I could see the tops of three motor homes, each with a dark SUV beside it. I'd found the Fellows' camp.

"Stay low," I said. Catherine ducked below the dash. I pulled all the way into the grounds, which seemed like a better option than parking on the shoulder of the road.

There was a second body beside the entrance to the nearest trailer. It was Fat Guy. He was sitting against the trailer wheel, his head slumped down over a bloody red hole in his breastbone. He didn't look so dangerous anymore, but no one did once a bullet or two had run through him. There was a third body, one I didn't recognize, beside the next trailer. Blood spatters from the exit wound had sprayed onto the white siding.

The shooter had fired from somewhere behind me, on the hill across the road. Someone was using a long gun and using it well.

I parked as far from the trailers as I could. Maybe the shooter, if he was still around, would assume I was alone in the car. Of course, the sniper had had plenty of time to take a shot while I'd stood over Stork Neck's body. Maybe he wasn't in position anymore. Maybe he was creeping closer in to inspect his handiwork.

"Stay as low as you can and keep out of sight. You're safest if no one knows you're here."

Catherine nodded and I climbed from the car, walking quickly away from it. I took the ghost knife from my pocket.

The closest trailer was dark and all the curtains were drawn. I didn't get any closer than ten yards as I trotted past. The second trailer was not lined up with the others—someone had hooked it up to a Yukon and tried to pull away. There was a bullet hole in the driver's window and blood on the windshield, but I couldn't see a body. I didn't look for it, either.

I did see the red-and-white card on the dashboard. It was a parking permit for the campgrounds. Damn. I'd told Regina exactly where to find them.

The last of the trailers was parked beneath the trees. It was also dark, but the curtains were open. Everyone still alive must have fled. Then I heard a woman shout a warning, saw movement in a darkened window, and heard the shot.

Strangely, I felt something tear at the front of my shirt before I saw the window burst open. It took a moment to realize I'd been shot in the chest and should play dead. I toppled sideways, letting my right hand fall across my chest to hide the spot where the bullet hole should have been.

I tried to stay completely still, although my heart was racing—in fact, my heart was speeding up as I lay there. Some asshole had just taken a shot at me, and if he'd gone for my head, I'd be as dead as Stork Neck.

It scared me, and being scared pissed me off. The freezing mud soaking into my clothes pissed me off. Somebody was going to have something unpleasant happen because of this.

For now, though, I put that out of my mind. I heard a thin screen door smack shut and the squish of approaching footsteps. I held my breath and kept still. Through my half-closed eyes, I could see the trailer. A figure with a white ski mask and a white sleeve peeked around the front of the RV and aimed a rifle at me. My arm was curled and ready to throw the ghost knife, but the gunman was twenty-five or thirty yards away. By the time the spell reached him, he'd have put two or three bullets into my brain.

After a few seconds, the figure decided I was dead and aimed at the car. I hoped Catherine was still keeping low.

The sniper stepped out from behind the truck. Despite the ski mask, I recognized her. It was Ursula. She was wearing the same clothes she'd had on when she held a gun on me in the guesthouse behind the Wilbur estate. I could even see the cuts the ghost knife had made in her white jacket.

I'd been thinking of the shooter as "he"; I should have learned better by now.

She walked directly toward the car, rifle to her shoulder like a soldier. She stepped around my feet and out of my line of sight. I counted four squishy, muddy steps after she'd passed, then a fifth and a sixth before I decided I was being a coward. I rolled over and threw the ghost knife.

She turned toward me, swinging the rifle around. The ghost knife cut through it, and the weapon came apart in her hands.

She gaped at the broken rifle for a few precious seconds while I rolled to my feet. Then she threw the halves aside and reached into her waistband.

There was no time to be gentle. I charged her and hit her once in the same spot I'd hit Esteban. She staggered but didn't go down. I did it again.

She fell into the mud, arms waving vaguely in the air, still trying to defend herself even though she was out. I pulled her handgun out of her belt and dropped it into my pocket.

She also had a knife, which I threw onto the top of the nearest trailer. Then I took her wallet and keys, just because she was annoying. In her inside jacket pocket, I found three pairs of handcuffs with keys.

I dragged her by the heel to the nearest trailer, wrapped her arms around a tire below the axle, and cuffed her.

I pressed my ear against the wet, freezing shell of the trailer. Someone had shouted a warning to me, and it sure hadn't been Ursula. I didn't hear anything, so I circled around to the door. One of the tires was flat. I knelt and saw a bullet hole in the rim. It was almost the same spot as the one on the tire of the overturned delivery truck on the estate. Ursula was quite a shot.

The trailer door was wide open. I reached in and felt for the light switch, flicked it on, and stepped back.

No gunshots zipped by me. I looked in, leaning farther into the doorway until I saw a woman's fur-trimmed leather boot and the leg that went with it.

I went inside. The boot belonged to Professor Solorov; she was slumped against the wall in the little booth that served as a dining area. Her eyes were half closed and her mouth was hanging open. Blood had soaked through her blouse on the lower left side. She did not look like the same woman who had taken Kripke at gunpoint, or who had threatened to kill his whole family if he didn't turn over his spell book.

The window above her had a bullet hole in it. I was standing where Ursula had stood when she shot at me. Solorov must have shouted the warning, although I doubted she knew who she was shouting at.

She looked at me, blinking sleepily as she tried to focus. "Did you kill her?"

"No. I'm going to call an ambulance, okay? Where's the phone?"

"Right there." She didn't have the energy to point, but I did follow her gaze to the cell on the floor. It had been smashed.

"Hold on," I said. I went outside and knelt beside the nearest corpse. It was Horace Alex; I took his cellphone again. The campground got one bar, but that was enough. I dialed 911. My headache flared and I said what I needed to say. I didn't give my name, but I didn't kid myself that it would be a secret for long. My headache faded as I went back inside. "Someone will be here soon."

"Let me out," a new voice said. "I don't want to be found here." It came from the back of the trailer. Through a tiny hallway I saw Stuart Kripke handcuffed to a narrow bed.

"Yes," Solorov said. "Get out. Both of you get out."

I went into the back. His cuffs matched the ones I'd taken off Ursula. I took the keys from my pocket and freed him. He rolled over onto his wide ass and sat rubbing his wrists. He looked me up and down. "You look like crap."

Charming. I went back into the other room and leaned close to Solorov. She had ordered Biker killed and tried to do the same to me, but I still felt sorry for her. "Is there anything I can do for you?"

"Yes," she answered weakly. "Go fuck yourself. I don't need your pity. Wait! Wait." She worked her carefully painted mouth, trying to call up enough spit to keep talking. "If you kill that Norwegian cow, I'll pay you ten thousand dollars."

"Why did she do all this?"

"Why do you think? That tattooed bastard told her we had the package. Of course it was a lie, but she didn't want to hear it." Solorov raised her other hand from beneath the table. Her fingers had been smashed crooked. "On second thought, don't kill her. I want to do it myself."

Kripke squeezed through the narrow hall. "I'll pay you five hundred dollars if you can get me out of town before the police arrive." His voice was too loud and too blunt. "Everyone else here is dead."

I didn't have time to deal with him. "Just a minute," I said.

He leaned over Solorov and flipped open her sport jacket. The professor didn't like that but couldn't do anything about it. "You keep your hands off, you fat creep."

"Hey!" His voice was bullish and thick. "You don't get to tell me what to do! Not after all this. You're lucky I don't fuck you right here and now."

I grabbed hold of his shirt. "That's enough out of you! You keep running your mouth and I'm going to cuff you again."

"And give up five hundred bucks?" he said, as if he was calling my bluff. There was something off about the guy, but I didn't know what it was. He seemed like a brainy guy who wasn't very smart. It wasn't until he looked at my face that he backed down, muttering something about *jocks*.

I turned back to the professor. "Where can I find the tattooed man?"

"Forget him," she answered. "He's a big, bad grown-up and you're just a little boy. And his boss is something else entirely."

"Let me worry about that. Where can I find them?"

"Hah. What's in it for me?"

"She can't tell you," Kripke interrupted. "She won't ever admit that she doesn't know something or that she's in over her head. That's how she ended up like this."

Solorov sighed and closed her eyes. For a moment I thought she'd died, but when she spoke, her voice was whisper quiet. "Get out. Both of you. I don't want you near me. Just go."

I grabbed Kripke's shirt and pulled him out of the trailer. He complained about the cold and the drizzle and the mud on his shoes. The sound of his voice put me on edge, but I didn't tell him to shut up. I wanted him in a talking mood.

Ursula had come around and was working furiously at her cuffs, scraping them back and forth along the bottom of the axle. She was tenacious, if nothing else.

I put Kripke in the backseat of my Neon and climbed behind the wheel. My muddy clothes were cold against my skin. Catherine sat up and looked at me in silence.

"Before the cops get here," Kripke said. "Five hundred bucks. I'm not kidding."

I took Ursula's handgun from my pocket and gave it to Catherine. "If he does anything stupid, shoot him."

"Okay," she answered.

He was silent as I pulled out of the campground. I didn't hear sirens.

I glanced into the rearview mirror at Kripke. He was sulking. I'd interrupted my search for the pastor and the sapphire dog, and he was all I had to show for it. He'd better be worth it.

I drove by the school and beyond that the little houses and cross streets. I looked at Kripke in the mirror again. "Where have you been staying?"

He rolled his eyes. "Nowhere. I came to the auction. I was kidnapped. That's where I've been staying, with my kidnappers."

I wanted to question him, but where? Steve Cardinal might look for me at the Sunset. The Grable was a wreck. It was late enough that the bar would have closed. I wondered how Steve would react if I showed up at his house.

Kripke blew out a long, slow breath. "I shouldn't have come anywhere near this place. I just want to go home and pretend none of this ever happened."

"What about your buddy?"

"Who? Oh. Paulie. We weren't close. Besides, he was *supposed* to be my bodyguard. It's not my fault he blew it. Look, if you can get me out of town, I can get you two hundred dollars right away. That's the ATM limit. I'll send you a check for the rest."

I parked in front of a narrow house with a lopsided porch. A six-foot-long baby Jesus had been mounted on the siding, and it watched us with big blue eyes. I turned off the engine, then turned around, took the gun from Catherine, and dropped it into my pocket. She went back to doing nothing. I wished I had the real Catherine here. This next part needed an investigator.

"I heard you talking to the professor outside the Wilbur house. Right before the floating storm was summoned. How much of that was true?"

He ran his fingers through the hair above his ears, fluffing the frizzy tangle. His motions were sharp and annoyed. "Oh, come on. Really? Are we going to do this here, on a public street? Are you going to threaten to shoot me in your own car? Please."

"You don't have to be impressed. Just answer my questions."

"What if I don't?"

"More people will die."

He snorted. "Oh, noes! More people like the kidnappers who killed my bodyguard! Let's do everything we can to prevent *that*!" His voice was raw with contempt.

I'd had more of him than I could stand. "I don't think you understand the situation you're in."

"You don't scare me any more than Paulie did," he said. "You think this is still high school? You may have been King Dick among the jocks back then, but I have the money, the house, and the job. What do you have except a Walmart name tag?"

For a moment I just stared at him, astonished. If he'd given that little speech to Arne or one of my old crew, he would have gotten a beating so ferocious he would never stand up straight again. He'd lived all his life in the straight world. He had no idea how to behave in mine.

I took the pistol from my pocket and fired off a round. It passed through the back window about a foot from his head, but I'm sure it felt much closer.

Catherine shrieked. Kripke slapped his hand over his face as if he'd been shot. He rubbed at his cheek, then checked his palm for blood. A fleck of gunpowder must have landed on his skin, but he couldn't tell the difference between a burning speck and an entrance wound.

"High school?" I said. "I didn't go to fucking high school. While you were carrying your books in the halls and complaining about homework, I was on the street stealing cars and getting high. I was doing time in juvie for *shooting my best friend.* Don't you brag to me about your money or your house, motherfucker. If I want anything you have, *I take it.* Understand?"

His eyes were wide and blank, but there seemed to be a little spark of understanding in there. "Everything I said to the professor was true, but there was some stuff I left out."

"I'm waiting."

"Okay, um. The guy who baited his way into our server and gave us all that information? He was logging on from somewhere in Bozeman, Montana. And he called himself TheLastKing."

King? I knew someone named King. I hoped to God it wasn't the same guy. "What was his real name?"

"I don't know. He always logged in from a public wireless network. We could never find out who he was. We were going to ban him, but his first posts were full of great stuff, so we voted against it."

"What did he teach you?"

"Well," Kripke said, and swallowed. He lifted his hand close to his chest and pointed at my gun hand. "That's the closed way on the back of your hand."

I felt goose bumps run down my back. He knew more about the spells Annalise put on me than I did. I scowled to hide my excitement. "He taught you to recognize spells? What did he tell you about the closed way?"

"That it stops physical attacks the way a washed-out road blocks a traveler. That when a primary casts it, the marks are invisible and the skin can feel anything unspelled skin can feel, but as you go down to secondary, tertiary, and so on, the spells become hard to hide and you lose sensation."

I stared at him. Months ago, during our time in Hammer Bay, Annalise had used the word *primary* to refer to a very powerful sorcerer, but at the time I couldn't press her for more information.

I couldn't press Kripke, either. As soon as he realized I wasn't testing him—that he had information I wanted—he'd want me to bargain for it.

"TheLastKing, huh? Did he give any idea who he might be or where he got the information?"

"Well, he had a spell book." Kripke's tone was almost disrespectful.

"Are you playing with me?"

"No," he answered, almost swallowing the word. "He said he had a pair of spell books. He said he stole them, and that if we bought the sapphire dog for him, he'd share six of the spells with us. He didn't say who he'd stolen them from."

"I want to meet him."

"I'll bet, but I'm not going to be able to arrange that. The guys on the server already know I lost the auction. I texted them as soon as the price got out of reach."

"All right," I said. "Then let's narrow it down by which spell books he has. Can you recognize any of these?" I set the gun on the seat and stripped off my jacket and my shirt. My bare skin prickled in the winter air, but I felt warmer with my wet clothes off. After glancing around to make sure there were no cars coming toward us, I turned on the dome light.

Kripke squinted at the spells on my chest. "Iron gate," he said and pointed just below my right collarbone. "It protects against different kinds of mental attacks."

"Is that it?"

He pointed low on my left side, just at the bottom edge of my ribs. "The twisted path. It's a shape-shifting spell for primaries, but as you go down the . . . um . . . chain, it doesn't do much more than alter your fingerprints and the way people remember you. And you can't control it. Um, hey, can you control it?"

This guy was unbelievable. "Still want to know about magic? I guess you haven't been kidnapped and shot at enough. There's a lesson to be learned, if you have the brains for it."

He didn't seem to get my point. "You're part of the society, aren't you? You're the reason TheLastKing couldn't come, because he said you were looking for him. You know who he is, don't you?"

"What about the rest?"

He glanced over my chest and stomach. "I recognize the closed way around the edges, but the other spells . . . he never went over those. Most of the spells he showed us were for summoning."

"What?" If Kripke knew a summoning spell, I was going to drive him out of town and put a bullet in him immediately. There was no way I'd trust this idiot with that much power.

"Only the written part!" he said quickly. "Only the visible part. He only gave us enough to recognize one. He said that summoning spells don't decay the way other kinds do, so we'd be seeing more of them."

I believed him. He was too brain-damaged to lie this well. I picked up the gun. He winced but stayed silent.

I laid my thumb against the safety. Should I kill him? A single predator loose in the world could call more of its kind and feed on us until there was nothing left. People who summoned them, or just wanted one, were risking everyone on the planet.

And Kripke here had tried to buy a predator.

So. Bullet to the head, right?

He'd failed here in Washaway, but what if he hunted down a new spell, or bought one directly from his anonymous Internet buddy? Kripke was like a guy who'd tried to buy an A-bomb or a vial of anthrax. I couldn't arrest him, but could I let him go?

Annalise had warned me about this. She'd told me that, because I was part of the society, it was my job to make corpses. And yeah, if I'd been ruthless with Ursula, no one would have known I was on the estate and the floating storm wouldn't have been summoned to hunt me down. I didn't like it, but being soft on these people had cost lives.

Kripke cleared his throat. "You're trying to decide whether you should kill me, right? Because I tried to buy the sapphire dog."

"Hell, yeah," I said.

"You don't have to," he said. "I can help you find TheLastKing. I can even connect you to the others in my group. Some of them claim to have a full spell or two."

"You're offering your friends to me to save your life?"

I expected him to make excuses, but all he said was: "Yes." At least he was as blunt with himself as he was with others.

Kripke had given me an excuse to spare him, and I grasped at it. If someone in the society wanted to kill him later, they could do it after they'd collected his buddies' spell books.

"Give me your wallet." He did. I took out his license and made a point of studying the address, then I tossed it back to him. "I'm not going to drive you out of town, and if you offer me money again, I'm going to punch you in the mouth, understand?"

"I do."

After putting my shirt and jacket back on, I drove through the winding streets until I hit one I recognized. From there I made my way to the Sunset B and B. They had a VACANCY sign in the window. Yin might expect me to turn up here, but I doubted they'd be looking for Kripke.

"What's this?" he asked.

"A place to hole up tonight. There's probably a bus in the morning. Ride down to Sea-Tac and catch a flight home. Get a lawyer and tell the cops you came up here because you heard about the festival, but you got robbed. They'll believe it. Just stick to your story."

"On Christmas Eve? I'll never catch a flight!"

"Then stay in Washaway. I don't care. In the airport you'd have to eat overpriced food and wait around a really long time. I'm sure you'd rather be kidnapped again."

"You're right," he said, and for the first time I heard a note of humility in his voice. "Of course you're right. I . . . I just . . ."

"I don't care," I told him. "Get out." He opened the door. "And Stuart? You'll be hearing from me. Do I need to tell you not to mention our deal to anyone?"

"No, sir," he said, which startled the hell out of me. He left the car and walked up the gravel path.

I did a quick U-turn and started back toward town. Did I have enough gas to keep driving around looking for Dolan?

A pickup started its engine and pulled up next to me. I was reaching for my ghost knife when I recognized the driver. It was Ford, Steve's friend with the Wilford Brimley mustache who had gone to check on Little Mark's head injury. "By God, it's about time!" he said. His voice was deep and clear like a country-music singer's.

"What's going on?"

"Chief asked me to fetch you. He said there's some dead Chinese millionaire fellas you need to identify. You want to follow me?"

That changed things. "Give me a minute." I turned to Catherine. She was still staring at me with cow eyes. I couldn't keep dragging her around with me. Ursula could have killed her, and Catherine would have sat there and let it happen. Not to mention what the sapphire dog would do to her.

But if Yin was dead, the Sunset would be safe for her again. "Go up to the room and get some sleep." I gave her my key. I was going to say more, but she opened the door, shut it, and walked up the front path without asking for an explanation. She'd do whatever I asked without question. It was creepy.

Ford had his cellphone to his ear. He held up one fat finger without looking at me. Then he said, "Okay," and switched it off. "Change of plans," he said to me. "Follow behind."

He backed up and did a three-point turn. I followed him around the block, past Hondo's darkened garage to a street I hadn't seen before. There was a shoe store, a gift shop, and what could only be the town hall Steve had mentioned. It was made of red brick, but the window ledges were marble, and at four stories, it towered over the other buildings on the block. Four round steps led up to a pair of unlikely stone columns and a single cramped door.

We parked in the adjoining lot. Ford waddled toward the back of the building and down concrete stairs to a basement door. We were going in the back entrance.

The room we entered had three more chairs and one more desk that it could comfortably hold. Papers were jumbled everywhere, and the corkboard on the wall was six deep with tattered flyers.

As Ford shut the door behind me, a heavy wooden door across the room opened. A black woman with Coke-bottle glasses came in. It was Sherisse again, who had gone with Ford to pick up Little Mark. She was younger than I'd first thought, and she trundled forward to give Ford a quick kiss on the lips. "Thank you for coming," she said in a ragged, whispery voice.

"Of course, sugar kitten. What do you need?"

"I couldn't get through to Steve," she answered. "And I need him to know about this. Come on." She looked at me. "You can come too, if you think you can be useful."

She needed three steps to turn herself around, then she led us through the back door. The next room had a single desk and a huge boiler in the far corner. When Sherisse closed the door, I saw the jail cell.

It was only about seven feet by four feet. Inside was a bare wooden bench that someone had taken from a picnic table. Penny lay on the bench, her face slack. She was dead. One glance told me that.

Little Mark sat slumped in the corner. He was dead, too. Within the confined space of the cell, he was as far from his mother as he could be.

"My God," Ford said. "What happened?"

"I thought they would want to be together, so when I brought Little Mark here, I put him with his mother. He didn't seem to mind, but they didn't even talk to each other. They wouldn't even look at each other."

Ford cleared his throat. "Honey song, how did they die?"

"Well, Penny started yelling at me, but it was all gibberish. Her left arm was hanging at her side like she couldn't move it, her left eye was partly closed, and she started drooling. My Auntie Gertie had a stroke while she was teaching me to make piecrust, so I knew what was happening. I called 911 right away, but it was already too late. They were both . . . like this."

"Strokes?" Ford said. "Well, Little Mark did bump his head. . . ."

"But both at the same time?" Sherisse said.

She was right. That wasn't a coincidence. "Have they had any visitors?" I was suddenly sure that Pratt had killed them both with one of his sigils, just to be careful.

Sherisse seemed surprised by my question. She glanced behind her. There were two doors beside the cell: one had a sign that said REST-ROOM hung on it, and the other was unmarked. She had glanced at the unmarked door. "No one that has anything to do with Penny or Little Mark."

"That's good," I said. "Who?"

Ford cleared his throat. "If Sheri says—"

I lunged between them, stepped up onto the chair, and jumped the desk. Neither of them reacted quickly enough to stop me. I rushed to the unmarked door and yanked it open.

The next room was dark, lit only by the glow of a small television. *Fantasia* was playing, and three small children sat in front of it, legs crossed, faces pale and serious.

The sudden light from the opened door made them all turn toward me. "Momma?" the smallest one said, but when he saw it was me, he turned back to the show. The sound was very low, and I realized that there were six or seven more kids bundled up in blankets and sleeping bags on the couch and carpet.

The child who looked oldest said: "It's you!" She jumped to her feet and came toward me. It was Shannon, the girl who had apologized for hiding from us. Staring up at me, her expression hidden in shadow, she grabbed hold of my wrist. "Did you kill it?" she asked. "Did you?"

"I'm sorry, but no. It got away from me. But I haven't given up. I'll keep after it."

"Please," she said. "*Please* kill it. I want my granma back. Please kill it."

"That's enough now," Sherisse said, and pulled me out of the doorway. "Shannon, this is the last video, okay? I need you to be the big girl and get the rest of them to sleep a little. Okay? Will you do that for me?"

"Please," Shannon said to me. "There's no one else I can ask. No one is listening. Please." She looked at Sherisse then, without saying anything else, and went back into the darkened room. Sherisse shut the door.

Ford's phone rang. He answered it, moving away from us.

I lowered my voice so no one but Sherisse could hear. "How many kids are in there? Is Shannon the oldest?"

"She is. There are nine in there right now. Most of them, their parents just vanished. They don't answer their cells, and no one knows where they are."

I was about to tell her to prepare for more when Ford cut in. "All right," he said in a sharper tone than I'd heard before. "That was Steve. You and I have to go right now."

I shrugged and followed him out to the cars.

We drove back toward the fairgrounds yet again, but well before we got there, the pickup turned onto a feeder road. Fallen trees made it looked blocked and abandoned, but Ford led me around a sudden turn and I followed him uphill.

The pickup was big enough that I couldn't see the road ahead, just a high back fender and cargo net. We turned sharply and drove up a switchback trail for another fifty yards or so before pulling into a small field. Steve's Crown Vic was parked at the far end, and there were two burgundy BMWs and the Maybach beside him. Ford pulled in behind Steve, blocking him in, but there weren't many other spaces left. I parked at the entrance, blocking everyone in.

The field wasn't very large, but it was tremendously muddy, even by Washaway's standards. To the left was a large log cabin with a shake roof. I'd have called it rustic if it hadn't been painted fire-engine red. A few dozen yards behind the cabin the mountains rose straight up for several hundred feet.

The front door swung open and Steve strode out. He moved quickly, but he looked tired. I was already walking toward him when he waved me over. As I slipped between the BMWs, I glanced inside. They were empty.

Before he could say anything, I called: "I don't know if they told you, but I found more dead bodies at the campground, and one woman who was near death. I haven't heard an ambulance, so you might want to have it checked out. One of Regina Wilbur's people, a woman named Ursula, shot up the place."

"Thank you for telling me. After we finish here, I'll head over there to look into the mess you . . . found."

For a moment I thought he was going to say *made*. I kept my mouth shut and took a deep, calming breath. "What did you want me to see?"

"Before we get to that: Why were you in the campground?"

"I was looking for the pastor, obviously."

"Who did you take away from the scene?"

Damn. He knew more than he'd let on. Well, to hell with him. "No one. I did have Catherine with me, though. Why?"

Steve turned to Ford. "Did you see a third person in his car?"

Ford's face flushed and he looked at the ground. "Um. I didn't see everything. . . ."

Which meant he'd been waiting for me at the Sunset and had fallen asleep. I sympathized with him. Steve looked even more irritated than he had been. "Ursula said you took a man out of the trailer and drove off with him."

"Maybe she thought Catherine was a dude. She never seemed all that sharp to me. Or maybe she's lying. I did knock her down and cuff her, after all."

He rubbed his chin. "She didn't mind admitting to mass murder. I find it hard to believe she'd lie after being honest about *that*."

I shrugged. "I did . . ." *Hit her pretty hard,* I was about to say. I felt dirty just thinking it.

"What about her gun?" He stared up at me squarely.

"Oh, you mean the handgun I took off her?" I laid my hand against my jacket pocket, then moved it away when I noticed Steve's sudden tension. "Do you want it?"

He held out his hand. "Please."

I had been aware this whole time that Ford was standing somewhere behind me and to the right, but I'd mostly ignored him. I felt his presence keenly as I took Ursula's pistol from my pocket. I handed it over slowly.

Steve accepted it. "This weapon has been fired."

I wouldn't be able to hide the bullet hole in the back of the Neon. "Yeah. I thought the safety was on." I shrugged again. "I'm not really a gun person."

"What about Ursula's rifle?"

I should have ditched it after I cut it apart. "What about it?"

"Ray, if I find you've been playing games with me—"

"Oh, for fuck's sake!" I shouted, my voice echoing off the mountains around us. Steve flinched, but I couldn't hold it in anymore. "Games? You think I'm having fun here? You think I want to hang around some strange town, tripping over gut-shot people? Over corpses?"

And yet, this *was* what I wanted. This was my part in the society. I'd sought it out and now it made me sick.

"Chief," I said, trying to give Steve a little respect because I wanted him on my side, "when all this happened to me that first time, it ruined my life. I can't sleep right anymore, can't focus at work, can't . . . I sit in my room with a book in my hand and stare out the window for hours. I think about this stuff all the time. I'm constantly on the watch for it, in the faces of people on the street and in the newspaper and . . . and now here I am again. I found it here and I'm trying to stop it, because it absolutely has to be stopped."

"I understand what you're saying, Ray. But that doesn't mean you've told me everything you know, does it?"

I saved you, I wanted to say, but I didn't. I hadn't saved him to earn a marker I could call in. Still, it would have been nice to have a little more trust, even if he was right.

Steve sighed and turned away from me. "I believe you're trying to do what's best, son, but if you hold back on me, I'll see you in jail, you hear?"

I nodded. I'd been in jail before and I'd expected to be back already. It wasn't much of a threat.

Steve led me into the log cabin, and Ford followed. For a moment I thought they were flanking me, but they were too relaxed for that.

Inside was a store, with racks of skiing, climbing, and camping gear, along with flyers promoting climbing lessons and kiddie camps. Yin's bodyguards lay around the room, handguns in their fists, their guts and brains all over the floor and walls. There'd been a gunfight. They'd lost.

Steve's voice was shaky. "Ford found a .32 slug in the wall, but these fellows are all carrying .45-caliber weapons. They fired them, too. See the casings all over the floor? Doesn't look like they hit what they were aiming at, does it?"

And I'd heard them, too, but I'd thought it was thunder. "What were they aiming at?" I asked, although I was pretty sure I already knew the answer.

"I was hoping you could tell me."

"Sorry. I can't."

"Then come look at this." He led me behind the counter, through the back office, past a very interesting little goosenecked desk lamp and out onto a weather-beaten wooden deck. There were three more bodies out here. Two were burned and shriveled, lying on scorched sections of the deck. The third was Yin himself. His thick tongue stuck out of his mouth, and his face was purplish. He'd been strangled.

Lying on the deck beside him was his soul sword. It had been broken into three pieces.

The smell of blood and burned flesh became too much. I stepped off the deck and vomited into the bushes, making a mental note not to eat greasy grilled cheese when I was on society business.

When I turned back, Steve and Ford were giving each other a significant look. I wasn't sure what it meant, and I didn't care.

Steve cleared his throat. "Don't feel bad, son. I did the same thing. Just I knew where the bathroom was."

I didn't answer because I didn't feel bad at all. I'd feel bad when a building full of burned and head-shot corpses *didn't* make me puke. I went back onto the deck.

"Do you know him?" Steve asked. It was a simple, dangerous question.

"Not personally," I said. "You know who he is, too."

"Sure, but I want to hear what you have to say."

"I already told you this. His name was Yin, and he was rich. He won the auction but let the sapphire dog get away. The people at the campground were some of the losers."

Steve's mouth was a thin, tense line. "Any other bidders I should know about?"

I sighed. If I really did want him on my side, I couldn't exactly say *no*. "There was a fat guy from California and an old man from, I think, Germany. I don't know whether they left town or are still here hunting for the sapphire dog."

"Any reason you didn't mention them before?" Steve's voice was sharp.

"Because this is what they do to people who know too much about them. And how did you know about the campground? I doubt 911 dispatched you."

"Justy found them. She talked to Ursula, then she called me and I called Bill and Sue direct. Then I called the staties. I gave up on the sheriff hours ago."

I looked at my watch. Steve looked at his. How long until they arrived? He took out his cell. "Let me get an ETA for the state police."

I felt a dull ache in the iron gate on my shoulder. It was a warning that someone was using a spell against me, but it didn't seem important.

"Hi, Marlis," Steve said into his phone. His voice suddenly sounded vague and dreamy. "Steve Cardinal over in Washaway. How're the kids? That's great news. I'm sorry you'll be working through the festival. We'd have loved to have had you." He paused a moment. I moved closer to listen. "Trouble? No," Steve said, "we're not having any trouble here. Just the usual Christmas spirit."

The ache in my shoulder became very strong, and I closed my eyes against it. I heard a woman's voice at the other end of the phone say: "Lots of you folks down in Washaway have been calling all day to wish me a happy Christmas. It's . . . it's . . ." She sounded a bit confused, as though she was trying to remember something important. "It's very sweet," she said at last.

Steve answered her in the only way that seemed logical to me: "Everything is just fine over here. You be sure to give a Christmas kiss to those kids of yours."

He hung up the phone, and the pain in my shoulder eased. He'd said what he needed to say. He nodded to Ford. "That should get them out here right quick."

I was glad Steve had made that call. I was glad the state cops knew about the trouble we were having.

I rubbed my face. "Where's the woman?"

Steve looked startled by that. He turned to Ford, who didn't have anything to add but a shrug. "Describe her."

"Short black hair and dark skin. She looked like she was from Indonesia or something. She wore dark suits and had her hair up in a bun like a librarian. She was maybe my age, just a little under thirty. She was part of Yin's entourage as some sort of researcher, I'd guess."

"Does she have a name?"

His tone was getting annoying. "Yeah, but I don't know it."

"We searched the whole grounds and didn't find any women. Could he have sent her home before all this?"

Steve was obviously a glass-half-full sort. "It's more likely that she's been reduced to a pile of greasy dust, or that she's gone to work for the people who won the gunfight."

Steve nodded. "There's one more thing I want to show you." He led me off the deck and across the muddy field. Ford was still trailing me. Now it did bother me to have him at my back.

I stopped, turned around, and said: "Hi. My name is Ray."

He looked a little surprised, but not much. "I'm Ford."

"Nice to meet you, Ford. This is ugly business, isn't it?"

"That it is," he said. He opened his jacket to show me his holstered gun. "Whoever's responsible for all this shit is going to be shut down." He gave me a hard stare as he said it, as though I was suspect number one and a wrong answer away from a beating.

"I agree completely," I said. Then I turned to follow Steve.

We passed a swing set and an open sandbox. As we walked, Steve spoke to me over his shoulder. "When this Yin character rented the Johnson place over on Outpost Road, Pippa did a little checking. He's so rich I can't even imagine it. Who could have tempted this missing Indonesian woman away from him?"

I remembered the pirate's expression on her face when she'd seen the tattoos on my hands. "Some things are more important than money."

He grunted his agreement.

Steve led me down a trail, which ran alongside the cliff face. The night air was cold enough to sting. After about thirty yards, he stopped.

"Know this fella?"

We were well away from the cabin lights by now, and there were very few stars out. Steve flicked on a heavy flashlight and shone it into the bushes.

At first I couldn't make sense of what I was looking at—it looked like a jumble of brown clothes. Then Steve played the light across a face.

I recognized the hat and the tan coat. It was Pratt.

Oh, shit.

"Well?" Steve prompted. "Do you know him?"

"Remember when I told you help was coming? Here it is."

CHAPTER FOURTEEN

Pratt looked like someone had laid a burning fern leaf on his face. "What happened?"

"I've seen this before," Ford said in an authoritative voice. "I spent a couple of years doing missionary work in the high places in the Congo. This man was struck by lightning."

That startled the hell out of me. I jumped up and scanned the skies around us. I didn't see any lights, and I didn't hear an electric hum.

Time to get the hell out of there.

"Settle down, son," Steve said. He shone the light in my face, blinding me. "We have a bit more jawing to do. Are you still armed?"

"I already gave you my only gun," I said.

"You'll have to forgive me if I don't take that at face value," he said. "You've been holding out on me from the start, haven't you? Who is this fella, and how was he really killed?"

What I needed was a time-travel spell that could send me back to the moment just before I told Steve help was coming so I could dummy-slap myself into silence. I'd wanted to give him hope, but all I'd done was make him curious.

But I sure as hell couldn't tell him about the Twenty Palace Society. *Information shared is information leaked.* "I can't answer that. I'm sorry."

I heard Ford pull back the hammer on a gun. I turned and saw that he was pointing a snub-nosed police .38 at me.

Steve rubbed his chin and glared at me. "I'm afraid I'm not giving you any choice, son. I'll admit that I don't know a thing about these people." He waved his arm toward Pratt's corpse and the cabin behind me. "For all I know, they're just a bunch of gangsters and crooks. But

Penny is my cousin. Isabelle nursed my wife through the final stages of cancer. I was godfather to the oldest Breakley girl. Do you understand what that means in a town like this?"

I didn't answer. He frowned at me. "Everything. That's what it means. Now, I want to know everything you know, and if I think you're holding back, I'm going to arrest you for murder. I'm sure I can make it stick. Do you want to talk to me here and now, or through the bars of a cell?"

"I'm not the enemy here."

"So you say."

Enough. I liked him, but I didn't have time to play these games. I turned my back on him.

Ford aimed his revolver at my breastbone, the way you're supposed to. But he was too close. "Ford, you realize that if you shoot me, the bullet will pass through and hit Steve, right?"

That startled him. He said: "Uh . . . ," and looked at Steve.

I rushed him, knocking the gun aside. It went off, and the shot echoed against the rocky cliffs around us like the "thunder" I'd heard earlier. I hit him once in the belly. He let out a huge *oof* and fell sideways into the thicket. His gun landed in the mud.

I spun around and saw Steve down on one knee, his left hand over his head like a child about to be beaten, his right fumbling at his holster. I was on him in two steps. I clamped my hand over his, trapping his weapon, and drew back a fist.

Steve flinched and bared his teeth in fear. Damn. I couldn't throw that punch.

After a couple of seconds he realized I wasn't going to hit him. I yanked his pistol out of his hand. He lost his balance and fell back onto the path. I took Ursula's gun from his pocket, then turned to Ford. He was lying in the thicket, moaning and holding his belly. I picked up his gun, too.

"I'm sorry, Steve," I said.

"Son—"

"Don't. I'll leave your weapons on the hood of your car." I wanted to say more—about the risk to him and to all of Washaway if he learned too much about magic—but the words wouldn't come together in my head. I ended up saying nothing.

I jogged back up the path and went around the cabin. There was a brick barbecue pit in the side yard and a stainless steel gas grill. Between them, I saw a tarp lying over something vaguely human-shaped. I knelt beside it and caught a whiff of an outhouse.

I lifted the tarp just enough to see that it was Frail. Blood had trickled from his mouth to his ear; he'd died on his back. On a hunch, I pulled the tarp back farther and saw what I'd expected to see: he'd been stabbed through the heart by something big, like a lightning rod.

"No one else handy, huh?" I asked him.

I left his face uncovered so Steve would notice him, then hustled to the car. I didn't see Well-Spoken, and I didn't see another body under a tarp. I tried to speculate who Frail had been—servant? apprentice? both?—and what he'd done, if anything, to make the old man stab him.

I set Steve's and Ford's weapons on the hood of the Crown Vic but slipped Ursula's gun into my pocket. Right now, Washaway wasn't a place for anyone to go unarmed. Using my taillights to guide me, I backed down the road.

I couldn't return to the Sunset—even if Yin was dead, Steve and Ford knew to look for me there, and they might bring friends. I'd end up in a cell while the sapphire dog ran loose, turning people into its pets.

But at least the cell would have a place to sleep. I blinked until my blurry vision cleared. The short naps I'd been getting weren't enough. I was weary. I'd lost the support of everyone, even Steve and Catherine. I didn't know what to do about the predator or the bidders, but there was one job I could still do.

I drove directly to Steve's house and kicked the back door in. He would be out looking for me, of course, but I didn't think he'd come here first. I pulled the patties out of the freezer, dropped them into a stainless steel mixing bowl, and rushed back to the car. Maybe I should have defrosted them first, but I couldn't imagine myself standing in Steve's kitchen, anxiously waiting for the microwave to ding.

I drove back to the cabin. Steve's and Ford's cars were gone. Good. I turned the Neon around so I wouldn't have to back down the feeder road, then carried the bowl of patties into the woods.

If Pratt was anything like Annalise, he could be healed from injury by eating meat. The fresher the better, but these frozen burgers would have to do.

I knelt in the wet moss beside him and cut a thin sliver from the column of meat. It didn't want to go down his throat, but I wiggled it in. Then I did it again and again. I had a hair-raising moment when I imagined Pratt clamping his teeth down on my fingers and swallowing them, but that was all imagination.

It didn't do any good. He didn't come alive. Damn. I'd seen other peers survive damage worse than this, but maybe there was some sort of magical *oomph* behind the floating storm's red lightning.

And while I didn't like Pratt, I could have used his help.

I left the last three patties defrosting in his mouth and tossed the bowl away. No other cars had come up the road to block the Neon. I drove down the hill and back onto the road.

I was alone again, and now I had no idea what I should do.

The sign for the school appeared in my headlights. On impulse, I pulled in and drove past the tiny playground. I switched off my headlights and parked behind a Dumpster.

I closed my eyes, but as tired as I was, I couldn't sleep. The smell of those dead bodies stuck with me, and my head was churning with thoughts of the sapphire dog. I leaned my head against the window and stared up at the blank night sky.

At first the sapphire dog seemed to want to get out of town, but something had changed. Esteban hadn't tried to drive it away from Washaway; he'd been a distraction. And how many hours had it spent hiding out at the stables? If I was going to figure out where it had gone, I needed to know what had happened.

My biggest problem was that I knew so little about it. It came from another place. I couldn't bring myself to use the word *dimension* or *universe*, even in the privacy of my own head. It was just too dorky.

Still, I'd seen that place—the Empty Spaces, as the society called it, although others called it the Deeps. It was a nothing, a void, but what did I know that could help me understand the sapphire dog?

Steve's Crown Vic drove by and was gone. I assumed he was after me, and I wondered where he would start his search. I didn't know a thing about Washaway except what I'd seen over the past couple of days, but if I'd been local, he would have known where to search for me. He would have gone to my home, my friends, my work, my hangouts. He would've had a place to start.

But I was a stranger. I didn't have any place to go, so I could have gone anywhere.

This was the same problem I had with the sapphire dog. The big difference was that the predator had the pastor to guide him. If I knew what the predator wanted, I could figure out how the pastor would try to give it to him.

But of course I already knew what the sapphire dog wanted. It wanted what every living thing wanted: to eat. And somehow, it fed itself by making people crazy. My ghost knife cut away every part of a personality except compliance. The sapphire dog took everything but love for it.

Until the stroke hit, that is.

The darkness and the cold became too much. I closed my eyes. Just for a moment.

When I opened them again, there was light in the eastern sky. It was Christmas Eve morning.

I rubbed my face, hard, to get the sleep out. Time to move. I climbed from the car and emptied my bladder against the back of the Dumpster. The temperature had dropped below freezing overnight. I was hungry. My back and neck ached. I needed a toothbrush. Worse, the job I had come here to do was not over yet.

I rubbed my arms, trying to make myself feel warm and awake. I was alone here, an ex-con with a couple of spells, trying to find a predator before a full sorcerer did. I was completely outclassed, up to my ass in corpses, and I had no leads at all.

I couldn't even talk to Catherine. Steve would be looking for me, and I had no way to contact her without running into Nadia and Nicholas.

Unless . . .

I climbed behind the wheel and started the engine. I had half a tank left, which was pretty good considering how much driving I'd done already. Then a motorcycle rumbled across the road ahead, headed toward the left. Toward the fairgrounds.

It was Tattoo. He was watching something mounted on his handlebars. If I wanted another shot at him, now was the time. This time I'd twist him until all his bones were broken.

And I just happened to be sitting in a car.

I drove to the mouth of the driveway. I was about to turn to follow him when a line of ten or twelve trucks and vans cruised by.

I cursed at them and wrung the steering wheel. The last pickup went by with a bed full of poinsettias, and I pulled out after it.

To me, the line of cars seemed as slow as a parade. I tried to peer around them, but I couldn't see the front vehicle, let alone Tattoo. Eventually, they all pulled into the fairgrounds. Had Tattoo pulled ahead and vanished around the next turn of the road, or was he in the fairgrounds?

I turned with the other vehicles and followed them in.

They drove to a low corner of the parking lot and onto the field. None got stuck in the mud, but it was a near thing for a couple of them. I parked at the edge of the grass and looked out over the grounds. People rushed around, setting up stalls in the early light. They were already selling things—Christmas ornaments, tiny jars of what looked like preserves, warm clothing, Yule logs, and model train kits.

The pickup with the poinsettias pulled up beside a tent, and a woman with long gray hair began carrying the plants inside. Three men followed her in with a big gas heater.

The snow machine was silent, and the ground beside the field house was coated with snow. I wondered what would happen if I ran out there and jumped around in it.

The people were smiling. There were no cards, no happy greetings, but I did see them shaking hands and hugging one another. Washaway, their community, had gone through a tough couple of days, but these folks were determined to keep going—to celebrate. If the hugs seemed to be more out of consolation than joy, and if a couple of the people wiped gloved hands across their cheeks while they spoke, that just showed their strength and connection to one another.

And I hadn't gotten inside any of it.

I didn't see Tattoo anywhere nearby, so I didn't belong here. I backed out of my spot and took the side road to the church. It was closed up tight, and the windows in Dolan's house were dark. The upstairs front window was still open. The pastor had not come back here.

I drove toward town. The sky was finally bright enough that I could turn off my headlights. I would be easily recognizable in the Neon, but short of stealing a new car there was nothing I could do about it.

In town no one stopped me, and I didn't come across any road-blocks. I drove by the Sunset B and B and pulled into a little gravel road. There was a space on the far side of a stand of trees, and I parked there. It didn't hide the Neon all that well, but it was better than park-ing on the street.

I ducked between the trees. The Sunset was encircled by a neatly mowed lawn, but beyond that was a fringe of heavy underbrush. I pushed through it, little chips of ice breaking off the branches and melt-ing against my clothes, until I reached the back of the building. Damn, it was cold.

The closest ground-floor window—in the kitchen—had a light in it, but all the windows in the upper floor were still dark. After a little figuring, I decided my room was the one on the far left. Catherine should be there; I hoped she was.

Movement in the lighted downstairs window made me duck low. Nadia entered the room with a bag of flour in her arms. She looked at the window, and for a moment I thought she was looking straight at me. Then she tucked some stray hairs behind her ears, and I realized that she was looking at her reflection.

She sighed, took a bowl from a high shelf, and moved away.

I breathed a sigh of relief and crept, shivering, along the edge of the property. I couldn't find a stone to throw at the window, but I did find a small piece of bark. That would do.

As I drew my arm back to throw it, the kitchen window darkened.

I ducked low again, but it wasn't Nadia blocking the light. It was an irregular spatter of red fluid.

Blood. There was blood on the window.

I threw the wood chip at Catherine's window and ran to the building. I couldn't see into the kitchen, but I could see shadows moving back and forth on the grass. I couldn't tell how many people were making those shapes, but it was more than one.

The upstairs window opened. "Catherine!" I hissed.

She stuck her head out and looked down. "Ray, what the—"

"Enemy in the building," I said. Maybe that wasn't the best way to say it, but her expression showed she understood. She leaned back and, after a few seconds, stuck her head out again.

"Get up here!" She tossed a heavy quilt out the window, letting it hang down to me.

At least the effects of the ghost knife had worn off. Was it because the spell wore off after a while, or did sleeping reset her personality? "Is that a joke? Come down before you get killed."

"Ray," she said, her voice harsh. "Get your skinny ass up here."

Fine. I stepped away from the building, took two running steps, and jumped up. I set my foot against the windowsill and grabbed hold of the quilt.

I knew Catherine hadn't had time to tie it to something solid—and how would you tie off a quilt, anyway?—so I expected it to come loose and drop me back onto the lawn. That didn't happen. I began pulling myself up hand over hand.

Suddenly, the quilt began to draw back through the window as though pulled by a winch. I was so startled I nearly let go. Instead, as I came to the open window, I let go of the cloth and grabbed hold of the sill.

"Christ, what the hell was that?"

Catherine stepped out of the darkness and pulled the sleeve of my jacket. It didn't help, but the thought was nice. I hauled myself through the opening, flopping into the dark room with all the grace of a drunk sneaking into his house.

"Come on," I said, as I got to my feet. "Let's get out of here."

Out of the corner of my eye I saw the quilt flutter onto the bed. I shouted in surprise and spun around. Another figure stood in the darkness well away from the window. A jumble of thoughts rushed through my head. At first I thought Catherine had brought a guy to her room, then, seeing how small the figure was, I assumed it was a boy, which would have been a screwed-up thing to go to jail for, and last night she'd been under the influence of my ghost knife, so that would have been another awful thing I was responsible for.

The figure spoke. "Ray, what the hell have you been doing here?" I knew that high, deadpan voice. The lamp snapped on.

"Boss!" I said, much too loudly. It was Annalise, the peer in the Twenty Palace Society who had bulletproofed my chest and arms, and who had led me through the whole mess in Hammer Bay.

I almost hugged her, but her ribs-backward, shoulders-forward body language made it clear she didn't want to be touched. I stopped myself after an impulsive step forward and let my hands drop to my sides.

"Boss, I've been screwing everything up from moment one."

Catherine started to protest, but then she noticed the ghost of a smile on Annalise's face.

Annalise moved toward the door and listened. She looked just the same as when I'd first met her—her dark red hair was clipped so short you couldn't grab a strand between thumb and forefinger, and she wore a new pair of black, steel-toed boots and a new firefighter's jacket. Her pale face was small and delicate. Black tattooed lines just like mine peeked out from the collar and sleeves of her shirt.

She looked to be about twenty-two years old, but she'd already lived longer than most people do, and the things she'd seen had made her hard and dangerous. One look into her eyes could tell you that.

That absurd little voice of hers sounded loud in the room. "Someone was killed downstairs, you said?" She glanced down at a scrap of lumber in her hand.

"Yeah, Nadia, the owner, I think. I couldn't see how. Just . . . blood. Is that why you guys were sitting in the dark?"

"No," Catherine said. "I was debriefing her, and we didn't want anyone to know I was up. Don't worry, Ray, you didn't interrupt anything."

I felt my face grow warm, and Catherine smirked at me. I said: "You're pretty comfortable, considering."

"I can't help it. It's a tremendous relief to have a peer right here with us. I feel safe for the first time in days."

Downstairs, something fell over with a muffled thump. "Okay," Annalise said. Her expression was serious. It was always serious. "You don't know who's in the building?"

I didn't answer right away. It could have been Tattoo, but I thought I'd have heard his Megamoto. Then I remembered the missing third Mercedes at the red cabin. "Whoever it is, they're working for the old man. He's the only one left. If I had to guess, I'd say it's the last of Yin's guys with a new boss."

Before the room fell into darkness again, I stepped closer and confirmed what I already expected: the scrap of wood had a spell drawn on it. It was a glyph that wriggled like a nest of snakes when certain kinds of magic were nearby.

It was dead still.

She tossed the scrap of lumber at me. I caught it. The sigil flashed silver as it reacted to the magic Annalise had put on me. On the other side of the door, we could hear the floorboards creaking.

Annalise said: "Look after yourselves." Then she yanked open the door and stepped into the hall.

Immediately, I heard a sound like a series of low sneezes. Something invisible tugged at Annalise's clothes. Someone was using silencers. She raised her arm to cover her eyes and charged forward.

"Stay low," I said to Catherine. "Count to thirty, and then follow Annalise out of the building."

I swung my leg out the window into cold morning air. Then I lowered myself as far as I could and dropped onto the grass. I didn't break my leg, and no one shot me. So far, so good.

I sprinted around the side of the building. The gun in my pocket bounced against my hip; I'd forgotten about it again. I could have used it against the gunmen inside, but Annalise could handle them better than I could. Killing people was her calling in life.

CHAPTER FIFTEEN

I came around the side of the house just as a man in a dark suit fled down the porch steps, firing desperation shots back into the doorway. He didn't see me come at him.

I hit him from behind at full speed, knocking him face-first into the gravel. He didn't make a sound as he scraped across the stones, but I hit him once behind the ear just to be certain.

I heard the *chunk* of a car door closing. Well-Spoken Woman charged out from behind a parked X6 and ran down the street in her expensive shoes.

The gunman's pistol had landed a few feet from me. I snatched it up. The slide was back; it was empty. I tossed it away and took out Ursula's gun, then I ran after Well-Spoken.

It felt good to run. I liked stretching my legs, and she was not fast at all. However, she *was* carrying a shotgun. I held Ursula's gun ready and stepped as quietly as I could.

When I was just five paces behind her, I slipped on a patch of black ice and fell hard on my hip. My whole body jolted under the impact and my gun fired, the round skipping off the asphalt into the air.

It took Well-Spoken seven or eight stutter steps to stop her run, turn, and point the shotgun at me. That was plenty of time for someone as motivated as I was to get to my knees and aim my gun at her.

I didn't shoot and neither did she.

"It appears we have a standoff," she said, trying to sound confident.

"Except only one of us is bulletproof," I answered. I showed her the damage to my jacket and shirt. Her mouth fell open. She didn't have an answer for that. I reached out with my left hand, and she walked toward me and laid the shotgun in my palm.

Thank God. She'd been aiming a little too low to hit my bullet-proof parts.

I stood and led her back to the B and B. Catherine and Annalise were standing over the man I'd knocked down. Well-Spoken stumbled and almost fell against me. I took her elbow to support her. "Thank you." She sounded grateful. "My name is Merpati." She looked up at me with wide, innocent eyes.

"I'm Ray. See that woman up ahead? She's a peer." I felt Merpati slow a little, but I urged her forward. "We have another few seconds before we say hi to her, and I want you to think about how you're going to present yourself. Helpful? Snotty? Pretty, wounded girl who needs a big guy to save her?"

She let go of my arm immediately. We walked together up the middle of the street toward the B and B. Townspeople stood in open doorways or in lighted windows, watching us.

We joined the others. Annalise had her foot on the gunman's back, holding him belly-down on the gravel. Catherine was kneeling beside him. He was talking in Chinese.

"I don't understand you, young man. I don't understand."

His wraparound shades had come off, and I was startled to see just how young he was. I didn't think he was old enough to buy a beer.

Merpati said: "He wants to go back to Hong Kong. He has a sister there who needs him."

I looked back at the B and B. A tall, slender young couple stood on the porch. Kripke stood beside them. They had the shell-shocked look of people who'd just been through a disaster. "How many dead bodies inside?"

Catherine stood. "Aside from this guy's friends? Five that I found right away. Nadia is one of them. I didn't see Nicholas, but I didn't search all that hard." She looked down at the kid on the gravel. "I wonder how many of them had sisters who needed them? Or kids?"

"Enough," Annalise said. She slapped the back of the kid's head. It made a sound like a cracking walnut, and he fell still.

Damn. Whether he deserved it or not, I didn't think we were the ones to dish out that sort of punishment.

Catherine gaped at Annalise. She didn't look relieved to have Annalise to keep her safe anymore. Suddenly, she looked afraid. She stepped toward Merpati, clasped her hands in front of her body, and spoke in a low, friendly voice: "Hello, honey. Did you order all this killing?" It was a new role for her.

"No!" Merpati responded. "Never. I was forced to come here by the man who killed my employer. The old man. He ordered this. They were going to leave me at the scene to take the blame."

This was the same voice that had bartered Kripke's murder in the Wilbur kitchen. Of course, now that she'd been caught, she was all shocked innocence.

"Who was the target?" I asked. I shouldn't have butted in on Catherine's shtick, but I was angry and I couldn't keep my mouth shut.

"I don't know," she answered, turning back to Catherine's friendly face. "I wasn't involved in the planning of this terrible, terrible crime."

"For Christ's sake," I said, my voice sharp. Merpati turned toward me quickly. If she was pretending to be afraid of me, she was doing a damn good job of it. I thought I might have been stepping on Catherine's work, but the expression on her face was encouraging. I waved my hand at the dead kid. "This guy spoke German, did he? Or did that tattooed bastard speak Chinese?"

"Cantonese," she corrected, with the habit of someone who corrected other people often.

"Whatever. I'll bet the only way they could have gotten their orders was through you. You're saying the old German guy didn't make you a better offer? You didn't switch teams and bring a couple of dumb young guys with you? You're going to be stuck with that story for a while, so you better be sure."

She turned back to Catherine. "I swear. I am telling the truth. I swear."

Catherine bent low so their faces were close together. "We know that's not true, honey. I don't want them to kill you, but I can't stop them if you don't help me."

Holy crap. I was the bad cop.

Unfortunately, Merpati wasn't sold. "It's the truth," she said. Her voice quavered as she spoke—she was afraid, but she wasn't going to change her story.

"We don't have time for this," Annalise said. She stepped forward.

"Wait!" Catherine snapped. She turned back to Merpati. "Honey, you have to give me something."

Merpati looked at her and shook her head. She had tears on her cheeks. She believed she was about to be killed, and she wasn't going to give us a thing. Whatever the old man had on her, it was strong.

Catherine sighed. "Okay," she said to me. "Go ahead."

I blinked at her. Go ahead and what? I hope she wasn't expecting me to start throwing punches. I had a shotgun in my hand. Was I supposed to use it on her, with little mobs of neighbors gathering down the street to watch us?

"Ray." Catherine sounded annoyed with me. "Quickly, or your *boss* is going to break this woman's neck."

"What?" I was completely at a loss.

"Lord," Catherine said. "You'll use it on me but not her?"

I suddenly understood what she was talking about. I tucked the pistol under my arm and took the ghost knife from my pocket. "I used it on you because you were trying to kill me." I grabbed Merpati's wrist and swept the ghost knife through her little finger. It cut a notch in her braided gold ring, but her flesh was unharmed.

She gasped. Her shoulders slumped and her hands drew up next to her chest in a frightened, defensive posture. "Both of you," she blurted out. "I'm sorry. He sent us to kill both of you, along with Mr. Kripke, if we could find him."

Catherine leaned toward her. "Who sent you to kill us?"

"His name is Zahn." I heard Annalise inhale sharply. That wasn't a good sign. Merpati kept talking. "He's what Mr. Yin has wanted to be his whole life. He's a real sorcerer. When his man approached me and offered to make me an apprentice, I couldn't refuse."

Catherine's voice was quiet. "So you double-crossed your employer for him."

"I . . . yes," Merpati said. "Mr. Yin . . ." Her voice trailed off.

Three of the townspeople, all men, began walking up the street toward us. One carried a rifle. The others were probably armed as well, but no weapons were visible. I lifted my empty hand to tell them to stop, and startled by the gesture, they did.

"Mr. Yin was the forty-sixth richest man in the world. He was ruthless and a little crazy, but he was a good man, in his way. He loved me. He even asked to marry me, and my solicitor assured me the terms of the prenup were excellent. Here I was, just a bank teller's daughter from Surabaya, and I would have been set to take care of my parents and siblings for life. And of course my association with him would have enabled me to pursue my only real interest: magic."

She glanced at the marks on the back of my hand. We were all quiet, waiting for her to continue.

She looked at Catherine again. "When we kidnapped you, I thought we were going to get everything we would ever want. But Mr. Yin . . ." She looked at me. "He wanted that spell you offered him so much that he lost all caution."

I didn't look at Annalise. I didn't want to see the expression on her face.

"When Herr Zahn approached me, I made the same mistake. Exactly the same. He promised me the secrets of the world behind the world, and I threw away everything. I lured Yin to his death. Me. When Zahn ordered me to take the few men I'd saved for myself and come after you, I knew he'd used me. He didn't care if I made it back, and if I had, he would have killed me. I betrayed a man who would have given me a good life for nothing. I'm so sorry."

She began to weep. A sorcerer had once promised to show me the world behind the world, but instead I had stolen his spell book and created my ghost knife. In the end, he had seemed like a decent guy—for a sorcerer—but I saw the world behind the world without his help. And just like Merpati, I wanted more.

With that thought, I couldn't help but look down at the dead gunman at my feet.

The townspeople were slowly moving closer to us again, and this time they had a crowd behind them. Whatever we were going to do with her, it would have to happen soon.

Annalise stepped over the boy's body and jostled Catherine aside. She laid the scrap of wood against Merpati's shoulder; the sigils didn't react. She wasn't carrying any magic.

Annalise's voice was quiet. "Where can we find Zahn?"

"He's been staying at a cabin near the fairgrounds. It's where he lured Mr. Yin and his men to kill them."

"I was just there last night," I said. "The chief of police discovered Yin's body—and the others—but the sorcerer was long gone."

"No," Merpati said. "He has a way of forcing you to think certain thoughts and turn away from certain places. Sometimes he can make people not see him when he's right there with you. He thinks it's funny."

"Merpati," I said.

"Yes?"

"I want you to tell those people"—I gestured toward the approaching townspeople—"that you came here with these gunmen to kill everyone in the building, and that you did it on Zahn's orders. You can say they forced you or whatever, but don't tell them about the magic. Make up a believable lie. Understand?"

"I will," she said. "Do I have to spend the rest of my life in jail? I'm afraid."

"No," Annalise said. "Someone will be along to debrief you and ease you out of this world. You're done, but if you talk about spells or predators to anyone—*anyone*—I'll personally kill your whole family. I promise."

Merpati's mouth dropped open, then shut. She nodded.

The three locals at the head of the crowd were about ten feet from us by then. "Excuse me," the man with the rifle said. "What's going on here?"

Merpati glanced at Annalise one more time. I knew she would do what I told her until the effects of my spell wore off, but the look she gave Annalise told me that she would stick to that story for as long as she had to.

Then she turned toward the three men. "These others are not involved. I will explain," she said in her perfectly accented English.

Annalise gave me a look. "Let's go." I followed her along the side of the road toward town, away from the throng of people gathering around Merpati.

"Hold it right there," one of the men said, hustling in front of us to block our path. He was a balding guy with a couple more chins than were strictly necessary, but the double-barrel shotgun in his hand was tough enough.

Annalise sighed. "Let me show you my identification," she said. She reached into her jacket.

"Boss—" I was suddenly afraid for Balding's life. But Annalise pulled out a white ribbon and showed him the sigil on the bottom. Balding suddenly closed his eyes and turned his back on us. Then he stretched out on the road and went to sleep.

She frowned up at me. "Did you think I was going to kill him?" We started walking again.

I glanced back at Kripke. He was watching me, his face pale and sweaty in the chilly morning air. He turned around and went back inside.

Catherine started to follow us.

"What did I hear about a spell?" Annalise asked. All trace of the tiny smile she'd greeted me with was gone. "You didn't ransom that investigator—"

"No," I said. "No way. I know better. I gave him a fake." I explained how I set up the arson, then got Yin to believe me when it came time to give him the spell.

Annalise nodded but still didn't smile. "That's all right, for this time. But don't do it again. People do crazy things for spells, Ray. If word started to spread that someone bartered with you for a spell, it could cause trouble for you."

I could imagine. "Gotcha. Can I ask a question?"

Information shared is information leaked. But Annalise turned to me and said: "You've earned it. Go ahead."

"Is Zahn a primary, whatever that is? Are you?"

"That's more than one question, but okay. No, Zahn isn't a primary. He's a quaternary, at best, but probably isn't even that high. And before you ask, I'm a senary. Now I'm guessing you want to know what that means."

"Pretty much, yeah."

"There are only three real spell books in the world. They're the source of all the magic on the planet, but they don't have any actual spells in them. They're also not really books, but never mind that. When you read one, you have visions. Dreams."

She fell silent for a moment. "After the visions are over," she continued, "the primary writes them down as clearly as possible, and that becomes what most of these idiots think of as a spell book."

We turned the corner. Annalise's battered Dodge Sprinter stood on the shoulder of the road. I was glad to see it again. I said: "So, if the primary passes the written-out spell book—one named after him, like, *Mowbray Book of Oceans*, to an apprentice, that apprentice becomes a secondary."

"Right."

"And the secondary casts the same spells, but they're weaker. Because, I guess, you can't pass on a vision to another person without having it change a little."

This time Annalise did smile, just a bit. "Very good."

"And the Twenty Palace Society doesn't have those three original spell books anymore, so you've been slowly losing power."

"We had two, but that's right. Several centuries ago, they were stolen. It's an ugly part of our history."

We reached the van. Annalise gave me the keys, and I got behind the wheel. It was just like old times.

Except I wasn't thrilled the way I had been when Catherine picked me up. It wasn't an adventure anymore. It was a job. An ugly job. I couldn't understand how I'd been so excited to come back to it a few days ago. "Are more peers coming?" I asked.

"No. Why would they?"

"First Pratt, then you—"

"Pratt was assigned by the peers. He won't be replaced until his death is confirmed."

"Then why did you come, boss?"

"Because I'm checking on you, Ray. You're my wooden man. You belong to me."

Catherine pulled the driver's door open. "Are you going to leave me behind?"

"Yes," Annalise answered.

"You can't. Not after all this."

"Hey," I said, "what happened to *this is not part of my job?*"

"I can't walk away from all this," she said. "Not now. All these years that I've been snooping around, making a phone call and then bugging out. I've been hiding, making the easy choice. . . . Last night, with the horses and that little girl . . . and I was watching those people set up for their festival, but I couldn't feel anything at all because of the ghost knife. They were working so hard in the dark and the cold—sometimes stopping to hold someone while they cried.

"But I couldn't feel anything, not until I woke up this morning when the effect had worn off. I haven't . . . God, that little girl *apologized for hiding*. I can't walk away from that. I need to do the right damn thing. Again."

Annalise leaned across the center of the van toward Catherine. "Will you be my wooden man?"

I mouthed *No!* "You're already an investigator. A good one."

Catherine frowned at me. "Pratt was a quinary, wasn't he? And Zahn killed him."

"Pratt was an arrogant ass," Annalise said. "He thought everyone would tremble at the sight of his big hat and long coat. I'm not as precious. And I have help."

"I want to help, too. I won't be a wooden man, but I'll do what you ask me to do."

"Get in," Annalise said.

I unbuckled and slid out of the driver's seat to let Catherine sit there. I gave her the keys. While she started the engine, I sat on the deck. The van was cold and my clothes were still wet.

"Ray, you've been to the cabin before?" Catherine asked. I gave her directions, and in a few moments we were on our way.

Annalise said: "Zahn isn't the only dangerous one here. Issler is trouble, too."

"Who's Issler?" I asked.

"Zahn's tattooed bodyguard. He's good. Three years ago, he took a hand off a full peer."

"A peer?" Catherine said. "Wow."

No one spoke again for a while. I thought about how close I'd come to killing him on the steps outside the Wilbur house. Things might have been simpler if I had succeeded. Or maybe not. At least I was going to get another chance.

I looked out the back window and saw a boy standing in the open doorway of a house. He was looking up and down the street, and I was pretty sure I knew what he was searching for. I hoped someone would call Sherisse about him soon.

"Is there a plan, boss?"

"Yes," Annalise said. "Catherine is going to drop us off at the entrance to the property, then drive into town to look for the predator."

Catherine stared at her. "Is that really what you want me to do?"

Annalise grunted. "When I brought Ray in, I had hours to put spells on him and prepare him to face a full sorcerer. With you, I have five minutes. You're not ready. You're still as soft as Jell-O."

Annalise looked back at me. "Here's our part of the plan. We sneak up on the cabin and kill Zahn and his people."

"I'm not sure I can remember all the steps," I said. "You know what would be useful? An Apache helicopter."

"Some peers use military equipment overseas. It draws too much attention in the U.S."

We were at the turnoff. Catherine slowed to a stop, and Annalise and I piled out.

"My cell is off," Annalise said. "If you find the predator, leave me a message. Use the one in the glove compartment."

Catherine opened the glove compartment, took a slender cellphone out, and dropped it into her pocket. "Can I try to kill it?" she asked.

"Sure, after you've left the message. Try not to get killed unless you can make it count."

I stepped back into the doorway and set the sawed-off shotgun on the passenger seat for her. Just in case. I closed the door and she drove off.

"What if Zahn already has the sapphire dog? What if both of them are up there?"

"What do you think?"

"Kill them both. I get it. But what if I have to choose?"

She stopped and stared at me. "Nervous, Ray? Asking questions you already know the answer to isn't going to make this easier. Now shut up. I don't know if Zahn has extra-sensitive hearing or not."

We started up the muddy drive. Of course I knew the answer to my own question: the sorcerer summoned predators, so he was top of the hit list. At least, that's how I saw it.

I was surprised that no one had strung police tape across the drive. I'd heard Steve call the state cops, although I was a little fuzzy on what he'd said. Still, considering what had happened, the National Guard should have been marching through.

Instead, there was only us.

I didn't care about Yin or his people. They were assholes. I did care about that housekeeper. She'd been murdered right in front of my eyes, and there was no one but me to make that right.

But this was a problem. I was the one who needed to believe the person I was going after was a murderer or worse. I was the one who needed more than "knows magic" as a reason to kill someone.

That wasn't the job I had come here to do. I wasn't here to kill a murderer; I was here to kill a sorcerer. Knowing he had killed, too, made this one job easier for me. But the next time—

"Your mind is clear, right?" Annalise asked.

"Absolutely." I forced myself to imagine the cabin and the land around it. I still wasn't sure Merpati was being straight with us about Zahn staying there. Somehow, I didn't think he was bedding down in the ski aisle.

I walked along the center of the path where the ground was relatively dry. All I could hear was the sound of my breathing, the wind rustling the trees, and our squelching footsteps. We were almost at the top of the drive when fat, wet snowflakes began to fall.

The BMWs and the Maybach were still in place. I kept low while I headed toward Yin's cars, leaving Annalise to slip into the underbrush.

The snowflakes melted on contact with the cabin windows, distorting the view inside, but I wasn't interested in the cabin. The second car had a strip of gray cloth hanging out of the trunk. I was certain it hadn't been there when I'd passed through last night.

The key for this car was probably on one of the dead gunmen. Assuming they were still inside, there was no way I was going to search them all unless I had to. And I didn't. I slid the ghost knife back and forth until it cut the latch. The trunk opened.

I loved my little spell.

Inside, I found empty halogen floodlight packages along with a car battery wired to an AC adapter and a three-pronged plug.

It had to be part of a carrier for the sapphire dog. The real question was simple: Where was the cage itself? I hoped Steve didn't have it. He'd be tempted to use it, and nothing good would come of that.

Or did Issler—I had to get used to thinking of Tattoo by that name—and Zahn have it? More important, were they still here, and could we kill them in their sleep?

I backed away from the trunk. It couldn't be closed again, so I left it up. That was a good thing, though. I was the wooden man. It was my job to draw attention to myself so Annalise could attack from behind.

I strolled back to the cars and the front of the cabin, doing my best to fake a casual calm I didn't feel. Issler might be aiming a gun at me from one of those darkened windows, or Zahn might have sent him to fetch the lightning rod.

Or maybe they were sitting in the back office playing cards. Why didn't I ever imagine good things?

I stepped up onto the wooden porch and tried the doorknob. The door wasn't locked. It swung inward, letting sunlight into the darkened store.

CHAPTER SIXTEEN

The smell had gotten worse—the door and windows had been shut for hours, letting the stink of blood, shit, and spoiling meat seep into everything. I flicked on the light switch by the door and saw that the bodies were still there. Steve had pulled camping blankets off the shelves to cover them, but no one had come to take them away.

What the hell did it take to get help in this town?

I looked around. Zahn and Issler were not napping among the dead. I went into the office. The interesting goosenecked lamp was on, which was strange, but there was no one there. I went out the back door and flicked on the porch light. Yin was covered with a heavy tarp weighted down at the edges with skis.

I shooed away the crows that were trying to get under there, and if the squawking they gave me didn't draw enemy fire, there was no fire to be drawn.

Annalise came out of the underbrush. "Nothing?"

"Nothing," I answered.

She stepped up onto the porch. "You came through the building pretty quickly. You checked the second floor, too?"

"There is no second floor," I said.

She gave me a funny look and went into the office. "What do you call that?" She pointed at the wall.

"A wall." If it had been anyone else, I would have thought she was joking. She gave me a funny look again, then her brow smoothed as if she'd had an idea. She went to the wall.

Whatever. The light over the desk was still on, which I still thought was strange. Something about the light was—

Wood cracked and splintered. I spun around, startled, feeling as if a huge weight had been lifted off me.

Annalise was standing beside a flight of wooden stairs. She pointed at the broken bottom step. Black steam fizzed out of it. "See that sigil?" I looked at it, although every time I did, I felt an unbearable urge to look away. The urge grew less and less powerful as the magic drained out of it, and I felt much less fascinated by the very ordinary desk lamp across the room. My iron gate ached.

"Oh, crap." I rubbed my face. Issler could have shot me from that step, and I wouldn't have seen it coming.

"These are on the roads in and out of town," Annalise said. "No one leaves and no one comes in, and they all think it's their own idea. Let's go."

I followed her up the creaking steps. She reached under her jacket and took out a green ribbon.

There was a yellow door at the top of the stairs. She pushed it open and went inside.

I followed her into a small living space. To the right was a kitchen that was little more than a dent in the wall and an open door that led to a bathroom. To the left was a chair and three mattresses on the floor. Blankets were bunched in the corner, but there were no suitcases or clothes nearby. A threadbare couch sat beneath the far window.

"Pretty spartan," Annalise said.

"Boss, could they still be here? Could they be watching us from a corner where we can't see them?"

"Yes," she answered. Then she sighed. "I think they're gone. There's no luggage, no vehicle out front. They might come back, but—"

"What's that?" I led her toward the kitchen. Beside the sink was a heavy tarp wrapped around something big. I peeled it back, expecting to find another body. It was just an oven.

Someone had bent the seal on the metal door so it would close over a thick black electrical cable. Light shone out through the dirty window on the oven door. An electric hum made the floorboards vibrate.

"What the hell have they done here?" Annalise asked. With one hand, she shifted the fridge to the side. It was unplugged; the heavy black cable had been plugged into that socket. Someone had put a powerful light—or several powerful lights—into the oven. I peered through the oven window, trying to see inside. It was no use. Then I remembered the halogen-lamp packages out in the car.

"The cage the sapphire dog was kept in for all those years was ringed with lights," I said.

She knelt and peered at the gaps in the door. She didn't have to ask the next question: *Was the sapphire dog in there right now?* She set her scrap lumber on the stovetop. The sigil on it twisted and writhed like an orgy of snakes. Whatever was inside, it was magic.

"Take the handle," Annalise said. "Don't open it until I say go."

I stepped around her and stood by the stove but kept my hands at my sides. She reached under her jacket and took out two more green ribbons. She closed her eyes.

I wondered if Catherine had told her everything about the sapphire dog, and whether I had told Catherine everything. Did she know it could pass through solid objects? Did she know about its tongue?

Annalise opened her eyes and nodded to me. I laid my hand on the handle. It was warm to the touch, but—

"Go!"

I yanked the door open and jumped back. The electric hum immediately stopped. The connection had been broken, but the light from inside didn't shut off. There were no halogen lights, but the oven seemed to be full of light anyway. At the bottom, I saw the blackened silhouette of a tiny rib cage and a human skull.

This wasn't the sapphire dog at all.

The churning light floated toward me just as Annalise threw her three green ribbons. The ribbons burst into flame—the same weird green hissing fire that I had seen her use to burn people down to their bones. I was already backing away.

The floating storm emerged from the wall of green fire, gases trailing behind it. Annalise said something, a curse, I think, and began throwing more ribbons.

Another billow of green flame struck the predator, then a brown ribbon flashed and the white-hot churning core of gasses I thought of as its face suddenly pointed the other way, moving toward the kitchen. Beams of blue light burst from a handful of thrown ribbons, some of them impaling the creature, all linking together to form a lattice. But the floating storm moved right through them, turning back to us.

Annalise's face was grim as she reached under her vest for another ribbon. The predator was closing in on her.

The stairs were right behind me. I could have sprinted down to the back door and been out on the road in three minutes. I knew the predator couldn't catch me out on the asphalt. But I couldn't leave Annalise. I was her wooden man, and this predator needed to be destroyed.

The pipes leading through the roof down to the sink told me where the water tank was. But I'd missed my chance. The predator was already too far away from it to replay the water-sprinkler trick.

An old set of skis and poles stood in the corner. The poles were pitted and crooked, but they were made of aluminum. I grabbed one and ran across the room.

Annalise had stopped throwing spells at the creature. She grabbed a mattress off the floor and heaved it. The fabric was already burning when it struck the floating storm, but it had no more effect than it would on a column of smoke. Pieces of mattress fell into the corner and set fire to the wall.

I threw the aluminum pole like a spear. It flew crookedly, striking the predator at an angle. That weird red lightning played along the pole's length as it passed through. Arcs jumped to other objects nearby, including the metal nails in the couch. The couch started burning.

The ski pole hit the floor, still sparking. The floating storm turned toward me. I backpedaled, drawing it away from Annalise as I went for the other ski pole.

Annalise picked up the burning couch and threw it. I think she was trying to kill the predator by breaking up the swirl of gases at its center, but all she managed to do was fan them out, set a new fire, and delay the thing for the few seconds it needed to pull itself back together.

I grabbed the other ski pole off the floor and, with two cuts from my ghost knife, shaved the end to a sharp point.

It was nearly on me. "Take this!" I shouted, and threw the pole through the predator. It sparked just like the other one did, shrinking the floating storm slightly. But not enough to kill it.

I backed toward the steps, the predator moving closer to me. Swirls of orange, yellow, and red curled around one another in sudden spirals and breaking wave fronts. It was like watching a half dozen small hurricanes collide in slow motion. In its own way, this thing was beautiful, too.

It passed over the burning couch, and now there was nothing between it and me. I backed down the stairs, well aware of what would happen if it got above me.

I hoped Annalise understood what I was doing.

Just as the predator moved into the stairwell, the ski pole shot through it and wedged into the wood paneling.

The floating storm froze in place. Red lightning flashed off it, draining into the wall studs. The paneling caught fire.

I bounded down the steps. The wall beside me groaned and the glass in the back door shattered. I turned away from the door and ran to the main part of the store.

There was a sudden, deafening blast from above. Hot air struck me from behind, followed a bare instant later by pieces of broken wood. I sprawled forward onto the trembling floor, feeling something huge and heavy land on my back. For a moment, I thought the terrible pressure of it wouldn't stop until my back was broken.

For once, I wasn't afraid. I pulled my knees under me and struggled to my feet, gratified that I still could. Firelight shone from behind me. I staggered toward the door but tripped over one of Yin's men.

My balance was shot and my ears were ringing. I stood anyway and looked back at the office. A section of the wall was missing, and everything was on fire. I could see fire upstairs through holes in the floor. I stripped off my jacket, but it wasn't burning.

The floating storm did not come through the doorway after me. I breathed a heavy sigh and leaned against a rack of winter coats. I needed to get out of this building, but for the moment, I didn't trust myself to cross the room without help. My head was still swimming and my skin felt scalded. I tried moving my arms and back—my ribs hurt, but I didn't think anything had been broken. Lucky.

Another explosion shattered the windows. This one sounded different from the one in the stairwell, but my ears were still ringing. I saw a sudden flare of light and stumbled toward the office.

I couldn't enter, but I could see into the backyard through a gap in the wall. Annalise was out there, and she was on fire. Another explosion struck the ground at her feet, and she was thrown back into the bushes. The cabin rattled with the blast.

The floating storm didn't attack like that. I ran to a side window.

Issler stood in the falling snowflakes. He held something that looked like a massive, two-handed revolver. As I reached for my ghost knife I heard him shoot it—*foof!*—and another blast of firelight erupted from the back of the house. He was smiling.

He didn't see me as he started toward the backyard. I threw my ghost knife at him.

The spell didn't go where I wanted it to go. It had never missed before, but it turned away from him just as I had turned away from the stairs in the office.

At the last moment, I willed it toward his weapon instead.

The ghost knife cut through the top of the barrel just before he squeezed the trigger. The gun burst apart in his hands, fire flashing over his face and neck. He screamed.

I turned and staggered toward the front door. Firelight shone down at me from the ceiling. The cabin groaned as if it was about to collapse. I yanked the door inward, feeling it scrape against the floor, and sprinted into the yard. The men inside would be getting a Viking funeral soon.

I *reached* for my ghost knife again. It was almost too far, but it came.

I held it ready to throw as I came around the barbecue pit, but it wasn't necessary. About fifteen feet away, Issler was kneeling in the dirt, squealing and grunting from the pain. With one hand he smeared mud into his left eye, and with his other he dug inside his mouth. I could hear meat sizzling.

I wondered if the ghost knife could hit him if I held it in my hand rather than throwing it. There was only one way to find out. I started toward him.

Suddenly, the shadows around us slid across the ground. The floating storm came over the top of the cabin and moved down toward Issler. It was small—no larger than a cantaloupe—but if it fed, it would get bigger.

I still had the gun in my pocket, but it was useless. I pressed my ghost knife to my lips. I didn't know what would happen to me if it was destroyed inside the floating storm, but I might have to chance it.

The only thing nearby was the barbecue pit and the stainless steel gas grill. I cut through the gas hose and dragged the tank out of the bottom. I couldn't tell if it was full or empty, and at the moment I didn't care. It was metal and it was handy.

But I was too slow. The floating storm was already directly above Issler and moving downward.

The tank snagged on something. I tugged and twisted it, trying to tear it free. It wouldn't come.

The floating storm was close enough to Issler that he could have reached up and touched it.

Red lightning never struck. The predator floated above him, swaying back and forth as though trying to find a way in. Maybe it was having the same trouble my ghost knife had had.

I shook the tank, making a horrendously loud noise but finally freeing it. The predator floated toward me.

I swung the tank once in a wide-armed circle and heaved it. It struck the floating storm dead center. I wished the propane had blown up like a bomb, but that didn't happen. I had to be satisfied with a couple of sparks and a slight delay in the chase.

Damn. Annalise was nowhere in sight, and I had no one to help me. For all I knew, she was dead in the bushes back there.

But that didn't mean I was out of ideas. Getting inside one of the cars out front would protect me from real lightning, and now seemed like a good time to try it against magic. I didn't know what I'd do after that, but maybe I'd have a chance for my head to stop spinning.

I ran to the front of the building. The firelight was bright and the heat was raw against the side of my face. Wood cracked and crashed somewhere nearby, followed by a roar of flame. The front wall of the cabin trembled and leaned toward me.

"Ray!"

That was Annalise's voice. I stopped and looked for her, letting the predator get uncomfortably close. I saw her silhouette waving at me from the far side of the cabin.

I angled back toward her and the heat. The little floating storm followed at about shoulder height. I could have sworn that it was having trouble staying in the air.

The wind changed, choking me with a gust of black smoke. I gave a wide berth to the porch, even though the fire hadn't reached there. The flames were flickering along the outside of the wall, slowly spreading downward.

I rounded the corner with tears streaming down my face and nearly ran headlong into Annalise. I dodged to the side as she stepped forward, and I could only catch a glimpse of the thing she was holding over her head as she tipped it over and slammed it onto the ground.

It was the water tank from the roof. She'd dumped it over the floating storm.

Scalding hot mud shot out from under the lip of the tank. It scalded me through my pants, and I dropped to my knees in the freezing mud to leach away the heat.

"Where did Issler go?" Annalise asked. Her clothes were in tatters, exposing pale skin from her chin to her ankles. She was completely covered with protective tattoos, as I had always suspected, but what I hadn't expected was how she looked. She always wore clothes that were large and loose, but I never expected to see all her ribs, her bony hips sticking out through her skin . . . I wasn't prepared for how *starved* she looked.

Then I saw that the sides and top of her head were burned nearly black. There was a section of undamaged skin on her face about the size of both her hands, but the flesh around it was actually smoking.

"Jesus Christ, boss," I said, with more fear in my voice than I'd intended. I jumped up and slipped out of my jacket. She let me wrap it around her shoulders. Her usual expression of stony anger turned a little sour, but she didn't shake it off. It looked as big as a quilt on her. The smell of her burns made my stomach twist into knots. "Is there something I can . . . Does that hurt?"

She pulled the jacket closed. "I hate it when they burn my clothes."

"Issler is on the other side of the building. He was still alive when I left him."

"I can fix that," she said, and started walking in that direction. "Get away from the building."

I sprinted for the line of cars and crouched behind the trunk of one of the BMWs. A few moments later, Annalise walked around the pit with Issler dragging behind her. His head hung at an awkward angle. Dead.

She lifted Issler's corpse in front of her like a shield and kicked the front door of the cabin open. Flames roared out. She threw him inside, then trotted toward me. My jacket was smoking, too.

"Well," she said when she reached me, "that was annoying."

As we walked down the switchback trail, Annalise stayed a few paces behind me. I didn't know whether she was sparing me the sight of her burned flesh, using me as a lookout so that no one would question her injuries, or using me as her wooden man again. It didn't matter. We walked in silence, and when I glanced back to see if she was about to go into shock or something, she glared at me.

Back at the road, Catherine was waiting for us in the van. She slid open the back door to let us climb in. I stepped aside to let Annalise get in first.

"I thought I told you to find the sapphire dog," Annalise snapped.

Catherine glanced at her, gasped, and shouted: "Oh my God!" She shoved her door open and fled into the road, running to the opposite shoulder to retch into the dirt.

Annalise knelt at a big plastic cooler behind the driver's seat. She took out a Tupperware tub and peeled off the lid. It was filled with little cubes of uncooked red meat. She popped one into her mouth.

That was it for me. I slid back out of the van and walked a few paces away, grateful for the clean, cold breeze.

Catherine had finished, but she stayed on the far side of the street. She looked spooked, so I moved toward her.

"What's she doing in there?" she asked.

"Healing her burns," I answered. "She has a spell that protects her, and when she needs to recover from an injury, she eats meat."

"She's . . . *eating*?" The look on her face showed that she was close to losing control again.

Raw and fresh, I almost said, but I didn't want to make either of us queasier than we already were. Instead, I went with: "Glamorous, isn't it? Don't worry, she'll be back to normal soon."

"What happened up there?"

That was a good question. Issler and Zahn had left a booby trap for us, and it had nearly worked. A normal gangster would have just left a bomb in that oven. It would have killed me in a blink. It wouldn't have killed Annalise, though, or any of the other peers I'd met. Zahn and Issler had gone to a lot of trouble to set up that disaster, and when I thought about the tiny bones in the bottom of that oven, I wanted to kill Issler all over again.

Not that it would be enough. Nothing would ever be enough to set right all the things that had happened in Washaway.

"Issler is dead," I told her. "We aren't." Then I remembered telling her *Stuff*. I gave her a quick rundown, making sure to mention what had happened to Penny and her son.

I shivered in the cold but didn't head for the van. I didn't care how warm it was, I didn't want to see Annalise's body—not the injured parts, not the uninjured parts.

The driver's door suddenly swung open. "Let's go!" Annalise called out. Her little voice had a nasty sharpness to it.

Catherine and I crossed back to the van. "I'm still driving," Catherine said. I laughed and went around to the side door.

Annalise had changed into heavy canvas pants and a heavy canvas jacket. Her head was pale and healthy and completely bald. She pulled a knit cap on, then opened her jacket and began alligator-clipping ribbons to the inside lining.

I knelt between the two seats. "You okay, boss?"

She tossed my jacket at me. I pulled it on. It stank of smoke and other things I didn't want to think about, but I was too cold to be fussy. "Except for all the spells I wasted, yes. Now, did you find the sapphire dog?"

Catherine started the engine. She wouldn't turn her head to look at Annalise. "I left you a message, but I guess you've been too busy to get it. I didn't get close enough to see it, but I'm pretty sure I know where it is."

"Then go."

Fat, damp snowflakes that wouldn't stick were still falling. Catherine pressed the gas and we pulled onto the road. I knelt on the metal deck and watched where we were heading. I didn't need to. I already knew.

We had to take the long way to the fairgrounds. The feeder road we had used to chase the plumber's truck was blocked by two pickup trucks and three men with deer rifles. We drove around the property into the main parking lot. There were men here, too, but they didn't display their weapons. I was sure they were close at hand, though.

Catherine stopped when one of the men raised a hand. She rolled down the window and said: "Is there a problem?"

"Not here," the man said. He wore a big, beautiful cowboy hat with a plastic rain cover. There was no white mark on his face. "But we've had some disturbances nearby."

"I've heard about that," Catherine said. "What's been going on?"

"Don't know," Waterproof Cowboy answered. "Outsiders have been causing trouble, and some of our own folks have suffered for it. We're being careful this year."

"Good Lord," Catherine said. "I wish people had the decency to keep their messes in their own yards."

"Me, too. Most of the outsiders have left Washaway, though. We're not seeing as many shoppers as we used to."

"Well, I hope you're not going to send me away without a poinsettia. And I have some last-minute gifts to buy."

Waterproof looked us over and nodded. "Be sure to try the sugar cookies. The proceeds help the food bank." He stepped back and we drove in.

We pulled ahead and parked. There were a lot of open spaces. Once Catherine had slipped the shotgun under her jacket, we climbed out of the van and started down the slope. The snow-making machine was off, and there was a quiet chill in the air. Catherine and Annalise spoke in low voices, pointing out toward the tents. I was about to join the discussion when movement off to the side caught my attention.

Six men marched toward Waterproof Cowboy and his pals. They carried hunting rifles, and one had a banana-clipped assault rifle. They spoke for a few minutes in a way that wasn't friendly or unfriendly. Waterproof tilted his head as though something puzzled him, but the newcomers stood in neutral positions with very little body language.

Finally, Waterproof shrugged and led his buddies toward the tents. The replacements took up their positions.

I jogged to catch up with Annalise and Catherine.

"This is a waste of time," Annalise said. "There's no evidence the predator is here. Just her guesses." She held out her hand.

Catherine sighed and gave her the van keys. "It wants victims. This is where the town is going to gather. Isn't it—"

"I'll go to a hotel until you have something solid."

"Boss, there *is* something weird going on here. Look."

The nearest tent was twenty yards away. A pair of heavyset women were beckoning for another to come out from behind her glasswares stall. Their persistence wore the other woman down. She followed them toward the cinder-block field house.

Annalise didn't respond, but Catherine said: "I'm guessing that's where we need to go."

We walked toward the field house. The stalls we passed were all set up but completely abandoned.

Finally, just a few dozen yards from the entrance to the field house, we came to an occupied stall. A little old gray-haired lady in a parka with a fur-lined hood stood in front of a huge display of gift chocolates and candies. ALL HOMEMADE, the sign said; she'd obviously spent a lot of time getting ready for this day.

She smiled pleasantly at us as we approached. "Excuse me—" Catherine said, but the woman interrupted.

"You should get out of here right now." She didn't let her smile falter, but the look in her eyes was fierce. "Right now. You're in terrible danger here. Go quickly."

"We're here to help," I said.

The woman glanced to the side, and her smile turned bitter. "Behind the table," she said. "Get in and get down. Quickly!"

Catherine rushed around the edge of the table and crouched behind the white tarp that covered it. I followed, herding Annalise in front of me. We hid.

"Why are we hiding?" Annalise asked. She sounded annoyed. "We should find the most heavily defended spot and attack."

I wanted to kill the sapphire dog with as little collateral damage as possible, but Annalise had other priorities. "The sapphire dog is fast," I said. "We have to sneak up on it, or it'll get away again."

The woman in the parka kicked me and said, "Hello, Rich. Back again so soon?"

"Come with me, Livia," a man's voice said.

"I'm not here to go to your town meeting, Rich. Whatever you have there, I'm not interested. I'm here to sell, not buy."

"I'm sorry to hear that." I heard his footsteps squish in the mud as he came around the stall. Then I saw his legs. He was wearing puffy snowsuit pants—the kind you'd see on a toddler. They were bright red with little candy canes on them.

I surged upward at him, but Catherine was faster. She slammed into his legs, knocking him to the mud. He fell facedown and was still. Weird. I grabbed the shoulder of his candy-cane jacket and rolled him over.

It was the bartender from the night before. He'd been holding a syringe and had fallen on it. The needle stuck out of his shoulder. I had no idea what was in it, but he was out cold.

I turned to Catherine. "Don't use up our good luck on mooks."

She was about to laugh when Livia hissed at us. "Get back under there and don't do that again! More are coming!"

She started pushing me down to the ground. I didn't want to fight her, so I got down on my knees and hid under the table.

"I've been hearing gunshots and explosions all morning," Livia said. "I think they've already killed a number of us. I can't get to my car, and I certainly can't walk out, not with my heart. But maybe I can distract them long enough for—well, if you're really here to help, maybe long enough for you to help."

I knelt in the mud and kept quiet. Annalise and Catherine did the same. If we raised a commotion here at Livia's stall, we'd draw every armed citizen in the fairgrounds. The sapphire dog would run, and we'd have to hunt it down all over again.

Besides, I wasn't keen on killing the sapphire dog's victims. I was hoping that, once the predator was dead, the townspeople would return to normal. Hey, it could happen.

There was a supermarket milk crate on the ground beside me. I looked inside and saw candies. My mouth watered and I wished I'd stolen a little time for breakfast.

More footsteps approached.

"Livia," a woman said. "Everyone is waiting. Join us."

"Thank you, Constance," Livia said, "but no."

"No one is coming today," Constance said. I wished I could see her face. "There's no one to sell to. You know I'm right."

"I'm still staying put."

"The pastor is asking for you."

"If he wants to buy some truffles, send him over."

Catherine was kneeling beside another of the plastic milk crates. She looked inside.

"I'm already here," a new voice said. It was Pastor Dolan.

From where we were hiding, I could see back to the church and the pastor's house. There was a sudden flash of reflected sunlight in an upstairs window. I tapped Annalise's shoulder and nodded toward the house. The flash came back, and she saw it. Someone was watching from there.

Livia's voice was strained but still pleasant. "Come to buy some chocolate-covered almonds, Pastor?"

I heard the distinctive double click of a revolver being cocked. "Livia," the pastor said, "if you don't come out right now, I'm going to shoot you in the stomach. Then we'll drag you back to join the others. You won't live long, just long enough. Now come on."

That was it. Whether we had to sneak up on the sapphire dog or not, I couldn't just cower here while this woman was led away at gunpoint. My ghost knife would be useless against them, but I still had the gun. And since they couldn't feel fear anymore, I couldn't control them at gunpoint. I'd have to shoot them.

I started to move out from under the table. Livia held her hand in front of my face. It wasn't visible to the people she was talking to, but she was telling me to stop.

God help me, I did.

Livia sighed. "I guess I don't have a choice." She walked around the edge of the stall.

"What about the strangers?" Dolan asked. "Rich said you were talking to them."

"I told them to get out of town." Livia sounded just as pleasant, but I couldn't see her face. I assumed she wasn't smiling anymore. "I warned them off, and they ran that way. They're out of your clutches, you self-righteous little fucker."

"Get her inside," the pastor said. Squelching footsteps receded.

"We don't have enough guns," Constance said. "You shouldn't have sent so many men into town."

"We need to gather everyone. He's hungry."

"*She* needs to be protected more than she needs to be fed," Constance responded. I guess they didn't like to call the sapphire dog *it,* or look under its tail.

"When the next missionary group returns, we'll keep them here. Better to be safe, I guess, until the outsiders are caught."

"I'll get some people together to search," Constance said, her voice flat.

More footsteps receded. Catherine turned toward me and said in a low voice: "We can't stay here. As soon as Livia is turned, she'll tell them everything."

"I'm leaving," Annalise said.

"What?" Catherine's voice was too loud.

I held up my hand to Catherine, and she calmed down. It had worked for Livia, and it worked for me. "Boss, do you want to go after Zahn right now?"

"I do. He's a slippery bastard, and I don't want to let him run back to whatever hole he hides in. What he did at the cabin is SOP for that fucker. It's not enough to keep the sapphire dog from him; he needs to be dead, and the society has been hunting him for fifty years. Besides, I bet he didn't bring any predators with him. We may not get a better shot."

"What about the sapphire dog?"

"I'm leaving that for you two."

It was my turn to be shocked. "What? You're going to face him without me? Boss . . ."

There really wasn't a delicate way for me to ask if she could take him in a fight. She was powerful, but she wasn't the *most* powerful. Besides, she'd used up a lot of her spells on the floating storm. She needed me.

She narrowed her eyes at me. As it turned out, I didn't have to ask that delicate question. She understood exactly what I was going to say. "Yeah, he's dangerous, Ray, but you know what? If he can be killed, I can kill him."

"Okay, boss."

Annalise turned to Catherine. "You follow his lead in this. You're good at what you do, but he knows this."

Catherine nodded and looked at her shoes. Annalise turned to me. "You just worry about taking care of that predator."

"Okay," I said. I didn't like it, but I didn't have much choice. Annalise rushed out of the booth and slipped into the tree line.

"What's the plan?" Catherine gave me a steady look.

I pulled the ghost knife from my pocket, then stuffed it down the front of my pants. I had an absurd moment when I worried it might slice off something I wanted to keep, but of course it didn't. It didn't cut through the bottom of my pocket, after all. "I'm going to get myself captured. I'll make a big enough distraction that you should be able to get to the parking lot and steal a car. Can you steal a car?"

"Yes, but Annalise—"

"Annalise told you to do what I say. The best way to get through all these people is to let them bring me to the sapphire dog. If I can kill it without hurting them, maybe they'll get better." I tried to say it with conviction, but I didn't have any. I'd never had much luck curing the victims of a predator. I didn't expect it to work, and I didn't expect to get out of there alive. But there was no need to say that aloud. "But you're an investigator. You got us where we need to be." I was tempted to say *You don't have to die, too.* "You have kids."

"A lot of these people here have kids. Somebody needs to stand up for them. Somebody has to be ready to pay the price, Ray, and I'd rather be good than safe."

It seemed the definition of *good* was more fluid than I thought. "I'm not doing this to save your life," I said. "Well, not only to save your life. Washaway is full of these bastards. Someone ought to report this—" I stopped talking for a moment as a sudden migraine overtook me. Catherine winced, too. *Don't think that thought.* Instead, I said: "I might be the one who makes it, not you."

Catherine sighed. "If we both survive, I'll buy you a beer. If you survive and I . . ." She took a deep breath. "I have two daughters, Ray. If something happens to me, I want you to stay away from them. You and the whole society. There's nothing you can tell them about me that they don't already know. Okay?"

"Absolutely. Here." I offered her Ursula's gun. "They'd take this off me anyway."

She took it. "Ray, I'm going to say this quickly and get out of here. You're a decent guy, but you'd better *do what you have to do*. You're sending me away, so I'm relying on you. Whatever it takes. Okay?" I wasn't sure if she was telling me to kill or be killed, and I don't think she knew, either. She turned and scrambled into the woods.

I took a candy out of the crate beside me. It was delicious. Then I stepped out from under the table and vaulted into the open.

CHAPTER SEVENTEEN

I sprinted through the stalls, dodging between the tents and hopping over cables. Someone shouted, "Hey!" and I turned at a right angle and ducked under a sign that said SNOWMAN CONTEST HERE!, then ran around a tarp covered with melting, machine-made snow into the open field. I heard shouts behind me and, because I wasn't really trying to get away, glanced back.

Men, women, and children raced across the field after me. They were slow, even the teenagers, and for a few moments I worried that they wouldn't be able to catch me. Then I saw a pickup bounce across the field in my direction. It was the guards who had replaced Waterproof.

I ran faster, knowing I would only reach the safety of the trees if the truck bottomed out or wrecked.

For a moment I thought they might try to run me down. I prepared to veer off to the side, but the driver slammed on the brakes a dozen yards away and the men in the back aimed their weapons at me. I stopped and raised my hands. "Don't move!" one of them shouted.

"What are you guys doing?" I shouted back, letting my voice crack with fear. Staring down the barrels of their guns, I didn't have to put much effort into acting. "I just want to leave!" I hate to be afraid, but they'd be suspicious if I didn't show some fear, and I hated them for it.

The driver climbed from the truck. Three dozen people were running toward me.

As I expected, they were complete amateurs—they stepped into the gunmen's line of fire and generally milled around me. When they patted me down, they missed the ghost knife.

One boy of about fourteen, sweat running from under his knit cap, took up a position behind me, knife in hand. I told them I would go peacefully, but they didn't care. They made me walk with them toward the field house and continued milling as we trudged through the mud. The smallest of them, a handful of kids that barely came up to my armpits, had enough energy to run wide, looping circles around me. A couple of them had guns, but most had knives, hammers, shovels, and other household tools.

I wanted to look over at the pastor's house, but I didn't. If Zahn was watching, and I suspected he was, I didn't want to give anything away.

Hondo was right beside me, a smear of auto grease on his forehead, and once I'd seen one familiar face, I saw more: one of the stilt walkers, Sue the paramedic, Justy Pivens. None had a white mark that I could see, but they all had the single-minded glare of the sapphire dog's pets.

One of the men walking beside me was a tall guy with a jaw like a train cowcatcher and sullen eyes. He stumbled slightly, then turned toward me, his left eye closing in a slow-motion wink. He said: "Buh buh guh glerr," then his mouth and left arm sagged and he fell onto the grass.

I lunged at him and turned him over. His hat fell off and a thick strand of drool hung from his lip. He was dying right in front of me—dying of a stroke just like Penny and Little Mark in their cells—and there was nothing I could do about it except watch.

I rubbed at the stubble of hair on the top of his head. It only took a moment to find a patch of white skin beneath his hair. The sapphire dog had learned to hide its mark.

The pets moved closer to me, and I held up my hands again. Seven or eight of them fell on me, pressing me down onto the wet grass. They bent my arms behind my back. I cursed at them and tried to struggle free, so they leaned on my arms until I thought my shoulder would pop. I stopped struggling and let them cuff me and pull me upright. Damn. The only way I could get to my ghost knife now would be to *call* it through my own body. No one tried to help Sullen Eyes.

Across the field, I saw a gray Volvo creep out of the parking lot. No one else seemed to notice. Go, Catherine, go.

They shoved me along. As we came near the field house, I saw Preston among the folks still standing guard. He was still holding his double-barreled shotgun, but he didn't seem interested in scaring me anymore.

Behind Preston I saw Pippa Wolfowitz and Graciela. I looked for Graciela's toddler with her tiny earrings, but I didn't see her nearby. Pippa was still wearing the same Santa cap and bulldog expression she'd worn outside Big Penny's house, but underneath her jacket she wore pajamas. She looked up at the sky as though she wanted to study the clouds, then fell over backward and was still. No one moved to help her.

Damn. They were dying all around me.

Pastor Dolan pushed through the crowd. "Where are the two women who were with you?"

The stone-cold way he looked at me gave me a chill, so I smirked at him. "They escaped while you dipshits were chasing me."

He wasn't insulted. Maybe he didn't know how to be insulted anymore. "You'll tell us more soon enough."

"Yeah, sure I will," I said. "Take me to your pet."

Everyone stopped and turned toward me. They looked to be a half second from stomping the life out of me. I felt a sudden nervous tingle on the back of my neck.

"He isn't a *pet*," the pastor said in a low voice. "Do you hear me? Don't use that word again."

"Sure, sure. But next time you threaten someone, stand on a box first."

He didn't react, just turned away. Hondo grabbed my right arm, and a man I didn't recognize grabbed my left. This was it. I wished my hands were free so I could grab my ghost knife. The entrance to the field house was just ten yards away.

A green light lit the sky on the right. Everyone turned toward it, and I stepped back to get a clear view through the tops of the festival tents.

Green fire had blasted a hole in the roof of the pastor's house. There was a loud boom, then a series of sharp cracks. It sounded almost like fireworks.

A nest of blue lights came through the wall. The whole house appeared to buckle, a piece of roof blasted upward, and we heard the explosion a second or two later.

There was another sudden flare of green flame. "Go, boss," I said under my breath. "Kick his ass."

A section of the downstairs wall suddenly blinked out of existence. The building sagged in on itself. There was a high-pitched sound almost like a scream. The walls shuddered and a column of white flame tore through the entire roof.

Burning wood rained down on the nearby lawn. I had a sick feeling in my gut. I'd never seen Annalise use white fire; maybe it was a spell she kept in reserve.

The walls twisted and collapsed into rubble. I stood in the crowd, watching the pieces of broken shingle and siding burn in the mud. I looked for a figure moving amid the wreckage, a glimpse of a dark coat, but I couldn't see anything.

Boss, please still be alive.

The pastor turned toward Waterproof. "Get together a dozen men and check that out." He glanced back at his house, his expression showing as much concern as he'd show for a toppled Porta Potti. "Actually, bring twenty. With guns. Kill anyone you find over there. We don't want to take any chances with his safety."

Waterproof took about a third of the crowd with him, maybe two dozen people, but these guys weren't operating under military discipline. They marched across the open field in a mob with their mismatched weapons.

I was hustled toward the open door. People stepped over Pippa's body as if she was a rotted log. "I'm cooperating," I snapped. "You don't have to hold my hand. I'm cooperating!"

They didn't let go. My stomach knotted up as I thought about being dragged in front of a predator with my arms pinned. Damn, did I feel stupid.

We went inside, passing a halogen floodlight set on a stand in the back corner. This was the same white room where I'd eaten the church lunch. The tables, chairs, and steam trays had been removed, and the room was flooded with light. I counted four halogens, each set into a corner and each shining onto a pedestal near the far wall. I nearly tripped over the fat black power cables that ran along the base of three of the walls.

And there on the pedestal was the sapphire dog, sitting on a big satin pillow like pampered royalty. Its tail wavered, sometimes weaving slowly and sometimes snapping from one position to the next too quickly for the eye to see.

Its back looked different than I remembered. The last time I'd seen it, it had been smooth like a snake, but now I saw a row of polyps.

It turned its weird, rotating eyes toward me.

My God.

I shut my eyes, trying to think. The floodlights didn't make sense. Regina and Yin had used lights to trap the thing, but the people it fed on—its pets—had never done that. At first they'd tried to get it out of town, then they'd kept it safe. But they'd never kept it *prisoner*. So maybe it wasn't a prisoner right now.

I felt a sudden rush of affection for it. It was trying to control me again. I shut my eyes and focused on the pain in my iron gate, but I couldn't keep them closed. I had to *look*.

"I love you!" I shouted, fear and hatred giving power to my voice. I lunged forward, breaking the grip Hondo and his buddy had on me, then pretending to fall onto the stone floor. I took most of the impact on my shoulder and a little on my forehead. The pain was sharp, but it reminded me why I was there.

Was I in range of the sapphire dog's tongue? The space where its mouth would be was still smooth and unmarked; it wasn't opening its "jaw." I had moved my my cuffed hands behind my knees when Hondo and his buddy caught my arms again.

There was a gunshot outside. Then more shots followed in a sudden rush, including the harsh pecking sound of automatic fire. It faded away, then surged again as people reloaded. I closed my eyes and refused to think about who they might be shooting.

There was a quick double honk of a car horn from outside. After a few seconds, I heard Steve's high, strained voice. "What the heavens is going on here? Who are those men shooting at?" He was trying to push into the room with his gun drawn. No one seemed afraid of it. He started calling people by name.

Of course. No one here had a visible white mark. Steve didn't know everyone had been turned into pets.

I heard him shout, then his gun went off. He cried out "Kerry!" in horror and was shoved into the room, unarmed. "What are you people *doing*?" He looked terrible, pale and drooping, with dark pouches under his eyes. He obviously hadn't even gotten the meager sleep I had. He scanned the room, then gasped when he noticed the sapphire dog. "Oh," he said quietly. "The lights. Good work, everyone."

They stared at him. I passed the cuffs under my feet, then rolled to my knees. I pulled the ghost knife out of the front of my pants and palmed it as best I could.

As soon as my hand touched the spell, the sapphire dog turned toward me. I had its full attention.

"I love you!" I shouted and lunged forward.

The sapphire dog jumped off the pedestal immediately. It knew.

Hondo and the other man pounced on me. I didn't even have time to throw the spell before they pinned me.

I cut a slot in the concrete and dropped the ghost knife into it. The pets would need a jackhammer to get it now.

The sapphire dog hurried toward the wall on its awkward, crumpled-leg gait. Steve had just come in through the door on that side, and he shuffled to intercept it. Neither were quick, but Steve managed to step into its path. He crouched low and held out his arms as though about to catch a running child.

None of the pets tried to stop him, and I knew something was wrong. I remembered the way the sapphire dog found us at the stables, and the way the pastor had immediately run from me when he had no way to know I was planning to kill it, and the way Hondo and his buddy had just pounced on me before they had any way of seeing my ghost knife—the sapphire dog was in their heads.

Not in the heads of the people it had controlled at a distance, like Regina and Ursula, but the heads of people it had fed on and marked.

And there was no way it would let them trap it here, no matter how much they loved it.

I shouted: "Get out of the way!" Steve looked at me in surprise, but it was too late.

The sapphire dog leaped up as if it was jumping into his arms. Its head struck Steve low on his torso and then *sank into him*. Its legs, body, and tail pulled back into a thin column behind that oversized head, like the tentacles of a jellyfish, and it slowly, excruciatingly, passed through Steve's body and the wall behind him.

It couldn't have taken longer than five or six seconds, but it seemed much longer. As it happened, Steve's mouth fell open and a sorrowful expression came over his face. He looked as though he realized he'd done a terrible wrong to someone he cared about.

Then the predator was through and gone. Steve's face went slack and he fell onto the floor in a sloppy mess.

I laid my forehead onto the freezing concrete floor and let out a long string of curses. The predator had not recognized me, or it would have had me shot out in the field. It had seen the ghost knife as soon as I touched it, though, and it had fled. Steve was dead because of me. The sapphire dog had not even bothered to feed on him.

I had failed.

Hondo and his pal still held on to me. I struggled, but they were using all of their weight. I was sure the next thing I was going to feel was a bullet punching through my skull.

"Move aside," someone said. The speaker's voice was low and gravelly and heavily accented. "You will move aside! I have only come to talk." He pronounced *will* as "vill" and *have* as "haf" like a cartoon villain.

They moved aside and Zahn limped in, the right side of his head scorched black and his right arm withered to the bone. His clothes were in tatters, and his left leg was a mess of raw meat. Annalise had hit him hard, and I was glad she'd gotten her licks in. Still, just seeing him walk in here instead of her filled me with an empty, grieving rage.

Zahn didn't act like a man with critical injuries, though. He didn't even walk like a scrawny old man. "Is it not here?" he shouted, his voice raw. "I will speak to it immediately!"

The sapphire dog's pets stared at him with the same inscrutable gaze the predator had given me.

"Very well," Zahn said. "I will speak to underlings." He walked up to a young woman in a long red coat, seemingly chosen at random. "I have sealed this town off from the rest of the world. Unless I lift this seal, no one will ever come here again, and no one but me will ever leave. You will be trapped—and starving—on a world teeming with food. Again."

From somewhere behind me, Pastor Dolan said: "What do you want?"

Zahn turned toward Dolan. "I will take you from this place," he said. "As my captive."

Everyone who had a gun raised it in unison and began shooting at Zahn. The old man's skull split open as a shotgun blast tore through it. He staggered, and bits of blood and flesh splashed off his body under the barrage. God, the sound was deafening.

Bullets ricocheted around us. One skipped off the floor near my hand, and Hondo collapsed heavily across my neck and shoulders.

The firing stopped after a few seconds. I glanced around the room. Six people lay dead or dying on the floor, and eight others were pressing their hands against bloody wounds. The nearest corpse had her face toward me. It was Karlene.

I had a sudden vision of her dog Chuckles, sitting on a blue tarp in the back of her truck. Was he still alive? If so, I hoped he'd find someone to care for him.

Someone behind me threw an empty nine-mil on the concrete floor. Preston's shotgun and a pair of rifles were discarded, too. Obviously, they hadn't brought enough spare ammunition.

The old man had fallen on his back into the corner. He raised his left arm and made a horrible choking sound. The woman in the long red coat lay on the floor beside him, a bright spray of arterial blood pulsing out of her thigh onto the wall. I shrugged Hondo's body off me and got to my knees. Zahn was still making that *hrk hrk hrk* noise.

Then I realized he was laughing.

He sat up. Most of his head and face were gone, and his body was riddled with bloody exit and entrance wounds. His only good eye rolled in his head as he looked around the room.

He saw the bleeding woman beside him and lunged at her wound, ruined mouth gaping.

I shut my eyes. My stomach felt sour, and my skin crawled. I wanted to run for the door, but I could hear a couple of the pets nearby reloading. The sounds the old man was making were revolting. They weren't the wet slurping noises you hear in a horror movie. They were the moans a connoisseur makes during a fine meal.

I couldn't help myself. I looked at him again.

As he gulped down the blood, his wounds were healing, even the ones Annalise had given him. *Raw and fresh,* I wanted to say again, but the thought made my stomach twist. Annalise used that same spell to heal herself, but at least she limited herself to meat bought at the supermarket.

The woman died before Zahn finished healing, so he started eating the meat.

"I don't understand," Pastor Dolan said, his voice flat and toneless. "Why didn't you die?"

"Of course you don't understand," the old man said between bites. "This world is full of things you and your food do not understand. Chief among them is me. You can't kill me with those guns, but they do hurt. If you hurt me again, I will leave you here to starve."

"I don't want to be captured again," Dolan said. I didn't want to look at him. I didn't want to see the expression on his face. I also didn't want to turn my back on Zahn.

"The people who held you captive before didn't understand what you are. They would have fed you if they knew how, but they didn't. I know more about you, and I can guarantee that you—and your new selves—will never starve again."

New selves? That didn't sound good.

"I don't want to be captured again. I nearly starved to death the last time." Pastor Dolan's singsong voice sounded a little closer to me.

"You have been captured already," Zahn said. "You and your food."

"I know this. I tried to escape many times."

"If you come away with me, I will see that you are fed. I don't want to destroy you, like this one does." He pointed at me. "I want to grow in power with you. Or you can starve here. The choice is yours."

"I don't really have a choice," Pastor Dolan said. "Isn't that right?"

The sapphire dog poked its head though the hole in the cinder block. Zahn looked at it and smiled. "It is right," he said as he tore a long muscle out of the runner's thigh. "You have belonged to me all along." He stuffed the meat into his mouth, opening his jaws unnaturally wide to make it fit.

The sapphire dog stepped through the opening in the wall and curled up on the floor. Four of the uninjured townspeople moved in front of it, blocking my view. Damn. I was probably too far to use my ghost knife anyway.

Then Zahn turned his bloody face to me. He smiled in a way I didn't like. "And now for you."

CHAPTER EIGHTEEN

Without Hondo, the man holding me couldn't keep me on the floor. He was strong, but I thrashed desperately. I knocked him down and moved away from the old man.

Unfortunately, the sapphire dog's pets had clustered in front of the exit, blocking it with their bodies. If I ran that way, they could simply grab me and hold me for Zahn.

So I moved away from him in a direct line. I only managed a few steps before three or four others took hold of me. I struggled but couldn't break free. My legs were kicked out from under me, and I fell to my knees again.

Someone stepped on my calf, pinning it to the stone floor. The pain in my kneecap was intense. I tried to glance back to see who it was, but I didn't have that much freedom of motion.

Zahn stood, took a linen napkin from his pocket, and delicately wiped the blood off his face. He began to resemble the little old man I'd seen on the Wilburs' back lawn.

"Damn," I said, trying to keep tremors of fear out of my voice. "You carry a napkin around? I guess cannibals never know when they'll need to freshen up."

"That word holds no revulsion for me. I have done many, many things that you would consider a horror, but to me they are the price of power and extended life. I do not even think of this"—he held up the bloody cloth—"as distasteful anymore, unless they soil themselves in fear.

"But you find many things to be a horror, yes?" He began walking toward me. I tried to move my pinned leg, but I didn't have the leverage. "I enjoy killing your people, Mr. Twenty Palace Society. I enjoy seeing your numbers dwindle. You were so close to winning, not so many decades ago, yes? Or maybe you don't know that. You were very close to making yourselves kings of the world."

He stopped in place and held his arms out as though a crowd was cheering for him. "But there were always some, like me, who refused to play by your rules. Individualists. Rebels. And how many palaces do you have left now? Eleven? Ten? Six, perhaps? And you have no more dreamers, yes? Soon your kind will be gone from the world, and free men will be free."

He started toward me again, taking his time. I didn't like seeing him so confident and relaxed. I wanted to shake him up. "Free to bring predators here to feed on other people . . ." Maybe he no longer thought of himself as human, but I pressed on. "And feeding on them yourself, too. The world would be better off without you."

Zahn smiled. He should have packed some floss along with his linen napkin. "What would the world be without magic?"

Then, finally, he stepped on the slot I'd cut in the floor.

I said: "What would this town be without magic?" I closed my eyes and *called* my ghost knife.

It cut through Zahn's foot and flew into my open hand. The old man gasped as a jet of black steam shot out of the top of his black leather shoe. I ducked low, letting it blast over me.

The people holding me cried out in shock and pain as the steam struck them, and I broke free. I kicked the leg of whoever was standing on me, knocking him into a pile, then dropped to the floor and rolled away from the scalding blast. With a twist of my wrist, I slid the ghost knife through the handcuff chain.

I scrambled to my feet as Zahn fell to one knee. He clasped his hands over the energy blasting out of his foot. I charged at him, grabbed him by his scrawny neck, and scraped the ghost knife down his spine.

Another, larger blast of black steam roared out of him. I gripped my spell in my teeth, grabbed Zahn's leather belt, and lifted his tiny, withered body off the ground.

I held him in front of me and ran at the human shield around the sapphire dog. The steam made the pets fall back, covering their faces and shrieking. They didn't break and run, but they did fall.

I spun Zahn behind me, dropping him to the floor in case more pets came at me from behind. He caught hold of the lapel of my jacket as I let him go, and I wasted precious seconds slipping out of it. Then the sapphire dog was right in front of me. I grabbed the ghost knife out of my teeth.

The predator split into three and vanished.

I wanted to roar in frustration, but I didn't have the time. The pets were all around me. I dropped to the floor next to Steve's legs. My hand fell on a gun lying against the wall, and I grabbed it, then scrambled through the hole the sapphire dog had made.

I heard shouting and commotion behind me. A hand grabbed at my pant leg, but I fought free. The second hole to the outside was just a couple of feet away. I scrambled through.

Then I was outside. I ran, holding the found gun by the barrel.

I heard two quick gunshots, but I had no idea if the shooter was aiming at me. I ran through the tents to make myself a more difficult target. I felt faster without my jacket, but that wasn't going to last. I was cold, wet, and hungry. The only real weapon I had was my ghost knife, which was useless against the pets. If the old man summoned another floating storm, I was dead.

I stole a cinnamon bun out of a booth and, still running, took a bite. It was sweet and sticky and exactly the fuel I needed.

There was movement ahead. A teenage boy stepped out from behind a plastic tent. He raised an old revolver, but I was too fast for him. I hit him hard and ripped the gun out of his hand as he fell.

I passed the last of the stalls and hit open ground. There were no more pets in front of me, but there were plenty behind. I could hear them yelling instructions to one another. I would have guessed that, with the predator in their heads, they wouldn't need to talk to one another, but that wasn't the way it worked, apparently.

I had five options: the two feeder roads across the open field; the parking-lot exit; the horse trail that connected the fairgrounds with the stables; and finally the pastor's church and ruined house. The feeder roads and parking lot pretty much guaranteed I'd be shot. The horse trail was the safest in the short term, but the locals knew the landscape and would run me to ground eventually.

The last choice had something the others didn't—Annalise. Even if she couldn't help me—and I hoped she was still alive and dangerous, even if only barely—I couldn't leave her behind. Besides, I hoped she would have something I needed.

So I ran toward the rubble of the pastor's house, swerving erratically in case someone took another shot.

At the edge of the field, I scrambled up the small hill bordering the church property. A bullet smacked into the dirt beside me, and goose bumps ran down my back.

When I made it to the top of the hill, I looked back. The people of Washaway, teen to senior citizen, ran toward me in a straggling mob, weaving between the stalls. A few carried guns, but most had other weapons.

I turned back toward the church. Waterproof Cowboy and his crew lay scattered across the grass. All of their guns were slag, and all of their heads were missing.

I ran toward the rubble of the pastor's collapsed house. I remembered the way parts of the building seemed to vanish and hoped Annalise hadn't vanished with it.

There. Annalise lay motionless beneath a pile of scorched wood. I stuffed both guns into the back of my waistband and hauled her out by the wrist. She was even smaller than Zahn, but the wood was heavy and the nails snagged on her clothes. It took three tries to heave her into my arms. She wasn't missing any limbs and I couldn't see any blood, but she looked like just another corpse.

Damn. Annalise couldn't help. The pets were nearly at the bottom of the hill.

The back door to the church was only a few yards away. I ran for it, cradling Annalise in my arms. "Wakey, boss." I lifted her onto my shoulder. "Now would be a good time to wake up."

The fastest of the pets had reached the bottom of the hill. I had the ghost knife in hand, ready to cut through the lock, but the door swung inward when I turned the knob. Thank God for country churches.

I rushed into the food bank and set Annalise on the floor, then I slammed the door and flipped the dead bolt lever to lock it.

The room was dark. I switched on the light. Hands jiggled the knob and fists pounded at the main door behind us. I put my shoulder against one of the metal shelves and tipped it against the door, pinning it shut.

I ran back across the room into the church. There was a dead bolt on the main door and I threw it closed, but the bright, beautiful stained-glass windows in here weren't going to keep anyone out.

I rushed back into the food bank and locked the door. After I wedged a high-backed wooden chair under the doorknob, I knelt by Annalise.

A gunshot blasted through the back door. I tipped over another shelf and wedged it against the upper part of the doorway.

Bullets pinged around me. The tilted shelf had spilled seven or eight fifty-pound bags of flour onto the floor, and I sprawled behind them. I kicked the pastor's desk against the wall to make room. Bags of dirt would have protected me better, but this was the best I could do.

I grabbed Annalise and dragged her across the floor toward my meager shelter. I had missed my chance to kill the sapphire dog, but I wasn't ready to give up. Unfortunately, I wasn't going to get at the predator until I'd gotten through its pets first. The two guns jabbing into my hip bones might have helped me with that, but I didn't want to start gunning down innocent people who couldn't control themselves because I couldn't do my fucking job. I didn't care what the sapphire dog had done to them, I didn't want to fight *them*.

What I wanted was the white ribbon Annalise had used to make that man outside the Sunset fall unconscious.

I searched through her jacket, remembering Penny and Little Mark lying dead on the floor of a tiny jail cell, and Pippa falling onto her back. Maybe if I killed the sapphire dog, the pets really could go back to being themselves again. Maybe, just maybe, they wouldn't fall over dead. But I had to be quick, because I didn't know how much time the pets had left, and bullets were still coming through the door.

Annalise looked uninjured, but she was completely still. I couldn't even tell if she was breathing or not. It was as if Zahn had switched her off.

The white ribbon wasn't there. I searched again. She only had two ribbons left. Both were green. I knew what they could do, and it was most definitely lethal.

I spit out a string of curses. The sounds of breaking glass came from the church, then a series of gunshots blew through the door. I knew they would be in the room in a minute or two, and I knew what that would mean.

I stuffed the green ribbons into my pocket. I wouldn't use them—I knew I wouldn't—but I wanted to have them just in case.

The gunshots stopped and the kicking began. The mob was trying to bash their way in—even the dead-bolted door that led into the church rattled under the assault. They were coming from all sides. I scrambled to my feet and shoved over the last of the shelves, tipping it against the interior church door just as it began to swing open. I ducked back under cover.

I took the guns out of the back of my pants, then laid Annalise on top of the bags of flour. Her tattoos made her bulletproof; the same spells that had protected her from Merpati's gunmen would protect her from the pets' guns—and they'd protect me, too, if I stayed low enough. That was as much barricade as I was likely to get.

I aimed the old revolver at the door. Damn. Was I really going to do this?

Do what you have to do, Catherine had said. *Whatever it takes.* I remembered little Shannon Conner looking up at me, pleading with me to kill the sapphire dog and give her grandmother back to her.

When was I going to stop holding back?

I squeezed off four shots. A return volley immediately blasted through the door and wall. The bullets poured through like hail, a terrifying mix of rifle and handgun and shotgun blasts.

My skin prickled as I lay flat. I'd never heard such a deafening wall of gunfire, and I thought the incredible, oppressive sound of it alone might kill me.

The volley ended quickly. My ears were ringing, but I could still hear the clicking of empty weapons.

Morning sunlight shone through the holes in the walls like a rack of spears, illuminating the floating plaster dust. I lifted both guns and squeezed the triggers until they were empty.

A second volley came through, but the gunfire was thinner and more scattered. A ricochet tugged at the heel of my shoe, but it didn't touch me. Finally, the shots petered out and all I could hear was the clicking of empty guns.

The pets began to smash through the walls with rifle butts, expanding the openings. I lifted Annalise onto the desk, taking care not to kick the cord of the portable stereo. The ceiling was unfinished, and I could see water pipes and BX cable running between the rafters. I jumped onto the desk and stood over her. With my ghost knife, I cut a two-and-a-half-foot length out of the water pipe. Water gushed freely onto the tile floor as I hefted it. It was heavy, but it would have to do.

More arms and legs were pushing through the growing gaps in the wall. The pets who had been smashing against the interior church door had quit, probably to come around the building. They kicked and bashed at the wall and door, then started trying to squirm through. All I could do was wait.

I reached down and pressed Play on Dolan's portable stereo. It was the old-fashioned kind that played CDs. After a couple of seconds, a Spanish guitar version of "Rudolph the Red-Nosed Reindeer" began to play. Holiday music? It was one more reason to hate the world. I watched the pets breaking in.

The waiting was miserable, and my helplessness and fear made me want to scream. I didn't. I stayed silent and still, and I funneled everything I had into a furious red rage.

If only I had Zahn in front of me, or Stroud, the man who gave the predator to Regina so many years ago. Whether I was a match for them or not, they were the ones I wanted to face. Because of them, the sapphire dog was here and alive, and maybe it would get free again and do this over and over all around the world. All this death and misery was the reason the society fought and killed. Because of this. *This.*

But I couldn't vent my rage at Zahn or Stroud because I didn't have them here; I only had the crazed, ruined people of Washaway. I knew the pets weren't in control of themselves. I knew the sapphire dog was really to blame for the death of Little Mark and so many others. But my anger wasn't logical, and it was so terribly, terribly strong.

Someone wrenched the bullet-ridden door open, shattering the hinges and opening a space big enough for a person to enter. It was Bushy Bill Stookie, and I was almost grateful to him that the fight would finally start.

He laid his meaty hands on the metal shelving and pushed at it, scraping it across the wet tile floor. Others pushed at him to get by, and by then one of the holes in the wall was large enough for more people to squeeze through.

They were all men in this first wave—all strong and heavy, with baseball bats and rifle butts and iron mallets. They sloshed through the water, climbing over the toppled metal shelves toward me. Someone outside let out a trilling, alien war cry, and everyone took it up. They howled as they came at me.

I kicked the portable stereo off the desk. It landed in the water still pouring out of the overhead pipe and splashed onto the tile floor.

Nine men froze in place, muscles twitching. I made sure to count them carefully, so I wouldn't forget. A big, brawny woman pushed through the crowd and stepped into the water. She grimaced and jolted up straight. Ten.

Then the room went dark and silent. Everyone collapsed over the metal shelves, and the woman fell backward through the doorway, bowling through the crowd behind her. So much for saving them from the sapphire dog.

The only light I had left was the daylight shining through the door and the damaged walls. The people pushing their way into the room now were little more than backlit silhouettes. At least I wouldn't have to see their faces.

They were coming with knives, woodworking tools, axe handles, and empty guns. I lifted the iron pipe high and held my left arm low. I didn't have a shield; the tattoos on my forearm would have to do. I put the ghost knife between my teeth. They let out another war scream—a piercing animalistic keening—and I felt like screaming right back at them, but I kept it inside instead, channeling that raw energy to my arms and eyes.

The first guy to get close tripped over Big Bill and fell to his knee in front of me, so I smashed the pipe against his shoulder, knocking him against the one behind him, then I hit the next one hard on the

edge of the wrist, sending his hammer bounding off the wall just as
two more came close, keeping their balance better this time, and I
smashed elbow and shoulder as fast and as hard as I could, blocking a
sharpened hoe with my protected arm, but now the pets were crowding in, stumbling sometimes but not enough for me to keep ahead of
every swing, of every hand reaching for me, of every sound they made,
because I wasn't even looking at their faces anymore, I didn't have time
to guess the attack they'd make based on their eyes or body position,
they were just a mass of bodies rushing at me, and I laid out with my
pipe, swinging everywhere with all my strength against people I'd told
Catherine I didn't want to hurt but here I was, breaking arms and collarbones, and the first time a bat struck the bony point of my hip, the
pain frightened and enraged me so much that I smashed the man wield-
ing it right on the side of his head, and then every dark shape seemed
to be tinged with red as I slapped away attacks with my forearm and
crushed bones with the pipe even though many of them didn't even
have weapons, just hands that reached to pull me down, so I smashed
those, too, watching for knives and swings for my head, and I smashed
wrists and elbows and collarbones and fragile, fragile skulls as the pets
kept coming for me, climbing over the ones I broke, stumbling, slipping
in water and blood and tripping over fallen bodies, then I felt a sudden
sharp pain in my calf and looked down to see a girl no older than thirteen stabbing a long knife into my leg, and my fury and adrenaline and
hatred and rage made it so easy—so easy!—to slam that iron pipe across
both her little arms and I know she screamed even though I couldn't hear
it over the noise the other pets were making but *God* I saw her expression and the whole world should have stopped right at that moment but
they kept coming and I kept fighting and I knew right then that it didn't
matter whether I lived through this, in fact better if I didn't because I was
becoming everything that was raw and evil in this world and I didn't
deserve to be in it anymore, so I screamed, finally, letting out all my anger
and hatred at predators and peers and most of all myself for what I was
doing, because I was not going to stop, not ever, until I had done this
damn job, and the ghost knife that fell out of my mouth began to zip
around the room with the speed of a sparrow, circling me like a rock on
a string, and I just kept hitting and hitting, because I wasn't tired at all,
evil men never tire of doing evil.

Then one of them—Ponytail Sue—finally got the idea to kick the
desk I was standing on. It skidded to the side and I overbalanced, falling
into the pets. They were crammed together as tightly as kids at the front
of a rock concert. I swung at the nearest one, but three or four people
caught my arm and the pipe was yanked out of my grip.

They grabbed me, hands everywhere, pulling my clothes, my hair, my skin, scratching me, screaming at me, bearing me to the floor. Two inches of water splashed up my nose and down my throat. With my free left hand, I reached into my pocket and pulled out one of Annalise's green ribbons, and as I sloshed on the floor, I looked up and saw two kids, neither older than sixteen, lunging for me with knives in their hands and cold, raging murder in their eyes. I slapped the ribbon onto the top of someone's red rubber boot, and I saw the green firelight shine on them.

I closed my eyes. What happened next was something I could not watch.

CHAPTER NINETEEN

When the sound of the fire and the throbbing of the protective spells on my chest finally died away, I opened my eyes again. The room was full of bones. The water sloshed back and forth, and soot and ash made a greasy film on top.

Some of those bones were small. Very small.

Annalise was still lying on top of the desk, and as I expected, she wasn't even singed. I kept looking at her, so small and frail-seeming, but so filled with power, because I didn't want to look at what I'd done.

A shadow moved on the wall. I turned back and saw another person at the door. There were two more behind him and who knows how many I couldn't see.

My dirty work wasn't finished. I moved my foot through the murky water until I found my length of pipe, then I pulled it out of a pile of bones. They came at me.

"They" were a skinny boy of about fourteen, a middle-aged woman with the hunched back of a vulture, and an old man with too much belly and too little biceps. They were all holding hatchets. I could see by their expressions that they weren't going to back down. I didn't need them to. I had my pipe.

It took less than half a minute for me to put all three on the ground. I left them alive because I could, but they wouldn't be bothering anyone for a while.

They screamed curses at me. I was the one who wanted to kill their beloved sapphire dog, and they were sure I deserved to die. I didn't bother to disagree. I felt my ghost knife nearby and *called* it to me. For once, it didn't feel good to have it back. I dragged the last three pets outside.

I carried Annalise to her van and laid her in the back. Then I found a tow truck near the edge of the parking lot with a full ashtray and a pile of fast-food wrappers on the floor. I cracked the ignition and backed it into the corner of the church, smashing through the wood frame and breaking partway inside.

Then I cut my way into the building with the ghost knife and made a slit in the truck's gas tank. I used a book of matches to set a grease-stained brown paper bag alight and let the flames spread. The pews were already engulfed when I ran back to the van.

Someone was going to investigate the deaths in Washaway. Someday. The fire was clumsy, but it would at least explain away the charred bones I'd left behind, as long as no one thought too hard about it.

I had Annalise and I had the van. Leaving town didn't make sense, but I could certainly hide inside Steve's house until another peer arrived. How long could that be? I'd failed to kill the sapphire dog more than once, and now it was with Zahn, a sorcerer strong enough to take out my boss. Sure, I'd surprised him once with a sucker punch, but he'd be ready for me next time. It wasn't as if I had a big bag of tricks.

I had every reason to run. I didn't even know where Zahn had gone, and I certainly wasn't going to drive around looking for his Mercedes with more pets on the loose.

But then I realized there was only one way to transport the sapphire dog.

I turned the key in the ignition and pulled into the road.

My calf started to ache. I looked down and saw blood on my pants. I'd been stabbed. I was also wet, jacketless, and a fucking child-killer. I began to shiver and had to pull to the shoulder of the road until the feeling passed.

I turned the heat on and held my fingers in front of the vent. Then I found a first-aid kit behind the seat and taped a wad of gauze over the stab wound. It wasn't a large cut, certainly not large enough to kill over. I rubbed my hands together to warm them. I'd think about those people tomorrow. Not today. Today I would think about the ones who still needed killing.

I drove past the Breakleys' home and up the long hill toward the Wilbur estate. The gate was wide open. I drove up the long empty driveway and parked just out of sight of the house.

"Don't go anywhere, boss."

I climbed from the van and closed the door as quietly as I could. There was no sound other than the wind through the trees. I jogged uphill toward the house, keeping low.

Beside the house, at the edge of the asphalt parking lot, I found

Esteban's plumbing truck. I went around to the other side and found a half dozen corpses. They were pets, and they had been beaten to death. The nearest one was the pastor—he had a dent in the side of his head about the size of Zahn's fist.

I couldn't beat Zahn in a fair fight, and I didn't see any reason to try. I ran to the corner of the building, squeezed between it and two well-trimmed bushes. The unlit woven Christmas lights snagged at my shirt. I peeked into the nearest window. The room had stacks of fabric and a little sewing machine set where it would catch the sun. No people, though.

I heard broken glass from the backyard. I hoped it was Zahn.

I was only going to get one chance. Jumping out of the bushes wasn't good enough. I needed to hit him before he knew he was being hit.

I cut the lock on the front door, then rushed into the entrance hall. The house was dark, quiet, and smelled like spoiled pork. I rushed to the nearest door on the left and pushed it open. The stink of rotting flesh washed over me. Stephanie Wilbur lay on the floor, still in her green-and-gold outfit, and it was clear she'd been there awhile. Someone had shot her in the chest and closed the door on her.

I hurried to the windows. There were three of them, each twice as tall as me and arched at the top, but made of individual squares of glass no larger than my hand. They gave me a good view of the open back of the truck. I crouched low and pressed my face against the glass, looking toward the backyard. I couldn't see far.

I heard them before I saw them. I stepped away from the window and curled my arm against my chest, ghost knife ready. They were talking very loudly, very excitedly. Or one of them was. Zahn spoke German in a low, somewhat bemused voice, while the other voice was loud but halting, as though the speaker was struggling with the language.

Then they came into view. Zahn was carrying the Plexiglas cage from the cottage, and Ursula was carrying a car battery. The sapphire dog lounged on the bottom of the pen, brightly lit by the floodlights at the corners. It was facing away from me. Ursula babbled enthusiastically.

They did not look up at the house and did not suspect I was watching. When they came about even with me, I threw the ghost knife.

There was only one target that made sense. Ursula wasn't important, and Zahn was too powerful for me to take on. Any fight between us would just set the predator free again and get me killed.

So I aimed straight for the back of the sapphire dog's neck. This time, the creature was facing away from me and trapped inside Zahn's cage. This time it couldn't get away. The ghost knife sliced through the window pane with only a slight *tik*, and then it was through the Plexi and the predator.

I immediately *called* it back. It zipped through the sapphire dog's neck a second time. The creature's head tipped forward and rolled free in the bottom of the cage.

The ghost knife landed in my hand at the same moment that Zahn reacted. He said: "Ah!" and gaped at the predator.

Both of them looked up at me. Ursula glanced at the predator, threw the car battery onto the wet lawn, and turned back at me, her face wild with hate. Then she took off toward the front of the building.

Zahn dropped the now-dark Plexiglas cage. *"Scheiss doch!"* he said, his voice seeming to come from everywhere at once. He raised his arm toward me and opened his palm.

Six shining, buzzing objects came at me, wavering like guided missiles and leaving glowing silver contrails behind them.

Time to go.

I ran for the door, hopping over Stephanie's corpse. The missiles punched through the window glass, and I saw they weren't missiles at all—they were some sort of worm as long and as thick as my thumb, and the little round opening at the front was ringed with tiny, jagged teeth.

Damn. Annalise was wrong. Zahn had brought predators with him.

I rushed into the main hall just as Ursula burst through the front door. She raised a rock the size of a woman's shoe above her head and charged at me, screaming. Guess she'd run out of guns.

I ran at her because I refused to run away. Two of the worms punched through the wall on the right, then two more came a moment behind. Three turned toward me, but the farthest one began to arc toward Ursula.

Damn. As they came close to me, I juked to the left. The worms zipped by, and just being near them made my skin feel sticky and hot. Ursula kept running straight at me—either she didn't notice the predator flying at her, or she didn't care.

I threw my ghost knife. It zipped across the room with astonishing speed and sliced through the worm as it came within inches of her flank. The worm disappeared and reappeared at the spot where it had punched through the wall. It went after her again, and since she was coming at me, it was flying at both of us.

I *reached* for my ghost knife again but didn't watch for it to come into my hand. I had predators on both sides of me and Ursula, too. Not good. And where were the other two worms?

There were stairs at the far side of the room, but I wasn't going to get to them without a fight. Ursula swung the rock in a vicious downward hammer swing, but she'd telegraphed it from ten feet away. I slipped it, grabbed hold of the collar of her ski jacket, and tugged her off course. She stumbled into the sewing room door, smashing through it and sprawling on the floor.

Right beside Stephanie's body. And there, sticking out of Stephanie's corpse, were the tail ends of two shiny worms, wriggling like they were burrowing into an apple. Just as I'd hoped.

I charged into the room and hauled Stephanie's body off the ground. It felt sluggish and heavy, and the room filled with a nasty wet odor. I forced myself to ignore all that and rushed toward the door, getting between Ursula and Zahn's predators.

All four worms zipped straight into the dead body, attracted to whatever meat they could find. And while I knew the society didn't want me to use them against a human enemy like Ursula, I didn't think they'd mind if I used a corpse as a shield.

Then Stephanie's head jerked up. She opened her rotted eyes and looked directly at me.

I screamed something unintelligible and shoved her, stumbling, into the main room. I heard Ursula getting to her feet behind me, and I ducked through the door. I didn't want my enemies on both sides of me.

Stephanie wobbled, barely able to keep her balance, as the worms disappeared under her stained clothes. Ursula had found a pair of scissors somewhere and was cursing at me in her native language, whatever it was, as she stumbled through the door. I backed away from them both, wondering how I would get to the hall, then the kitchen, and finally the back door, because I expected Zahn to step through the open front door at any moment. And I knew I'd be a dead man if he found me here.

A blast of white fire tore through the wall near the front door. The flames looked like they were roaring through an invisible hose four feet thick, and the spell came from the same spot where Zahn had been standing when I hit the sapphire dog. Maybe he wasn't coming through the front door after all.

The white fire began to sweep slowly across the room like a flashlight beam, incinerating doors, walls, and support posts. I heard, again, the sound of screaming that I'd heard when the pastor's house had been destroyed, but because I was close to the spell, I could tell that it wasn't just one scream but dozens, maybe hundreds of voices—as if the fire still held the deaths of all the lives it had taken.

I jumped back, hitting the edge of the stairs, then vaulted up onto them. Ursula threw herself to the floor as the beam of fire reached her, and Stephanie—or the creatures inside her—didn't have the same control. It seemed to suddenly lose all strength and collapsed to the floor.

The fire churned through the opposite wall, then dipped down through the floor. I retreated upstairs, watching the bottom of the staircase burn to ashes.

Then the fire stopped. The scorched edges of the wooden floor and walls sputtered with pale flames for a moment but quickly went out. A loud crash from the left drew my attention, and I saw the wall buckle.

Ursula stared up at me from the floor. Her face was pale and her eyes wide with shock. Death had come awfully close to her. She turned and scrambled on her hands and knees toward the front door. Stephanie was nowhere in sight. Hopefully, she'd burned to cinders.

I glanced to my right and looked through the hole that blast of fire had bored through the house. There was Zahn, still standing just where I'd left him, Plexi cage on the ground at his side. The cage looked different—rounder—but I didn't have the time to study it. Zahn smiled, drew his arm back, and made a throwing motion. A chunk of the wall disappeared at the edge of the fire-blasted hole, then another, larger piece of the wall between the sewing room and the room I was in popped out of existence.

Whatever it was, it was coming right at me.

I sprinted up the stairs and leaped to the left. The invisible thing he'd thrown passed behind me, erasing the steps and wiping away part of the upstairs floor. And it had grown larger, too. I looked through the hole it left at the open mountainside and wondered just how far it would go before the spell stopped turning something into nothing.

Just ahead was the servants' stairs leading down to the back door. I ran to the top as another jet of white fire swept through the floor below, destroying the lower flight and wall beyond the way a lazy hand might clear fog off a misty window.

I turned and ran back the other way, leaping over the gap in the floor. The whole building shifted and jolted, and I fell to the threadbare carpet. Somewhere close, lumber cracked and splintered, making noises as loud as gunshots. I needed to get out of this house and out of Zahn's sights as fast as I could, and the most direct way was through the big arching front windows.

The room with the white sheets over the furniture was just ahead. I lunged upward and threw my shoulder against the door. It didn't open—it broke into pieces, already cracked from the collapsing jamb above it.

Once through, I fell to the floor, sliding on my knees along the sloping floorboards. The room was collapsing toward a huge hole in the center, and I could see the piles of basement clutter all the way down at the bottom.

The whole house shuddered. A wardrobe tilted away from the wall and slammed to the floor. I struggled to my feet as it slid at me, and I tried to jump up and run along the flat back of it but ended up clumsily stumbling across it instead.

I sprawled on the floor again as the entire house lurched. Plaster dust fell onto the back of my neck, and I managed to stand. I did not want to die in here. Not like this. Another blast of white fire sliced upward through the floor, cutting the wall with the tall front windows from the rest of the house.

Everything *leaned* toward the front, and I thought the whole building might fold up right then, pinching me into jelly. There was no way to get out by the front—the gaps were too iffy to jump, and I couldn't trust the floor to hold me even if I made it across. I had to try the back of the house.

The floor dropped beneath me—just a foot—but it was enough to slam me to my knees again. I imagined myself falling backward onto all that clutter below: the overturned chairs, furniture corners, everything. At this height I'd be lucky to only break my back. Goose bumps ran down my back and arms, and I scrambled on my hands and knees toward the door.

Stephanie came toward me.

God, the smell was awful. I struggled to my feet, determined not to die on my knees. She was standing on a cloud of silver smoke a foot or two off the buckled floorboards. Where her eyes should have been, two worms wagged back and forth, their mouths gaping wide enough to show little teeth.

The wall behind her suddenly vanished, and I knew another spell was coming. I lunged at her just as she reached me, but I was faster. Her ankle squished like a bag of jelly when I grabbed it, but I squeezed tight and pulled, tipping her off balance. She fell back as the spell advanced, and I leapt up toward the broken doorway.

Zahn's spell swept over her and erased her from the world. I grabbed the edge of the doorframe and pulled myself through, barely clearing the edge of the spell.

I scurried along the hall toward Regina's room. She had a window in there, even if getting out that way would leave me on the wrong side of the house. The floor was so crooked that I had to run along the corner where it met the wall. The building groaned and shuddered, and something somewhere close snapped. The sound was as loud as a sledgehammer's blow.

Regina's door was already open, although her bed had slid against the crooked frame. I climbed over it, kicking at the covers as they tried to tangle my legs. I tread on Regina's framed photos, smashing the glass.

The exterior wall leaned above me. When I lifted the window, it slid open like a blessing. I caught hold of the bottom of the sill and started to pull myself through just as everything began to come apart with a sound like a series of small explosions. My footing fell away and the wall rushed toward me. In a burst of desperate strength, I pulled myself through the open window, ignoring the sawdust billowing into my face and the shards of glass striking it.

The wall plummeted around me as I lurched through it. I tumbled down the outside of the house, feeling as though I had used the last of my strength and willpower. I fell into the grass, and somehow landed on the side of the house, practically right on the spot where Fat Guy had been crouching when I'd cut his shotgun apart.

I forced myself to sit up. I was exhausted, and when I looked up, I saw Zahn and Ursula standing where I'd left them. Both were staring at me; Ursula looked pale and shell-shocked; Zahn had a grim smile on his face.

I couldn't make myself care anymore. I'd destroyed the sapphire dog, just as I'd said I would, and I didn't have any more willpower left. Not after everything I'd done. I was finished, and they could see it on my face.

The Plexiglas cage behind Ursula and Zahn had somehow shrunk. I looked at it more closely and saw that it wasn't only the cage that had changed shape. Everything—space itself—had bent toward the cut in the sapphire dog's neck. The cage, the battery, and the ground they rested on bowed inward as though the world was being pulled into the predator's body.

But Zahn didn't see it because he was focused on me. He opened his coat and drew a playing card from an inside pocket with well-practiced ease. The warp suddenly expanded, and the edges trembled as though under tremendous strain. I could feel the distortion inside me, like an urge to scream.

Zahn turned toward it, surprised. Ursula gasped. The warp suddenly swelled and both of their bodies twisted as though they had stepped into a funhouse mirror.

Then the warp released in a single overwhelming blast.

I remember the light, but I don't think there was any sound. I felt myself silently lifted up and thrown across the grass.

The light was bright and pure. It filled everything, and it seemed to be full of watching eyes.

I woke on the grass at the base of the hill a couple of dozen feet from where I'd been. Nothing seemed to be broken. I snapped my fingers and heard the sound, which was a tremendous relief.

I checked that I still had my ghost knife, then moved toward the house. Ursula and Zahn lay on the lawn. They weren't whole, though. You couldn't have made a whole body out of both of them combined. There was no blood anywhere, just a lack of parts.

Then I saw a flash of blue near the front of the house. I walked around the bodies, trying not to look at them. I felt hollowed out, and I wasn't ready to fill that empty space with the sight of more dead people, even these.

On the front lawn, the two halves of the sapphire dog's body were fading in and out, appearing here and there in a seemingly random way. It wasn't until I realized that the ghost knife had cut through the predator's eyes, blinding it, that I understood that the two parts were trying to find each other.

The hedge closest to the truck had been spared the collapse of the Wilbur house. I quietly took a set of the woven Christmas lights off the top. There was an electric outlet set in the back of the cube truck. I plugged the lights into it, and they lit up dimly.

I clicked my tongue. The ears on the creature's head suddenly turned toward me, then the head vanished and appeared beside me. I draped the lights over it, then folded it twice for good measure. It stopped vanishing and reappearing. I had trapped it. It wasn't the lights—it liked the light—it was the live wires that the predator couldn't cross. The cages had been spiderwebbed with wires, and the pets had been careful to run cables along only three walls in the field house, leaving one open for an escape route.

I held my hand away from my body and snapped my fingers. When the predator shot its tongue toward the sound, I sliced it off with the ghost knife. The severed tongue fell into the mud and shriveled there. Its body staggered, then crumpled to the ground and lay still.

The head could only twitch its ears. I wondered if it could understand me. "Stay away from my world," I whispered to it. The ears twitched back and forth as though it couldn't find the source of my voice. "There are monsters here."

The head shrunk and bowed in on itself. I backpedaled, but there was no second explosion. The head, tongue, and body each seemed to be sucked into a tiny spot, and then they were gone.

There was still another job to do. I walked to the side of the house. All that was left of Ursula was a pair of legs and the hips to hold them together. The rest of her body was simply gone. Even stranger was that there was no gore or exposed organs at the severed part of her torso. That part of her was covered with smooth, unmarked skin, as though she had grown that way naturally.

Zahn was missing his body from the ribs down. He was also missing one arm from just below the shoulder and the other from just below the elbow. When I bent to see if he also had skin over the severed part of his torso, he called me an asshole.

Yeah, I was startled. I knew sorcerers were tough, but this was a bit much.

"Feed me, and I will teach you," he said. His voice sounded low and strained. "I will show you the world behind the world."

"Pass. I've seen how you treat your people. No loyalty."

"They were simpletons and they failed me. But you are something else, yes? Not even a true sorcerer, and look what you did."

"That's what I do," I told him. My voice sounded flat, and it scared me a little. "I kill."

"I do not believe you. I can see it. You have killed, but you are not a natural killer. You *care* too much for that. The Twenty Palace Society has lied to you, the way they lie to everyone."

"Is this conversation going to take long? Because my socks are wet."

"And you want *power*. For three hundred years I have been looking for someone clever enough to pass my secrets to. I think that could be you. I need meat. Care enough to save my life, and you save three hundred years of history. In return, I will show you real power the *Hosenscheisser* in the society cannot. Come on, boy. Care enough to save one more life."

I couldn't help it. I laughed at him. "You don't get it, do you? I killed kids today because of the deal you made with that predator. *Kids!* If you think I'm going to . . ."

Why was I talking to him?

I dragged the ghost knife through his torso. Black steam blasted out of him. The smooth skin over the bottom of his rib cage where the rest of his body should have been suddenly burst open. He lost blood and magic in a tremendous rush.

I hit him again and again, and it took me a few seconds to realize that he was laughing as well as screaming.

"A ghost knife!" he wheezed. "You are killing me with a ghost knife, and you cast it on a piece of paper!" He screamed, then laughed again, straining every muscle. "I'll bet you do not even realize what you've done!"

I didn't feel like being laughed at just then. I dragged my spell through his face and head, then stuffed Annalise's last green ribbon into his mouth. That was it for him.

Once Zahn was dead, I suddenly thought it might be a good idea to call someone outside Washaway who could help. I took a deep breath and let relief flood through me. The town was no longer sealed. Help would be coming very soon.

I gave his three-hundred-year-old bones a kick for the hell of it.

In the truck I found the lightning rod Zahn had used to summon the floating storms, along with a carpetbag loaded with candles, jars, amulets, and other suspicious crap, all in a mixed-up jumble.

I set all that stuff at the top of the driveway. Then I dragged the bodies into an opening in the side of the house, dropping them into the basement. That was an ugly job, but I didn't have much choice. I wondered whether Regina had gotten away, or was crushed under a beam in the wreckage or rotting in a ditch somewhere, feeding the crows. Maybe I'd never know.

I parked the truck next to the house and lit them both on fire.

It started to rain again as I made my way to the van. The wind was cold. Annalise was as still as before. I loaded the old man's gear into the back of the van and drove away.

EPILOGUE

I hit Redial on Annalise's cell and told the tweedy-sounding guy who answered what was going on. He seemed pissed that I'd called, but to hell with him. After I disconnected the call, I had an itch to call all the hospitals in the area to ask about my mother. It made no sense at all, but the urge was there.

I drove home. It took four hours, but another society investigator was already waiting for me there. I told him and his recorder everything that happened and showed him the stuff I'd taken from Zahn. He seemed impressed for about three seconds, then called up his poker face again.

When I asked about Annalise, he told me not to worry, they had someone who would be able to find her. I was about to tell him to look in the back of the van, because the search was over, but maybe he meant something I didn't understand.

After that, he left. I half expected him to offer me a ride to a safe house or something, but he didn't. I didn't ask.

I didn't deserve to be safe.

I reported my credit cards stolen and called Harvey. I told him I could work my usual shift after the holiday, and he didn't even ask about my mom. Maybe he heard something in my voice and thought better of it.

The fires and violence in Washaway made the national news, of course, but it took a while for the authorities to settle on a story they liked. While they were hashing it out, the remaining pets died. As I'd expected, killing the predator hadn't saved them. Whatever the sapphire dog did to their brains had cut their lives short. None of them survived to the end of the week.

Maybe that should have made me feel better about what I'd done in the food bank, but it didn't.

The state cops, the FBI, Homeland Security, and news crews from every part of the world descended on Washaway. The feds quashed talk of a terrorist attack, but it took a while before they decided to blame it all on international drug violence and the brave local citizens who were killed in the crossfire. Hanging those accusations on Yin and Zahn was a stretch for some folks, but no one had a better explanation. As for Kripke and Solorov, they were inconveniently alive and spent a fortune on lawyers trying to stay out of prison.

Two full shifts of 911 dispatchers lost their jobs for small-talking when they should have been raising alarm bells. Steve Cardinal was singled out for special scorn—they even played a couple of his friendly calls to the state police on the TV. It was unfair to him, but he was past caring.

But I didn't follow any of this from the comfort of my apartment. By Christmas morning, the cops had found my name and brought me in.

I disappeared from the world.

ACKNOWLEDGMENTS

This was not an easy book to write, and I'm tremendously grateful to the people who helped me put it together: Betsy Mitchell, Caitlin Blasdell, Liza Dawson, Beth Pearson, Margaret Wimberger, and many, many others. Thank you all.

CIRCLE
OF
ENEMIES

For my son, who isn't old enough to read it yet

CHAPTER ONE

It was August in Seattle, when the city enjoyed actual sunshine and temperatures in the eighties. I'd spent the day working, which made for a nice change. I'd just finished a forty-hour temp landscaping job; dirt and dried sweat made my face and arms itch. I hated the feeling, but even worse was that I didn't have anything lined up for next week.

As I walked up the alley toward home, I passed a pair of older women standing beside a scraggly vegetable garden. One kept saying she was sweltering, *sweltering,* but her friend didn't seem sympathetic. Neither was I. I was used to summers in the desert.

When they noticed me, they fell silent. The unsympathetic one took her friend's hand and led her toward the back door, keeping a wary eye on me. That didn't bother me, either.

I stumped up the stairs to my apartment above my aunt's garage. It was too late to call the temp agency tonight. I'd have to try them early Monday morning. Not that I had much hope. It was hard for an ex-con to find work, especially an ex-con with my name.

I'm Raymond Lilly, and I've lost track of the number of people I've killed.

My ancient garage-sale answering machine was blinking. I played the messages. Two were from reporters, one from a journalist-blogger, and one from a writer. They offered me the chance to tell my side of what happened in Washaway last Christmas. Except for the writer's, I recognized all the voices—they'd called often over the last few weeks, sometimes several times a day.

I absentmindedly rubbed the tattoos on the back of my hands. They looked like artless jailhouse squiggles, but in reality they were magic spells, and without them I'd be behind bars. None of the survivors in

Washaway could pick me out of a lineup, and none of the fingerprint or DNA evidence I'd left behind pointed to me anymore. I was on the twisted path.

I erased the messages. There was no point in calling them back. None of them understood the meaning of the words *fuck off*.

The sounds of their voices had triggered a low, buzzing anger that made me feel slightly out of control. I showered, then dropped my work clothes into the bottom of the tub, scrubbed them clean, and hung them from the curtain rod. I felt much better after that.

I wiped steam from the bathroom window and looked out. My aunt had not hung a paper angel in her kitchen window. That meant I could order in a sandwich for dinner. I put on my sleeping clothes: a T-shirt and a pair of cutoff sweatpants. I could eat alone, in silence, without someone asking how I was sleeping, how I was eating, and wouldn't things be better if I went to talk to someone?

I wouldn't have to say *Thank you, but I can't* a half dozen times. My aunt was right; I'd probably sleep better if I could talk about the nightmares—and what I'd done to bring them on—but I'd be bedding down in a padded room.

I opened the bathroom door to dispel the steam, even though an unlocked door felt like a gun at my back. Then I turned to the mirror and looked carefully. Damn. I was wasting away.

A voice behind me said: "You look like shit."

I yelped and spun around. In an instant, my heart was pounding in my chest as my hand fumbled across the sink for something to use as a weapon.

Caramella was standing in the bathroom doorway, and I was so startled to see her that everything went still for a moment. My adrenaline eased, and I could hear my harsh breath in the silence. It had been more than five years, and she'd changed quite a bit. Her skin, which had once been so dark, seemed lighter, as though she spent all her time indoors, and while she still straightened her hair, now she had it up in a bun. She wore orange pants with an elastic waistband and a white halter. She'd gained some weight and she seemed taller somehow.

But she didn't belong here in Seattle. She belonged down in L.A., hanging at the Bigfoot Room with Arne, Robbie, and the rest.

I almost asked her what she was doing here, but I didn't want her to think she wasn't welcome. In truth, I didn't know how I felt about her. "Welcome to my bathroom," I said.

"Thanks. I hate it."

I nodded but didn't respond right away. Her hands were empty, although she might have stuffed a gun into the back of her waistband.

Not that I could imagine why she'd want to kill me, but that was how my mind worked now.

"I'm guessing you're not here for old times' sake."

"We don't have any old times, Ray." She turned and walked into the other room.

I followed her, noting that she didn't have a weapon under her waistband. "Then why are you here?" I kept my tone as neutral as I could, although I had less self-control than I used to.

"I'm paying a debt," she said, as though it was the most bitter thing in the world. "I have to deliver a message to you. In person." She stopped beside the efficiency stove.

"Okay. Here I am."

She looked away. Her lip curled and she blinked several times. Christ, she was about to cry. "You killed me, Ray."

I gaped at her, astonished. She turned and slapped me on the shoulder. Then she did it again. That still wasn't enough, so she slapped my face and head four or five times. I didn't try to stop her.

Finally, she stopped on her own. Hitting me wasn't bringing her any satisfaction. "You killed me," she said again. "And you killed Arne, and Lenard, and Ty, and all the others, too. We're all going to die because we knew you."

"Melly, what are you talking about?"

"Sorry," she said with a wet sniffle. I looked for tears on her face, but her cheeks were dry. "That's the message. That's all you get."

She swung at my face again. I flinched, but the blow never struck. When I opened my eyes a moment later, I was alone in the room.

I had been standing between Caramella and the door; she couldn't have gotten around me and gotten out, not in the time it took me to flinch. I walked around the little studio anyway. She was gone—vanished in the blink of an eye.

Magic. She had magic. Damn.

My cheek and scalp were sticky where she'd slapped me, and the stickiness was starting to burn. I went into the bathroom and washed my face and head. I could feel a smear of acidic goop that was so thin I couldn't even see it. Plain water washed it away completely. My clean skin was slightly tender, but the pain had eased.

I checked the washrag, but it didn't have any unusual stains or smells. I hung it over the kitchen faucet.

Crossing the room, I took my ghost knife from its hiding place on my bookshelf. It was only a piece of scrap paper, smaller than the palm of my hand, with a layer of mailing tape over it and some laminate over that. On the paper itself was a sigil I had drawn with a ballpoint pen. It felt alive, and it felt like a part of me, too. The other magic I had, the tattoos on my chest, arms, and neck, were protections that had been cast on me by someone else. The ghost knife was my spell, the only one I had.

Then I took my cellphone out of my sock drawer. After the mess in Washaway, an investigator for the Twenty Palace Society met me on the street and slipped me a phone number. They trusted me enough to give me a way to contact them, which was damned rare and I knew it.

The society was a group of sorcerers committed to one end: hunting down magic spells and the people who used them, then destroying both. They were especially determined to find summoning spells, which could call strange creatures to our world from a place referred to as, variously, the Empty Spaces or the Deeps. These creatures, called predators, could grant strange powers, if the summoner knew how to properly control them. Too often, the summoner didn't know, and the predator got loose in the world to hunt.

I was a low-level member of that society, but except for my boss, Annalise, who had put the magical tattoos on me, I knew very little about it. How many peers were there? How many investigators? How many wooden men, besides me, did they have? Where were they based? Where did their money come from?

I had no idea and no way to find out. The Twenty Palace Society took its secrecy seriously. I hadn't been invited to secret headquarters, hadn't trained at a secret camp, hadn't been given a secret handbook with an organizational flow chart at the back. When they wanted me to do something, they contacted me, and they told me as little as they could.

What I did know was this: peers live a very long time—centuries, in some cases—and the magic they use has left them barely human. Oh, they look human enough, but they have become something else.

And they were bastards, too—ruthless killers who took a scorched-earth policy when it came to predators and enemy sorcerers. As a group, they didn't seem to care much about collateral damage.

They had their reasons. A single predator, let loose in the world, could strip it of life. I'd visited the Empty Spaces once and seen it happen. So maybe the peers were justified in their "kill a hundred to save six billion" attitude, but it was a slim consolation if your loved one was among the hundred.

Which was why I set the cell back on the bureau. Caramella had vanished right in front of me. It was magic, yeah, but calling the Twenty Palace Society and asking Annalise to meet me in L.A. was as good as taking a hit out on Melly and everyone else I knew. Annalise would first determine who, where, and how they had been touched by magic—spells didn't strike people out of the sky like lightning. Magic powers, enchantments, and hungry predators were things people *did* to one another.

After that, Annalise would kill them all just to be safe, and I would be the one who'd hung a bull's-eye on their backs.

God, I couldn't kill more people. It was too soon.

An overwhelming weariness came over me. Too little sleep and a full day's work in the sun had left me exhausted. I smeared peanut butter on a slice of bread and ate it with all the enthusiasm you would expect, then climbed into bed. I wasn't ready for a long trip south. I didn't have the energy for it.

I closed my eyes and fell into a dead sleep. I dreamed of fire, and mobs of people coming at me in the darkness, and brutal violence. I woke screaming at five in the morning.

I grabbed my ready bag, my ghost knife, and my cellphone. I wrote a note to my aunt explaining that I would be away for a few days. Then I went out into the summer darkness, climbed into my rusty Ford Escort, and drove south.

It was a long trip, and I had plenty of time to think. Too much time, really. It had surprised me when Melly had said we didn't have old times. I'd met her when I was seventeen, still stealing cars for Arne and feeling a little cocky about it. She'd been a couple of years older, and I'd tried to smooth talk her. It was the first time a woman had ever laughed at me without making me angry or ashamed. She took me under her wing, sort of, and we became friends.

Until then, I hadn't thought men and women could really be friends—not that I'd become a man yet, no matter what I'd thought of myself. She had been kind to me when she didn't have to, and she had yanked on my leash whenever I got too full of myself. I'd done things for her, too: fixed her car a dozen times, helped her move, and the one time an ex-boyfriend had threatened her, I'd broken his thumbs as an important lesson in good manners.

Never mind the times she'd lifted cash from my wallet. That's how we'd lived back then. I always felt I'd never done enough to repay her for the things she'd done for me. And now she'd denied we'd had good times at all.

Maybe it should have stung more, but it didn't. I'd spent three years in Chino, and the two years after that had been centered on the society and its work. Caramella was like a ghost from another life come to haunt me—a life where we'd told one another we were brothers and sisters but I'd had to sleep with my wallet in my pocket. I could barely remember how that felt.

I drove straight through, taking twenty-three hours with meals and bathroom breaks. Most of the time I was in a trance, but as I approached the city, passing through dry, brown hills wrinkled like unfolded laundry, I could feel my anxieties gathering strength.

Then I was inside the city in the cool, dry predawn, riding on an elevated highway with barriers along both sides. I could see treetops and the roofs of houses laid out around me; I was skimming above the city, and felt it beneath and around me. It gave me the same tingle I got standing outside a lion's cage at the zoo.

I was exhausted. I pulled off the freeway into the parking lot of an IKEA, drove up to the top level, and shut everything down. I slumped in the seat and shut my eyes.

Everything was wrong. I was back in L.A., but I felt like a pod-person imitation of the man I used to be. Stealing cars, getting high, spending hours on the PlayStation or hitting the bag at the gym—none of that matched who I was now. Now I had bulletproof tattoos on my chest, neck, and arms. Now I had tattooed spells that obscured evidence of crimes I'd committed, plus others that did who knows what. Now I was a killer of men, women, and children.

Sleep overtook me and I woke up around ten-thirty feeling sore but without my usual parade of bad dreams. This level of the parking lot was still empty. Already sweating from the morning heat, I started the engine, filled the gas tank at a station on the corner, and drove to the Bigfoot Room.

It wasn't really called the Bigfoot Room. It had changed names several times over the dozen or so years I'd spent as a member of Arne's crew, and the latest name was the Dingaling Bar. I nearly laughed. I couldn't imagine Arne in a bar called the Dingaling. I parked in the lot beside it and walked around to the front. The wall above the door was recessed slightly, and coated with dust. Years ago, Arne had brought a bar stool out front, climbed up, and written BIGFOOT ROOM in the dust with his finger.

"That's our sign, just for us," he'd said. And while the bar had changed hands three times, no one had ever noticed his writing or tried to wash it away.

It was gone now. Someone had swiped a hand through the dust, erasing the words.

I went inside anyway. The place had been remodeled, but there were still booths in the back corner. Arne wasn't there, and neither were Robbie, Summer, or any of the others.

A brief conversation with the bartender confirmed that he didn't know Arne. This wasn't the Bigfoot Room anymore. I recognized the barfly sitting by the jukebox, but he didn't recognize me. He claimed not to remember Arne, either, even though Arne had bought him drinks many times over the years. He had the flat, burned-out eyes of a mannequin.

I ordered an egg sandwich and coffee, mainly so I could use the dirty bathroom. When the bill came, I asked for a phone book. Violet Johnson's name was in there. I paid and left.

Vi still lived in the same place in Studio City. I drove over there, feeling vaguely sick at the idea of seeing her again. Or maybe it was the egg sandwich. Melly had been like a big sister to me, but Violet was the girl I wanted for keeps. I'd wanted us to buy a house together, the whole deal. The three years I did in Chino were because of a punch I threw while defending her kid brother. She was also the one who dumped me just before my arraignment, and I hadn't even heard her name since.

I had to park two blocks from her place, but I managed to find a spot. Her neighborhood was so familiar that it felt eerie. Walking down this same sidewalk felt like wearing a costume, as though I was disguising myself as a younger me. I went up her same front walk to her same row of mailbox slots. I even remembered her apartment code. I buzzed her. Her voice, when she answered, sounded thin.

"Who is it?"

"It's Ray," I said, the way I'd said it many times before. Then I remembered there were five years between us, and I added, "Ray Lilly."

She didn't answer right away. She did press the gate buzzer. I pushed the gate open and went inside. The courtyard and little pool looked the same; no one was swimming. She was on the third floor, and I headed up the stairs.

She was already standing in the open doorway, waiting for me. It took me a moment to recognize her. She looked smaller and thinner than I remembered. Her thick brown curls were pulled back into a simple ponytail, and she wore no makeup at all. Like Melly's, her skin looked lighter than it had, although she'd always been lighter than Melly. She no longer wore the little stud in the left side of her nose.

I used to tease her when she looked this way; I'd always liked the hair, makeup, and shoes—what Vi had called hyper-girly. Now I felt embarrassed by the memory, but I didn't feel much else.

"Melly warned me you might show up here."

Warned her? I didn't have any reaction to that. After a second look, I realized she had dark circles under her eyes.

"Ray, you look terrible."

"It was a long drive," I said.

"Do you want to come in? You can't stay, but . . ."

"I can't stay, no, but I would like to come in."

The first thing I noticed was how cool it was in the air-conditioned apartment. The second thing was the toys. There were several different types of dolls lying about: rag dolls, Barbies, baby dolls in diapers. A huge dollhouse stood in the corner. Beneath the toys, all the furniture was the same threadbare yard-sale stuff she'd had years before.

I glanced at the couch, remembering all the things we'd done there. Then a little girl came out of the kitchen, a half-eaten peanut butter and jelly sandwich in her hand. Her skin was much lighter than Vi's—nearly golden—and her hair was just a little too dark to be called blond.

"Mommy, can I have a hot dog?"

Vi bent down to her. "You already have your lunch, sweetie. Right in your hand."

"So?"

"Don't answer me that way," Vi said, a note of warning in her voice.

The girl stepped around her mom. "Hi, I'm Jasmin. Who are you?"

"My name is Ray. You're a very big girl, aren't you?" My voice sounded hollow and strange.

"Yes, I'm five."

Vi bent down to steer her toward the kitchen. "Jazzy, eat at the table, okay? If you're still hungry after your sandwich, you can have some raisins. If you behave."

Raisins were the only incentive she needed. She turned and ran into the kitchen.

Vi looked me in the eye. "She's not yours."

I didn't know what to say to that. "No?"

"No. And I know you can do the math, Ray, but it was a long time ago."

If I added nine months onto five years, it was pretty clear that she *could* have been mine. Vi had always been careful with me, saying she wanted to wait for kids, but apparently she'd had someone else on the side. Someone she was not so careful with. "Okay."

"That's it? *Okay?* Two years we were together, and you're not going to shout at me? Call me a whore with my little girl in the next room to hear? You're not going to take a swing at me? You're not angry or hurt or nothing?"

"When did I ever take a swing at you?" But I knew that wasn't what she meant, exactly. Maybe I should have been angry or hurt— she was the woman I'd planned to spend the rest of my life with—but I was secretly relieved. If Vi had stuck with me, she might have been caught up in the society, too. She'd dodged a bullet when she dumped me. "It's been a long time for me, too."

She crossed her arms over her chest, a sure sign that I was pissing her off. "Fair enough. What did you come here for?"

"Melly came to me and told me she and Arne and everyone was in trouble, and that it's my fault." I almost said *I want to save them.* "I need to find out what's going on."

"Well, I don't know anything about it. I'm not a part of that anymore."

"Fair enough. Where can I find Arne?"

She scowled and looked around the little apartment. For a moment I thought she would throw me out without an answer. Instead, she said: "You could have called me, you know. You could have written me a letter."

"I thought you didn't want me to call" was the only answer I had. I didn't mention the three years I'd spent in jail without hearing a word from her, or that she'd specifically told me to go away.

"You could have tried anyway." When I didn't respond, she shrugged her bony shoulders and dismissed all of it. "He has a new Bigfoot Room. I don't know where it is, though. I have a straight job now, and I'm a goddamn citizen. You should ask Tyalee. I think he's still in touch with all of them."

"Where—"

"Ty has a straight job, too. He's a trainer at a gym now."

"Do you know the name of the place?"

"Nope. But it's across the street from that jungle restaurant. Remember that place you took me to, where everything came with sweet potatoes and mangoes?"

"I remember."

"His gym is in the shopping mall across the street. Don't ask me about the others. I have nothing to do with those people now."

"Thank you." There should have been more for me to say, but I wasn't sure how to come at it. "How's Mouse? I mean, how's Tommy?" Mouse was Violet's younger brother, and I'd forgotten that we weren't supposed to use his nickname anymore.

"Gone," she said. "He skipped town."

I knew her well enough to know she was holding something back, but if she didn't want to talk, I couldn't force her. I supposed I didn't have the right, not after five years, but I was still concerned about her. "Are you doing okay?"

"I'm fine," she said. "You're the one who looks like a hungry ghost."

As I went to the door, Jasmin came out of the kitchen. She watched me leave with a careful expression and, just before the door shut behind me, I heard her say very clearly: "That man scared me."

It was nearly noon, and L.A. felt like a blast furnace. I walked slowly to my car. There was no way I could avoid a ring of sweat under my arms and back, but I could keep it small by going slow.

Unfortunately, my Escort was a Seattle car. The wiper blades were brand new, but it didn't have air-conditioning.

It was a short two miles to the restaurant, and the gym was exactly where she'd said it'd be. The name was EVERYTHING ATHLETIC, and a sign in the glass door announced that it was the home of the founder of the original "Cardio-eira" classes. There were no windows, so I just pushed my way inside.

A sign at the front desk said that all of Justin Gage's Cardio-eira classes had been canceled until the end of the month. As I was reading it, a pale young woman with dyed-black hair at the front desk asked if she could help me. Her eyes were rimmed with red, and her face was puffy. She had been crying.

"What's wrong?" I asked, more out of surprise than concern.

"Oh, I'm sorry," she said. "I just . . . Are you a member?"

"I'm not. I've never been here before."

"Okay. You should know that the Cardio-eira classes have been canceled, and we don't know when they'll be starting again. If ever."

"What happened?" I asked, because she seemed to expect me to.

"Justin was assaulted last night. Right out in the parking lot. He's in the hospital, and we don't know . . . he's in bad shape."

"I'm very sorry," I said. "Did they catch the guy who did it?"

"No," she said. "They have no idea who did it."

A heavily muscled black woman stepped in to join the conversation. "We do have other trainers here." I noticed that her name tag read MANAGER along the bottom. "And while they may not have the same infomercial cachet that Justin has, they're really quite excellent."

"What about Tyalee Murphy? Is he here?"

The manager was carefully neutral. "He's finishing up with a member at the moment. Are you a friend of his?"

"I'd like to talk to him, if I could."

"Why don't you have a seat?"

She gestured toward an overstuffed little couch beside a rack of swim goggles. I sat. The manager typed something into a handheld device without looking at me. The weepy employee handed out keys and towels to people who entered, and collected them from people who left. I heard the sad tale of Justin Gage several more times over the course of five minutes. He was apparently a much-loved figure, and no one had any idea what had happened to him, and wasn't this city just awful?

Eventually, a tall black man rushed into the lobby and said: "You paged me?"

The manager pointed toward me, but I was already standing out of the chair. Ty turned toward me and looked me up and down. He didn't recognize me.

He looked different, too. He'd shaved his head and his chin and, while he'd always been addicted to the gym, now he was almost a parody of fitness. His uniform—a black polyester shirt with the gym logo over the heart—was tight enough to show off all the curves of his muscles.

"Ty, it's me. Ray Lilly."

"Ray!" He almost shouted. He stepped toward me, and for a moment I thought he'd hug me. Instead, he wrapped his gloved hand around mine and pumped, smiling broadly. "Good to see you again, man. Good to see you. What brings you back to town?"

I was almost sorry to answer him. "A little trouble, unfortunately." Melly had said I'd killed him, but he didn't look unhappy. I needed to find out what he knew, especially where the magic had come from, but I couldn't do it in a crowded gym.

"Hey, if there's anything I can do, name it." He glanced back through the door to the workout area beyond, as though he hadn't meant to promise so much. "I mean, things are a little busy *right now* . . ."

I wasn't sure what to make of him. We'd always gotten along, but I didn't think we were close enough for him to be so glad to see me again. "Ty, I'm looking for the new Bigfoot Room."

"No problem! It's at a place called the Roasted Seal over on Kalibel Ave. Remember that Baja Fresh where Mouse puked in the toilet? Right there. I'm not part of that scene anymore, you understand. I still *know* the guys, but I don't do stuff with them anymore. Not much, anyway."

Everyone had grown up and turned into citizens. Except me. "Thanks."

"Listen, um . . ." He glanced back into the workout area. "I'm a little busy right now. We're short-handed today and I'm covering another dude's clients. Plus, I *really* need the money." He laughed a little at himself, and at the slightly desperate note in his voice. "But I'll catch up with you soon, okay? You're okay, aren't you? You look a little worn thin. Take care of yourself in this heat. And thank you, man. Thank you."

He checked his watch and rushed back inside. I headed out to my car.

I sat behind the wheel and closed my eyes. I'd taken Vi to the Baja

Fresh many times and I could picture the intersection clearly, but I needed a moment to remember where that intersection was in relation to this one.

Then I remembered and I opened my eyes. Out of perverse curiosity, I angled the rearview mirror so I could see myself. Jasmin and Ty were right; I looked bad. I needed a week's worth of sleep, but I wasn't going to get it.

Ten minutes later, I was parking outside a church. The Baja Fresh was gone, but the other businesses—a sushi place, a dry cleaners, a shoe store—were the same. The Roasted Seal was just down the street. The front was made entirely of glass, but the view inside was blocked by an amateurish painting of a sad-faced seal perched on jagged rocks. The seal looked at me as if I'd ruined its day with hairspray and car exhaust. In the dust above the door, someone had traced BIGFOOT ROOM.

I pushed the door open and went inside.

It wasn't as dark as I expected. In fact, the place was almost nice. There were circular black tables seeded around the main floor with a surprising amount of space between them. Each table had a little light shining down on it. Ambiance.

There was a row of booths at the far end of the room and a bar against the wall behind me. Everything was polished black stone and hexagonal floor tiles. There was also sawdust on the floor, which didn't seem to fit.

I glanced at the bartender and realized he was watching me with a tight expression. Maybe I didn't look like the trustworthy type. He only had one other customer: a rumpled-looking guy who must have run out of shampoo a month before. He was also watching me, but at least he tried to be subtle about it.

I walked farther into the room and saw him.

Arne sat in a back booth just beside the fire exit. He had a cup of coffee and a smart phone in front of him. He wore a black button-down shirt and chinos, and his curly blond hair was cropped short. Near as I could tell, he was alone and he wasn't surprised to see me.

I started toward him. Lenard suddenly stepped out of a wait station that had been built like an alcove. Before I could react, he had his hands on me, shaking me roughly as he patted me down. I tensed up but held myself rigidly still. I wasn't here to fight.

Time had not been kind to Lenard. He had smoker's wrinkles around his eyes and mouth, and his whole body had gone pear-shaped. "Well, well, Raymundo," he said. "Imagine seeing you here." I looked down at the shaved stubble over his scalp; he was going bald in little patches near his forehead.

He finished by checking for an ankle holster. Of course he didn't find anything. He stood and shrugged to Arne. I was cleared to go.

"Good to see you, Lenard," I said.

He looked at me sidelong as he backed into his alcove. "You look like shit, baby."

"I know it."

I walked by him. Arne was sitting in his booth with his arms folded across his chest. He wasn't even going to shake my hand.

"Arne," I said. "You don't look surprised to see me."

He smiled without a trace of good feeling. "You always had a pretty good sense of direction, Ray. How'd it take you two years to get from the gates of Chino to me?"

"I got on the wrong bus."

"The bus to Seattle. I heard. I've been following your name in the news. It's very interesting, all the scrapes you've gotten into. What happened in Washaway? You can tell me, buddy."

"Caramella said you were in trouble."

He didn't like that I'd changed the subject. "Do I have to remind you? You used to be smarter than that. I spent two hundred and fifty a month on you while you were inside. Every month, I sent a check to a sweet little lady in Boyle Heights so her son and his pals would babysit you."

And now he was challenging me. The funny thing was that I didn't feel like playing that game anymore. I'd seen too much to be afraid of Arne, and he knew it. "Arne—"

"Because I knew prison would *break* you." He was letting his anger show openly now. "I knew you couldn't handle the misery. You were never tough enough up here for that." He tapped his temple with his index finger.

I let him have his say. After he finished, we stared at each other for a second. Then I said: "Caramella said it was my fault."

Arne laughed. There was something desperate and helpless in it. "Jesus. Ray. *Ray.*" He looked at the phone on the table, then slipped it into his pocket. "Okay. It's time. Come on, Ray. You're going to do a job for me."

CHAPTER TWO

Lenard came up behind me. "You're taking *him*?"

"He's here and Ty isn't," Arne said, "so yeah. I sure as hell can't take you. Stay here just in case. He only has to drive a car—as long as he doesn't point the grill at Seattle and take off, he'll be fine. Besides, if I show up with you, they'll probably make us mow the lawn or something."

Lenard laughed. "Fuck you. Those guys have Japs do their landscaping. They'd make me patch the roof."

"I'll be two hours at least. Probably three. Go into the kitchen while I'm gone and wash some dishes. Make yourself useful."

"Hey, I was born in this country, just like you. I'll do a day's work when I see you do one."

"Don't hold your breath," Arne said. "No shit, Lenard. Be careful."

"Always."

Arne turned to me. "Let's go for a drive, Ray. You owe me."

He started toward the front door, and I followed. I'd always trailed after him, going from one place to another. It felt natural to let him lead me around, and the feeling—that if I did what he wanted he'd eventually give me what I needed—was startlingly familiar.

And he was right. I did owe him.

We went into the street. Arne was more watchful than he'd ever been, and I wondered why. We walked to a Land Rover, and he circled it carefully before he got in. I sat in the passenger seat and aimed the air-conditioning vents at my face. He pulled into traffic.

"Where are we going?" I asked.

"You'll see."

"No. Seriously. Where?"

"You know what I always liked about you, Ray? Timing. You always had good timing. For instance, here you are today of all days. Remember Rufus Sceopeola?"

I did. He was a weight lifter and amateur boxer who'd tried to take over the Bigfoot Room some years ago. He was used to intimidating people with his size, but he wasn't as tough as he'd thought. "Of course."

"You remember how you took him out?"

"A couple punches."

Arne laughed at me as he swerved onto a freeway onramp. "You don't even realize you do it, do you? Anybody can throw a couple punches, Ray. You threw the right punches. Rufus thought he had defenses—I ran into him later, and he talked about you. He said he'd never been taken apart so fast, in the ring or out. He said you had a good eye. When I told him you were in jail, he dropped into a deep funk. I think he wanted to invite you to his gym."

None of this interested me, but I asked anyway. "What ever happened to Rufus?"

Arne slapped his hand on my chest, then crumpled my shirt. I couldn't feel anything where the tattoos covered my skin, but I didn't like being searched anyway. "I'm not wearing a wire, and Lenard already checked me once."

He finished searching anyway. "The asshole is doing a stint at Corcoran. Some bastard took his gun and mailed it to the LAPD in a shoe box. Funny thing. They had his fingerprints on file, and the gun matched a shooting in North Hollywood from the year before. Attempted homicide." He glanced at me. "That's what I heard, anyway."

I didn't answer right away. For Arne, *asshole* had a specific meaning. Assholes were criminals who liked to hurt people—or who tried to mess with his business—which was pretty much every criminal we met.

Arne hated assholes. He had always kept us low-key—we dressed like college students and did "safe" jobs—but there was always someone who heard about the money he was making and tried to muscle in. Arne hadn't blustered or threatened, but those guys generally never came back a second time. We'd always wondered what he'd done to drive them off. Had he been turning them in to the cops? The idea made me a little sick.

But I hadn't come here to talk about old times. "Arne—"

"No questions, Ray. You don't have the right."

"Yes, I do. I'm in this car. I came down here to find you, and I can help, maybe."

"Maybe," he said. And laughed to himself. "Do you know why I asked you to go to the bar with Mouse that night?"

That startled me. I'd forgotten that he'd asked me to watch Mouse's back. "No."

"Okay. Do you know why I paid that protection money for you while you were inside?"

"Because you thought I would try to make a deal for a lighter sentence."

"Ray, Ray. You're such a beautiful idiot. And now I'm glad you took off for Seattle. At first my feelings were hurt, but now I think it's better you weren't around when everything went to shit."

He wanted me to ask him about Mouse and the protection money, but I wouldn't give him the satisfaction. "How did things go to shit?"

"We got old," Arne said, sounding annoyed. "When you're stealing cars and getting high at sixteen, it's like an adventure. Hell, even when you're twenty-two you can tell yourself you're a hard and dangerous dude, out on the streets taking what you want. But as you get older, it changes. The life starts to go sour. Even I wanted a house, a wife, and a kid, Ray."

I noticed he said *wanted* instead of *want*. "Caramella said someone had killed you."

"Well, here I am," he said. His tone was difficult to read. I'd always found Arne hard to read; maybe that was why I'd always been willing to follow him.

"She said it was my fault." But I'd said this already, and it didn't pry the truth out of him this time, either. Arne stared into the harsh desert sunlight, staying with traffic. He never drove faster or slower, preferring to hide in the crowd.

We were heading east. Las Vegas? But he'd said three hours at most, so it couldn't be. "Where are we going?" I asked again.

"Ray, have you noticed that I'm not answering your fucking questions?"

I looked over at him. He was shorter than me and built heavier, but he was quick. And I knew he was tough, but I was a wooden man with the Twenty Palace Society. I'd faced scarier things than Arne Sadler. "That's why I have to keep asking."

He smiled at me then, and I truly couldn't read his intent. Then he turned his attention to the road. We drove in silence for a while.

For more than ten years, Arne had been the most important person in my life.

I met him in juvie, when I believed I was going to spend the rest of my life in prison. He was three years older, and while he wasn't the first person to tell me that the shooting wasn't my fault, he was the first one

I believed even halfway. And he told me to come find him when the time was right.

I did. Arne taught me to steal cars, to fight, to live as a criminal without being an asshole, to tell victims from non-victims, and how to treat them both.

But I'd turned my back on him. When I walked out of Chino, I couldn't go back to that old life. I just couldn't. I wouldn't have chosen the society in its place, but that didn't change how I felt about being in L.A. again.

And yet, here I was. Worse, I had already gotten swept up into one of Arne's jobs.

I was seriously considering cutting him with my ghost knife—he'd tell me whatever I wanted to know after that, and he'd apologize for making me wait, too—when he suddenly sighed.

"Ray, how about this? You help me finish this job, and I'll help you with your thing. Okay? Melly was right. Things are in a bad way for me, and for Robbie, Summer, Lenard, even Bud, if that matters. But this job we're on is too important, and if I start talking about this shit, I'm going to lose my game face. You get me, don't you?"

"I get you."

He smiled at me. "Thanks, man."

We cruised the freeway eastward. The houses and strip malls gave way to warehouses and industrial, which eventually gave way to rough, low desert hills. The car was silent. Arne hated to play music when he was on a job.

The hum and movement of the car had lulled me to a dreamless sleep. I heard the tires roll over gravel and jolted awake. "This is it," Arne said. The sun was in my face; we'd turned around, and I'd slept through it.

Arne pulled off the highway onto a flat gravel path. There was a dry streambed directly beside us—if the car swerved a foot to the right, we'd tumble into it. Directly in front of us was a low hill, no different from any other low desert hill in Southern California. I honestly had no idea where we were, or even if that was the 15 back there. The gravel gave way to a dirt track as we drove northwest, following the trail around the hill.

At a wide part, nearly out of sight of the freeway, Arne did a quick two-point turn. "Get behind the wheel and wait here for me," he said. "I have to pick up a ride from just around the bend there." That meant he was about to steal a car. I held out my hand. Arne smirked at me, then took out his key ring. He had dozens of keys, along with a little flashlight, carabiner, Swiss Army knife, and who knows what else. He detached the Land Rover key and gave it to me.

He got out of the car into the scorching desert heat. The Land Rover was pretty roomy, but I was too tall to climb over the shifter. I got out, too, and walked around the front. "Expecting trouble?" I asked.

"We'll see." I must have reacted to that, because he smirked again and said, "The place should be empty. It's a hell of an August out here. But if someone's home, it won't be a problem. Wait here and be ready to pull out fast, just in case." He turned his back to me and walked away. After a few steps, he glanced back. The expression on his face suggested I was not doing my job. I climbed into the car and shut the door.

It was cool inside. I rubbed the sleep out of my eyes. Considering the way I'd been sleeping, it shouldn't have been a surprise that I'd nodded off, but I felt pissed off and ashamed anyway. If something dangerous had happened—hell, if Arne had decided to shove me out of the car at freeway speeds—I couldn't have done much about it.

I watched Arne as he moved away. He didn't look tense, but maybe he'd gotten more relaxed when he stole cars in the years I'd been away. Maybe he'd lost his edge. Or maybe he didn't expect any trouble out here at all.

After forty yards or so, he disappeared around the side of the hill. Without really thinking about it, I opened the driver door as quietly as I could and slipped into the afternoon heat. I shut the door gently, hoping the sound of car tires on the nearby freeway would mask the noise.

Arne didn't peek back around the edge of the hill at me. I felt absurdly like a disobedient teenager as I followed after him, walking on the dry, hard ground to avoid the crunch of footsteps on gravel.

At the bend in the path, I crouched low behind an outcropping of rock and spied on Arne. He had stopped at the end of the gravel path and was fiddling with a padlock on a gate. The hill concealed a fenced area, and inside the fence was a prefab sheet-metal building.

The gate was on the western part of the property. The building faced south, with a peaked roof and a row of closed windows set high on the walls. The huge front doors slid open on runners.

The building was deep enough that a tractor trailer could have driven through the front and pulled all the way inside without turning, and it was three times wider than it was deep.

Whatever Arne was doing with the gates, he got them unlocked and pushed them both all the way open. Then he started toward the big front doors. He moved casually, but his head turned back and forth as he scanned the area, making sure he was alone.

He spent much less time fiddling with the latch at the two big front doors before sliding them open and walking into the darkness. Damn, it must have been like an oven in there. Sweat prickled on my back at the thought of it.

There was a sign on the open gate, but I was too far away to read it. If the society had brought me in as an investigator, I'd probably have a pair of binoculars, or maybe a camera with a telephoto lens that would not only let me read the sign but would record it for the benefit of the people who recovered my body.

But I was just a wooden man, and this was not even an official mission.

Still, I couldn't help but wonder what Arne was doing all the way out here in the middle of nowhere. When I'd been with him, we'd stolen cars and driven them to a dealer in Long Beach. He'd fake up papers for them and ship them out of the country for resale. It hadn't made any of us rich, but it had been better than throwing trash into the back of a municipal truck, or mopping floors, or clearing dirty plates from restaurant tables. At least, we'd thought so. Maybe we'd have made more money if Arne had been more willing to take risks, but he'd kept most of us out of jail.

A car rolled slowly out of the big double doors of the building below. I didn't recognize it for a moment. Then Arne got out to close the hangar doors.

A Bugatti. Arne was stealing a Bugatti.

They were worth a quarter million dollars, and they were completely out of the range of cars we usually handled. Hell, he'd told us not to steal Ferraris because they were too high-profile. But a Bugatti?

He shut the building. I'd seen enough. I slipped away from the outcropping of rock and hustled back to the car. It was several minutes before Arne pulled up alongside me.

I rolled the driver's window down, but he only gave me a thumbs-up as he crept by. I followed him back to the freeway, watching him drive at a crawl. The Bugatti scraped its bottom on the gravel, but it had made it in, and it made it out, too. Arne gunned the engine and zipped into traffic. I hurried after him. Together we headed west again toward the setting sun.

I made note of the first sign that told me how many miles we were from L.A. Figuring quickly, the sheet-metal building was almost as far as Bakersfield, but not quite. That meant the desert on the other side of the highway had to be the Mohave.

I hoped Arne would let me drive that damn Bugatti, just for a few miles.

That didn't happen, of course. Instead, we drove through the last remaining hours of the evening rush and swung over to Bel Air.

Arne pulled up to a white marble mansion ringed by a black iron fence like a wall of spears. The lawn was as neat as a putting green, and the driveway was lined with white pillars. As L.A. mansions went, it was nearly moderate in its splendor. The place across the street was little more than a long driveway with a gate at the end. Nothing of the house itself was visible except for the Mediterranean-style roof.

I'd always liked driving through the rich neighborhoods of Los Angeles to look at the houses. There's a kind of sick fascination about it, like looking at a car accident.

Arne honked the Bugatti's horn and stepped out of the car. I rolled down his window as he came over. He dropped his fat roll of keys into a little pocket on the driver's-side door. "Wait out here, okay?" He was rubbing his hands together. "I'll be a couple minutes." He'd never been this excited on jobs in the old days, and I didn't like to see it now. I didn't trust it.

"What are we doing here?"

"Recovering stolen property," he answered. "Some guys have been operating out of the Valley, mostly, crowding my turf. I made a point of learning all their wheres, whens, and hows, and now they're going to make me a couple of bucks."

"That doesn't sound like your style."

"You've been gone a long time, baby. Things change."

He got back behind the wheel as the gate rolled open. He drove through the pillars while I shut off the engine and settled in.

I didn't stay settled in for long. After about three minutes, four men walked through the gate toward me. The one in the lead was a white man of about fifty, with a bull neck and a face like a plate of lumpy mashed potatoes. One of the men behind him looked familiar, but I couldn't place him. He was a black man, my height but bigger in the shoulders. His broad forehead was furrowed with a resentful scowl.

I rolled down the window a few inches. Potato Face crooked his finger at me, signaling me to come with him. There was nothing bullying or arrogant in his expression, but I didn't like being treated like a misbehaving first-grader.

"Why?" I asked.

Mr. Familiar didn't like my question. He tried to come around Potato Face at me, but the old man laid a hand on his chest to stop him, and Familiar stopped. Nice to know who was in charge.

Potato looked at me again. "Your buddy needs your help."

I didn't believe that for a second, but I opened the door and climbed out anyway, mainly because I could see they'd force me out if I didn't. There was no sense in scuffling in the street.

Potato walked toward the house, and I fell in behind him. Familiar walked on my left, and the two other guys, both bulky, pale-skinned, and as expressive as boulders, flanked me on my right and from behind.

"I recognize you," Familiar blurted out. "You're the Flower." Suddenly I recognized him right back. He was Wardell Shoops, a former wide receiver for the Chiefs. He'd been drafted out of UCLA and, during bye week of his rookie year, he'd flown home to have dinner with his mother and to beat the hell out of his business manager, who'd lost half his money on a Louisiana alligator farm. He'd pleaded guilty and did a year in Chino while I was there.

I looked at him and at his aggressive smile. He looked at me like I was an apple about to be plucked and eaten. I didn't like that look. "I remember the man you used to be," I said. "What happened to that guy? He was something else."

Wardell's smile vanished. He cursed and stepped toward me, but Potato stopped him with one backward glance. We all walked up the driveway while the gate rolled closed behind us.

The inside of the house was bright with natural light. Nearly everything was white—the carpet, the chairs, even the narrow hall tables with white princess telephones. White picture frames with no pictures hung on the walls. The ceiling was made of squares of glass with black framework in between.

Potato led us into a sunken living room at the back of the building. Arne was there, standing by a pair of French doors, with two more heavyset creeps next to him. Through the doors, I could see a broad lawn with a flower garden along one side and a little Jacuzzi on the other. Two men were on their hands and knees digging in the garden, but I couldn't see them well enough to tell if they were Japanese, Mexican, or something else.

"Come on," a man said impatiently. "There's no reason to be afraid."

Potato led me down into the room, and there, seated on an overstuffed couch in the corner, was the man who thought I was frightened of him. He was narrow-shouldered and as thin as a boy, and just about as tall, too. His face was weathered by sun, but his two-hundred-dollar haircut and open-necked linen shirt suggested he'd gotten his tan in a deck chair. His blue eyes were watery, and his thin hair was the color of sand. A tall, bony Asian woman in a purple bikini lounged on a couch beside him, a magazine in her hand.

Potato jerked a thumb back at me. "This is him."

Linen Shirt was about to speak when Wardell said: "I know him. His last name is Daffodil or something. Something flowery. He was in Chino a couple years back, and someone on the outside had to pay for his protection, 'cause he couldn't do it himself."

Linen waited for Wardell to finish. Everyone else was silent, and I had the impression that Wardell had stepped on his boss's line, and not for the first time. Then he glanced at me. "What are you doing here, Mr. Daffodil?"

Arne spoke up. "I needed someone to drive my car."

"I wasn't asking you," Linen said, his voice sharp. He turned away from me. "Well? Is this him?"

The Asian woman regarded me with a sleepy, careless self-confidence. Her skin was dark and her face broad and beautiful. "Nope," she said. She took a swizzle stick off the table beside her and began moving it through her hair as though she was stirring her scalp. "I told you it was a spic."

Linen sighed. "Don't say *spic*. It's low-class." She shrugged and went back to reading.

"I told you before," Arne said, "I didn't steal your car. I thought I knew who'd done it, and I was right. I took a real risk retrieving it for you."

Another one of the interchangeable beefheads came into the room. He held up a DVD inside a paper sleeve. "It was right where you left it."

Linen opened a cabinet, revealing a little screen. The beefhead loaded the disc and pressed PLAY.

Swizzle Stick found the energy to stand and look at the screen. We all watched the video of her and Linen naked and grunting on a white bed in a white room—probably one right upstairs. No one seemed the least bit embarrassed or awkward.

"I look hot," Swizzle said.

Linen sighed again and turned the show off. "Did you see this?" he asked Arne.

"No, I didn't." Arne sounded very casual.

Linen turned toward me. "You?"

"No, but maybe if you play more, I'll recognize it."

Arne laughed suddenly. It felt so good to have him smile at me that I almost laughed with him. We had been friends once.

Linen turned to Potato Face. "Make sure."

Wardell grabbed my arms and held me while one of the other men patted me down. Arne got the same treatment. Potato stood watch over us. They found my ghost knife and cellphone, but no one objected when

I took them back. No one found any discs, so Potato took Arne's satchel and dumped it out onto the table.

"Hey!" Arne shouted. I heard the dangerous tone in his voice, but no one else seemed to care.

They picked through his things, bending them and ripping the pockets of his bag. Linen opened the French doors, and one of the men pitched Arne's laptop into the Jacuzzi.

Arne glowered at them.

Linen took a checkbook from a little drawer, filled out a check, and gave it to Arne. I noticed a wedding ring on his tanned finger. Swizzle Stick didn't have one.

Arne glanced at the check. "What's this?"

"That's your payment," Linen said. He sounded bored with us, as though we'd stayed too long at his party.

"Half the price," Arne said. "That was the deal. I'd get the car back for you, and you would pay me half what it cost."

"But did you get that in writing? That disc was valuable; the car . . . meh. The Bugatti is insured. My marriage isn't. That check will buy two laptops to replace the one that just took a swim, with a little left over for a lazy day's work."

"Are you sure you want to do this?" Arne asked, his voice quiet. "Are you sure you want to break a deal with me?"

Linen turned to Potato. "He sounds feisty."

Wardell immediately sank a hard right into my midsection, while one of the other men did the same to Arne. It didn't hurt me; I could barely feel the pressure of it through the protective tattoos Annalise had put on me.

I threw a quick uppercut at Wardell, but one of the other men tangled my arm with one of his punches, blunting the force.

I caught another painless shot in the guts, then the men on either side of me drove their knees into the outside of my thighs. The pain was intense, and I fell onto the cool tile floor. The beating continued.

I didn't have to take this shit. My ghost knife was in my pocket. All I had to do was cut one of these bruisers with the edge of my spell to take them out of the fight. In less than a minute, I could take control of this room and everyone in it.

I took the beating anyway. I wasn't going to use a spell in front of Linen; he might decide to search for magic of his own, and I was sick of the messes that came of that.

A punch grazed the edge of my chin—nothing serious, just a scrape—and Potato stepped in and backed Wardell off. "Not the face," he said. "You know better."

That was the end of the beating. Arne rolled onto his side, cursing, but he didn't look too bad. Linen picked the check up and stuffed it into Arne's shirt pocket. "No need to be feisty anymore, right? Because now you know how lucky you are. Be glad our deal is the only thing I'm breaking. Get out, and tell your car-stealing buddy he was smart to stay away from me."

The guards lifted us to our feet. One of them swept Arne's things into his satchel, being careful to get everything but not being careful in any other way, then hung it around Arne's neck like a gold medal. We were hustled out of the house and down to the street. I could hear Wardell behind me, laughing.

Once released, Arne stripped the satchel off his neck and collapsed onto his hands and knees. He puked onto the street. There was no red in it. I picked up his satchel. A few things had fallen out when he'd dropped it, and I examined each as I put them back, hoping I'd find something useful.

"What's this?" Wardell said. He was facing a wall of bodies. Potato Face and his men were barring Wardell from returning to the house. One of the men held out a tan sports jacket for Wardell to take, but he wouldn't accept it.

"You have the wrong temperament for this work," Potato said. "You think this is about you. It ain't. You're fired. Don't let me see you again, or you won't be happy about it."

Wardell stared at them, simmering. I hadn't known him personally in Chino, but everyone had known who he was: a pro athlete who'd done a TV commercial or two. He was used to being the big man in the room, and he didn't seem to be adjusting to his new life all that well.

"Come on, Arne," I said, helping him up. He staggered as he went toward the driver's door, but I wanted him to move faster. "Let's get out of here and find a place we can talk."

"I don't think they broke anything," Arne said. "Jesus, can you believe that guy called me a liar?"

I glanced back. Wardell was still staring at Potato. Potato stared back. Beefy guy still held his arm extended toward Wardell, jacket in hand. Finally, he got tired of waiting for Wardell to take it, so he tossed it. Wardell was forced to catch it against his chest or let it fall into the street. Potato and his men went back through the gate and shut it with a sharp *clang*.

Arne made his key chain chirp and popped the locks on his car. Wardell turned his head toward the sound. Shit.

Arne got behind the wheel. "I don't have time to talk to you right now, Ray."

"Arne, no. This is too important—"

"No." Arne glanced through the windshield at Wardell, who was stalking toward us. "After the job, remember? The job isn't over until I get paid. Besides, your boyfriend wants to talk to you."

"Hey!" Wardell shouted. "Flower!"

Damn. I hated being called that.

Arne started his car. He gave me a crooked smile. "Take care of this, would you, Ray? I have work to do."

Wardell grabbed my shirt and shoved me against Arne's car. I tipped back over the hood, my feet coming off the ground. Christ, he was strong.

I drew my ghost knife from my back pocket.

Arne's car began to back down the street, and I slid along the hood of the car until I dropped backward. I heard my shirt tear just a little in Wardell's grip.

"You just cost me a job, Flower. A good job that paid okay. There ain't a lot of places a guy like me can get paid to have my fun. So now you're going to hire me."

Arne backed away down the street. I saw him grimace as he twisted to look through the back window, but he didn't glance at me at all.

"Don't you look at him," Wardell said. "You look at me now. Just like you paid those barrio motherfuckers to watch your back in Chino, you're going to pay me to watch your back out here."

"I wouldn't pay you to watch a pot of chili," I said, and slid the ghost knife through his ribs.

According to the spell book I'd cast it from, the ghost knife could cut "ghosts, magic, and dead things." Its edge could split a steel door, destroy the sigils that made spells work, and on living people, it could cut their "ghosts."

Whatever that meant. I'd never seen an actual ghost, but trial and error had taught me that the ghost knife took away a person's anger and hostility, turning them docile and apologetic but without doing them any physical harm. At least, no harm I could see.

Wardell was no exception. He gasped as the spell passed through him and his eyes went wide like deer eyes. He lifted me to my feet— the spell didn't take his strength away. "I'm sorry," he said. "I shouldn't have said those things."

"You're right. You shouldn't have." Arne was long gone. I sighed and turned to Wardell. "Where's your car?"

He led me to it. It was just around the corner, parked beneath an old oak. It was an older Nissan Pathfinder, and it had probably been his run-around-town vehicle before he went inside. He asked me if I wanted to drive.

I did. Traffic was heavy on the way back to the Bigfoot Room. Wardell talked most of the way, mostly about what he was doing now that he was outside and people we'd known inside. An unsurprising number of them had gotten themselves out and gotten themselves thrown right back in again. Wardell was of the opinion that that would happen to him soon, too.

He also told me that Linen's real name was Steve Francois, and that he'd inherited his money from some South American paper mills and banks in Texas. Mostly banks. Steve liked having badasses around, and Wardell was an ex-con and ex-NFL, so he was hired.

I couldn't even begin to guess why Arne was running errands for a guy like Francois.

I liked Wardell better when he wasn't desperate to be alpha male, but not much better. Even with his aggression cut out of him, he was still arrogant enough to think he should dominate the conversation. I was tempted to make him turn himself in to the cops until he said he had a wife at home who was sticking by him—so far. "She wants me to go to anger-management classes," he said.

"Why haven't you?"

"I didn't want to," he answered. "I'm sorry about the buttons on your shirt. Do you want me to ask her to sew them back on? She would, I think."

I looked down. He had popped off a button from my shirt, second from my top. "No, thanks," I said, being polite because of the ghost knife, and I didn't feel like taking anything else from him. "Do you beat on her?"

"No! I would never hit my lady." He sounded honestly surprised that I'd asked.

"Good. You should take her advice." I remembered waking from nightmares in the middle of the night. "If your shit isn't under control, you should get help."

I pulled up to the curb at a corner near the Bigfoot Room and climbed out. My legs and back were getting stiff and achy from sitting so long. I was glad Potato and his men had landed most of their punches on my chest and stomach, where I was protected. My car was still where I had left it.

"Thanks for the ride," I said.

Wardell climbed into the driver's seat. He was a big guy, but he was limber enough to make it without knocking the stick shift out of PARK.

"Thank you," Wardell said. I shut the door. He hit the turn signal and pulled into traffic.

I watched him go, wondering what I could do if my own stress got so bad I lost control of it. Not therapy; as soon as I talked about predators, the therapist would think I was delusional. And if the therapist found out about the people I'd killed . . .

It didn't matter. None of it mattered.

Wardell disappeared into traffic, so I crossed the street and entered the Roasted Seal. The sawdust was still on the floor and the rumpled guy was still sitting at the bar, a beer and a cup of coffee beside him.

And Arne was sitting in the same booth. He was tapping at a different laptop.

I moved toward him, holding out my hand to block Lenard as I came around the wait station. "Are you going to pat me down again?"

Lenard slammed a little locker door shut and spun the combination lock. Then he glanced at Arne. Arne shrugged. Lenard backed toward the booth, and his body language told me not to approach.

"I hope," Arne said, "you're not pissed that I took off without telling you what's what or caring one shit what was going on with you."

"Of course not. What kind of petty bastard do you think I am?" And it was true. I wasn't pissed. In fact, I'd expected him to abandon me somewhere—that's why I'd held out my hand for the Land Rover keys when Arne asked me to drive it. It's one thing to be stranded in Bel Air and another to be stranded in the middle of the desert. "Bought yourself a replacement already?"

"Oh, no. This is my real computer. The other was the one I take on jobs, just in case."

"Arne, what happened to Melly? What happened to you?"

"Just a minute. Busy." He turned back to the computer and started typing.

"Busy with what?" My voice sounded sharper than I'd intended. I wanted to say more, but everything I could think of sounded ridiculous.

"Destroying a man's life," he said. "Ray, what do you know about porn on the Internet?"

"There's porn on the Internet?"

Arne laughed loudly, and I could feel some of the tension going out of the room. I needed him on my side, but somehow I'd lost the knack of winning people over.

"My favorite is where people make their own and put it up online. It's crazy popular, even if most of the content is videos some dude made with a hooker or revenge postings by the recently dumped. Sometimes it's even weirder. Check it out."

He turned the laptop toward me. A video was playing, and it took me a moment to realize it was the same video I'd seen in Francois's house. Except that someone had added a timer to it.

"Why is there a . . ." Then I saw why. By the time the counter reached 27, Francois had finished.

"See, Francois has a wife somewhere—Park Avenue or something—and she is a litigation powerhouse. Her whole clan is. Once word starts to spread about this video, he's going to have a very expensive divorce on his hands. Plus the twenty-seven-second thing."

He turned the laptop toward himself again. There was a jangle of keys, and I noticed that his big key ring was hanging off the side of the machine. Arne pulled at it, unplugging a memory stick, and pocketed it. He must have found the DVD in the Bugatti right away, copied the file during the drive back to the city, and put the disc back.

But that was his deal. I had other problems.

"Arne, Melly said you were dead. She said you'd been killed and it was my fault."

Arne gave me a steady look. This was it. He was about to break down and give me what I needed. "Well, he was your buddy, wasn't he?"

I didn't have any buddies. Not anymore. "Who?"

"Wally King."

Oh, God. Wally Fucking King.

CHAPTER THREE

Lenard touched Arne's shoulder as though he'd just seen something they'd both been waiting for. "Hold that thought," Arne said.

I heard a foot scuffle behind me. Arne glanced at the floor behind me. I turned, but there was no one there.

A heavy metal canister clanged near my feet and let out a wet hiss. A plume of tear gas billowed around my legs.

I turned to shout a warning to Arne, but he was no longer in his booth. I shut my mouth and clamped my hand over my nose before I caught a whiff, then soccer-kicked it toward the front door. Damn, it was hot already—I could feel the heat of it against my ankle. It struck something on the floor I couldn't see and skittered sideways toward Rumpled Guy.

I shut my eyes just as the stinging started. Something moved very close to me, and the gunfire started.

I dropped flat onto the floor. The tattoos on my chest and the outside of my forearms are bulletproof thanks to a spell called the closed way, but my head, back, legs, and sides were completely exposed. The guns sounded very loud and very close, but nothing hit me.

I crawled blindly toward the fire exit. Sawdust stuck to my skin, and my chest felt tight. I hadn't caught a good breath, and my oxygen was running out. Fortunately, the gunfire had already stopped. It takes very little time to empty a magazine.

I heard the sounds of clips being ejected from pistols and slammed back in. There were two gunmen, at least, and now I was sure they were close. Someone was hacking and choking on the gas, but it didn't sound like anyone near me. Were the gunmen wearing masks?

I was sure they could see me—the gas couldn't have been that thick—and I expected a bullet in the back. I hoped they'd have the decency to shoot at my head; at least it would be quick.

But I didn't stop crawling, and the bullet never came. I finally made it to the wall and, reaching to my right, found the doorway. Arne was right about my sense of direction. The door was open, but I was barely across the threshold when it swung shut, slamming against my head and making me gasp.

I crawled into the alley, gagging on the wisp of tear gas I'd inhaled. I didn't know if it was heavier than air, but I wanted to be on my feet; I stood and stumbled against a dumpster. Time to live dangerously; I opened my eyes.

Immediately, they started to burn. Tears flooded my cheeks, and I couldn't stop coughing.

Arne and Lenard weren't there, but Rumpled stumbled through the door just behind me. He was coughing so hard I thought he'd convulse.

My eyes were burning stronger now, as though the tears were washing the chemicals into my eyes rather than out, but he had it worse. He kept saying: "Ah, God! God!" between retches.

We were helpless. If the shooters inside the bar came out here, they could have put bullets into us without breaking stride. Of course, they could have done that inside, too.

I blinked through my tears and saw a short, slender figure knock Rumpled to the ground. A second, larger figure stepped up close to me. "Well, well," he drawled. "If it ain't old Ray Lilly himself. Howsdoin', Raymond?"

"Bud?" I asked, suddenly recognizing his voice. "Someone just tried to kill Arne. I didn't see who, though. Is he around?"

"I don't see Arne," Bud answered. "He musta lit out."

Again.

I could almost hear a smile in Bud's voice. I blinked to clear my vision, and it worked a little. The slender figure moved toward us. "He's gone," she said. "We should go, too." That was Summer, another member of Arne's crew.

Bud and Summer each grabbed one of my sleeves and steered me down the alley toward the sidewalk. I let them. While I could see—barely—I couldn't see well enough to drive. And my tears were still flowing, my nose was running, and I was still trying to blink the pain away. If the cops found me here, they'd snatch me right off the street.

I heard Bud reassure a passing pedestrian that I'd just had my heart broken. I didn't know where we were going. "Someone tried to kill Arne. We have to look for him."

"Oh, we'll look for him, all right," Bud said.

Something was wrong. Bud and Summer were part of Arne's crew, just like Lenard, and just like I used to be, and right now they were being too casual.

A bad feeling came over me. I turned toward Summer. She'd let her hair grow out so that it almost reached her shoulders. Her face was broad and tanned, her pale blue eyes sullen in the heat. Her sleeveless jogging shirt was damp with sweat and hung untucked over a pair of shorts with an elastic waistband. Had she been one of the shooters? She could certainly conceal a gun at her back, but a gas mask, too? I didn't believe it.

Bud was the same. He had a loose T-shirt over belted shorts, and while he'd cut off his mullet, he still wore that stupid bolo tie. He could have hidden a gun at the small of his back—or maybe under his growing beer belly—but not a gas mask.

Arne had taught them better than to dump something like that right at the scene of the crime, so I figured they weren't the shooters. Of course, they could have been lookouts or backup. "Where are we going?" I asked.

"Tear gas is toxic," Summer said. "There's a Ralphs up the street. We'll pick up some stuff that will help there."

"At a supermarket?" I asked. "How do you know—" A fit of coughing cut off the rest of my question, and a rolling drop of sweat suddenly blinded my right eye.

"Are you seriously asking me how I know what to do about tear gas?" I'd forgotten that Summer's hippie parents—her hated, hated parents—had marched in dozens of street protests over the years, and Summer herself had probably been dosed with the stuff several times.

"Then we'll get out of here," Bud added. "Robbie is going to want to talk to you."

Robbie was Arne's second-in-command, and we had always gotten along well—better, in fact, than I'd gotten along with anyone. I wanted to talk to him, too.

But first I needed to get away from Bud and Summer. Arne had said Wally King's name, and that meant bad things were happening. He was the reason I was mixed up with the Twenty Palace Society. The spell book he'd stolen, the predators he'd summoned, and the deaths he'd caused almost two years before had ruined my life.

I needed to call the society, and I needed to do it in private. Those bastards take their secrecy seriously. And I needed my boss. I needed Annalise. I didn't want to face Wally King without her again.

"We're parked just up here in the lot," Bud said as we turned a corner. I blinked my eyes clear again and saw a field of colored metal gleaming in the sun. They led me to a white pickup and let me sit on the gate.

Summer stepped away from me. "Bud, go inside and get what he needs."

"You sure?" he asked, as though nervous about leaving her with me.

"Go." She sounded irritated. He went.

I squinted in her direction. I wanted privacy to make my call, but she didn't seem ready to give it to me. "I'm glad you and Bud are still together," I said.

"We're married now," she answered, her voice flat.

"That's great." There was nowhere for the conversation to go after that, so it just sat there. Now that we had stopped moving, my eyes began to sting even more. I raised my hands to rub them but thought better of it. "I need to make a call," I said. "In private."

She didn't move. "To who?"

"Nobody you know." Since she wasn't moving away, I hopped off the gate and walked along the side of the truck to the wall. Then I started toward the sidewalk.

She trailed behind me.

"Wait by the truck, Summer," I said. "I'm not kidding. This is a private call."

"You're calling the cops, aren't you?"

Out of reflex, I cursed at her. If that's who she thought I was now, she couldn't be trusted. It was the same as saying *We are enemies*.

My reaction must have mollified her a little. She sulkily stepped back, but not because she was afraid of me. I'd never known her to be afraid of anyone.

A young mother came toward me, navigating her baby stroller through the narrow space between the whitewashed wall and parked cars. I stepped around her, then looked toward the truck.

Summer wasn't there. I glanced around the lot and inside the truck. Nothing. I dropped to the ground and peered under the cars. Nothing, again. She'd vanished.

I walked to the sidewalk, darting through a line of cars pulling in from the street. The store was too far for her to have gone inside, but where was she? I didn't like that she seemed to have blinked out of existence within ten feet of me. Just like Caramella. Had she transported herself far away? Where?

Even now, as evening was coming on, the traffic noise was ever present. I stepped into a bus shelter for some relative quiet and took out my phone. It had speed-dial buttons, but none had the number I needed. That was only in my memory.

I was feeling jumpy as I dialed. Something was wrong, but I couldn't figure out what. The phone picked up after four rings.

"Hello? This is Mariana." She had an accent I couldn't place, but I was never good with accents.

"This is Ray Lilly. I need my boss."

"Mr. Lilly, this isn't how you are supposed to make this request. What is the situation?"

I knew I was breaking the rules, but my instincts were ringing like fire alarms, and I couldn't ignore them. "I can't go into it on the phone."

"Mr. Lilly," she said in a tone that was almost scolding, "you aren't calling from an unsecure location, I hope."

"Considering what I've been seeing here, I don't think a secure location is possible."

"I understand." She had dropped the scolding tone. "The phone GPS has given me your location. Return to that location at this time each day for the next four days." I glanced at my watch. It was just after seven-thirty. "You will be met."

She hung up and so did I. There was a trash receptacle right next to me, but I was supposed to ditch the phone where no one would notice. And while I couldn't see anyone nearby . . .

I swept my right arm away from me and struck something invisible a foot from my elbow. It was sticky, just like Caramella's slap. I heard a hiss and the scuffle of shoes on concrete.

I grabbed the invisible shape, shoving it toward the bench and knocking it off balance. It suddenly darkened, becoming an outline with a misty blackness inside, just like the Empty Spaces.

Damn. That's exactly what it was. I was looking into the Empty Spaces.

I would have freaked out if I'd had the time, but the vision vanished suddenly, and I was holding Summer by the shoulders. She was staring at me with wild, dangerous eyes. "Let go of me, Ray," she said, and grabbed my wrist with her bare hand. My skin began to itch and burn under her grip.

I pulled her to her feet and spun her around. She tried to resist—and she was strong—but she wasn't as strong as me. I yanked a pistol out of the back of her waistband, then patted the pockets of her gym shorts. They were empty.

The urge to run was unbearable, but I knew it would be useless.

They still had Bud's truck. "Keep away, Summer." My breath was coming in gasps. I barely recognized my own voice. "Don't make a bigger mistake than you already have."

I backed toward the lot, holding the gun on her. My mind was racing. There were no other pedestrians nearby, but someone in a passing car might see me and call the cops. For a moment I tried to imagine what I would say if a patrol car suddenly pulled up to the curb, but I couldn't focus on it.

Summer stood in the bus shelter with her arms at her sides, watching me. I bolted back into the lot.

Bud was standing beside his pickup, scanning the lot for us. He had a little shopping bag in his hand. I ran toward him. Once he spotted me, he patted the truck bed.

"Back here, Ray. You're giving off fumes. We'll get you showered and changed as soon as we can, but first"—he held up the shopping bag—"we'll mix these and—"

I came up next to him, and he saw the gun in my hand. "Give me the keys, Bud."

His good-ole-boy grin twisted with disappointment. "I thought you were out of the car-stealing business."

"Keep back. Don't touch me. Give me the keys. I'll drop your truck within a few blocks of the Bigfoot Room, but I'm not going anywhere with you. And don't touch me. Get it? Don't touch me! I'm not going anywhere with you!"

"Don't get all wigged out, Ray. All right? Don't. Here's the stuff you need for your skin." He tossed the grocery bag onto the passenger seat. "Just mix it one to one. And don't scratch my truck." He set his keys on the hood.

While he backed away, I picked them up. I wondered where Summer was—I should have made her come with me. I should have made her stay visible. I imagined her behind me, knife in hand. I imagined the point digging into the back of my neck or into my kidneys, and my skin prickled all over. My breath rushed in and out of me, and even though everything was different I felt that same urge to scream that I'd felt that last night in Wash-away, just before the killing started. My finger tightened on the trigger.

No. No, I wasn't going to shoot Bud. I was in control of myself. I was in control.

I climbed into the truck. Bud stood with his hands at his sides. If he'd been one of the shooters inside the Bigfoot Room, and I was ready to believe he was, he had a gun on him that I'd forgotten to take. I was screwing up, and that was going to get me killed. Either that, or

I was going to have to kill him. I wasn't ready for that. I started the engine and lurched out of the spot.

In a mild voice, Bud said: "My apartment keys are on that ring, you know."

"Within a few blocks," I told him, fighting the urge to *flee flee flee.* "You fucked up, Bud."

"Robbie will still want to talk to you."

"And I want to talk to him," I said, and raced out of the lot. Summer stood by the entrance, watching me impassively. She was still there when I drove down the street.

I forced myself to take long, slow breaths. I looked down at my wrist. My skin had turned red and gotten inflamed where Summer's little hand had touched me.

An idea occurred to me, and I lifted my arm toward the rearview mirror when I stopped at the next stoplight. My shirt was a henley, three buttons at the neck, no collar, and sleeves that reached just past my elbow. Both Summer and Bud had grabbed my arm where the sleeve covered it, but I couldn't see any effect on my clothes. They weren't sticky, discolored, or slowly dissolving.

The light turned green and I drove on. Could Bud turn invisible? I hadn't seen him do it, and I hadn't touched his skin, but something about the way he'd acted—as though he'd expected my reaction, just not so soon—made me think he could.

And Caramella. I thought she'd transported herself out of my room after that last, aborted slap, but maybe she'd hung around for a while, watching me sleep.

The idea gave me the shivers, and I almost blew through the next red light. Instead, I forced myself to calm down. Potato Face and his men hadn't triggered this kind of response when they'd swarmed around me, but why should they? They were men. All they could do was kill me.

When the light changed, I parked the truck. I was only a block and a half away from the Bigfoot Room, and that was close enough. I didn't like the idea of driving Bud's truck when another drop of sweat could blind me.

I wiped my fingerprints off Summer's gun. There was no reason to—the twisted-path spell on my chest altered the physical evidence I left behind, like fingerprints and DNA, making it impossible to pin me to a crime scene. It still felt good. Then I stuffed the weapon under the seat.

I opened the glove compartment. Sure enough, there was Summer's purse. I flipped through it. There was no makeup—the only thing she had in common with her mother was her refusal to wear it.

There was an address book and a billfold with a little cash inside. I was tempted to take the money to teach her a lesson about fooling around with magic, but I didn't. Class hadn't started yet.

I did take her address book. I flipped to the *H* and read the entry for Caramella Harris. She lived in Silver Lake.

There was only one more thing to do. I still had the cellphone the society had given me. If I turned it on and stuffed it into the back of the seat, the society would be able to locate them the same way they'd located me.

I didn't do it. The risk that Bud or Robbie or someone else in the crew would find it and press REDIAL may have been slim, but I still wasn't going to take the chance. Secrecy came first. I pocketed it, tossed the keys under the front seat, and picked up the grocery bag. Then I climbed out, leaving the driver's window rolled down.

I walked back to the church and my car. There were police cars with flashing lights parked in front of the bar, and plenty of yellow tape on the sidewalk. I stopped at the corner to gawk a little; it would have looked suspicious if I hadn't. A patrol cop looked at me, then looked away, uninterested.

I went to my car and drove away before a cop came close enough to smell the tear gas.

Summer and Caramella could turn invisible. Probably Bud could, too. I tried to figure who else should be on that list, but I didn't know enough yet. I was sure Arne knew about it, even if he couldn't vanish himself. I suddenly understood why there was sawdust on the floor of the Bigfoot Room.

But that wasn't the worst of it. The worst part was the way Summer had looked when she'd dropped her invisibility—she'd looked like a doorway into the Empty Spaces. Nearly two years earlier, when I'd first come face-to-face with predators, magic, the Twenty Palace Society, and all the rest, I'd cast a spell that let me look into the Empty Spaces.

That had only been a peek, though. I'd learned enough to scare the hell out of myself, but not much more. And it wasn't like the society was going to explain things to me; they didn't exactly offer night classes.

What little I understood about the Empty Spaces was this: it surrounds the world we live on and is, at the same time, beside it. It's a void of mist and darkness, and *creatures* live there.

The society calls them predators, but they aren't like the animals you find here on the earth. Coming from this other, alternate space, they have their own physics and their own biology. Some are living wheels of fire, some swarms of lights, some massive serpents in which every scale is the face of one of its meals, some schools of moving, singing boulders. When they come to our world, they are "only partly real," as my boss once explained. They're creatures of magic, and can be used to do all sorts of strange and dangerous things . . . if the summoner can control them.

So they're out there in that vast expanse, right beside us but unable to find us. And they're hungry. One of them, allowed to run loose on our planet, would feed and feed and feed, possibly calling more of its kind, until there was nothing left but barren rock.

The entire reason the Twenty Palace Society existed, as far as I could tell, was to search out and destroy the summoning magic that called predators to our world, along with anyone who used that magic. They also kill predators when they find them.

But a human taking on a predator is like a field mouse trying to kill a barn owl. That's why the society uses magic of its own. They don't call predators—summoning magic is a killing offense, even for them—but as far as I could tell, everything else was fair game. The spells tattooed on my body and the ghost knife in my pocket were prime examples of that.

A car behind me honked, and I realized I'd been sitting at a stop sign for nearly a minute, lost in thought. I pulled through the intersection, blinking my eyes clear.

And although it had been nearly two years, I'd instantly recognized the Empty Spaces when Summer had dropped her invisibility. If she'd gotten this ability through non-summoning magic like mine, that would be bad enough. The society would want to check her out and hunt down the spell book she'd used. And . . . damn, I hated to think it, but they would probably kill her just to be safe.

When people learned magic was real they often became obsessed with the power it gave them, and they did dangerous things to get it, like summon predators they couldn't control. I'd seen it more than once, and it was why I was so alarmed when Arne had said Wally King's name. Wally hadn't just summoned predators; he'd killed people to steal spells from them.

But were Caramella and Summer his accomplices or his victims?

In the end, that might not even matter. That vision of the Empty Spaces suggested that Summer got her power from a predator. Maybe it was inside her body like a parasite, maybe nearby, but it was connected to her somehow. I'd seen both. Maybe she didn't know how dangerous it was, or even that it was there.

That predator, if that's what it was, had to be destroyed. The big question was: could I destroy it, whatever it was, without killing my friends?

I kept driving west and pulled into the second park I saw. The grass was dead brown, but what did that matter to me? I carried the Ralphs grocery bag to a bench beneath a tree. There were two bottles inside: a liter bottle of water and a little blue bottle of liquid Maalox. The first thing I did was pour water over my wrist, washing away whatever acids Summer had left there. It didn't stop hurting, but it stopped getting worse.

Then I guzzled some of the water. The heat was oppressive, and the sweat on my face made my eyes sting.

Once the water bottle had as much fluid as the Maalox did, I poured the antacid in and shook it up. It worked surprisingly well, and soon I'd rinsed off my face and hands completely.

I stood. It wasn't enough. The faint, choking stink of tear gas still clung to my clothes, and my skin was beginning to crawl.

I used a clean shirt from my jump bag to wipe the drying Maalox from my face. The empty bottles went back into the grocery bag along with the cellphone. I wrapped them up and dumped them into the trash.

I drove back toward the freeway until I came to a Best Western half a block from an exit. The vacancy sign was lit.

My shirt still stank, but the clerk didn't care. I don't think she cared about anything except her air-conditioning. I rented a room on the second floor and trudged upstairs.

The room was clean and plain. I stood by the bed with the TV remote in my hand for a full two minutes and tried to convince myself to shower. The temptation to sit in front of the tube in a trance state was so strong it was like a death wish. I closed my eyes and tried to imagine myself watching TV while predators spread through the city, killing people. I couldn't do that, no matter how much I wanted to rest. I carried my bag into the bathroom.

I stripped down and threw my clothes into the bottom of the tub. I had brought a small bottle of laundry detergent, and I scrubbed the sweat, stomach medicine, and tear gas by hand. The cold water felt good on my hands. Then I hung them by the window, turning off the air just below them.

Then I took a shower of my own. My skin was raw and red where Summer had touched me. I switched to cold water. It was uncomfortable, but I wanted it that way. I'd seen a predator on Summer and I'd backed off. I had to stand up and stay in the fight. I had to endure.

My clothes were not even close to dry when I finished. I took my last clean shirt, a white button-down, from the bag and put it on. Then I looked at myself in the mirror. I didn't look like a hungry ghost anymore, just a guy who needed a good night's sleep. At least I had cleaned the sweat off my face. I've always hated the feel of dried sweat.

I got back into my car and drove to Silver Lake, giving a wide berth to the Bigfoot Room and the street where I'd parked Bud's truck. I wasn't ready to run into them again.

Caramella's place was a little house, which surprised me. It had a lawn about the size of two postage stamps and a lot of Spanish stucco on the outside. As on just about every street in L.A., the houses on the block were a mishmash of styles, but hers was a basic A-frame that had been troweled over with a pueblo exterior. I took out my ghost knife.

A Corolla was parked in the driveway. There were two tall windows at the front of the house, and I nearly walked into the tiny flower garden to peep through the glass. It was just after 9 P.M., and I was planning to break and enter a friend's house.

Instead, I pocketed the ghost knife and rang the doorbell.

No one answered. I fidgeted a little, then rang it again. Again there was no answer. My Escort was parked at the curb, but the idea of driving away felt like defeat. Where would I go after this? I didn't know where Caramella worked. I didn't know where she hung out. A detective might have started walking around the neighborhood, asking about her at every diner, deli, and bar, but I wasn't a detective. I was a criminal.

I took out my ghost knife and slid it through the lock. The front door opened easily, and I let myself in, pushing the door closed behind me.

The house looked even smaller on the inside, but it was nicely furnished. Everything I owned had come out of a yard sale, but Melly's tables and chairs were new if not fancy. The plaid couch and recliner matched the curtains, and there were tiny white throw pillows everywhere. A pair of lamps on either side of the couch threw a pale blue light around the room, and the ceiling light in the bathroom was on.

But while the room looked tidy and homey, it was sweltering hot and stank of garbage. The smell made my eyes water. It wasn't a dead body, I didn't think. I'd smelled bodies before.

It felt strange to stand in Melly's empty house, but what the hell. She had walked into mine without knocking.

First, I wandered around the room. I was concerned that the garbage smell would hide the stink of a dead body, but I didn't find one behind the furniture and there were no blood splashes against the walls. The bedroom was empty—the bed was neatly made, in fact, and the little desk in the corner was tidy.

Then I went into the bathroom. The medicine cabinet was standing open. I pushed it closed, getting a glimpse of the dark circles under my eyes. The shower curtain was drawn, and a couple of the rings had been pulled free. I peeked through the gap into the tub. I couldn't see anything in the bottom of the tub, not even droplets of water.

I went back to the living room and noticed a mail slot just beside the front door. Below it there was a small wicker basket full of mail. It looked like a couple of days' worth, but I couldn't tell exactly. I fanned through it and saw that most of it was addressed to Luther Olive.

There was a list of phone numbers on a notepad by the phone. I picked up the receiver and dialed the one at the top, labeled WORK. The woman who answered announced that it was a hospice-care facility, but she wouldn't answer any questions about Caramella and she wouldn't transfer me to her voice mail. I left my real name and a fake call-back number and hung up.

Finally, I went into the kitchen. There was a pink ceramic bowl full of rotting chicken on the counter, but most of the stink was coming from the open garbage can. I looked around without touching anything, then went back into the living room.

I was alone and it was obvious that I was the first person to stand in this room for a couple of days. I picked up a framed photo on the end table.

It was a picture of two faces close together. One was Melly and she was laughing. She looked older than I remembered, and more beautiful. She had little wrinkles at the corners of her eyes, and seeing her open-mouthed smile brought back the memory of her laugh.

The man laughing with her, his cheek pressed against hers, was a black man with a short haircut, a scar below his eye, and a crooked nose. He had a beefy, solid look about him—the kind of muscular guy who would get fat at the first sign of comfort. He also gave the impression of puppy-dog earnestness, as though he was eager to please out of habit. That must have been Luther.

I liked the friendly roughneck look of him, and I was a little jealous, too. Not because I wanted Caramella—we hadn't had that sort of relationship—but because he had happiness and love and a home. I hoped I would be able to save whatever he and Melly had.

There were other pictures on the mantel, and I studied them one by one. Here were pictures of Melly and her guy with her mom and sister in a lush forest somewhere. Next was an old bridal picture of a black couple, both looking heavenward. Next was a picture of Luther with Ty, Lenard, and Arne. They were all smiling. Most of the rest were Melly and her guy at various events—parties, picnics, carousels.

The last showed Melly and Violet laughing while they baked Christmas cookies. I was surprised to see them together. They hadn't been close when I was around, but apparently things had changed.

Suddenly, I couldn't stand it anymore. I rushed into the kitchen, dumped the rotting chicken, bowl and all, into the trash can, then carried the garbage out the back door.

There was a plastic bin in the little backyard. I upended the trash can into it, letting a plume of stink blow over me. I tossed the can onto the parched lawn and went inside, leaving the back door open. I went to the bathroom and threw open the window, then opened the bedroom and living room windows. A mild crosscurrent blew across me. It wasn't enough to clear the stink, but it was better than the stale, oppressive heat.

Then I got to work.

I searched the house from top to bottom, taking special care to put things back where they belonged. I was careful out of respect for Caramella more than a desire to trick her, although if she never found out I'd broken in, I'd be happy.

I was looking for spell books, of course. Barring that, I wanted to find single spells, either instructions for casting them or a spell itself—a sigil drawn, carved, or stitched onto another object. If I couldn't find that, I hoped to find something to tell me where to look for Caramella next. An open phone book with a secluded Big Bear resort circled in red ink, maybe. I wasn't that lucky.

I searched every drawer, beneath every cushion, inside the pocket of every jacket and pair of pants. I opened every box and chest, looked inside every lamp, and ran my hand along the underside of every piece of furniture. I even unscrewed the grates over the air vents for their central heating. Nothing.

Caramella had a laptop on a tiny sewing desk in her room, but I hadn't done more than search around it so far. I didn't have a computer of my own, and I didn't know much about them.

I opened it and it came to life. I was surprised that it was sitting there, already turned on. Had Caramella been here recently, using it? She could have come and gone invisibly, of course. In fact, she could have followed me around the house while I searched it.

I felt a surge of anxiety as that thought grew larger in my mind, but I took several deep breaths. No one was there. Not with that garbage smell. No one was there.

Once the computer had fully come to life again, it began to download four days' worth of emails. It had been sitting there, switched on, for several days, and no one had used it recently.

I read the five dozen new emails as well as a couple of days' worth of old ones. Most were useless: supposedly funny stories about squabbling married couples, ads for natural Viagra, and attempts to organize a group of friends for a Friday movie date.

Only in the last day's messages did I notice anything unusual. Her mother had sent a note asking where she was, and telling her to please call. She had similar notes from her supervisor and co-worker, and from Arne.

I tried to find out more, but everything I did on her computer caused something inexplicable to happen, so I closed it.

I went back into the living room and looked at the clock. It had been just over two hours since I'd snuck in, and I had nothing to show for my time. Predators were on the loose, and I had no idea what to do next. Tomorrow at seven-thirty I'd go back to Ralphs and hope to meet Annalise, but until then I had nothing.

But there was nothing left to do here. If I went back to my motel, I could have another shower and sleep—maybe—but I would have run out of options. There was nowhere else for me to go but back to Arne, and I wasn't ready for that yet. I needed to talk to Caramella first.

So I stood there, my indecision making the choice for me. Finally, I decided I might as well wait. I wanted to talk to her, and I was more likely to find her here than at my motel.

I dug out the remote and turned on the local news, hoping there would be a segment about a mysterious invisible assailant, but I was out of luck there, too. The first segment covered the president's plan to visit L.A.

Then the newscasters switched to extended reports of a break-in at a movie star's Beverly Hills home. Her name was Ellen Egan-Jade; she'd been in Minnesota filming her latest romantic thriller, but her live-in housekeeper had been beaten, raped, and left for dead. The only thing the asshole took was her Oscar. The cops didn't have any leads.

There was a pizza box with three slices of pepperoni in the fridge. The house didn't smell so bad anymore—or maybe I'd gotten used to it—so I took the pizza into the living room to eat at the coffee table. It was dry and tight, like jerky.

The announcer started speculating what would have happened if the actress had been home at the time of the break-in, while they showed pictures of her beautiful face. The whole thing made me feel a little sick, so I turned it off and ate in silence.

After finishing the pizza, I leaned back on the couch. My eyes started to fall closed, so I jumped up and walked around. I peeked out the front window, then the back. No one was in sight.

The heat and food were making me drowsy. I shut the front and back doors and propped a chair under each knob. I shut all the windows and turned the thermostat to eighty-five. Cool air hissed into the room. That would help with the heat. I just needed to keep myself awake.

I paced until I grew tired, then sat on the couch with my arms folded. Just as I told myself I could stay up as late as I needed to, I nodded off.

I dreamed I was standing on a ship on a stormy sea. Everything below deck had been taken over by a huge beehive—the buzzing was incredibly loud—and waves against the wooden hull were making it groan and crack.

Then I realized I was sleeping and that the sounds were coming from outside my dream. I snapped awake in a living room full of noise. I jolted to my feet, looking around.

The buzzing, cracking sounds were coming from the bathroom.

CHAPTER FOUR

I raced to the bathroom door. The windows were dark; it was still nighttime, but how late was it? I took my ghost knife out of my pocket.

I glanced around the room. No one else was here—not that I'd expected Caramella or Luther to come home and leave me sleeping quietly on the couch. I rubbed my eyes, trying to get them to focus.

The buzzing became hollow, as though it was echoing down a long tube, and was followed by a series of cracks that sounded like the bathroom was falling off the building. I pushed the door open just as a terrible silence fell.

The bathtub seemed to be full of darkness. I took a step into the room so I could see the bottom, but there didn't seem to be one. All I could see was swirling black, and slightly darker shapes moving far, far away.

An opening to the Empty Spaces had appeared in the bathtub. It wasn't a vision this time; I could feel the *absence* there.

Something floated through the opening into our world. It was little more than a colorless, shapeless shimmer, strung out like pulled taffy, and it hovered seven feet off the floor.

A bad feeling came over me, and I backed out of the room while lifting the ghost knife. A second form began to rise out of the tub.

The first shimmer rushed at my face. I instinctively held up my empty hand to ward it off. It struck my palm and flowed around it like a thick jelly. Tendrils struck my mouth and nose. It was sticky, just like Summer's hand when she grabbed my wrist. I kept my mouth tightly shut, but it seemed to be trying to squirm into my nostrils.

My iron gate, one of the spells Annalise had put on my chest, suddenly felt burning hot. For a moment, I felt a strange, heavy blankness in my thoughts, as though something was erasing my mind.

I slashed my ghost knife through the tendrils, splitting it apart. The blankness vanished. I yanked the bathroom door shut. Whatever the hell I was dealing with, I wanted to face them one at a time. I slashed again, and the stuff let out a strange keening that bypassed my ears and went directly to my guts.

This goop was alive. It was a predator and it was after me.

My ghost knife can kill predators, though. I slashed it across the shimmer again, dragging it along my face and around my mouth and nose. More keening, which was just what I wanted. I cut it again.

But I had to be careful: I know little about magic, and only slightly more about this spell I'd cast. My ghost knife has a powerful effect on living creatures, and I'd never cut myself with the spell, for fear of what might happen. At best I'd lose my will to fight, like Wardell. I didn't want to imagine the worst thing.

So I held the laminated edge of the paper close and smeared it through the sticky liquid slime spreading over my neck and shoulder.

The creature flexed, twisting me off balance and knocking me to the carpet. I reached out to the table to break my fall, stupidly dropping my ghost knife. The predator wrenched me flat on my back. I could still feel it pushing despair into me, trying to make me surrender. With a quick exertion of will, I *reached* for my spell and called it back into my hand.

The creature flowed over my face, and I squeezed my eyes shut. I blasted air out of my nose to clear it, then clamped it shut with my free hand. My skin . . . Everywhere it touched me, my skin burned. The thing was like acid.

My iron gate flared again. The despair grew stronger and my thoughts were sluggish and dull. Without that protective spell, I would have been comatose.

The creature flexed again, trying to pull my hand away from my face. Damn, it was strong. It took everything I had to hold my fingers over my nose. Eventually, it would realize it could bend back my fingers until they broke. For now, though, I was new prey and it wasn't quite sure how to deal with me.

I brought the ghost knife toward my face, but the predator pushed it back, slamming my wrist to the floor. I couldn't move that arm.

It had me pinned, and eventually it would find a way inside my body. Then the acid burning would be on my insides. With the right leverage, I might be stronger than it, but I was on my back, my air was

running out, and I couldn't see. I had to do something quickly—I had
to think quickly—or I was going to die.

I flexed my right arm with all my strength, trying to bring the
ghost knife near my face with a sudden burst of power. It almost
worked, but I couldn't quite reach. I moved the paper back and forth
along my wrist as much as I could. It made tiny cuts in the predator,
but I felt it peeling away from my hand and the spell.

Then my burst of power was over, and the predator slammed my
arm back against the carpet.

I was failing. Bad enough that I was going to be killed by this
damn predator here on the floor of Melly's pretty little house, but
Caramella would have a predator in her home, waiting for her. God,
no, I could not do that to her. I could not be responsible for that.

I *reached* for my ghost knife again, even though it was already in
my hand. I could feel it, like a part of me, ready to do what I wanted
it to do. I'd learned months ago that I could "throw" it without moving my body at all; the spell went where I wanted it to go—there was
no other way to explain its uncanny accuracy. But while the throwing
motion helped me picture where I wanted it to go and made the spell
faster, I didn't need it.

I willed the spell out of my hand, imagining it zipping across my
body and over my face. I felt the edge of it strike the predator several
times, and the creature keened in its soundless way again. Its body
peeled back where it had been cut, and the tension suddenly went out
of it.

I kicked out, rolling myself onto my knees while *calling* my ghost
knife back to me.

There was a sudden pressure against my ears; it was trying to get
inside me by going through my eardrums. I scraped the ghost knife
over one side of my head, and the creature suddenly leapt away from
me.

I gasped, taking in air. My hands and head stung all the way up
into my nostrils. I opened my eyes, feeling my eyelids burning where
they folded.

The predator moved away from me, dragging parts of itself on the
carpet. Instead of being a liquid shimmer, it was frayed, like torn rags
blowing in the wind.

I threw my ghost knife at it, willing it to hit the center. It did. The
thing split apart, turned pallid gray, and fell to the carpet with a
*squerch*ing sound. Dead.

I felt a sudden rush of triumph and fury. I'd faced another creature
from the Empty Spaces, and I'd beaten it. My mind seemed to rev into

overdrive, but after a moment I realized I was just coming back to myself—the predator had tried to take my mind along with my body, but my iron gate had partly blocked it, and now I could think clearly again.

My whole body was drenched with sweat, and I gasped in heavy, ragged breaths. Damn, my whole head was really starting to burn.

I moved toward the bathroom. I'd definitely seen a second predator coming out of the tub, but was there a third, and a fourth? Was there a thousandth? As much as I was ready to take my victory and retreat, there was no one else here. I was the only one who could stop these predators. I had to open that bathroom door and fight.

The knob trembled slightly as something on the other side moved against the door. I reached out just as I saw a flicker of movement near the floor.

I jumped back. Another predator had pushed under the door, flowing through the narrow crack and protruding toward me. And I'd nearly stepped in it. I'd been so focused on the doorknob that I had missed the threat below me.

It struck at me like a hungry snake.

There was no time to think. I grabbed hold of the creature's farthest end—it felt strangely like a muscle—and slashed the ghost knife through it. The predator collapsed, almost splashing onto the carpet, then vanished.

In a panic, I fell to my knees, gouging and slashing with my spell. I'd thought it had escaped somehow, and that I'd let a predator get loose in the world. Then the strange keening returned. The thing was still below me, but it had turned invisible. I kept cutting. After several more slashes, it turned a pallid gray and died.

Were there only two? If I opened the door, predators might flood out at me like a breaking dam. I crouched low, waiting to see if another predator would try to squeeze under, but I didn't see anything. I swiped my ghost knife through the crack but didn't connect with anything.

Fine. If there were more inside, they weren't coming out. The stinging on my face and hands had become worse—it felt like every patch of bare skin the creature had touched was coated with a film of weak acid. The pain grew and grew, and eventually I had to act, because waiting made me think about the pain too much.

I shoved the bathroom door open, darted inside, and slammed it shut. The predators weren't fast enough to have gotten out—at least, I hoped not. I yanked a towel off the rack and kicked it against the bottom of the door.

In the tub, I saw only a faint bath ring. The vast, deep darkness of the Empty Spaces was gone. Good. I didn't have a way to close a portal into another universe.

But had more predators come through? I couldn't see anything, but I hadn't seen that second one after it went flat on the floor.

I bent down and swiped my ghost knife against the floor, barely splitting the linoleum, then I did it again and again. The marks spiraled out one from another, covering the whole floor and moving up the walls and cabinets. I made long vertical slashes six inches apart, then I stepped up onto the toilet and did the same to the ceiling.

I was especially careful with the window. I didn't want to cut it open, in case a predator was looking for a way out. I did scrape through the wooden jamb and latch, though.

Then I fell to my knees and opened the cabinet under the sink. I cut through all of it, including the drainpipe. There was no keening sound, and while one of these predators might have escaped down the drain, I doubted it. The space under the door was much larger than the pipe, and it would have been a struggle to squeeze through.

Two. There had only been two. I was blearily glad that I'd turned on the air-conditioning and closed the bathroom window.

And I couldn't stand the burning on my skin anymore. I'd forced myself to stay and search the bathroom carefully, but the pain had become unbearable.

I ran into the kitchen, stuck my head in the sink, and sprayed cold water into my hair. The effect was sudden and wonderful—my skin was still hurting, but the acid film dissolved and washed away on contact with the water.

I did my hands, my neck, and my face. Finally, I got a turkey baster out of a drawer, filled it with water, and sprayed the water into my nostrils several times.

Better. Better. I still felt the pain, but at least it wasn't getting any worse.

I wandered back into the bathroom. It was all ruined, of course. Melly would need a contractor to come in here to fix what I'd done, but I couldn't bring myself to feel sorry. The pain was still there, and my fear was too recent. I picked up a bottle of aloe gel and began dabbing the stuff onto my face. It dulled the pain even more.

I glanced down at my sleeve. It was wet but perfectly clean. The predator had wrapped itself around my arm, but it hadn't left a stain on my clothes.

The predators had hurt my skin in exactly the same way that Summer's handprint had, and Caramella's slaps. They were hard to see, too. When they were attacking they looked a lot like heat shimmers in the air. But the predator that had squeezed under the door had gone flat and vanished. I'd looked right at it and hadn't seen it.

It was invisible. Just like Summer.

Summer had to have one of these predators on her, and she must have been protected from it somehow. Well, "somehow" wasn't really much of a mystery. Someone had cast a spell on her. She was wrapped up by a predator that wanted to devour her but couldn't.

The thought gave me shivers.

My face felt a little stiff and I looked like I had a bit of sunburn, but that was all. I'd gotten off easy.

Back in the living room, the pile of goop on the floor looked smaller. Was my mind playing a trick, or was the dead predator dissolving? I took a sock from a drawer in the bedroom and laid it beside the gray mess. Slowly, the goop receded from it. It was vanishing on its own. How considerate.

I took a chair from the desk and sat beside it. My hands were shaking. It was strange that my hands were shaking so long after the fight. I kept control. I breathed as slowly and as evenly as I could while the predator's corpse vanished in front of me.

Under normal circumstances, I would have burned Melly's house to the ground. These weren't normal circumstances because *this was Melly's house*. When she and her guy returned . . .

I looked around. The faint garbage stink was still there. The place felt empty. They weren't coming back—I knew they weren't—and to hell with this pretty little house.

I fetched a cotton robe, a candle, and a lighter from the bathroom, then closed all the curtains. I lit the candle and arranged it and the robe beside the edge of the couch. Then I lit the robe. The flames spread down to the throw pillows, and I knew that it would soon spread to the curtains and carpet.

The lock on the front door was still broken. I went out the back way, walked down the block, and got into my car. I didn't drive by Melly's house. I wouldn't have been able to see the flames behind the curtains, and I didn't want to try.

Five years ago, Melly had been a good friend to me. We'd been part of the same crew, had joked and laughed together. Now, as a wooden man in the society, I was burning her house down.

I didn't want to think about that, but I felt like a complete bastard.

What to do next? It was after three in the morning; the sun wouldn't rise for hours, and I'd never be able to sleep. There was no

use going to Violet's place. If Arne had gone out looking for cars to
steal, he would have already quit for the night. At best, he'd be at
Long Beach, loading stolen SUVs into shipping containers. The very
early morning hours were no good for boosting cars, he'd always said.
No one else was on the street, and it was too easy to get noticed.

I drove back to the Bigfoot Room. The bar was closed, of course.
I parked down the block and walked by the outside. There were no
bullet holes in the glass front. None of the shots had gone in that direction. I checked the top of the door; someone had already wiped the
words BIGFOOT ROOM away.

I walked around to the alley, half expecting to find stinking clouds
of tear gas there, but of course there weren't. Even the smell was gone.

The security light above the bar's back door gave me enough light
to look around, but first I waved my arms and kicked my feet along
the walls in case an invisible person was standing there. I didn't find
any.

The fire exit had a half dozen bullet holes punched through it. My
eyes had been closed for most of the gunfire, but it appeared that the
bullets had gone in one direction—toward Arne.

Then I noticed my name. I stepped closer to the door and saw that
someone had written my name in black Sharpie. It read: RAY LOVES TO
HANG AT THE QUILL AND TYRANT ANY TIME OF DAY OR NIGHT.

I touched the ink; it wasn't wet. It could have been graffiti written
by a disgruntled customer, but the way it was phrased made me think
it was a message for me, in case I came back. Arne would never have
been sloppy enough to leave a message right where the cops would see
it, but maybe Bud or Robbie would.

I returned to my car. I knew people could look up addresses with
their computers or with more expensive phones than the one I'd thrown
away, but I was going to have to make do with the yellow pages.

I went back to my motel room and looked up the Quill and Tyrant. The address was in North Hollywood; I had to drive back the
way I'd just come.

The Quill was just a door in a cinder-block box, and of course the
lights were out. It was after 5 A.M. I went up to the door anyway and
looked through the window. Everything was pitch-black inside, except
for one lone beer sign.

When I turned around, there was a cop car at the curb, with a cop
inside it asking me what I thought I was doing. I told him I'd lost my
credit card and started looking around on the sidewalk. He grunted,
looked me over once, and drove away without wishing me luck.

When he'd turned the corner, I walked around the building to the back. There was a dumpster back there along with a row of recycling bins. Behind that, by the cellar door, was a heavily tattooed Mexican man with a crooked nose and full beard. He was smoking a reefer, and he had a .45 S&W in his lap. He looked so stoned he was nearly comatose. "You got lost," he said.

"I'm looking for Robbie. Is this the right place?"

He laid his hand on his weapon. "Ain't no Robbie here."

"My mistake," I said, and started to leave.

"Hey! I didn't say you could go. Who're you?"

I turned back and looked him in the eye. It had been a couple years since I left prison and this life behind me, but I knew better than to show fear or try to make friends. "I'm Ray," I said, keeping my voice flat.

He pursed his lips in a parody of thought. He really was amazingly stoned. I wondered, briefly, if I could rush him if I had to. "Ray Lilly?" he asked.

"That's right."

He rolled his eyes. "Well, you should have said so. Go ahead down. Fidel is waiting for you."

Fidel? I didn't know anyone named Fidel. But Stoned had waved at the cellar door, so I stepped toward it and lifted it open.

Light and music came through the opening, but no voices. I walked down the stairs, letting the door fall closed behind me. There were two more young guys on my left, both tattooed and bearded like Stoned. Bud and Summer sat on a low couch on my right. Robbie stood at the far end of the room with a very short, very muscular man with a shaved head. He was covered with jailhouse tattoos, including one along the side of his neck that said THUG in Gothic letters.

And everyone was watching me.

Robbie smiled. "Ray! You got my message."

He didn't walk toward me, so I walked toward him. "Good to see you again, Robbie."

His smile faltered a little. "That ain't my name anymore, dude. It never was. It's Fidel Robles."

"Really?" I said. "All those years we knew each other and you never told me your real name?"

He shrugged and smiled more broadly. His teeth were straight and white, his face full. He looked healthier than anyone in the crew, myself included. "I used to be embarrassed, man. My parents named me after an enemy of America! Oh no! The shame!" He laughed, and I laughed with him. "Then one day I realized I had brown skin just like Castro, and a nasty habit of taking things from rich people. Then I realized, hey, I'm an enemy of America, too. And proud of it."

I laughed and held out my hand. "It's good to see you again, Fidel."

He glanced down at my hand but didn't take it. His expression told me that he thought it was a test he didn't want to take, which it was. "I know you know," he said.

CHAPTER FIVE

I let my hand and my smile drop. "We gotta talk about this," I said.

"I agree." Robbie waved toward the room. It was just basement storage—a couple of stools with torn seat covers in the corner, a massive beer fridge against one wall, with stacks of whiskey crates beside it. There was a tatty carpet on the far side of the room, and a yard-sale couch set on it. Bud and Summer were all alone over there. "Humble beginnings, huh? But we're tired of being humble. We're ready to move into the big time."

Arne had looked at me with resentment and anger. But Robbie looked ready to thank me. "What happened to you?" I asked.

"I got a super power! Want to hear my origin story? It's pretty fucked up."

"Actually, I do. I really, really do."

"That's cool, Ray, but later. I need something from you first. Okay? We got more important things to talk about. What did Arne say when he called you back to L.A.?"

"It wasn't Arne," I told him. His smile became a little strained, as though he didn't believe me. "It was Caramella. She said she was in trouble."

"Come on, Ray. Are you kidding me?"

"Of course not. Caramella came to see me in Seattle. She said everyone was in trouble and that it was all my fault."

"Well, she was wrong. I'm not sure I'll ever be in trouble again." He rubbed his chin, thinking of a new way to come at me. "Ray, you know that Arne was never really your friend."

"I know it." Robbie had been the closest thing I had to a friend. Still, though: only the *closest* thing. "And you were his second-in-command."

"Yeah, but he *trusted* you. He always thought you were smart."

"And he kept food in our bellies and games in the PlayStation. So why aren't you with him anymore?"

"I already told you, dude. We're through playing it safe. No more stealing cars, no more tiny payouts. We jumped the fence. No one can touch us now, so we're moving up."

"To what?"

"Anything we want! If I want to rob a bank, I can do it. If I want to kill a guy—even the best-protected guy in the world—I can do that, too. How much you want to pay me to kill the royal family in England? I could fly over there and fly back in a couple days and the job would be done. Me, I'd have the money in my Swiss bank account."

I stared at him, trying to decide if he was joking. I was pretty sure everything Robbie knew about being an international hit man came from the movies.

"You don't look all that convinced, Ray."

"Can I hear that origin story now?"

"Don't you get it? You could be in with us. I'm going to take my cousins over to see your boy later, and you could come with us."

"Wally King isn't my boy."

"Oh yeah? He told us he was your friend."

I couldn't talk for a moment because my jaw wouldn't unclench. Wally had murdered a woman to steal spells from her. He'd claimed to be able to cure any disease or injury, when all he could really do was implant predators into people—including the oldest friend I had in the world. He'd turned my friend Jon into a monster, and God help me, when Annalise came to put a stop to it, I'd fought her.

And now he was telling people we were friends? "Rob—I mean, Fidel, the last time I saw Wally I tried to kill him." And I'd try again, as soon as I could.

"Does he know about that? 'Cause he's still talking about you like you're his bestest pal."

"Can I hear that origin story now?"

He sighed, sounding a little irritated, then turned into a silhouette. I caught a brief glimpse of the Empty Spaces, and he vanished. I held myself completely still, listening. What the hell should I do?

Before I could come up with a good idea, he suddenly reappeared in the same spot, but now he was pointing a gun at my face.

I jumped back and ducked low, my heart pounding. The door was too far for me to run to with a gun on me, and there were too many of them for me to start swinging. I had to fight an overwhelming urge to *attack! attack!*

Fidel laughed and his cousins laughed with him. Summer and Bud watched me quietly from the couch, their expressions closed. The laughter made me furious, made me want to blow myself up like a bomb, but I swallowed it. It was time to stop thinking of him as Robbie, the guy who could never beat me at Mortal Kombat but always made me laugh. This was someone else.

The jeering laughs slowly died down. Fidel seemed sorry they had to end. "Damn, Ray. Living easy up in Seattle has made you soft. You're jumpy. I was just showing you my new piece. It's a SIG Sauer, just like those Blackwater guys in Iraq use." He slid his gun into the waistband of his pants. "But I'm not sure you can really appreciate it from all the way down there."

I was still crouched down. It took all the willpower I had, but I made myself stand straight. "Guess so."

"Are you joking about trying to kill your pal Wally? 'Cause I was hoping you could help me out with him."

It took me a second to catch up. "I get it. You want super powers for your cousins, and you want me to talk Wally into giving them an origin story of their own."

"Not just that, Ray. I want you on my side. Arne was right about you. You're a sharp guy. You always got your eyes open. I want you on my team, not his."

"What about that origin story?" I asked.

Fidel shook his head and came close to me. He still wore that broad, perfect smile. "Didn't your boss tell you all of that? You came to town and ran straight to him. We saw you there."

"Caramella contacted me, not Arne," I said again.

"He was never really your friend, Ray," he said, as if trying to convince me to stop lying. "You were his loyal guy, and look how he paid you back with Violet."

I stepped back, startled. Violet and Arne? So Jasmin—

"That's right, dude." Fidel stepped close to me, but not close enough to touch. "You did everything he told you to do, and he went behind your back with your girl."

I flinched. I couldn't help it—the image of Arne and Vi together in her bed was sudden and sharp. Fidel could have been lying, but I didn't believe it. Arne and Vi—I knew it was true. It was like a secret I was keeping from myself.

I closed my eyes and imagined Annalise beside me. Would she think this mattered? Those relationships were five years in the past. I'd come out of prison and turned my back on all of it. Did it matter? Of course not. It hurt, yeah, but I wasn't here to settle that sort of score.

"Fidel," I said. "Where can I find Wally?"

Fidel smiled and turned sideways. "I don't think that's such a good idea, Ray. You haven't even signed up with me yet. You're still on Arne's side."

"Sign up with you, Fidel? Wally King already killed you."

He didn't like that, but he smiled through it. "I don't think so."

"You think I've been living easy in Seattle? Wally King put a curse on my oldest friend up there, and . . ." I wasn't sure how to say this next part, so I just said it. "And now he's dead."

Fidel's cousins were focused on me. They didn't like what I was saying, and Fidel didn't like the attention I was getting. "C'mon, Ray. Don't try that shit with me. Are you ready to make your choice? Me or Arne?"

I absentmindedly rubbed the back of my hand. The tattoos there made my skin dead to the touch. I had a new boss now, and I couldn't talk about her. "I'm here for both of you, Fidel. Against Wally King. I'm here to save your life, if I can." I glanced over at Bud and Summer. "All your lives."

The short, muscular cousin stepped close to Fidel and said something in Spanish. I couldn't understand him, but I knew it wasn't friendly. "No, no," Fidel said to him, then turned to me. "Ray, why don't you go visit Arne? Talk to him about Violet and about his plans for the future. Then you can decide if you want to come back to me. Tell me what he has planned, and decide if you want to be safe with him or rich with us. Go ahead, and think about what I said."

I started backing toward the door. "You should think about what I said, too."

Fidel watched me with a look on his face that I'd never seen before. He looked confident and wise, like a king sending a messenger on a particularly clever errand. I wanted to hit him. His cousins glared at me, but Summer and Bud had peculiar expressions. Had I gotten through to them, at least?

I backed to the stairs, then forced myself to turn around and walk away. No one shot me. I went outside. It was still cool, and the sun wasn't up yet, but I could see a faint glow along the horizon. Traffic had already started to pick up.

It was nearly 6 A.M. I should have been tired. It was unfair that I couldn't drive back to my rented room and close my eyes for a little while. I'd been in L.A. barely a day, and I was already back on a car thief's schedule.

Where could I go next? Was it late enough to stop at Violet's place to ask her about Caramella again? Probably not, but I didn't know where to find anyone else, so I thought I'd try it.

I drove back through the Valley with my windows down. The temperature was perfect, but I knew the heat would roast me later. I had no idea what to do about Robbie—Fidel, I meant. He had magic, almost certainly from a predator—he and Summer and Bud, and probably Arne and Lenard, too.

My boss, Annalise, would know what to do. She would have killed everyone in that room just because they had magic and wanted more. And having worked against her on one incident and with her on two, I could see where she was coming from. People could be crazy about magic. I'd seen it.

But I didn't want to kill them. Not if I could avoid it. In fact, even if I couldn't avoid it, I didn't want to do it. I hoped Annalise would be there to meet me outside the Ralphs tonight, so I could hand off the job to her. Maybe it was unfair, but there it was. I'd done my share of killing in Washaway, and I wasn't ready for more.

If it was not a predator that gave Fidel his invisibility—if it was just a spell, like the spells on my chest that blocked bullets or obscured evidence I left behind—then I was sure I could take care of it without killing anyone. My ghost knife cuts "ghosts, magic and dead things," and I could slash it through whatever spell they had on them and put an end to it.

The odds that their magic came from a spell were so low they were practically nonexistent, but I had to have hope, or I wouldn't be able to keep going.

Aside from that, I'd have to find Wally King. I owed him something, and it was long past due for him to get it. Him, I didn't feel squeamish about killing. Not at all.

The lights in Violet's apartment were dark, which didn't surprise me. I found a parking space just a block away, pulling in behind a woman who was obviously on her way to work, and closed my eyes for a while. I was ready to sleep after all.

The sun woke me around 8 A.M. I rubbed my face, climbed from the car, and rang the doorbell.

Jasmin answered. I introduced myself again, reminding her that I'd visited the day before, but she buzzed me in before I could finish.

It wasn't Violet who answered the door; it was her mother. "Raymundo," she said, squinting at me from behind her drugstore glasses. "Vi isn't here. But come in! Come in! Have a cup of tea."

"Thank you, Mrs. Johnson. I'd love some."

I followed her into the kitchen, where Jasmin was sloppily spooning cereal into her mouth. Mrs. Johnson put the kettle on the burner. "Please," she said. "Call me Maria. You are a grown man now. You can talk to me like one. I don't mind."

"Thank you, Maria." I was careful to keep my tone respectful.

She leaned against the cutting board and looked me over like an unexpected second chance. "So how have you been? Where are you working?"

"Things have been difficult," I told her. That was true, but the next thing I said was a white lie: "I got laid off from one job and haven't been able to find another." She looked disappointed at that, and I suddenly remembered that she could talk about jobs and the finding of them endlessly. I changed the subject. "How have you been? How is Mr. Johnson?"

"Oh," she said, and waved my question away. "I'm the same as always, but older. Mr. Johnson, he is off in Florida now, fighting for the unions. I tell him, 'Why go there? They hate unions!' but he don't listen. So, Ray, can you tell me what happened to my Tommy?"

That startled me. "Vi said he left town, although the way she said it made me think there was more to the story. I'm sorry, Maria. I haven't heard a thing about him."

"Can you ask around for me? I tried, but nobody does anything for an old Mexican lady. You're the only one who ever showed me any real respect. And Tommy . . . He don't call me or his father. Mr. Johnson, he blames me. He thinks I drove Tommy away from the family. You went to jail for Tommy, yes? You'll do this for me?"

"If I can, I will," I said. "But I'll need to talk to Violet again. Where—"

From the other room, Jasmin shouted: "*Abuela*, the ghost is still here!"

I hadn't realized she'd left. I rushed into the other room, Maria close behind me. Jasmin was kneeling on the couch, looking down into the space behind it.

"Jazzy! You come away from there and finish your breakfast. Then we can go to the park. And stop this foolishness about ghosts."

I went close to her. There was nothing behind the couch except dust bunnies. "What kind of ghost is it?" I asked. The window was right beside us; I glanced through it and saw a man in a red shirt with long camo pants standing on the sidewalk, looking up at the building.

"It's a fire ghost," Jasmin said. "It burns you if you touch it."

I knelt on the cushion beside her and reached into the space between the couch and the wall. I touched something wet and sticky that I couldn't see. Almost immediately, my fingertips began to burn. I yanked my hand back and pulled the little girl off the couch. "Hold her," I said to Maria, and the tone of my voice surprised her. She took the little girl in hand.

I rushed to the kitchen and ran my fingers under the tap. The pain washed away quickly, leaving my skin a little red. I filled a tall glass with water and went back into the living room.

Maria had pulled the couch away from the wall. "Go to your room, Jazzy," she said, but she didn't object when the girl ignored her by jumping onto the couch and peering over the back.

Maria reached into the space in front of the wall. "Ah! Holy Maria!" She held up her fingers, trying to see what had hurt them.

"Don't wipe it on your clothes," I told her. "Dip your fingers in here, quickly. That will help." I gave her the glass and she wet her hand, cleaning it off.

"And I didn't believe Jazzy when she said she saw a ghost. What is it, Raymundo? What's in my daughter's home?"

"I don't know yet." But that wasn't true. I knew damn well it was one of the predators that had attacked me at Caramella's house, but why was it lying inert behind Violet's couch?

I knelt and poured the water behind the couch. It struck something, then flowed over it onto the carpet. Water could wash off the burning effect but not the invisibility.

"What is it?" Maria asked.

I didn't know how to answer. It was an irregular shape, and rounded. Was it lying in wait? "You have to get Jasmin out of here. Right away."

"But what is it?" Maria asked again. "You didn't tell me."

"Because I'm not sure, but you're not safe here. Please."

"You brought this, didn't you?" She looked at me with narrowed eyes. "Is this some fancy plastic you put here?"

Jasmin hopped off the couch and ran into the back of the apartment. I turned to Maria, incredulous. "How could I have put something behind the couch? And why?"

"You should know already we don't have nothing to take," she said. "I know that's what all of you boys do. You and Arne and the rest—I know you got Tommy into it, too, before he vanished."

There was nothing I could say to that. I was good enough to search for her son but couldn't otherwise be trusted. Maybe she would have liked me more if I'd lied about having a job.

Jasmin ran back into the room with a roll of toilet paper, the loose end trailing behind her like a streamer. She leaped back up onto the couch and offered the roll to me.

The end of the paper fell onto the invisible whatever-it-was and stuck there. Damn. Smart kid. I took the roll and laid the paper over the invisible shape, doubling it back when it reached the end closest to me.

The paper stuck into place, showing the contours of the object. All at once, I realized what I was looking at. It was a human face, its eyes closed, its mouth open in a soundless scream.

Maria gasped. "Oh, my Melly!"

I jumped back, nearly knocking Maria over. Christ, she was right. It was Caramella. I stared at her, stunned. What had happened to her?

"You brought this here," Maria said. The way she said it made me think she was trying to convince herself rather than accuse me. "This is because of you!"

I felt a sudden flash of anger. "You don't know what you're saying!" Her eyes went wide, and she stepped away from me. I took a deep breath, pulling back my anger. Of course Maria wasn't accusing me of feeding Melly to a predator. Of course not.

I swallowed my anger and panic, trying to get a rational thought out of my brain. "Do you really think I brought invisible acid plastic here? Sculpted to look like Melly?"

"I—"

"Take your granddaughter out of here. Something dangerous is going on."

"That's really . . . her, isn't it?" Maria looked back over at Caramella. Jasmin was still kneeling on the back of the couch, but she was now laying toilet paper along the invisible form on the floor, outlining Caramella's breasts, belly, and arms. I didn't even realize I'd dropped the roll.

"Hey!" Jasmin said. "Her lips are moving."

My guts turned into a tight knot. I knelt close to Melly's face. It was true; her lips were quivering as though she was in tremendous pain.

She was still alive.

"Why is she doing that?" Jasmin asked.

I lunged at her, caught her by the arms, and lifted her off the couch. I felt like I was violating a taboo—*never touch someone else's child*—but I wanted to startle Maria. I wanted her to get the hell out.

As I pivoted to hand the little girl to her, she was already moving to take her. I pressed Jasmin into her arms, then forcibly steered her toward the door. She let me. "I can't tell you what's going on because I'm not sure myself. I only know that, whatever it is, it's not safe for little girls."

Jasmin pleaded as they left. "I want to see Melly some more! I want to see!" I closed the door but didn't lock it in case I needed to get away quickly.

I went into the kitchen and grabbed a sheet of cheesecloth from the bottom drawer by the oven, silently thanking Violet for keeping everything the way I remembered it. Back in the living room, I tore the toilet paper away; Caramella didn't deserve to have that stuff over her face. I laid the cheesecloth in its place. Then I laid a second sheet over her neck and chest, then a third over her stomach. I could see it move very slightly as she breathed.

My throat felt tight and my breathing was shallow. Melly was obviously in agony, and I was sure I knew why. This predator had draped itself over her and started to feed. Whatever had been protecting her when she'd visited me in Seattle—whatever was protecting Summer right now—must have worn off or been taken away. Now she was feeling the full extent of the creature's acid touch. It covered her entire body, was up her nose and down her throat, and it was slowly dissolving her while she was still alive.

As if I needed another reason to hate Wally King.

I took out my ghost knife. When I killed the predator in Melly's house, I'd had to cut it ten or twelve times before it died. Maybe it had a weak spot, but I didn't know how to find it.

I took a deep breath; I'd need steady hands for this. Judging by the cheesecloth, the creature was spread thin over her skin. There was no way I could cut it without also cutting her. That was okay. The ghost knife wouldn't hurt her while she was alive—it would just alter her personality for a while. The predator—this drape—was made partly of magic, so it *would* be hurt.

I heard movement somewhere nearby—this was an apartment building full of people. I imagined the Twenty Palace Society arriving and airlifting Caramella to a secret base in the desert somewhere, where a team of scientists in hazmat suits waited to save her life. Too bad I didn't have a copter or a desert lab. I didn't even have a pair of safety goggles. And the society, even though it was still hours away, would rather burn her to cinders than try to save her.

It was just me, and if Melly was going to come through this, I would have to cut the predator off of her by myself.

No more stalling. I moved the ghost knife close to her face, thinking I would scrape it along the skin of her cheek, possibly over her lips to clear her airway. How long had it been blocking her mouth and nose, or was it breathing for her?

The drape seemed to tense as I came close, and when the ghost knife plunged into it, the cheesecloth over Caramella's rib cage suddenly jerked upward. I heard her bones crack, and beneath the cloth her mouth opened in a silent scream.

Then she seemed to sag, and her lips stopped trembling. Her head rolled slightly to the side. It wasn't a big change in position, but it looked as though the strength had gone out of her. The predator had killed her.

I closed my eyes and lowered my head. Melly had just died in front of me—had just died *because* of me, in fact. I had failed her. I remembered her slapping my face just two days before, her face twisted with misery but without tears. Had the drape taken those from her, too?

I wanted to tear the cheesecloth off her—she deserved a more dignified shroud, but if I did that, there would be no evidence of her at all. I heard more voices outside, and I quashed the urge to yell at them to shut up. People shouldn't be shouting at their kids. They should have respect for the dead.

A strange buzzing voice spoke from somewhere near me. Then I heard a second and a third. Something groaned and creaked like a ship in heavy seas. Then there was another crack—this time not coming from Caramella's body. This one sounded like the world was breaking open.

I slashed the ghost knife through Caramella's head. A pale gray line appeared where I cut the predator.

I felt that strange keening again, and I took a savage joy in it. I slashed a second and third time, as the buzzing voices grew around me until they became that furious beehive noise I'd heard in Melly's home. Was this drape calling to others like it?

There was a sudden thump on the couch above me, and for one terrified moment I thought another predator had landed beside me. But it wasn't a drape; it was Jasmin. She'd broken away from her grandmother and run back inside.

"What's that noise?!" she shouted.

Beneath Caramella, the floor vanished, revealing an opening into the swirling black mists of the Empty Spaces.

The shrouded figure of Melly dropped into the darkness, and I fought for balance at the edge of the portal. The back legs of the couch were also over the void. The couch tipped downward and began to slide into the opening, scraping the edge of the wooden floor.

Jasmin screamed as she pitched forward. I lunged at her, throwing all my weight over the gap. I didn't think about it; I had no plan or courage. I just moved.

The couch pitched over backward as the front legs caught on the edge of the floor. I clamped my hand on Jasmin's wrist, my knee slamming onto the arm of the chair, my ghost knife slipping from my grasp and tumbling into the darkness.

I wish I could say I'd been graceful about it, that I'd grabbed her arm and hopped lightly to safety. But in truth I scrambled across the tumbling couch, snagging my shoe on the arm and trying desperately to throw some of my body weight onto the solid part of the floor.

It didn't happen. The couch floated away from me as my weight pressed on it. I slammed my left hand down on the carpeted living room floor and tried to keep my left foot in the solid world, too, but it slipped free and I swung out over the void.

My hand pressed down on the floor, stopping my fall. Once my body weight dropped below the level of the room, I wasn't falling anymore. Like the couch, I had momentum, but the void didn't pull me downward because there was nothing to fall toward. The friction of my left hand against Vi's carpet held me in place, and I started to pull myself back up. I glanced down at Jasmin. She stared at me with huge, terrified eyes.

Suddenly, a strange pulse pulled me downward. It wasn't like the tug of gravity—this felt as though something huge was trying to breathe me in. My mind only had room for one gigantic thought: *Hold on hold on.* The pull subsided, then came back again, and again, and again, with the regularity of a beating heart. *Hold on.*

Something grabbed my left wrist, and I cried out in panic. I pulled myself high enough to see Maria on her knees holding my forearm like a baseball bat. For a moment I had an absurd fear that she was going to lift my hand and fling me into the void, but instead she pressed down, anchoring me in this world.

"*¡Santa madre de Dios! ¿Que pasa aqui?*" she shouted.

"Here!" I lifted Jasmin as high as I could.

Maria let go, snatched her granddaughter, and dragged her into the world. She pushed the little girl toward the door and, bless her, started toward me again.

"Get out of here!"

She grabbed my wrist again. "What's happening? What's happening?"

I glanced down and saw pale, shapeless forms swirling in the darkness below. "Get out of here and close the door behind you! Run for your lives!"

It was a ridiculous thing to say, but it worked. Maria rolled to her feet and scooped Jasmin off the floor. With both hands free, I lifted myself halfway into the room. The door slammed shut.

My ghost knife was gone. I tried to *reach* for it with my thoughts the way I've always *called* it back to me, but I was scrambling out of the hole in the floor, and the shapes below were getting closer, and I was frightened, and I hated myself for my fear. I couldn't concentrate.

I'd lifted one leg out of the void and onto the solid floor when one of the sudden pulses dragged me back. They hadn't let up the whole time, but just as I was about to be free I was hit with one so much stronger than the ones before that it nearly sucked me in.

I cursed and scrambled upward again. I had one leg out when something heavy and soft struck my trailing foot. I rolled onto the floor, outside the void, just as another, even stronger pull started. I'd made it back into the world, but I wasn't safe.

There was a pale glob on the lower half of my left leg, like a small blanket bundled around my foot and ankle. And it was creeping upward.

I leaned over the opening into the Empty Spaces. The shapes were closer than ever now, and two were very, very close. I held my hand over the darkness and closed my eyes. *There.* I could feel my ghost knife in the darkness below. I *called* for it, desperately.

God, I had a predator on me, and it was already making the skin on my leg burn. I didn't even have to watch it move; I could feel it.

One of the drapes rushing out of the void faltered, and a moment after that I had my spell in my hand again.

Just as I rolled away from the opening in the floor, a drape rose out of it and rushed at my face. I shut my eyes and slapped my free hand over my nose and mouth.

The predator hit me and knocked me back; my iron gate suddenly burned white hot. A sudden rush of despair sapped my strength and my thoughts became confused, but I knew it was something the drape was doing to me, and I did my best to shake it off.

The first one creeping up my leg suddenly *squeezed* so hard that I almost gasped in a mouthful of slime. They began to pull in opposite directions. *Christ, they're fighting over me.*

I laid the edge of the ghost knife against my cheek and began to slash at the drape. It flared back, clearing a space from my mouth and nose, but I didn't dare take a breath. Not yet. I could feel it holding on to my head and neck, burning my already tender skin.

If one broke my neck, would another opening appear in the floor?

I scraped my spell across my throat just as the predator tried to squeeze. It pulled away, releasing me, and the one on my leg began to drag me across the floor. I opened my eyes in time to see the drape float away from my face. A third came through the gap in the floor, then the gap closed. The opening to the Empty Spaces was gone.

There were still three predators in the room with me. The third one moved unsteadily. It took me a moment to realize my ghost knife had already passed through it once when I *called* it from the void.

I twisted onto my stomach and slashed my ghost knife through the one that had just let go of my face. I swiped through it four, five, six times, but it wasn't dying fast enough. It retreated along the floor, too badly wounded to fly.

But the first drape around my leg was still pulling me in the other direction. I scrabbled with my elbows after the second one, then dug my untrapped foot into the carpet and launched myself after it.

I plunged the ghost knife into it. The drape tried to wrap itself around my hand, but I was already twisting and wiggling my spell, cutting it with every tiny move, and it quickly turned to sludge and died.

I spared a second to look at it closely, hoping to see a brain or an eye or some other vulnerable spot on its now visible body. I wanted a way to kill the thing in one shot, but I couldn't see anything

I rolled onto my back. The first predator had reached higher than my mid-thigh, but the effort it had put into dragging me away from its competition had slowed its progress. Still, it was much too close to my crotch. There was no way I was going to let this damn thing crush and dissolve my nuts.

I scanned the room for the telltale shimmer of the other one, knowing that it would be invisible if it had landed on something solid.

It hadn't. It hovered at the edges of the apartment door as though trying to figure out how to get through. I had to kill the third predator before it reached open air and a victim of its own, but first I had to give this first one something to think about. I sat up and slashed at it with my ghost knife.

But pain and panic had made me sloppy. I saw the edge of the spell cut through the thin flesh of the drape, and I saw my pants split apart, and I felt the ghost knife cut my leg.

My iron gate flared with white-hot pain—every tattooed spell on my body, even the two tiny ones on my neck that I never think about, suddenly burned as though they were made of napalm. A scream erupted from my throat.

My head was filled with roaring: *Cut cut cut cut* it screamed, over and over. It was a compulsion—a fury—to slash and splinter and tear and slice. The ghost knife had a desperate hunger to cut and destroy, and it ached to cut the spells on my chest, the spells Annalise had put on me.

I moved the spell toward my stomach.

A tiny voice in my head resisted. Those spells were precious. They'd saved my life many times, and I wouldn't last long without them. The burning of my iron gate slowly brought me back to myself.

But the compulsion from the ghost knife was unbearable. It had a powerful will of its own, and it needed to destroy *everything,* especially the magic on my body and in the predators.

One of those predators was getting away. I turned my attention toward it, trying to turn the will of the ghost knife toward it, too. I couldn't hold out much longer against the compulsion; I had to distract it. The spells on my body weren't going anywhere, but that predator would escape if I didn't destroy it first.

The ghost knife turned toward the drape. I threw it. It flashed across the room faster than I'd ever seen it move and cut through the creature.

I *called* it back immediately. I couldn't deny its hunger for the predator, and now that I'd opened myself to its will, it ran wild. The spell returned to me and I threw it again. *Called* it back. Threw it. I struggled to my knees, scrambling clumsily toward the drape, suddenly feeling as though I was as hungry as the predator I was destroying. *Called* it back, threw it.

The drape collapsed onto the carpet. I grasped my spell and fell on the creature, slashing and tearing at it in a mindless frenzy. I might have screamed, but I wasn't aware of myself at the moment, only of the growing pain of my iron gate and the ghost knife's unbearable urge to destroy.

Finally, the predator was dead, and my attacks against it felt empty and useless. The urge to *cut* was still strong, but the iron gate under my collarbone was blocking it with pain.

It would have been so easy—so easy!—to surrender to that need and slash through all the spells on my chest.

Instead, I turned to the drape on my leg. My hand trembled as I laid the edge of the spell against it. The predator wrenched at me and squeezed, but I didn't even notice. All my perceptions had narrowed to a tunnel, with the compulsion of the ghost knife at the center and pain everywhere else. It wanted to jump out of my hand and cut me, but I held on to it like it was a rattlesnake. It slashed into the drape.

The predator recoiled, and I felt the ghost knife's hunger for it. I couldn't fight my own spell, so I let it pursue the drape, using all my will and strength to redirect it from my body.

The drape peeled off me, and I cut it until it died. At the end, I could barely feel the ghost knife's compulsion anymore. The pain from my iron gate had grown large enough to fill my whole mind and will. It burned away the spell's influence, and I was in control of myself again.

I rolled over onto my stomach, gasping for air, waiting for the pain to ease. My mouth lay open against the carpet, and I inhaled enough dust and hair to make me hack. The pain wouldn't subside—my iron gate kept burning and growing, and I finally cried out pitifully, feeling tears running down my cheeks. Maybe it would never stop. Maybe it would go on and on until I lost my mind or ate a bullet or I really did slash it with my spell.

Then, finally, it began to subside. I struggled to my knees, not ready to stand yet. My ghost knife lay on the carpet beside me. It was mine. I'd created it. I'd used it against other people.

I shuddered. The pain from my iron gate had been so overwhelming that I thought it would destroy me, but I'd needed it to scour away the influence of the ghost knife. The spell hadn't affected other people the way it affected me, but I had no idea why. I also didn't have a coherent thought in my head; this was something I'd have to puzzle out later, if ever.

But my own spell had been just as hungry as the predators I fought, and by cutting myself I'd let it take control of me. I could never let that happen again. Never.

The pain wasn't entirely gone. My face, neck, and head were burning, just as they had the first time a drape attacked me, and so was my leg. I struggled to my feet. Exhaustion made me unsteady, and my leg felt stiff and swollen. I needed to wash away the sticky acid the predators left on their victims. Maybe a shower?

I stepped onto the section of the floor that had closed over the gap, feeling miserable enough to risk my life. It felt solid—I didn't fall through into the Empty Spaces, at least. Was it safe to bring Maria and Jasmin back into the room?

I glanced out the window. The big guy in the red shirt and camo pants was back, and he was looking right up at me. He took something long and thin from a hockey bag at his feet. One end was vaguely spear-shaped.

He lifted it to his shoulder and pointed it at me.

Oh, shit. I spun and hustled for the apartment door. It was seven or eight strides away—too far. I was never going to be able to run that far before the explosion hit. I ran anyway, because the only other option was waiting to die.

My stiff leg made me lurch across the room like a wounded drunk. I was halfway there and the explosion hadn't come. Then I had my hand on the knob, then I was pulling the door open, knowing that would only make it easier for the flames to blast out into the hall. Then I shut the door behind me, threw my leg over the railing, and jumped toward the pool below.

The explosion, when it came, was loud but not as loud as I expected. The flames never reached me; I struck the water with a painful slap and was shocked by how cold it was.

The pain on my face and leg eased immediately, and I struck the bottom gently. For one disorienting moment, I lost my bearings, but I saw light above and struggled back to the air.

The building was burning. Fire alarms blared and doors around the complex swung open. What were all these people doing here so late in the morning? Didn't they have jobs?

I saw Maria and Jasmin standing beneath a set of concrete stairs. They both had a shell-shocked look about them. I paddled to them and pulled myself out of the water.

"Take her out the back way," I said, straining to keep my voice low.

Maria grabbed my hand. "What—"

"Don't ask me questions!" I snapped at her. "It's not the time! Take Jasmin out the back way and get her someplace public. She's still not safe here."

Maria snapped her mouth shut. Jasmin tugged at her arm. "*Abuela,* I want to go."

They both hustled toward the little door on the far side of the pool, leaving me dripping water onto the pavement. People were charging around the complex, shouting at one another, demanding to know what had happened.

Me, I turned toward the front gate. I should have been exhausted, but my anger gave me a surge of energy. Someone had just fired a grenade at me, and I was going to kick his ass.

I ran out to the sidewalk. The asshole in camo pants was nowhere in sight. I looked up the street both ways; a Jeep Cherokee was driving away in one direction, a Dodge Ram truck in the other. Which one should I chase?

I had no reason to choose either, then the choice was gone. Both vehicles turned corners and vanished. Neither had been driving fast, like they would if they were fleeing the scene of a crime. Which meant the asshole could still be here.

And I was standing out in the street like a target at a gun range. I ran toward the spot where he'd stood, but I wasn't quite sure where it was. I turned around and surveyed Violet's burning building.

The flames were already shining through the windows of the apartment above, and the smoke was billowing out in two heavy black columns. I heard sirens in the distance, and people were rushing out of the courtyard with cats in their arms, or baby gear. One woman ran across the street toward me and set a milk crate full of paperbacks on the lawn, then sprinted back to the building.

Things would get very crowded soon. I tried to remember everything about Camo Pants that I could. I had seen the hockey bag at his feet, so I moved away from the line of parked cars. Had the telephone pole been on the right or the left? Had he stood on grass or the pavement?

I walked around the area, looking for something that looked like a clue. In Chino, I knew a guy who'd left his wallet on the front seat of a Lexus he'd jacked. Camo Pants wasn't so considerate. I couldn't find anything but cigarette butts and food wrappers. Maybe TV cops could spend hours going over all this trash in some lab and finger the guy, but it was useless to me. And I'd forgotten to ask where I could find Violet.

The sirens were getting closer, and that made me itch to leave the scene. But as I turned toward my car, someone behind me said: "Hey, Mr. Lilly."

I turned slowly and saw a homeless man walking toward me. His clothes were tattered and stiff with dirt, and even at this distance I could smell a year's worth of cheap cigarettes on him. "Hey, Mr. Lilly," he said again, his pale blue eyes wide and blank. "Your sick friend asked me to give you this." He held out a cellphone.

I didn't move to take it. "Who gave it to you?"

"Come on," he said, "he paid me ten bucks." He sounded a little nervous, as though he'd have to give back the money if I didn't accept it.

The phone rang.

"Who?" I asked again. I still didn't move to take it.

"I don't know his name, but he looks like a cancer patient or something. He said he's your friend. Come on."

Okay. I can come on with the best of them. I took the phone from him. He bustled away, looking relieved.

The phone was a cheap flip-closed type. It stopped ringing as the call went to voice mail. I opened it and looked at the number. It was an 818 area code, so it was coming from somewhere nearby. As expected, it started ringing again a few seconds later. I answered. "This is Ray."

"Ray! It's been so long. Remember me?"

"I remember you, Wally. Why don't we get together? We can talk about old times."

"Heh. I'm sure you'd like that, Ray, but I haven't forgotten that you tried to kill me. I mean, some stuff is hard to remember, but not that."

He sounded different, almost dreamy. Wally had never been the sharpest guy, but he'd never sounded like this. "I'm a different person now," I said.

"I'll bet. Listen, Ray, I do want to meet with you. Right now. Walk west about three blocks. There's a little diner that serves a nice breakfast. My treat."

I didn't know what to say to that. "Do you think I'm stupid, Wally?"

"Not at all, buddy. I know you still want to kill me. But I haven't forgotten what you did for me over the years. I still owe you. So we'll meet in a public place, and you'll give me a chance to talk for, say, sixty seconds before you try to kill me again. Okay? After that, we'll see what happens. The place is called the Sugar Shaker. Okay?"

"Okay." I closed the phone and started walking west. The fire engines drove by me as I went, and I saw bystanders and lookie-loos helping tenants unload their apartments or stand guard over their stuff.

At the corner I dropped Wally's cell into a trash can. It was painful to throw away resources, but it was Wally's. I didn't want any gifts from him.

I had three blocks to figure out what he wanted, but I couldn't put it together. In junior high, a couple of guys from the baseball team had picked on Wally until I told them to lay off. It wasn't that I liked him, but I hated to see the misery they were making.

Then I'd played with a handgun, and my life changed forever. I never went back to school and didn't hear from Wally again until just before I got out of Chino. He wrote to me, offering me a joe job at his copy shop. I tried to remember how it felt to be grateful to him, but it was too long ago. Too much had happened since.

So I wasn't sure what Wally owed me. An apology for what happened to Jon? For the predators he'd unleashed? As far as I was concerned, all Wally King owed me was his spell book and his miserable fucking life.

The Sugar Shaker turned out to be a storefront café with a counter along the back wall and ten round tables.

I took hold of my ghost knife before I walked through the door. The spell was quiet—just a sheet of laminated paper that I could sense—as it had always been. But if it still wanted someone to cut, Wally would do just fine.

A man sitting by the wall near the newspaper rack waved to me, and it took me a moment to recognize him. It was Wally, and he looked bad. His sallow skin sagged off his body. His skull seemed slightly misshapen, and his body was a formless mass. He'd always been fat, but now he looked lumpy, as though he was riddled with tumors. He wore green sweats that needed to be thrown into a hamper, but he'd spent a long time brushing and blow-drying his hair.

There were a dozen other people inside, talking, eating breakfast, or just reading. My adrenaline was still running, and I was jumpy and pissed off. Annalise, if she were here, would have smashed in Wally's skull and burned him down to cinders without a second thought, and she would have written off anyone killed in the crossfire as an acceptable loss. I wasn't ready to do that. While Wally needed killing—oh, how he needed killing, no one knew that better than I did—this wasn't the place.

Unless it had to become the place.

Wally held up his pale, flabby hands. "Sixty seconds, right?"

"You don't deserve sixty seconds."

"But they do." He gestured toward the crowd around him.

"You look terrible."

"But I feel fantastic." He rubbed at a piece of peeling skin on the end of his ear. "Ray, I know what you want to do—it's written all over your face and I can see it in your glow—but I'm a different person, too. If you make your move here, all these people are going to suffer."

I stared at him, picturing him with a split skull. Could I do it quickly enough? My ghost knife felt alive in my pocket. I remembered how it had felt when it tried to control me, and the killing urge dimmed just a little.

"Can't we just talk?" Wally asked. "Have a seat."

I sat and placed my hands on the table. "My friend died today because of you."

"Which one?" I nearly snatched a knife off the table and stabbed him in the eye, but he kept talking, oblivious. "Was it the cute one with the big butt? I knew we were getting close to her time. She gave you my message, right? I mean, you're here."

"Why, Wally? What are you trying to get out of this?"

He sighed. "I'm not much for schemes, Ray. I think you know that. Some guys can come up with complicated plans to get what they want, but I'm not like that. I need things to be simple."

A waitress stepped up to the table. She was a tall Asian woman with a broad forehead and long, straight black hair. She did her best not to look at Wally and didn't seem all that impressed by my soaking wet clothes. "Can I take your orders?"

"I thought this table was in the other waitress's section," Wally said. He sounded a little whiny about it.

"Nope, I'm your waitress," she answered in a tone that suggested she wasn't happy about it and didn't want to argue.

Wally sighed again. "I'd like three hard-boiled eggs, a side of bacon, and a side of sausage. And water. Ray? It's on me."

"Black coffee," I said, knowing I wouldn't drink a drop of it. I didn't want to accept anything from him.

The waitress hurried away. "I thought this table was in the other waitress's section," he told me, as though I hadn't heard him the first time he said it. His lips were rubbery and his teeth were gray. "I'm not into Asian chicks. I know some guys are crazy for them, but I like curly hair."

I closed my eyes. I was not going to sit here and talk about women with him. "You need things to be simple," I prompted.

"Right. I needed invisible people for my thing, and I wanted to do it in a way to get your attention."

"What 'thing' are you talking about?"

"I'm trying to get my hands on a puzzle. . . . Actually, never mind about the thing," he said. "I blew that, anyway. This is about you now. You remember what I told you last time, right before you tried to kill me? Well, nothing has changed. Bad shit is coming, Ray. Really, really bad shit."

"But why is this about me?"

"I owe you, for all the good things you did for me growing up."

"That doesn't make us friends."

"Oh, no. I'm well aware of that. Still, you did good things for me when no one else would, not even the actual friends I had at the time. Besides, I like knowing you. It's like being pals with Stalin's deadliest assassin or something."

Even I knew who Stalin was. "What the hell are you talking about?"

"The Twenty Palace Society, natch. They used to be really scary, you know, back in the day. I've spoken to some of the people who were around back when. Everyone was terrified of them, and hid like field mice. But they lost their spell books—the original spell books—and can't produce primaries anymore. They've been in decline ever since."

I knew all this. Zahn had bragged, and Annalise confirmed, that the society had once had and had lost two of the three "original" spell books. According to Annalise, they were the source of all magic in the world, and they weren't really books with spells written in them.

Why they were still called spell books was beyond me. I learned the names of two of them—the Book of Grooves and the Book of Oceans—during the disaster in Washaway. I had no idea where they were, and as far as I could tell, no one else did, either.

Annalise said that anyone who read them had visions. The visions turned them into a "primary"—the most powerful kind of sorcerer—and they recorded their visions by writing them out as spells in an actual book. Those secondhand spells were what everyone thought of as spell books, and they were traditionally named after the primary and the source: Smith Book of Oceans or Jones Book of Grooves.

I'd seen one of those secondary books. Well, in truth I'd stolen it. I'd cast my ghost knife out of it and nearly died in the attempt. Annalise had taken it back, but I had a copy hidden away. In fact, it was so well hidden that I hadn't gone near it since.

When a second person laid hands on the Jones Book of Whatever, that person became a "secondary." The third person became a "tertiary." Every time a book of spells passed from one hand to the next, the spells became weaker, because each new person was further and further from the original vision. It didn't take many generations for them to become useless.

That's why sorcerers guarded their spell books so carefully, because sharing them made them decay. Unfortunately, the spells that held on to their potency the longest were summoning spells.

I knew the society was losing power as their sorcerers died and their spell books were handed down, but it didn't really matter to me. That was long-term thinking. I was in this game for the short-term fight. I was here for this enemy, and this danger. Someone else would have to worry about the next few centuries.

Wally watched my face, waiting. For a moment, I thought he might try to sell me something.

I said: "You're not telling me anything new."

"You're the first real threat they've been able to put into the field in decades."

I looked away. Annalise, my boss, was ten times more dangerous than I was. She could tear my head off with one hand, and she wasn't the most powerful member of the society by any means. I was a guppy in a shark tank. "That's bullshit and bullshit won't work on me."

He laughed. "You would think so, dude, but I'm one hundred percent serious. You killed Ansel Zahn, man!" The rail-thin old woman at the next table looked up from her book at that, but Wally was oblivious. "You killed the last of the Hammers. You took out a whole swarm of cousins, too. And those were just the top-of-the-marquee names. Do you understand how badass that is?"

I glanced at the woman beside us. She watched us warily and looked about to bolt from her seat. "He's talking about videogames," I said. She sighed and returned to her book.

Wally grinned at me with his gray smile. "And then there are all the *regular* folks. I didn't know you had it in you. I tried to get my hands on the police report—"

"Shut up."

"No, really! I wanted to find out how many bystanders you killed in Washa—"

"*Shut up.*" I wanted to hit him so bad I could barely breathe, but I didn't know what would happen to the people around me. They would be just like the people I'd killed in Washaway, innocent victims—only this time it wouldn't be self-defense, it would be sloppiness.

Luckily, Wally wasn't interested in pushing me. "Okay, dude. Be cool. I'm just saying it's like I went to grade school with the Seahawks' quarterback. People are talking about you."

That, I didn't like. "Tell me about the 'thing' Melly was supposed to help you with."

"Why else would you want an invisible person? I wanted to steal something that's moderately well guarded."

"A puzzle," I prompted. He smiled and shrugged. "But you couldn't get it." His gaze became a little distracted, as if I was boring him. Either he didn't want to talk about it or there wasn't anything to say. "You're TheLast-King,' right? That was you last Christmas in Washaway, right?"

He focused on me. I had his attention again. "I was never in Washaway."

"But you were the one feeding information to . . ." The faces of dead people came back to my memory, and I stopped talking. I couldn't say the names of those dead men out loud.

Wally held up his hand, his thumb and index finger almost touching. "Teeny, teeny bits of information, but it was enough to get them running out there with their checkbooks and shotguns. They didn't matter, though. Not really. They were in the way."

"Wally, tell me about the thing you're planning. What part did Caramella have in it?"

He laughed. "Forget about the thing. I wish I could. Anyway, she already did her part."

"You . . ." I'd almost said *killed her,* but the woman with the book was still too close. "The drape already took her, and it almost got me, too."

"That's the risk we face when we call these things," Wally said, absentmindedly touching a lump on his chin. "But wait, what did you call it?"

I shrugged, feeling vaguely embarrassed. "I had to call them something, so I've been thinking of them as drapes."

"Hah! In the book, they're called Wings of Air and Hunger, but I like your name better. Less ridiculous."

The word *book* pushed one of my buttons. "Wally, I want you to turn over your spell book and all copies—"

"Ray! I can't believe you'd try that shit with me."

"Excuse me," the waitress said. She set a plate in front of Wally and a cup in front of me. "You can't use that language in here. If you do it again, you'll have to leave."

Wally beamed up at her with his sickly face. It was a nasty smile. "I hear you."

She left. Wally picked up a hard-boiled egg and popped it into his mouth—he didn't even peel the shell off first—then gulped it down like a snake. "Ray," he said, as he cut his sausage patties in quarters and stacked them. "Don't try that 'turn over your books' crap with me, okay? It's insulting. First of all, I'm not one of the powercrazy jagoffs you're used to dealing with. I'm trying to do some good here."

"Tell that to Caramella."

"And her boyfriend, too, probably." He looked at his watch. "Should have happened for him first. And the rest of them soon enough. But I'm sorry about that. Seriously. I know that drapes are painful, and I'm not looking to cause a lot of pain."

I laughed at him. He shrugged and looked sheepish. I said: "They're bringing more of their kind."

Wally stabbed the stack of sausages with his fork, stuck them into his mouth, and swallowed them all without chewing. I wondered how his throat could squeeze them all down. "Good thing I brought you and your buddies down to take care of it, then."

"I'm going to take care of you, too."

The lumps on Wally's face suddenly shifted position, as though something under his skin was moving around. His body hunched up, bulking around his neck and shoulders.

"Whoa," he said. "Hold on, let me deal with something." He closed his eyes and took deep breaths as though fighting the urge to puke. After a few seconds, he smiled again. "My passengers didn't like that you said that. Don't, okay? It'd be embarrassing to call you here under a white flag and break the truce myself."

"Christ, Wally. You have predators inside you."

"Oh, yeah, Ray. You'd be surprised by how many. I'm a different thing than you're used to facing. Man, the whole world looks different to me now. Literally. Did you know that some outsiders don't use light to see? Now I'm sharing that gift, too, and it's wild."

"You're carrying predators for their abilities? Are you fucked in the head? What could be worth that?"

"Oh, well, they let me fly like Superman, and I can hork Chubby Hubby ice cream through my nostrils. Right? Dude. Come on. You expect me to just *tell* you? We're not exactly pals—for now, anyway—so I'm not going to tell you everything I can, you know, *do*. That would be showing my hand."

"Showing your . . . Have you looked in a mirror lately? You look like you're dying right in front of me."

"Looks bad, feels good; that's what I say."

"Christ. You're so fucking stupid."

"Hey now," Wally said. He didn't seem offended at all. "I have power, Ray. Not Ansel Zahn levels, but I don't have to take the risks his type takes, either. All I had to do was put a protective spell on myself—a permanent one—and summon a couple something-somethings into myself. I keep them fed, and they share their little tricks with me."

My hand twitched as I resisted the urge to grab my ghost knife and start cutting. It could destroy the mark that protected Wally from his predators—wherever it was—turning them loose on him.

Except that was absolutely forbidden. No one in the Twenty Palace Society was allowed to feed a predator, ever. When I killed Wally, I was going to have to do it some other way.

He kept talking, oblivious. "Ray, I'm sure *you* could find a way to kill me if you really tried, but it would not be easy. Then, if you survived, you'd have my little buddies to deal with. But you shouldn't try. You want to know why?" He gestured toward his face and neck. "Because I'm making sacrifices to do some good here."

"You're trying to kill everybody."

"Everybody dies anyway, Ray. I've seen it. If things keep going the way they are, what happened to Caramella will look like passing peacefully in your sleep. And you know what? Drapes and cousins and sapphire dogs—that shit is really painful and scary for people. But I'm not about that. Just because I plan to euthanize the world doesn't mean I want to be a dick about it. My plan is supposed to make things easier. Make it, you know, quick and painless."

"Don't do me any favors," I said.

"Too late. I already decided. Ray, do you want to know why the outsiders are so anxious to get here, to our world? Do you know why they're desperate to escape the Deeps?"

"What outsiders are you talking about?"

Wally touched a lump on his face. "The society calls them predators, which is correct but doesn't really describe everything they are, and calls their home the Empty Spaces, which is a pretty stupid name for a place that's so full of weirdness. Ray, do you know why they want to get here so badly?"

I didn't like being instructed by Wally, but no one else ever wanted to explain things to me. Certainly not Annalise. "Tell me."

"Because there's no death there. I'm serious. The Deeps are teeming with outsiders, but they can't feed on each other because they can't kill and eat each other, because nothing there can die. So they're stuck out there, desperate and *starving*. You think what happened to your friend was bad? She probably had a couple days of pain before she died. Maybe less. The outsiders hurt for decades—centuries, maybe—waiting for a chance to feed again."

"And you want to help them to a snack."

He sagged and looked disappointed. "No, Ray. I'm trying to save everyone from . . ." He stopped and looked around the room. The woman with the book had left, and no one had taken her place. In fact, the diner was only half as full as it was when I entered.

Wally sighed again. "Never mind. I had to try, okay? I owed you that. I know the Twenty Palace Society has brainwashed you, but I still think of you as the guy who stood between me and Rocky Downing at the edge of the basketball court. I know you have your heart in the right place, you just need to get your head there, too. Keep your eyes open, Ray. That's all I'm saying. You can't trust those society people. And you may decide soon that you want to stand between me and the bullies again."

Wally swallowed the remaining two eggs, again without peeling them. Then he folded his soggy bacon, speared it with his fork, and gulped it down, too.

"Don't get up," he said as he stood. "I'm serious. You're a great guy, but the truce only lasts while we're here. I'm skipping town now anyway, so you should deal with the, uh, drapes. We'll see each other again." He laid a couple of bills on the table. It was more than enough to cover the check. "And I wish Curly-Head had waited on us. That was supposed to be part of the plan."

Damn. He was leaving, and I hadn't gotten anything truly useful out of him. "Wally, at least tell me how to stop the drapes."

He snorted. "Is that how you've been doing it? *Please please tell me what to do?* Come on, I want to see some of your mad skills."

I stood out of my chair and turned toward him. He stepped back, looking up at me in surprise and delight as though I was a plot twist in an exciting TV show. I reached into my pocket for my ghost knife.

But Wally had already placed his fingers in his mouth. He pulled out something small, wet, and red as blood. It was round like a Ping-Pong ball and gleamed like metal. Then it unfolded legs as long and slender as needles.

Wally tossed it over the counter into the kitchen. "Choices, choices," he said and took one step backward. He passed through the wall like a phantom.

CHAPTER SEVEN

Damn. I was tempted to run out the front door after him, but a scream from the kitchen changed my mind. I vaulted over the counter.

The tile on the other side hadn't been mopped recently. I landed on grease and nearly fell on my ass. I heard a clatter of shell on stone and a man's cry of fear and disgust from the kitchen. I pushed through the door into the back.

It was a kitchen much like any restaurant kitchen. Everything was stainless steel, and the three Hispanic men at the stove were dressed in white with black hairnets. The tallest of them shrieked like a little girl and staggered back, away from the creature that was scuttling across the floor at him.

A short man snatched a huge pot of water off the stove and dropped it onto the creature. Boiling water splashed into the air, and the heavy pot clanged like a muffled bell.

Then it fell on its side. Steaming water rushed at me, and I jumped back too slowly. It sloshed through the fabric of my shoes, scalding my feet.

The little predator wasn't affected. It charged at the man who'd dropped a pot on it and jumped onto his leg. Then it began to dig.

The man screamed and grabbed a ladle. He hit the predator with all his strength, trying to knock it away, but the ladle crumpled and the predator didn't move an inch.

Blood splashed onto the floor and the predator burrowed deep into his flesh. The man fell, screaming full-throated now. His co-workers backed away in terror, screaming themselves.

I charged through the scalding water, grabbed the cook's torn pants, and ripped them up to his thigh. The predator was visible as a bulge moving under his skin. I took my ghost knife and slashed through it.

My spell passed through the man's flesh without damaging it, but the creature inside him was another matter. It exploded into a fireball as large as a basketball.

The cook, mercifully, fainted. I snatched a pot off a hook and filled it at the sink. Then I poured it over his burning clothes. The other cooks stared at me, dumbfounded. I said: "What do you think? Ambulance?" One of them blinked and lunged for a phone.

Wally's waitress was standing at the edge of the kitchen, her body hunched in shock, her mouth hanging open. Behind her, also dressed in a waitress uniform, was Violet. "Vi, check your voice mail!"

I didn't wait for a response. I ran out the back door into the parking lot, desperate to find Wally again.

I sprinted to the side of the building where Wally would have come through the wall, but there was no sign of him. I scanned the area, looking for a blob of a man in green. Nothing. The predator he'd thrown into the kitchen had distracted me, but not for more than a minute or so. I didn't think he'd had enough time to get into a car and get away.

Unless he'd brought a driver. That would have been a smart play, but I didn't believe for a moment that Wally had a friend in the whole world. Which would mean he was still on foot. Was he in one of the other stores, watching me? Was he walking through them, building after building, wall after wall, down the entire block in a place I couldn't see him?

Did you know that some outsiders don't use light to see? Now I'm sharing that gift, too, and it's wild. Maybe he was watching me through a brick wall, waiting to see what I'd do. My skin tingled at the thought of it.

Violet came outside and edged toward me. She looked afraid of me. "Ray, what the hell is going on?"

"How well do you know the guy I was sitting with?"

Under other circumstances, she would have snapped at me for answering a question with another question. I wondered what my expression looked like. "Not at all," she said. "He's just a creep who's been coming around lately."

She was lying again, but I didn't have time to press her on it. "All right. Listen: I think he's still nearby, watching. I think he's going to make sure he lost me before he goes back to wherever he's staying. So I'm going to walk away, and you're going to stand in the window of the café and watch for him. Understand? I'll be back in five minutes or so."

"What happened to my apartment, Ray?"

"I'll explain what I know later, but I can't let this guy get away." She didn't look convinced. "Vi, all you have to do is stand in the window and watch."

I could see she didn't want to do it. She didn't want anything to do with Wally King at all, and I didn't blame her. But then she nodded and looked away from me. Thank God.

I ran to the sidewalk. If Wally had kept going in a straight line, he would have gone back toward Vi's apartment and my car. After one quick look around, just in case I got lucky, I headed in the opposite direction.

I wasn't sure how far I should go. I wanted Wally to have enough time to feel safe and hit the sidewalk again, but not so long that I couldn't catch up to him. As long as he didn't have a car stashed nearby . . . I didn't want to think about that.

I'd planned to jog two blocks, but I'd only gone a block and a half before I felt too anxious and tense to continue. I hurried toward the Sugar Shaker, sweat prickling my back.

Violet met me at the door. "He was just here, not a minute ago," she said. "The creep walked by the window and winked at me." She shuddered a little and pointed down the street toward her apartment. "Then he took off that way and turned right at the corner. Ray—"

I ran off before she could finish that thought. Whatever she had to tell me, it would have to wait until after I'd found Wally. Found him and killed him.

"Ray!" Vi followed me onto the street. "Ray! You wait for me!"

"Vi, dammit, he's going to hear you."

"Don't you tell me to shut up! You're going to tell me what's going on!" So much for being afraid of me.

"If Wally hears you, he'll come back here and kill us both."

"You don't play that shit with me! You're going to tell me who this asshole is, or you're going to regret it."

We couldn't stand out on the sidewalk hashing this out while Wally walked away. "Come on, and keep your voice down."

I led her down the sidewalk. In the distance, I could see a column of black smoke stretching into the sky. It gave me a weird, jangly feeling to see the destruction that was following me around.

"I'm waiting," she said.

"Wally is from Seattle."

"Duh."

I remember this mood very well. She wanted me to talk to her, and she wanted to be nasty about it. If I let her turn it into a fight, I'd lose

my shot at Wally. "Don't, okay? Just let me finish. I knew Wally from
school. We weren't friends, but I made a couple of bullies leave him
alone, so now he likes me. But we're not friends," I added quickly, because I could see she was about to talk.

"That's not what he says."

"Fuck him." We reached the corner and I peeked around it. Wally
was almost to the end of the block, walking with a strange, stiff-legged
limp on the other side of the street. He wasn't moving very fast, and I
figured he'd be easy to catch on foot.

And I was ready. I was ready to kill him right there on the sidewalk, if I could. But not in front of Vi.

"He did something to a friend of mine," I said. I didn't want to
explain further, but I knew she wouldn't be satisfied with that. "He
hurt the oldest, best friend I had in this world. Understand? Nobody
in my whole life ever meant as much to me as that friend did."

She seemed taken aback, but I pressed on. "Wally . . ." *Wally put a
predator inside him.* "Wally poisoned him. He gave him some kind of
experimental drug that drove him crazy—"

"And he ate people. Right? That was all over the news."

Of course. "I tried to save my friend . . ." *From the Twenty Palace
Society.* "I tried to bring back the old him, the guy I knew. I protected
him. But in the end, he wouldn't stop, so . . ." *I killed him.*

No. I couldn't say that. I didn't believe in confession.

She didn't need me to say it. Something in my voice had blunted
her anger. "So Wally's after you and you're after him, and me and my
daughter are caught in the middle."

"At least you're still alive," I said. "So far."

She turned her back on me and walked away. Finally. I peered
back around the corner and saw Wally farther up the street, close to
the intersection. Maybe I'd do something for Vi later, if I survived, but
I couldn't imagine what. I couldn't think about her, not when Wally
was right there.

I took out my ghost knife. Wally didn't change his pace or turn
around as I crossed the street and fell in behind him. Whatever X-ray
vision he might have had, he still couldn't see behind him. Good. If he
was as full of predators as he said, I was going to need to ambush him.

And God, it felt so good to have that clarity. It was calming, almost, even as I felt my heartbeat quicken and my body grow warm. I
was going to rush at this bastard, and I was finally going to kill him.

I walked faster. My spell would hit whatever I wanted it to hit, but
I'd have to call it back between each attack, and the distance between
us meant there would be a lot of time between hits. I had to get closer.

He crossed the street and slumped up the next block. Suddenly, all the doors of a 4Runner opened just as Wally came near it. Five guys piled out and stepped up to him, blocking the sidewalk. Wally didn't seem startled by them at all.

I had been about to cross the street, but I ducked into the loading dock of an appliance store at the last moment. I peeked at them from behind a stack of pallets.

One of the men who'd stepped out of the 4Runner looked up and down the street warily. I recognized him immediately as the shortest and most muscular of Fidel's cousins. Then I immediately recognized the others, including Fidel himself.

I couldn't hear what they were saying at this distance, but I could see their body language. Fidel was smiling and making broad gestures with his hands—he was trying to look like a magnanimous gangster, the guy who asked for things in a friendly way while the gunmen around him made sure you knew what the correct answer was supposed to be.

Something Fidel said made Wally throw back his head and laugh. He didn't seem nervous or intimidated at all.

They were standing in front of a hotel, and Wally waved for them to follow him up the walkway. They did, glancing around warily as they went.

"Hey! What are you doing there?" a voice behind me said.

The man who'd challenged me had a belly like a wine barrel, a wiry beard, and tiny round glasses. He'd just come out of the back door onto the loading dock. "Duh," I said. "I'm spying on someone."

He opened his mouth to respond, then shrugged and went back inside.

Wally, Fidel, and all his people were gone. I crossed the street, approaching the building slowly. There was an arched opening in the middle of the building and a driveway for cars to pull through. On one side of the arch was the lobby and reception area, and on the other was a diner.

The building was stucco, with tall sliding glass doors, and even from the street I could see how dirty it was. The little diner was mostly deserted, with a few scattered people-watchers on plastic furniture eating out of red plastic baskets. None of them looked like Fidel's crew.

A sliding glass door opened somewhere above me, and I glanced up. The stoned guy from the alley last night stepped onto a balcony. It was the lowest floor and nearly at the north end of the building. I quickly turned my back.

I walked away from him until I heard the door close again, then risked a glance back and saw that the balcony was empty. Thank God for a criminal's paranoia. I'd never have found them otherwise.

The windows and balconies alternated along the length of the building—window, balcony, balcony, window, window, balcony, balcony, window. That meant there were four units on each floor in opposing pairs that let the architects set their bathrooms back-to-back.

How to get there was the problem. I wasn't keen on the idea of kicking the door down, and no one had left a ladder conveniently leaning against the building. I went into the office.

The man behind the desk was small, dark, and narrow-shouldered; he had a thin mustache like a movie star from the thirties. "How may I help you?" He had a slight British accent.

"I need a room."

"Of course, sir. Do you have luggage?"

"In my car," I said. "I'm looking for something specific. I need the lowest room you have, and I need it to be in the northeast corner of the building."

"Ah. Are you concerned about feng shui?"

"No, I'm interested in the flow of energy in my living space." He couldn't quite suppress a smile, and I was happy to let him laugh at me. Being underestimated has saved my life more than once.

"We do have such a room." He brought out the paperwork.

"Can I check it out first? For a few minutes alone? I'd like to meditate on it."

He pursed his lips and shook his head. I wasn't *that* amusing. I paid for the room and promised to get my luggage after I checked out the flow. He gave me a plastic card to unlock the door.

I went up the stairs, gambling that if Fidel didn't place a guy in the diner, he wouldn't have one in the hall. And I was right. I paused at the door to Wally's room and heard Fidel say that he couldn't use that place anymore and they needed a new place. His voice was raised, as though he was arguing.

I didn't listen for long. Getting caught with my ear at the door would be a bad thing. I walked quietly down the hall, feeling the sweat prickle on my back. The gold-painted walls and wine-colored carpet made me feel stifled, even if it was cooler inside than out.

I let myself into my room. It was two steps above utilitarian, with a floral print on the covers.

My hands started shaking. I clenched them into fists and pressed them against the dead flesh over my heart to control them. Wally was just on the other side of that wall, and my chance to kill him was coming soon. I had no idea what he was capable of, aside from walking through walls and puking a tiny monster onto me. I took a deep breath, trying to calm myself down. It would have been nice to have a better plan than *Move fast hit hard,* but what the hell. I would give it a shot, and if I failed, so be it. I just hoped I wouldn't see any more of his *tricks,* if he had them.

I went to the balcony and looked across at the adjacent one. I could jump it and be close enough to eavesdrop, but I knew someone would catch me.

The ground was about fifteen feet below. If I missed the jump, I'd land just outside the manager's office. I think he'd find me much less amusing after that.

I hurried into the bathroom to splash water on my face, then grabbed a glass off the sink and returned to the main room.

By my standards, the room was comfortable, but the walls were not terribly thick. I laid the glass against the wall and pressed my ear to it.

I'd seen this work on TV, but it wasn't doing me a bit of good here. The voices in the next room were too muffled to understand, although I could tell that the argument was over.

"Seriously, Ray? A glass against the wall?"

I pivoted in surprise, dropping the glass onto the carpet. Arne was standing just behind me. He sat on the edge of the bed. "If you want to spy on people, you ought to order the right tool for the job. On the Internet you can get a pretty good listening device for a hundred bucks."

My heart was racing, but I did my best to act calm. "Sure, but can you drink iced tea out of it, too?"

"You got me there."

"I guess you finished your job?"

He rubbed his hands on his thighs. "No. This is just a quiet moment while I wait for the stupid people to catch up, so I thought I'd check on other things. What happened with that big guy?"

"Wardell? We're best buds. He invited me over for a *Golden Girls* marathon."

"I'll bet." He sighed. "You've developed a knack for slipping out of trouble, haven't you? Didn't you get snapped up by Uncle Sam a few months ago? After Wash-away?"

I became very still. "Yes."

"And what? They let you go?"

Not really. "Yes."

"I guess they had to, huh? How'd you manage that?"

I'm on the twisted path. "They caught the real assholes. Nothing to do with me."

Arne seemed amused by that. "You know what turns people into monsters, Ray? Knowing they can get away with anything. Once they realize they aren't going to be punished for anything they do, the masks come off, baby, and the devils run free."

I didn't need anyone to tell me this. This was my life. I said: "It's time to help me with my thing, right?" Arne spread his hands to say *Why not?* "Tell me how this started. Tell me about Wally."

"But it didn't start with Wally. It started with Luther."

"He's the guy you brought in to replace me, right?"

"Nobody replaced you, Ray. Your spot was open and waiting for you. Luther was just extra help. He was big, strong, and friendly—not that bright, but how many bright people do the work we do? Mostly he was loyal, as long as you put a couple of bucks in his pocket.

"Luther was hanging at the Bigfoot Room all by himself when Wally walked in. Wally dropped your name, which Luther recognized. After I don't know how long, Luther called all of us at once: me, Fidel, Summer, the whole crew. Everyone but Vi and Melly met up at the Bigfoot Room. Wally made his pitch—he offered us a super power—and Luther was the living proof that it was real. He vanished right in front of us. All we had to do in return was a single favor. Luther's excitement was infectious.

"I had a bad feeling about it, though, and I put him off for twenty-four hours. You know why."

"Wally looks like a walking tumor and you didn't want to end up like him."

"Hell yeah. I'm a good-looking man. I can't throw away a face like this. But Luther said that the powers Wally had were different from the invisibility thing. Bigger. He said Wally couldn't vanish himself, which was why he needed our help."

My mouth suddenly felt dry. "What powers does Wally have?"

Arne shrugged. "I don't have a lot to tell you. You'd have to ask Lenard."

"Why?"

"Well, Lenard doesn't like victims to feel too comfortable around him. He likes them wide-eyed and sweating, right? And he starts thinking that your buddy Wally is too cheerful, so out of the blue he rushes the guy and knocks him over, right into the dirt. Then he starts screaming at him like a nutcase, 'Don't you dare smile at me! Don't you fucking smile!' And the rest of us are rolling our eyes at him.

"But your buddy just got to his feet and smiled at Lenard again, like a big *fuck you.* And Lenard, now he has to step up or he'll look like he wimped out. So he gives Wally another shove.

"Except this time, your boy was ready and it didn't even move him. It was like Lenard was pushing against an office building—he couldn't even make a dent in the guy's flabby man-titties. Almost like . . ."

I remembered the way the cook had hit the little red predator with his ladle, and how the creature didn't move an inch. *I keep them fed, and they share their little tricks with me.* "Almost like nothing could move him if he didn't want it to."

"Yeah, and then there was this wave that came out of him—I'm not sure what to call it. It was like one of those old kung fu movies, where one dude shoves another without touching him. Lenard had his ass lifted off the ground and dropped into the dirt ten feet away. He didn't know what to do about that, but Ty and Fidel took the heat off by making a joke of it. You'd have to talk to Lenard to find out what it felt like. I was just standing there watching."

"Right."

"Not much, is it? It's like he's the patron saint of shoving. He acted like he could do more, but then, he would."

I nodded. I didn't want to thank Arne; he might have told me I was welcome and walked out. "What favor did Wally want?"

"He hasn't asked for one. Not from me. By the time Luther came to us, his debt was paid in full. I asked him what he'd done, and he took me to the—"

A gunshot popped in the next room. Arne's expression became weary, and he vanished.

Damn. My questions would have to wait. I ran into the hall and cut the lock on Wally's door with my ghost knife.

The door swung inward. A bearded man pivoted toward me, raising his arm. I threw myself to the floor, but there was no gunfire. Fidel laid a hand on the gunman's shoulder, and he lowered his weapon. Fidel had his SIG Sauer in his other hand.

"Ray?"

They all had the same gun. I left the ghost knife on the floor and raised my hands to show that they were empty. Then I got to my knees, letting my hand fall on my spell and picking it up. Wally lay on the bed, his arms wide, his feet on the floor. There was a single bullet hole in his chest. He looked like a lumpy bundle of old clothes.

Was he dead? I'd assumed he'd be as hard to kill as a sorcerer, especially with normal weapons. Ansel Zahn had been reduced to a bloody mess by an amateur firing squad, and he'd laughed about it. And Wally had said he was full of predators.

But now he had a hole in his chest, and he wasn't moving at all. Had they done my job for me?

I didn't believe it. I couldn't believe it.

"That's not cool, man," Stoned said. He pointed at me. "This guy's a witness."

"You saved me the trouble," I said. My hand brushed against something on the table. It was a wallet, bulging with paper receipts and cash. One of those scraps of paper might lead me to his spell books, and damn if I didn't want to steal his money.

"He laughed at me," Fidel said, staring down at Wally's body. The hammer of his pistol was cocked. I looked at the other guns, but their hammers were all uncocked. Stoned rolled his eyes and shared a glance with the others. The three of them looked disappointed.

In the moment they looked away, I pocketed the wallet.

Fidel chewed his lip as though he was trying to work out a tough math problem. "First, he refused me. Then he laughed at me."

"What now, Fidel?" The short, muscular man with the heavy beard stepped close. "You promised us something. How you gonna deliver now that this guy is dead?"

Wally's shirt moved.

"You guys should get out of here," I said.

Muscular pointed his gun at me again. "You ain't calling the shots here."

"It's not about who's the shot caller," I said. I pointed to Wally. "This guy isn't as dead as you think."

Wally's shirt twitched and shifted. One of the guys cursed in surprise, and they were behind me all of a sudden, because I'd moved toward Wally's body without even realizing I was doing it. The clean, cold certainty I'd felt while I was stalking him had evaporated. More predators were about to get loose, and there was nothing between them and the world except me. I raised my ghost knife.

A gleaming red ball pushed its way out of the hole in Wally's shirt. Then another, then four, five, six more were coming out as if they were being pushed through the opening. They tumbled down the sides of Wally's body like golf balls and stopped in the folds of the blankets or in the nest of his crotch. A couple struck the floor with a heavy thunk.

Spiny metallic needles extended from their bodies, and they began to scramble toward us. I gripped my ghost knife tightly and moved forward to meet them.

Pop-pop-pop-pop-pop-pop came from behind me, as Fidel's family cut loose with their SIGs. Bullets zinged around me, some punching through the floor, others ricocheting in unpredictable ways. I turned to shout at them to stop, but as I did I saw Muscular lean down to fire at the closest predator.

The sound of the shot, the spark on the creature's shell, and the bloody wound on his leg all seemed to appear in the same instant.

He fell back against the wall as the predator advanced on him. The bullet's impact had as much effect as it would against a bank vault.

There were a dozen predators fanning across the room toward us and more coming every moment. Three were a second or two away from my own ankle, and I swept my ghost knife through the lead.

It burst into flames as I leapt back. The fire touched the two behind it, and they burst apart as well.

The sudden flares stopped the gunfire, at least. Fidel and his cousins backed toward the door, leaving Muscular cut off against the wall. Stoned drew back his leg and kicked at one of the scuttling little balls, but it was like kicking a metal post anchored into the ground.

I had to move away from the burning spot on the carpet. Stoned fell backward toward the doorway, cursing. Fidel and one of his cousins grabbed at him, but they were so spooked and frantic that they worked against each other. I could hear Muscular behind me, shouting in Spanish, his voice going high with fear.

Everything was loud and bright and hot. The carpet was burning, streaming thin black smoke that smelled like burned plastic. It was all too much. I couldn't think clearly.

I moved toward Stoned, Fidel, and the others and cut through one of the predators pursuing them, then drew back. The creature burst into flames, then the others began to go up in a chain reaction, spreading the fire from the wall to the dresser and cutting off my path to the door. I turned my back on the popping sounds and the growing firelight.

Muscular had scrambled into a corner. He'd tucked his injured leg behind him and hammered at the closest of the predators with the butt of his pistol, but there was no effect at all. His teeth were bared in raw terror, and I rushed toward him, ghost knife in hand.

The nearest of the predators began to tear through his leather shoe with its needle-sharp forelegs. I saw blood, but Muscular didn't do anything more than grunt. I swept my spell through the creature, and this time I saw that the predator didn't split apart—its shell and limbs seemed to vanish, revealing the expanding fire from inside it.

Now Muscular screamed as the flames engulfed his leg. A second predator burst into flames nearby, and I fell away from the heat. There were no other creatures close enough to go up with it.

Christ, the things were still coming through the hole in Wally's chest, as though he had an inexhaustible supply of them. The flames blocking the way toward the door had spread with startling speed; the front half of the dresser was wrapped in fire. Black smoke flowed along the ceiling and out into the hall through the door that Fidel had left open. The smoke alarm shrieked out in the hall, but I could still hear predators popping like caps in the fire.

The way out of the room was blocked by burning carpet, so the predators were trapped on the far side of the bed, piling up against the wall, testing it with their sharp legs. Apparently, they didn't like digging through something that wasn't flesh.

Another stream of predators came toward us from the balcony side of the room. Muscular tried to pull farther back into the corner. He slammed his elbow against the wall, trying to break through to safety, but he had no leverage and no time.

I stepped over him and crouched low, swiping my ghost knife through the lead predator. It burst, igniting the other creatures beside and behind it. The fire spread backward along the sliding glass door and ignited the polyester blankets hanging off the bed.

The flames had already reached the other side of the bed. I dropped to my knees, beneath the thickening cloud of black smoke. The fire on the carpet was only as high as my calves, but the doorway was already wreathed in flames. The covers, still just starting to burn, dripped liquid fire onto the carpet.

And damn, it was so *loud*.

I lifted Muscular to his feet, but we both stayed well below the billows of smoke. The fire moved toward us, and the carpet at the edge of it was giving off white smoke. God, it had gotten so hot in the room so quickly. I felt like I'd been thrown into an oven.

But predators were still pouring out of the hole in Wally's chest. They were tumbling away from the flames, swarming in thick piles along the headboard and wall. I could see some of the predators digging at the drywall, trying to escape into the next room.

The only real weapon I had was my ghost knife, and it was just a piece of paper—covered by laminate and mailing tape—but still just paper. I'd been hitting the predators as quickly as I could—like flicking a finger through a candle flame—to keep the fire from damaging it, but I couldn't hold back anymore. My spell was precious, but stopping these predators was more important.

I threw my ghost knife toward the opening in Wally's chest. At the same time, I willed it to move as fast as it could, putting my fear and adrenaline behind it. It zipped away from me like a rocket.

I lunged across Muscular's body toward the curtain.

The ghost knife passed through the bulge in Wally's stomach. Fire blasted out of his body like water from a fire hose. I tore the curtain from the rod, letting it fall over us. Predators went off like little fire-bombs. I slapped my hand across Muscular's mouth and nose as the flames roared around us.

God, the heat! Muscular's face was inches from mine, and his eyes were bulging with terror. I'm sure I looked the same.

The roar of flames subsided. The curtain scorched my back, so I threw it away, letting it fall on the carpet between the sliding glass door and us. I'd hoped it would smother the flames a little, but actually it added fuel.

At the other end of the room, fire climbed the wall and rolled against the ceiling. The bed was completely aflame, and I couldn't see anything of Wally except his feet.

I hefted Muscular onto my shoulder. He was heavy, but my adrenaline was flowing. Time seemed sluggish, my chest felt tight, and my skin was steaming as sweat poured out of me. There was no way I could get to the door, but the balcony was only three feet away. I just had to walk through the fire.

Eight thick midnight-blue tendrils suddenly rose up out of the flames where Wally's body lay. They arced and pressed down against the floor, lifting Wally's corpse toward the ceiling. He was still on his back, his arms flopping loose, his nasty green sweat suit burning against his skin. A thick sludge bubbled out of the hole in his chest and flowed over his body, extinguishing the flames. He—it—something turned so its face was toward me.

Wally's eyes were open. "Damn, Ray. That actually hurt."

Moving like spiders' legs, the tendrils walked him through the wall as though he were a phantom.

My blood was rushing in my ears, and Muscular was clutching at me, digging his fingers into my shoulder blade. I ran through the flames, staying as low as I could. The heat against the bottom of my shoes and up my legs was intense, but it was just pain. Just pain. I slammed my elbow against the door handle, and thank God it opened. Then I was through the doorway and onto the concrete balcony.

I swung Muscular off my shoulder, setting him on the far side of the iron rail. We both gasped for fresh air, and he suddenly began slapping at me. For a moment I was furious and drew back my fist, but then I realized he was beating out the flames on my clothes.

I stood still, listening to the roaring fire behind me and the sirens in the distance. My legs and feet didn't hurt anymore, which was a huge surprise.

Muscular stopped swatting the flames out and looked me directly in the eye. "*Mi hermano,*" he said.

Adrenaline buzzed in my head and made it hard to focus on what he'd said. We gripped each other's wrists as though we were actors in a sword-fighting movie, then I lowered him to the grass below. I bent over the rail as far as I could, but just as I thought it was still too high, he let go.

He struck the ground with a cry of pain, rolling on the grass and clutching at his burned and bloody legs. Then he struggled upright and began hopping toward the sidewalk.

The wind changed, blowing the choking black smoke toward me. The temptation to follow Muscular down to the grass was strong, but I couldn't flee the scene yet. My head still buzzed; it was hard to think, but I knew I needed to look for predators. I had no idea what I'd do once I found them, but that had never stopped me before.

I swung my leg over the railing. I felt stiff, but it didn't register why. The other balcony was only about six feet away, but when I jumped for it, my legs had no strength in them. I barely managed to catch the top of the rail opposite and pull myself up onto the ledge.

Something was wrong with my legs. No, not something. I was burned, and worse than I realized. Maybe I was in shock, too. I staggered into my room. The wall between mine and Wally's was dark at the top and giving off wisps of smoke. I felt the door; it was cool. I pulled it open and staggered into the hall.

Just a few feet to my left, the doorway to Wally's room was open. Black smoke flowed out and the flames ran all the way up to the ceiling. The smoke alarm blared an awful noise. Where were the other guests? Long gone, I hoped.

There was a staircase on the other side of the flames, but I knew it led down to the front office. Instead, I turned to the stair at the other end of the hall. The door was propped open. As I stumbled toward it, choking and coughing, I saw that it was blocked by a pair of legs.

I pushed the door open. Stoned lay on his back on the stairs, his head hanging down and his mouth open. His face was bloody, as though he'd puked blood on himself, and there was a ragged hole where his windpipe was supposed to be. His shirt rippled—something moved under there.

Damn. I had screwed up again. At least one of Wally's predators had escaped, and Stoned had died. I dragged him by the belt into the hall and let the metal door close. Fidel and his other two cousins were nowhere to be seen.

I stood over Stoned's body, feeling dizzy and weak. I couldn't breathe deeply without gagging. The sirens were getting closer, but they didn't sound close enough. Stoned's pant leg rippled then, and his shirt in two places. Did he have three of those nasty little bastards in him? I reached for my ghost knife, but it wasn't there and I couldn't remember where I'd left it.

To hell with it. I pulled him down the hall by the pant cuff. The dragging on the carpet caused his green plaid shirt to slide up, and I saw lumps under his skin moving down his body toward my hand, as though they could smell living flesh where it brushed his. I moved faster.

By the time the nearest predator was at Stoned's knee, I was close enough to the fire to feel it scorching my back. I let go of his ankle and shuffled around to the other side of him. The bulges under his skin stopped moving toward his foot as though they'd lost the scent.

I didn't want to give them the chance to find it again. I grabbed Stoned under the armpits and hoisted him up and through the doorway. I had to get so close that it felt like being on fire again, but I managed to drop him well into the flames.

I staggered back against the wall, coughing and choking. I crouched there, staying low where the air was still breathable, and watched to see if any of the little iron creatures came scuttling out of the flames. There was nothing I could do about it if they did, but I had to know.

My back and legs began to hurt in earnest now, and my wooziness grew stronger. I wanted to puke and take a nap but forced myself to wait and watch.

The flames spread, the sirens of fire trucks roared outside, and the smoke grew thick. No creatures came out of the fire toward me, but did that mean they'd been destroyed? I couldn't think about it. My head was too muzzy.

Time to go. I crawled along the wall toward the metal door at the end of the hall. Saturday-morning public-service announcements had told me that I would find clean air at knee level, but I coughed and hacked on the stink of burning polyester. Just as I reached the edge of the door, it swung open.

Two firefighters rushed by me. They wore helmets and bulky masks, and I suspect they didn't even see me there on the floor. I slipped into the stairwell and let the door close behind me.

The stairs were difficult. What smoke had gotten through rose up to the top of the stairwell, making the air breathable, but my legs did not want to move. I didn't know how I was going to get to my car, or what I would do after that. A sudden wave of nausea almost made me slide down the final six steps.

On the ground floor, I fell against the door and went out into the sunlight. The heat of the day was raw against my burns. I didn't look down at them, though. I didn't want to see how bad they were, because then the pain would hit me like a tidal wave.

Not that it wasn't already coming on. I tried to breathe slowly to control the pain, but every breath caught in my throat. I circled around the back of the building, leaning on parked cars while I passed between them. A firefighter yelled at me to get out of there, and a slender black woman in gray pinstripes rushed by me with car keys in her hand.

Suddenly, Bud was beside me. "Hey there, Ray."

I staggered away from him and fell against the hood of a Lumina. "Damn," I said, my voice slurred. "Scared me. Give me a hand, Bud."

He laughed. Summer was standing beside him. She never laughed. Neither moved to help me. "You said you were going to save us, Ray." There was a touch of contempt in her voice. "How you gonna manage that?"

I didn't have the energy to spar with them. I was helpless, and that made me furious. "Vanish!" I shouted. The word made me choke. "VANISH!"

Summer sneered at me. Bud smirked. Both of them turned their backs and walked away.

I didn't care, because my anger had given me focus and I'd suddenly remembered what I'd done with my spell.

I'd thrown my ghost knife but hadn't *called* it back, not through those flames. It should have passed through the wall, but I didn't know how far it could go. I staggered toward the far end of the building—the south? I was all turned around—determined that I would not leave a magic spell lying around for anyone to find. I had to get it back.

At the far side of the building was a narrow alley with a high fence. The chain-link fence had plastic slats threaded through it, so I couldn't see what was on the other side. The pain grew stronger, stealing my life force away.

There was not very much trash in the passageway, but I didn't see my ghost knife anywhere. The only places left to go were back into the building and out to the front, where the fire trucks had gathered.

I didn't need to do that. I closed my eyes and *reached* for my ghost knife. It was nearby—still inside the building and above me, and as I focused on it, I felt myself wavering. My body wanted to shut down, and I was barely able to feel my spell and *call* it to me. The world seemed to be growing dark, but I did see the ghost knife slice through the wall to land in my open palm.

I slapped it against my chest and fell against the side of the building. Whatever it was and whatever it wanted, it was part of me, and I was glad to have it close. I slid it into the back pocket of my pants, miraculously hitting the target on my first try.

I was about to fall when I felt a pair of hands grab me roughly. Damn, I had been caught by one of the firefighters, which meant an ambulance, then cops, then jail. I tried to convince myself it was better than dying, but I couldn't make those thoughts come together in my head. The hands were strong; they lifted me and propped me against the fence.

I looked up but didn't see a firefighter's jacket and helmet. It was the guy in the red T-shirt and the camo pants. He seemed happy to see me. "Hey!" he said. "Here you are!"

I punched him in the mouth with all my strength, but I knew it wouldn't be enough. The whole world turned dark, and I went down into it, knowing that I might never see daylight again.

CHAPTER EIGHT

PAIN WOKE ME. I was lying on my stomach in a darkened room; my legs were stiff and my back felt like it had a turtle shell attached. I put my arms underneath me and raised myself slowly—I couldn't see any people, but if Camo Pants was nearby, I wanted him to think I was fall-down weak right up to the moment I jumped him.

Unfortunately, I *was* weak. My back and legs hurt beyond belief. Every movement I made was like being burned all over again.

Still, I had to move. I didn't know anything about this place except that Camo Pants had brought me here, but that was enough. I had to get out.

Most of my burns were below the knee, so I lifted my feet off the bed and did my best to roll over into a seated position.

I didn't make a sound. It took every bit of restraint I had, but I didn't make a single sound.

When the spots faded from my vision, I looked around. In the dim light from the window, I could see a little lamp on a table by the bed. I snapped it on. I was in a little room—a hotel room, by the look of it—with white paper on the walls, gleaming silver in the fixtures, and pale, ghostly furniture.

I wasn't wearing a shirt. My clothes were gone and my lower legs were covered with gauze and gauze pads. Now that I was finally ready to look at my burns, they were hidden. I glanced around the room again and saw burned, ragged black cloth on the little table by the window. My pants.

My head was pounding and my mouth was parched. I peeled the edge of the gauze away from my leg just enough to peek underneath.

It looked red, swollen, and wet. Had they smeared some kind of gel on me, or was that a huge blister? I hoped it was gel.

I stood. The pain was blinding. I gritted my teeth to hold back a scream and dropped back onto the bed. God, the power of it made me nauseous. What the hell had I done to myself?

I had only walked a few steps through a fire. A magic fire.

Dammit. I was out of commission. How was I supposed to help Arne and the others with these drapes on them? How was I supposed to find Wally again? How was I supposed to find out what happened to Mouse?

I put my feet on the floor. They felt swollen and the pain was agonizing, but it was only pain. Only pain. I staggered to the little table and searched my pants pockets. I found my wallet, my keys, and my ghost knife. The wallet even had my money inside. What this said about Camo Pants, I didn't know and didn't care.

I put my wallet in my teeth, biting down hard on it to distract myself from the pain. I slid the key ring over the little finger of my left hand and used my ghost knife to cut the corner of the table. The table leg came free, with enough of the top still attached that it made a dull wooden pick. I stared at my ghost knife for a few seconds, wondering how I was going to take it with me. Eventually, I slid it inside my wallet and put the wallet back in my mouth. It didn't fit but I didn't care. I just needed to get to a place where I could call an ambulance.

I used the table leg as a cane while I crossed the room, then I pushed the door open and staggered through.

It was a hotel suite, as I'd thought, and an expensive one. There was more white, silver, and platinum out here. My feet felt like they were soaking wet through the gauze, and I was sure I was seeping onto the snowy carpet.

A gleaming silver phone sat on a tiny table at the far side of the suite. My original plan had been to get out of the building to get help, but suddenly I wasn't sure I could cross the room. My vision was swirling and my head throbbed. I nearly lost my balance, which would have gotten me off my feet, but I didn't think I could get back up.

Then I noticed a small figure sitting at a marble-topped table in the center of the room. Its back was turned to me, and it was wrapped in black lace and hunched over like a vulture. It couldn't have been Camo Pants, could it? He was too large for this small shape.

It didn't matter. I couldn't get to the phone without passing him. I hefted the table leg like a club and moved forward. The pain made it hard to think, but maybe this little person all wrapped up in black fabric was Camo after all.

It was just pain. Just pain. It made me dizzy and sick, and it clouded my vision at the edges, but I could push through it. I raised the table leg, feeling bleary and angry. I was hurting and I was ready to share that hurt.

"Ray."

I stopped, confused, and turned toward the voice. Annalise stood beside a small desk in the corner, watching me carefully.

Annalise Powliss was my boss, a peer in the Twenty Palace Society, and she was incredibly powerful. Although she was just barely over five feet tall and as thin as a rail, she was covered with tattoos—spells—that gave her extraordinary strength and toughness. She could tear a car door off its hinges with one hand and could shrug off a bullet through the eye. I'd seen her do both.

She wasn't wearing her usual gear—there was no outsized fireman's jacket, no vest covered with alligator-clipped spells. She wore a pair of plain blue drawstring pants and a white button-down shirt. Her tattoo-covered feet were bare. I'd never seen her dressed in such flimsy clothes.

Like mine, her tattoos were spells, but hers covered her whole body from her collarbones down—I'd seen them one time after her clothes had burned on a job.

Finally her face, which was pale and delicate—almost childlike—was set in the most curious expression I'd ever seen. She had always been difficult to read, but for the first time since I'd met her, she seemed nervous.

"Ray," she said again in her funny high voice, "that's a peer in the society you're threatening."

I turned back to the shrouded figure. It had turned toward me, and I saw that it was a little old woman with olive skin and gray streaks in her hair. Her face was impassive and her eyes were dreamy.

How had I mistaken her for Camo Pants? I let the table leg fall from my hands, then immediately wished I had it back so I could lean on it again. The little old woman was a peer? If so, she was probably just as powerful as Annalise—maybe more so. Hitting her with a hunk of pine wouldn't have done more than tear some lace.

The world began to go dark.

"Talbot!" Annalise called. Her voice seemed to come from far away. Suddenly, I felt hands lift me up and steady me. I leaned against a body—not Annalise's, a large one—and fought my way back to consciousness.

"Hey hey now," a man beside me said. He smelled of Old Spice and dry sweat. "You shouldn't be out of bed yet. You ain't ready."

I looked up at him. He wasn't wearing his red shirt anymore, but it was Camo Pants. I was happy to see he had a fat lip. He was holding my wallet and ghost knife; I reached for them and he let me take them.

"Get off me," I said. "You tried to kill me."

"Is that right? Maybe I did, although most of the guys I've tried to kill were wearing a keffiyeh at the time."

"You fired a rocket at me today." Had that happened today? I had no idea how long I'd been out.

"Guess I should apologize then. Guess I should be glad I missed." He must have guessed wrong, because the apology never came. He led me back into the small room and eased me into the bed facedown. "My name is Talbot, by the way. I'm a wooden man, just like you. Do you want some kind of painkiller?"

"*Yes.*"

"No," Annalise said from somewhere behind me, and in that moment I hated her and everything about her. "Talbot, go out to the fridge and bring the blue container."

Talbot left the room. My face was turned toward the window. I didn't want to look at Annalise. I was badly hurt, helpless, and ashamed of it.

"Ray, what the hell am I going to do with you?"

I almost said *Put me out of my misery,* but I was afraid she'd do it. "Water, boss. I need water."

"No, you don't." She took my wallet and ghost knife. Damn. I thought we were past that. I didn't have the strength to object.

The door opened again. I turned my head and saw Annalise intercept Talbot and take something from him. He left, closing the door behind him. I felt my ghost knife getting farther away from me, until I could no longer sense it through my pain and misery.

Annalise pulled up a chair and sat by the bed. She looked absurdly small, but I was glad she was nearby. She held a big plastic bowl in her lap. "You know you belong to me, right, Ray?"

I didn't like the sound of that. "I'm your wooden man, boss." She didn't respond. "You're not going to sell me, are you?"

"No, I don't want to sell you," she said, as if it was a legitimate possibility that didn't interest her for the moment. "But I have changed you."

I almost laughed. Yes, a lot about me had changed since I met her.

"Ray, you're not paying attention." She popped open the lid on the plastic bin and held it close to me. Inside were tiny cubes of raw, red meat. Beef, probably. They smelled like blood—I'd been cooked more than they had. The smell made me dizzy and sick.

I stared into the bin and at her. She moved them closer to my face. Carefully, I reached in and picked up one of the cubes. It was cold.

"Don't bother chewing," she said. "It doesn't help. Just swallow it down."

I put it in my mouth. It felt wrong. Wrong wrong wrong, as though it were a dog turd. I spit it into my hand.

"No, Ray. Try again."

I didn't like the way she was looking at me. I put the cube back in my mouth. Was it poison? No, and I knew it wasn't. Annalise would crack my skull open or throw me through a window before she'd poison me. I tried to swallow it three times, but it wouldn't go down. The fourth time, it finally slid down my throat.

Annalise quickly set the bin down and lunged at me. She clamped one hand over my mouth and grabbed the back of my head with the other. Her strength was enormous; she held my head in place, my mouth closed, while my guts wrenched and my body bucked. My legs scraped against the sheets, bringing out a whole new level of agony—fierce and wild and utterly in control of me. Blisters burst and flooded the gauze. The pain was so overwhelming that it felt like madness.

Eventually, whatever was happening inside me eased. My body stopped writhing and I lay on the sheets, soaked in sweat and exhausted.

Annalise had a spell on her body somewhere that healed her when she ate meat, especially meat that was raw and fresh. Not only had I seen her do it, I'd saved her life once by cramming tiny slices of raw beef down her throat.

But it hadn't been like this. She hadn't tried to puke up what she ate. Her body had accepted it. Mine didn't. Mine wasn't healing. If she'd put a spell on me like the one she had, she'd screwed it up. It didn't work.

I lay still because I didn't have a choice. Annalise let go of me and picked up the plastic tub again.

"No."

"Yes, Ray. Another."

"No. I don't belong to you."

"Yes, you do, Ray. You wanted to be my wooden man, so you do. You're mine."

She held the bin closer to my face. I swatted at it, but I was too weak to knock it away. I doubt I could have knocked it out of her grip if I'd been at full strength. "Fuck you."

"Ray," she said, leaning close to me. Her voice was still absurdly high, like a cartoon animal. "Ray, you gave yourself to me. You're mine. The golem flesh spell is on you because *I* wanted it there; you don't get a say. If I have to, I can break your jaw open and force this crap down your throat. Why not? Enough meat would just heal you again. Now, are you going to take it, or am I going to make you take it?"

God, I hated her. She scared the living hell out of me, and I hate to show my fear. "Boss, go fu—"

In a blink, her thumb was in my mouth. It tasted gritty—of course she hadn't washed her hands—and she forced another cube of meat past my teeth. I tried to bite down on her, but it was like biting the tread of a tractor tire. If it hurt, she didn't show it.

She forced that cube down my throat, then another, then another. After a while, I didn't have the strength to buck and thrash anymore. I sprawled on the bed, sweating and miserable. When I tried to puke, Annalise clamped her hands over my mouth and nose. I choked. I shuddered. Finally, I wept like a child.

She forced it all down me. It took almost two hours, but she put the whole contents of the tub into me.

When she was done, she tossed the bin onto the carpet behind her.

"Boss," I said weakly. I wanted to die, and I thought I could make her do it for me. "Annalise. I'm going to kill you for this."

"That wouldn't surprise me at all," she said as she sat back in the chair. She took a white ribbon from her pocket and held it up. I knew what her white ribbons did, and I was hungry for it. I looked at the sigil at the bottom and fell into unconsciousness.

When I awoke, it was daylight. Annalise was sitting beside me.

And my pain was gone. I sat up and looked down at my legs. There were no bandages on them, and the skin looked pale and healthy. And hairless.

"We have clean clothes for you," Annalise said. "Still want to kill me?"

"Boss, I . . ."

"Forget about it. You handled it better than I did, that first time."

"Golem flesh?"

"I hate the name," she said. "I don't know who called it that, but it's the name that stuck. Remember when I took that bullet in the eye?"

I did remember. She'd gone on talking and walking around with a huge hole in her head. My throat felt thick at the memory. I nodded.

"Well, you won't be that tough. Not for a long time. Golem flesh takes a while to have its full effect. The spell is still changing for me, too. But here's the deal: you need to eat meat every day. Your body will break down if you don't. Also, you can heal injuries by eating flesh—the more recently killed, the more effective it will be. Over time—over decades, really—you'll have less pain and less impairment from each wound. Eventually, massive injuries won't do much more than make you look like an extra in a shitty horror movie. That'll take a long time, but when it happens you'll be like a person made of clay. Sort of."

I didn't say anything to that. My hands were resting on my bare legs, and I pinched myself. Annalise noticed.

"You aren't dreaming. And I didn't put this spell on you. Csilla did. I don't have the power for it." She took a long breath. "I called in a favor for this."

She had put another spell on me. She'd healed me. It had been hellish, but it wasn't as bad as skin grafts, physical therapy, and a lifetime of scars. "Boss, we have a lot to talk about."

She gave me a quick nod and stood briskly from her chair. "Your new clothes are on the table. Put them on and come out to debrief us."

They were white briefs, faded blue jeans, a green T-shirt, and white socks and sneakers. The briefs would cramp my style, but what the hell. Beside them was a brand-new cellphone. Annalise hadn't said it was mine, but she hadn't said it wasn't. I slipped it into the pocket of my new jeans; if she didn't want me to take things, she was going to have to put them away.

My room had a little bathroom, so I went inside for some water. I thought I really ought to be shaking and unsteady, but I felt strong. I felt like a man who'd slept. I touched my bare face and leg; it felt like skin, not clay. For now.

There was a drinking glass on the sink, and when I unwrapped it, I realized it was made of actual glass, not plastic. I filled it, drained it, and filled it again.

In the mirror, I found the new mark on my ribs under my left arm. It was in black, like my others, and the swoops and curls suggested images of . . .

I looked away. It was dangerous to study magic too closely.

My face was covered with dry sweat, so I brought my new clothes into the bathroom and took a quick shower.

When I finally went out to the main room, Annalise, Talbot, and the old woman in the black shawl were sitting at the table under the chandelier. They were serving themselves from a platter of bacon, hard-boiled eggs, sausage patties, fried potatoes, and toast. No one spoke to me as I approached the table and began to serve myself, too.

"Thank you, Csilla," I said to the old woman.

She looked up at me with a vague expression. "You'd better be worth it."

Worth what? I didn't know what it had cost her to cast the spell on me, and I squelched the urge to ask. She had already started staring dreamily at an empty spot on the wall. I sat, cut a small piece of bacon, and put it into my mouth. I didn't vomit or have a seizure. The flavor seemed muted, but I didn't have the urge to spit it out.

While I chewed, I tried to decide what to tell Annalise and the other peer. I knew them well enough to know what would happen if I told them about the drapes. It'd be like putting out a contract on Arne and the others.

But what could I leave out? It wasn't just that Annalise would kill me if I tried to shield another friend—she would, but that wasn't the important part. The important part was that protecting my friends would almost certainly unleash more predators on the world.

And there was the thought that had been lurking in my mind ever since Melly was carried away. Luther had been lying at the bottom of the tub in his house the whole time I'd been there, and when he died, his drape carried him away and two more came through.

That had to have been what happened, because that's what happened to Melly. The only difference was that three drapes had come through when she died. Did that mean four would come through when the next one died? Five for the one after that?

I tried to do some quick math, but the others were staring at me and the numbers jumbled in my head. Damn. I'd been lucky that the first two victims had died indoors and close to me. If Summer, Ty, or one of the others keeled over in a subway station, or outside a Starbucks, the drapes would be free to hunt in secret. In no time, people would vanish by the thousands until the whole world was empty.

My friends were important to me, but were they more important than the survival of every living thing on the planet?

I told Annalise, Csilla, and Talbot everything. I didn't sugarcoat it, and I didn't hold back any names. I even told them about the Bugatti, Wardell, and Steve Francois.

While I spoke, Annalise stared at me the way a cat stares at a mouse hole. Talbot kept eating; he was paying careful attention, but he was trying to be casual about it. Csilla stared off into space and didn't seem to know I was there.

When I was done, I realized I still didn't have my ghost knife. I asked for it. Annalise nodded at Talbot, and he resentfully fetched it for me.

"These 'drapes' are minor stuff," Annalise said.

I was startled. "What do you mean, boss?"

"The big question is this: Why is your old buddy Wally King making operatives in L.A.?"

It was hard to imagine Arne or Fidel as an operative of Wally's, but they owed him, and he could collect at any time.

"He's trying to end the world," I said.

"Seriously?" Talbot said, a crooked, swollen-lipped smirk on his face. "I'm sitting here squirting ketchup on home fries, and we're talking about a guy who wants to destroy the world?"

"He thinks it's a mercy killing," I said. "He thinks something worse is going to happen to us. He thinks the whole world is going to be—" Talbot was still smirking. "Is this funny to you?"

"No no!" he said, smiling wide enough to show teeth. "It's just . . ."

"I know." Talbot didn't have to say it. He felt like a hero, fighting to save the world, and he loved it.

"There is a dream in my eye," Csilla suddenly said. "I see strangers and darkness and a thought as large as the universe."

After a moment of awkward silence, Annalise said: "We know what he wants. Why does he think he can make it happen here, in Los Angeles?"

"I pressed him to find out what he was doing, but . . ." What was I supposed to say? He started calling me a rock star and I got distracted? "I'm sorry. I was focused on the predators. All he told me is that he needed people to get a puzzle. He had a simple plan to steal it, but he blew it."

Annalise put down her fork. "He had a *simple* plan?"

"He's not a smart guy, boss. I don't think he could plan a meal, let alone an elaborate crime."

"Have you seen this?" Talbot asked between bites of toast. He slid a newspaper across the table toward me. At the top was a notice about security preparations for the president to speak at the L.A. Convention Center about renewable energy or something. But below that was a follow-up article on the movie star break-in. Ms. Egan-Jade's spokesperson said the actress was going to sell her house without returning to it. She'd also set aside a trust fund for the murdered housecleaner's children. Apparently, the woman had died. To Egan-Jade's credit, she also blasted unnamed media personalities who had expressed relief that "only" a housekeeper had been killed.

I liked her just for that. At the bottom of the article, it stated that police had no leads but were investigating puzzling aspects of the case.

I glanced up at the others. They were watching me, waiting impatiently for me to finish. "Puzzling aspects?" I asked.

Csilla narrowed her eyes. "So many dreams that they come to life. Puzzling." I couldn't tell if she was responding to me or not.

Talbot smiled. If it stretched and hurt his fat lip, he didn't show it.

"See, that's what *I've* been doing. It's surprisingly hard to get information out of the cops in this town. Easy to get them to crack you on the head with a stick, but hard to get them to take a bribe." He spoke like he was giving a performance, and he was so snide about it that I wanted to punch him again.

"We are beautiful children swimming in the belly of the great fish," Csilla said.

"I found out some interesting things, though," Talbot continued. I glanced at Annalise; she watched Talbot carefully, absorbed by what he was saying. Not two years ago, she had refused to tell me anything about the job we were on, and now I was allowed to sit at the grown-up table for the grown-up talk. It was a big change, and it felt good. Talbot kept talking: "For instance, Ms. Egan-Jade's home had a state-of-the-art security system. Cameras everywhere, and even a guard with a twelve-gauge to look over things. The cameras were running, too. The cops have a digital video of the break-in."

"Who did it?" I asked.

"Nobody," he said, and he smiled as though he was pleased with himself. "I've seen the video. The lock on the front gate breaks apart and swings open a few feet, but no one is there. When the guard shows up to check it out, he collapses from no apparent cause. It was an hour before the cops found him, stretched out in some bushes. He's in a coma now. Brain damage. They don't think he'll wake up, and you don't hear anyone talking about him on the news, or his kids, but hey, he's just a white male.

"Anyway, the cops don't have a recording of the attack, but it's not the only one. There have been several different break-ins around the city—women's homes, banks, jewelry stores, all sorts of places."

"Where? Do you have a map or something?"

Talbot snorted. "No. I don't have pushpins, either. But some of them take place at different locations at pretty much the same time, so we know it's more than one of your friends doing it. The cops think someone has a new, superfast version of Photoshop, and the burglars are bringing a laptop to erase themselves from the video files, somehow. There were two break-ins last night, in fact. A jewelry store and a convent. Two women were killed."

I nodded. Was this Wally's plan? To create people who could break in anywhere, stir up the cops with these crimes, and . . . And what? What would he get out of that?

Nothing. Wally wasn't the type to create chaos. Events were hard enough to predict under normal circumstances, and I couldn't imagine him drawing more danger to himself.

But he had brought me down to L.A., knowing I wanted to kill him. Caramella had said she was doing a favor by visiting me, and Arne said favors were what Wally expected in return for his "super powers." Wally wanted me and the Twenty Palace Society to take care of the drapes, yeah, and the drapes allowed people to break in anywhere without getting caught, but what if Wally expected to be long gone by the time we got here?

"Where was the first break-in?" I asked.

For ONCE, we didn't drive in Annalise's battered Dodge Sprinter. Csilla had a black Grand Vitara, which was a little embarrassing, but at least Talbot had to drive. I sat in back.

We skirted a country club, got lost for a short while as Talbot drove in circles, then finally pulled up to a house in Hancock Park. There were iron gates along the front, with heavy green foliage blocking the view of the house.

"This is it," Talbot said, sounding relieved.

"What's the story?" I asked.

"This one we don't know as much about, because my source wasn't that interested. There was a break-in, same as the others, but the video was shut off two minutes in, which no one bothered with in later invasions. Another difference was that there was no one home at the time; the guy who lives here was in San Diego. The cops checked him out like they always do but couldn't find anything suspicious. They think the invaders hit the wrong house, waited around for the person they expected, got bored, and finally split."

That sounded like crap to me. I opened the door.

Csilla roused herself. "Where are you going?"

"Where do you think?" I turned to Annalise. She had put on her fireman's jacket and heavy boots; they were her fighting clothes, and they made her look a little wacky. "Um, boss—"

"Ray, I'm going to wait here. I'll keep Csilla company."

"Go with him," Csilla told Talbot. She seemed almost lucid.

"Ray." Annalise stared at me intently. "Be extremely careful in there."

I nodded, wondering what the hell was going on.

Talbot followed me to the front gate. The lock had been broken—I could see the marks of the crowbar—and it hadn't been repaired yet. A blue supermarket twist tie held the two halves of the gate together.

I undid them and pushed the gate open. The heavy bushes and trees were as thick as a jungle. I was sure the owner received regular visits from the city to discuss his water use.

"Smells nice," Talbot said. "Big-money Los Angeleeze house. Comes with its own perfume." He sounded as though he disapproved, but I didn't know why and I didn't care.

The house had a stone foundation and green-painted wood above that. I couldn't say exactly why, but the place looked like a haunted house. There were pry marks on the doorjamb by the dead bolt. That hadn't been repaired yet, either.

The trees and bushes were growing close enough to the house that I could have climbed up and broken in through an unlocked window upstairs. There was a thin trail that led to the side of the house. I didn't circle around. Instead I knocked four times with the knocker, then looked up into the camera above the door. I didn't feel like smiling.

After a few moments, the door creaked open a few inches and a man put his face in the gap. He was short, with a trim black mustache and a flabby face. He squinted at us a bit, his dark eyes straining against the sun.

"Can I help you?" he asked. He sounded nervous.

"We'd like to talk to you about the break-in that happened at your house," I said.

"Are you police?" he asked, but it was clear he already knew the answer.

Talbot started to say something that might have been *yes,* but I cut him off. "No. Can we talk? It could be important."

He looked uncomfortable. He didn't like the idea, but he opened the door anyway. We followed him inside.

Instead of opening into a room, the door led to a narrow hallway. The place was underlit, making everything seem dark and faintly unclean. The air smelled of unvacuumed carpet and Szechwan spices. "Thank you for giving us your time." I extended my hand. "I'm Ray Lilly." Someday, I was going to have to come up with a decent alias for society missions.

He shook it. "Lino Vela. I don't understand who you guys are or why you're here. The police are already working on this."

This time, it was Talbot who cut me off. "Anyone else in the house?"

Lino was startled and alarmed by the question. "What?"

"That's not important," I said to Talbot.

He gave me an annoyed look. "Experience tells me it is. So how about it? Anyone else here?"

"No," Lino said out of politeness, but I could tell he resented it. *Victim*, I thought, but I shook that off. Those thoughts were a habit I didn't need anymore.

I tried to steer the conversation back to the job. "I understand nothing was taken?"

"Who are you guys? Why are you here?"

"That's not important," Talbot said.

"We've been asked to look into these break-ins. We're not with the police, and you don't have any obligation to talk to us. But we're hoping you'll help us put a stop to this."

He'd been about to ask us to leave, which would have ruined my chance to get information from him, not to mention that I couldn't tell how Talbot would react. Now he hesitated.

"Who are you working for? Is it Jade?" The familiarity of his tone threw me for a second, until I realized we were talking about a movie star. He probably thought of her as a part of his extended family.

"That's not something we can talk about. I'm sorry. And if the police knew we were asking questions, that would make things hard for certain parties."

"It's not her, I guess. Or is it?"

I made an expression of regret. "Will you help us?"

He sighed. "Let's go sit down."

He led us into a front room. The lights in there were brighter, and there was so much furniture—chairs, shelves, desks, cupboards—that the room felt cramped. All of it was old, made of dark wood, and just about every horizontal surface had something on it. I walked past hand-painted plates, battered oil lamps, fabric dolls, hand-stitched leather balls, and an antique sewing machine with a foot pedal. It was all crammed together as though this was a showcase instead of a home.

Lino offered us tea, but we declined. "Why don't you guys take the sofa?" he said. He settled into a creaky wooden rocking chair beside the curtained window. Talbot and I sat on the red couch. The velvet had been worn shiny, but it was comfortable. Opposite us were the only modern touches in the room: a flat-screen TV, a mini-fridge, and an Xbox. A tiny end table was covered with coasters but nothing else. In the back corner was a desk littered with papers and stacks of books.

"Thank you," I said. "It's our understanding that nothing was taken?"

"That's right."

"Are you sure?"

"Well, as I told the cops, if I'd been robbed, there'd be someplace to put down a drink. But it's not just that. I double-checked against the list."

"The list?"

"The list of antiques," Lino said, waving reluctantly toward the room as though he was obligated to show it. "It's what I do."

"What do you mean?" Talbot asked. "How is it what you do?"

He folded his hands over his little paunch as though holding his guts in. "I'm something of a curator—a historian by training. I earned my Ph.D. at a little Texas college you probably never heard of, then fell off the tenure track. I came to L.A. for . . . actually, I'm not sure why I came. Hope, I guess. Hope for something better. Not that I found it. I was about to take a job teaching for the L.A. Unified when I noticed an ad in the paper for this place.

"This is my home, but I don't own it. It's the official residence of another man—I just live and work here. His inheritance is in the form of a trust—it's a great deal of money, but to access it, he has to maintain this family antique collection in his own home."

"He lives here, too?" Talbot asked.

Lino looked a little uncomfortable. "As I mentioned, this is officially his home. In reality, he spends three hundred sixty-five days out of the year traveling, often to his vacation home in Bel Air. The trustee turns a blind eye to it, if you understand my meaning. The owner visits once a month to check on things. It's my job to keep the house and make sure the antiques are maintained."

"That's it?" Talbot said.

Lino spread his palms as though he couldn't believe it, either. "The terms of the trust require my services, so I am here. I'm not paid very much, but my duties give me ample free time to work on personal projects—"

"That's what you do for a living?" Talbot let his scorn show. "Dust all this shit and play the latest Splinter Cell?"

"Talbot," I said, trying to cut in.

"Oh, I'll bet the chicks just love you, Mr. Inheritance—"

Lino sprang to his feet, and so did Talbot. I found myself between them, right in Talbot's face.

"You get out of here *right now*," I said. My voice was low, but every other part of me was burning adrenaline. Did he have a gun? A spell like my ghost knife? I imagined myself going for his eyes and balls—hell, I had golem flesh now. I could lean in to his throat and start chewing. Anything—*anything*—to get him to shut up and back off.

"You don't scare me." He tried to stare me down. There was something odd in his expression. He seemed angry and confused, as though we were doing something dangerous he didn't understand.

"You are fucking this job up," I said, "and you don't even know why. Get out of here. This part isn't for you."

He stepped back and held up his hands. "You know what? You're right. Sitting around chatting isn't what I'm on this job for. I'll leave that to you."

He walked out of the room. I followed him into the hall and watched him slam the door behind him.

He was gone. I took deep breaths, trying to pull in my anger.

"I do not have an inheritance!" Lino said. "No! I worked very hard for my degrees. Many hours! Many late nights! I still work hard on other work!" He waved at the desk in the corner. "Is it so wrong to have a good job? I'm asking you. Is it wrong to have a good job and to own a game console?"

"No," I said. My voice sounded strangled. Lino's raised voice was making my adrenaline pump harder. It took all my concentration to not punch him in the mouth so he would *shut the fuck up*. But I couldn't do that, because I needed information from him and because he had a right to be angry.

"Yes, I play games sometimes. It's a very relaxing thing to shoot zombies in the head." A note of humor came back into his voice as his anger subsided. I kept my mouth shut. I kept my control. "What I shouldn't do is jump from my chair when I'm insulted by someone bigger, fitter, and fifteen years younger. Thank you for getting between us. I think you saved me from a thorough beating."

"I'm sorry for bringing him here. I didn't know."

Lino looked at me and his whole expression changed. "Are you all right? Do you want a glass of water?"

I said yes, so he would leave the room for a couple of moments while I got myself together. When he returned with a tall glass of chlorine-scented water, I took a long pull. He gestured for us to return to our seats, and I made a point of using the coaster.

"Thank you," I said. "And thank you for not throwing me out."

"You're welcome. We were talking about the list, weren't we? Would you like to see it?"

"I don't know yet. I don't think so. Did the burglar take any money?"

Lino sighed heavily. "I wish I had money to take."

He had gone right back into the interview, which helped me steady myself again. I was grateful. "Does a woman live here with you?"

"What?"

"You know that some of these . . . odd break-ins have been attacks on women."

"Rapes, you mean." He said it with the air of a man who didn't like comforting euphemisms. "No. There are no women here. The trust has provisions for spouses and such, but I live alone. I'm an introvert and I find the quiet soothing. I don't even open the curtains that often. I do have a partner, but he doesn't like the collection. He finds it unsettling."

That made things clear enough. "Does the owner ever have people stay here? Friends or relatives visiting from out of town, maybe?"

"Not here. Mr. Francois doesn't even bring his wife here. He has nicer accommodations across town."

"Wait. What was that name?"

Lino stood and crossed to the mantel. "Mr. Steven Francois," he said. He took down a framed photo and handed it to me. "That is him there, with his wife. He keeps personal items here as part of the ruse that this is his home."

The photo showed Linen—Steve Francois—on a beach somewhere with a towel over his bony shoulder. The woman beside him, his wife, was tall, thin, and blond, with a Doris Day haircut. Her smile had the cool superiority of self-righteous affluence.

"I don't know where that was taken," Lino said as he returned it to the mantel. "I don't like to ask personal questions of my employer. His manner doesn't encourage it."

I tried to imagine how Swizzle Stick fit in. "Do they travel together a lot?"

"Sometimes. Not always." Lino shrugged. "They are both quite rich—her more than him, even. They live unusual lives."

I gestured toward the picture. "She looks tough. Are they having any problems? Money or marriage?"

He gave me a look. "I don't pry into his personal life."

"I have to ask," I said. "If she wanted to hurt him, could she do something to violate the terms of the trust? Hire someone to steal something and break up the collection?"

"I don't believe so, but I don't know all the details of the trust. Also, I don't see why she'd bother. Her family runs a successful law firm, and she is one of the top litigators in the country. If there was a problem between them, it would be played out in a courtroom, I think. Not here."

I could see that he was uncomfortable with the subject, so I changed it. "What about the video? I saw the marks on the door out front and the camera."

"Yes." He sounded grateful to talk about it. "The police collected the disc and the machine as evidence. The camera isn't plugged into anything anymore. Sorry. I did watch the video before I reported the break-in, obviously."

"Tell me what happened."

"Nothing to tell. I came home from my trip. I was surprised to see the front gate standing open. I didn't even realize it had been broken until later; I thought I'd forgotten to lock it. The door was open slightly. I saw the scratches and pushed it wide. When I walked in . . . it felt weird, you know? I was suddenly really afraid, as if I would find a burglar waiting for me. I went inside anyway. Only one . . . nothing was missing. I checked the security camera, and it had been turned off. I played the last fifteen minutes that it had recorded and . . ."

"What did you see?"

"Nothing. The video showed the front stair and front walk, but there was nothing to see. After a while, the door burst inward suddenly as though it was hit by the wind. A minute or so later the video ended."

Something was off about this story, but I couldn't figure what. "Can I see where the machine was set up?"

Lino shrugged and led me into the hall. On the other side of the house was a small library, although it had more knickknacks than books. He opened a little closet and showed me a bare shelf with a bundle of wires running out of the wood. "The insurance company lowered the rates when the trustee put this in, for all the good it did."

"Could someone have been standing to the side when—"

"No," Lino answered, as though he'd answered that question many times. "The video showed the whole door. You saw how the camera was placed. I haven't moved it since it was installed."

"What did you see that made you afraid? Why did you say 'Only one'?"

He looked uncomfortable for a moment, then shuffled his feet. "Come with me."

He led me to the dining room at the end of the hall. There were cupboards along each wall, with more plates and odd objects displayed on shelves. There was a place setting at the table, with a bowl of pita chips sitting out. Lino snacked on one as he walked by.

"See this?" He indicated a not-quite-square mirror about two feet wide. "The frame is walnut with gold leaf."

I expected him to tell me he had seen a reflection in the mirror, but it wasn't positioned where he could see it from the front hall. Next he showed me a surgeon's kit—a wooden case filled with knives, saws, and needles. Then he showed me a battered copper kettle, a drum with an eagle on the side, an apothecary balance that predated the Revolutionary War, and a daguerreotype of a husband and wife who had been friends of the owner's great-great-grandfather.

Why was he giving me the tour? I leaned close to the picture and studied the faces. I half expected to recognize them. "They don't look like anyone's friends."

"Dour, aren't they? And over here—"

"Lino, you were going to show me something." He was standing next to a wooden object that I could never have guessed the purpose of. He looked both confused and secretive. He glanced down at the shelf beside him, and I followed his gaze.

There was a little metal sculpture on the shelf near the items Lino had been describing to me. It showed a seated man with an open book in his lap, while a second man behind him chopped off his head with a sword. In fact, the figure was in midstroke, and only a little bit of the seated man's neck still connected his head to his shoulders.

I leaned in close, even though it seemed like an unbearable imposition on Lino's privacy to do it. The swordsman didn't have a face— was he wearing a hood? It didn't seem so. The seated man's face looked serene. I guessed he'd finished the book.

"When I came into the house after the break-in," Lino said, "this little statue had been moved into the hall. Someone had taken it off the shelf and set it down right in the middle of the floor over there."

Lino offered me another glass of water, and I gratefully accepted. I wasn't thirsty, but it felt good to follow him into the kitchen away from the statue—it felt profoundly wrong to pay attention to it.

This had happened to me before, I suddenly realized. Some kinds of magic—very powerful magic—could make you think certain thoughts. Every time I looked at that statue, I felt like I was intruding on someone's privacy, and it was unbearable.

Which was ridiculous. I used to be a car thief, after all. I've intruded on quite a few private spaces in my time, and I never gave a damn. I'd also spent time in prison, where guys did every private thing you can imagine in full view, from crying like a baby over a letter scrawled in crayon to beating off to rape. Now that I was outside, I was protective of my privacy and happy to let others have theirs, but I didn't have shame. Not that kind, anyway.

Which meant I was being magically controlled. I reached up and touched the space under my right collarbone where Annalise had put an iron-gate spell. It was supposed to protect me from mental attacks, but it hadn't even twinged. I didn't know what that meant, but it made me nervous.

And it told me that damn statue was important.

"Tell me about the statue," I said. It took an effort.

Lino turned away from me and picked up a little pot on the stove. He moved to a makeshift plastic funnel by the side window and emptied the pot into it. I heard the water run through the pipe and out the window.

"There's a drought on," he said. "I have a rain barrel in the back and a drip irrigation system for the plants. All my tea, pasta water, and such flows into the yard. Very water-efficient. I even have a pump for the bathtub."

"Lino," I said, keeping myself focused and my gaze direct. "Tell me about the statue."

Lino glanced at the door, as though the little statue might be standing there watching him. "It's part of the collection."

"Nothing unusual about it?"

"I don't like it," he said. "Some of the antiques are gross or disturbing. There's a room in the upstairs back that has some ugly stuff in it: pictures of lynchings, heads in jars . . . weird, awful stuff. I enter that room only when the maintenance schedule requires. This statue . . . I would have put it up there, too, but it fits better where it is."

That was it. We talked about his friends, whether he thought the statue was put there as a threat, who might want to threaten him, new people he'd met recently, and so on. It was all an excuse to find out if he'd met Wally King, and what he might know about him, but he never mentioned Wally, and with the way Wally looked, he would have. He did admit that he wondered if the statue had been moved to frighten him, because it had worked. He couldn't imagine who would do that, though.

I thanked him for his time, and he led me out. As I passed the statue, I wondered why it was so heavily enchanted, but really, that was none of my business, was it?

Outside in the car, Annalise was still sitting in the back, with Talbot behind the wheel and Csilla beside him. I had the impression they had been silent for a long time. At least they had air-conditioning.

Talbot pulled into the road before I could buckle up. Annalise turned to me. "Well?"

I almost said I *didn't learn anything*, but the way Annalise was staring at me let me know that was a bad idea. And that was the enchantment at work, still controlling me. I didn't like to be controlled. "Steve Francois has a little statue with a spell on it. Actually, I should say I noticed one statue with a spell—the spell may be on his whole collection. You know I'm no expert, boss, but it seemed really powerful."

Csilla turned to look at me, then at Annalise. She seemed impressed. Annalise said: "That's right, but not everyone makes note of it. We've known about that statue for years, but there isn't a lot we can do about it. It can't be stolen, bought, or given away."

"How did you get him to talk about it?" Csilla asked.

"It wasn't too difficult," I said. "He was nervous about it. Someone had moved it during the break-in."

Csilla and Annalise looked at each other, and I could tell I'd just said something important.

No one spoke for a while. Csilla seemed to drift off into her own thoughts. Finally, Talbot said: "Where do I go?" No one answered. "Ms. Foldes?"

Csilla didn't answer him. She just stared at a spot on the dash. Annalise spoke up. "Back to the hotel."

I stared out the window while we drove. Steve Francois was mixed up in this mess, and I didn't think he knew it. Just before the gunshots started in Wally's motel, Arne had said, *By the time Luther came to us, his debt was paid in full. I asked him what he'd done, and he took me to the—*

Took him where? It had to have been Lino Vela's house. Before Wally even offered the predators to Arne and the rest, he'd sent Luther into Lino's house to shut off the video surveillance system, then he'd tried to steal that statue. Tried and failed.

Later, Luther had brought Arne to the house. They probably saw Francois show up in his damn Bugatti to check on the break-in, and Arne, buzzing with the idea that he was about to get a super power, threw away all his usual cautions and went after him.

In the underground hotel parking lot, Talbot had to help Csilla out of the car. She didn't seem infirm, but she moved like a sleepwalker. Annalise hung back and so did I.

"What's going on with her?" I asked.

"Nothing," Annalise said. "Not really. She's just very old. Peers that survive a long, long time sometimes begin to withdraw from the world. She has lucid moments and can still do magic—I couldn't have laid golem flesh on you; it's not in my book and it would have been such a weak spell that it would have been useless. But it's hard for her to stay engaged. I don't know if it's because of the spells or because they're centuries old, but it happens."

"Should she even be out here?"

"No. I'd planned to ask her to help clean up Hammer Bay, but now that I look at her . . ."

Uh-oh. Hammer Bay was the first job Annalise and I had ever

gone on. She'd been injured and I'd been forced to leave a huge, scary predator alive, trapped in a circle, because I had no way to kill it. That was nearly a year and a half ago. "Boss, what needs to be cleaned up in Hammer Bay?"

"The predator there is still alive, obviously. No one in the society is quite sure how to kill it without a risk of escape."

My stomach suddenly felt like it was full of lead. "Really?"

"Really. And that's not the only one." She sighed. "The society isn't what it used to be. Which reminds me: don't ask Csilla any questions. Be careful around her. If she doesn't recognize you during one of her bad moments, she might attack. You don't want that." Before I could respond, she asked: "How did Talbot do?"

Time to change the subject, apparently. "He's a smacked ass. I don't like him and I don't want him around. He insulted the guy in that house for no reason and almost blew my chance to find out anything."

"And you kicked him out."

"Yeah. I was surprised he went, too. I didn't take him for the type to knuckle under."

"He's not, but he's worried about you. He knows you're the reason he's here, and he wants your approval."

"Um, what's that again, boss?"

"You, Ray. You're a wooden man, and you're still out here fighting."

I looked away from her. A wooden man was a term the Twenty Palace Society used for low-powered underlings who distract the enemy while peers hit them from behind. We were supposed to have the longevity of an ice cube on a hot desert rock.

And I had volunteered for the position. I hadn't really known what I was doing, but when do I ever? "Boss, how is this guy my fault?"

"Because you're successful at a time when the society has been struggling. We've been falling behind in this fight, Ray, for a long time. You've given us some rare victories lately. The peers never thought they could get this sort of success from a mere wooden man, but here you are. And they want more of you."

"And they picked Talbot? The guy's an asshole."

"They're peers. What do you expect?"

True. When it came to the society, I couldn't keep my expectations low enough. They were killers—vigilantes, really—hunting for the Wally Kings and Caramella Harrises of the world, and they didn't care what sort of person you were. All that mattered to them were the predators; the people killed in the crossfire were acceptable losses.

Naturally, they recruited a guy willing to fire an RPG into a crowded apartment building in L.A.

"Boss, I've been . . ." *I've been having trouble sleeping. I have nightmares.* I couldn't say it, not to her. She wasn't here to listen to my problems.

"I know, Ray," she said. She kept her voice low, as though afraid someone might overhear. "You have the look. You're constantly afraid. It's hard to control your temper. You continually think about the things you've done and will have to do again."

I nodded. Annalise wasn't nice to me all that often. I thought I should pay attention.

She studied my face, then turned away. "Lots of things in this job will kill you, not just predators, sorcerers, or mundane threats. You can win every fight and be destroyed by the victories. A guy like that doesn't last long."

I took a deep breath and let it out slowly. The garage smelled of damp concrete and exhaust. That was a perspective I hadn't considered. *Of course* the society was full of assholes; those were the only people who could stand it.

"Did Vela say anything else important?"

"I don't think so, boss, but there's magic there, and I may have heard something important without realizing it." I remembered Steve Francois saying *He sounds feisty.* "The guy who owns that collection, he's not a sorcerer, is he?" Annalise snorted as though the idea was ridiculous. "Who is he?"

She gave me a measuring look. "Remember when I told you that the society used to have two original spell books but lost them? Well, Georges Francois was one of the peers who went missing with the books."

"Meaning what?" I wasn't sure how far I could push the brand-new Share Time aspect of our relationship, but I was going to find out.

"Eleven peers vanished overnight along with the original books. No one knows what happened to them. Most people think two of them stole the books and betrayed the other nine. Maybe they were killed and their bodies dumped somewhere. Maybe they were banished from the planet altogether. Then each of the two took a book and went into hiding."

"But no one knows which two."

"No one is even certain that's what happened. It's possible that one or more rogue sorcerers took the books and killed all eleven peers. Or that one peer killed the other ten. Or that a predator took them. Or maybe the books left our world in some way and dragged the peers away with them. No one believes that one, though, because they don't want to.

"What we do know is this: the peers who vanished left behind odd objects and secrets—these were damn powerful sorcerers, you know—and the Francois collection is just one of them. Some people think it contains clues to the locations of the books."

"And these would be which books?" In Washaway, I'd heard the names of a couple of these spell books, but nothing more. "The Book of Oceans, right? Because that's your book. And the other is the Book of Grooves?"

"I cast spells out of the Mowbray Book of Oceans, yes, but the society never had the Book of Grooves. We could never find it. We had the Book of Motes."

"Uh, Moats? Like a castle?"

"No, motes. As in *And why beholdest thou the mote that is in thy brother's eye, but considerest not the beam that is in thine own eye?*"

I had no idea what she was talking about. "Okay."

"Like dust motes, Ray."

"Oh. Boss, has anyone ever come across the Francois Book of Motes or something?"

She squinted up at me. "No. No one ever has. As far as anyone knows, there hasn't been a new primary since those books vanished. In fact, there don't seem to be any primaries left."

"And Wally wants to be the next. Could Wally get what he wants as a primary? Could he destroy everything?"

"He's a dipshit, Ray. Any of us could destroy everything. All it would take is a summoning spell. You don't have to be a primary for that. That's the whole point."

"But he doesn't want to kill us all with predators. He wants to be gentle. He wants to euthanize us."

"And he thinks becoming a primary would give him the power to wipe the world clean. All these assholes are like that. They have power, but it's never enough. If they could just find one more spell, if they could just become a quinary, a tertiary, a secondary, if they could just find the real Book of Grooves, they're sure they could do whatever they want. All they think about is their limitations, and they're sure they'd be able to do anything at all if they could just get a little more power.

"Except it's bullshit. There's never enough power, not for that kind. What's more, primaries were damned scary, but they weren't powerful enough to make us all extinct. It's not like they crapped A-bombs."

"Okay, then." I scratched at the spells on the back of my hand. "I guess that means that Wally already has the power to kill everyone, but he wants the power to do it a certain way. So his euthanasia plan is on hold. But if he becomes a primary, he's going to realize he's wasting his time and fall back on option b: summoning one predator after another."

"Except by then he'll be really hard to kill. So let's hope he doesn't wise up." She glanced at her watch. "We should get back to Csilla. We don't want to keep her waiting. But . . . go easy on yourself. Okay? Remind me sometime to tell you the story of how I got into this life."

She started toward the elevator doors, and I followed. I wanted to hear that story. I just hoped I lived long enough to have the chance.

In the room, Csilla was back in her place at the table. Talbot hovered over her, draping a shawl over her shoulders, then setting a plate of crackers and cheese before her. She was oblivious to him, staring blankly into space. Talbot smeared a blue-and-white-speckled cheese on a cracker and passed it back and forth under her nose. She didn't react.

He dropped the cracker onto the tray in disgust. He was trying to be a loyal flunky, but he was beneath notice.

Annalise waved him away as she sat opposite Csilla. Talbot suddenly had nothing to do, and I turned my back so he wouldn't approach me. The suite had a balcony. I went out onto it.

A breeze off the ocean made the sun and dry heat tolerable. We were getting toward the middle of the day, but the air was actually pleasant.

Talbot ruined it by joining me. He closed the door behind him. I had the idea that he was going to tip me over the rail, and I backed away from the edge.

"Whoa," he said. "I'm not your enemy here."

"Okay."

"I got off to a bad start, didn't I?"

"Twice."

"Yeah. Sorry about the RPG. I knew there was magic in the apartment, and I wanted to really take care of it."

I didn't respond to that. It would be great to have a way to destroy predators by hitting them from a safe distance, but I didn't have a weapon that could do it. And neither did Talbot, probably. Predators were part real, part magic. Normal weapons didn't hurt them—most of the time, anyway. Would the drapes be vulnerable to shrapnel or concussion? What about fire? It was possible, I guessed, but not likely.

Never mind that he could have killed Jasmin, Maria, or Violet. Never mind that I should be tipping *him* over the rail.

Talbot exhaled through pursed lips. I guess I should have responded right away. "I don't know if an RPG would affect those predators," I said. "I mean, we'll never know until we try, but from what I've seen, most predators can only be killed with magic. Did they give you any?"

"Nope. Not a weapon, anyway. I got these, though." He lifted his shirt and showed me a circle of tattoos on his chest centered over his heart. I didn't recognize them, but I knew the same spells could look different depending on which spell book they came from. He dropped his shirt and looked at me. He seemed to be waiting for something.

I lifted my shirt, too. My spells were more extensive than his, but they were also darker and thicker, making my torso look like a nest of black lines. He looked down at them with a calculating expression, like a batter studying the positions of the opposing team's fielders.

I dropped my shirt and turned away. I wished I had resisted the temptation to share my spells with him. No way was I going to show him my ghost knife.

"Hey," he said. "A few years ago, do you know where I was?"

"No."

"Iraq. I was serving over there. We had some real scary shit go down, stuff you don't even want to think about. One time— Do you mind if I tell you this?"

"Go ahead."

"One time, we had word that there was a dude with bomb-making equipment in his house. Not that he was making it himself, supposedly he let insurgents visit him for tea and explosives lessons, right? So we made a forced entry in the middle of the night, the way we do, and we're shouting at them, scaring the crap out of them to intimidate them. Which is for their own good, really, because if they're not intimidated, they might do something stupid, and that'll get them killed.

"Anyway, we drag them out of their beds, and they're screaming and pleading with us, but we have no fucking idea what they're saying. And the mom is yelling at the kids, and it's all the usual chaos.

"But one of the guys on my squad, a dude from Oregon named Park, was trying to control a fifteen-year-old kid, and the kid suddenly did a jumping, spinning kick at him. I saw it, and it surprised the hell out of me. Park lost his grip on his weapon—it didn't fly up in the air like in the movies, but he did let it get out of his hands. Crazy, right?

"And see, when I come across a snobby fag like that Vela dude, who earns a living by wiggling a feather duster back and forth, I get pissed off. He's doing nothing, and I'm out here feeling like a fucking teenage hajji in my pajamas taking on trained soldiers with nothing but moves I learned from a cabinetful of Jackie Chan DVDs."

"Talk to Csilla about that."

He smiled, measuring me. "You didn't like my story, huh?"

"At least you got some Jackie Chan movies out of it, right?"

"Damn straight," he said. "The reason I tell you that story is that

I'm ready to do whatever now that I'm in this society. I'll be that hajji. I'm ready to do whatever it takes."

"To accomplish what?"

His head quirked to one side. "To live forever, man. Well, I know it's not forever, but it's what, five hundred years?"

Great. Now the society wasn't just hunting down people looking for magic and power, they were recruiting them. I took a deep breath to ease the anger building in my gut.

Talbot laughed a little at himself. "That was the wrong answer, wasn't it?"

"Pretty much, yeah."

"Well, I figured the whole 'I'm happy to be saving the world' thing was a given. Guess not."

I started toward the doorway. The balcony felt very cramped. "You'll meet some of the people we're going against, and you'll see why it's not a given at all."

"Hey." Talbot caught my elbow. "You don't have to tell me. I was there. I saw it. Some guys, you take away all consequences, and they turn into monsters. Like being a human being is just a mask for them. I saw it."

"I believe you."

"Listen." There was a hunger in his expression that I didn't trust. "I just want you to know I'm committed. If these guys"—he tilted his head toward the inside of the suite—"do things the smart way, they'll make you a DI, and I want you to know where I stand."

"I don't even know what a DI is."

"DI? It's a drill instructor."

Goose bumps ran down my back. I yanked the door open and went into the hotel suite. No way was I going to teach anyone anything, least of all a roomful of Talbots. Let the society make them into a useful part of the crew—it would be easy to find people who knew more about hunting, fighting, and killing than I did. The only real difference was in what we cared most about, and I'd spent too long in prison to think I could change that part of a person.

Annalise stood across the room, holding the fancy silver phone to her ear. She held up her hand to signal for me to wait a moment. The platter in front of Csilla had a long hunk of salami on it, and I had a sudden craving for it. I cut it in half and began eating it like a bread stick.

Annalise hung up the phone. "Gear up, both of you," she said. "The plane is prepped and ready, and we'll have a boat waiting for us at the other end."

"Okay. Where are we going?"

"Your friend Wally said he was skipping town, didn't he?"

"Boss, don't call him my friend. But yeah."

"Well, thanks to you, we know where he's going." She pointed to a wallet on the corner of the marble tabletop.

I walked toward it. It was brown leather and stuffed with paper. It was also singed at the edges. I felt I should remember it, but I had no idea where it came from.

"It's Wally King's wallet," Talbot said. "We took it out of your pocket when we brought you here."

I suddenly remembered snatching it off the dresser in his room. "I forgot. I was distracted by being on fire."

Talbot laughed. Annalise picked it up and dropped it into an envelope. "He had a punch card from a lunch cart in there. It belongs to a little place on Slostich Island. If King left town, it's likely that he went there."

"Boss, how big is this island? Because I never heard of it."

"It's in *Canada*," Talbot said, as though it was something shameful.

Annalise added: "Thirteen months ago a cabin on the north end was bought by a man named Walter Roi. With a wire transfer."

"That's it? You have an address and a name?"

Annalise shook her head. "There isn't time for anything else. We don't even have time to send an investigator. We're going to follow up on it ourselves. You know that *roi* is French for king, don't you?"

I didn't know that. Something about this felt wrong. Wally knew he was being hunted, and although the guy was no genius, he wasn't *entirely* stupid, either. Was he stupid enough to use a comic-book alias?

"Gear up," Annalise said again. My jump bag was still sitting on the floor by a bed at the Best Western, but it had nothing I needed, except maybe a toothbrush.

Someone knocked on the door and pushed it open. Talbot started talking about the drapes. He thought we should take them on first, then move on to the next target. His back was to the door and he was blocking Annalise's view, so neither noticed the housekeeper as she entered. She looked to be middle-aged and of Southeast Asian ancestry, maybe Vietnamese.

Talbot's voice was loud; I couldn't hear what she said to Csilla. From her body language, she appeared to be asking if she could come in to clean up.

Csilla stood without answering and walked around the corner of the table. The maid stood politely with her hands folded in front of her. Csilla didn't move fast, but it didn't take more than a few seconds for her to stagger up to the woman.

In one quick move, Csilla clamped her small hand over the maid's windpipe. The woman's face twisted in sudden pain and shock as Csilla twisted.

"Hey!" I shouted stupidly. Talbot and Annalise turned toward the center of the room.

Csilla yanked the maid onto the floor, then took something out of her pocket with her free hand; it was small—about the size of a raspberry—but dark and shiny like a stone. She stuffed it into the maid's gaping mouth.

I started forward, ready to throw myself at her, ready to slash into her with the ghost knife, but Annalise caught my wrist. I struggled, but she was too damn strong.

The maid bucked and her eyes rolled back. Csilla leaned down onto her, pinning her to the white carpet. A horrible wet rattle came from the maid's throat.

I couldn't stand it anymore. I twisted against Annalise, using my body weight to knock her off balance. She was strong as hell, but she weighed as much as a pile of brooms. I'd carry her across the room, if I had to.

But it was already too late. The maid's body burst as though she'd swallowed a grenade. Her legs, arms, and head split open in a ragged confusion, but there was no blood. In fact, there was no red in it at all, just a strange charcoal gray and smudge brown, and her body held together like a shredded blanket waving in front of a fan.

The maid's body was gone, transformed into something that fluttered to the ground as Csilla's spell spent itself. Her flesh, bones, clothes, and shoes had vanished, and in their place was a pile of something I couldn't make out. My brain was looking for a corpse; it couldn't recognize the dark, shiny stuff on the carpet.

I wasn't struggling against Annalise anymore—what would have been the point?—but she was still squeezing my wrist, much harder than she realized.

Csilla stood without letting go of what had been the maid's throat, lifting something that shimmered like raw silk. It hung from her hand like fabric, splotchy and wet-looking. She draped it over her shoulders as though it would keep her warm, and among the discolored blotches and ragged ends of that cloth, I could make out the shadow of an agonized face. Csilla returned to her chair and stared into space.

My hands were shaking and I felt sick to my stomach. A fury was building in me, and I didn't know what to do with it.

I turned to Annalise. "Boss." I looked down at my wrist and so did she. She let go. Her face was pinched and pale. I didn't want to think about what my expression looked like.

Talbot was breathing heavily. "That was fucked up."

"We're going to be fucked up if we don't move quickly," I said. I moved toward the door. The housekeeping cart was parked just outside the room, but there was no one else in the hall. "Talbot, pull that cart all the way back to the elevator. Then get back in here and close the door."

He looked jumpy. "What if . . ." *What if I get caught?*

I held his gaze with my own. "If someone sees you, tell them it was in the way. Just be cool."

He hurried out the door, taking a tissue from a silver box by the phone. He laid the tissue over the handle before pulling it away.

I spun on Annalise. "Boss, aren't predators just magical beings that kill people?" My voice was a harsh whisper, although I felt like shouting.

She understood what I was saying right away. "No." Her voice was low and urgent, as though she was afraid she'd be overheard. She glanced at Csilla. "Predators are a new link in the food chain. They're alligators in the rabbit hutch. The society doesn't hunt down *murderers*."

"I can see why."

She stepped close to me, her teeth bared. "Don't you *dare* talk to me about killing. Do you think I've never killed an innocent person by accident? What about you? Are you sure your hands are *completely* clean?" Talbot hurried back inside. He shut the door with both hands and his shoulder, as though it weighed as much as a bank-vault door.

"This isn't even her fault," Annalise said. "It's mine. The peers wanted her out here for him." She pointed at Talbot. "I was supposed to look after her."

Don't ask Csilla any questions, Annalise had said. I paced back and forth. Wally King, Arne's crew, and the drapes were all running around the city, and I had Csilla on my side. I felt just as dirty as the people we were after.

Csilla was still sitting in the same chair on the other side of the room, staring at the same piece of nothing. "The universe . . . we think its thoughts and . . . ," she said, her voice trailing off. "We . . . we . . . we . . ." She seemed agitated. Maybe she knew she'd done something wrong.

Annalise said: "We'll have to move her."

"What about me?" Talbot asked.

Annalise scowled at him. "You're with me now. Don't fuck up."

We packed quickly, throwing all the clothes into suitcases without folding them. Annalise checked us out, and a valet brought the Grand Vitara to the front door. We moved to a Best Western in Canoga Park, throwing all Csilla's things onto the bed and parking her in a little chair by the window. Annalise went into the bathroom to make a call.

When she emerged, she said: "An investigator will be here before tomorrow morning to escort her home. Let's go."

We went straight to the airport in Burbank, boarded a private jet, and lifted off. Predators were on the loose with more coming anytime, but we were leaving for Canada to go after the guy who was bringing them here. I was sure we were making a terrible mistake.

During the flight, Talbot tried to talk about the mission, but Annalise didn't answer any of his questions, and I certainly didn't know anything. Eventually, he stopped talking and stared out the window. I closed my eyes and slept heavily for an hour and a half. We landed at a small airport in Everett, Washington.

At the airport, we were met by a woman who didn't want to know our names. She was nearly my height, and was as skinny as a mop handle. Her hair was a nest of tight black curls with a good bit of gray mixed in, and her muscles were long and ropy. Annalise handed her an unsealed envelope, which she tucked into the satchel she carried.

She piled us into a pickup truck—Talbot and I sat in the bed. I peered into the cab to see if Annalise had something to say to the driver, but I didn't see them talking.

The truck ride ended at the docks. We had to detour through waterfront construction, but we eventually pulled into a long parking lot and stopped at the back.

Annalise followed the tall woman, and Talbot and I followed Annalise. The driver unlocked a gate and we followed her down the dock. The boats on either side of us were pleasure craft of one kind or another—some sailboats, but mostly they were tall motorboats with enclosed cabins and tinted windows. They looked like expensive condos with a hull, or maybe oversized SUVs. A little thrill went through me. I had never liked the ocean, but I liked a high-class ride as much as any car thief.

Unfortunately, the boat we stopped at was the smallest of the bunch. It was a little more than twenty feet long, I guessed, and completely open to the weather. BAYLINER was written along the side, but it looked like a brand name, not the name of the boat.

Annalise stopped short. "This isn't a sailboat."

"There wasn't time," the tall woman said.

"Wasn't time for what? This is a deck boat."

The woman sighed in exasperation. "Wasn't time for you to find someone else. I'm not doing this for you people in a sailboat. Not again."

I had an uncomfortable moment waiting for Annalise's reaction, but after a few seconds she nodded. "You're the expert."

The captain led us aboard. She cast off and carefully motored out of the slip.

"Do you have our folder?" Annalise asked.

"After we pass Jetty Island," Captain answered.

It was about thirty minutes before she opened her satchel and handed Annalise a folder. By that time, we were all stretched out on the long cushions that ringed the small deck area. Talbot went to sit out at the bow, but Annalise and I stayed near Captain.

Annalise opened the folder and took out three sheets of paper in plastic slipcovers. She handed one to Talbot and one to me. It was a map. I laid it flat on the cushion beside me to make it easier to read—we weren't going that fast, but there was enough of a breeze that the ride was rough.

"This is Slostich Island," Annalise said. "The little *a* is Walter Roi's cabin. That's where we expect to find Wally King. For once, there are no other residences nearby, although it's not *completely* isolated. The southern end of the island is where all the people are. The north end is scattered cabins, a few retreats, and protected forest. Memorize that map, because we're not bringing it ashore. With luck, we'll reach the cabin, kill the target, and be back on the water in two hours with no one the wiser."

There was a little mark on the paper where we were coming ashore. It was some sort of park, and it looked to be about a mile from the cabin. "Will there be a car for us, boss?"

"Not unless we steal one. There was no time to arrange it."

I nodded, but I didn't like it. A mile wasn't far to walk if you're going for pad thai, but fleeing the scene of a murder—and probably an arson—was another thing entirely, especially on a long strip of land with what appeared to be two north/south roads running through heavy woods.

Talbot looked at us, irritated. He waved the plastic sheet cover at me. "In the service, we had blue-force tracking. We had computers and . . . not fucking Google maps! We flew here on a private jet, but we can't afford a GPS?"

"Who's 'we'?" Annalise snapped. "The jet is Csilla's. She spent a couple of centuries killing people and taking their shit. You haven't. We're lucky we have someone in place to take us by boat."

"We could do better, is all I'm saying. Do we really have to go the whole way by boat?"

"Did you bring your passport?" Captain asked.

Talbot took a deep breath. "No."

"I'm a convicted felon," I said. "There's no way they'd let me through a checkpoint."

Annalise scowled at Talbot. "So we cross the border. We surprise King in his home, hopefully while he's asleep. We kill the hell out of him. We cross back into U.S. waters and fly east before anyone even knows about the body."

East? I almost corrected her, when I noticed Captain take the unsealed envelope out of her satchel. She opened it and unfolded the single sheet of paper inside. I couldn't read it, but I saw that it was a short, printed letter. Captain looked it over grimly, then put it back into the envelope and shut it inside a compartment below the steering wheel.

We cruised for about an hour. I studied the map off and on. I'd never been much for learning things off paper, but I went back to it several times until I was sure I had it down.

Finally, Captain turned off the engine. We floated a thousand feet off the Washington coast, gently rolling with the waves. Talbot looked alarmed. "Why did we stop?"

"We'll cross into Canadian waters after dark. Sunset's just after eight P.M., which is . . . two hours from now. Try to act like we're out for some summer sun. Maybe no one will pay attention to us."

I closed my eyes and lay back on the cushions. I was going to see Wally King again. Did he sleep with all those predators inside him? I hoped so. We could destroy the creatures and him at the same time.

How simple that seemed. How right. I closed my eyes, but I couldn't sleep.

After night fell, Captain started the engines again. We puttered forward, obviously in no hurry. She told us we had another five hours, more or less, before we reached our target.

We rode in silence. After three hours, Captain brought out a cooler and slid it to Annalise. She took out four bags of fast-food burgers, fries, and soda. The drinks were watery and the food was cold and greasy. I was hungry enough not to care.

I kept my eye out for patrol boats, but no one approached us. The trip was smooth and easy right up to the moment Captain pointed out our landing spot, and Annalise took out the guns.

They were revolvers, old Magnum .44s like the ones Clint Eastwood used to carry, and they were sealed in gallon-sized Ziploc baggies. There were two speed loaders in the bag, too. Talbot looked at his as though he'd been asked to dig a grave with a soup ladle, but I took mine without comment. I didn't expect it to be much use, but I appreciated the thought.

There were only two, of course. Annalise didn't need one.

Captain killed the engines and let momentum carry the boat toward the shore. There was a steep beach ahead and a line of trees at the top of the hill. Captain turned the wheel, letting the boat swing around. Annalise, Talbot, and I jumped off the port side into water up to our thighs—on Annalise it was up to her navel. Damn, it was cold, but no one else complained, so I kept my mouth shut.

Talbot ran ahead, yanking the gun out of the baggie as he left the water and charging up the sand as if he was storming the beach at Normandy. I hissed at him, but he ignored me.

I was surprised to come out of the water onto a flat, grainy tan rock. In the starlight it had looked like a stretch of sand, but it was actually solid and smooth like a boat-launch ramp. Annalise and I walked slowly up the hill, as though it was the most natural thing in the world, and Talbot came out of the trees to join us.

I took the gun from the baggie, folded the plastic and put it into my back pocket, then stuffed the speed loaders into my hip pocket. I wasn't wearing a jacket, and no way would I slip this blaster into my waistband. Life was too chancy. I carried it by the barrel instead.

It was about three hundred feet to the road, then we turned toward the south. It was almost midnight, and of course there were no streetlights. The starlight was bright enough for what we were doing, but flashlights would have been better.

We jogged along the side of the road. Talbot ran ahead, although I'm sure he thought of it as taking point. There was no sidewalk, of course, so we trotted along the asphalt. I turned around every ten steps, watching for headlights behind us. Not that it mattered: the gully along the road was choked with bush and brambles. We couldn't exactly dive for cover.

We didn't need to. No one came. The moon rose over the trees, lighting the roadway. I ran toward my own faint shadow.

At the mouth of a driveway, Talbot stopped and looked back at us. He made some sort of hand signal I didn't recognize, but Annalise beckoned him toward us impatiently. When he came close, she said: "This is it, isn't it?"

I'd forgotten that Annalise was hopeless with maps. Talbot said: "Yeah. Shouldn't we get off the road?"

Annalise shrugged, and the three of us started moving up the drive. I felt a twinge on my right collarbone.

"We shouldn't be here," Talbot suddenly said, rubbing the top of his breastbone with two fingers. "This is the wrong place."

I felt it, too. I was suddenly sure this was the wrong path. Why hadn't I studied the map better? My iron gate throbbed.

Talbot began backing down toward the road. "Let's try somewhere else."

"Talbot," I said, "are any of your spells hurting?"

He was still rubbing the spot on his chest. "Yeah."

"There's a spell on this place," I said. "Some kinds of magic can make you think or feel certain things. Pay attention to the spells on you. They're painful for a reason."

Talbot looked embarrassed and walked with me toward Annalise. "Want me to lead the way?" he asked.

A cloud moved across the moon, and things were suddenly very dark. "Is that how you want it?" Annalise asked. She took a scrap of wood out of her pocket and lit a Bic lighter. I recognized the scrap as one of her Geiger counters for magic, but the sigil was dark and inert.

The cloud moved away from the moon. I looked around. Everything seemed completely normal. "Shouldn't you be getting a reading from that thing, boss?" If magic was making my iron gate throb, her detector should show it.

"Yeah," she answered. "Unless I'm not."

"Boss, let me take the lead here," I said, without even realizing I was about to speak. "I owe this guy."

"No offense, Ray," Talbot said. "But I was the one kicking down doors for Uncle Sam. I should lead the team into the house."

Annalise turned to him. "We don't work that way. We don't bunch up; we don't charge in together."

"But . . . what about covering each other?"

"These are sorcerers," she said. "Taking them down is like taking down a suicide bomber, except without the suicide. This is how we do it: one wooden man comes at them from the front, and the others hit their flank."

"Boss, you know I have history with this guy. I want him."

"Ray, if you have history with him," Talbot said, trying to be reasonable, "if it's personal, you should probably not even be on this mission. Just saying."

Annalise waved that off. "With Ray, everything's personal." She turned to me. "Go ahead."

I started up the gravel driveway, wondering if I should feel stung. I shifted the gun to my left hand, holding it properly now. With my right, I took my ghost knife out of my back pocket. The revolver was loud, clumsy, and very, very solid, but the ghost knife was my weapon.

I wanted to head back to the boat. I wanted to be in L.A. Nothing was right and everything was wrong. My iron gate was aching like an old bruise. The spell on this property, Wally's or not, was getting stronger. I lowered my head and bulled forward, determined not to let feelings I couldn't control drive me away.

The brambles on either side of me were tall, well over my head. The path curved to the right, and after following it a few dozen yards, I saw a light in the trees up ahead. It was bright, not a lamp in a window—probably a security light.

I suddenly hit a spot where my iron gate flared with sharp pain. I flinched, bending over slightly as the pain hit. "Something is different here."

Annalise hurried forward, and I could see she felt it, too. Talbot also flinched, but less than I had. Annalise took out her scrap of wood and held it in front of her. Immediately, the design started moving. A shower of dull gray sparks shot out, along with a jet of black steam.

Something had changed drastically in just a few steps. I had stepped from a magic-free area into one that set off Annalise's detector like a siren. When I moved toward the house, my iron gate eased. I backed toward the spot where the pain had first started and moved side to side, trying to find out if whatever was hurting me was a single spot or if it had a shape.

It turned out to be a line that went across the driveway, down the stony gully into the brambles.

"The plants look thinner here," Talbot said. He was right. Not only were the brambles thinner, they were shorter. They had been cut or burned away some time ago up. I knelt in the rocky dirt and tried to peer through the underbrush, but it was too dark even with this bright moon.

"It's a circle," Annalise said. "He surrounded the house with a circle and buried it."

I scraped at the ground at the base of the gully, dragging my fingers through the loose and not-so-loose stones. Eventually I came to a piece of brick. I dug around it, exposing it and the two next to it. They had been broken at odd angles and fitted together . . .

"Leave it," Annalise said. "We have more important things."

I stood and brushed the dirt off my pants. "Are you sure it's a circle, boss? It seems like a straight line to me."

"It's some kind of closed shape," she said. She held up the scrap of wood. "It has to be to do this."

We looked through the trees toward the single lonely light. It was about fifty yards away up the hill. Did Wally really make a circle this huge?

"Boss, do you want me to destroy it?"

"I told you to leave it. There's no telling what he has trapped in here. Let's go."

Talbot bent his knees to lower his center of gravity as he raised his weapon. I started back up the driveway, my grip on my ghost knife tight.

After a few seconds, I heard Annalise say something to Talbot, and they both left the driveway, pushing through a stand of trees. I could hear their shoes quietly scraping on a wooden walkway.

Sound traveled far at night. I kept moving toward the house, trying to empty my thoughts of everything except what I could see, hear, and smell. When my iron gate twinged at the bottom of the drive, I'd been sure a sorcerer of some kind lived here. I was less sure it was Wally; it would have been just like him to lead us here to collide with some jackass he didn't like.

But now that I'd crossed the circle—and knew what it could do—I felt more certain that this was Wally's place after all. A huge buried circle a hundred yards across seemed like just the kind of crazy move he'd make. He was lazy and obsessive in nearly equal measures, and I believed a guy who would load himself with predators would set aside a private reserve for them, too.

I was letting myself get distracted. I focused my attention out-ward. I didn't see or hear anything unusual as I approached the house.

He wasn't here. The house was small, with a space beside it for a car and trees growing close behind it. The parking space was empty, and I couldn't imagine Wally walking all the way here from the nearest ferry.

The real question was whether he had left predators behind to guard the place or taken them all with him.

And there was something else. During our little talk, Wally had said *Don't try that "turn over your books" crap with me, okay? It's insulting.* He'd said "books." Plural. It had taken a while for me to realize what that meant, but I wasn't here just to find him and pay him back. He had spell books, and spell books had to be destroyed.

The cabin had wooden walls that had been painted the color of bricks. It was bigger than I'd expected. The outside light was a flood-light, one of the newer ones that use very little electricity but give off a thin, bluish light. It lit the front door and two windows. One of the windows was shuttered, and the other was boarded over.

I almost knocked at the door, which was absurd. Instead, I held the gun so my index finger rested beside the trigger, then I pushed the corner of the ghost knife into the door between the knob and the jamb and slid it up and down.

My spell cut through the door and locks as though they were made of smoke. I pressed gently on the wood, and it swung inward a couple of inches. The physical locks had been cut, but did Wally have magical protection, too?

I forced myself to take a deep breath. Whatever was going to hap-pen to me here would happen, and I'd live or I'd die, and there was nothing for me to do but get started.

I pushed the door all the way open. The light from the security lamp showed no one else was in the room. I turned on a table lamp by the couch.

The lamp was expensive, and so were the couch, table, and rug. I'd expected yard-sale furniture like the castoffs I had in my room, but the end table was made of solid dark wood. The couch was plump and new, and the rug was a mix of deep, beautiful colors. I supposed if I ever learned how to walk through walls the way Wally could, I'd have as much cash as I could carry.

Sometimes an empty house *feels* empty. Everything seems inert, like a vacant tomb. But I couldn't tell with Wally's place. It didn't feel empty or full; it was just a space.

A quick scan of the room didn't show any sigils or other signs of a spell. I kicked over the corner of the fancy rug, but it was just unmarked floorboards underneath.

To the left I saw a doorway to a room with counters and a tiled floor. I went in. It was a small kitchen, but it wasn't lacking for gear. It had a four-burner gas stove top and a full-sized fridge. I went through and opened another door to a little mudroom, complete with washer and dryer.

The only other door here obviously led outside. I wasn't ready to leave yet, but I did peek out the window. Having light sources close by made the darkness outside look like black paint on the glass. If Annalise and Talbot were out there, I couldn't see them.

On my way out of the kitchen, I opened the fridge. Part of me was convinced it would be full of human heads, but all I found were spoiled chicken parts and discolored steaks still in the packaging. The unit was just as cold as it should be; Wally hadn't been here for a while. This was the second abandoned home in as many days, and it made me feel like I was in a race but so far behind the pack that I couldn't see the other runners.

I went back into the living room, and more details jumped out at me. There was no TV, but there was a stack of newspapers in the corner and a pile of magazines beside that. A small stack of mail sat on the table, but when I flipped through it, I didn't see anything interesting. No brochures for Vegas hotels or train schedules, at least. It was all addressed to Wally King.

I lifted a framed photo off the table. It showed Wally at about eighteen, wearing a life jacket and standing next to a wide stretch of white-water rapids somewhere. He was smiling and giving a thumbs-up, as though excited about his new adventure. There was no one else in the picture, and there were no other photos in the room—not family, not friends, nothing.

In the back corner there was another doorway. It led to a short hallway with a door at the end and another just on my left. I figured the one on my left was a bathroom, and opening it proved me right. I looked around quickly but didn't find anything unusual, unless you counted a bottle of Vicodin with no doctor or patient's name on it, which I didn't.

When I put my hand on the knob of the other door, though, goose bumps ran up my arms and back. I've learned to trust those sudden intuitions, and I held both my weapons at the ready as I opened it.

This was the bedroom, naturally. It was empty. I stood in the doorway, my heart pounding. No one was there. I flicked the light switch.

The bulb in the center of the ceiling struggled to life. It barely lit the room. The dresser against the back wall was made of mahogany, and the sheets on the bed were satin. Between the dresser and the wall was a pair of sliding closet doors.

I crossed the room to the dresser, hearing the floor creak under my feet. I took each drawer out of the dresser and dumped the contents onto the bed. All of his clothes were triple-X sweat suits in various colors, plus gray boxers and white socks. There was nothing else in the drawers or taped to the bottom. There was nothing in or under the bed, either.

Then I opened the closet.

The only thing hanging inside was a heavy winter coat. I took it off the hanger and tossed it onto the bed. I'd search the pockets, but that could wait.

Because inside the empty closet, Wally had drawn something on the wall in black Sharpie. I couldn't see the whole thing at once because the sliding doors blocked half the closet. Gripping the bottom of the door, I lifted it up and out like the door to a DeLorean until the wheels burst out of the tracks. Then I did it again, tossing both onto the bed.

I squatted low, because the light was weak and I was throwing a shadow. "Well, well," I said aloud. The sound of my own voice surprised me.

In the upper left corner of the closet was a drawing of the earth. There was a crude energy to it—it wasn't pretty, but I could see Florida and the eastern edge of South America along one side of the circle. On the other, I could see West Africa and southern Europe. Two heavy black lines ran along the continents and oceans like cracks in an eggshell.

To the right of that drawing and a little lower on the wall was a second drawing of the earth, but while the first was made by someone who couldn't form a perfect freehand circle, this one was obviously meant to be bulging and malformed. Billows of steam shrouded most of the planet like a blanket of clouds, but something was just coming through them—something alive. Wally had drawn a single eye on a face that might have been liquid, or partially liquid, and in other places something else was rising out. Were they tentacles? The curves of a serpent?

To the right of that drawing and still lower on the wall was a crude image of a city. In the foreground, people fled toward me, their arms over their heads in a stick-figure depiction of blind panic. In the background was a towering *something*—a thing so huge that the city skyscrapers looked like pencil stubs next to a grown man's leg. I had the impression that it was dragging across the ground like a tongue licking a lollipop, and inside it I could see objects rising up: buildings, trees, and tiny screaming people.

The last image was almost down at the carpet, and at first it was difficult to make out in the shadowy corner of the closet. I got onto my hands and knees to peer at it.

The sun—our sun, presumably—was way down in the bottom right corner. There were a few broken specks to the left of that, and it took me a moment to realize that they must have been asteroids or loose rock. Maybe the broken pieces of the earth?

On the left edge of this picture was a drawing of something obviously meant to be very much in the foreground. It was a ragged piece of something that was moving out of sight on the left, and all I could see was the rear part trailing behind like a corner of wet laundry. Inside it, as though trapped in an amoeba, were people, and they were screaming with all their might. I got the impression that they had been screaming for a long time, and would still be screaming an eternity from now.

I took out the cell Annalise had left for me. I had to noodle with it a little, but eventually I figured out how to take a picture of all four pictures together, then I took a close-up of each one. What the hell. Someone might care.

On the floor by this final sketch was an open book. It was a thin hardcover, one of those kids' books that come in series with each featuring a different animal. This page showed a wasp laying eggs inside a caterpillar, and what I could read of the caption in the bad light said the eggs would hatch inside the living animal and begin to feed.

There was a Post-it note sticking out of the book. Wally must have bookmarked a page. I grabbed the book off the floor and flipped through it.

Immediately, the darkness began to deepen as though someone was dialing down a dimmer switch. At the same time, I heard a sound that was part hiss, part electrical crackle.

Damn. When I'd moved the book, I'd uncovered a small sigil on the closet floor. Now, with the spell exposed, something around me was waking up.

CHAPTER ELEVEN

I slapped the book back down over the sigil, covering it again. It didn't work. The room kept getting darker, and the hissing grew louder.

I swept the edge of my ghost knife through the sigil, cutting the spell in half. It came apart in a jet of black steam and iron-gray sparks—for all the good it did.

The darkness started to feel solid, like a thickening gel. I put my back against the wall, desperately afraid of being trapped. A dark line hovered in the air in the center of the room, as though something I couldn't see was blocking the light. It was dull black at the top and progressively lighter gray down toward the floor, and it was between me and the door. Things were getting darker every moment, and the line was moving slowly upward toward the bulb.

Inside the line, something moved. Then, from the very darkest spot, an arm reached into the room.

I squeezed off two shots at it, as much to sound the alarm for Annalise as to injure it. One of the bullets must have struck home, because the thing drew back.

Incredible. A predator that could be hurt by a mundane weapon. I turned back to the wall and slashed my ghost knife through the plasterboard in one large circle. I shoved at it, trying to bull my way through, but the air was so thick I could barely use half my strength on it. I held my breath. Whatever this stuff was, I didn't want it in my lungs. The darkness pressed against me; it had weight.

Something suddenly clamped down on my right biceps. It looked like an eagle's talon, but it was huge—easily bigger than my own hand—and it was mottled, greenish, and flaking. It squeezed, and the pressure was enormous.

My ghost knife was trapped in my right hand. I placed the revolver against the thing's wrist and fired off another shot. The sound of the gunshot near my face was like a whole new kind of punishment, and burning gunpowder struck my lips and ear.

The bullet deflected off the thing's bones, but not before tearing through its thin flesh. The pain must have startled it, because it released me. I pivoted into the corner of the closet. The room was still dim and gray at the edges, and I could see the talon where it had reached out of the darkness. I swung the ghost knife up at it, but my arm wouldn't work right, and I struck it along one talon instead of straight through the leg.

The end of the talon fell away, clunking onto the floor, and the crackling hiss turned into a sort of grinding shriek.

The darkness was flowing around and against me now, and I could barely see. The weight of it held me against the wall and made it difficult to lift my arms. The section of the wall I'd cut burst with a loud *crack,* and I felt the darkness moving toward it like a current of water. I pushed toward it, almost blind now, desperate to get out into clean, breathable air. As it grew heavier, the shadow around me began to feel like worms crawling on my skin. The darkness was not an effect, like a squid's ink cloud. It was part of this thing's body.

I grabbed the edge of the hole, but the plaster broke off in my hand. At that moment, I heard and felt the whole wall buckle outward. The predator, whatever it was, was entering our world, and it was too big to fit in Wally's bedroom.

I reached the hole in the wall just as a talon scraped along my back. I cried out; each talon was like a slashing knife, and I could feel the darkness inside my nose and sinuses, wriggling and alive. I shot at it again, but my grip was all wrong and the recoil knocked the gun out of my hand.

Then I was through the hole, stumbling across the back of a toppled shelving unit and falling to my hands and knees. This predator had gotten inside me, and it *hurt*; I had to get outside. At least I'd be able to breathe out there, and run.

A talon caught my right ankle. I spun immediately to swipe the ghost knife through its wrist, but it was so strong that it was already dragging me back. Fast, so fast—I knew I'd be pulled into that dark line before I could cut myself free.

The back door burst open and Talbot charged in, revolver at the ready. I could barely see him through the gray, but I shouted: "It's got me! Shoot it!"

There was nothing to shoot, not really. There was only a hole in

the wall and a growing shadow spreading through it, but Talbot
aimed his weapon into the darkness and squeezed off five shots, handling the recoil better than I had, and sending each round at a slightly
different angle.

The talon released me after the third shot. "Let's go!" I shouted.
He pulled me through the door, my injured ankle banging painfully
across the back of the metal shelves. I struggled to get my good left
foot under me and hopped along beside him, fleeing the house as fast
as I could.

Annalise was running toward us. "Boss—" I yelled, but I didn't get
to finish because just then the washing machine smashed through the
wall and flew by me like it had been flung by a tornado.

Talbot jumped away, even though it had already gone by. I lost my
balance, stepped onto my injured foot, and fell.

All the windows along the front burst outward, shutters and
boards along with the glass. The whole cabin buckled out like an
aboveground pool overfilled with water. I heard the groans of straining wood along with the bursts and cracks of breaking beams. The
roof split and began to spread apart.

Annalise plucked a green ribbon from her vest and threw it into
the open doorway.

At the same moment, that claw came rushing out of the darkness.
The ribbon fluttered between the predator's fingers and disappeared
into the darkness. With her left hand, Annalise caught the middle of
the creature's three talons, holding it at arm's length.

But although she had the strength to hold the predator off, she
didn't have the mass. Her boots slid in the gravel as the thing pushed
at her. The other talons tried to scrape at her.

Green light flared inside the house. Annalise leaned back, pulling
on the predator's talon just as it tried to retreat. She braced against the
crooked doorjamb with her right hand, holding the creature in place
while the fire burned. The hissing crackle became a grinding shriek
again, but this time it was three times as loud.

The green light shone on her face, and I'll never forget her expression. She was fierce and joyful, her eyes wide and wild, her teeth bared.

Then the darkness spilling out of the doorway retreated back inside. The talon went limp in her hands, and the limb it was attached to
dropped as though someone had let go of the other end. Annalise
tossed the talon behind her without looking back, and it nearly landed
on me. The thing had been burned off above the elbow. The talons
twitched, scraping at the gravel, and for a moment I was sure it was
going to start crawling at me, like a hand from an old horror movie.

But it didn't. Annalise walked into the house. The building groaned and shifted, but it didn't collapse on her. Yet.

I turned and saw Talbot standing at the edge of the gravel lot. He stared at the house—at us—in amazement, his mouth hanging open. If this was his first real experience with spells and predators, he was having pretty much the same reaction I'd had—stunned disbelief.

Of course, I'd been a citizen. Talbot was already a wooden man; he should have been better prepared. Had the society warned him what this was going to be like? I doubt Csilla would have, but somebody should have.

Something moved in the woods behind him. "Talbot!" I said in a harsh whisper. "Come here!"

He stared at me as if I was a talking dog. A shadow behind him moved against a darker shadow.

"Wake up! Get over here!"

He didn't want to come any closer to the house than he already was. Then he realized I was glancing over his shoulder and turned, taking a few tentative steps toward me. The wind hissed through the trees, but suddenly it didn't sound very much like wind at all.

Damn. There was another one out there.

Talbot hurried to me and crouched low. "Call your boss out here," he said, as though he wasn't allowed to talk to her.

"Shh!" I struggled to my feet, using Talbot as a support. I hadn't seen any eyes on the one inside, but that wasn't necessarily unusual. Did it hunt by sound? By smell? Maybe it could feel its prey with its expanding shadow. Then again maybe it saw "with something other than light." Whatever, I wanted to be as still and quiet as possible until Annalise finished whatever she was doing inside.

The security light at the front of the house flickered and went out, making the whole area clear in the moonlight. To the left, I saw another dark patch moving against the faintly lit background. Then another and another.

Christ, how many of these damn things had Wally summoned?

I watched them, hoping they were moving away from us. Maybe there was a deer or something they could hunt. It wasn't happening. The darkness was getting larger, blocking out the moonlit leaves and underbrush. Were they growing or just moving closer to us?

Either way, to hell with keeping still and quiet. "Boss!" I shouted. "There are more out here!"

Talbot backed toward the house, and I hopped to keep up with him so I'd have someone to lean on. I didn't trust my ankle enough to walk on it. Annalise still hadn't come out. "Boss!" I shouted again.

The creatures were close to us now, blocking the woods as they glided out of them. There were three—no, four. That I could see, at least.

I readied my ghost knife.

Talbot pivoted away from me, and I had to step on my injured ankle to avoid a fall. I hissed in pain as he broke into a sprint, running for the driveway.

Damn. I hopped in place, ghost knife in my hand. One of the predators changed direction, moving toward Talbot. I threw the ghost knife just as a claw reached toward him.

The spell sliced through two of the creature's fingers. That horrible grinding shriek sounded out again, and the limb retreated into darkness. Talbot juked toward it to avoid another of the predators, then leaped over a low wall and sprinted down the gravel path toward the edge of the circle.

The bastard. I hoped he'd make it.

I closed my eyes and cleared my mind, then *reached* for my spell. Annalise came up next to me just as the spell returned.

"Ray, how badly are you hurt?"

"I can't put any weight on that foot. Sorry, boss."

"There are five that I can see, and one of them followed Talbot. I only have four more of these." She held up the green ribbon with the sigil drawn at the end. It was the spell she used to call up her green fire, and I'd never heard her call it by name. Was it a secret?

The predators hovered at the edge of the forest. The darkness that shrouded them stopped expanding when they touched. "You can see them better than I can, boss. Do you know what they are?"

"Claw-in-Shadow. There are only a couple of predators that we could call common, but this is one of them. The summoning spell for it turns up in a lot of spell books, and it's a popular guardian predator among a certain sort of sorcerer."

"But . . . six of them? With only four more ribbons? Are you, um, going to carry me outside the circle?"

She turned toward me suddenly, scowling. "Run? Now?"

"So they're not . . ." *Dangerous?* I almost said.

"Oh, they'll kill you. They'll hunt you like a pack, tear you apart, and drag the pieces into the Empty Spaces. And they're not stupid. They know what I did to the one inside. That's why they're hesitating."

The predators were trapped inside the buried circle, and if Wally was right, they were starving. They wouldn't pass up a meal, but they were being careful. I needed to make them a little reckless.

I hopped away from Annalise, nearly falling over. I took a deep breath to relax my shoulders and kept my balance better as I went out in front of the house. I'd played decoy for Annalise before—that's what a wooden man was for—but I'd never done it in full wounded-bird mode.

The predators at the edge of the gravel seemed to be moving back and forth. I was no expert on living spots of darkness, but they looked agitated. Their hunting instincts must have been screaming at them.

I hopped toward them again and almost lost my balance. The predators moved toward me, then stopped. I needed to draw them in, so Annalise could take out more than one with each ribbon. As long as they were careful and keeping their distance, we were never going to kill them all.

It occurred to me that I might have been thinking of this all wrong. What if Wally's spell had simply created an opening between our world and the Empty Spaces? What if it wasn't six predators we were facing but one?

One of the talons emerged from the darkness ahead of me. I could see them better now as my eyes adjusted—there were five curving shapes, blotting out the moonlit landscape behind them. And they were getting closer. I tried to spot the one I'd mangled with my ghost knife, but I couldn't.

Five? The edge of the circle wasn't *that* far. Talbot should have reached freedom by now—or been killed—and the predator should have had enough time to get back up the hill.

Goose bumps ran down my back. I turned to Annalise just in time to see a dark shape come over the top of the ruined cabin and fall on her. I didn't even have time to shout a warning.

The hissing sound grew louder. I turned again and saw the other predators rushing at me. Instinctively, I reared back and, having only one good leg, fell sprawling onto the stones.

A predator clamped down on my wrecked ankle, and the pain made me scream with a high, shameful voice.

I sat up, reaching for that claw with my injured arm and wishing I'd switched my ghost knife to my left, and another predator clamped down on my other ankle.

Just as they were about to tear me apart like a wishbone, I swept my spell through the talon on my injured leg, severing it at the wrist. If the predator shrieked with that metal-grinding sound again, I couldn't hear it, because I was too full of my own screaming—the pain wouldn't quit, and my fear was tearing through me.

Before I could swipe at the claw on my left leg, another grabbed at my left arm. I swung the ghost knife at it, feeling something long and sharp slash through my right biceps as another talon barely missed me. I cut my arm free, but the pressure against my left leg was hurting like crazy and I couldn't see a damn thing.

Something slammed down on the left side of my chest, pinning me to the ground. Another talon caught my right wrist. I could still throw my ghost knife with a flick of my fingers, but I had to concentrate to aim it, and damn, they were already pulling me apart. The talon on my chest slid up onto my face and neck, and it was too much all at once; I couldn't concentrate. They were going to kill me, and my brain was screaming at me *This is it this is it oh thank God . . .*

Then green firelight flooded around me. The iron-gate spell beneath my right collarbone flared with pain as it protected me from Annalise's spell. The predators released me immediately, and I slapped my spell against my chest. It was only made of laminated paper, and Annalise's green fire could burn a human being down to the bones in seconds.

Then the fire was gone. There was no hissing and no grinding shriek. I blinked at the darkness around me, but my vision was full of spots. Were they all gone?

"How badly are you hurt?" Annalise asked. Her high, funny voice startled me, although it shouldn't have.

"Boss, I . . ." I started to shake. I'd come close to death yet again. Damn, did people really get off on this?

I pushed myself to my knees. "I think I'll live, boss, but I'm going to need some help."

She grabbed my left arm and raised me up. Her grip hurt, but I hid the pain as best I could. My left ankle was going to be bruised, swollen, and stiff by morning.

Annalise led me to a tree at the edge of the tiny gravel lot. "Did you get them all?" I asked. My vision hadn't quite cleared, and I wasn't sure if I should still be on alert.

"Yep," she said as she walked toward the house. "We'll get you fixed up soon. Good job."

Well. A compliment. I nearly fell over from the shock.

My ghost knife was still in my hand, and it appeared to be undamaged, as best as I could tell in the moonlight. I tried to consider what that meant, about her spell and mine. Was the ghost knife protected by my iron gate? Did her green fire affect everything but spells? Or was something else going on?

I kept turning it over in my head, anything to avoid thinking about that moment of relief I'd had when I thought I was going to die.

Annalise set a fire in the cabin, then I leaned on her while we returned down the long gravel drive. I hopped, she stayed close to me, and we went very slowly. It was exhausting, and it would have been so easy to fall flat on my face, but to hell with that.

Of course, Annalise could have carried me as easily as I'd carry a loaf of bread, but to hell with that, too.

On the way down, I showed her the pictures I'd taken of the drawings in Wally's closet. The phone's screen lit her face, but I couldn't read her expression. I wanted to ask if this was news to her or if it was goofball conspiracy stuff, but I was afraid she'd give me an answer I didn't want to hear.

Instead I asked what we should do about this place. She said she'd file a report and let another peer check it out. We'd leave the circle intact to deter locals from coming up to investigate, just in case there was something we missed in the darkness. She put my cellphone into her pocket.

Then we crossed the circle. Talbot hurried out from under the cover of a stand of trees and came toward us.

"I tried to lead them away," he said. Annalise laughed at him, but I didn't have the heart. If I'd had two good legs, I might have run with him. Well, probably not, but that didn't mean it was a bad idea.

He looked at me closely. "I saved your life."

Before I could respond, a pair of headlights swept around the corner. Police lights flashed on the roof. I had my ghost knife ready, but Talbot's hand moved toward the back of his waistband, a gesture I recognized immediately. As the driver's door opened, Talbot drew a gun.

I slammed my left arm across his hand and nudged him off balance. His gun went off, the bullet striking the stony dirt in front of the car, and he stumbled. I would have fallen over completely, but Annalise had a tight grip on my shirttail. With my right hand, I flicked the ghost knife.

A normal piece of paper would have fallen at my feet, but my spell went where I wanted it to go. It fluttered upward and passed right through the space between the car and the open driver's door just as the silhouette there drew a weapon.

He didn't get off a shot. I couldn't see him clearly, but I'd managed to hit him anyway. The gun fell from his hands, and he reached into the car and switched off the headlights. Annalise let go of my shirt, and I hopped toward the car, bracing myself on the hood.

"Put that away," Annalise said. I knew she wasn't talking to me.

I hopped around the front of the car. "I'm sorry," the silhouette said.

"Turn around and close your eyes," I told him. He did. "Did you get a good look at us?" I picked up his gun, a Glock, and tossed it into the car. My ghost knife was nearby. I *reached* for it and it zipped into my open hand. I put it away.

"I did," he said.

"That's all right. Just don't do it again. Call in to the fire department. They'll be responding to this fire soon, and you should warn them that ammunition inside the building is cooking off. Tell them to keep well away for now. And tell them there's no one here."

"Okay." He did that while I turned to Annalise and Talbot.

I patted the roof of the car. "This is going to be our ride back to the beach."

Annalise shrugged. It was all fine by her. Talbot stared down at the cop. "What did you do to him?"

We piled into the car. I couldn't drive with my injured ankle, so Talbot drove instead, and I sat in the back with Constable Shayholter.

That was how he introduced himself. He was a little under six feet and built like a high diver. He had a thick head of black hair and the kind of face you see on the covers of romance novels. And he sat beside me, obediently keeping his eyes shut tight.

The drive back to the park was so quick we almost missed the turnoff. Talbot drove us into the parking lot and parked at a wooden rail. The weird stone beach and night water lay open before us.

Annalise and Talbot got out. I turned to the constable. "Don't open your eyes yet. But listen carefully. I'm not going to cuff you or take your gun. In fact, I'm not going to do anything that would give you an excuse for letting us go. I want you to wait for a slow count of six hundred, then drive back to the fire and do your cop thing. Don't tell anyone you saw us. You'll remember all this tomorrow, but you won't be able to explain to anyone why you let three suspects leave the scene of an arson. You certainly won't be able to explain it to yourself. Think how it would look if you tried."

"I understand."

"Start counting," I said. He did. I hobbled out of the car. Annalise led me down to the bay, and it was a relief to float out into the cold, cold water.

Captain was waiting for us. Annalise muscled us into the boat and we sped away. I lay back by Captain, stretched out on the padded bench, and let the cool night air blow my clothes dry.

After about an hour, Captain turned to me and asked if I would hold the wheel steady. "Don't turn at all," she said as if talking to a child. "Like this." I struggled into the pilot's seat, my ankle stiff and screaming, and did as she asked.

She went to the front of the boat to fuss over something. While her back was turned, I opened that cabinet beneath the wheel and took out the envelope in there. I took out the note Annalise had given her. It was printed on generic printer paper. I held it up to the lighted dials. It read: DO WHATEVER THE BEARER OF THIS ENVELOPE TELLS YOU TO DO IF YOU EVER WANT TO SEE YOUR SON ALIVE AGAIN.

Oh, shit.

CHAPTER TWELVE

The SUN was rising when we docked in Everett. By that time, my ankle was swollen and unbearably tender. It had to be broken. Walking was impossible; Talbot and Captain had to practically carry me to the truck. They laid me in the bed, and Talbot sat beside me. He looked as though he wanted to talk but wisely kept his mouth shut.

We stopped off at a supermarket on our way to wherever we were going. While we waited in the parking lot, I closed my eyes and fell asleep almost immediately. I woke again instantly when we pulled out of our parking space.

Not long afterward, we were back in the plane and in the air, heading south. I wanted a chance to talk to Captain—to apologize—but I never got it. Then it was too late, and I knew I'd never get another chance. I didn't even know her real name.

I sat on the plane, miserable and tired. I wanted to lie down, but there was no space.

Annalise sat next to me. She held a plastic bag full of sliced meat. "Remember how bad it was to heal those burns?" she asked. "Broken bones are worse."

She was right.

When we landed in Burbank again I was shaky and sick to my stomach, but I could walk again and my bruises were gone. I rode back to the hotel with Annalise and Talbot, but I couldn't look at them. I was wrung out and tired, and pissed off at the world.

Annalise had Talbot drive us to my Escort. "Stay here," she told him. Talbot gave us an unhappy look as we climbed out and went to my car. There was no pain in my ankle at all. It was completely healed.

Annalise stood beside the driver's door. The heat roasted us. "Well, he was useless."

"He wasn't wrong to run, boss," I said. I sighed. This wasn't a conversation I wanted to have. "Csilla didn't give him a useful weapon. He'd have fed a predator, and there would have been two victims to draw them in. You might not have gotten them all with your green fire." She shrugged. I was boring her. "What's next?"

"Same thing we've been doing: find your buddy Wally King. I want you to get out there. Here." She gave the cellphone back to me. A quick check showed that the pictures I'd taken had been erased. "My number is in there. Call me when we have some killing to do."

"What about the predators he's been summoning?"

"Wally King is our top priority. If I find out anything about those pictures, I'll let you know. The predators . . ." It was her turn to sigh. "You knew these people, yeah? If you confirm they have predators in them but you can't bring yourself to cure them, give their names and addresses to me." I knew what she meant by *cure*. "I can make it quick, Ray." There was no kindness in her voice, and I was glad of it. The woman who'd given Captain that note shouldn't play at kindness.

She turned and walked back to her van. Did I want to see Annalise burn Fidel down to a pile of bones? Did I want to sit alone in a motel room, TV blaring, while I knew she was out there killing him, or any of them?

Hell, no.

I drove back to my motel.

Annalise had promised to tell me what she learned about Wally's pictures. She had never offered to pass me information without prompting before. Now, just as she was trusting me, I wanted to be far away from her.

My duffel was still in my room; I was glad I'd paid for the week. Then I showered and lay on the bed. I dreamed of a huge mob of women, all of them clones of Captain, weeping on their knees beside tiny caskets.

When I woke up, it was just six o'clock. The air-conditioning had turned the place into a fridge. My throat was raw from the dry air. I went into the bathroom and ran cold water over my hands.

I'd nearly died the night before.

It seemed like such a small thing. *I nearly forgot my keys. I nearly bought new shoes. I nearly died.* I looked at my face in the mirror, re-membering the way the talon had clamped down on me, and trying to picture how it would look in the light.

I also remembered the Iraqi kid with the Jackie Chan DVDs—maybe he would have made it if he'd had an Annalise of his own at his back—an Annalise who threatened a woman's son.

I left the room and got into my car. The filling station was packed; cars were lined up three deep at each of the pumps. After I topped the tank, I drove aimlessly for a while.

Annalise had offered to kill my old crew for me. I knew she thought she was doing me a favor, but I couldn't turn the responsibility over to her. I had come here because my old crew was in trouble. I wanted to save them.

That was the hard part. I wanted to be a guy who saved people. I wanted to protect them from sorcerers and predators, but that wasn't how this game was played. Arne and the others were being eaten alive by predators, and I had no idea how to save them. In fact, I was nearly certain it couldn't be done.

I knew what I had to do. I had to kill them. Because it didn't matter what they'd done, and it didn't matter if they had people who loved them and kids to look after. Only the predators mattered. Not the people.

I said it aloud in my car: "Only the predators matter. Nothing else." It was easy to say when I was here alone. It was a lot harder when I was holding a gun to someone's head, or swinging a length of pipe in a crowded room. I had killed people to get at predators, and if I had to be honest with myself, I knew I'd do it again.

But I couldn't kill a woman's kid because she refused to give me a boat ride.

The Twenty Palace Society had changed me, but maybe I needed to do more to change the society.

I parked a block away from the Roasted Seal. I didn't have a conscious reason to go there, but it was as good a place as any to take the next step. I walked through the back alley to confirm that it was empty before I went to the front.

The bar was busier than it had been, which meant it had ten or twelve people in booths or sitting at the bar. The bartender was new, but he looked enough like the other guy to be his brother. A pair of middle-aged women gave me the once-over as I scanned the room, but Arne wasn't there, and neither was Lenard, or anyone I knew. One thick-necked guy with a crew cut looked vaguely familiar, but I couldn't place him. He was talking on his cell and looking down at his beer, not at me at all.

Most of the crowd were watching Mexican soccer on two flat-screen TVs mounted high on the wall. The surging white noise of the crowd was the loudest sound in the room.

Three tall, slender men occupied Arne's booth. They wore wait-staff black and had stylish haircuts. They were victims; they wouldn't know where to find Arne.

The back door had already been replaced, and the wall was patched with fresh spackle. Soon it would be painted over, I was sure, and all traces of that incident would disappear.

Behind me was the alcove Lenard had been standing in. It was a wait station, but there were no waiters here. The plastic tub was dusty, and the notepad on the counter had yellowed at the edges. Only the bar stool looked as if it had been used lately.

Lenard's small locker was there, painted the same dark color as the wall. The lock had a little slot for a key, but I had something almost as good.

The urge to look around the room to check who was watching me was powerful, but I knew it would just draw attention. I took the ghost knife from my back pocket and sliced through the lock. The door squeaked as it swung open.

Right at the front was a Nintendo DS; Lenard liked his video-games, especially when he needed to kill some time. Beside that was a roll of cash no thicker than the cord of a vacuum cleaner. But in the back, hidden in the shadows, was a foot-high gold statue of a hairless man standing on a black base. The base was made to look like a spool of film, and a nameplate had Ellen Egan-Jade's name on it.

Oh, shit. Was this what Lenard did when he thought he could get away with anything? This?

I snapped up the roll of cash. If he'd been standing beside me, I could have beaten the hell out of him. I could have kicked him in the nuts. I even, for a few moments, considered calling the cops. But no. I couldn't do any of that. I took his money—let that be an expensive lesson. Then I'd tell Arne one of his people was keeping evidence of a rape and murder at the Bigfoot Room. I'm sure that would go over beautifully.

"Hey, what are you doing?"

It was the bartender. I shut the locker as I turned around. "I'm looking for a guy," I said, unsure if I should use Lenard's name or how best to describe him.

"Try a bar in West Hollywood," he said, to general laughter. "This place is for people who want drinks."

Now every face in the room was turned toward me. Only Crew

Cut wasn't smiling. Suddenly, I recognized him. He had been the one who tossed Wardell's jacket at him in front of Steve Francois's fancy white house. He shut his cellphone off and put it into his pocket.

At that moment the front door opened, and I saw several large figures backlit by the desert sun as they entered. Crew Cut slid off his stool.

I sprinted to the back door, slamming it open. This time an alarm sounded.

The alley smelled of garbage and concrete. I vaulted onto the dumpster, then jumped for the edge of the bar roof. Crew Cut and the rest of Potato's crew weren't idiots, even if they looked like they were. I was sure they'd have someone at the mouth of the alley.

I scrambled onto the roof, feeling like a coward. Which I was. Ghost knife or not, I didn't want to tangle with anyone in Potato's crew. The door banged open a second time, and I heard heavy treads scraping against the ground.

"Dammit," a man said. Despite the alarm, I recognized the voice as Potato's. "Gone."

"He didn't come this way," a second voice shouted. It sounded farther away.

Another voice came from a good distance away. "Not this way, either." I'd been right about the entrance to the alleys.

Someone opened the dumpster lid and let it fall shut again.

"How do they *do* that?" Potato didn't sound annoyed at all. In fact, he sounded almost admiring. "Okay. This fucking alarm is going to bring cops. Let's get gone."

I risked a peek over the lip of the roof and saw them moving away. Good. Just as they turned the corner, I threw my leg over the sheet-metal roofing and hung by my fingers. It was a three-foot drop to the concrete, and when I hit the asphalt, I was face-to-face with the bartender. He scowled at me from the open doorway, the Oscar statuette in his hand like a bell.

"What the hell do you call this?" With the door open, he had to shout to be heard over the alarm.

"Evidence," I shouted back. "And you're putting your fingerprints all over it."

His hand sprang open and the award clattered to the ground. I turned and ran toward the end of the alley that Potato and his men had not taken. Once I hit the sidewalk, I slowed to a casual stroll.

I should have asked Wardell to drop me off a mile from my car and walked back to it. I should have realized that Francois would send Potato and his men after me once he found out about the video Arne posted, and that Wardell could tell them where he'd dropped me off.

But had they already grabbed Arne off the street? Judging by what I'd just heard, I'd bet against it.

Still, if Arne wasn't at the Bigfoot Room, I didn't know where to find him, and I didn't have as many friends as I used to.

I unrolled Lenard's money and spread it flat under the floor mat. A cop would find it two minutes into a determined search of the car, but this was the best I could do. I drove back into Studio City and parked outside Ty's gym.

Six people pushed through the doors in a rush just as I reached them, but the last, a muscular woman who couldn't seem to stand up straight, held them open for me. The front desk was swarmed with people turning in locker keys and receiving plastic cards in return. I waited for things to thin out, watching people get processed at the desk and exit. Leaving work, rushing home to make dinner, pick up their kids, or go on dates, they were nothing like me. And God, there were so many of them.

When things had slowed enough that the supervisor could pay attention to me, I stepped forward. She was the same one I'd spoken to a couple of days before, but she didn't recognize me. I had to explain myself again. Ty wasn't here, she told me, and no, I couldn't have his address or phone number.

A customer at the counter turned to me and said: "You mean Ty-alee Murphy? He's just around the corner. I'll show you."

I followed him outside. We stood at the edge of the parking lot together. He gestured toward an intersection like a man karate chopping an imaginary opponent. "That street there beside the pet-supply store is Cartwell. I think. Whatever the name, you go that way one block and take the very first left. Ty lives on that block, on the left side, in a building with two beautiful jacarandas out front."

I had no idea what a jacaranda was, but I could figure it out. "That's great. Thanks."

"No problem. You're a friend of his?"

"Actually, I'm a hit man hunting him down."

We laughed and went our separate ways.

It was early evening, so parking on Ty's residential street was impossible, but I did luck into a space around the corner. There were three buildings with two trees out front, and I found Ty's name in the second one. I rang the buzzer and spent a few seconds studying the tiny fernlike leaves of the whatever tree out front. The security gate squawked at me like a mechanical crow, without anyone trying to speak to me first.

I went inside and up the stairs, then knocked on the apartment door. It was yanked open by a short, slim Korean man. He had small features on a broad, smooth face, and he was so fit his collarbones showed at the opening of his polo shirt. Like the client who'd given me directions, he had hair that had been cut very recently, and it had a lot of mousse in it.

Something about me startled him, and he laid his fingertips next to his throat. "You're not the guy."

"No," I answered. "I'm a different guy."

"I mean the pizza guy." He looked me over, as though I might be hiding a pizza box somewhere.

"I'm looking for Ty," I said. "Is he here?"

He moved his weight onto his back foot and put his hand on his hip. His expression suggested he thought I had a lot of nerve saying that to him.

"It's not like that," I said. "I'm an old friend and I think he's in trouble."

He started to say something but stopped himself to think about it. Then he let out a long, relieved sigh. "Come in come in," he said, as though I was a doctor making a house call. "What's your name?"

"Ray."

"I'm Dale. I'm glad you came here and said what you said. I've been thinking something has been wrong for days, but . . . Ray Lilly? Tyalee told me about you."

All my old crew were talking about me. It made me feel odd; I never talked about them. "What did he tell you?"

Dale looked around the room as though he was going to offer me a chair, but my question had made him rethink it. "He said you were the most honest thief he had ever seen, and that he could never trust you. What does that mean, anyway? Are you really some kind of thief?"

Ty and I had been thieves together, but I wasn't going to be the one to break the news. "Let's stay focused on Ty. Why do think something has been wrong?"

"He won't touch me," Dale said, looking distinctly uncomfortable. "He wears those gloves, and when I touch his skin . . ."

"It burns."

"Yeah. And he gets angry, like he's afraid for me. What happened to him?"

I wasn't going to go there. "Is he here?"

"I don't know where he is."

That wasn't a good sign. Ty could have been lying somewhere in the apartment the way Caramella had.

The buzzer sounded. I stepped aside to let Dale access the intercom, but all he did was press the security button. He was a victim waiting to happen, and I wondered what Ty saw in him.

"Oh my God," he said. "I haven't even asked you to sit down. Come in, please, and be comfortable. Can I get you something? Beer?"

"I'd rather have water."

"Of course, it's so hot." He hurried into the kitchen and filled a glass. I looked around the room. Their apartment had been furnished right off the showroom floor of IKEA, which made the place feel like a robot habitat. On the end table beside me there were two little spaceships facing each other. One was from *Star Trek,* but I couldn't recognize the other. I had the sudden urge to smash them both.

As Dale handed me the glass of water, there was a knock at the door. He opened it without looking through the peephole first, signed the pizza guy's slip, and shut the door. I took the pizza box from him.

"There's something we need to do first."

Together, we searched the apartment. He looked in cabinets and cupboards, and above them, too, searching for a clue to Ty's odd behavior. I went through the motions with him, but what I really wanted to do was check every corner and behind every bit of furniture for a shape that could be touched but not seen. We didn't find that, but in the bedroom, Dale showed me something else.

"I wasn't sure if I should, but . . ." He dragged a stainless-steel suitcase out from under the bed. I knew what was in it even before he opened it.

Cash. It was bundles of twenties and hundreds, all thrown in randomly, and all bound up in paper wrappers.

I shut my eyes and took a deep breath. The urge to slug Dale, hard, and run out the door with this money was incredible. So many of my problems could be solved with this suitcase. And he was a guy who didn't even look through the peephole before opening his door. It would be a useful lesson for him. . . .

"Look at this! It's just like a *movie!*" Dale made that sound like an insult. "I don't even know where it came from!"

I held up one of the bundles. The name of the bank was printed on it. "Yes, you do."

He plopped down onto the corner of the bed. "Okay. I do. But Ty, he . . . Okay. Once, about a year and a half ago, I had a flat on my car, and I couldn't afford a new tire. I was really, really broke, and he and I had just gotten together, okay? And I was upset because I'm in frickin' L.A. without a car, okay?

"The next day, Ty had put four new sidewalls on it. He thought I would be happy, but he had even less money than I did. He hadn't even started to cover his facility fee at the gym. I'm not stupid, okay? I knew he hadn't bought them. But I made him promise not to steal again."

"But you kept the tires," a voice behind us said. I spun around, my pulse already racing. Ty stood in the doorway, his hands empty. He looked at Dale, then at me, then back at Dale again, as though he wanted to make us unmeet each other.

"Why is this here?" Dale demanded. "In my home!"

Ty glanced at the suitcase without much interest. "I need it," he said. "I need to offer it to someone to get him to do something for me."

"Who?" I asked. "Wally King?"

"Yeah," he said to me. "You've been putting it together."

"I still have a couple of blank spots in the story. Help me with the rest of it." He laughed at me. It was a cynical sound; he wasn't so glad to see me anymore. "All right, then," I said. "Help me get the guy who did this to you. No one else can."

"You're the one who did this to me."

"That's bullshit, Ty."

"Well, *what do you expect from me?!*"

His shout echoed in the tiny room. Dale bolted to his feet and retreated toward the corner. I held myself absolutely still, and I knew right then I would have to kill him.

"What do you expect from me, Ray? This guy shows up out of the blue at the Bigfoot Room saying he knows you. He says he can do things for us, and Luther is right there to say it's true, it's all true. He promises us power, and he delivers, too. All he asks is one favor in return, and he hasn't even collected from me yet."

"I don't think he'll bother, Ty." *You're just a distraction. You're his wooden man.* "Tell me what happened."

He sighed. "What's the use?"

I thought about Wally's cabin and my iron gate. Maybe I didn't need him to explain it all to me. "I'll tell you, then. You went somewhere secluded. Wally had a circle or square or something painted on the floor—maybe it was drawn in chalk—and it had symbols around it. Then he put a symbol on you, too, and you got into the circle. What was next? Chanting? Music? Did he draw another symbol?"

Ty wasn't in the mood to answer questions. "How did you know he drew a symbol on me?"

"Because he put a *thing* on you. Something alive, and the only reason it hasn't killed you yet is that you're protected."

Ty lifted his shirt, exposing ab muscles that gave me a twinge of envy. And a sigil.

It wasn't large, barely as wide across as seven quarters arranged in a circle, all touching. Three squiggles had been drawn inside a slender ring, but this time I couldn't figure out what those squiggles might represent.

Then I realized that the ink was fading. The outer ring especially was wearing away.

Dale had leaned in close to me so he could look, too. "It's henna," he said. "But fading."

Ty dropped his shirt to cover the sigil. It occurred to me that I had Annalise's cell in my pocket. I took it out and lifted Ty's shirt again. He went stiff and awkward when I touched him. I snapped the picture quickly and backed away. Ty frowned at me and straightened his shirt. "Yeah. The ink was diluted, I think, and when it wears out, I'm history, right?"

I looked him in the eye. "Caramella is already dead."

"Damn." He turned his back and stepped over to the bureau. There was another unrecognizable spaceship on it. Ty flicked it with his fingers. It slid across the painted wood and fell to the carpet with a fragile plastic sound.

"Ty," I said, pointing my thumb at Dale. I chose my words carefully. "Do you care about this victim?"

Dale looked at me, shocked. "Victim?"

Ty laughed sadly. "Oh, Ray, you have no idea. You don't know how many times I've had to pick up a credit card he's left forgotten on a restaurant table. Or car keys. You don't even know. But yeah. I love him."

"Then you have to get away from him."

"No!" Dale shouted. "Ty, I don't know what's going on, okay, but—"

"Shut up," Ty said. His tone wasn't unkind, just sad. "I mean it."

"When Caramella went," I pushed on, "she nearly took Vi's daughter with her."

"Vi's daughter?" he said, as though it was hilarious that I'd called her that.

"Yes. And not just her, either. When this thing takes you, it's going to take whoever is nearby, too. Ty, I can—"

"You can what, Ray? What? Tell me what you can do?"

"I can get you away from people—"

"Fuck that. I want to live." Ty bared his teeth at me as he said it, letting anger give him strength. "I'm not going to give up now! I'm going to find this Wally King, and I'll offer him the money. If that doesn't work, I'll offer him his own damn life. He'll show me a way—"

"Ty—"

"No, Ray, shut up! He'll show me how to take it off and put it on when I want, and—"

"Ty, it's not a goddamn jacket! It's down in your lungs, isn't it? It's breathing for you, and it's up your nose and in your head. And it's strong, I know. It's not going to let you put it on and take it off like a hat."

"What can you offer that's better, Ray? I wouldn't even be in this mess if it wasn't for you, and you want to take me somewhere quiet to die?"

My ghost knife was in my pocket, but if I used it, the drape on him would kill him, and who knows how many more would come through. Ty wouldn't be happy to see me reaching into my pocket just then, either.

"You were wrong about one thing, Ray. Wally King *did* ask me to do a little something for him, but I wasn't going to do it. I think I changed my mind."

He turned into a silhouette, giving me a glimpse of the Empty Spaces, then he vanished.

I spun and tore the covers off the bed, throwing them at him. I didn't have to bother; he wasn't hiding from me, he was charging. The striped sheet flopped over Ty's head just before he slammed me off my feet into the wall.

I was pinned, the wooden bedpost digging into my low ribs and kidney. Damn, he was strong. I felt his right hand release my shirt, saw the blanket flutter as it slid off him. I raised my left hand to protect my head.

His first punch glanced off my triceps and the top of my head. It probably hurt him as much as it hurt me. His second struck the part of my forearm protected by spells. That one didn't hurt me at all.

His weight shifted and I twisted to the left. His third punch landed right on my solar plexus. He might have killed me with it if not for the spells there.

My feet were off the floor, and I didn't have room to lift them onto the bed. Instead, I kicked low, hoping to hit Ty's knee. I missed. I had no idea where he was. All I could see was Dale standing in the corner with a horrified expression.

I tucked my chin and protected my face as well as I could. Even though I couldn't see him, I could feel him. He was still holding me with his left hand. I reached out with my right, trying to find his eyes, but he wrenched himself away and slammed me down on his bed.

I could hear his breathing, ragged and furious, but I looked straight through him at Dale. While he rained down punches on me, I curled my legs and kicked at him again. I needed to get him off balance. I needed leverage.

Ty switched his grip on my shirt so his knuckles would grind into my throat. I finally managed to get a good kick against his knee and made him stagger. He didn't let me up, but the pressure eased, and I had a moment's break from the beating I was taking on my ribs and my left arm.

His grip on my throat loosened. I caught his thumb in my right hand and started to peel it back. He wouldn't let me break it, though. He ripped his hand away and backed off.

For a moment I was afraid he'd gotten smart. If he'd let go of me and hit me with a bit more distance, I'd never have been able to protect myself. I pushed my way off the bed toward him, determined to keep him close.

I hadn't yet gotten all the way upright when a fat ceramic lamp floated off the bedside table and rushed at me. I swung at it with my protected forearm and shattered it. Broken bits of clay clattered against my face and chest, and the heavy base struck my lip painfully.

I felt something kick against my feet, and I was on my back again. Ty fumbled at my shirt, trying to get control of me and pin me again—he could turn invisible, but he couldn't break his fighting habits. He had to stick with what he was comfortable with.

Shards of broken ceramic jabbed painfully into my back, and the twisted metal workings of the lamp lay across my chest. I grabbed it. The shade had come off, but the bulb had not broken. I felt Ty heave his weight on me, about to throw more punches, and I jabbed upward.

It wasn't hard to guess where he was. The thin glass of the bulb shattered with a muffled *shink* sound, and I pushed.

I heard Ty back away, cursing. The bulb was broken almost down to the socket, with a couple of nasty glass shards sticking out. I'd expected to see blood on them, but there was nothing, just a faint, slimy sheen. I tossed it aside and sat up off the bed. Ty didn't come at me again.

He cursed again, and I oriented myself on the sound. The left side of my body below my arm was bruised, and I had several spots on my face and head that felt painful and inflamed. If he'd been planning to beat me to death, it would have taken him a long time, but he was capable of it.

Ty cursed again, and this time his voice had gone high with fear. Had I hit a vital spot like a throat or an eye? I couldn't say I was sorry if I had, but I didn't want to deal with the consequences of killing him here. I wasn't ready to face four drapes, or to defend Dale from them.

Ty let out a wordless cry, then said: "It's like a tongue!"

"What's happening?" Dale cried.

"Ty!" I said. "Show yourself."

He did. There was a tiny drop of blood on his shoulder. It didn't look serious to me, but Ty shuddered and twitched back and forth. "Ah! Omigodomigodomigod . . ."

I moved toward him at the same time Dale did. There was still a delicate sliver of glass protruding from his skin. While I watched, it slowly backed out of the cut as though pulled by an invisible hand, then fell. I picked it up off the carpet. There wasn't a drop of blood on it.

Dale grabbed Ty's bare arm, then let go with a hiss. Ty grimaced and turned his face to the ceiling. The cut on his shoulder didn't look serious. It barely seemed to be bleeding.

"Shit!" Ty gasped. "It's digging in and squeezing—Ah, God!" He grimaced and staggered as though the right side of his body was paralyzed. "It's milking the blood out of me!"

I grabbed his gloved hand. It was bone dry, while my clothes were soaked with sweat. "This way," I said. "Quickly."

Dale struck my hand away. He was stronger and faster than he seemed. "You're the one who hurt him! Get out! Get the fuck out!"

"I'm the only one who knows what's going on!" I shouted, surprising myself with my sudden anger. My face was in pain and felt swollen. Not to mention, I was trying to help a guy who had been beating the crap out of me a minute earlier.

"This is my place!" Dale shouted, and he was angry enough to let a Georgia accent show. "Mine!"

"Stop fighting," Ty said, "and do something about this leech."

Dale and I looked at each other. I waited for him to lay out a plan, but it was pretty obvious he had nothing. After a couple of seconds, I turned to Ty.

"All right, asshole," I said. "That thing on you is starving."

"Jesus, *shit*!" Ty said, as the blood welled up around his little scratch and vanished. "It's *drinking* my blood?"

"It won't be satisfied with your blood. It wants your skin and your guts and all the thoughts in your head, too. It wants everything, and like I said, it's starving. Now, it can't feed on you while Wally's spell is in place, but—"

"But it's taking the parts that come out of me. I'm not stupid."

I led the two of them into the other room, fighting very hard against the urge to tell him just how incredibly stupid he was. It was hard to raise my left arm, and my upper left incisor felt loose in my mouth. Ty parked himself on a chair at the little dining room table.

Dale said he was going to the bathroom for bandages and disinfectant. I went into the kitchen, set a small cast-iron skillet on the stove, and turned the gas under it as high as it would go.

"Ray." Ty's voice came from the other room. I didn't think he could see what I was doing, because I don't think he could have been so calm. "I'm sorry."

I told him what he could do with himself.

"Then why are you helping me?"

There were gel packs in the freezer. I took two, pinning one against my ribs with my elbow and laying the other on the side of my face. "Because you may be a selfish, self-justifying asshole who thinks he can buy his way out of this mess, but that thing on you is worse."

"It's really alive, isn't it? It's a monster."

I sighed and closed my eyes. Predators killed people, and so did I. "It's an animal," I said. "And it's probably a person, too. I think it's smart—maybe as smart as a human, but in a different way." The dry skillet had begun to smoke faintly.

"I don't even know what you're talking about. Listen, if it's hungry, and it can't eat me, can't I get it to go to someone else? You know? Agh!" He paused while the drape worked on him. "Why can't I just, I don't know, transfer it?"

The packs were too cold. I tossed them into the sink on top of a pair of tiny bowls. "We don't do that," I said as I went into the other room.

Dale returned with a roll of bandages and a squeeze tube of disinfectant. He crouched in front of Ty and tried to squeeze gel onto the cuts. Ty looked me in the eyes, and for the first time I saw desperation there. "Ray, there's got to be a way."

I looked directly at Dale. "Ty, who do you have in mind?"

"No," Ty said. "There has to be someone else. Some bum off the street maybe. Somebody worthless." He winced and clutched at his shoulder. "Hey! There's a guy at the gym who smacks his wife around sometimes. He's the one."

"Even if I knew a way, I wouldn't do it," I said.

"Why not?" Ty demanded, as Dale flung the squeeze tube onto the table with an annoyed hiss. The drape was not letting him put the disinfectant on. "Why does it have to be me? If this thing is going to kill somebody, why can't it be him? Why me?"

I thought about the rape souvenir Lenard kept in the locker at the Bigfoot Room, and Maria's endless talk about finding a job, and Ty himself holding me down while he was hitting me. Why do any of us do anything? It's not like we put a lot of rational thought into things.

"You two have slept together in the last few days, right? I mean, in the same bed."

Ty saw what I was saying immediately. "Shit."

Dale laid a bandage over Ty's shoulder and placed some tape on it. Then he looked back at me. "What?"

"This thing's been on him for days, waiting for the chance to feed. If it was going to jump to another unprotected victim, it would have done that already while you were sleeping. Wally didn't put a mark on you, did he?"

"I don't know any Wally."

I turned my attention back to Ty. "It has a meal and it's not letting go. Ever."

"Goddammit!" Dale said. The bandage had slid to the side and bunched up, and the tape had peeled away. He started to lay another one in place, and Ty helped him hold it still.

I went into the kitchen. The skillet was smoking hot now, and slightly grayish at the center. I wrapped an oven pad around the handle and picked it up.

"What's that smell?" Dale asked as I came back into the room. I shoved him aside and jammed the hot metal against Ty's wound.

He screamed. Oh, how he screamed. His voice almost covered the sound of the meat hissing against metal, but nothing could mask the smell of burning flesh and polyester shirt.

After a couple of seconds, I took it off him. Then I grabbed Dale by the elbow and pulled him back. If the drape killed Ty, I wanted Dale and me to be far enough back that we didn't fall into the Empty Spaces.

It didn't kill him, though. Instead, Ty slid off the chair onto his knees, cursing and promising to kill me.

Dale tore out of my grip and rushed to him. "Oh my God, you—"

"At least he won't bleed to death from a scratch," I said. Of course, he would die soon enough anyway, but now I figured it was safe to take him outdoors. I went into the bedroom and slid open the closet doors. Half a dozen belts hung from a hook. I chose an army-surplus web belt.

And there on the floor was the open suitcase. I picked up a packet of hundred-dollar bills. The wrapper helpfully told me, in ink the color of spicy brown mustard, that the bundle was worth ten thousand dollars.

A suitcase full of money was a new thing for me. I'd always stolen cars, not cash. At least, not in piles. I didn't have a job and I'd just taken a beating from a friend—I wanted this money so much that it made me angry. I tore the wrapper off and stuffed the folded bills into my back pocket. I could have made things hard for Ty and Dale by tossing the wrapper behind the bureau where the cops might find it, but I dropped it into the suitcase instead. I wasn't put on this earth to help cops.

Back in the other room, Ty was smearing aloe on his shoulder. Dale stood between us, a butcher knife in his hand. I'm sure it was the biggest one he could find.

"You're leaving," Dale said. "Now."

"I know. And I'm taking Ty with me."

"I don't think so."

"What are you gonna do? Stab me so my guts fall out on the carpet? Right here in your own apartment, with a suitcase full of stolen money in the other room?"

That was all he needed to hear. He sagged and turned toward Ty, letting the knife hang low at his side. "Ty . . ." His voice had an air of finality about it.

"Don't say it," Ty said. "I already know." He stood. "I tried to do things the right way. I tried a regular job and taxes and everything, but I just couldn't work it out."

"Are you going to be okay?"

"I'm not going to go down without a fight." Ty turned to me. "How much of the money did you take?"

"Less than all of it, but enough that I don't feel like killing you anymore."

Dale was staring at me. "Can you . . ." He couldn't finish the question. I didn't think he was even sure what he was asking for.

"I don't know, but no one else is even going to try."

Ty laid his hand on Dale's shoulder. "Take the money and get out of town for a while. Take a week, drive up the coast. Use up some of that vacation time. If you spend the money slowly, no one will notice."

"Tear off the wrappers," I said. "Order something at a drive-through McDonald's or something. Take the food out of the bag, stuff the wrappers into the bottom, and roll it up tight. Then stuff the bag into a trash can right there at the restaurant."

Dale moved toward Ty. "Don't," Ty said, and stepped back. "It'll burn you."

Dale kissed him.

I looked away, but I didn't turn my back. Dale still had that damn knife. After a short while, I heard Dale go into the bathroom. He closed the door and turned on the water to wash.

I wrapped the belt around Ty's right wrist and tightened it as far as it would go. He let me. We left the apartment and went down the rough concrete stairs. I held the end of the belt like a leash. It made me feel like an asshole.

"I'm through playing games," I said. "If you take that belt off or"—I couldn't say it in a public stairwell—"do your thing, I'll kill you, and to hell with the consequences."

"I was the one who beat the hell out of Justin Gage, you know."

I couldn't remember who he was talking about, and I said so.

He laughed a little. "Guess you wouldn't. He's a big figure in *my* life, but . . . He's the Cardio-eira guy at the gym where I work. You know, like Tae-Bo, but with capoeira? Never mind. It's a new fitness thing that's been getting pretty popular, even though it's really stupid. Everyone who went to the gym wanted Gage—I couldn't even pick up the guy's sloppy seconds. And to make it worse, he was always being nice to me about it. Encouraging me that I was good enough and telling me how it all takes time . . . like I needed attaboys from him. Do you know how much the gym charged me to work there?"

"No." I tried to sound like I cared, but I failed. He glanced at me. He could see how I felt, but he was too busy feeling sorry for himself to drop it.

"Well, it's a lot. After I kicked his dancey little capoeira ass, I took over a bunch of his clients, but I could tell they weren't going to switch permanently. It was just a waste. Maybe I should have killed him. He was just lying there, at the end—I could have stamped on his neck, you know? But I wasn't desperate enough for that. That's what I told myself. I wasn't desperate enough. I thought I could be a straight arrow, you know? Like Dale. Such a waste, man."

He didn't sound sorry about what he'd done. I guess that would have been too much to expect. We reached my Escort and I opened the door for him. He sat and I shut the door. I went around to the driver's side and climbed in.

"I should have taken that money," he said. "I had hopes for it."

"Wally doesn't need your money."

"Maybe he wants it."

"For God's sake! It should have been obvious to you a long time ago that you cannot pull the usual shit here. You can't buy off or bully these people. There's no way to blackmail them. They have their own little world, and it only comes into contact with ours when they need to kill someone or find a patsy."

"Fuck you. I'm nobody's patsy."

"Fuck me? You have a living stomach lining over your whole body, and it's going to start eating you soon. You're a patsy. Deal with it. Whatever Wally really needed, he tried to get it with Luther. You weren't involved."

Ty turned toward me suddenly. "Tried? At that house?"

I didn't like the look on his face. "Dude—"

A Range Rover screeched to a halt right in front of my car. I jammed the key into the ignition at the same moment that Ty opened the passenger door and turned invisible. The engine started as I lunged toward Ty but missed him. He was gone.

The doors of the Range Rover swung open. Meatheads One, Two, and Three piled out.

To hell with this. I threw it into reverse and tried to back out of my spot. One of the meatheads fired three rounds into my engine block.

Immediately, the engine started grinding and lost power. I cut the wheel, backing up anyway, but I didn't have the space to make the turn, and I plowed into the street-side taillight of the car parked behind me.

By then, a man was standing by my window, tapping a pistol against the glass.

I turned off the engine and opened the door. Their ugly faces were all around me, thick, pouchy, scarred with acne. Hands pressed me against my car and patted me down the way a cop would. They found my cell and ghost knife, and this time they kept both. They also found the ten grand. Damn, I hadn't even gotten to the end of the block with it, and now I had to listen to them laugh as they split it between them.

A woman on the sidewalk held up her cellphone and snapped a picture of us. I stared straight at her, knowing my face would be recorded. Too bad I was on the twisted path; by the time she showed the photo to someone, it would no longer look like me.

"Let's go," one of the men said. They dragged me into the Range Rover and shoved me into the back, where I sat squeezed between two guys who smelled like sweat and enchilada sauce.

Potato Face sat in the front seat. He looked me over and turned away. He'd caught me, but he didn't look happy about it.

We pulled away, leaving my car with the money under the floor mats jutting into the street. An embarrassing pang of grief went through me. I'd killed too many people to be moved by the loss of an old vehicle, but I was anyway.

We drove on Beverly Glen Boulevard much too fast. The windows were open, but the freeway air blowing into my face was dry and hot—there was nothing cooling about it. I asked for water, but no one acknowledged me. I was forced to sit quietly and wonder how I was going to track down Ty again, not to mention the others, and how much time I had before he fell out of this world and let more predators in.

We pulled up to Francois's big white house and parked at the curb. There was a blue panel van in the drive, and its back doors swung open as we got out of the car. Two more meatheads climbed out, with Arne and Lenard at gunpoint.

Arne had a nasty smile on his face. "God, it's a beautiful day. Am I right?"

Lenard snorted. I wondered why the two of them let themselves be captured. Were they trying to keep their power a secret? I thought I was the only one concerned about that.

The three of us let ourselves be herded up the front walk toward the house.

CHAPTER THIRTEEN

Each of us had two meatheads assigned to him, with two more in back and Potato leading the way. When we entered the clean white house, the air-conditioning was so startling that I gasped aloud. It must have been 65 degrees inside, and the sweat on my face and back immediately chilled.

Lenard turned toward me, smiling at the way I gasped. "I know, huh? Let's move in."

One of the meatheads shoved him roughly, and we ran out of things to say. I could feel my ghost knife nearby, in the pocket of one of the men, but I didn't call it. If Arne and Lenard were hiding their tricks, so would I.

We were taken to the same room as the last time. The sliding doors were closed, and blinds were drawn across them. The only light came from a pair of lamps in opposite corners, and they cast a sickly yellow tint over the white furniture.

Swizzle Stick sat in a plush chair in the corner. She wore the same purple bikini, but her legs and arms were crossed, and her chin tucked low, as though she didn't want to be noticed.

Beside her chair, Francois paced back and forth. His suit this time was midnight black—maybe it made him feel tough.

He never took his eyes off Arne. Potato stopped us five feet from him. The meatheads were all around, standing so close together they were practically in one another's way. There was a door behind Francois, another that we came through, and of course the sliding doors. The meatheads would catch me if I bolted toward Francois, and there was too much heavy flesh to shove aside to get to either of the other exits.

"Well?" Francois suddenly barked.

"Yeah," Swizzle Stick answered. Her confidence had drained away. "It was the middle one." She lifted her chin toward Lenard. "He was the sp—"

"Watch your fucking mouth," Francois said. "Now get your things and call a cab."

Her crossed arms and legs slid apart. "What?"

Francois spun toward her. "What did you think would happen? Get out!"

She pushed her long, lanky body out of the chair. I stepped to the side to give her room to pass—and to better position myself to rush the door—but the meatheads took hold of me in a very convincing way. Swizzle went out the far door anyway.

"Bad enough," Francois said to us, "that you steal my fucking car and try to sell it back to me, but you had to put that fucking video on the Internet? And then you tell *my wife*?!"

Arne was still smiling. "That's Web two point oh, baby."

Francois stepped up close to him. "You think I'm being funny?" There was something unconvincing about Francois's performance. He wasn't used to threatening people, and he didn't have the knack. I snuck a glance at Potato Face. His expression was not quite blank, and he had turned his body away from his employer. I didn't think he'd be murdering anyone for this boss.

Francois shifted his feet. This wasn't turning out how he'd planned, and he was growing frustrated. "Do you know what I do to people who cross me?"

I said: "You make them leave this air-conditioned room?"

Arne and Lenard both laughed. Francois spun and came toward me. He got very close to my face. "You think you're someone, don't you? But you're nobody, and I'm going to prove it.

"What's the matter, *gallito*?" Lenard said. "Are you a man or not? Tell your wife you wanted to fuck somebody new for a change, and if she don't like it, tough."

"The only problem with that," Arne said, "is that most of the money is hers. Right?"

"That's bullshit! I have my own money. All my own."

"That's good," Arne said, his voice full of bad ideas. "It's good for a man to have his own."

"For now, at least," I said. "I hear your wife is one hell of a lawyer."

Francois licked his lips. "You guys are nothing. Mosquitoes. You have no idea what kind of enemies I have."

Arne grinned at him nastily. "Baby, *you* don't even know what kind of enemies you have."

He turned into a silhouette and vanished.

Francois shrieked—actually shrieked like a little girl—in shock. The meatheads shouted curses or little prayers, and suddenly no one was holding me at all. Lenard smiled and shrugged, then he vanished, too.

Potato suddenly grunted and doubled over as though he'd been kicked in the crotch. The door behind me banged open, and I could hear heavy footsteps stomping through it. Potato staggered toward Francois and fell against him, pinning him against the door and shielding him with his body. "Shut that damn door!" Potato rasped, and his heavy, low voice had the authority to stop everyone still. I heard the door slam shut.

My ghost knife was still nearby. I *called* it and it zipped out of one of the meatheads' breast pocket into my hand. He gaped at me, but no one else seemed to notice.

There were five of the meatheads left, plus Potato, Francois, and presumably Arne and Lenard. And me. Three meatheads backed against the glass doors blocking them. One stood against the door we'd come in, and the last one kicked the back of my knees and drove me to the floor.

I hated kneeling, but before I could do anything about it, Potato yelled, "Guns!"

The meatheads drew their pistols. Everything suddenly fell silent. We all listened for some sign of Arne and Lenard but couldn't hear anything. Were they being completely still, or had they already left the room?

Potato fished a Zippo out of his pants pocket and tossed it to one of the men at the sliding doors. "Newspapers," he said. The meathead grabbed a section off the coffee table and set fire to it, then held it out in front of him.

"Wave it around," Potato said. "Spread that smoke." He turned to me. "How the fuck are they doing this?"

"They were bitten by a radioactive chameleon."

He scowled at me but didn't press further. He had other problems to focus on.

The smoke filled the room quickly. I stared at it, eyes unfocused to take in as much as possible, looking for swirls that didn't have any obvious source. I couldn't see any.

"Let me out," Francois said, his voice a low, terrified whisper. "Let me out. Let me out."

"When I'm sure we have both of them trapped in here, I'll open the door. Until then, shaddup."

The central air-conditioning suddenly turned on with a low hum. Smoke swirled in every direction, and at the same moment, the guard holding the burning paper grimaced and clutched at his chest. Blood welled up under his left breast, and he collapsed forward onto the carpet, smothering the flames with his body.

"No, no!" one of the other men yelled, but Potato hissed at him. He shut up.

"Do you know what kind of enemies I have?"

It was Lenard's voice, and it came in a low whisper, making it hard to trace. I had a strange feeling, though, that he was very near me—just a couple of feet away. It was the same feeling that had led me to the spell on Sugar Dubois's back, a lifetime ago. It felt like magic, pulling me toward him.

"Gimme those," Potato said, pointing at the newspapers. One of the men tossed him a couple of sections. He shook them out, letting the pages fall onto the carpet around him. His men did the same.

Within seconds, each was surrounded by four or five feet's worth of paper.

"All right," Potato said. "You guys don't have guns. I know, because I took them from you. And I got your buddy right here." He pointed a pistol at me. "You can't get close to us without stepping on the paper and giving yourself away. And getting shot. So I'm gonna count to three, and if you don't show yourself, I'm putting a bullet in your pal here."

Potato aimed the gun at my forehead. Why couldn't he have chosen a part of me that was bulletproof?

"Go ahead," Lenard whispered. "So what?"

The smoke alarm suddenly went off; everyone winced except Potato. "Fire department's on its way!" he shouted. "Time is running out!"

"You're right, it is!" Arne shouted. He suddenly became visible just behind me. Damn if he didn't have a gun of his own in his hand, although I had no idea where he got it.

He pointed his pistol at Potato or Francois—it was hard to tell which. The meatheads all pointed their weapons at him. He was outnumbered and outgunned, and I couldn't figure out what his play was supposed to be. If he had the gun . . .

"Lenard!" Arne shouted. Lenard became visible just a few feet in front of me, crouching beside a low table. He shrugged, his smiling expression suggesting that he was playing along in a game that was beneath him. The meathead who'd been standing guard over me moved toward him.

Arne shifted his aim and fired a single shot at Lenard. The meathead jumped back. Lenard looked at his old friend in shock. There was a bloody hole in his shirt over his heart. Behind him, red was spattered against the wall; the drape was strong, but not strong enough to hold an exit wound closed.

Arne laughed and vanished again.

"No!" I shouted. There was a loud cracking sound, and beneath the piercing alarm I could hear a droning buzz.

It took a moment or two for Lenard to drop. I grabbed the meathead who'd been guarding me and pulled him away from Lenard's body. He twisted, thinking I was attacking him, and laid a heavy, door-busting right hook to the side of my face. I tried to roll with it, but it still had enough power to bounce me off the wall and lay me flat.

The noise was oppressive, but the awful mix of sounds helped me stay conscious. I struggled up onto my elbow, trying to clear the blinking white spots from my vision. Two meatheads moved toward Lenard—damn, they were close. I tried to warn them back, but all I could manage was a harsh croak and a vague wave of my arm.

Potato stepped toward them. "Back!" he shouted over the noise. He pulled one back and the other moved, too, as though they were tethered. Just then, the floor turned dark and vanished. Lenard's corpse dropped away into the void, and the meatheads began screaming.

Five drapes floated through the opening like balloons rising out of a manhole. The yellow light from Francois's lamps made them look like phlegm. The meatheads gaped, frozen in place.

Potato Face stepped back, and the first of the drapes rushed him. It flopped over him like a net, and he struggled for a couple of moments before toppling to the floor.

The two men he'd pulled away from Lenard's body turned to run, but drapes were on them before they could take a second step. One fell against a lamp and end table. The other landed on the middle of the floor.

One drape moved toward the guard who'd laid me out, and he fired four quick shots into it. The bullets tore through the predator's body, looking like clean spots on smeary glass, but the holes sealed over immediately. I tried to stand and push him away, but I was too slow. The man had time to scream once before it wrapped itself over his face and head.

The opening into the Empty Spaces disappeared. The couch jolted to the side as one of the guards thrashed against it, but Potato and his three men had vanished. I reached toward the space where the fourth man had fallen. He was there, invisible and trembling, just like Melly after her protective spell wore off.

Where was the fifth drape? I tried to remember how many men had fled the room and how many should have been here still. The only other person I could see was a lone blond beefhead crouching by the French doors. He stretched his hand out and touched the air at the base of the glass, then yanked his hand back and wiped it on his polo shirt.

Was that the fifth? I touched the one that fell near me, then crossed the room to touch that one. One man had fallen closer to me than I thought, and I nearly tripped over him in my search. Then I found Potato by the back door and the last beside the broken end table.

That was five. If one of the drapes had escaped the building, I didn't know what I'd do. Luckily, it hadn't become an issue. There were enough victims right here when they attacked.

And I'd had my ghost knife in my hand the whole time. I'd failed them all.

Worse, now I had to find a way to kill them safely.

That last guard stood. "You!" I shouted, trying to be heard over the blare of the alarm. "Stay here so we can help your friends!"

He stared at me for just a second, then barreled out the door. So much for my leadership abilities.

The alarm set my teeth on edge, and I suddenly remembered what Potato had said about the fire department coming. I rolled to my feet, bumping against one of the invisible bodies. My arm started to itch from the contact, but I pushed it toward the wall anyway. If firefighters chopped the door down and tripped over one of these invisible bodies . . .

I couldn't think with that damn alarm going, so I pushed a chair to the middle of the room and stood on it. The alarm was mounted on the center of the ceiling, and the cover came off with a quarter-twist.

It was nothing more than a thirty-dollar drugstore model. I yanked out the nine-volt battery, and the unit fell silent. There were no wires connecting if to the rest of the house, and no way for it to call emergency services when it went off. Potato had been bluffing.

First things first. I went through the open door into the kitchen, which looked like a smaller version of the kitchen at the Sugar Shaker, but without the men in white caps. I rinsed off my hands and searched the house as quickly as I could.

Francois was gone. So were Swizzle Stick, the two guards, and the Bugatti. Had Arne taken Francois and the car, or had one of the others? I wouldn't have a chance to drive it after all.

Beside the blank space where the Bugatti should have been parked was an H2 Hummer in a grotesque blue-green color. It was a big, stupid vehicle, but it was perfect for what I needed. A set of keys hung from a hook by the door.

There were also gardening gloves in the garage, but nothing I could use to move those bodies. Damn. I needed to find something, because there was no way I could leave those drapes and their victims here in the house.

Even if the fire department never came, *somebody* would. Maybe the guard would come back, or Swizzle, or even a process server for Francois's soon-to-be-ex-wife. Eventually, someone was going to want to know what happened to Francois—in fact, they could be placing a call to the cops right now.

These drapes couldn't be left here; I had to take them with me. I would either have to find Annalise and hope that one of her spells—the green fire?—could kill the predators without opening a passage to let more in, or I was going to have to figure out where they'd been summoned.

I didn't have what you'd call encyclopedic knowledge of predators or magic, but I had seen a couple of summonings. They took place inside circles—usually—sometimes painted, sometimes made of a particular material. They were like the circle around Wally King's cabin, only not usually so huge, and they could imprison the predator in our world.

I needed to know where Wally had summoned the drapes for Arne and his crew. Maybe, if I was lucky, the circle would still be intact. If a guard died inside it, the next group of predators—more than five of them, I guessed—would be contained.

I needed to catch up with Arne or one of the others. I needed a way to get that information out of them, and I needed to get them inside the circle, too.

The first thing I did was search the invisible bodies. One of them had taken the cellphone Annalise had given me, and I couldn't contact her without it. The drapes, strangely, seemed to be both under and over the guard's clothes. I could touch and move the fabric freely, but it was completely hidden by the predator's invisibility.

I searched all five bodies and couldn't find the phone. Damn. It was probably forgotten in the pocket of that meathead speeding toward Mexico.

That meant I would have to find Annalise or the circle—not an easy thing to do with ten million people in L.A. County, but I had a couple of leads.

There was a little shed out by the pool, but when I opened it I found nothing but towels and water toys. Apparently, Francois was too rich to own a wheelbarrow.

I took an office chair from a back bedroom, laid the bodyguards into it one by one, and wheeled each of them into the garage. The cargo area of the H2 was huge, but so were the guards. I had to slide out the last row of seats to make room for them.

Damn, they were heavy. At least they hadn't gone limp—each man was still fighting the effect of the predator, and all their muscles were clenched. I wished the blond guard hadn't run off. I could have used help getting the bodies up into the SUV.

I stopped myself. They weren't *bodies*. Not yet. They were still living men, and I wanted to treat them that way, not least of all because if one of them died in the back of this SUV, I was going to have drapes all over me.

I tried to lay them side by side; if one of them was pinned at the bottom, the weight of the others might suffocate him. The last two went into the backseat, tipped at an angle to fit.

By the time I was finished, I had slime all over my arms and on my neck. The burning and itching was intense. I skipped the sink and the shower and went straight out to the pool. After dropping my wallet and ghost knife on the grass, I toppled into the water.

I climbed out dripping wet, feeling like a guest who'd overstayed his welcome. I made a last stop at the fridge to steal six finger sandwiches, then it was time to go. I opened the back of the H2 to tap around the interior with a broom handle, just to reassure myself that everyone was still there. Then I climbed dripping wet into the driver's seat.

A button above the rearview mirror opened both the garage door and the driveway gate. I pulled out into the street, threw the switch to close them both again, and drove away.

There were more predators out there for me to find.

CHAPTER FOURTEEN

There was only one place to start my search: Ty had been much too excited to hear about Lino Vela's house. I didn't like the idea of Ty—or anyone in Arne's crew—finding a spell book. I didn't even want them to hear the words "Book of Oceans."

I drove toward Hancock Park, trying to be careful on the highway. The Hummer felt as wide as a traffic lane, and I didn't want to get into a fender bender in a stolen car. Luckily, other drivers assumed I was a jackass and gave me a lot of space.

I pulled up outside Lino Vela's address. Everything seemed quiet, but of course the greenery hid most of the property. I found a parking spot a block away and around the corner and pulled in.

Annalise's Dodge Sprinter sat parked across the street from Vela's gate. I tapped on the window. Annalise was in the passenger seat. She opened the driver's door and I climbed behind the wheel.

I didn't fit. The seat had been moved forward as far as it would go. Annalise had driven herself. "Talbot didn't come with you?"

"No," she said. "Have you accomplished anything?"

"I have five predators in the back of an SUV." She seemed surprised. "They have victims. Want to destroy them?"

She looked uncomfortable. She wanted to, always, but she didn't want to leave her post. I told her the drapes take a long time to feed, and what happens when the victim finally dies.

She asked how long we had until they actually killed their victims. I thought about the garbage stink in Melly's house, and the big pile of mail, and I said it seemed to take time, maybe a day or two.

Annalise nodded. "Normally I wouldn't wait to take out a couple of predators, but this is an unusual circumstance. If Wally King thinks there's a way to get a spell book from this house, he'll be back, I have to be here when he shows up. I can't let him get a lead on the Book of Motes or the Book of Oceans."

There was a note of desperation in her voice. Was she worried that Wally would become a primary? I was sure of it. But that wasn't all. The original spell books were a tremendous source of power, and she wanted them for herself.

But that was above me. I was just a guy with some invisible monsters in the back of his stolen Hummer. "Boss, these guys are dying slowly and badly. We need to . . . Wouldn't Wally have needed a circle to summon these things? A barrier, like the one in Canada?"

"Yes. Get one of your buddies to tell us where it is. If we can find that, we'll kill them there. If we can't, we'll try to get our hands on his book; it would have instructions on making the circle ourselves. If that falls through, we'll have to risk it. We won't have a choice. And yeah, those guys are suffering, but we're not here to make things easier for people."

She was looking away from me as she said it, and I was glad. She wouldn't have been happy if she'd seen my reaction—and maybe that's why she was looking away. Because in a sense, she was right; the most important thing was stopping the predators. Still, the suffering those men were going through had to count for *something*.

"So you're just going to sit here, waiting for Wally King?"

She still didn't look at me. "Looks that way."

"What if one of the invisibles turns up? How will you know?" She shrugged. "What if the guy who lives here is in danger?"

She turned and looked me in the eye. Her pale face was serene and still. "We're not here for him, either."

Before I had a chance to think about it, I was pushing the car door open and climbing out. I didn't want to be near her right then. Annalise had the power to kill predators *and* help people. The only thing she lacked was the will to do it. She just didn't give a shit.

I jogged across the street and went through the gate. The grounds were as overgrown as they'd been before, and it was quiet. The sun was still burning hot, and my clothes were drying quickly. I jogged toward the door. It was closed.

As I came closer, I saw a tall patch of natural wood on the painted green door. It had been repaired while I was in Canada, then broken open again. Someone had kicked the door in.

I could have gone back for Annalise, but I didn't. Ty might be in there, and who knows how many others from my old crew. They had predators on them, yes, and they would have to be killed, yes—and damn if that wasn't a hard thought to take and hold—but I didn't want Annalise anywhere near them. She didn't care about making things easier for people. She didn't care, period, and I didn't want her anywhere near my people.

I laid my hand on the door but didn't open it. Maybe there would be a better way. I went back down the steps to the narrow path between the bushes and went around the house.

It was impossible to move without rustling bushes, and the noise made me feel incredibly exposed. The windows were as high as my shoulder, and the bushes had grown slightly higher than the sill. There was no way I was getting through a window, or even getting a good look inside.

I went around a tall tree to the next set of windows when someone walked past the glass, moving away from me.

I ducked low. It was Bud, and while his face was turned away, I could see his jaw moving. He was also scratching furiously at the back of his neck. Was he talking to Lino or to one of the guys in the crew?

I crouched low, squeezing between some sort of thorny bush and the tall wooden fence that marked the edge of the property. I reached the backyard and the lush vegetable garden. It was empty. A rain barrel sat beneath a back window, with a PVC pipe leading out of the house and through the lid. I moved toward the back steps.

"Good to see you, Ray."

Damn. I turned toward the sound of that voice and saw Summer sitting on a little bench by the tomato vines. She held a gun on me. For a moment, I thought it was a toy ray gun, then I realized it had a silencer on it.

With her empty hand, she rubbed at her nose. My ghost knife was in my pocket, but could I reach for it without being shot?

"Don't," she said. "I can see your spongy little brain working—it's right there on your face—and if you try something stupid, I'll kill you and make my excuses to the new boss."

"Who's the new boss?" I asked. I already knew the answer.

"He can introduce himself."

She nodded toward the back door and stood. I went up the steps with her behind me. I pulled the door open, thinking I might spin around and snatch the gun from her, but when I looked back she'd gone invisible again.

I couldn't steal what I couldn't see. I wondered whether the predator would feel pain when the bullet left the barrel, or if the gun became very hot. I went inside.

The house was stuffy; Lino needed to turn on his air-conditioning.

There was a small entryway with a long room off to the side—it held gardening equipment, piles of sports gear, and the laundry machines. The door behind me didn't swing shut right away; Summer was staying close enough to catch the door, but not too close. I went up the next step into the kitchen.

As I entered the room, I let my hand fall on the door and slammed it shut behind me. I twisted to the side, bumping against the stove and the handle of a bubbling pot of water as a single gunshot punched through the door. My ghost knife was in my hand, but I couldn't use it. Not unless I wanted the drape to kill Summer and bring more of its kind.

I took the handle of the pot—there were three eggs bubbling in about a quart of water—and lifted it off the stove.

As the door swung open, I threw the water into the gap. I felt like a monster as I did it, but that didn't stop me. The steaming water passed through the open space where she should have been but struck the wall beyond. Summer was too smart to rush through a door face first; I'd missed. She became visible and glared at me, her teeth bared.

She lifted the gun.

"Stop!" someone shouted. Fidel stood in the doorway to the next room. He wore a green silk suit that I guessed was tailor-made. It looked sharp, but how could he stand it in this heat?

"Fuck that," Summer said. "I owe him a bullet."

Fidel put his finger into a hole in the cabinet. "You gave it, now knock it off. The boss wants to talk to him."

Summer made a face when she heard the word *boss*, but she didn't pull the trigger. Fidel waved at me and I followed him, wishing I could keep the bulletproof tattoos on my chest toward Summer.

We went into the dining room, where the statues and other antiques lined the walls. Ty was standing beside the window, and Bud entered from the front hall at the same time I did. The table was on its side against the wall, and Lino Vela was sitting in one of the chairs. He looked exposed and vulnerable, and he was sweating freely. His thermal coffee cup lay on the floor beside him, and I was absurdly glad it wasn't leaking. *Focus, focus.*

"You brought these people here?" Lino blurted at me.

Wally King was standing in the corner. "Hi, Ray," he said without looking at me. He stared at the little statue he'd tried to steal, running his fingers along the place where the little figure's head was coming off. "I have to say I'm disappointed."

Was he expecting me to sneak up in a ninja costume? Drive through the front wall in a half-track? I didn't care; I wasn't in the mood to play his games.

And damn if Annalise wasn't just a few dozen yards away. He'd gotten here without her noticing, or before she'd set up her stakeout. I needed to get to the front door and shout for her—somehow—as soon as I found out where Wally's summoning circle was, and whether he'd erased it.

I turned away from him toward the others. "You can't be working with this guy," I told them. "You don't realize what he's done."

"I think we got a pretty good idea," Bud drawled. He scratched at a spot on his leg.

"He's killed you."

"You're the one who wants to kill us," Ty said. "He explained it."

Fidel cut in. "Why we gotta be your enemy? You remember the old times, don't you, Ray? Shit, I feel like an old man just talking this way, but we have history."

"I remember. It's good stuff and bad, just like any family. That's why I'm here." Fidel scratched the back of his hand, and I couldn't look away. "What he's done to you is going to get bad soon. Very bad. And after it kills you, it'll bring more of those things into L.A. I have the proof right outside—"

"Outside where your peer is?" Wally said. He looked at Fidel. "She's the killer he works for, and she'd burn down this whole city block, killing all the kids and mothers and old people, to get to us. That's what they do."

"She's here for *him*," I told Fidel. "I want to help you."

Wally laughed. "I don't think they believe you, Ray."

I looked at their faces and knew he was right. They'd seen through me, but I had to keep trying. "We can go outside without her seeing you. I have something to show you in the trunk of a Hummer. Guys, you don't realize what he's done."

"Yes, we do," Summer said. "We're not stupid."

Ty held out his arm as though he wanted to show it to me. "We know these things are like a poison. But he's the only one who can offer an antidote."

Fidel was still smiling. "We aren't into euthanasia, baby."

I reminded myself that none of them had seen a drape as it fed. "Lenard is dead," I told them.

That hit them hard. There was silence for a moment, until Bud said: "How?"

"How do you think?" I snapped back, because I didn't want to put the finger on Arne, not even now. "The creature that was wrapped around him opened a hole in our universe and carried him off. He's gone."

"Opened a hole . . . ," Summer said with contempt. "What bullshit."

I spun on her. "How perfect is this: Vanishing Girl doesn't believe in magic. Wake the fuck up. There's more going on here than you understand, no matter what he's told you." I spoke to the group of them. "It killed Lenard and carried him back to its home, and more of them came through the opening. I have them, *and the people they're eating*, in a car outside. All I need is for you to be willing to look at what's going to happen when the symbols he put on you wear off."

"Crazy," Lino muttered. "You're all crazy." Wally laughed again.

The others thought about what I'd said. Summer's face was closed and angry—she didn't trust me, but she was willing to let the others think things through. Fidel smirked at me; he'd been trying to win me over, talking about old friendships, but that didn't mean he was open to what I was saying. Just the opposite, really.

Before I could judge Ty and Bud's responses, Wally broke in. "Why don't you tell them why you're here, Ray?"

I turned to him. He looked so grotesque that I wanted to look away, but I didn't. "Because a friend came to my apartment in Seattle and told me that you'd killed her."

"I don't mean why you're in *Los Angeles*." Wally sounded annoyed. "I mean why you're here in this house. Surrounded by all this crap."

"Because I knew Ty was coming here, and I needed to find these guys."

"You're a liar and you're not even good at it." He reached out to the head-chopping statue, wrapped his hand around it as though he was going to pick it up, then let it go. "You're here for the same reason I am, for the same reason your boss is. For the same reason your own secret society pays the people across the street to keep video security cameras pointed at this house at all times."

Lino glanced up at that. "What?"

Wally liked being the focus of attention. He kept talking. "Georges Francois, the owner's great-great-something-grandfather, had a real spell book. One of the three originals. And when he vanished, he left behind this collection."

If he was talking, he wasn't killing me. I gave him a prompt. "A collection that can't be broken up."

"Nobody can break apart this collection. I have some wild and weird outsiders in here with me, but not even they can resist the compulsion to leave it all alone. You think the sapphire dog sold for a high price? This stuff would bring treasure beyond imagining at auction. At least five of the richest men in the world would literally give everything they own for it."

"Beyond imagining?" Ty asked. He looked around the room.

"Try to steal something," Wally said. "See how far you get. Anyway, the real point is that Francois—the original—had one of the three most powerful magical items in the world, and it's been missing and presumed lost for over two hundred years.

Ty tried to pick up an old candlestick shaped like a gas-lamp post but apparently decided against it. His hand fell to his side. He tried to touch it again, didn't, then shrugged and walked away. The compulsion was strong.

"But this," Wally continued, waving his arms around. "This is a clue farm right here. I think Georges Francois hid the Book of Oceans, and I think this unbreakable collection contains the clues we need to find it. What's more, I think this head-chopped statue is the key to the mystery."

I stared at him. "What the hell are you talking about?"

"It's true, man! I'm sure of it! It's how these people think! They want to pass their power to someone who's earned it. And I'm not the first person to believe this, let me tell you. Not by a long shot."

"Why would he hide it and leave clues? You said he vanished, right? How do you know it didn't vanish with him?"

"Then why would he create this collection, huh?"

"Because he was an egotistical asshole." I turned to Fidel, Summer, and the others. "You're signing on with this guy?"

They looked dubious. "Apparently," Fidel admitted.

"Ray, don't doubt me." Wally shuffled his bulk into the center of the room. "I know you think you're hot shit, but I gotta tell you, I haven't seen it. Neither have these guys. I have no idea how you got this rep as a badass killer, but I suspect you're just a front.

"And I admit, I'm not really big on thinking up plans. But you know what? I don't have to be. I am damn good at finding out secrets. I solved every version of Myst without ever looking at a walk-through."

I couldn't help it. I laughed at him.

He smirked and shrugged. "Go ahead, buddy. Have a chuckle. But I'm telling you, I see things in ways you can't understand. These objects are all bound together, and they're all connected to him." Wally waved a hand at Lino. "I know a little desert retreat that's going to be abandoned soon, and I *was* going to ask you to join me while I worked this out. Why should you be killing all these people for the Twenty Palace Society when you could be killing for an old friend? Huh?" He sounded almost hurt. "I was hoping that, if nothing else, your rep would keep some of those assholes off my back while I figured these clues."

"Why would you think I'd help you?"

"The King Book of Oceans," he said. "The Lilly Book of Motes."
He moved toward the statue, his expression blank.

"No."

"I know. It's too late for that anyway. Kill him."

I held up my empty hands, thinking my old friends might hesitate
to kill me in cold blood.

Summer raised her gun.

I *reached* for the ghost knife and it zipped out of my back pocket.
Summer sighted on my chest and fired two quick shots. Then I had my
spell in my hand.

I whipped my arm down as I lunged at her, slashing the ghost
knife through the barrel of her gun. It cut at an angle, slicing it close to
her hand but not touching her. The silencer and front end of the barrel
thunked to the floor, then the slide shot toward me and bounced off
my leg.

Summer gaped at the ruined weapon in her hand, then at the two
holes in my shirt.

I spun on Wally. He stepped backward, passing through the wall
like a phantom. I threw my spell at him.

The ghost knife plunged through the plasterboard after him, zipping right between the head-chopping statue and a brass cow rearing
up like a lion. It couldn't have missed, I was sure, and a moment later
I was proven right when a jet of flame burst through the wall, blasting
plaster, wood splinters, and knickknacks toward me.

I stumbled, struck something with my heel, and fell backward
onto jagged wood and broken plaster. Lino was on the floor next to
me, curled up on his hands and knees and covering his head.

Wally screamed as the flames roared out of him and through the
hole in the wall. I must have hit one of his little iron bugs and ignited
the others. They tumbled, still burning, out of a hole in his belly.

I grabbed Lino's flabby biceps and hauled him to his feet. "Let's
save your life." I dragged him from the room.

Summer was still standing by the back door with Ty beside her.
Fidel was standing in the doorway with Bud right behind him, almost
ready to push his way into the room. Only Fidel was looking at me; he
gaped at the bullet holes in my shirt.

"Shit, Ray," Fidel said. "Are you bulletproof?" I could see the hunger in his eyes.

His expression made me furious. I threw a punch at him, but he
retreated toward the front door and vanished. My fist slammed into the
doorjamb, and I cursed at the pain. I'd split my knuckles wide open.

Stupid. I moved toward the hall. I couldn't see Fidel or Bud; they had to be between me and the front door at the end of the hall. There were stairs on the right, and I shoved Lino toward them. We stumbled up.

The knowledge that Fidel or Summer could be inches away from me with a knife made me so shaky that I could barely lift my legs. Lino pounded up the steps, and I did my best to follow him.

"Front room," I said, but he was already headed there.

I entered after him and slammed the door. At least we'd know when one of the invisibles tried to come in.

Lino ran to the bedside table and yanked open a drawer. He pulled out an old revolver with a carved pearl handle. I grabbed it and twisted it out of his hand. "No."

"How can you say *no*?" His voice was high with stress. "These criminals broke into my home! If I can't shoot the hell out of them, please explain why not!"

The bedroom we were standing in was carefully arranged and covered with a thin layer of dust, like a museum exhibit. I went to the window and looked out. The greenery was heavy, but we were pretty high up. I could see the Dodge Sprinter parked across the street. There was also a sloping roof just outside the window, with a low gutter at the edge.

"Because nothing they're doing here is worth you losing your life." I snatched a baseball off the bureau. It felt small in my hand—it had been many years since I played ball, but in my freaked-out adrenaline high, the long throw felt entirely natural. The ball punched a hole in the window, soared out through the tree branches, and struck the side of Annalise's van.

"That was Mr. Francois's Mickey Mantle!"

"Well, why don't you go get it, then?" I opened the window. There was glass on the shingles, but he was wearing shoes. Lino hesitated. Just as I was about to point out the tree he should climb down, the bedroom door burst open.

I tore the curtain rod off the wall, then spun and threw it toward the door. The curtain fell on an invisible form there, and I charged at it, knowing I couldn't use my ghost knife or Lino's gun. I drew back my bloody right hand, hoping that the punch I was about to throw wouldn't hurt too much.

"I have a gun!" It was Bud's voice. I stopped where I was. The curtains bounced to the floor, and I heard him move away from me. Damn. I stepped toward the sound, but Bud shouted, "Don't!"

"Show me the gun."

He obliged by becoming visible. I had no idea why he did what I told him, but he definitely had a gun, which looked so ungainly because of the silencer. He was pale and trembling, so scared I thought he might crap himself. I knew how he felt.

But he didn't squeeze the trigger. Wally had been completely casual when he told them to murder me, but Bud wasn't a killer. He was a tough thief and a little mean, but killing someone in cold blood was deeper waters than he liked. I could see that he was trying to work himself up to it.

"Happy now?" he asked. "I'm bringing this loser back downstairs. Him, we want alive."

"Bud, you have to let me go downstairs to meet my boss. She's on her way into the building"—in fact, she should have arrived already. Where was she?—"and she's coming for Wally. I need to tell her to lay off you guys."

Bud scratched at the side of his neck. The pale skin there looked red. "They have guns."

I pulled at the holes in the front of my shirt. "So what?"

"You ain't bulletproof," Bud said, as if trying to convince himself. "Not with that face."

"Bud, you have it all wrong. We need to get you—all of you—back to the place where you got this creature." There was something at the back of my mind, something I was missing, but now wasn't the time to think it out. "We—"

"Shut up, Ray," he said through clenched teeth. "You think I'm going to listen to you? *You stole my truck!*"

He was working himself up to pull the trigger, and he was very, very close.

Lino stepped up from the side, almost from behind Bud, and slammed a golf club down on his forearm.

The gun didn't go off. I rushed Bud and slammed my right elbow into his mouth while I groped for the gun. I clamped my left hand onto his right, but it was empty. He'd dropped the gun and I hadn't even heard it hit the floor.

I spun him around and pushed him against the wall. The fight had gone out of him, and when I grabbed his forearm, he hissed sharply in pain. Lino must have broken a bone.

"Sorry, Bud," I said, although I was suddenly unsure how much that apology was supposed to cover. I looked down to pick up the gun, but it was missing.

So was Lino. Had he gone out the window? Somehow I didn't think he was spry enough to get out and down so quickly. The bedroom door was standing open.

There was a loud crash downstairs. Annalise had finally arrived.

A sound like water flowing through a tunnel came from the first floor, and I shoved Bud through the door toward it. He let me. An eerie orange light shone up the stairs; was the building on fire? I hurried toward it. Bud curled his arm across his body and moved his feet as fast as I pushed him, but the vitality had gone out of him.

At the foot of the stairs, we found the ground-floor hall blocked by a weird twist of the air, an orange glow that made the air seem to flow toward the front of the house. I didn't know what the hell it was, but it felt fundamentally *wrong*, the way some predators do when I get too close.

Bud drew back, not wanting to touch it. The weird flow was close to the bottom step, but I couldn't judge how close. It was coming from somewhere in the front room and flowing toward the front door— from Wally toward Annalise, I assumed—but I didn't want to get close enough to look down the hall to confirm it.

Then the flow reversed and I felt a weird pressure wash over me. I started rethinking all my thoughts of the last few seconds, but backward. I fell against the stairs, disoriented, feeling unmade in some odd way I couldn't understand.

My skin crawled. Whatever strange magic had been flowing toward the door, it had been turned back on itself, and I'd felt the effects. The flow faltered and stopped.

I tried to raise my hand, but it swung downward instead of up and I banged my wrist against the edge of the stair. The spell Annalise had used to turn Wally's magic back on itself was still affecting me, making me move in the wrong direction and sporadically think backward.

Bud's drape must have shielded him from the effects, because he stepped off the bottom stair, turned toward the front of the house, and raised his good left hand. He was holding a tiny pistol, and I had no idea where he'd gotten it. He looked tired and sad, as though he'd given up any hope of living out the day. Annalise strode into view. Bud aimed the gun at her throat and, from barely six inches away, shot her.

She didn't even flinch. She swatted his hand away, and his face came alive with sudden, startled pain. Annalise grabbed him by the belt and collar, then raised him over her head.

"Boss, no!" I hadn't gotten the words out of my mouth when she threw him down onto the floor with such force that the whole house shook and the floorboards cracked.

Bud suddenly turned crimson—all the blood that would have splashed out of his shattered body washed over his skin, held in by the drape. Someone was screaming and the wooden floor kept cracking, although part of my disoriented brain knew the sound wasn't coming from the floor.

Annalise stared at Bud's corpse, her brow furrowed as she watched his blood disappear. A buzzing noise grew louder and I struggled to my feet. Annalise reached toward her vest.

I tried to move toward her but took two steps back instead. Damn, her reversal spell still had me all turned around. I let myself fall toward her—she grew larger in my vision, at least—just as the floor vanished.

Bud and Annalise both dropped into the darkness below. Annalise gasped in surprise just before I caught her sleeve. The Nomex was slick; for a moment I thought it might slip out of my injured hand, but it didn't.

I jammed my foot between banister posts so I wouldn't slide in after her. Annalise slid out of the oversized jacket—it wasn't fastened, and she didn't fit into it anyway—but she caught hold of the hem and swung out over the void. She looked up at me, and God, for the first time ever she looked genuinely afraid.

And there, below her, was a huge mass of drapes moving toward us.

Just as I was about to start hauling Annalise in, she did it herself, scrambling hand over hand up the length of her jacket, then over me. She hopped up onto the stair behind me and said: "Don't lose my jacket."

The drapes were coming, and not in small numbers. Not five, not six . . . This was a swarm of thousands. I scrambled to the side, trying to get away, but I was too slow. Too slow! The drapes were already here.

The predators burst up through the opening in the floor just as a ribbon zipped over my head and burst into a huge bubble of green flame.

There was no keening this time, no death cries. The drapes died suddenly and violently.

When the green flames faded, I saw the predators swirling around the opening—close enough that I could have rolled over and slapped one—but not coming through. Then the floor reappeared and became solid, sealing over the opening.

Thick wads of gray sludge covered the baseboard and wall. Damn if we hadn't just found a way to kill the drapes without letting more into our world. I saw Annalise pluck another green ribbon from her vest. It was her last one.

"Boss, don't kill the ones who can turn invisible."

"He didn't look invisible to me." Police sirens grew louder. "Remember what I said about the police."

She stepped onto the hall floor, one hand on the banister just in case the portal reopened. It didn't. I stepped out behind her. Wally stood at the end of the hall, with an open door behind him that led to the backyard. The front of his shirt was torn, and his swollen belly had burst open. I could see dark, wet things moving inside.

He held Lino Vela beside him. Lino looked at me, gasping for air. He was so freaked out that any of us could have controlled him with a gentle word. At the edge of the room stood Summer and Fidel, and they looked just as shaken and helpless as Lino. Flickering light from a fire I couldn't see played against their faces.

"This guy," Wally said, his voice quavering a little, "can help us find the Book of Oceans. We can make a deal. Your people are looking for it, too, and—"

Annalise lowered her shoulder and ran through the gray sludge at him.

Summer and Fidel vanished.

Wally shoved Lino in front of him. "Listen! Wait!" he said, but that wasn't going to stop Annalise. Lino cringed.

"Boss!" I shouted, moving toward her, but it was too late. She threw a ribbon into the room. A greenish black tentacle whipped out of the open wound in Wally's gut and slapped Lino toward it.

Lino and the ribbon touched. For an instant, green fire lit his terrified expression. He didn't scream. He didn't have time.

Wally, though, screamed high and loud. Annalise charged into the room just as the flames died. Lino's smoking bones hadn't even had time to fall to the floor before she knocked them around the room.

I followed. Wally stumbled and fell onto his side. He raised his left hand to protect himself; everything from the middle of his forearm to the tips of his fingers had burned down to a stiff, gleaming, resinous bone.

Annalise grabbed him just above the elbow and stomped on his thigh.

His leg flattened and buckled. Wally shrieked, and the sound of it stopped me in my tracks. I stood in the doorway, horror-struck at the noise he was making. Goose bumps ran down my back, and I flushed with shame. I hated Wally, but no man should ever be reduced to making a sound like that.

Annalise, her face utterly blank, like that of a skilled worker with a complicated job, twisted Wally's burned arm like a chicken wing and tore it off at the shoulder.

There was no blood for some reason, but I could see the awful knobby end of Wally's upper-arm bone. Annalise crammed that raw bone into his open, screaming mouth.

I didn't want to see any more. I didn't want to see the breaking teeth or the way she nearly pushed the bone out the back of his head. This was her work. I didn't want to see any more, but I couldn't look away, either.

This was who *we* were.

Something greenish black inside Wally's body lashed out at Annalise, but she caught it with her other hand. More tentacles flashed out at her, battering her and knocking her away, but she had hold of her victim and there was no way she'd give up now.

God, she was winning.

The strange orange flow erupted out of him, and Annalise was thrown back and her body curled to the side as though gravity was bending around her. The distorted flow suddenly changed direction, shredding the tentacle in her hand.

Annalise staggered. The torn flesh on Wally's belly opened again, showing more of the formless, writhing thing inside him. A limb flashed out, slapping Annalise away. The flowing orange distortion struck her again, lifting her off her feet and blasting her into the living room.

I rushed after her to keep her in view. She flew in a straight line, smashed through the plate-glass window, and passed through the greenery out of sight.

Damn. I ran toward her as though she had me on a leash. I had to make sure she hadn't been turned inside out or something.

She lay tangled in the bushes by the front gate, and two LAPD uniforms struggled toward her, guns drawn. Her expression was furious and frustrated.

A cop turned toward the house, and I ducked out of sight.

Wally was gone.

I ᴦᴀɴ ɪɴᴛᴏ the kitchen. Ty, Summer, and Fidel were gone, and so was Wally. Had they carried him away? I doubted it. They wouldn't have stuck around for the whole of that beating.

Lino Vela was still here—his bones were all over the floor. And there was his coffee thermos, and the little statue that Wally had wanted so badly. A burning piece of table lay against the wall, and there was a small fire on the wooden counter. Goose bumps ran down my back as I went near it, but it wasn't spreading like the fire that had burned me a few days earlier. No polyester.

I picked up the statue. The urge to return it to the shelf was strong, even though the shelf didn't exist anymore.

Someone pounded on the front door. The cops were about to bust in, and here I was standing in a ruined house beside a dead man's bones. Even better, Lino's gun lay in the corner.

I picked it up and fired two shots into the floor. The pounding changed to cursing and retreating voices. That may have bought me a few seconds, but when the cops came, they were going to come in force.

The compulsion to put the statue down was strong. Instead, I laid the edge of my ghost knife against the cut part of the man's neck.

And damn if that wasn't the easiest thing in the world. The enchantment on the statue demanded that I ignore it, but the ghost knife cut right through all that. The ghost knife *wanted* to cut the statue. I slid it through the metal, and the head fell, thunking to the ground.

I picked up the head—there was nothing usual about it—and set it on the counter. On the statue, there was a tiny hole on the cut stump of the neck.

It was small, less than half the size of the mouth of a soda straw. I angled it toward the window, hoping daylight might show a sliver of paper inside, and something blue spilled out.

The liquid dangled from the statue like a long, thin line of mucus. I righted the figurine and the stream zipped back up into the opening. Damn. What was that?

I grabbed Lino's coffee thermos off the floor and spun the lid off.

The liquid poured out of the statue in a thin, milky-blue stream. I tossed the statue away, and the spell's effects faded. The compulsion had been laid on the statue, not on this strange fluid. In fact, there was an odd feeling to the liquid—an absence, almost, as though it wasn't really there.

Whatever. I twisted the lid on tight. Time to go.

I snatched a big bottle of corn oil off the counter and splashed it onto the floor, then onto the hall carpet. In the other room, the phone rang. I tossed the oil onto the floor beside the spreading fire. Then I grabbed an antique lantern off the floor and smashed it against the burning wood. Firelight chased me out the back door.

No one shouted, "FREEZE! POLICE!" I vaulted over the back fence into the next yard. A huge brown mastiff raised his head to look at me, then lowered it again. It was too damn hot to bark.

I ran around the side of the house and let myself through the gate onto the sidewalk. There were no cop cars racing down the block, although I could hear more approaching.

I crossed the street and walked to the corner, keeping my pace slow and steady. People were coming out of their houses, and I stood at the curb in a knot of them as a cop car went by, sirens screaming. Sweat ran down my back, and my mouth was dry.

An old lady gave me a suspicious look as I stepped off the curb—I'd taken too many punches to be truly anonymous. I crossed the street, slipping through a crowd of lookie-loos, then I got into the Hummer and drove away. I took a deep breath for what felt like the first time in hours.

If those patrol cars had gotten there a few minutes sooner, I would have been trapped. For once I'd had a bit of luck.

But something was nagging at me, and I couldn't figure out what it was. Something Arne had said? I turned my attention to other things to let my subconscious work on it. Ty, Summer, and Fidel were on the loose, and whatever was left of Wally had gotten away. I couldn't even catch a thought, let alone predators . . .

In a panic, I pulled into a strip mall and parked. I threw open the back door and poked into the empty cargo space with the base of the thermos. It wasn't empty after all; the bodies of the guards were still there. All of them, I hoped, but I couldn't tell unless I climbed in and started moving them around with my bare hands, and I wasn't going to do that.

I took another deep breath and pressed my trembling hands on the back door. Annalise wasn't around to burn the drapes to ash, which meant I needed to find the circle Wally had used to summon them, if it still existed. If it didn't, I didn't know what the hell I'd do. Could I stash them somewhere until Annalise got herself released? Although I was pretty sure she had run out of green ribbons and had no idea how long it took her to make new ones.

I leaned against the bumper and wiped my face with my shirttail. God, I hated sweat on my face. And I was thirsty, too. Of course Wally had come here in August; it was like he wanted to give me extra reasons to hate him. Why couldn't he have holed up in that cabin in the woods? The breeze was cool there.

There was a Starbucks in the shopping mall, so I ducked inside and bought a bottle of water. It cost too much, but a little sign by the fridge promised that some of the money would go to help people somewhere get something. Clean water, apparently.

I was happy to spend some money on a well or whatever. I sure as hell wasn't doing any good as a wooden man. Wally had gotten away, and so had all the others. I went back out to the car and sat behind the wheel, drinking the cool water slowly and thinking about all the things I didn't do to stop them. I hadn't threatened anyone's children or torn someone's limbs off. I hadn't burned an innocent man to death.

Annalise was as ruthless as ever, and remembering what she'd done to Lino and Wally made me shiver in the sweltering car. Then again, next to Csilla she was practically a hero.

Damn, I was tired. The thermos lay on the seat next to me. I unscrewed the cap. The liquid was the same milky-blue color I'd seen in the fire-lit kitchen, even though it was at the bottom of the dark thermos. It was as though it had one color, no matter what light hit it.

For a moment I was tempted to gulp it down. Wasn't that what people did on hot summer days? I swirled it around the cup instead. Whatever this was, it had been sealed in an iron container for decades, possibly longer, and I didn't even like to drink a Coke that had been left out open overnight.

I poured a little into my cupped hand. It pooled like mercury—although it obviously wasn't that—but even stranger was the thin line of milky blue that connected the stuff in my hand with the stuff in the now upright thermos.

It wouldn't be divided. It flowed like a liquid but held together. I was glad I hadn't drunk it. I still had my ghost knife, of course, but I left it in my pocket. I suspected that using it against this "clue" was another bad idea.

Now that I was touching the stuff—looking at it, too—I could feel the weird absence of it again. It was almost as if it wasn't really there.

Actually, that wasn't quite right. Just as the drapes' portals were openings to another place, this liquid looked like an *intrusion* from another place. It felt oddly like it was pressing against me—against everything around me.

I was getting used to receiving strange impressions from magic, but I wished I understood them better.

The tiny pool of liquid in my hand swirled and rippled. I peered closer, trying to see what was making it move. Was something alive in there, but so small that I couldn't see it?

I should have poured it back into the thermos, but I didn't. There was something about the way it flowed upward from my hand to the thermos and back again that captured my attention. I was entranced.

My thoughts began to run free, growing and changing into something alien. It was as if they'd broken out of shackles that I hadn't known were there. My mind felt huge and monstrous . . .

Then the world turned to darkness.

For a moment I thought I'd gone blind. A strange whistling trill of panic blasted at me from somewhere, and the weird echo it made told me I wasn't in the Hummer anymore. I made myself still, trying to figure out what had happened. Where had that sound come from? What was I seeing?

Because I was seeing *something*, but I couldn't get a mental grip on what it was. I could feel myself floating. Once, years before, I'd cast a spell that had sent me into the Empty Spaces. I'd floated then, too, but I could still see dark mist against an even darker background, huge predators gliding past, and whole worlds spinning below, obscured by darkness.

This wasn't that. I could hear a continuous, confused trilling, and there were moving shapes nearby. I tried to reach forward with my hands, hoping to grab the steering wheel of Francois's stupid Hummer, but there was nothing in front of me.

The shapes moved away, and I realized I was perceiving them with senses that were completely new. It was as though I was seeing and feeling them at once, and not just the edges, either. I almost laughed, and the trilling suddenly changed.

The noise was coming from me; with a sudden, dreamlike certainty, I understood that it was an expression of my own thoughts—my confusion, analysis, and emotional responses. I was broadcasting like a radio tower.

I forced myself to be silent, which wasn't easy. My "arms" wavered in front of me like the tails of kites, if kite tails had large hooks on their ends. The other shapes had long arms with hooks for hands, but they kept them around their middles.

The shapes were round and soft, and they floated by without paying me much notice. Only one, darker and more dense than the others, approached me. It trilled a greeting, and hearing its voice was like thinking its thoughts. I knew my vision had changed, but obviously my hearing had as well.

It was surprisingly easy to send a greeting in return; I only had to think it without trying to hold it back. The sound left me and became a thought in the other creature's head.

I was dreaming, obviously. Only a dream—and a fucked-up one at that—would have this kind of absurd certainty.

The dark, dense creature opposite me thought a warning into me, letting me know that calling someone unreal or absurd was a serious insult. I sent back an apology.

It moved away from me, trilling a burst of notes that told me it was my host and I should stay close. I complied without hesitation. Having someone else's words appear in my mind as though they were my own thoughts made for a damn compelling request. After a moment of trying out my new body, I floated in its trail.

I was getting used to my new perceptions. I sensed that my host was dark and dense because he was scarred. I realized, with the sudden certainty that you get in a dream, that he'd fought in a war. My host had hooked arms, too, but only six of them. I had nine. I felt a twinge of envy at that, but it felt like someone else's emotion and I held it in.

I willed my arms to wrap around my midsection the way my host wrapped his, tucking them in place. It was probably bad manners to walk around with sharp blades at the ready, like walking through a shopping mall with a bowie knife in your hand. Other creatures like us floated by, trilling conversations about math that I couldn't understand.

A sudden stabbing pain in my guts startled me. Was I sick? I slowed down. My host matched my new pace and played a short melody of sympathy. I knew immediately that this body was dying, and it was impossible to tell the difference between my host's pity and self-pity.

What kind of screwed-up dream turned other people's opinion of you into your own thoughts? I didn't want to be here anymore. Maybe it would be better to wake up in the Hummer now.

We quickly reached a narrow opening in the ground. To my dream senses it was as impenetrable as any well or cave. My host told me to enter. Before I realized that it had been his thought, not mine, I was too close. Suction caught hold of me and dragged me inside, into the darkness.

Then I popped out like a kid at the bottom of a slide. I scuffed along the gritty stone floor and painfully managed to rise into the air again. My host popped out of the tube behind me with more grace. I felt clumsy and vulnerable, and that made me angry.

My host asked if I was well, and I snapped back that I was fine. It wasn't offended. Maybe that's what it meant for one of these creatures to go to war; it'd had other people's dying thoughts in its head without dying itself.

It led me down a tunnel into a room as large as a tennis court. I stopped just inside the entrance at the top of a long slope. Indirect "light" shone through gaps in the wall, but the room was dim to my dream senses.

Then other creatures like me entered the room, although the dim light made them little more than silhouettes. They filed in from somewhere, casually falling into ranks like soldiers.

God, it was so much like the food bank in Washaway that I couldn't breathe. My dream body wanted to broadcast my panic but held it in. I'd had dozens of nightmares about the pets—no, *people*—I killed in Washaway, but none of them had been like this. This was too much. I backed toward the entrance.

One of the creatures moved toward me just the way the pets had, and I lost control.

The hooks around my torso untwined, and a loud trill whistled out of me. I knew I was beaming fear, fury, and the memory of what I'd done in Washaway directly into the minds of the creatures below me. I backed away from them, holding my "arms" out like a cobra's hood to warn them away.

They fell into a panic, crowding toward the exits and trilling in fear.

My host came toward me and, over the blare of panic and confusion, unleashed a single blast of noise. It was almost above my range of hearing, and it turned my mind into a still, dark nothingness.

I awoke in the same alien body, feeling myself being pulled down the hall. I felt the gritty stone floor and suddenly knew that this wasn't a dream—it wasn't a vision. I was here, somehow, in this body and in this place. The liquid I'd found in that statue had transported me here, and . . .

My host loomed above me. It placed a single barb on the center of my body and at the same moment made a sound like a soothing, sustained note. It was telling me I had nothing to fear, unless I lashed out. I understood and was still.

Then it asked for the story at the source of my fear, and the tones it used were impossible to resist. I answered, and the sounds that came out of me told everything—every nuance—in a startlingly short time. It felt like opening up my mind.

My host kept putting questions into me, and I kept responding. I couldn't hold back. These creatures didn't seem to understand secrets, and they certainly didn't understand shame.

It stole my entire life story within ten minutes, maybe less. I tried to make it stop, but it pressed its long spike a little harder against my flesh and urged me on. It couldn't understand that it was *taking* something from me.

Then it promised to "fix" me.

It told me that I could keep my memory of the pets—of the *people* I'd killed, but it was going to erase the awful feelings that came with it. It couldn't grasp why humans felt guilt or shame, and it was certain I'd be better off without it.

The Twenty Palace Society would make me its new poster boy.

No, I told it. No. I was a human being and I didn't want to be changed into something else.

It said I was too damaged to make this choice for myself.

I swung one of my hooked arms at it, aiming for its center. I knew my attack was feeble, but I didn't expect to kill the creature. I expected the creature to kill me.

And that's what it did. There was a sudden sharp pain as the hook went in, then I was back inside the Hummer, staring down at the milky-blue liquid in my hand.

I carefully poured the liquid into the thermos and twisted the lid back on. I set the thermos into the cup holder. Spilling any of it would be a terrible thing. Terrible.

Then I began to scream.

I didɴ'т scream for long. For one thing, it didn't make me feel better, not even a little bit. For another, it was a waste of time. I had predators in the back of my car. I didn't have time to freak out.

I looked over at the thermos on the seat next to me. What the hell had just happened?

There was a sudden knock on my window. A chubby guy with a thick Vandyke was standing by my door.

The windows on the Hummer were electric, and I didn't want to fumble with the controls trying to lower them—that would be a sure sign that the vehicle wasn't mine. I opened the door a crack.

"Hey, man," he said. "You okay?"

And here I thought nobody in L.A. cared. "No," I answered. "I just got fired."

"Oh. Um . . ."

"Thanks for asking."

He accepted that and, his good deed accomplished, walked away. I was going to have to be more careful where I had my meltdowns.

I put my hand on the key in the ignition, then put it back into my lap. Where was I going to go? I had no plan, and no idea where to find Wally, Arne, or the others. I picked up the thermos again.

The liquid inside had sent me to some other place. Not the Empty Spaces, though—there was no air, no stone chambers, no caves there. It was all mists and nothingness. Another planet? This planet in the distant past or far future? I had no way to know for sure. What I did know is that those creatures were going to put thoughts into my head.

I have the Book of Oceans. The realization hit me like a medicine ball in the gut. The statue wasn't a clue; it was a container. Every sorcerer and wannabe sorcerer in the world was looking for this, and 98 percent of them would be willing to nuke the city and sift the ashes for it.

Annalise wanted it most of all. The Twenty Palace Society was fading without its spell books; it was losing ground against sorcerers who summoned predators. If Annalise got her hands on this, she'd share it with the other peers. She'd share it with Csilla.

And she'd killed Lino without a second thought. She'd threatened the boat captain's son. She wasn't as big an asshole as Wally or Ansel Zahn, but could I hand over the spell book to her?

Hell, no.

I gripped the steering wheel with my left hand, rubbing it against the leather. That was my skin, touching. My face itched from the sweat and heat. My hair was damp. It felt good to be back in my own bones, and I was tempted to step out into the parking lot to dance, just to make sure everything worked. And yet, I could still feel those nine hooks wrapped snug around my middle, like phantom limbs.

I closed my eyes and tried to remember how I'd "seen" in my vision. Those alien creatures had been about to tell me something important. They'd brought me to that private place, and they were all about to share something with me at once.

Maybe that's how the original spell books worked—they didn't really give you visions, they sent you out of your body, where those *things* dumped the knowledge of the universe into your brain the way I'd throw old newspapers into a recycling bin. And Christ, they'd almost given that knowledge to me.

I set the thermos on the seat next to me, but when I realized I was about to belt it in, I moved it to the cup holder. The L.A. River was just a few blocks away. I could dump the contents of the thermos into the thin stream and watch it flow out to the Pacific. Hell, I could take the advice I gave Dale and stuff the whole thermos into a trash can by the curb. The book would vanish into a landfill somewhere.

Would that be enough to get it away from everyone, including myself? Part of the reason I wanted to trash it was that I wanted it so much. "Reading" the Book of Oceans would turn me into a primary, one of the most powerful sorcerers in the world. I would live for centuries. I could go back to Hammer Bay and destroy the predator I'd left behind. I could do things I couldn't even imagine.

But if I didn't trust Annalise with that much power, I certainly didn't trust myself. Not that I was sure those aliens would accept me if I tried again. I laughed, and the sound echoed in the confines of the SUV. I hadn't lied to the chubby guy after all. My alien host had taken me into a room to become a full sorcerer, and I'd gotten myself fired.

I was going to have to get by on what abilities I already had . . .

And suddenly I knew where to go. Wally had said: *I know a little desert retreat that's going to be abandoned soon.* Arne had "broken into" a building in the desert—a building with security cameras on the outside—to steal that Bugatti, but he hadn't bothered to go invisible first. The building must have been his.

And once Arne vanished into the Empty Spaces . . .

I started the engine and pulled out of the parking lot. I drove aimlessly for ten full minutes, trying to remember the best way to get to the 15. Francois had been right all along; Arne was ransoming the man's car back to him, not recovering it.

I followed the 15 through Barstow into the desert. Somewhere out here was the turnoff to that little dirt road and metal warehouse, and I spent at least twenty minutes convinced that I'd missed it when it suddenly appeared in front of me.

To my right was the Mohave. To my left, across the median and the westbound lanes, was the dirt road. If I was lucky, I'd also find the circle Wally had used to summon the drapes. It was the only way he'd know about the building. I hoped.

Traffic was thin. I slowed and swerved onto the dirt median. When the way was clear, I drove across the westbound lanes onto the raised gravel pathway. Once I passed the rough ground by the dry stream, the gravel gave way to a dirt track.

After about a mile, I passed the spot where I'd spied on Arne, then came to the fenced gate. It was standing open, always a bad sign. A battered sign on the chain-link read QUAKEWATER REFRIGERATOR RECYCLING. I drove straight to the run-down sheet-metal building.

A piece of yellow metal stood out from the far corner, and I decided it would be best to drive around the building once, just in case a SWAT team was hiding back there. As I came closer, I saw that the cameras were pointing right at me, and that the front doors, each as wide as an airplane-hangar door, were wide open.

I drove down the path and coasted by the open doors. It was dark inside, unsurprisingly, and all I could see was a concrete floor and a row of unlit headlights.

Then it was once around the building. On the far side from the gate, I saw a digging machine, almost certainly stolen. There was a scraper on one end and a scoop on the other. Behind the building was a low berm that prevented me from driving out into the desert, which I didn't want to do anyway. The dirt out there had been disturbed in a few places, as though someone was digging for treasure.

At the front of the building, I turned the Hummer around and backed in. I was barely inside before a tremendous anxiety washed through me—I couldn't turn my back to all that darkness. I jumped from the vehicle and wandered into the room, wishing I had kept Lino's gun. I kept my hand close to my ghost knife.

Once I was out of the sun, the room didn't seem so dark. Against the far wall was a row of cars, mostly German makes. Those were always popular in South America, and Arne made most of his real money with them. In the dimly lit corner at the far right of the building was a small workbench and a radio playing norteño music. God, I hated those accordions.

To the left was a set of desks and tables, including a much larger bench covered with tools. There was also a huge blue plastic water jug mounted atop a cooler.

Against the right wall, off into the darkness, was a red circle on the floor.

I moved toward it. It had been made with red paint—in fact, an open bucket was set in the corner—and it was much bigger than I'd anticipated, more than fifteen feet across.

There were sigils along the inner ring. I compared them to the ones on the back of my hand, but they were not the same, of course. These were rounder and more filled with open space . . . which was appropriate, I guessed.

This was it. This was where Wally brought the drapes into our world, and killed my friends.

Time to work. I went to the tool area and found a long-handled shovel. The blade was sharp and heavy; it could kill someone if I put my back into it, but it was too crude. I kept searching, but the best option I found was a long flat-head screwdriver. There was duct tape, too, which would suffocate someone, but no. That's an ugly way to die.

Then I noticed a little shelf loaded with soup cans and packages labeled MRE. They were army rations; I could only wonder where Arne had stolen them. Beside them, in the back corner, was a knife block. I found a long, sharp boning knife there. It would have to do.

I got into the Hummer and backed it closer to the circle but not too close. I didn't want any part of it extending over the red paint when I opened the back hatch.

I opened the rear door and laid my hand on something I couldn't see. I caught hold of it—it felt like an arm—and pulled it toward me. My skin began to itch, but that couldn't be helped. I jostled the body until I managed to roll it onto its back and grasp it under the arms. As I dragged it, it whispered.

I jumped back, startled. Had the drapes learned to talk? I heard the sound again, and it didn't sound like something a drape would make. It sounded terribly human.

I leaned in close to listen. It was Potato Face's voice, and he was begging me to kill him.

I hauled him out of the vehicle, doing my best to keep him from flopping onto the concrete floor. He still fell heavily, and I apologized to him. I knew he was in terrible pain, and maybe thumping his heels on the ground was minor by comparison, but I owed him a bit of dignity before I did what I had to do.

I dragged him across the red circle, then set him down and checked the paint. It was undamaged. My brain was working quickly, and I didn't try to slow it down. How much time did I have before these men started dying? It could have been two weeks, or it could have been two minutes. I had no way to know, except that they'd been stuck in the back of a car for hours in desert heat, so probably not two weeks.

But I couldn't put them all into the circle at once. If I did, the first to die would drag the others into the Empty Spaces. If Wally was right about there being no death there, those four men would never have an end to their suffering.

So it would have to be one at a time. I taped the knife to the butt of the shovel handle. I probably used more tape than necessary, but I didn't want it to fall into the void.

Then I took a handful of dirty rags out of a bucket. I was ready, even though I really, really wasn't.

I laid my makeshift spear on the ground outside the circle. Then I found Potato's body and felt around for his throat. Once I had that, I laid one of the dirty rags near it, pointing away like a beam of light from a kindergartener's drawing of the sun.

Then I went outside the circle and hefted the shovel. The first time I'd killed someone in cold blood, Annalise had been standing over me. This time, I couldn't even see the guy's face. It didn't make things easier.

I slid the knife forward just above the ground. I suddenly felt resistance and shoved forward, sawing back and forth. I hoped I was hitting him just below the ear—that's where I pointed with the towel, at least. But I couldn't see blood. I couldn't see anything.

There were no sounds, either. I yanked the shovel handle back, pulling it outside the circle. The blade was clean, but . . .

A portal suddenly opened. There was no buzzing or cracking noise this time. The entire floor inside the red circle just vanished. The shop rag fluttered down into the Empty Spaces.

A swarm of drapes flooded up through the hole, swirling at the edges of the circle but unable to cross it. I stepped back to see how high they could go. It looked to be about twelve feet, well below the ceiling above.

I stepped back farther. It was like looking at a giant aquarium filled with drapes instead of water—minus the aquarium. I didn't want to be anywhere near it.

With my ghost knife in hand, I watched them swarm, hoping the circle could hold them all and knowing there was little I could do if it didn't. It held, and after a few seconds, the drapes dropped out of our world and the floor reappeared. From off in the corner, a man sang in Spanish about love and death, with accordion and sax accompanying him.

The next man wasn't easier, but it was quicker. I made sure to turn him the other way so the knife would enter below his left ear rather than his right. I had the idea that that would make it quicker, and I was right.

When the drapes swarmed in again, I turned my back on them and went for the third man, because fuck them. They scared the crap out of me, and I was tired of being afraid.

My hands were itching badly. The watercooler was just across the room, but I didn't wash the slime away. It seemed right that I should suffer during this job. These men were. Somewhere, somehow, I'd acquired a taste for penance.

Once the last man had vanished into the Empty Spaces, I walked to the back of the room toward the watercooler. It was half full. I dribbled the water over my hands and forearms; the slime the drapes left behind vanished at the water's touch, but my skin was still raw. Sweat ran down my back. The radio played another song with lyrics I couldn't understand. I felt terribly, painfully lonely and, at the same time, grateful to be alone while I worked.

"Is that what you plan for us?"

I yelped and jumped to the side, backing against the wall. A push broom and other long-handled wooden tools clattered to the floor.

It was Fidel. He was three feet from me, scratching furiously at his neck. He'd stripped down to a sleeveless undershirt and those fancy green linen suit pants. I didn't like the bitter, desperate smile on his face.

Summer and Ty appeared beside him. Summer's expression was fierce, but her eyes were red, as though she'd been crying. Ty gaped at me.

"Let me ask again, Ray." Fidel's voice was quiet. "Is that what you planned for us all along?"

"We could see them," Ty said. He held his injured shoulder high and his arm close to his chest. The burn must have been bothering him badly. "Mostly. We know what they were."

"And you killed them," Fidel said. He scratched furiously at his arm. Summer did the same. "I didn't think you had it in you, baby. But why did you put them in that summoning circle, hey? You calling up more of these creatures?"

"That's not what the circle is for," I said, but Summer didn't let me continue.

"You tried to stop that woman from hurting Bud, but you weren't trying to save his life. Right? You just wanted to kill him here so you could call up more of these things."

"Summer—"

"I'm right, Ray. Just admit that I'm right."

"You don't understand," I said. "As soon as that symbol wears off, you're going to be like those guys I pulled out of the SUV. How long have you been itching?" Summer stopped scratching her arm.

Ty glanced at Fidel. "He said they would start eating us."

"What bullshit," Fidel said.

"Once you're dead, they carry you away and let more into our world. If you die outside the circle—"

"This is bullshit, Ray!"

"They get loose!" I shouted at him. "And they do this to other people!"

"Fuck other people!" Fidel leaned into my face. "I got to watch out for myself!"

I almost said: *There's nothing left of you to see*, but I didn't. He'd backed himself into a dangerous spot, and he couldn't see a way out. I sympathized.

Ty's expression was uncertain. I thought I'd had him convinced that the drape was killing him, but it was pretty clear he wanted to be unconvinced. He was still looking for a way out. "Did Arne tell you to say that?"

"Where is Arne?"

Fidel and Summer rolled their eyes. Ty said: "He said we should meet him up here. He said he could make things right."

Arne had brought them running to him by giving them false hope. Maybe I should have done the same thing. Maybe I should have lied. It would have been easier than this.

But what had I expected? They weren't going to line up inside the circle like victims of a firing squad.

"Ray." Fidel's voice was low and urgent. "Did your good friend Wally make you bulletproof?"

"No," I blurted out with more anger than I'd intended.

"It wouldn't work anyway," Ty said.

"What wouldn't work?" I asked.

"Ain't nobody else offering another plan, so why not?" Fidel said. "Where did you get that magic, Raymundo? Hey? How did you get so well protected? Who hooked you up?"

Damn. He wanted a closed-way spell to protect him from the drape. "It won't work, believe me."

Fidel sighed and turned to Summer. "He don't know how to answer a question."

Summer glared at me. "Maybe we should raise our voices."

"Guys, these creatures are in your mouths and down your—"

"I got a better idea," Fidel said, raising his voice to talk over me. "Ray might be bulletproof, but we can all see he'll still take a beating, hey?" He stepped over to the table and picked up a hammer.

Oh, shit. He snatched a screwdriver off the workbench and tossed it to Summer. She caught it, and they both vanished.

Ty gave me a helpless look, and he vanished, too.

I grabbed a tool from the wall behind me—it was a curved metal piece at the end of a twenty-foot wooden handle—and swung it. The metal tip struck something soft, and I backed along the wall. I swung the handle again, this time not hitting anything except wall.

The radio at the far end of the room suddenly switched off.

In the silence, I listened for footsteps. Nothing. I moved toward the middle of the floor, which maybe wasn't a good idea, but it was the only way to get to the Hummer.

I swung the handle again. They were keeping their distance. Good. I glanced at the metal piece and realized it was used to open and close the transom windows at the top of the wall.

Not that it mattered. I swung again, struck something at two o'clock, then swung overhand at that spot.

I hit nothing but concrete, breaking off the metal tip. The splintered wood and metal end flipped up and over my shoulder—too high to hit me, but I ducked away from it just as something struck the outside edge of my ear.

I snapped my head to the side; it felt like my ear had been torn off. I didn't pause to check it, though. I swung the broken handle, and it moved much faster now that it was shorter. I struck something and heard Fidel grunt in pain.

Then something dull scraped against my shoulder blade.

I stabbed backward with the splintered end of the wood, but I missed whoever it was behind me—Summer? Which was a good thing, since we weren't even close to the red circle yet.

I sidestepped, swinging the handle low in a full circle. Summ hissed when I hit her shin. Contact. I charged at her, my arms wide to make sure I caught her.

I did, by her hair. She yelped in pain and I felt a sudden rush of shame. I had to kill her, but I didn't want to hurt her. Was this how Wally felt?

Whatever. I caught her around the neck and knocked her to the floor. I couldn't see her, but I could feel that she was facing away from me. I guessed she had the screwdriver in her right hand and grappled for it blindly. It clattered to the floor.

Scuffling footsteps approached from behind. I wrenched Summer off the floor and spun to put her between me and whoever was getting close. Nothing bashed my skull open.

Sweat stung my eyes as I backed toward the red circle. If I could get her inside, I could use my ghost knife on her. The drape would kill her, quickly, and that would be that. It would almost be like mercy.

But she was struggling furiously, and even though I was stronger and heavier, I couldn't contain her. She was fighting for her life, and in my heart I wanted her to win.

Ty became visible in the middle of the room; his expression had so much sorrow in it that it stole my energy away and I stopped fighting.

Summer tore free of my grip. "Fuck!" she shouted, letting herself become visible. "This is bullshit."

"Yeah," Fidel said from just behind her. He became visible, too. "Let's try shooting some more."

Summer moved her hand toward her lower back. I grabbed her and half lifted, half shoved her into Fidel. We were too far from the red circle for me to try to wrestle her inside, not if people were drawing guns.

I sprinted toward the open door. The Hummer was right there, but there was no time to get in, start the engine, and pull away.

A barrel beside the door suddenly toppled on its side, and a wash of dirty black oil flowed toward me. I jumped, clearing it before it spread too far, and landed in the doorway.

I went through the doorway and turned the corner out of sight. A gunshot went off, but I didn't feel any sudden, crippling pain, and I didn't fall over dead.

At the corner of the building, I crouched behind the digger. No one came out of the building—not that I could see, anyway—but if someone did, the machine would give me some cover.

Who had tipped over that barrel? I hadn't seen anyone, but Ty had been at the other end of the room, by the toolbench, and I'd just left Summer and Fidel behind me.

It had to be Arne. If it wasn't, there was another person running around with a drape, and I didn't want to think about that. Had he turned off the radio, too?

Was he helping me?

I still couldn't see anyone leaving the building, and I thought I would at least see a smear of oil or loose dirt stirred up by their footsteps, even if they were invisible.

There. A smear of black appeared on the concrete lip of the building foundation, then a scuff of dirt.

The footsteps headed toward the gate, away from me. I scrabbled toward the back of the building.

The ground was packed hard with a fine layer of dirt on top. I sprinted across the open area in back of the building, my feet scraping through the faint tracks Francois's Hummer had laid down. Would they be able to find me with those footprints? They looked pretty faint, but I didn't like the idea of leaving a trail. Not that I had a choice.

I scrambled over the top of the berm and slid down the other side. This dirt was loose, as though it had been moved recently, but it was the nearest cover. I left huge footprints, but the dirt would stop a bullet.

There was a deep, broad hole in front of me. I hopped over it, but the dirt crumbled. I tipped into the hole, landing on my hands and knees.

I heard flies buzzing, and that smell . . . The hole was just a bit over five feet long, and right beside me was someone stretched out, lying in wait.

My throat was too tight to let me scream; instead I hissed like a leaky bicycle tire. I panicked for a moment, convinced that Ty or Summer had gotten here before me and was stretched out with a gun trained on me.

But they weren't. The figure beside me wasn't moving at all. I leaned closer to it, to the smell and the flies, and I saw that it was Francois. He had been shot once in the head.

"You're lucky," Arne said from somewhere nearby. I spun and saw him crouching in the open space above me. "Some of the older holes have rattlesnakes in them."

He extended his hand. I clasped it, letting him lift me out of the hole. He stood upright, visible above the top of the berm beside us. I stood upright, too.

He slapped a .38 revolver into my hand. "Don't get busted with this."

I opened the cylinder. One round had been fired—and I was pretty sure I knew where that bullet was—leaving five shots. For all the good it would do me.

"I can't use this."

"Oh no?" Arne gave me a look that was difficult to read. "I thought that was what you did now."

"It is," I said, hating the words as they came out of my mouth. I had never admitted it aloud before. Arne was still giving me that look. "But I can't kill them unless I can get them in the circle first. Otherwise—"

"No need to explain. I know. I was in the building, too." He scratched at his neck, then lowered his hand with a visible exertion of will. "I saw."

"You can see them when they're invisible?" It was hard to believe

he was really on my side. It seemed impossible that he'd help me, knowing that I would have to kill him, too.

He broke eye contact, looking toward the building as though scanning for the others. "Yeah, if I really concentrate." If he saw something,
he didn't say. "Well, I said I would help you with your thing when I was
done with mine, didn't I?" He waved toward Francois's corpse. "I have
one more problem to bury, but I guess I won't have time for that."

I looked away, determined not to think about patches of disturbed
dirt behind me. "I didn't know," I said.

"I didn't want you to know. There are some problems that can
only be solved by a grave in the desert, but I couldn't trust you with
that. Don't take that hard; I couldn't trust anyone."

Graves. And I had thought that disturbed dirt had come from digging for treasure.

We heard the sound of an engine, a low-horsepower motorbike approaching. I grabbed Arne's elbow and pulled him low, so we were just
peeking over the berm. The bike came into view and passed through the
gate. It was a small thing, baby blue, with the minimum cc's necessary
for highway travel.

Wally was riding it. His green sweats had been replaced by a pair of
huge purple M. C. Hammer pants and a gigantic dashiki. His left hand
was encased in a mitten, and he had a pair of expensive mountain-
climbing shades on.

I pulled Arne all the way down out of sight. He resisted at first, then
turned invisible. I caught his elbow and looked at him, shaking my head
at where I hoped his face was. *I can see with more than just light.*

I sat with my back against the dirt, silently cursing at myself. I'd
known Wally wasn't dead—yeah, his injuries would have killed most
people, including me, but I had learned to expect a certain *toughness*
from the people the society went after.

But I didn't want him here. I still didn't know what I was going to
do about Fidel and Summer—putting Wally on the to-do list just made
me feel tired.

The scooter engine idled. Was Wally coming over the berm at me? I
took my ghost knife from my pocket and held it in my right hand.
Arne's gun was in my left. I was as ready for him as I'd ever be, and that
wasn't ready enough.

Then the engine started again, and I heard the bike putter away.
The sound became muffled as it moved to the other side of the building, then shut off.

I turned to Arne, who had become visible again. "Shall we?" We
stood.

"Ray, two things." Arne took a deep breath and scratched furiously at his neck for a second or two. The drape must have been getting to him. "First, I saw the way you did those five guys in there. I want you to make it quick for me, too. Humane. Okay?" I nodded. He looked out over the desert. "Second thing, about Jasmin . . ."

Damn. Was he going to apologize, finally, for stealing my girlfriend while I was in prison? It didn't seem like the time, but part of me was hungry for it.

"She's relying on you to stop these things." He wouldn't look at me. "You're the guy who handles this stuff, right? That's what Wally said, anyway. Jasmin—my daughter—needs you to clean this mess up, okay?"

I almost laughed at myself. Had I really expected him to apologize? Shame washed over me like a wave. Arne didn't give a damn about my hurt feelings; he had more important things to think about.

So did I. "Okay," I answered. He vanished.

And so did I, in a way. My fears, my guilt over the crimes I committed in Washaway, my desire to do the right thing, whatever that was, all seemed to shrink down so small that I couldn't even tell they were there.

Arne's clarity had copied itself onto me. Wally was here, along with all my remaining friends, and best of all, they'd brought their predators with them. It was as if they'd gathered together in one place as a gift, to give me another chance to murder them all.

There was a scuff of dirt to my left; Arne was circling the building.

I crept toward the back corner. The radio and workbench should have been just on the other side of that wall, along with the line of stolen cars.

I took out my ghost knife and cut a horizontal stroke across the sheet metal an inch above the ground and again two feet higher. Then I sliced two vertical lines and caught the panel gently as it fell to me.

I ducked low and eased myself inside, nearly hitting my head on the rear bumper of a black Lexus LX 570. I stayed low, creeping along the bumper toward the bench. The red circle was a few feet from the front fender, just ahead on my left.

People were talking. I raised my head to peer through the Lexus's windshield. The driver's-side window was busted, and I caught the faint, nasty stink of old cigarette smoke.

Wally stood in the center of the room, facing away from me. The red circle was several yards to his left. Fidel, Summer, and Ty all faced him. Any of them could have seen my silhouette just by glancing over at me, but they were too focused on Wally.

The high, metal ceiling created muffling echoes; I couldn't make out what they were saying, but it sounded as though Fidel and Ty were trying to convince Wally that they could be useful to him. Wally's answers were mild, and the others seemed to find them frustrating.

I backed away from the window and bumped against the bench. Jars behind me rattled like wind chimes, and I dropped to the concrete floor.

The Lexus had a high clearance, but the car beside it was a Dodge Viper. A pair of black sneakers—Summer's, I was sure—moved toward me, then stopped. If she took a few paces to her right, she would see me.

After five long seconds, Fidel spat out a string of curses, and she went back to the others.

I eased into a crouch and turned around. A disordered row of mason jars stood on the long, pressure-board table. I took two of them, choosing ones that were empty and had lids. Then I set them carefully on the concrete.

I edged a little higher, peeking into the Lexus. There, in the cup holder behind the gearshift, was a Bic lighter.

I wanted it, but there was no way to open the door and get it without everyone hearing. And although the window was already broken, the lighter was out of reach. I was going to have to lean in with my whole head and shoulders.

Summer and Ty were focused on Wally, but I could see their faces. If I made too big a movement, I'd catch their attention, and I wasn't ready for that. I crouched down, unsure what to do.

"You're being ridiculous!" Wally suddenly said in a loud, clear voice. "I can see you, you know."

My hands immediately went to Arne's gun in my waistband and my ghost knife. But it was Arne who spoke next. "So you can. So what? You're still an asshole."

I peeked through the SUV's windshield again. Arne was standing by the doorway, and everyone had turned their backs to me to face him.

I lunged through the open window, grabbed the lighter, and ducked out of sight again. No one yelled out my name or shouted "What was that!" I snatched a rag off the floor, grabbed both jars, and scurried behind the Lexus.

Arne stood in the sunlight, talking shit at Wally. The urge to stop what I was doing and listen was strong. It was stupid, too, so I ignored it.

The underside of the Lexus had skid plates on it, for reasons known only to the idiot who'd bought them, and I couldn't remember where the gas tank was. Beside it, the Viper was too low to the ground to fit the large jars beneath it comfortably. The third vehicle was a silver Audi A8. I unscrewed the lids and set them aside, then crawled under it. At the other end of the building, Arne talked a fast patter of insult and abuse at Wally, who only laughed in response.

With my ghost knife, I cut the corner of the Audi's tank. Gas streamed into a jar. The noise seemed unbearably loud to me, but Arne raised his voice, seemingly in anger.

Damn. He was holding their attention. He was acting as my wooden man.

It didn't take long for the first jar to fill. I swapped it for the second, then used my ghost knife to cut a small gap in the metal lids. I slashed the rag in half and began stuffing the pieces into the gap.

The gasoline slowed to a trickle and ran out when the second jar was two-thirds full. The tank had less than half a gallon in it. Arne must have drained the tanks after stashing the vehicles here. I screwed on the lids.

I was still afraid. I hated to admit it, but I was. But Arne was running out of time, too, and I couldn't let Wally kill him, not outside the circle. I set jars beside one another so the rags would touch, then I lit them.

"For God's sake!" Arne yelled, his tirade getting louder. "You should have gone and gotten yourself laid, you stupid shit!"

I stood and threw the ghost knife.

It zipped across the room silently. Wally, Fidel, Ty, and Summer had no idea it was coming, but Arne saw it and, not knowing what it was, jumped aside at the last moment.

The spell struck Wally in the back of his neck. His skin split open, and from the other side of him where the exit wound would be, a huge splatter of thick green gushed out of him.

I *reached* for the spell. It passed through Wally's chest, causing another splash of nasty green liquid. He started choking, then collapsed onto his knees.

The ghost knife returned to my hand all slimy. I stuffed it into my pocket, knowing I'd be burning these pants soon.

"No!" Fidel yelled. "We need him!"

Fidel ran at me, reaching into his waistband.

I bent down and reached around the flaming wick. The fire was scorching, but I wouldn't be holding it long. I straightened and threw the jar across the room.

It landed just short of Wally's foot. Flaming liquid splashed up onto his back and sloshed around his leg. I grabbed the second jar—not so carefully this time, because Fidel was getting close—and threw it on instinct.

This time my throw was perfect. The jar shattered between his calves, and the fire roared under his crotch and belly. Wally went up like a bonfire.

I couldn't see Fidel, but I could hear his scuffling shoes nearby. A tiny black hole appeared in front of me, and just as I realized I was looking at a gun barrel, it went off.

I didn't feel the bullet strike. Fidel did, though. He turned visible, not three feet away. There was blood on the front of his shirt, and his mouth fell open. His bullet had hit me over my heart, then ricocheted back through his breastbone.

He dropped the gun and collapsed onto the floor. I shouted his name and grabbed his shirt, hoisting him up again. His eyes grew dim, but he had enough life in him to look at me hopefully, as though I could save him somehow.

I lifted him as high as I could, his drape eating at the skin of my hands, then bum-rushed him between the cars toward the red circle. I bumped against something I couldn't see, but it only took a moment to regain my balance and momentum.

Fidel sighed and his eyes closed just as I crossed the line with him. I dumped him onto the concrete—not gently, but he was already dead—and leaped back across the red line.

The drape carried him away and brought another huge swarm into our world. The red circle held them until they fled.

God, I was tired. I was drenched in sweat and had no energy left.

Ty stood by the grill of the Viper, Fidel's gun in his hand. He bared his teeth at me. "I didn't want this, Ray."

"I know you didn't."

He walked across the front of the car toward the Lexus, circling me and scowling. He could lift that gun in a moment, but my ghost knife was in my pocket and Arne's gun was back in my waistband. We weren't going to have a quick draw.

I glanced at the others. Arne had turned invisible again—or he'd run. Wally was rolling in green slime, trying to extinguish the flames. It was working, too, a little. Summer stood in the middle of the room, a look of blank shock on her face. She'd gone as far as she could go. She was done.

I turned back to Ty just as he stepped across the edge of the red circle. I reached for my waistband, hungry for the chance to kill my friend.

Ty pointed Fidel's gun at his head.

"I didn't want this," he said. "I had plans, Ray! I had plans!"

"We all give up our—" The gunshot cut me off. He didn't hear me. He'd already pulled the trigger. I watched his drape carry him away.

I turned to the others. Wally was on his feet. A long black tentacle stretched across the room and pulled the watercooler tank off its base, then held it over his head. Stale water gushed over him, extinguishing most of the flames. His left hand burned like a torch at the end of his arm. He slapped at his shoulder with it, trying to put it out. He looked smaller.

Wally's face was a horror of blackened flesh. "Dammit, Ray," he said, his voice as clear as ever. "You really are a pain in the ass."

I had no idea how he was talking with that scorched and ruined throat. Maybe his voice was a hallucination and had been since we met at the Sugar Shaker.

"Well, your ass is such a big target—"

"Shut up, dude. Seriously. I had to eat a *whole family* to heal the injuries your boss gave me. Now I'm going to have to do it again, and that's on you."

A tentacle suddenly shot out of his belly and wrapped around Summer's neck. She squawked as Wally yanked her off her feet. Wally's belly split open like a huge mouth, the roasted flesh tearing, and a green, puckered funnel that looked like a large flower petal pushed toward Summer. She tried to scream as the tentacle stuffed her into the funnel, but her neck snapped. More bones broke as Wally crammed her inside.

I backed away, goose bumps running over my whole body. It didn't seem imaginable that Wally could stuff a hundred and thirty pounds of human being into himself, but I had just seen it. His flesh seemed to fill out, and some of the blackened skin began flaking off. No portal opened beneath him. It wasn't just Summer he had killed and eaten; he'd gotten her drape, too.

"Better," he said. He rolled his neck around once to loosen it up. More black flakes fell. "Better, but not enough."

He took another step toward me.

I backed toward the Lexus, then around it to the work area. There were plenty of things there I could use as a weapon, but not against someone like him. I took out my ghost knife.

Wally laughed at it. From under his shirt, a half-dozen tendrils appeared, coiled like snakes. Would they catch my ghost knife or slap it away? I wasn't sure which would be worse.

Wally floated upward as though he was being lifted off his feet. He looked pretty startled as he tumbled onto his side. At the same moment, Arne dropped his invisibility.

Wally fell inside the red circle. Arne fell on top of him.

I already had Arne's gun in my hand. He turned toward me— maybe he wanted to say something, or maybe he wanted to meet my gaze one last time, the way friends do.

I didn't give him the chance. I put a bullet into his head.

Skull and brain splashed out of the exit wound onto Wally's ruined face. He laughed. "Oh, gross," he said, "but it's just what the doctor ordered," then made as if to lick it.

He realized his error a moment too late. The floor vanished. Wally gasped as he fell into the upsurge of drapes. I could see his gaping expression of horror dropping away, distorted through a filmy screen of fast-moving predators.

Gone. Thank God.

Suddenly, a tentacle shot out of the swirling mass of drapes, crossed the red circle, and slammed down on the hood of the Lexus. The breeze it made as it zipped by my face ruffled my hair. I stumbled back, almost falling, as a second limb shot out of the dark and lodged itself on the undercarriage.

The Lexus lurched forward, knocking me onto the ground. One of the tentacles had punched through the underbody at just the right spot to grab the front axle. A third punched through the grill and secured itself against something inside.

I jumped to my feet and slashed the ghost knife through the nearest tentacle. It parted like smoke, then joined together again. A fourth tentacle snaked under the body, and all of them flexed, pulling themselves out of the Empty Spaces.

I ran to the passenger door just as the Lexus slid forward again, straining against its brakes. Damn if I wasn't on the wrong side of the car, but there was no time to run around.

I yanked the door open and dove inside. I slammed the gearshift into neutral, then grabbed the parking-brake release.

I pressed the button and slammed it down; it let go and the Lexus wrenched forward. Metal under the hood strained and groaned. I scrambled backward, the idea of falling into the Empty Spaces in this ridiculous car giving me frantic speed. My feet hit the ground and my upper body spun as the SUV glided forward, the frame scraping across the concrete lip as the front wheels fell into the void.

Then I was out, on my hands and knees on the concrete, as the Lexus tipped into the opening and disappeared. The drapes retreated and the floor became concrete again.

Alone. I began to laugh.

CHAPTER EIGHTEEN

My laughter didn't last long. It only took a few moments before a terrible lonely silence came over me. I rolled onto my back and stared at the ceiling overhead. It would be full dark soon. Maybe I could shut my eyes and sleep on the concrete.

I stood and walked out into the center of the circle. My feet scuffed against the concrete. A sudden bout of vertigo made me stagger, as if one misstep would topple me into the void after my friends.

But of course that wasn't going to happen. The hole had sealed over and they were gone. Arne, Ty, Robbie, Summer, Bud, and, oh God, Melly . . . They had all gone down into a grave as deep as the universe, into a darkness where I could never follow, and I was left standing there breathing parched air and squinting against the light of the setting sun. The ground beneath me was unyielding, and I was alone.

Wandering through the building, I found, among other things, a suitcase with a bunch of clean unfolded laundry inside and a case of bottled water—Arne's jump bag? I stripped off my pants and tossed them aside in favor of a pair of long plaid surfer shorts. They looked stupid, but they didn't have Wally's predator puke all over them.

I rinsed the ghost knife with a couple of bottles of water. The green goop stuck to the plastic, but I managed to wipe it off on a clean spot of my ruined pants. When that was done, I tossed my pants into the oil Arne had spilled.

Arne had said he'd run out of time to finish what he had to do, and now he was dead. I walked around the building to the digger and started it up. I had no idea how to use it, but a little trial and error made the basics clear.

I lurched the machine around to the back of the building and spent the next half hour scraping loose dirt out of the berm over Francois's body. It was hard going at first, but I managed to finish just before sundown. It wouldn't fool the cops if they decided to search, of course, but I thought it would pass a casual inspection.

The building was metal and concrete; I couldn't exactly burn it down the way Annalise always did. Sure, there were plenty of flammable liquids, and cars burn real nice, but it wouldn't totally wreck the place. It would, however, draw firefighters and cops.

I found an oil pan and slid it beneath the Audi, then cut the brake line and collected the dripping fluid.

There was a shop broom by the front door. I dipped the bristles into the brake fluid and scraped it over the painted floor. While I couldn't burn the place down, I didn't have to leave a functioning circle. I scraped at it until it was nothing but faint smears of red. Then I threw a bunch of Arne's old clothes onto the floor and pushed them around with the broom until they were ruined and the circle was barely visible.

After that, I swept the spilled oil from the barrel across the floor until it washed around the green glop Wally had puked on himself. Cement building or not, that crap would have to burn. I tossed my ruined pants into the pile.

What was left?

Nothing. Nothing was left.

I went outside. The sun was well below the horizon by now. Only a faint red glow in the west remained, but the moon was overhead, and its dim white light was soothing.

I didn't want to take Francois's SUV back into town. The bodyguards who'd fled the house should have notified the police hours ago, and I didn't want to be caught in his car. Arne's Land Rover was there, and so were Fidel's and Summer's cars. There were no keys, though; those would have been in their pockets when they fell into the Empty Spaces.

The Dodge Viper, however, had the keys inside. I got behind the wheel and drove it out of the building. I siphoned enough gas from Arne's SUV to fill the tank halfway. Once I got back to the city, I'd ditch it somewhere. The cops would return it to the guy Arne stole it from—hell, I'd be doing someone a favor.

I took the coffee thermos from Francois's vehicle. The Book of Oceans was still in the bottom, but I didn't look at it very long. I wasn't ready for another "dream."

I tore the boning knife off the shovel and dropped it into the oil. Then I set fire to the oil and shut the huge doors. The building wasn't visible from the highway, and the darkness would hide whatever smoke the oil gave off. Sure, the smell would be strong, but the wind seemed to be in my favor.

Not that it mattered. The last of the green crap would be burned up by then. The rest was just details.

I drove the Viper along the gravel bed back to the highway, wondering how Arne had managed to steal gravel.

About forty feet from the shoulder of the highway, I waited until I couldn't see any headlights in either direction, then pulled out. In no time, I was up to sixty, headed back to L.A.

I went to Violet's place, partly because I didn't want to see anyone from the society right away, and partly because I wanted to see what I'd done to her life. The building was still there, and it still had a gaping hole in the side, as though a giant had put a fist through the wall.

Violet was there, too. She was leaning against the hood of her own car, smoking and staring up at the ruined apartment. I parked at the end of the block and walked up to her.

Her cigarette smelled rank, so I walked to her upwind side. "You okay?" I asked. "Where's Jasmin?"

"With my mom. They're hiding with a friend of a friend of a friend. I don't even know where they are."

"I'm glad they're okay." It was a stupid thing to say, but it felt like an obligation.

She threw her half-finished cigarette away as though it wasn't doing what she wanted. "Mom said she asked you to find Mouse."

"We shouldn't talk about it here."

She got into her car and I got into mine. I followed her out to Cahuenga Pass. In one of the sharpest bends of the road, she swerved up someone's driveway. I thought she'd jumped the curb for a moment, until she parked. I pulled in beside her. Lino's thermos stayed in the cup holder, but I got out.

Vi held a package under her arm as she led me inside.

The house was small but tasteful—wood paneling, dark couches made of fake leather, and hunting rifles on the wall. Very male. As I followed her into the kitchen I wondered whose place this was. New boyfriend? I realized I didn't care.

Then I laid my hand on the couch and realized that the leather wasn't fake.

Violet dropped the package onto the counter. "Come here," she said, and led me to the bathroom. "Get yourself showered up. I'll get you some clean clothes." She shut the door.

I showered in a stranger's tiny tiled bathroom. I lathered up with translucent blue soap and dried off with rough white towels. The clothes were too big for me, but there was a belt, too.

Violet was in the kitchen when I returned. There was a lot of glassware and copper. She opened the fridge, took out two beer bottles, and popped the caps on them. She set one on the counter for me.

I walked close to the package to examine it. It was a brown leather folder with a black ribbon tied around it. SHIMMERMAN & PENOBSCOTT had been printed in gold leaf along the edge. I didn't touch it.

"Whose place is this?" I asked.

"Mine, if you can believe it. Arne gave it to me this afternoon." She held up her bottle. We clinked them together and drank.

"He did, huh?" My brain was racing through the events of the previous few days. Arne had a house? Like this? I never would have guessed.

"He really fixed it up. He got it from a guy who owed him money. That was right before I got the court order. Did you know I had a restraining order against him?" Violet's voice was soft. "He kicked my door down once, the second time I broke up with him. The cops came and everything. All those crimes he did, over all those years, and he'd never been picked up by the cops before. He was furious with me, as though it was my fault he had a record."

"He was always careful."

"I always thought he was too careful." She took a long pull. "And I thought he should grow up and get something legit. But he used to laugh at that."

"Why did he give you the house?"

"The guy explained it to me. Penobscott, although I think it was Penobscott's kid, really, not the one with his name in gold. Arne said he was going away, shedding all his worldly possessions and simplifying. He was going to find himself. It's all in a trust or something. I don't know. This snotty-faced kid was sitting behind a big desk in a suit that cost more than I earn in a month, and he's telling me all about the terms of the trust and what I have to do to maintain it for Jasmin. But I couldn't hear a thing he said. We must have talked for half an hour, and I walked out of there like I'd been hypnotized to forget it all. But Arne left me and Jazzy a bunch of offshore accounts, properties, and stocks."

I had no idea how to respond to that. I'd been living above my aunt's garage carrying rocks down a hill, and Arne had been squirreling it all away.

I wondered how much he'd gotten from Francois before he killed him.

"Vi, how long has the Bigfoot Room been at the Roasted Seal? When was the last time he moved it?"

She shrugged. "Years. A few weeks after your sentencing, actually. When you were busted, he pulled up stakes and didn't set them down again until he was sure you were going to do the time without naming him."

"He didn't pull up stakes when Mouse disappeared, though, right?"

"Right. Now, what about him? Where is Mouse?"

"In the properties Arne just gave you, is one of them out near the Mohave? A little patch of desert and rock, maybe, with a prefab building on it? A place called Quake-water."

"Maybe," she said. "I think . . . maybe."

"Don't go out there, understand? Not if you want to keep what Arne left for you and your daughter."

She set the bottle down and picked it up again. In one long pull, she drained it. She understood what I meant, and she wasn't surprised. "Oh, God, Ray," she said, her shoulders slumped and her head bowed. "What did I do?"

I went around the counter and put my arms around her. She cried against my chest, soaking Arne's shirt with her tears. When she was done, she grabbed a fistful of his shirt and pulled me into the bedroom.

Arne's bedroom, and it hadn't even been five hours since I'd put a bullet through his brain. I kissed her, then she pulled his clothes off me. Arne was dead and gone, and there was nothing left of him but memories and a lot of expensive crap. Violet and I were still alive, and together again.

Whatever she and I had was in the past; this was something new. Everything between us was different except the sounds she made. It felt like new life, and a new chance at happiness.

But when we both had finished and she lay against my shoulder, I knew I was not about to get a new life. I had a life already, and it was inescapable. A few moments later, when Vi rolled away from me, I didn't try to draw her back.

"I think I'm going to move away," she said. "I think I'm going to meet with that guy in the suit again, get him to explain everything again, and then get the fuck out of here."

"You want to leave L.A.?" I was surprised to hear it. People leave the city all the time, of course, but I didn't think Vi would be one of them.

"I mean leave America. I've never met any of my mother's family in Oaxaca. I could . . ." Her voice trailed off. I waited for her, and eventually she said, "Better yet, we could go to Canada. They let you in if you have enough money, right? Live up in Canada with all that cold, clean snow."

Something about the way she said that made me think that *we* didn't include me. I rolled out of bed and began to dress again. They were Arne's clothes, and she was the mother of his child, but I'd never had any qualms about stealing things before.

"Ray . . . ," she said, as though she was about to make a confession.

"I already know," I said as I pulled on the shirt.

"No, you don't."

"Yes, I do." I sat in a little cloth chair in the corner and put on my socks. "You're the one who connected Wally with Arne, and with Caramella and Luther and Fidel and the rest. Wally wouldn't have known about the Bigfoot Room or about Arne, but he would have been able to find you, the girl I was living with when I was busted. You're the one who told him how to find the Bigfoot Room."

Violet pulled the blankets off the bed and wrapped them around herself. She didn't turn toward me.

"Wally as much as told me so himself," I continued. "He was disappointed by our waitress at the Sugar Shaker. He wanted to sit in your section. I'll bet he was, actually, and you asked the other girl to take his order, yeah?"

"Yeah."

"Wally wanted me to know he was connected to you. And Arne . . . well, Arne moved the Bigfoot Room when I went to prison because he was afraid I'd turn him in. He didn't move when Mouse disappeared, though, did he? You knew your brother was dead. You didn't exactly gasp in surprise in the other room when I told you. I think I must be the only idiot who didn't realized that Arne had a place to dump the bodies of people who were dangerous to him. That's why Fidel tried to have him killed before striking out on his own; Arne didn't like the idea of his crew getting busted for stupid jobs and easing their sentences by naming him.

"So, Wally must have looked you up. You didn't know him, but anyone who took one look would know the guy was trouble. You thought about your missing brother, and your suspicions about what happened to him, and you pointed Wally King straight at—"

"Do you think Arne knew what I did?" she asked, breaking in as if she couldn't stand to listen anymore.

I remembered the expression on his face as we stood out behind the berm. Hell yeah, he knew. "No."

"Okay," she said. Vi had always told me I was a terrible liar, but she seemed to believe me now. Maybe she wanted to. She still didn't turn around. "But what does that make me?"

I almost answered *Nothing*, but I held it back. She would have misunderstood. "Someone with a secret. A secret you should never ever admit to anyone."

And that was all we had to say to each other. She was silent and wouldn't even turn her head to look at me. I finished tying my shoelaces and stood. She slowly tipped sideways until she nestled on the pillow. Maybe she was going to sleep.

I let myself out. The stolen Viper was still parked in her drive, and there were no cops clustered around it, checking the plates. There was only one place to go. The thermos and I went back to the supermarket.

I parked the Viper a block away, making sure I overlapped the marked fire-hydrant zone. The car would collect tickets until someone ran the plates. I tossed the keys under the seat. Even if I couldn't find Annalise, I didn't want to drive it again. I didn't feel sporty.

I wandered out to the bus shelter where I'd called the society and spoken with Mariana. No one was there. I sat on the bench and waited.

It took about five minutes for Annalise to pull up in her van. She must have been nearby, watching for me.

She opened the driver's door and climbed into the passenger side. I got behind the wheel, adjusted the mirrors and seat, then started the engine. The thermos went into the cup holder beside me.

"Where have you been?" she asked me.

"Finishing a job."

"Tell me about it when we get onto the freeway."

"What about Csilla? What about Talbot?"

"Csilla is gone, back to wherever she goes. And we're not going to see Talbot again. He's out."

"Out?" I couldn't hide my surprise. "I don't understand. Why is he out? Because he ran?"

"No," Annalise said. "Because you said he was useless."

That wasn't how I remembered it.

I didn't much like Talbot, but I hoped whoever caught up with him killed him quickly. "I don't know, boss. The guy probably needs a little training. Hell, he could probably design the training. He might still be useful."

She grunted as though I'd made a good point. And that was all I could do for Talbot. Maybe she'd send word not to kill him. I hoped so.

Annalise hadn't told me where to go, so I got on the 10 heading east. She didn't object. Maybe she didn't care. As we rolled along with traffic, I told her everything that happened after she went through Lino

Vela's front window. The only thing I left out was finding the Book of Oceans inside the statue, the vision I had, and the fact that it was sitting in the thermos between us.

By the time I'd finished, we were northbound on the 15, heading for Barstow. She told me briefly about her time with the cops. They'd been gentle with her from the first moment they'd fished her out of the bushes. She told them that she was trying to reach Steve Francois to convince him to donate to her foundation, and within half an hour they'd received confirmation that she did exactly that with her time. She gave them a statement and asked to be released. They let her go.

I shook my head in disbelief. Even with her tattoos, she still got the middle-class white-woman treatment. Or did she have help from one of the spells on her body?

"Boss," I said. "What would you have done if we had found the Book of Motes? Or one of the other original spell books?"

Her response surprised me. She sighed heavily. "That's a hard question. The long-standing rule of the society is that anyone who finds one of the three original spell books is to bring it to the peers directly without 'reading' it first. All the peers would gather together and decide what to do."

"You wouldn't want to check it out before you turned it over? Become a primary yourself?" She didn't answer right away. "Boss?"

"You're damn right I would. I want to finish the job in Hammer Bay *myself*. I want to . . . We're falling behind in this fight, Ray, because we're losing focus and power by the year, while the predators are as dangerous as ever. But the peers want to decide as a group who should have access to it."

"I'm guessing you don't think they'd let all the peers have a turn."

"I know they wouldn't. A few of them don't even think a woman can become a primary. They're sure the visions would corrupt her and maybe damage the book. Also, aside from me, one Brazilian, and one Arab, the other peers are all white Europeans; they don't trust the rest of us with that kind of power."

"What if you read it anyway, then gave it to them?"

She sighed again. "Civil war? Again? The problem is that I *believe* in the work the Twenty Palace Society does. I couldn't live with the terrible things I've done otherwise. But the society itself has become a nest of serpents. If I could do this work without them, I'd kill them all."

"I saw the letter you gave to Captain." Dammit. I didn't want to go there next, but the words had slipped out.

"Who? Oh, our friend who took us to Canada? Is that why you've been such a crabby bastard? The letter was for her protection in case we were arrested, genius."

"Okay."

"I know this is leading somewhere, Ray. Get on with it."

"When I asked you if you wanted to become a primary . . ." *You blinked.* I wasn't sure how to ask Annalise if she was frightened or uncertain, and it turned out I didn't have to.

"I hesitated. I know. Ray, what was that guy's name? You know the one I mean."

I did. "Lino Vela."

"Lino Vela. As apprentices, we're trained to attack rogues at the first opportunity. No matter where we are, or who's in the line of fire, we *go*. Becoming a primary, having all that power, well, that would make things easier. But there's a part of me that doesn't think what happened to Lino Vela should ever be easy."

Well, damn. I knew she trusted me enough to share information, but not that she was ready to share this.

She kept talking: "So, you asked, and I hesitated. But the answer is always going to be *yes,* because there's too much at stake."

We drove in silence for a while.

I needed to be careful with this next part. "What if we—I mean, just us two—went out to find one of those original spell books? What if you had the visions, and to hell with the society? You'd be a primary, right? Couldn't you take over? Change the training? Couldn't you just . . ." *Wipe them out?* I couldn't finish the sentence.

"Fight the whole society? Take on not just all the peers but the allies, too? Plus whatever rogues they decided to point at me? Without support? I don't know. I don't think so. And the society has financiers, lawyers, and investigators, too. They can strip away an enemy's resources before a fight, if they know who they're targeting, and they know me. I'm not saying it's a terrible idea. I'd be happy to get my hands on a spell book just to keep it away from assholes like your—like Wally King. But if I became a primary, I think the Twenty Palace Society would kill me—would kill us both. And even if we won the fight, we'd lose the infrastructure of the society. As a primary I'd kick ass, yeah, but I'd need investigators to tell me where to go, and financiers to cover the bills, and so on. *If* we won, and I doubt we would."

"What if the peers got their hands on a book?"

"Incredible power for the most vicious serpents in the nest. These aren't men who worry about the job being easy; it's already easy for them, because they love it. They love the brutality. They pride themselves on their willingness to kill. With society resources backing them, they'd have the world behind the world under their heel."

"You've thought about this."

"Of course I have. This is my life and my future. Either the society loses this fight and the world is overrun with predators, or I become a primary and lose a fight with the society, or the assholes become primaries and I get demoted to . . . what? Wooden man? Errand girl? None of them are good options, but the last one is the least awful."

"To hell with that." I picked up the thermos and swirled the liquid. I couldn't hear it over the rumble of the engine, but I could feel it slosh around. "Boss, here. I found the Book of Oceans."

She stared at me silently for a moment, trying to judge if I was being serious or if she was going to start breaking my bones for playing a prank. I pushed the thermos at her, and she took it. She screwed off the top.

"Oh" was all she said.

I laid my hand over the top. "You're not going to go back on everything you just said, are you?"

She gently moved my hand away and looked into the bottom of the thermos for another few seconds. Then she screwed the cap back on and held the thermos in her lap. "You bastard." She sounded almost as though she wanted to laugh. "You goddamn son of a bitch. You're really good at this job, aren't you?" I shrugged. "Where are you driving us?"

"East," I said.

We drove to Barstow in the dark, and I switched to the 40. "The Mohave Desert?" Annalise asked.

"Can you think of a better place to hide the Book of Oceans?"

"Death Valley."

I laughed. I couldn't help it. "Don't be annoying, boss."

"We're going to hide it?"

For a moment, she sounded unsure of herself. I hadn't thought that was possible. "You said it wouldn't be safe for us to use it, and I sure as hell won't give it to the serpents. I have a better idea."

We took the 40 to the 95. The sign said that Las Vegas was 103 miles away. As we passed the freeway entrance sign for the westbound on-ramp, I made note of the odometer. We counted off a random number of miles, then pulled onto the shoulder.

"Shovel's in back," Annalise said.

We climbed out into the darkness. I couldn't see a car in either direction.

There was a shovel mounted on a rack in the back of the van. Only one, though. I knew who would be using it. I took it down and followed Annalise into the desert.

We walked at least a quarter mile away from the asphalt before Annalise pointed at the ground. "Here."

I dug a shallow hole. She tossed the thermos in without hesitation. It was long life and power beyond anything I could imagine, but I shoveled dirt over it. Annalise picked up a rock as large as a beach ball and set it down to mark the spot. Then she found two more large flat rocks, each the size of a trash-can lid, and laid them beside the beach ball.

"I think we'll be able to find it now, boss. If we have to."

She nodded. We started back to the van. No other cars passed by on the road. "Ray, this only works if we trust each other. You understand? Because either one of us could come back later and move that thermos. Either one of us could cut the other out."

"Boss, if I wanted to cut you out, I wouldn't have handed you that thermos. The truth is, I need your help. It's not enough to hide the Book of Oceans from the Wally Kings of the world—or from the other peers, either. There are two more books out there, and I don't trust anyone with that power—"

"Neither do I."

"Not even the two of us. I don't think we're ready for it."

Her answer was quieter this time. "Because of what you did in Washaway. And Lino Vela."

"Yeah. We will be ready for it, someday, but not yet. Like I said, stashing one book isn't good enough. We need to hunt down the other two."

"That's all, huh? Just go out and find them?"

"That's all."

"And what then? You and I form a new, kinder, gentler society?"

"Yes. We clean the serpents out of the nest. This whole legion-of-brutal-killers thing isn't working. It's a losing strategy. We can do better."

She didn't respond, and I couldn't read her expression in the dark. We returned to the van.

"Ray, this is incredibly dangerous. You don't even understand how dangerous it is. You're just my stupid wooden man."

"All they think about is their limitations," I said to her.

"Don't throw my own words in my face—"

"Some things should never be easy."

"Dammit, Ray! I'm the peer and you're my wooden man! You belong to me!"

"I know I do, boss. You're in, though, right?"

"Fuck, yeah."

I started the engine and pulled onto the highway. It took a long while to get up to speed.

"Where to, boss?"

"Straight through to Vegas," she said. "You look like you could use some sleep. Then we're headed east. You're going to the First Palace. The peers want to meet you."

"Um, really?"

I wasn't sure if I should be pleased about that or not, so I changed the subject. "Can you convince the society to work with Talbot? He's an asshole, but he saved my life."

"I'll make a call. It probably won't do any good, but I'll call."

"Damn. He was really looking forward to living a century or three."

"Not everyone earns a golem-flesh spell."

I turned to her. "What?"

"Not everyone earns that spell," she snapped, annoyed at having to repeat herself. "Especially in the last few years. Only older peers like Csilla can even manage it anymore."

I touched the spell Csilla had put under my left arm, the one that healed me when I ate meat. Annalise had called that mark golem flesh.

For once, she understood my expression. "Didn't I explain that part?"

"Jesus." I wasn't sure what to say. I was going to live to be, what? Five hundred? Older? "How long until I talk gibberish like Csilla?"

"Gibberish? She was telling you the secrets of the universe."

ABOUT THE AUTHOR

Photo: © Maryann Kuchera

HARRY CONNOLLY spent two years writing his first novel, *Child of Fire*. He has held a variety of jobs in the past, from customer service to stay-at-home dad. He lives in Seattle.